DARRELL YATES RIST is well known for his articles on politics, gay activism, AIDS, and the arts, which have appeared in many publications, including *The Nation*, *The Village Voice*, *New York Native*, *Christopher Street*, and *Harper's*. He lives in New York City.

DARRELL YATES RIST

HEARTLANDS

A
GAY
MAN'S
ODYSSEY
ACROSS
AMERICA

Ⓟ
A PLUME BOOK

PLUME
Published by the Penguin Group
Penguin Books USA Inc., 375 Hudson Street, New York, New York 10014, U.S.A.
Penguin Books Ltd, 27 Wrights Lane, London W8 5TZ, England
Penguin Books Australia Ltd, Ringwood, Victoria, Australia
Penguin Books Canada Ltd, 10 Alcorn Avenue, Toronto, Ontario, Canada M4V 3B2
Penguin Books (N.Z.) Ltd, 182-190 Wairau Road, Auckland 10, New Zealand

Penguin Books Ltd, Registered Offices:
Harmondsworth, Middlesex, England

Published by Plume, an imprint of Dutton Signet,
a division of Penguin Books USA Inc. Previously published in a Dutton edition.

First Plume Printing, November, 1993
10 9 8 7 6 5 4 3 2 1

For permissions please turn to page 486.

 REGISTERED TRADEMARK—MARCA REGISTRADA

LIBRARY OF CONGRESS CATALOGING IN PUBLICATION DATA
Rist, Darrell Yates.
    Heartlands: a gay man's odyssey across America / Darrell Yates
    Rist
        p. cm.
    ISBN 0-452-27037-5
    1. Gays—United States. 2. Homosexuality—United States.
I. Title.
HQ76.3.U5R57 1993
305.38'966—dc20   93–16026
                                                                      CIP

Printed in the United States of America

CONTENTS

ACKNOWLEDGMENTS

WHEN THE IDEA FOR AN AMERICAN JOURNEY FIRST OCCURRED TO me in 1985, I could not have imagined how, in time, my travels would shape themselves in this book, or how many of my family and friends, both old and new, would wonderfully contribute to its creation. The devotion of some has been constant:

Robert Michael Cataldo, my lifemate, who gave me courage and spiritual sustenance when mine were depleted, who has always sacrificed to keep me writing; and Buddha, my Lhasa apso, who curled at my feet.

My parents, Louis Raymond and Geraldine Yates Rist, and my sister, Jerolyn Rist-Szuch, whose ardent belief in me has been unwavering; whose love knows no bounds.

My editors, Margaret Blackstone and Matthew Carnicelli, who have not been merely literary advisers, but tireless, wise, and sensitive friends.

My agents, Carol Mann, whose unselfishness brought the proposal for this book to fruition, and Victoria Sanders, whose remarkable dedication guided the manuscript to publication and beyond.

Heartlands is yours as much as mine. I am a new man on account of you.

And though I would inevitably fail if I tried to name everyone who has been a friend to me and supportive of the completion of this odyssey, I would be unforgivably remiss were I not to thank especially a community of men and women who in countless ways have enlightened me and sustained me.

Doctor Stuart E. Nichols, Dr. Sharon Lewin, and Dr. Michael Rendel, who are healers. Mariette Pathy Allen, a photographer and dear friend whose genius and vision inspired me to see men differently. Peter Ginsberg, whose amused, sympathetic counsel has been my steady guide. The late Robert Chesley, Raymond Jacobs, George Dudley, Brett Averill, Carolyn Parqueth, Terezinha Gomes Lage Zamudio, Dr. Paula Murphy, DeLys Mullis, and all the men and women I met across the country, whose lives have transformed mine.

This book is a testament to your spirit.

Without the generous support of the Fund for Human Dignity, the Center for American Culture Studies at Columbia University, and the New York State Council on the Arts, these many years of writing would not have been possible. I am grateful.

FOREWORD

THIS BOOK IS A JOURNEY THROUGH SEXUAL DESIRE AND IDENTITY. It is the story of American men in the last years of the twentieth century—men who are sometimes, at least, homosexual, not always "gay."

For three years—but really much longer—I traveled through the heart of male America, discovering the roots and expression of homosexual need in the vast geographies that shape and nurture them. From Puerto Rico to the northernmost nipple of Alaska, from Hawaii to the urban sprawl of the northeast coast—more than one hundred thousand miles—I have wandered through the masculine soul of a nation to learn what shades of yearning woo it.

This is a spiritual tale, of survival and liberation in a man's world. It is a tale of release from exile, from the self-imposed bonds of bigotry. This odyssey is true and an allegory. It is my story and the story of a continent of men in the age of AIDS, behind the proclamations of prejudice and gay politics.

Ultimately, this book is the story of every man.

THE TROPIC
OF
DESIRE

I DON'T KNOW HOW IT WAS THAT I FIRST HEARD OF VILLA CAIMITO. Its existence seemed to be whispered on the Caribbean breeze those first few days I spent in Puerto Rico in the winter of 1987. It was like a mythic haven the *conquistadores* might have sought. Everyone spoke of it. No one knew how to get there. *"¿Villa Caimito?"* answered Luis. Luis was *dueño* of the La Princesa guest house in the east end of San Juan, where I was staying. I had come late in the morning to the patio to have a continental breakfast. "Oh, jes! I know of it." His English, like his Spanish, was as gossipy as castanets. "That is where the truly local *maricones* go. No *turistas*, no San Juaneros, no Nuyoricans—only campesinos, country people, go there. It's in the mountains, maybe twenty minutes from here. I cannot exactly tell you where.

"¡Oye! ¡Tú eres un maricón! You're an old fag!" Luis teased the elderly man who worked the bar. *"¿Dónde está Villa Caimito?"*

"¡Ay, Virgen! I was young when I was there—so long ago! I do not know the road."

The fan suspended from the veranda turned slowly, wobbling

its stem. The morning air was dead and heavy. A high concrete wall, dripping with barbed wire and scarlet hibiscus, surrounded the compound. Over the top of the barricade, palm leaves lay lifeless, like heat-stricken lizards. A waterfall, spouting from the wall by the pool, gurgled sleepily. A cock crowed repeatedly, distant dogs barked. I drank a second cup of coffee, *con leche*. It was sometime around ten. A short, round gentleman and his slender wife, with their little boy, sipped wine and piña coladas at the end of the bar. In a moment of silence, the husband said, as if rhetorically—as if the answer to my quandary were apparent— "You want to find the way to Villa Caimito?"

He lifted a map from a holder on the bar and introduced himself, Dr. Ramón Alfredo Santos-Ortiz. With his finger he wordlessly drew the route, confident and vague. Reaching the jungled peaks of the mountains somewhere past Caguas, he tapped at a spot where gray one-lane roads wound about each other like vines and finally said, "And then you will be there. I was there with a friend once—an older, professional man who wouldn't want to be seen in the bars in San Juan. It's a magical place." His wife had shining black eyes and straight, raven hair pulled tight in a bun—a pure Spanish lady. She lifted her chin and smiled in assent, named a number of other bars that might interest me, then slipped from the stool to play dominoes at a table with her son. The couple, I guessed, were in their fifties.

"A lot of our friends are gay," the doctor continued. "Gays are very cultivated people. They love good music, art—that's why we're drawn to them. They are the most kind, loyal people I know. I think they have often been treated so badly that when you accept them they are your friends forever."

Luis, all this while, was busy about himself, making coffee and toast for the few other guests, tidying the veranda, chattering at his dogs—keeping an ear on my conversation. Now, he slapped down a stack of English and Spanish newspapers on the bar. The headlines were all of AIDS. "Here in San Juan, it's always all over the news," he declared smugly as if to defend San Juan's status among the worst of the nation's ravaged cities. "We're *third* after New York and San Francisco, you know! Young boys—mostly drug users, the rest gays. Gay life in San Juan is like New York. Maybe even wilder than that! You can do what you want to here, just like the States."

"Is there any kind of gay politics here? Gay community life?" I asked.

"Oh, *sure!*" He was insulted. "We have an organization, a group for AIDS . . . I don't know its name. In San Juan, we have everything!" That was all.

I had lived in Puerto Rico as an adolescent. On New Year's Day 1963, my family moved there from Tennessee along the Alabama border. My father was an industrialist who went to the island to open a baseball factory for Wilson Sporting Goods in the United States' Caribbean colony, for cheap labor and ten years' exemption from corporate taxes. The project was part of Operation Bootstrap, a joint U.S. and Puerto Rican program begun in the late 1940s to lure American industry to the poverty-ridden island. The purpose of this effort was certainly to supply jobs, but just as certainly, behind the goodwill, to subvert the radical independence movement, which sought to reconstitute Puerto Rico as a free nation. In fact, in the late nineteenth century Puerto Rico had been close to full independence, having negotiated with its then ruler, Spain, autonomous self-government as well as full representation in the Spanish parliament. Its sort of freedom lasted only eight days, however. The United States invaded the southern coast at Guánica on July 25, 1898—and the American conquest of Puerto Rico had begun.

In 1963 Puerto Rico was a shock to me—and then an adventure of confusion and troubled delight. My family were hillbillies, really, ecstatically Christian, solidly patriotic, family people, the boundary of whose world extended little beyond my like-minded grandparents, uncles and aunts, hordes of cousins, and unending nights of tearful prayer meetings. I was fifteen when we left the States. In my school in Tennessee, only the slow kids took Spanish, and no one could fathom the purpose of French. I took Latin. Now I found myself in a Spanish-speaking school—a *Catholic* school. We'd always thought Catholics to be alien, dangerous creatures of black-magical intent. My mother cried when she learned I had to take catechism classes and attend mass with the rest. I was drawn to the ritual of the Church like something beautiful, secret, and dirty.

I learned Spanish quickly and, in that, first glimpsed the befuddlement of Puerto Rico. We studied, and were made to practice, Castilian Spanish in school. But what we spoke on the street was something less than another Spanish dialect, it was a confounding of languages—part misunderstood English, part solipsistic Spanish: "Spanglish," a vulgar colonial mix of no linguistic consistency because it depended on what pieces of English one picked up from school or tourists or Puerto Ricans returned from New York or the influx of North American settlers like me. I saw the confusion too in the conflict of patriotisms—in the exuberant singing of "La Borinqueña," the Puerto Rican national anthem, each day at school, and the daily sullen pledge to the American flag, as feeble as the Santa Marías we were made to pray. But my schoolmates would cry out in insult at the vaguest suggestion that persons born on the continent were Americans and that Puerto Ricans were something other than that. "We are Americans, too!" they corrected with acid indignation. So to distinguish us from themselves, they called us *continentales*, not *americanos*. Declared Puerto Rican nationalists, particularly the ones heard from at the Universidad de Puerto Rico, were starker. They called us *imperialistas*, intruders. I grew fascinated by the *independentistas*, defiant and sometimes violent, worrisome to "continentals" like my father.

In the States, my mind had been a childish, settled thing—I was sure about God, my obligations to my family, the freedom for which my country stood. In Puerto Rico, for the first time in my life, it startlingly occurred to me that some lands, some people, under the American flag in fact might not be free, but captive. And I wondered at this confusion of identities, for who I was had always been for me a destiny, given at birth, unchangeable, surely not something one struggled with, an oppression one could bow to, a liberation one could pursue—a choice.

Adolescence, I'm quite sure, fueled my wonderment for, my

love of, Puerto Rico. For newly urgent needs burned inside me, so all my settled thoughts and ways smoldered into question. I'd bloomed, surely enough, on time—but didn't realize the pleasures of my new estate until our second month in the Caribbean, on my sixteenth birthday. We were living in Mayagüez then, on the western end of the island, though all of our household belongings were still stuck on the docks of New York on account of a long-shoremen's strike. For the while, we roomed in the dormitories of the College of Agricultural and Mechanical Arts. My sister bunked with a single woman who'd come from the States to work with my father. Her room was adjoined, like mine, by a balcony to our parents' quarters. I bunked with Paul—a manly bachelor, thirtyish, another Wilson employee—directly on the other side of my parents. Paul always showered with the bathroom door ajar. Feverish with fascination, I watched nightly from my bed. He slept naked. I lay sleepless with the thought of his unconscious, unclothed body in the bed across from mine.

Each night the family gathered in the center room to take turns bathing—too private a thing for my sister and me to enact in a room with strangers. Then we held our religious devotions. On my birthday night, in my shower, a miracle happened: I soaped myself the right way. I was thinking of Paul. Ecstatic droplets of pearly, hot liquid spat from my body and lathered my stomach and legs. No sooner did the pleasure grip me than I knew it had to be iniquitous. Moments later, on my knees, I led evening prayers and before my mystified family sobbed, impassioned, while traces of my sticky sin still gummed my flesh.

So simply may a rebellious life begin. We moved to the north shore city of Arecibo soon after that, for a better school. My pals, who taught me "Spanglish" on the playground, taught me as well what were the tools of pubescent arousal: in the locker room of the country club, boys frustrated by the Latin custom of a chaperone on every legitimate date jerked off in a circle, my friend Daniel told me, dropping their loads in a towel. Ramón—a strong, good-looking Nuyorican, our neighborhood's star baseball player—gave blow jobs. My family were not members of the country club. I enjoyed none of this except in fantasy; I was crippled with shame. These masculine boys were dark, slender, muscular, with black curly hair, and smelled perpetually of the mischievous sweat of sexual power. Their swagger was spontaneous. They appeared to me to be everything I was not. I longed for them and eroticized the teasing trills of their language.

Under the heat-bleached skies of tropical noons each school day, I walked home for lunch. The Arecibo Sport Shop was on the way. To be sure, it vended sports equipment, but it also carried such pornography as was available in Puerto Rico then. Each noon I stopped and, mesmerized, gazed at the colorful pages of "muscle magazines." The models all wore G-strings, the soft Victorian folds of the pouch concealing the sexual outlines. In the lower outside corner of every page, there was a small pencil drawing of the model naked. I studied these sketches closely, then, panicked with desire, ran two blocks home to lock myself in the bathroom. When ten or fifteen minutes had passed and my lunch sat tepid, my mother would rap on the door, anxious with suspicion, and, whispering, I'd start to cry and pray, promising Jesus I'd forsake my sin, terrified it already had marked me for life, that my depravity was already inexorable. One day as I stood in the sultry air of the sport shop, a young clerk took the magazine from my hands and held it up for his customers. "¡Mira!" He laughed. "¡Un pato!" ("Look! A duck!"—a feather-tailed swish, a faggot.) And for the first time in my life, I intimately understood how identities could change. I'd been given a new one that strangled me—that wholly contained me like a locked airless room. I learned I was "queer."

And now, more than twenty-five years later—and before setting out on my journeys across the continental United States—it seemed to me only appropriate to return to the place where my sense of sexual identity began, where I learned that such identities could sum us up with their tight definitions, secure and also confound us.

Michael, my lover, is Sicilian and therefore, among all the other needs he meets, he fulfills my adolescent Latin fantasies. He had joined me on this return of mine to Puerto Rico, for this reclamation of my past. One night in San Juan we ate at a gay restaurant on the beachfront—one geared, not to locals, but to "Americans." Business that night was slow—the whole season had been. The restaurant's owner and chef blamed it on the terrible fire at the Dupont Plaza Hotel in December. The resultant deaths, he thought, had generally scared away tourists. The hulk, still smelling of moist ash, sat blackened and boarded down the street. The sea wind carried the odor to us.

This owner-chef, quintessentially a New Yorker, knew little of homosexuality in Puerto Rico. "Could care less," he said. "I come here for the winters, that's all. The weather's perfect." But Puerto Rico itself? "Puerto Ricans are all crazy," he spat. Michael and I slowly forked the overbroiled fish he had served us personally. Everything on the plate tasted musty. "Liars and thieves, all of 'em. In the ten years I've been coming down here, I haven't met one exception. And the food? *You know the food?* Rice and beans—*slop!* Just a mess on the plate. Forget about presentation! What can you *possibly* do with it?"

And I wondered, was he a "gay brother" whose desire for men made him just like me? I despised him as a colonial blight on the island, no one I felt a kinship with. He did volunteer that he'd heard of Villa Caimito but couldn't tell us how to get there. Nor could he begin to imagine why anyone would go to a place where nothing but Spanish was spoken. He led us instead to Vibrations, a San Juan sex bar that catered to tourists and banned, he believed, Puerto Ricans. I was curious—both about the sex and the banning.

The chef was wrong. There were a number of Puerto Ricans there—half of the clientele, maybe. The bar consisted of three dark rooms, all on the second story of a two-story building. They were wholly enclosed, no outside light or tropical air, muskily air-conditioned. They might have been moved intact from a sex parlor in New York. The first chamber was the bar itself, the second a drearily lit poolroom. The third was the sort of black space, with several blacker nooks for intimacy, where pleasure and place are sensed only by the sightless press of skin.

Michael was drawn by a man he met into the back. I drew

another. He'd been standing opposite the bar with a beer when I first saw him—wiry black hair, mocha skin, a handsome mustached face, a small tight body. I judged him to be in his twenties. His shirt was pale blue and of shimmering polyester, a fabric of choice among a common class of Puerto Ricans. His shoes were thin blue loafers of the Italian style. His sharply pressed shorts were khaki. I moved past him to the dark-room, clasping him with my eyes. He followed. Invisible along the wall beside the door, this young man and I embraced.

In time, full of foreplay, I invited my dark-room partner back with me to the guest house. Miguel was his name. In the front room bar, I offered an option: "Do you have a place?"

"*Mi familia está en casa,*" he said without elaboration—"My family's at home."

I found Michael and arranged to leave the rental car with him. Miguel and I hailed a taxi. Once in my room, he grew anxious and closely watched the clock until past two. Michael, having had sex with his trick at the bar, had come back home by then and joined us when at last Miguel confessed, "My wife thinks I am working late"—he was a carpenter and house painter—"but at such an hour she will start to wonder. I must go." We talked no more about it then, but Miguel promised to return in the afternoon and bring his children. He said, "To play in the pool." Given the nervousness I had known in married men, I doubted that I would ever see him again.

The next afternoon he knocked on my door, as arranged, sharply at one—with two beautiful little ones in tow, Alexis and Ramses, girl and boy. He was an attentive, gentle father, firm nonetheless. His dark eyes never left them as they entered the shallowest water, squealing and laughing. Their presence precipitated his story. Miguel and his wife were Pentecostals. They'd been raised that way and still were deeply religious. When Miguel was almost eighteen—he was now twenty-four—he'd attended a church camp in the mountains as a counselor. There he'd been raped by the senior counselor of his cabin, a man some ten years older. At first, shamed and terrified, he told no one. But the rectal bleeding didn't stop, and the sharp pain began. He turned to his grandparents, who'd raised him, and after their doctor examined him he was hospitalized for surgery. The doctor was Pentecostal as well and suggested Miguel undergo pastoral counseling and psychotherapy to exorcise the trauma he'd suffered. He recommended a preacher-psychologist, whom Miguel agreed to see.

It was early in his therapy that Miguel married—a girl whom he'd known from church since childhood and had sometimes dated. Both of his children were born within two years. "I needed to win my manhood back," he told me.

But it wasn't long after the birth of their first child that, in therapy still, he began to discover desire beneath the brutality of his first homosexual experience. He remembered—and recalled for me now—the weight and shape of his assailant's body over him, the masculine smell of his skin, his seductive breath, the strong handsome face, the exciting roughness of his beard, his strength of movement. Despite the frightening force with which the man had pinned him to the bed, he had also been solicitous of Miguel's comfort as he'd entered him—that is, before passion carried him away. Miguel had never *known* homosexual longings before then, he was certain—no dreams or witting attraction. But now, so awakened, he wondered if he'd been, not raped, in the strictest sense, but taken upon subtle invitation. He questioned whether, in fact, he'd not all the while wanted the man to have him, though not at all so hurtfully. Now, spiritually faithful to his wife, he mostly allowed himself just this with men: to have sex in bars or parks, always standing. Rarely had he gone home with his partner. Never had he submitted to intercourse again, but he often fantasized about it, he said.

"Why don't you *leave* your wife," I asked, "if you're really attracted to men?" I was more tendentious, I think, than sympathetic, though I know I had a sympathetic air about me. Ten years before, I had divorced my wife and dogmatically become a gay activist. And I wondered why any self-respecting homosexual wouldn't do the same.

"I made a *compromiso* when I married," he answered, and seemed taken aback by my question, "a promise to God and to my wife. Now I have my children, too. It is what I chose for myself then. I cannot go back on it just because I change my mind. *No sería justo*," he said—"That would not be right."

Perhaps his sense of ethics was more highly developed than mine, perhaps my love of men was more encompassing. Though the two of us shared a kind of desire, we were dissimilar in all other ways, it seemed at the moment. And though I believed I could never have made the choice he had made, I mightily admired him for it—even in spite of myself.

Miguel had only vaguely heard of Villa Caimito and certainly could not tell me how to get there. Finding it became an obsession. In its elusiveness, it became for me the metaphorical key to some happy state of belonging I had always been seeking, to the ideal of gay brotherhood I think I was hoping to find on my American trips. I set out single-mindedly to discover this mountain haven, conjuring it as a utopia, where men and women could be both wholly Latin in this Latin land and freely gay—a homosexual El Dorado. Luis, the guest house owner, assured me that one of his bartenders, Pedro, could tell me everything about gay life here I wanted to know. I awaited Pedro's arrival at noon on Saturday, when he worked at La Princesa. Otherwise he was too busy to be gotten hold of.

He arrived in a furious rain that had worked its course northeast across the mountains and rushed, in twirling silver streamers, upon the patio and pool. Large-leafed schefflera slapped madly at low palms—a pattering merengue—while bright hibiscus blossoms shivered with the steamy rhythm. This untamed rain created a shimmering, splashing hatchwork upon the ground and a raging sound—like quick-witted fingers on the drum roof of the veranda—as peaceful as silence. The stereo and human noise were drowned. Pedro and I tried to introduce ourselves above this music of the tropics but, deafened, might as well have been mute. We read lips in salutation. "Do you know the way to Villa Caimito?" I mimed.

The storm died as suddenly as it had erupted. A magnificent breathlessness fell; from the wet earth, a white, hot mist rose. I repeated the question. Pedro had never been to the mountain resort but knew of it well. "Pepito," he said, "will know the road exactly. His family lives in a village near there. I will introduce you to him."

Pedro "Peters," as he was known, had been born in Puerto Rico and raised in Philadelphia. It was there that friends had given him this new surname, simply translating his Christian name into English, befuddling its roots. He'd liked the nickname—he said, "because everyone knew me that way"—so he kept it after coming back home to the island. His bartending job was part-time, a hobby, really. Full-time he was an aide to the Puerto Rican legislature and adviser to the house committee on health. He invited me to visit him at his office—at the Capitolio del Estado Libre de Puerto Rico—on the Friday before I left the island.

On that day, I took the number 2 bus down Loíza, past the beach hotels of the swank Condado, through Viejo San Juan with its ancient Spanish nunneries—half a conquered millennium old—which stood, brown as parchment, among walls of bright-shuttered windows and doors on the hills. The sunlight was pure white, the sea blue as crystal. The old buildings gleamed with the fruity hues of exotic flowers. It was as if the architecture were all glass casks, shining with the brilliance of an inner treasure. Such an illusionist is the sunshine of the tropics.

The marble-domed Capitol rose white by the sea. Glistening ocean winds swept inside the great rotunda and stirred down the high hallways, entering through monumental portals. Pedro's office was on the ground floor, where soaring windows overlooked the triumphal statue of San Cristóbal and, beyond that, the South Atlantic. The roar of the surf was resonant in the room. As I entered, Joaquín Corona-Rodríguez, a public aid lawyer—and openly homosexual—stood before Pedro's great baroque desk with livid complaints against colonial degradation still on his lips. Yet another report of George Bush's vice-presidential push for Puerto Rican statehood had reached the local press. Joaquín practiced law in federal courts, where the imposed tongue was English, the participants nearly all Spanish-speaking, the proceedings interpreted aloud—continuously and laboriously—in

both directions. "An American circus!" Joaquín declared resent-
fully as he left.

"But we have a law to protect us!" Pedro insisted. He'd been
angrily searching an index of commonwealth statutes. *"Ley seis
ciento—we* alone have the right to decide. But I doubt Bush knows
the law. He is dumb and stupid." Still, I knew that the real power
behind life in Puerto Rico was its American rulers. Inhabitants of
a mere protectorate, Puerto Ricans were bound by federal law
and most federal obligations but remained without all the rights
enjoyed by full U.S. citizens. They were forced to register for the
Selective Service but could not vote in federal elections and had
no voting representation in Congress. And in this, the island's
population seemed to me not unlike homosexually inclined citizens of the continental United States, who had to pay taxes and
go to war for their country but were denied the legal right to
practice same-sex love without discrimination—and in half the
states without the threat of arrest and imprisonment. Not all people under the American flag, I was reminded again, enjoyed full
citizenship.

The man—the boy—whom Pedro had brought me here to meet
was Pepito, who was sure to know the road to Villa Caimito, having been raised nearby. He was living in San Juan now, attending
chefs' school. He'd be coming today from class at twelve. At noon
exactly, he arrived. He was a vision in the ornate framework of
the door. Long, thin, brown, with a handsome cockscomb of
black hair and a whisper of a mustache—he was a willow of a boy,
a child. His wide eyes glistened like black gems. His shirt was
ripely papaya-colored, with hot red trim, his safari jeans were as
blue as a coral sea. He moved with awkward self-assurance. He
was smoking. He might have been a lost jungle bird, endangered
species. He was sixteen.

"*¡Ya tú tienes un nuevo* look! ...*" Pedro cried. "You have a
new look! More punk since I saw you!" It had been months since
Pedro saw him last, when Pepito began school. He announced,
"You must understand that Pepito is a *líder!*"

"I am the best cook in my school!" Pepito said in Spanish,

beaming. He spoke only the palest English so didn't try. He was doing a course at a *panadería*, a bakery. He wanted to work in a hotel kitchen when he graduated in the spring. "It is the best way to better yourself," he explained. He took a chair beside me before Pedro's desk—an elaborately carved chair, thronelike—and lit a long cigarette. Then, slipping one lithe foot from its flame red loafer, he dangled the other nimbly on his toe.

Pepito was delirious with perfected recipes. His specialties were lasagne and classic rice and beans. He chattered on enthusiastically, then, as a boy will before his elders, fell abruptly shy. In the lull he bounced his shoe and sighed. Then suddenly he remembered brightly some news Pedro wouldn't know yet. *"En julio me caso,"* he stated—"I'm getting married in July."

I glanced at Pedro in surprise. Pedro furrowed his brow, disbelief having dulled his eyes. "To a *woman?*" he asked finally.

"To my boyfriend!" Pepito scolded. "I will cook for the ceremony, we will sign a paper, we will give rings. He is older than I, twenty-seven. He is in school to be a surgeon. My mother is proud of me. The best man will be a doctor, too, my maid of honor will be a nurse. The wedding will be at my mother's house on Saturday, two days after I become seventeen. I will have a chower the week before. Rafael will have a bachelor party at his friend's." Pedro and I sat speechless. Pepito paused, then said, "I'm wearing white. To here. . . ." He pointed to his feet. "I was going to wear a dress, a veil, *everything*, but that got too expensive. Now I am wearing *pantalones* white—white pants—and a little crown of flowers in my hair."

Pedro, stunned by the story till now, ventured a joke here, in the manner of an old queen. *"White*, my dear? How long now have you been *doing it* with this man?"

Pepito's face went tight. He answered dryly, "We are not married yet. We don't have sex." Pedro's eyes grew wide. I sat there, bemused. "We talk, we kiss—that is everything. We will wait till our honeymoon—as we should—when we live in our new house. We have bought one!" he exclaimed. "Oh! There is so much furniture I must buy before the wedding!" Then, for a moment, Pepito again fell suddenly serious while Pedro and I, stricken with still greater wonderment, waited. "There are still some problems that remain," Pepito considered. "We want to have kids. Our friends Carlos and Manuel adopted a boy who's seven now and soon are adopting a baby girl. Both of them stay working. And I will want to keep my profession too when the baby comes and hire day care. But my boyfriend says I can't, *no puedo*, our child should not be raised by strangers. So this is a big decision we must make."

Pepito had, throughout, kept an eye on his watch. He checked it now. "I have a class," he said. "I am never late." As he rose from the chair, he pulled a folded paper from his pocket and placed it on Pedro's desk. "This is the map to Villa Caimito you asked me for."

"I'm in shock!" Pedro squealed when Pepito left, and continued to stare through the door.

Pepito's map contained a big dot for San Juan, double lines for the *autopista* out of the city, zigzags for the mountains, where a crossroads was marked with an "X" and an arrow to a curious note that read *"Aquí hay que parar....* Here you must stop and ask for directions. Then you must find it for yourself."

Michael and I set out in the midafternoon on Sunday, the day before our departure. The *autopista* ascended for nearly thirty minutes. Then, in fact, it did intersect with another road of notable size, which we took to be Pepito's "X." I asked a campesino on an old brown horse, who said, *"¡Oh, sí!* I know the club! Past the arena for cockfights, there is a banana grove, then a tiny road. Turn and you will soon be there! *¡Por seguro!"*

This road was a narrow lane that climbed through a dark, raining jungle, where enormous philodendron leaves slapped at the car like hands. Only one sign of humanity lay along this path—El Ojo del Tigre, the Tiger's Eye, a cafe whose rippled tin door was locked tight and window shuttered. Within a half hour the road circled back to the fork at the cockfighting ring where we'd begun. The air was raw with cheers and desperate wings and shrieks that chilled the spine.

In the wet forest nearby stood a blue, stilted house—no bigger than twenty by twenty—with bamboo poles running from its windows for plumbing. Three small children played naked in the tiny yard, where an old woman gathered colorful laundry from the gnarly limbs of bushes. "One mile more down this highway, past the wrecked green bus," she answered, stooped and toothless and grinning. "Great place! Wonderful fun!"

About an hour later two ancient men playing dominoes by a lush clump of bamboo beside the road directed us to a fork where the tent for a Pentecostal revival meeting had stood until last week. The sign, they said, was still standing. Close by, we would find a dump of automobile wheel covers and a turnoff, six or seven minutes beyond, that descended into a valley, then up the far mountainside. "It is a very popular place!" one exclaimed. We would see at least one hundred cars!

The roads were skinny and rough. Crawling roots and vines roped the tenuous black earth. A constant mist fell. Deep, green pillows of fog settled onto the mossy tops of trees, then in a breath disappeared. Daylight waned early. The flame orange blossoms of a flamboyant tree lay like a wound on the gangrenous gray of the sky. A stalk of bananas, cut to ripen, flashed yellow as passion at the blackening edge of the forest, while its winy blossom swung from the end like the swollen head of a penis.

Had we been on this road before? The night wind shifted and carried the fluttering steel voices of drums. How many times had we passed here? The distant music swelled spicily, then weakened and died. Memory hung on the air. Had we ever known such sounds? Like spirits, they now seemed everywhere. A dissolving cloud unveiled two lots of cars, beside the road on either side. On the sloping edge of the cliff, a large pavilion sat in failing silhouette, etched into the liquid orange globe of the sun. We watched while the dim sun set and this glimpse of Villa Caimito flashed out.

The afternoon party was at its peak, wonderfully crowded. The dance floor, under a ceiling of tiny Christmas lights, was a glittering torrent of gyrations. Castanets chattered high in the air, tambourines drummed and rattled above the deejay's trumpet merengue. Quick wrists snapped; fervid, embraced hips churned the cool night's darkness. Both the old and young were here. There were men of a respectable age in white straw hats and pressed slacks, and younger men in shimmering outfits. The women, of every age, pulsed with the music in slender dresses and steep heels that teased the wooden floor with their rhythms.

Two boys, their arms mutually clasped, took to the dance floor with skittering thighs, then two girls with their young breasts pressed tightly against each other. *"¡Arriba! ¡Baile! ¡Baile! Keep it going! Dance! Dance!"* The music was glowing and sweaty. The dancers were aglow with smiles. Same-sex and opposite couples moved among each other freely, some swapping—all fluid and united. Seldom had I seen such unbridled spirit. I noticed— because it struck me as a rarity in a gay bar—that lovers held hands here. There was no hard-eyed cruising. Sexual pursuit seemed beside the point, though the night was charged. The darkness was electrically romantic.

Even the last of the twilight faded. I grew anxious that we would lose our way. We left quickly. The roads submerged themselves in jungle blackness. All remembered signs of the route lay beguiled. Had the journey been worth so brief a stay? The road back home is always changing. All paradises fade. Only the longing lasts. Why do we go on journeys, anyway? An adventure into one new moment's happiness and some chance fear. There are wordless understandings that reshape our souls: a deeper vision, the salsa dance of unknown truths. In the bursting smile or grief on a face we had never known before, we find ourselves.

Sometimes we may travel together, our paths intersecting or parallel. We will gaze upon a common thing and see it differently, and then a second time. We can never see the same. If we care about each other, we will share our peculiar insight and grow wise.

Twenty-five years before, my journey through homosexual longing had begun in Puerto Rico. Now it began again. I had far to go.

PART ONE

A SPRING
OF
DEPARTURES

CHAPTER 1

THE GAY JERUSALEM

THESE ARE THE WINTER DAYS OF 1987—THE LONG, COLD, BLEAK-gray New York days when I say to myself, "I will begin."

I have been numb.

I am one elbow on the floor. Maps of America fan wide before me, atlases of possibility—the red-, blue-, and gray-veined webs of hidden lives. I lie with them as I might with a man, ecstatic. Geographies redraw anatomies upon the page: masculine faces, strong arms, legs, the tight stateline of a stomach, twin Kansas Cities' tangled pubic tufts. Vermont hangs uncut, lubricated by a lake. Upright New Hampshire rubs beside it, foreskin crested in Quebec—*coucher à trois*. Through the desert of Nevada, a lone red road throbs like the artery of a lover's burning thigh.

I have taken many turns in life, some precipitous, no *wrong* turns, all necessities of accident and choice—though they are roads I would not keep to now. Which route shall I take? I plan a course of fifty thousand miles. They reproduce—they are promiscuous—become one hundred thousand miles, then more.

They are their own creation. The miles don't count. I will journey through light-years of the spirit.

Who am I as I set out?

By birth, I am mountain Irish, Appalachian, maddened
Pentecostal—searing claims on life that won't let go. Musician,
polemicist, dogmatist, scholar, teacher, wanderer, linguist, writer.
Married once and bitterly divorced. I'm the committed lover of
one man now, still fiery with desire: no army of men can quench
this need. Hurt son, social exile. How is it that so natural a thing
as same-sex love, longing for love, can dig so hot an abyss between some men and the rest of the world?

I am yet an angry activist—known "personality" in the gay
rights movement, unknown quantity—self-devouring. I am every
man I've ever known or touched. I'm anguished. I am afraid—of
dying in the sexual plague, of living when the gay world my
"brothers" and I created has ended. I cannot tell you, now, *why*
I'm going—or what I'm looking for. The yearning is desperate,
dull and blind. I have political propositions in mind, but I can't
articulate my heart. I know only this for sure: I must go.

I wait—for the money to travel, for the destined moment. Winter
will turn to spring before I leave to cross the continent. Then I
will begin a circle through the West, arriving in San Francisco in
the dawn of May Day. My plane will depart New York at midnight.

The plane—like a fat, winged snake—crawls up to the concourse
window, screaming. Two jocks become the first in line. There are
scowls, but no one argues—frontier law. I merge into the
roundup. My bags lock on to others', and I'm carried away. Michael, my lover, waves. I am swallowed by the gate.

It is four A.M. The San Francisco airport is desolate at this
pale hour. Delirious with fatigue, I ride the moving walkway at
the speed of dreams. In panchos and sombreros, an artist's salsa
band of skeletons stands beneath a dome of Plexiglas—
motionless, soundless, white as death. A William Wiley canvas
hangs above the baggage claim, "VOID" scrawled across its ab-

stract face—and a vague tombstone is inscribed, "is form, is void." The caption on the painting reads "One might see . . . ALL have a lot . . . in common after the dust settles . . . the glittering—remains."

It was a "San Francisco kind of day," as San Franciscans are apt to say. The sky was a lamp of azure. The breeze was crisp. Towering clouds, like an architect's dreams, blew in from the ocean.

Robert Chesley, a gay playwright, had lent me his apartment for the month while he was in Greece and so helped to determine the time of my California visit, proposing San Francisco again as first, the queen among gay cities. The apartment building perched on the sharp east slope of Buena Vista Hill, like a watchtower over a fortressed state. The view from his rooms was Mediterranean. Cypresses feathered the park at the top of the hill with emerald and lithe shadows. The white town below glistened tropically—sunlight bursting from a million facets. In the northwest valley, the roof tiles of the University of San Franciso, a Catholic school, burned blood red—Spanish mission style, antique passions. At the Golden Gate, the high-heeled towers of the bridge, shorn of fog, glistened scarlet. It was May Day in a metropolis of brilliants. From the window that faced southeast, I watched morning rise on Castro Street, where the pavement cut a steep path between sharp, ascending rows of motley gingerbread and gabled roofs—a bar line in a polychromatic score of syncopated rhythms.

The Castro is San Francisco's gay neighborhood, its *gayest* district. Nowhere else on earth do so many professed homosexuals live porch to porch. The area is a powerful voting block, the smoky back room of gay politics, the center of gay attention from the city's politicians and the press. The opening shots of the gay revolution may well have been fired at the Stonewall riots in New York's Greenwich Village, but the deepest aspirations of homosexual liberation had already long settled here, in the Castro—the all-American gay hometown.

Castro Street begins where precipitous Waller Street meets
Divisadero, down the hill from Buena Vista Park, around the corner from the Haight, the old hippie enclave. From there, it gently
dips and swells, surprised (at the rise at 14th Street) by the distant
valley, where the Castro Theater's tall marquee of neon filigree
bills campy, rerun movies—the stuff queens' dreams are made of.
It is here, at the bottom of this valley, that the Castro itself becomes a place, where Market Street—running out of the heart of
the financial district and past City Hall, following the route of the
yearly Gay Pride parade—penetrates Castro Street, and Harvey
Milk Plaza sits like a gate to the gay homeland.

I was in graduate school at the University of Chicago in 1977
when Harvey Milk was elected a San Francisco city supervisor—
the first openly homosexual official of such stature in the country.
I knew little of the burgeoning gayness of San Francisco then and
paid Milk's election no attention. Few in the heartlands did, I
think. Chicago was still creeping out of the McCarthy era. There
was little public display of homosexuality for so large a city. At U
of C, though the school had a long, liberal history—pinko and
defiant of red baiting—I had professors who glibly referred to
"faggots" in class. No one protested. Homosexuals hid. I was recently divorced then and fearfully, angrily finding my place as a
homosexual man. Then, in the fall of 1978, Milk, along with
progay Mayor George Mascone, was shot to death, assassinated in
his office at City Hall by Dan White, an ex-cop and antigay
former city supervisor. And many of us in Chicago, for the first
time, were startled out of our silent self-pity: bigotry no longer
meant some mere social inconvenience we could learn to dodge
deftly; it meant bloodshed. We rallied in the streets.

The gunshots that killed Harvey Milk that day gave shape to
San Francisco in our minds, not so much as a place by the bay,
but as the idea of freedom. It became the place of martyrs—the
Promised Land we longed to create wherever we lived. We
danced to the Village People's ecstatic "San Francisco" in the
Northside bars and raised our arms like men who'd at last seen a
vision of heaven.

Heaven was not just sex, but the comfort of honesty in the

workday world. Early on weekday mornings in the Castro, expertly groomed gay male brigades could be seen descending the hills in pin-striped streams and draining into the subway at Harvey Milk Plaza, washing away to legitimate jobs downtown. I'd slept late, on this my first day, and didn't make it down to the village till lunchtime. At noon the sidewalks were filled with the leisure crowd—off for the day, going to work late, the unemployed and unemployable, gay pilgrims to the only place in the civilized world truly tolerant of homosexuality. There were AIDS-stricken men on the arms of caretakers. By far, most of the strollers and shoppers were male. Counterculture eccentricities—frizzed hippie or biker's beards, a case or two of punk-spiked hair—cropped up here and there. But the general look was tidy: haircuts sharp as cadets', mustaches trimmed tightly, trim bodies, T-shirts and 501 jeans worn to leave no pectoral or pelvic contour unexplained. The gay "clone" of the 1970s remained.

The gay bars had been packed since breakfast. But little these days survived of the heavy cruising. The eyes on the street at noon seemed dulled, distracted. I had actually never known the Castro as a sexual paradise, except by exuberant secondhand stories. By the time I first visited here in 1982, the air was already poisoned with the terror of disease. Now the fog had settled down more deeply. Homoeroticism, for the time, had foundered tragically on the ground where its expression had been most fertile—an abrupt, deadly swing of the pendulum.

The lunchers today, in the diner where I ate, pored over the *Sentinel* and the *Bay Area Reporter,* free gay weeklies, with a devotion with which only the *Times* is read in New York. There was news of homosexual participation in Contragate. Carl R. "Spitz" Channell and several right-wing collaborators—their taste for men known all along to the CIA—had raised more than two million dollars for military aid to the Nicaraguan rebels: perversion condoned in the extremes of patriotism. Trenchant, campy comments hissed table to table.

And further headlines revealed that the last of San Francisco's now infamous bathhouses had been closed the previous weekend, victim to the politics of AIDS. This report drew murmurs of dissent—a matter that had once hotly divided the gay community.

The *Sentinel* reported a sharp two-year rise in antihomosexual crime in San Francisco. The *BAR* ran a story, buried deep in the back, on a fag-bashing victim left partly blind. This report drew no notice from the talkative diners, inured as homosexuals were, even here, to such violence, too much an American habit to be news.

One couple sat at a window table, intent on each other instead of the papers. The first man was tall and slender, his cropped, sand-brown hair growing thin. His cloud blue eyes were solicitous of his partner's, always smiling. Sometimes he spoke, as softly as rain. Mostly he listened.

His partner was his complement, of sorts, could well have been his lover—or his twin brother, in such a way do homosexual couples often self-select. His scrappy flattop was heavily moussed—unkempt more than conscious. A vacant row of earring holes ran up each ear. His face was strong, but in the window's white glare he looked worn out. His T-shirt sagged at the neck but drew at the sleeves, much too small for his shoulders. His biceps had no tone. The skin of his arms was mottled by purplish stains, the lesions of Kaposi's sarcoma, AIDS-related cancer.

I watched a bumblebee buzz about his head, as though to find some bloom in this weed patch. He fanned it away absently, but the bee persisted. In time, taking a napkin, he lined his hand, and, waiting until the intruder fluttered in place, he nabbed it. He was fast but not abrupt, like a dancer. Then he drew back his chair and went outside, where he rose on his tiptoes and balanced. In a moment he leapt, with his arm in the air, and with a flash of his palm set the bee free. The napkin gleamed in the sun, a startled spirit. The arching, painted sign on the restaurant's window crowned his head like a backward nimbus: "WITHOUT RESERVATIONS."

The Castro had always represented to me the very beginning of American gayness—the starting place and greatest achievement of gay self-definition. So it had seemed to me that there was no apter place to begin my gay transcontinental travels than this idealized enclave. Here gay life came as close as it could to the hometown domesticity many homosexuals had believed was forever denied them. Still, I was by nature wary of ideals and had always felt an inexorable need to parse them. How close did any of our fantasies come to fulfillment?

I had visited the Castro many times before but knew only one home-owning Castro couple well. I called Jason Thomas and Martin Peters, my longtime friends. Jason fairly squeaked with enthusiasm on the phone, after a customary, surprised pretense of caution. "Is this *really* you? Have you really come again to see our little gingerbread house in the city by the bay that *all* of our friends who don't live in San Francisco want to visit, with a real yard in the back with flowers and trees?" Jason sometimes spoke this way to me—the ritual silly speech of intimate friendship. "And I suppose you *also* want to see Blueberry, the sweetest little bird in the world, and the smartest, too?" I'd been present at Blueberry's purchase, in Chicago ten years earlier.

Jason was breathless, not nelly. He was not a queen, but more of a boyish innocent in this playful role, really, which still fit him at thirty-nine. His body was boyishly slender. He had big brown boyish eyes. His lover of eleven years was Martin, whom he'd pet-named "Humpo." "*Oh!*" Jason cried suddenly. "You've called at a *most* fortunate time! I hear him now! And he's parking his brand-new car that he just drove home from the dealer. He said we'd had old Whiskers long enough—two years is a long time for Humpo not to buy a new car."

Jason, Martin, and I had met in the early seventies in a graduate Chaucer seminar at the University of Chicago. Jason had been sullen in class. A Vermont Yankee and laconic Colgate graduate, he was disdainful of the university's British-y pretenses—its Oxford-like quads in the midst of the Southside's ghetto, its stuffy intellectualism. Martin was likewise condescending, though combative—if diffidently, irksomely proper about it. I couldn't help but take especial note of him. He was a graduate of Rice, a kind of aristocratic Texan with some Yankee influence somewhere in his childhood. Small and impeccably mannered, he sported a tidy black beard. His voice was soft and arrogant.

"Do you remember what it looks like, with so much fur on the chest for such a small creature?" Jason asked as Martin, fresh from buying the car, entered the living room. "Oh, *here* it is!"

In graduate school Martin had been perfectly Edwardian in his homosexuality—a gentleman bachelor of cultivated tastes, an academic and an aesthete. Despite his perch on the third floor of Regenstein Library—known as a gathering place for homosexuals—and the fact that he had a male lover, he was reticent to divulge his proclivities too apparently. I was still married then, and nonetheless more public. Martin, I could see, took surprised and disapproving notice of my wedding band but said nothing about it until he saw it consistently off my finger. He offered his condolences. I smartly told him that divorce was my release.

We argued over everything. Soon after leaving my wife, I became an apologist for gay rights. Martin was offended in those days, on principle, adducing all sorts of constitutional arguments to defend the private individual's right to discriminate, and the government's as well. He was enormously bright and sent me flying under the force of his intellect to reread Hamilton to save myself. "We're an *oppressed people*," I had insisted.

"You can't argue for change in American law from mere sentimentality," he would scold. Our disagreements were often bitter. And I wonder now if we'd have remained friends if Martin hadn't also met Jason that year and fallen madly in love.

"What a *cute* thing he is to have for my very own!" Jason squeaked into the phone, then grew mock sober. "Oh, no! Now it won't talk to me! I've embarrassed it, in its very own home. No one in the Castro's supposed to know about him and me."

The summer after Jason and Martin had met and moved in together, I met Michael, my mate, at the Belmont Rocks, a cruisy beach and former missile site on Chicago's Northside. And within the year the four of us newlyweds cemented a friendship in the mold of the Ricardos and Mertzes. We rented in the same building. But not even then had some intellectual or political alliance developed between Martin and me. I'd become more unforgivably ideological, a purist propagandizing homosexualist views still repugnant to Martin—and I think to Jason, too. But the dearest of friendships are built in spite of such conflicts, upon some indefinable sense of common journey. None of the four of us knew other same-sex couples well. Like most homosexual men and women as recently as the 1970s, we were striking out in the frightening, exciting terrain of committed same-sex love patternless and alone. Having been taught for a lifetime that homosexual love was, at best, illusory and fleeting, our relationships were a courageous experiment that our very lives depended upon. We became each other's intimate models. However much we disagreed about gay rights, we believed deeply in love and marriage. On that shared belief, more than anything else, we built a friendship—full of love that was contrary, deep, and lasting.

Jason and Martin's San Francisco house was within easy walking distance of where I was staying. Still, when they invited me for breakfast the very next morning, Martin insisted on picking me up—seizing every opportunity to parade his new car. He buzzed from the lobby at eight—always an early riser—then waited outside, leaning against his dark blue Mercedes like a man who'd bought an expensive toy and then gotten suddenly bashful about it. We hugged, he beamed, the Mercedes shined. Its insides smelled fresh of the showroom. The dashboard blinked, a scoreboard of digital panels. A blue, plastic ring around the ignition switch lit up for the key. Symbols flashed and soft buzzers and bells sounded commands and warnings.

Martin was full of warnings. "Don't buy *The New York Times* while you're in San Francisco. Don't compare San Francisco and New York: one of them is *not* noisy and dirty and full of people who say they want to leave and don't. And," he added, with futility in his voice, as I gestured to a thicket in Buena Vista Park where I'd seen young men trysting, "don't do anything illegal in the park."

Martin and Jason lived midway up a mercilessly steep street, easy, even by car, only to practiced San Franciscans. Martin had gotten the climb down well. They'd lived here only three years.

From Chicago they'd first moved to Philadelphia. Then—though they'd never been sexual liberationists, certainly not gay rights activists, and had never cultivated many close gay friends or even been that "out," really—they suddenly announced that Philadelphia was not gay enough for them, left good jobs, and immigrated to the Castro. I'd known other friends whose "gay identity" was a kind of religion to them who'd moved here and been happy. But Martin and Jason's comfort in this gayest city had always puzzled me. Perhaps it was simply the modern need not merely to accept, but to *understand* the people we love that kept me obsessed about their motivation. I found countless, oblique—and irritating—ways to get at it.

Jason was waiting for us at the head of the two steep flights of steps that led from a scarlet bed of geraniums to their front door. His hands were folded in front, like an eager child's. His eyes were wide. He wore a smile of anticipation. "You can*not* stay away from our pretty little house very long at all, can you?" he said as I topped the stairs. I had visited them the previous autumn.

Pausing inside the door, Jason silently guided my eyes with his to the music stand of the piano, an antique mahogany Steinway grand that sat by the bay window, where he'd opened the score of "San Francisco." Then, scurrying into the kitchen by Blueberry's cage, he turned on a tape deck and played an old rendition of the song, miming Jeanette MacDonald's every change of mood and flourish. The City Council, he explained—I think, facetiously—had voted "San Francisco" the city anthem, to please the Castro's campy homosexuals. "I Left My Heart in San Francisco" was elected the official ballad to please "straights." "San Francisco," he stated, "always keeps everybody happy. That's an important fact to remember while you're here."

Breakfast was served in the garden in the back, which was a high-fenced enclave, their Eden. The flowers were brilliant and delicate—camellias, purple cineraria, roses, carnations, gopher purge, petunias, a host of herbs, a heavenly chorus of impatiens. Jason and I took the settee, in the shade of the ginkgo tree. Martin set a chair in the sun, then, wincing—oddly, painfully—moved it out again and below the ornamental cherry. We began to gossip, plundering two black lacquer trays of sliced strawberries, Jason's own recipe for blueberry muffins—hot from the oven and laden with butter—juice, and white fluted cups of coffee.

We dished old friends. Martin and Jason had been deeply offended by two from Chicago who'd come to visit and criticized everything they'd found here. One of them, Arnold, had irksomely pressed them to build a rental apartment in their basement garage, for extra income. "I had to explain to him," Jason began, "that *we* live in San Francisco so we can live in a *house*, and their house in Chicago is really just an apartment because they rent part of it out to someone else.

"Of course," he conceded, now on a roll, "*some* people in San Francisco *do* turn their garages into mother-in-law apartments"—as they call such flats here. I must have seemed distracted. "I'm not telling you idle gossip about friends," he reprimanded me. "This is an important story."

Jim, from Chicago, had met a Chinese man, Chung Wing Yee, while vacationing in San Francisco. He'd returned to Chicago, packed, and moved here for love, carrying a very large dog and five cats with him. The lovers bought a house, but no sooner had they settled in than Wing Yee's mother, the wife of a former ambassador to the United States, arrived unannounced from Taiwan, intending to take up permanent residence with her son. "She didn't speak English and she wouldn't leave. So they built her a little home of her own in the basement. In a case like *that*, you just *have* to do that sort of thing."

I was fascinated, but not by Jason's argument for building mother-in-law apartments. What, I wondered, could Mother Chung think of her son's relationship? "It must be something of a culture shock for a little old lady from Taiwan," I stated.

Martin began, peremptorily, to gather dishes on a tray and take them back indoors. He paused icily, while the rainbow flag of gay liberation shuddered in the branches above him. "They *don't talk* about it," he answered. I snatched a final muffin from the bowl and intimately picked at the strawberries with my fingers.

This issue of parents and their sons' male lovers had always been, by far, the most forbidden topic between us.

"I know you think we're just being evasive," Jason challenged.

From the beginning of our friendship, I'd pressured them to "come out" to their parents. For all these years, the issue had been as clear as sin and righteousness to me: the cardinal law of gay liberation was, "Come out!" To me, and an army of other activists, that had meant angrily forcing the acceptance not merely of our same-sex desire, but of every turn of our sexual lives. To reject any aspect of our gay identity or sexual expression was to reject us wholly. I'd demanded that my parents proudly announce my homosexuality among family and friends and freely introduce Michael as my lover. They hadn't, of course. They wouldn't. Under the weight of my insistence, we'd fought bitterly again and again—and then they'd grown sullenly unresponsive to my diatribes. Certainly, over the years, they'd come more and more to accept Michael as my spouse but in other ways they had grown more recalcitrant. They refused to accept my politics wholesale. "I think," I complained to Jason, "that the word *gay* still gags them!" I was growing less cocksure, I told him, about my tactics, if not my goals. *"They still just can't say 'gay'!"*

He snapped. "Why *should* they?"

My politics having failed, I had no answer. "And *your* mother?" I parried. Margaret, Jason's mother, came for an annual visit, January through April. "Haven't the two of *you* talked yet?"

Martin's and Jason's faces hardened, stone against assault. I fell headlong. In Chicago there had always been a terrible rearrangement of rooms before Margaret's yearly stay, for discretion's sake. "One of you moved into the study and made it look like a bedroom when she came," I recalled. Their eyes froze and glared. "Well, *here* she's right in the middle of the gayest place on earth! How can you *not* talk?" Unspoken understandings seemed to me a form of cheating—and when it came to being gay and gay relationships, just another closet. Was that why they'd moved to San Francisco after all—*not* to talk?

"Darrell"—Jason was stern with me—"she *knows* we've lived

together all these years, she knows we sleep in the same bedroom and in the same bed, she knows we own this house together, and she still comes to visit. What *is* there to *talk* about? She doesn't need to know what we do in bed! She was coming to San Francisco before we ever *thought* of moving here. Every day she goes to the coffee shop on Castro Street and sits with all the guys. She knows about AIDS.

"She *sees* things. We took her to visit this couple. One of them is a real queen and crochets all this stuff. I mean, she's met *him*—and he's one of the most *exotic* creatures you could ever want to know. Now they share sewing secrets. You should see these wonderful aprons she embroidered for us—one for me and one for Martin—with our names."

"Well, that's *some* sort of recognition," I said cruelly. Sometimes we live out our own disappointments on the backs of our friends.

All of a sudden Martin turned his head toward the flower bed with a look of quick delight. "Look at the robin. That's unusual. The swallows usually keep them away. *Oh,*" he whispered, "he's listening for worms."

Its chest feathers burned fire orange. Sporadically it hopped, as brightly as if its feet were springs. It cocked its ear to the ground, then hopped again for finer tuning. In a moment it stopped dead, suspending its head a breath above the earth. Listening to rumblings human ears can't hear, it beaked the dirt with a lightning snap and missed.

Before I left their house that day, while Jason was showing me a new pair of running shorts that came in a little tote bag, Martin unbuttoned his jeans without warning and lowered his underwear. A crusted band of shingles blisters wrapped his waist, then descended into his crotch and down his thigh. "Being in the sun makes it sting," he said. The stress he was under at work, he insisted, had caused it. I was startled and suddenly, horribly sad. His message, I knew, was meant to be tacit. Illness was one of those things we could never talk about. In young gay men, shingles is presumptive of AIDS.

Over the next two years I followed the course of Martin's decline as best I could, though he remained typically quiet about it. Then some months after the earthquake of 1989 had devastated parts of the city and shaken lives, Jason called me in New York to say that Martin was again in the hospital and would not live much longer. I made the sudden trip to San Francisco and held him in my arms only hours before he died. *Dear Martin!* He was wasted, painful, aphasic, his once brilliant mind struggling to make sense of this world. For a moment I would have died with him if I could, a traveling companion to ease his journey. "Don't cry, it's okay," was all he could say as I stood beside him, grieving. Half in the other sphere, he seemed mystified by my anguish.

In Martin's final days I saw things about his life—about his and Jason's—that I'd never seen before, not that they hadn't been there all along to see. The closeness of death sharpens our failed vision. Nor was there any particular witnessed act that jolted me, but quiet revelations in the steady routine of my friend's dying. Jason's mother was always there for her son and for her son-in-law, as if her devotion could draw no distinction between them. And though they lived at a great distance, Martin's mother and father had been there, too, off and on, during the last, long, desperate weeks of their son's illness. Never had Martin spoken to them explicitly about his life with Jason, but if there were problems now between Jason and them, it had nothing to do with homosexuality. Martin's mother had kept a scapula beneath his pillow and had summoned a priest against her son's stated wishes—and so had infuriated Jason. But these were vaguer, smaller differences. "My son's life has been too short," Martin's mother told me, "but I know he's known a lot of love with Jason, maybe more than most men know in a long lifetime."

Jason was in a netherland of grief and disbelief. "Since the day Martin was diagnosed," he said, "death was never an option." Martin and Jason had been best buddies, inseparable friends, lovers, mind mates, soul mates with a separate world around them—they'd needed few other people in their lives. They fascinated each other. I had never known life partners happier together than they. Now I was watching their married life end—this wedded union between two friends with whom my lover and I had begun.

I watched Martin's face slip farther away, with his families gathered around him.

Only then did it strike me how narrowly I'd judged him and Jason all these years, in a time when such judgments seemed to carry much less consequence. Theirs, I came to believe, had simply been a different vision of the way the world must work—more ideal than the politically correct one. For Jason and Martin, the very act of "coming out," it occurred to me, lent credence to a denigrated difference between "gay" love and "straight" and claimed the bondage of labeling their love as heterosexual lovers are never required to do. They had moved to San Francisco, perhaps after all, *not* to talk about their homosexuality—to live in a sacred place that allowed their love to be tacitly understood and subverted the need to declare themselves. Their lives, it seemed to me then, were far more utopic, perhaps, than my politics had ever been.

If I saw the Castro as the best starting place for my travels, I also saw it as an apt place of departure. How far did any utopia extend? The Castro was white, male, educated, and affluent—not a cross section at all—and seemed to revel in its sameness and segregation from heterosexual society. Were there uncloseted homosexuals in San Francisco untouched by the Castro's gay ideal? Were there in the rest of America?

Robert Goldstein was my guide to the city's homosexuality outside the Castro. A poor man, he despised the gay middle class. He lectured me mercilessly about it: "They think if they buy a house and a couple of cars and mimic a heterosexual marriage, *then* they'll be accepted like straight men. But none of that changes the fact that to straights they're still queers. After all, that's what *queer* means." And here he quoted the dictionary by heart. Rob was a writer. " 'Of dubious character,' 'counterfeit,' " he stated. "They're not prepared to deal with their oppression as gay men. Their only choice is to fit in." Rob believed fervently in a debt of commonality that all homosexual men owed one another. The problem was simply that most of them, still benighted, had yet to recognize and embrace it for themselves. And I would say that this belief was one of the few Rob held in common with the Castro.

We met at the Cafe Flore on a Sunday evening at six. Rob had thick black wiry hair with threads of gray, a strong, slender nose, moist, brown eyes, a dark beard, soft lips, a well-carved chin. He was seated at a table for two in the garden, whose walls climbed with vines. Other patrons conversed animatedly, read serious books, wrote in journals, stared thoughtfully. The Cafe Flore was a bohemian, bourgeois place. Rob smiled knowingly, his plaid shirt buttoned to the neck. The heavy metal buckle of his thick black belt guarded the fly of his black Levi's. Black boots. His jacket, deep forest green—a delivery man's or a gas station attendant's—was pinned with a nameplate that announced "Troublemaker."

We'd met just once before, in April in New York—at a forum I had co-organized on the theater's response to AIDS. Bob Chesley, Bill Hoffman, Larry Kramer, Colleen Dewhurst, Joseph Papp—an all-star cast of playwrights, actors, and producers—had all spoken. Rob was distraught by what he saw.

"Coffee?" he asked, and brought me a cup from the self-serve counter. I took it back for more cream. His voice was soothing, wooing, though he was in a frenzy to talk. Ideas frantically leapt from him as if I had to agree to the whole disparate agenda of his politics before he'd take me anywhere. "We're abandoning our gay children," he insisted, "and neglecting our poor and elderly, while AIDS activists fight among themselves for fame."

It wasn't that all the playwrights in New York had attacked each other on stage or any such thing, not at all. It was the loss of common ground that had upset Rob most deeply. Playwright Larry Kramer, the pope among AIDS activists, had vilified every writer, gay or straight, whose work during the epidemic dealt with anything but AIDS—there being no greater grief in the world for him and no joy now imaginable.

"When will we care about more than AIDS?" Rob asked, and sipped his coffee slowly. He'd been raised in a public housing project in the South. He was dyslexic and had laboriously taught himself to read. He was severely manic-depressive, and so at high risk for suicide. Strong medications continued to fail him. Much of his life was spent in and out of psychiatric wards now. When he was out, he lived on public assistance, indigently. "When will gays start to really care about class oppression and the way we use it among ourselves?" he stated.

When I had nodded my agreement sufficiently, we set out. Rob had set this night up for me as though it were a giant canvas in a city of anxious images. I was to see the gay San Francisco of his disenfranchised experience. He walked me up Market Street and dismissively through the Castro. We walked—talking, mesmerized by talk—across 18th and 17th to the Arabs' market in the Mission, to buy a soda and a beer. Rob's room was in the largely Latin Mission district, nearby on Albion. Short, snug trees overreached the narrow street. A bottlebrush tree, its scarlet bristles tipped green, lazily swung its blooms in front of his building.

His lodging was in the back courtyard, secret through a whitewashed wooden passageway of padlocked storage locker doors. There sat the dilapidated clapboard cottage he shared with the beat poet Harold Norse, his mentor and muse. Rob's room lay to the left inside, opposite the curtained kitchen transom. Harold, who was elderly, went to bed every day at sundown. We whispered so as not to wake him. At home Rob lived with whispers.

A bare ceiling bulb lit the clutter. Secondhand paperbacks squeezed each other out on two low shelves. Genet and Ginsberg lay open, belly down. The dust jacket flap marked the place in *Naked Lunch*. There were literary journals, mostly poetry, in a falling stack, volumes flying loose at their hinges, creased pages, crinkled covers, ravaged reading, assault on authors, the plunder strewn around the room; the explosion of ideas settled everywhere.

Wretched furniture, all found objects, made a maze of the space in front of tall purple curtains hanging on the window like a reredos. Nothing Rob owned was new. A teddy bear, pale with age, sat like a Buddha overlooking the mess.

"Do you want to smoke?" Rob asked, reaching for his pipe and stash. He sat on a bed piled high with mattresses and toked, legs spread wide. "This thing in New York was rare for me," he offered. "I've stopped thinking of myself as sexual." He was reminiscing about a trick named Nick, not the gay playwrights. "Not because of AIDS," he added. "It's something very different from that. I'm just someplace else on sex." He made a sassy smile: "*Well*, *that* sounded very California, didn't it?"

The boy—the young man—he'd met was beautiful, he said: slender, nineteen or twenty, dark eyes, black hair, Latino or Italian. They'd met in the Village on gay Christopher Street at Boots & Saddles, a cowboy bar in name only. Nick had had his earphones on. "Which is the way he receives *all* his information," Rob said. "I asked him to let me hear what he was listening to. *You* wanta hear it?" He bounced off the bed. "It's *great* stuff!

"Nick's a hustler, you know," he suddenly added while searching futilely for the tape. "White trash, low-rent boy, street kid—like me. He didn't ask me to pay."

Nick lived on a subway grate at the Port Authority bus terminal on 42nd Street, where his every belonging was stowed in a locker. "He really didn't know how to take what I was giving him," Rob remembered. "You know . . . being with him that way and not demanding sex. He was used to being meat for men who go right for the ass." When Rob had taken him home, Nick had curled up with his face on Rob's chest and slept.

The next day Rob took Nick to "Epidemic, Center Stage," the forum where Rob and I met. Nick tuned it out, listening to a tape through his earphones. "I had to ask him to take them off and pay attention," Rob recalled. "Larry Kramer incensed him."

Nick wrote Rob notes: "This guy is an asshole." Rob wrote back: "These guys are your brothers. They're the leaders of your community. You have a lot to learn from them. Listen." Rob kept these pages from a notepad.

"Nick is somewhere *before* you see yourself as gay," Rob said.

It was lives like Nick's he would tour me through during the evening.

In the corner behind Rob's bed leaned a flimsy cross with a collection of 3D Jesus cards nailed upon it: Jesus with a bleeding heart and a saccharine, simian face; Jesus walking on water; a cutout Jesus with a succoring, outstretched hand. A soiled set of plastic tits hung by a thread from the middle. Nearby, a mournful plaster Blessed Virgin Mary stood in front of a poster of Marilyn Monroe. With sunglasses hooked at the back on her nimbus, she shielded her eyes from the Crucifixion. At her side stood her Son, the plastic Jesus. A black yarmulke covered his head, a huge sombrero. He gazed at the makeshift Calvary stolidly. A placard announced "Jesus Is Who He Says He Is" like a heavenly sign behind him.

"Were you Bar Mitzvahed?" I asked.

Rob picked through his stash. "Like I told you," he rasped melodramatically, "we were *white trash!*" He'd grown up in the Charleston, South Carolina, public housing projects. "Getting me Bar Mitzvahed wasn't one of our priorities," he said, choking on the grass. "It was important to my grandmother, though." She and the rest of the family, who lived on Long Island, were wealthy. "She arranged everything for me," Rob said. "I'm glad she did that. It was a wonderful gift."

He paused and smoked between his statements. His mother, he said, had always been the black sheep in the family. She'd married a laborer instead of a businessman and left home in New York to move south with him. Rob's father stayed unemployed. "So my mother had to earn all the money," Rob stated. As he toked, Jesus' yarmulke seemed to float like a black crescent moon behind his head. "She was a prostitute for most of my childhood." He confessed this matter-of-factly.

"Did you know that *then*?" I asked. I was aghast, not so much at the fact as at his easy admission of it.

"*Oh, yeah!* How *couldn't* I? She turned tricks in the apartment."

In the sixth grade, Rob quit school and became a sissy with hair to his waist, a street queen. He thought he wanted to become a woman and contemplated a surgical transformation. "I mean, that's what I thought I was supposed to be. That's what it meant to be a poor Charleston queer in the sixties," he said. Then suddenly he leapt from the bed, grabbing his jacket from a hook on the door. "You ready to go?" It was past midnight.

I sat a moment more, like a child curled up with a raconteur. I asked whether he ever saw his mother now and what she thought about his homosexuality.

"She's dead," he answered, and urged me from my chair. "She was beaten to death by a trick several years ago. It's only been the last few months I've been able to deal with that."

Even so abruptly we left on our tour and went first to Los Portales, a bar in the Mission district. Rob said no more about his family.

You enter Los Portales below a lighted Pepsi sign and past the white gloss glare of a food stand, where a steam table fumes like an oracle. A bouncer guards the narrow hallway. There, behind a window of protective glass, a young Latina, pallid with fluorescence, takes your dollar.

At the end of the barroom, across from the door, stiff gray curtains are gathered in fringe balls, framing an empty stage. To the left, debonair, dark men drink at a bar along the wall. Some chat. One lights another's cigarette. Most court the queens who, sleek in their shiny party dresses, sit shaded below potted palms. Their legs are crossed at the knee on the chrome-legged stools. Slick slacks, nylons, and patent-leather shoes catch tiny stars from a colorful string of lights beneath the counter.

In the center of the room, the tables are taken two by two by rougher *compañeros*. They survey the space impassively, aggressively spreading their legs. They smoke and swig beers—Coronas with lime—tipping the hand, keeping the elbow planted. The second hand grabs the thigh below the crotch. When a *chica* passes, they pout their lips in "her" direction, signaling their buddies. Two boys in the corner play pinball, slamming the front of the ringing machine with the heel of their palms.

"Don't cruise those guys," Rob warns, seeing me stare.

"They don't think of themselves as queer. Only the sissies are *maricón* here. Don't look too long at their 'girls,' either. I've seen some real rough brawls. The *real* fights are always over the 'women'! Now doesn't *that* sound like a bunch of drunk straight men?"

The jukebox plays a quick two-beat quartet: guitar, accordion, muted trumpet, maracas or castanets. A mirror ball above the dance floor—blue, green, orange, red—glitters the dancers' faces, which are coupled male and female in appearance only. Elbows, wrists, and hips swirl in the spicy air. The high wooden heels of cowboy boots pound the floor and flutter to the fiery rhythm of a Spanish guitar. Two brown men, their sombreros aloft, tightly dance around one "lady," sweating and competing for her hand. "*¡Rrrrrrr-ah!*" "*¡A-ha-a-a!*" "*¡Baile, baile!*" "Dance, dance!"

A mocha-colored drag queen enters the stage. The music stops. She nods her head unsmilingly from side to side, acknowledging the yodels, the stomping boots, the wild applause. She stands six feet—or more. Her ample back is disguised by the lavish, ballooning shoulders of her gown, which sharply cuts the outline of her breasts and cinches her tight waist. White, billowing yards of lace sweep the floor: a sort of wedding dress. Her head is luxuriously heaped with pitch black curls that fall in cascades. Her eyes are black, her lids are blue, her lips and high cheekbones are ruby. She flourishes her Spanish fan like a threat.

"*Es buen sacrificio de complacerles,*" she begins, and is interrupted by applause. She begins again, battling the ruffles around her chin. Her accent is richly dramatic, almost Castilian. She lifts her hands. "It is a great and good sacrifice for us to bring you pleasure here on this stage tonight—with all our miraculous talent and energies, all of our love, all of our devotion, *for* all of you, *with* all of you, *among* all of you. . . ." Her audience is rapt.

She welcomes "Marita" on stage, now clapping her hands above her head to cue applause, circling her arm to prime the music. Marita's lip-synched song starts without her. She hurries to catch up. "*Cuando calienta el sol . . .*" An admirer offers her three dollars. She stoops to seize them and kiss his lips—and loses three words of her song in the process.

Beside me, a boy with a dark Mayan face and raven hair stands uninterested, gossiping drunkenly with a group of friends. "*¡Lo vi!*" he exclaims. "I saw him in his little red Mazda and I said, '*Look* at that blond hair!' *¡Señor!*"

From the crowd, a woman approaches. She's boyishly thin. Hanging her hands by the thumbs in her waistband, she pins back the flaps of an old suit jacket. Her jeans cuff above her high-top tennies. She has thick wavy hair, mannishly cut and rich with tonic. She's a butch, carefully drawn—Jimmy Dean with the cheeks of an Andes Indian. Earlier she'd danced hip to hip with a buxom chick in steep red heels. Now her smile is sheepish, her face turned shyly. Seductive Marita—all-encompassing male/female—has stepped offstage to present her padded breasts for money. Her admirer gawks like a boy, abashed. Stricken, she tucks the false cleavage with cash and runs back to the arms of her girlfriend.

Suddenly a young, handsome man appears to dance before Marita, a smooth-skinned offering of flesh before the altar of the stage. Oblivious of the crowd, he has stripped to his underpants and, heatedly, ritually, back and forth, he runs his T-shirt through his legs. He grows erect. He wears white socks and white shiny shoes that flash like poltergeists against the floor. In his self-made myth he is the mad devotee of an Aztec goddess. He gazes upon the drag queen's face—like all men enthralled by the power of androgynes.

Rob and I return to his house to get stoned. We play five minutes of a Steve Grossman album—"*Where is he now? He's disappeared. . . .*"—then walk downtown past the housing projects. We keep an inviolable distance between us now—the exiled space of masculinity. Our steps are brusque. We callous our eye contact. Our voices are dead: we become straight men to protect ourselves.

After an hour we continue on. In a sheet of black sky above Market Street, a yellow half-moon lies naked on its belly and washes the dome of City Hall in platinum. Putrid in orange streetlight, derelicts search the plaza for handouts and a place to rest. A body lies curled on the pavement below the marquee of a dark theater. "That's a brother," Rob says, and stops me. "I used to see him at the bars." He is young, blond in the passing light of cars. His hair is a filthy nest. His clothes are rancid. Still handsome, he hugs himself asleep. "That man," Rob says, "is abandoned by his gay brothers—left to die by his own community."

A few doors down, an ink blue mural wraps a black-lit room at the Starlight. It's a maudlin memory of the San Francisco skyline. Old queens pose on stools around an island bar, under a faded, pink velvet canopy. Their bellies are bulbous with liquor and age and swell against the polyester tightness of their clothing. Their thin hair is puffed up on top of their heads, sprayed in place like domes of cotton candy. There burgeons a forest of toupees. At this late hour they sit as stiff as mannequins, lost in time.

Across the street in a rectangle of grass at a federal building, the ARC/AIDS Vigil is almost asleep—their line of defense gone weak in the darkness. Illegally, the vigilantes have bivouacked here for years against the plague and the government's indifference. Several lie enclosed in tents. In a bed barricading the courthouse door, one man sacks out fetally. A lesbian named Carol—back for the first time today from trying to live at home again in Tennessee—sits night guard duty. She reads by the pulsing light of a Coleman lantern. It is an article on AIDS from an obscure foreign journal. "D'you read this yet?" she asks. She is eager with belief: in a field of dying hope, another straw to grasp at. She has made AIDS the center of her world. "If ya wanna drop by tomorrow, I can get you a copy."

Within the blacker darkness of a huge, reaching tree, an ancient woman sits mummified in swathes of rags and foul clothing. Suddenly, in a wheelchair where she seemed to sleep, she propels herself from the night shade to the Vigil table. Stolidly she stuffs the contribution jar with fistfuls of bills, then, feeding the Vigil's hungry mascot dog a morsel, wheels wordless back to her treehouse. The vigilantes have long grown used to her charities. John, who's lived in a Vigil tent for two years, believes she may be an heiress. He hands me a rubber, with safe sex instructions, before I go, and a big button that reads "ARC/AIDS Vigil. A Civil Disobedience. We Rely on Love."

"I was in this porn shop once," Rob says as we walk across the plaza, "where some queen wrote on the wall by a glory hole, 'Please have safe sex. *Please!*' Queens are very busy right now getting out their message. *'Please!'* " He laughs to himself, adopting a tone of facetious eloquence. "Queens feel *so* misunderstood!"

The movie house at Golden Gate and Jones Street, in the Tenderloin, is open twenty-four hours a day. A ticket costs three dollars. The musty smell of urine, sweat, and semen curtains the door. Along one wall lighted cigarettes string the darkness, like a necklace of hot amber beads. The stench is filigreed with smoke and sultry. Your shoes stick to the floor. In pornographic bursts of silver from the screen, men's faces explode like grenades, and sudden, lustful eyes search for partners. White, black, Latino, Asian—a rainbow coalition of the desperate.

The dusty projector beam fires above two men embraced in their seats, while their frantic bodies flicker as fast as film clips. One, a "daddy," is chunky and bearded. Sitting erect, he holds his "boy," whose legs are propped on the row in front of them with his sweat pants gathered around his ankles. They kiss before the boy's face dips and disappears into the blackness. A close-up cock consumes the screen. A huge dripping mouth devours the phallus. The daddy stares at the film as he arches tightly. In the violent light he convulses terribly, then falls motionless. His nervous slave boy skitters away like a silent movie.

Several rows behind, a young man crawls, all fours in the scum on the floor, in a daze. After minutes he hides his head beneath a seat, turns in on himself, and lies quiet. "This place," Rob says, "has a reputation among the homeless for sex and cheap all-night shelter. Three dollars is something affordable." Rob has spent countless hours here in the writer's role, watching the degradation. These derelict men, he insists, are so reduced to their animal needs that gay identity is nothing more to them than cock sucking. "One of the few pleasures they have left," he states. AIDS is a less awful threat than their destitution. "Do you know about the homeless men with AIDS in Golden Gate Park?" Rob asks. "There's a camp of about twenty-five of them."

Back at Rob's house, we take a break, sit in silence before going to breakfast at Church Street Station, an all-night diner on Market and Church streets, a hostel for eccentrics. On the way, an excited redhead with a flattop—a friend of Rob's—approaches us, flailing his arms. "Richard's a theater person," Rob whispers wryly. "Writer, producer, director. *Too much!*"

Richard scurries across the street, grinning loudly. "Did you see Bette Davis on the Emmys?" he erupts, clutching, at *this* unlikely hour, an armful of scripts. *"Poor thing!* Going on and on and *on* till they . . . *Well!*" he gasps. "They simply had to take her offstage. *None* of the nominees got introduced!" He jams the heel of his palm in his teeth, dramatizing his exuberant, stifled outburst.

"Maybe," Rob says, "they should have considered how cruel it was to put her up there like that in the first place."

"Well . . . with her *stroke* and all . . . !" Richard answers.

Behind us, in the entrance to an apartment house, a young Latino holds the door open with his shoulder. He's handsome and slender. His T-shirt is cut off just below his chest, unveiling the fine, hairless musculature of his stomach. The three of us acknowledge his presence in turn, glancing obliquely, bouncing our eyebrows salaciously as we keep talking.

"Faggots!" he combusts, slamming the door. He runs to within several feet of us, fists up. We jump the curb. He jumps after us, swinging his leg, stabbing the air, missing my head by inches. *"Fa-gotes!"* he screams, thick with Spanish. "Shote ope! I kill you! *I kill you!*"

We cross the street briskly—refusing to fight, refusing to run—taking refuge from the streetlight in the shadow of a tree.

"Jesus!" Richard heaves. "Where did *that* come from? Did you see that guy's face? He's an *animal!*"

Rob leans against the tree, exhaling relief, watching our assailant go inside before he speaks. "All he has is his angry masculinity," he states breathlessly, preempting our terror with gender politics. "Look at this neighborhood! He's Latino, poor, he can barely speak English. Machismo's his last defense. *We* created him," Rob accuses inclusively. "The white middle class created a monster!"

"We *might* have fought back!" I spit acidly. I am shaking from fear and the insult. "There *are* three of us!"

"We *were* awfully loud. We woke him up."

"He *might* have just asked us to leave!"

"He didn't care about the noise. He *cared* about the *faggots*!"

"*Well*, that *certainly* was a calculated shirt, I think, to go queer bashing in."

"He *knew* fags won't fight back. *Three fags won't fight back!*"

"We *are* in *his* neighborhood."

Richard begins his walk home nervously. Rob continues his rap. "We want to believe that violence like that is always just another case of homophobia," he tells me. "It isn't. A lot of it's just low-rent boys getting back at the middle class—and *we're* the easiest target. That's what we mean by 'gay community'—white, male, privileged. When we get bashed, we're just keeping the dogs away from bourgeois straight men's doors."

However politically astute he seems to be, I cannot react so sympathetically. I've been badly beaten several times and called "fag." I've been called "fag" since childhood. It is like *nigger, spic, kike, cunt*—always a violent wound, a brutal epithet. It makes me rage.

As we sit at the diner for breakfast, an "empress of some importance in San Francisco"—a huge drag queen—stands at the counter to pay her check, grasping a cigarette and a takeout coffee. She scratches at the bottom of her bag, pursing her lips, searching for coins exasperatedly. Her makeup is exhausted, her eyes are red. A red nail breaks. Her face is stripped of unreality. It is daybreak.

It seems to me that what I've seen of this other homosexual life this night—the frenzied worship of maudlin femininity in the Latin bar, the degraded sexual use of bodies in the porn shop—is not all that different, really, from what I know of straight men. That it all involves the same sex is insignificant.

| | |

I took a long way home that morning, in the wake of a bevy of black-leather lesbians on huge motorbikes. I followed the distant path of their jet stream: past Gay Cleaners, the Chinese laundry; past the house at States Street where some vile soul had blackly scrawled, "Kill all Fag," and some more precise bigot had added a green plural "s"; past the yellow house at 15th Street where the thick warm taste of honeysuckle flavored the air; past the playground wall draped with red hibiscus where graffiti read "Straight AIDS is here"; past the quivering bottlebrush bush at the head of Castro Street. At the park at the top of the hill sat the borrowed apartment that had been my home for nearly a month now.

Perched like a tree dweller above the city, I watched the fog come in. Northwest, at the Golden Gate, its cloud slithered across the water's bed and swallowed the towers of the giant bridge like a great ghost snake. Eating for an hour, it lay full— then exploded, spilling itself into the breeze and across the hills until this once great thing became nothing.

The afternoon was hot and cloudless. The air lay corpse still—uncommon heat for San Francisco. The sun sucked out the sweetness of the cypresses. South from my window, in the park on a hill by the tennis court, a young man hid in the underbrush, naked. He played with his cock, watching another young man practice volleys. This vision attracted me outside early, but the voyeur was gone when I got there.

Soon yet another young man—brown, not past twenty, with a feather of a black mustache—climbed the slope, over and under the gnarling limbs of bushes. Dust, like clever Mercury's wings, plumed golden from beneath his feet. On arriving, he leaned on a fallen tree to catch his breath. He was shirtless. The crotch of his jeans, precisely where the head of his penis lay, was crosshatched with dark blue thread, a tempting jail window. His waistband was unbuttoned. "I am Fernando," he trilled. "Where are dju from?"

I was surprised he so quickly assumed I was not a San Franciscan.

"*Everybody* here is from *somewhere* else," he said, laughing. His English was good, the color of Spanish. "*¡Nalgas bonitas!* Pretty butts!" he said, craning to examine mine.

We sat on a log in the sun. Fernando was from El Salvador. He'd come here two and a half years before. He was studying to be a nurse. "I studied to be a doctor in my country, like my brother," he explained. "He treats the prostitutes with AIDS." Then why did he not go to medical school here? I wondered. Money. The language. "I cannot spell English very fast. So I must be what I can."

"And will you go home to work then?" I asked.

His face flashed. He answered sharply. "*No!* I will not go back to my country. I paid much money to stay here. I have all the documents now. There is too much fighting with guns over there. I am not political. I don't like to talk about that." His brother—the doctor—still lived in the capital, San Salvador, and remained under threat by death squads. "He is alone in my house. My other family—they all have left, or they are killed now."

He'd lost any certain count, but he thought either "fifteen or seventeen" of his family had already died in the civil war, murdered by U.S.-backed Salvadoran army men, in ambushes to exterminate leftists. "They shot my uncles on the beach," Fernando said. "One was just twenty-five years old. The other was twenty-six. I saw them die. There was no reason. They were not Communists." His young aunt, a schoolteacher, had been killed, too, for teaching her students *los sistemas políticos*, the various political systems and forms of government. "They said she was against El Salvador, but that was not true. The soldiers came into her house and cut her in the throat." He sliced his finger across his neck. "And also her daughters and sons. There were five. One boy was only six years old.

"They died together, the children."

Fernando had come to the United States to flee war, not to be gay, but he'd discovered gayness soon enough when he got here. He began quickly, seductively, to talk about that now, to leave the stories of horror behind him. His T-shirt hung from the hip of his jeans. He pulled it out, draped it on his head, to shield himself from the fierce sunshine. It advertised a bagel shop and read "We serve in bed." "What bars do dju go to?" he asked me.

I told him I'd been to Los Portales and La India Bonita and aimed to flatter him, speaking Spanish.

"Oh!" He was disappointed. "They are Latino. I don't go to them. I do not find what I want there." He grinned and dropped an arm around my shoulder. "I am looking for tall gringos!"

Fernando insisted that he'd only made love with one Latin—a Mexican lover. They'd met in San Francisco. "He was the only man who took my butts," he said. "He was not gay. He never got fucked. In my country, the gays are all drags. You have to be a *maricón* to be gay there."

But like a straight man, he seemed to think of making love only in terms of intercourse with consummation. In fact, one other man—a Salvadoran friend and a drag queen—had started to reverse the roles one time—tried to fuck him—but failed. Fernando ecstatically lapsed into Spanish when he spoke of him— Raul, who frequented the resort hotels in Los Chorros, in the Salvadoran mountains. There, married men, as Fernando put it, "went with the *maricones* into the jungle and took their *nalgas* from them. Everybody," he said, "knew Raul was a *maricón*. He wore dresses in the streets. *¡Estaba bien coludo!* So hung! *¡Dios!* Soch a meat. He tried to stick it in me, but I couldn't. It just went . . . *whoosh!*" He darted his finger, missing a small, rotted hole in our log. "And such a skinny boy! *¡Que placer, dolor, rico! ¡Papacito!* What pleasure! The pain! How rich it is! *¡Papi!*"

Fernando was much happier with homosexuality here. He told me, "I am gay and can still be a man"—and it sounded some-how like a warning. Then he said, "But I was not a gay when I was in my country. I was—how do you call it?—in a closet there. I didn't have anyone to be gay with. You have to have love to be gay." Through a clearing in the cypress trees, he motioned far downhill toward another, distant park, in the valley. "I live near that," he said earnestly. "It's a very gay place. We can go there all the afternoon and have love together."

Fernando was all alone in the United States. His mother had escaped several years before he did, to Guatemala with an American man. She'd gone there for love—and a ticket to freedom. Who could say which counted more? He had a sister in Los Angeles, but she'd long ago rejected him. She'd caught him, soon before they fled El Salvador, having sex with a boyfriend. "*I* was hafing *his* butts," Fernando protested. "But she couldn't see me good, so she was not sure I was being the man. I was going to live with her when we came here. Now she will not let me in her house again. I have told her I am gay like American men. Maybe she still thinks that if I am gay, I am a *maricón*, the woman. She will not see me anymore. I am sad for that."

Fernando and the men I met on Rob's tour might have represented, it appeared to me, a hidden homosexual population equal to—or even exceeding—the devoted membership of the Castro crowd. More than one kind of homosexuality survived in San Francisco. And it seemed that the gay identity of the Castro was perhaps a model of mainstream American culture and economic privilege as much as it was any natural fulfillment of homosexual desire. Still, I didn't want to judge the Castro and its ideals unfairly, and one evening soon after my night with Rob, I returned to have dinner with Benjamin Schatz—mid-twenties, handsome, Jewish, Harvard Law, an attorney with National Gay Rights Advocates, Zionistically gay. He was the quintessential man of the Castro. We'd met once, the spring before, in Atlanta at a Centers for Disease Control policy conference on testing "risk groups" for antibodies to the "AIDS virus." Most gay activists there seemed meek in the presence of the CDC's powerful bureaucrats. Almost alone, Ben had fiercely demanded more secure safeguards for confidentiality. I admired his courage.

Unlike many of San Francisco's gay immigrants, Ben hadn't moved here to flee intolerance, really. He'd immigrated in the heat of the AIDS epidemic to defend gay gains in the Promised Land—a soldierly volunteer in a continuing wave of young reinforcements, he stated.

I met him at his Castro office. He'd just returned from a

downtown press conference, announcing an antidiscrimination case NGRA had won somewhere in the American outback. He was dressing down—jeans and a maroon knit shirt—scribbling notes on a legal pad, putting his earring back in. His suit hung on the back of the door. "Both the media and the right wing," he said, "are desperate to say that all our emotional and political latitude has diminished in the epidemic, that our *power* is gone. But all of us aren't dead or dying. I know a *lot* of young men who've moved into San Francisco since the epidemic began. *I* did."

Ben had been raised in an accepting family, who knew of his homosexuality early on. "I mean," he qualified, "when I told them I was gay it wasn't like they said, 'Thank *God*! We were *hoping*!' But . . ." In 1962, when he was a toddler, his mother had found him dancing in his sister's dress to a recording of Beethoven. She'd gone to his father and said, "I'm worried Ben might be a homosexual." "My father," Ben said, "told her, 'So what? If this is what Ben's like, it must be good.' In college they were very proud of my involvement." Ben organized Harvard's first Gay & Lesbian Awareness Day.

What had drawn him here was a moral sense of obligation to his "own kind," as he would have it—an ethic he learned from his family's history. "We always understood suffering and oppression," he stated. His grandmother's family had been burned alive in a pogrom in Ukraine. "Part of this I look at as my heritage," he said. "Not just Jewish, but a *liberal* Jewish heritage that says, 'I've got to do something to stop this bigoted cruelty, wherever it happens.' For me the Holocaust has been the great educator. My standard since I was a kid was, 'Who will hide me?' I always hope for the best, but I have a genetic memory. There will always be cruelty."

At Luisa's Restaurant on Castro Street, we took a garden table in the back. Several smartly dressed gay pairs held hands, inmates of this paradisiacal American neighborhood where same-sex couples can show affection naturally. I watched the quiet conversations, envious of their ease, still wondering at the limits of this freedom. "Who," I asked Ben, "is gay liberation for—all the laws, the lawsuits, the educational campaigns?" I thought of the poor and alien men I'd met in the Mission and the Tenderloin. I thought of Rob, who'd introduced me to them. I thought of Ben's humane commitment. "What good does all that do for men and women who don't possess the white middle-class protections to begin with?"

He seemed genuinely stung by the question, but not at all unprepared to answer it. "Our community is so young. At this point we're just trying to create an atmosphere where the people who have the external trappings of power can survive antigay oppression. It's easier for us who wear Lacoste shirts and have read and traveled. In the black civil rights movements," he proposed, "wasn't it the middle class that marched first and defied segregation? People have to have a taste of possibility before they can get anywhere."

On the other hand, he believed, the gay rights movement held the same comfortable values as the rest of the affluent society. "I'd like to think it's inherently revolutionary," he said, "but that's not true. It's hard enough for people who are struggling to help others just like themselves, let alone reach out to people who are different."

I picked at the anchovies on my plate, thinking that Ben's statement was, as well, a facile justification for liberal heterosexuals who shied from homosexual causes. Ben called me back from my reverie. "I don't think that San Francisco's perfect," he conceded. "There's major bigotry here and callousness—from straights, and from gay men and lesbians toward other minorities, even if some of their members are gay, too. But I *can* say this: It's the best place I've found yet."

"The gay Jerusalem," I murmured absently, and for the moment perhaps not uncynically.

"I can't *believe* you say that!" Ben effused, drawing some attention to our table. "*I've* been saying that for a long time. It's a city on a hill, a divided city, a place for refugees. There are more Jewish people in New York than in Jerusalem, but you go as a Jew to Jerusalem for your *pride*. Gay people, wherever I travel, tell me, 'I lived in San Francisco and I loved it there.' When they move from here, they take home some of that pride with them.

"With all our problems, San Francisco's still a gathering place for the gay Diaspora. We have to keep gays coming here. *All* of us need to live for a while in a place where being gay is normal."

For Ben, as perhaps for most of the Castro's inhabitants, the enclave represented homosexual normalcy in a way that did not exist elsewhere. The Castro life was the natural model of homosexuality to which all homosexually desirous men were expected to conform—and by which they could be judged.

One of my last nights in San Francisco, I called Rob Goldstein to invite him on a tour, a piece of my gay journey through his city. I'd selected several Castro bars and the country-and-western Rawhide Bar downtown, where once a week for the month I'd been taking two-stepping lessons, preparing to meet gay cowboys in my travels toward the Rockies. I met him at the Pendulum. He was talking to Bill, a young Boston man on vacation. We sat on a bench at the end of the room. Bill was transfixed by the madness of the dancing. It was his final evening out before going home.

One white, built guy danced shirtless, his rhythms as strained as his torso. He jerked and ground his hard, sweating flesh. He was brittle. His eyes were closed. He was alone, stoned, working through his image of a man. A scrawny old man danced near him, lonely and shirtless, too, his failing skin tanned darkly with the desiccate color of youth. He angrily thrashed the air with feeble arms. He pouted, eyes in a squint, flailing to the fevered music ever more frantically. No one on the dance floor seemed to notice him. On the wall above his head there hung a huge framed poster of an Olympian physique, naked and smooth as a baby but for a bulging jock strap. The old man glared and shadow-boxed in front of him, spiteful with worship. Suddenly he struck his blow. The giant athlete staggered, his frame swaying dizzily against the wall. The codger, futile with success, hit again and again and again, till he slumped away exhausted, merely leaving the despised young god off balance.

When the deejay slipped into "El Dorado," a thin black adolescent dived from the bench onto the dance floor. He discoed, fisting the air, did salsa, stirring it with his hips. Bending over at the waist, he shimmied his shoulders like hummingbirds' wings. He crunched on the floor, jumped wild, threw back his head, skulked, stalked, clawed with his fingers, pawed and hoofed, crunched down to begin again, his face lit with a smile. Bird, animal and man, shaman in a rite, light spirit—he was lucid, precise, whatever the music told him to be. Pure joy.

"This, I think, is what we fight for," Bill said when the song had ended. "The possibilities. This kid is who we are when we're becoming free." Then he added thoughtfully, "I don't know what I'd do if I lived here. I wouldn't have a place, a role. I'm so used to running around being the outsider in Boston, always yelling, 'I'm gay. Gay rights! I'm gay!' It always seems so much of an *issue*. But in San Francisco, it seems more like a fact first and an issue second, if at all. That's what I love. We're free to move emotionally. We can play so many roles."

Outside, Rob and I got stoned and might have lost the night bingeing on political talk, as we were wont to do, dissecting the world. The munchies, however, saved us from ourselves, propelling us toward the Fourth Anniversary Chile Cook-off at the Rawhide Bar.

By the time we'd walked down Market Street to 7th and over to Harrison, a crowd of cowboys were already airing their meals outside, hats pushed back, one boot flat-soled against the wall, proudly rubbing their bellies for comfort. Inside, from a TV screen that overhung the bar, Dolly Parton watched competing men stand by their chile. Her volume turned down, she sang mum: the announcement of prizes had begun. "Gentlemen!" the emcee sang rhapsodically. "*Please* stay by your dishes!" There was a gritty shuffling of boots as the anxious audience arranged itself around a pool table converted to buffet.

Number two was thick, chunky with beef, and mild. Number five, in the metal bowl, was sweet. Number seven, the big iron pot, was spiced Mexican. Number twelve was Puerto Rican, a Crockpot soupy with sliced green peppers, tomatoes, onions, and beans—sweet when it hit the lips, tangy in the aftertaste.

"Number twelve, where are you? *Please* step up!" Manuel took his place behind his kettle, received one hundred dollars with a hard handshake, smiled as the flash went off—*first place!*

The music twanged Shelly West's cowgirl contralto. *"José Cuervo, you are a friend of mine. I'd like to drink you with a little salt and lime. . . ."* The dancing began with a rapid scuffle, in a swirling, two-stepping circle of paired straw hats, followers' brims angled to accommodate the leaders'.

"Did I kiss all the cowboys? Did I shoot out the lights? Did I dance on the bar? Did I start any fights? . . ." Backs stretched as straight as ranch hands', clasped hands held high, taut arms lassoing waists and shoulders, trots as nimble as horses' legs. Riding heels drummed the floor.

"Who's the cowboy who's sleepin' beside me? He's awful cute. How'd I get his shirt on? I had too much tequila last night. . . ." A short, chubby couple moved together perfectly, leg for leg, crotch for crotch, their boots stomping, sliding, kicking, pivoting. It was the flawless rhythm of a cowboy pirouette, partner turning partner round and round—mating's manly rite. *"All those little shooters, how I love to drink 'em down!"* Their fat red faces shined.

"*Look* at their faces!" Rob elbowed me excitedly. "Do you have any doubt what real power is when you see that?" As though distracted by the thought, he stared a moment more and spoke too softly.

"*What?*" I asked.

"I think our survivors," he said, still watching the couple take the floor, "the ones who survive this epidemic—will possess all the magic of wizards."

"You're my friend. You're the best, mi amigo. . . ."

Across from me, a little old man's white hair turned pink and blue, orange, green, and silver in the light from the mirror ball above the dance floor. In time he stood beside me. He had a handsome, slender face and luminous, sky blue eyes. He wore a string tie clasped by a silver brooch, from which a blue stone gleamed like a moon. The collar points of his blood red shirt were clamped in starlight silver. His leather-fringed jacket was red, his boots were of red lizard skin. His name was Eric, he said.

"Do you dance?" he asked.

"Not as well as these guys," I replied.

"Would you like a partner?" I nodded. "I'll have to strap this to my bike," he answered then, turning to reveal the bright red helmet he held beneath his arm. "Would you like to join me outside?" Curious, I followed.

A huge black Honda Gold Wing was hitched in front of the bar. Cowboys were admiring it while its round, shiny gas tank beamed their faces back like a midnight crystal ball. "You're not a regular here," Eric said, excusing his path through the crowd. "You from out of town?"

"New York," I answered. "I take it you come here often?"

He rode in once or twice a week to dance from across the bay, where he'd lived since boyhood. He hadn't lived in San Francisco proper since the 1906 quake, when he was four. "Our house didn't burn," he reassured me, waving his hand northwest toward where it stood. "But the place was shaking so bad you could feel it slamming against the house next door. I can remember my French governess at the time. She'd run frantic throughout the house, waving her arms and screaming, 'Le fin du monde vient!' Right away we moved across the bay to Marin," he recalled, "because the rest of the city was burning and you had no idea how things would end."

After the quake, most of the rest of his childhood was spent in schools in Europe—Bern, Zurich, Toledo. As a young man he moved to Germany. "Oh . . ." He sighed, wistful. "The Berlin gay bars in those days . . . the *dance* halls! You could rent private boxes to visit with a beau. Everything was very open then—until Hitler came to power."

Eric's lover, Heinrich, had courageously opposed the Nazis in Königsberg. In 1933, when Hitler was handed the chancellorship, they fled to France and began an odyssey of exile around the world. In time they ventured to Tahiti. The White Angel, as she was known—a San Francisco lady—offered to take them to the States aboard her yacht. They were three months at sea aboard her small ketch. But there were problems with the German's papers, and he couldn't stay in the United States. In between the cowboys' mechanical questions about Eric's bike, I heard him say, "We started looking for places in the world where he could go."

In 1935 the men went to Shanghai to live, where Eric performed as a pianist and singer in Sir Victor Sassoon's club. "People lived like royalty in Shanghai then," he remembered. "Summer houses and winter houses with fifteen or twenty servants. Everyone had cars and yachts. The club was crowded every night. And I had the most *wonderful* lovers! The Corps of Marines was over there." His romantic eyes gleamed wide. "I always had a marine sitting next to me at my piano."

It was in 1937 when this cosmopolitan idyll ended, when the Japanese started bombing Shanghai. The tourist ships stopped, nightlife died, fear settled in. Eric came back to the States in 1938 and consoled himself with a six-month bicycle trip through Mexico. Heinrich returned to visit Germany in 1939, and the Nazis caught him. "Shortly before the Nazis walked into Poland," Eric said, "I found out they'd forced him to fight with the Luftwaffe or go to prison. I got in touch with him once right after the war—but I didn't see him again until two years ago."

In 1985 Eric traveled to East Germany to visit Heinrich and his wife. "Of course," he explained quickly, "he's not gay anymore. He married a Hungarian actress. They have grown children. But there's no catch with the family whatsoever—they don't know. He and I can still talk about it, though, when the two of us are alone. It's just that I know he was my lover more than fifty years ago and a friend since 1931." For a moment he looked off, tranquil with amazement. Then suddenly he checked his watch and cried, "And *now* I have a lover sixty years younger than I! He's six feet four inches. I have to meet him soon. Would you like to dance?"

He ushered me through the crowd of cowboys and back onto the floor. "Do you want to lead?" he asked.

"I'm still learning," I said. The top of his snow white head was just below my eyes.

"Stand tall and keep your shoulders quiet," he instructed. "I'll guide you with my hand." He grasped my right hand high, hugged my waist tightly, covering the small of my back with the heart of his palm. "Slow, slow, quick-quick, slow, slow, quick-quick," he chanted the two-step softly to me, stepping off. With the warmest pressure from his fingertips at the bottom of my spine, he began to sweep me through the counterpoint of couples on the floor. Or, lifting his arm lyrically, he turned me away on the sole of my boot, then swirled me back through the arch again to his embrace.

When that dance ended he was brief and left, roaring across the Bay Bridge on his motorbike to meet his young lover on his. Eric had five motorcycles, all of different hues and powers.

Never had I visited San Francisco that I didn't leave feeling I'd been to no place real. I felt that way this time. For all its touted freedom, it was not a geography I could ever make my home. The Castro itself seemed too pat to me, too sure, ignorant of the possibilities that lay outside itself. I had never seen that more clearly than in my nights and days among the city's Latin homosexuals—these men for whom all top men were straight and only the effeminate (bottoms) were considered faggots. The Castro's brand of gay pride—gay men mutually loving gay men—could hardly embrace such a cultural vision. Nor might many self-respecting homosexuals long to be included in the particular gay ideas that made the Castro famous. For the first time it seemed to me that perhaps gay brotherhood was a cultural identity more than a natural one, that gay community had its limits. For years the Castro's all-American model of gay identity had been like religious dogma to me—a faith to which all homosexually desirous men should subscribe. Now I was beginning to learn that like all religions, the Castro could not fulfill its promise.

Still, there is a peculiar thing about the gayest of America's neighborhoods: every time I'm there I feel my heart move keenly—every elated emotion springing forth. My eyes watch, surprised at everything I see, on the edge of tears. I think it is the permission there to live a utopic vision that strikes me so sharply. In those brief moments the limits do not matter.

I am torn by the extremes. Perhaps that is what we mean by freedom.

CHAPTER 2

A DESERT
GAMBLE

ON THE FRIDAY BEFORE MEMORIAL DAY—A WEEK BEFORE THE Golden Gate Bridge's fiftieth birthday party—I rented a white Suzuki hatchback at the airport and practiced driving around the parking lot. A taxi- and subway-bound Manhattanite, I hadn't been behind a steering wheel in years. I tested the steering, pumped the brakes, then got out and kicked the tires, exorcising my worst anxieties with ritual. At the ramp to the Bayshore Freeway, I hesitated again, then flowed into the traffic with the radio up and all four windows down, suddenly exhilarated by the freedom of an automobile.

Within two hours I was sailing across the inland mountains at three thousand feet above San Francisco Bay. The snow-capped Sierras swept a valley dark with firs, and a tumbling cloud bank crashed in on top of itself. The trees on the lee grew thirsty and thin. Except at their very tops, their brittle limbs were broken off. They were skeletons with green toupees. The mountain peaks turned brusque and speared small clouds, which, like asphyxiating birds, flew by too slowly. Above Donner Summit, a lake sat trapped in a pass at five thousand feet and played on the edge of a precipice. The skirt of dirt below was strewn with the bone white trunks of fallen trees. The ridge was patched silver with snow. Rocks blanched in the cold: white rock, white earth, white trees, white sky. My white car glared in the light, changed gears, and groaned.

There was a sharp descent toward a railroad track and a river smooth as mercury. Far below, cabins stood around a mossy lake, where rowboats, tethered to shore, tested the water like frostbitten fingers. The mountains began to calm down. From a black umbrella of throbbing clouds, a sudden rain came. In the basin, where the mountains bottomed out, the sky dried dusk blue, and the horizon lit up like blue neon. Here, log cabins, cheap motels, and trailer parks placed among parched trees guarded the road and the railroad tracks that ran through Reno, Nevada.

The *Gayellow Pages* listed Dave's, which was closed, and the Hi-Ho Motor Lodge, which had no vacancy. The Hi-Ho clerk recommended the Fireside Inn, across the street from Harrah's. "Pro'ly," she said, "the only place with somethin' left till Monday."

"Is the Fireside gay, too?" I asked.

"*Gay?*" she gasped, stupefied. "It ain't *gay*, and *this-s-s*," she hissed, "ain't gay neither." A mistake in my source.

When I had checked in at the Fireside, I called "Rev. Ralph," a pastor at Reno's Metropolitan Community Church, which ministered mainly to gay men and lesbians. I'd gotten his number from the *Gayellow Pages* and talked to him once from San Francisco. He and his ex, a song leader at the church, shared a mobile home some distance from town. When I phoned they were leaving "the house" to drive in for the graveyard shift at the casinos where they moonlighted. Rev. Ralph was a maintenance man. Jamie, his ex, ran a roulette wheel. "Most everybody's on graveyard," the preacher said.

Jamie was going to the church to nap until work time. He invited me to meet him at the casino at 2:15 A.M. "I got my nametag on," he instructed me. "I'll be standin' by the wheel. I'm short and chubby, but still pretty cute. I cain't talk to you much tonight, but tomorrow I can sit with you during the morning service. I don't have nothin' to do, 'cept for opening prayer and sing-spiration. But I can still sit with you," he concluded, jubilant. "We got about thirty guys at the church," he volunteered, "and a couple drag queens that drops in sometimes. Other than them there's not usually any women. The lesbians are hard-nosed around here. They don't believe in Christ," he explained.

We ended our chat as the 6:59 whistled through town and set the crossing bells to clanging. I had seven hours' wait before my date with Jamie and set out to discover Reno alone. The downtown streets were rutted and unpaved, mazed with barricades and detours. Squat cement block buildings—white, with nervous, blinking signs—hunkered beneath roofs that were jungle gyms of ducts and vents and fans for air-conditioning. On the walls of the few high-rise hotels, their great names winked—Sundowner, Harrah's, Sands—while their lit perimeters scampered like hookers, frenzied with allure. Every building, great and small, hawked lodging, fast food, liquor, and gambling.

The strip—twenty minutes up and down—dazzled the town with the gaudy lure of its gambling holes, whose shimmering entrances gaped like mouths with rattling slot machines for teeth. I stopped at a Denny's to eat. All of the patrons but me played $50,000 Keno while they ate, then upped the ante to stronger drinks and higher stakes in the casino beside the dining room. In Reno, a chance on the future takes all. There were cocktail girls to ease you in, if easing was what you needed. Over their tops their breasts burst free, like an avalanche over a mountain, while a fleshy crescent moon of their buttocks escaped their tiny black skirts and panties. In steep black heels they pranced the room, dispensing a twenty-four-hour communion of liquid promise. A clattering chorus of coins made the slot machines sing. Congregations of cowboys primed the loud gods, staring at plums and oranges like pictographic answers to prayer, waiting for three cherries to appear. For gamblers the drinks were free.

Late in the evening, I explored the gay bars. The Rumpus Room, on a dark end of East 4th Street, was slow: a tough woman and four fey men watching a ballgame on TV. The Chute was jammed. Men skittered in by twos and threes through an entrance that did not announce itself. It might have been the facade for anything—a lone shark office or a bookie joint, except that either of those might have been more likely to have a window than a Reno gay bar.

An old white Cadillac cruised by, almost stopping. Out of all the windows, young rednecks hung contorted faces and their torsos like gruesome jack-in-the-boxes, all the way down to the waist. *"Faggots!"* they roared. "Get your faggot ass outa town!" Then they gunned it a block up the street and made a screeching U-turn for another pass. On the sidewalk, a terrified patron fell over himself to get inside.

The front rooms of the Chute were a mini–shopping center—an erotic bookstore and boutique and a Laundromat for laundering while you cruised. A poster warned, "Don't dye *anything* in these washers!"

Customers cramped shoulder to shoulder at the bar in crisp outfits—flats, slacks, and baggy cotton shirts with their collars up and long tails out, neck chains, bracelets, and overwrought rings. There was a clique of cowboys. Five mirror balls revolved above the dance floor, where a lone boy and a "fag hag" did "routines"—side by side, then one behind the other, action and stop action, mirrored motions, their sequences all doubled by the mirror on the wall, which fascinated them. Their shoulders shimmied. Her long hair lashed the air. His hair was spiked. He wore mascara. Satisfied with the look, they arched their eyebrows smugly. Delighted with himself, the boy screamed like a grade-school girl, and his girlfriend echoed him. In all the world there was room only for them.

When I left at one, a red Camaro cased the street, its furious passengers crying, *"Perverts! Faggots!"*

Downtown, Virginia Street was in a shambles of repairs, dirt that would make a bronco happy. Mountain men with whiskers and long, shaggy hair strutted between saloons. The lucky ones had ladies on their arms, who picked at the earth with their sharp heels like prospectors. The cold black air was cluttered with neon, the echoes of bells and coins, and melodic quips from video games. Disco brawled with country and western. Whoops and hollers staggered into the street. The Cal Neva's Pasta Place offered all-you-can-eat spaghetti for $2.75. In ten minutes on the slot machines at the Horseshoe, I won twenty dollars.

At the Nugget, where Jamie ran the wheel, the faces of the barkeeps had all worn out—long years or short, hard lives. Their ragged hair was just long enough to curtain the tops of their ears. They mixed drinks in glasses the size of cereal bowls for $1.25. I took a stool by a middle-aged dame with two-toned hair—brown at the skull, platinum from there to her shoulders. She was a Seattle gal. "I'm drinkin' for my birthday," she told me, the statement sloshing on her lips. Blearily she shuffled through her batch of Wheel of Fortune tickets. Excited at her prospects, she guffawed and slapped my back.

The bartender fed her with drinks on the house. He was campy as a queen. "I'm treatin' her as good as I would m'own mother," he said, grinning.

"I'm not *that* old!" she yodeled, and walloped me again.

I took my second pint of vodka to the slot machines and glibly lost my winnings and another ten dollars before Jamie came in, to a minute, at two-fifteen. I checked his nametag. He was maybe five feet six inches and carried a tummy. His chubby red face had a little red nose. His wavy red hair fluffed up like cotton candy. He shook my hand, then quickly went to work. He spun a barrel, drew out a stub, and announced the winning number. The gal from Seattle won. She whooped and bet on the wheel. It whirled past the jackpot of $699 and landed on $6. "*Damn!*" she cried, and, free of hope now, drank bottoms up.

Jamie rested against a nickel slot machine and, grinning, drawled right to the point of his gay life. "I'm forty-one. Ralph's fifty-nine. We was lovers. Not anymore. We just live together like roommates now. That's fine with me. And that's all there is to know."

A man passing out free Wheel of Fortune tickets went by again. I'd already tipped him two silver dollars. He strolled by lazily, a slow smile in his eyes. Was he bored, coming on to me, just hustling another silver dollar? I couldn't tell. From his apron he handed me a thicker stash this time. The maintenance woman had cowpoke short hair and wore heavy boots with overalls. Her wide leather belt held all her tools. She grabbed Jamie by the bicep to say hello. A firehouse of bells went off, a "bonanza" beginning. The woman announcer in the cashier's box was a baritone in the mike.

"Is *everyone* that works here gay?" I asked.

Jamie was startled. "Well, none of *them's* gay," he whispered back. "And none of them knows I am. O-o-oh," he guessed, "I think maybe there's thirty or forty percent of us that works the casinos. But not so many talks about it. You gotta be careful in Nevada, 'cause they'll fire you, you know. Being gay is against the law. Don't you think that's screwin' you around in a state that allows prostitutes?" His anger was timid. "I heard a few years back they caught a gay man and hung him. They can *hang* you here for that!"

(The next day at Sunday dinner, Rev. Ralph corrected the history. "That was back in the thirties," he said. "Not these days.")

Jamie's eyes were on the clock while a hungry mob milled around his wheel, desperate for round two. We arranged to meet in the morning again, right after Sunday school. He would just be getting off work.

The Metropolitan Community Church met in a borrowed basement across the street from the Wish House, where antiques and collectibles were sold. "I want to talk about my baptism in the spirit," the Sunday school teacher told his all-men's class. All of these men were casino employees and had worked all night. "When I get overcome by the spirit," the teacher confessed, "I cry a lot. Don, I've seen *you* on your knees during the service, raising your hands. Now, I was baptized by the spirit first, then later on had to get my water baptism done."

"It's gotta be both," said Don, sure as a Baptist. He had been baptized as a child but then backslid. "I need to be baptized again—*very badly*," he claimed.

"Darrell, have *you* been baptized?" the teacher asked.

I felt tight and breathless, but, disguising my mood, I effervesced. "By immersion!" swam out. I'd been baptized in the Church of the Nazarene when I was a child, in the oily Ohio River where it meets Ice Creek. I had suffered salvation back then and didn't want to say anything that would egg the class on to save me now. I played born-again. Everyone looked at me. Everyone smiled. To the last one, they wore sports jackets and slacks and wash-and-wear shirts with the collar folded out over the lapel. They all crossed their legs at the knee, with their Hush Puppies swinging like pendulums in a circle of folding chairs. I was wearing tennis shoes and jeans. I was suspect, I think.

At the end of the hour the teacher exclaimed, "Praise God!" then, sighing at his watch, wound down. There was to be a pool party at the deacon's house next Sunday. "Now if somebody wants to be baptized in the pool, that's fine with me. Just don't get me cryin'!" These men's weepy faith was a stream in the desert, watering their gambled lives. With our arms embracing our neighbors' shoulders, we stood in a circle to pray. "Jesus, thank you for bonding us with you," the teacher said, "and bringing us together as brothers this morning to love and worship in our own way. *Thank* you, Jesus!"

And everyone said, "Amen."

The whole of the church was in one room. A little Hammond organ warbled a call to worship. Jamie came up from behind and gave me a bear cub hug. "I couldn't do that last night," he said. He was all angelically changed, dressed in white— white pants, white vest over a pale pink shirt. With whispers and muffled laughs, the congregation greeted itself, hugging and squeezing their brothers' hands. The "pews" were rows of folding chairs. At the front a young man sat with an arm around his lover while they read from a Bible as big as their laps. A handsome heterosexual couple nodded and waved. "They come *all* the way from Sacramento," Jamie told me. I guessed that one of them at least swung both ways or was formerly gay. Jamie introduced me to a friend, a middle-aged woman in a blazer and slacks, who grasped my hand like a longtime friend. "Kathy," Jamie said, "had some trouble for a while with her church fam'ly here, but now she's come home." Her eyes welled with tears.

In the corner an old upright piano now quickened the spirit, banging the dotted polka rhythms of a gospel song. Jamie took his place to the side of the pulpit and led the singing. Rev. Ralph marched the aisle with a tambourine. *"I have a song that Jesus gave me. It was sent from heav'n above. There never was a sweeter me-lo-dy than the melody of love. . . ."* Jamie held the tone long on "love," building spiritual tension for the runaway refrain. *"In my heart there r-r-rings a me-lo-dy. There r-r-rings a me-lo-dy with heaven's har-mo-ny. . . . There rings a melody of love."* The people clapped rhythmically and lifted their arms toward heaven with their palms up to receive.

The sermon played on the use of "in" and "inn" in the Scripture. "There was no room *in* the *inn* for Jesus," panted the preacher. "And he still stands at our doors and knocks to get *in* and fill us with his *in*dwelling presence." Behind a pulpit shiny with shellac, the reverend paced. He had on a Roman collar and a clerical bib that was fuchsia instead of black. A pewter cross swept back and forth across his chest. A gold ring hooped his ear like a pirate's or a renegade's. His was an odd pasticcio, Pentecostal fire cloaked in gay and popish vestments. He had to appeal to everyone, it seemed to me. Gay exiles from every faith came to church here.

"Eleven years back, when Jamie and I first came to town," the reverend recalled, "God's dark-skinned children knew they belonged to the kingdom of heaven, but they knew they were getting left out awful bad down here." He remembered an arch in a park back then warning niggers to get out of town by sundown. It was painted out now but shone through when the sun hit it right. "That was a time not long ago when they couldn't get jobs or a place to live or even go to church where they wanted to.

"They were people like us! We're left out, too!"

Amens burst from the congregation.

"Now I hope none of those barriers are there," he continued, "because of un-Christian acts us gay people's done. I know some of our lives aren't led by Christ. You can be proud of yourself for comin' out the closet. But bein' outa the closet ain't enough," he thundered, and threw a curve. "Maybe once in a while you should go back *in*to a closet and spend some time alone in there with your soul.

"When I have an opportunity to go into our bars," he said sadly, "I don't find our young men and women there because they're happy. They aren't there because they're thirsty, neither—they've got Pepsi to drink at *home*. They're *lonely, empty!*

"I hear some of our brothers in those bars bragging about all the lovers they have. They're not ashamed of all that sex. We ought not to be ashamed of Christ, neither, our lover and friend. Christ's breast is big enough for all men to put their head on, like the apostle John." Suddenly he was struck by a reminiscence and laughed to himself. He recalled, "Years ago, before the Baptist church cast me out, I preached about being the bride of Christ. Ever see a bunch of straight men squirm, thinking of Jesus as their bride? With our gay men, you can talk like that, about marrying Jesus.

"That's one way we're different from straight people, I guess. But when we have the *in*dwelling spirit, we're *all* one family in Christ. Now we'd *better* start living in peace with each other while we're still on earth—black and white, the men and the women, gay and straight—because one of the things we'll have in heaven is an end to all this hatred and ill feelings and these terrible separations we've built up. God's straight children's gonna *have* to love us then."

"Thank you, Jesus!" someone wailed.

When the sermon had ended, the pastor and his deacons served communion—which, in spite of some Romanish maneuvers, contained Protestant grape juice Blood—and rebaptized Don from a flower vase in the midst of it. At the final prayer, the congregation spilled from its chairs and encircled the altar. Some fell to their knees, some stood, all prayed out loud, a homosexual Pentecost. They "lifted up" the navy boys killed when Iraq attacked the *Stark* and all the folk of Reno, Carson City, and

Sparks. They prayed for the sister of a man named Fred, "that she'll come to understand that all of us have lost loved ones to AIDS and allow us to put our arm around her. Let her know, dear Lord, that God's love comes through gay people, too. Don't let her lose out on that."

Rev. Ralph then took my face in his hands and, with his people gathered round him, prayed, "Thank you, Lord, for bringing this brother to Reno this morning to worship with us. Teach him to open his eyes and ears, but most of all his heart, as he crosses this great nation. Teach him to understand his people and to love 'em as they are. And, dear Jesus, let this book he writes help break down the things that separate us. Amen."

Growing up in this kind of faith, I had known the cruel side of it—the guilt, the self-hatred, the fearful exile of my desires. There had also been a generous and loving side that—in the bitter years of freeing myself from the Church—I had forgotten. This was not my faith now, nor could it ever be again. Still, it was an inexorable part of my life. Each Sunday these men at the MCC came together to heal the breach between their spirit and their sexuality in a way that had always eluded me. As we sang the gospel songs of my childhood and fervidly prayed, there were tears on my cheeks. I began to embrace my religious past and reconcile myself with it. From that day, I had one less war to fight.

CHAPTER 3

ROCKY
MOUNTAIN
RIDE

AN HOUR BEFORE DAWN ON MEMORIAL DAY, I WAS BACK AT Denny's breakfasting on a greasy plate of eggs, pork patties, hash browns, and biscuits. Using my atlas, I studied lonely Highway 50 through Nevada. My finger hiked over mountains and deserts to the melodies of electronic slot machines. Screens spinning with bars and fruits winked at bleary-eyed, all-night gamblers.

Suddenly a round of bells startled me out of my reverie. A woman in a ruffled party dress began to scream and swig down Kahlúa. She had won the jackpot on a slot machine. Across the street, a freight train wailed through town. It was six-thirty. I left a pond of yellow coagulating on my plate and set out across the Wild West's desolation for Colorado Springs, Colorado.

Dr. Thomas O'Reilly lived in Colorado Springs and was an officer and M.D. in the army. Sometimes he claimed to be gay and sometimes not. He claimed he had never had sex with a man, though his social life was almost without exception among gay men. At Fort Carson, the army base where he was stationed, he specialized in treating HIV-infected men and women. A friend of mine in New York, an AIDS educator, had met him through a gay AIDS organization, which Dr. O'Reilly had contacted to make new friends. It struck me as macabre that a man should seek out an AIDS organization as his primary source of friends. My friend told me, "You've *got* to meet this one!" and arranged for me to visit.

I called Tom before I left Reno and told him my plans: I would leave on Tuesday morning and arrive at his house by dinnertime. I had not yet looked at a map and figured mileage. To my back east mind, two and a half states was one day's drive. There was a baffled silence on the phone.

"Are you *flying?*" he asked. "Have you looked at a map?" He was as forbearing as a boot camp sergeant might be. "Count it up!" he commanded. "You're in the *West!*" It would take me two or three days to get past the Rockies. I adjusted my schedule and determined to do it in two.

The scrawl on an overpass outside Reno demanded, "Trust Jesus." There I picked up the two-lane U.S. 50, which ran some one thousand miles from Reno to the lee of the Rockies, where Colorado Springs sat on knolls in the Plains. A cow lay in the highway, which was only two cows wide. Salt licks glistened by the road like corroded mirrors.

The dusty land was a tapestry of rock and sagebrush. High, barren, brown-green mounds rose and fell on the flatness like the giant spines of sleeping lizards. A low, blue haze of mountains scalloped the far horizon, toward which the rough road ran straight as a ruler and empty of cars. A yellow, shotgunned sign staggered to one side and warned, "Cattle on Highway Next 110 Miles." Occasionally dirt roads to abandoned mines ran straight, like silver threads, toward the horizon and then disappeared.

I had never been in a desert before. I stopped and lay on my stomach in the middle of the road to photograph the endless yellow line. Turning on my back, I sunned in the dry, cold air till my fears of desolate places conjured snakes. I leapt up and ran back to my car ahead of the phantom rattlers, wincing from their fangs. Mammoth rocks, sharp as arrowheads, speared the sand.

The highway began to climb. "Marie Osmond and the Osmond Brothers in concert!" the radio hissed, then gasped its last breath and died out.

A gate hung free on a post by one rusty hinge, fenceless on both sides. Bone white fences, their decaying circuits incomplete, fenced in nothing. To the north a cold, wet cloud ceiling fell to the desert floor. New snow painted the mountaintops ahead.

At Cold Spring Station—a circle of stones that once was a telegraph station for the Pony Express—snow powdered the pale green sagebrush. Then suddenly, between the Desatoyas and New Pass Summit, a blizzard blinded the road, and it took me three hours to reach Austin Summit, little more than thirty miles. At the summit—7,484 feet—the snow stopped suddenly. Pale clouds tumbled down the mountainside, shivering against the cliffs. Over the desert floor below huge white plumes hung death still, misty cathedrals suspended in blue breath. Far to the east, the Toquima Mountains trudged the wilderness, packing thunderheads on their backs, black and stung with lightning. A beam of sunlight seared a cloud bank to the north. Below it a platinum circle of earth lay as brilliant as Canaan.

Late that cold afternoon I groggily stopped at a gas station cum tavern that seemed barely to hang on a high cliff. From here one could watch the wide abandon of Nevada exit into derelict Utah. I asked for coffee.

"You're gonna have a wait," the lone attendant grunted, wiping oil off her fingers with an oily rag. "Ain't none brewed." She wore a pair of oily overalls and an oily rawhide jacket. She smelled of gasoline and oil.

"How long?"

"Tomorrow mornin'," she snapped.

The mountain curves had grown sharp. I needed caffeine. I would lose my battle against my eyelids in a couple of miles. "Could you make more now?" I begged.

"For *one cup*?" she bellowed angrily, and walked away.

I pleaded my case. "Won't you have some with me?"

She stood in the door of the tavern and growled, "I don't drink coffee 'fore I go to bed." It was not four-thirty yet, but the sun was beginning to set. "You can git some at my neighbor's down the road. The Y. It's right in the Y of the road."

"How far?"

" 'Bout forty miles," she barked, and slammed the door. Like a cold pup, I watched her windows for a while but didn't dare.

The Y was a lime green cement block pit stop, with a peeling lime green mobile home beside it, one room long. It sat a few miles west of the Utah line, where a sign by the rocky road pointed toward Snake Valley and a crudely paved road crawled south toward Snake Creek. These eponyms brought reptiles to my mind. Over coffee I asked about snakes and nervously watched the floor, which lay open to the desert through the gap around the door.

"Rattlers!" rasped the waitress, who wore a cowgirl shirt and weathered jeans. She sat on the stool next to mine, spread her knees, and planted her elbows on them. I drew my knees together and hooked my boots on the highest rung. "Up here in town a ways," she whispered, looking me in the eye, "a flash flood'll drag 'em down the mountain and wash 'em into your yard. Now you can kill the damn things pretty good if you got yourself a hoe." She chopped at the floor beside me, grasping the imaginary handle with her fists. "But you cain't bury the ends too close together or they'll find each other and grow back together again. Then they get even madder. That's what an Indian told me."

The light was grim. I scanned the floor. "How far *are* we from town, anyway?" I asked, grimacing.

A codger, drunk in the corner, chimed in. "In miles or *beers?*" He slapped his thigh and belched. "Miles out here is measured in six-packs, son. Town's about three-ee cans—unless the troopers catch you. Then *you* get *canned.*" He guffawed at his pun.

The waitress slid from her stool and stoked the potbellied stove. Its mouth pulsed orange and ate a log. A white-haired grandma came out of the back with a fresh tray of cinnamon rolls. She stacked them by a shoebox that served as a mailbox, where mail was picked up once a day. I ate two buns. They were hot and chewy, sticky with swirls of cinnamon. There was a heavy silence. These people made me nervous.

"These are wonderful!" I sang, and sounded New Yorkish or gay. They stared. I calmed down. "I'd love to have the recipe." They stared again. "Family secret?" I suggested.

"I got no family secrets," the old woman said. Her voice was guarded but kind. "My hands just know what to do. Now, I got a neighbor," she offered, "she's got a gas station 'bout forty miles back. *She* might have a recipe of some kind. That's if you really gotta have one." I declined.

At the Utah border, a Mormon farm town sat where nothing but cold and breathless dustlands glowed rose in the failing sun. This was a no-man's-land, a geographic truce between Utah's ascetic Mormons and depraved Nevada's gamblers and whores. In the north, protected by the great gray wings of a thundercloud, a white stone mountain soared all alone, carved by the wind into battlements and Mormon temple towers, bossed with mossy rocks as gnarled as gargoyles. High cliffs, as though scarred by tears, walled the road, a narrow moat yielding no approach. Far to the east, the Cricket Mountains, round and low, shined hot pink beside the cobalt stain of Sevier Lake, which my atlas insisted was dry. I explored it for myself. A long road strewn with fang-sharp rocks and serpents' holes ended in a swath of sand before it reached the water. The lake rolled shallow, foam-fringed waves ashore—they were thick and slow with salt—and misted the evening air with indigo.

By the time I reached the first range of the central Utah Mountains, they were submerged in the midnight sky. I found a room in Salinas, where there were no traffic lights and one intersection boasted four-way stop signs. It was one A.M. I had been on the road more than eighteen hours. I built a bunker of blankets on my bed and defended myself against the late spring cold.

The second day I again began my journey at daybreak. The mountains here were stony and steep. Poplars and firs stood laced with May snow. A sign threatened, "Next Services 107 miles." There was one rest stop on this road, where a plea in the men's room read, "Stretch my shit hole as far as you can. Let's do it! When? Where?" (And a paranoid hand wrote, "AIDS is genocide.") There is no barren land from which such desire won't spring—not even Utah's Mormon desolation. I have come to believe that all men nurture it in some deep canyon of their longing. Above a urinal, a trucker's message offered love: "18-wheelers with a *head*ache Call for 'Slick' on CB/12 for a world Trip & T.L.C." Another man offered his wife. He wrote, "I'll watch." Men are tutored from boyhood by these john stall personals and learn their possibilities. We hold the privilege close among ourselves. Returning to his wife from a piss, the husband and father does not divulge the pleasure he takes in this network news while perching on a public pot, nor whether he sought relief by his own hand or another's. It is a shamed and sacred secret, a bond in all men's mute fraternity.

Up the road the slopes turned calm and khaki, nubbed with sagebrush, juniper, and piñon like a chenille bedspread. Gray clouds, thin as veils, whispered shadows on the sand, then, angered by a sudden wind, swelled up and silenced the hills in a blizzard. After a sweeping curve and a sharp descent, the storm stopped as suddenly as it had begun, and in a burst of sun the mountains fell through the desert floor so fast they took my stomach. Here, canyons ate the earth. Buttes and mesas built of crumbling plates of copper—orange, red, green—stood like the ruined catacombs of prehistoric giants and their monster pets.

Along this high plateau, a black wind soon blew furious. Tumbleweeds, shivering with speed, played chicken with the car. As if shaken by the confrontation, it ran in nervous swerves. A rush of hail, white as locusts, swarmed the road. In the east, the pluming head of a thundercloud split open like a judgment. Between its rolling halves, a summit gleamed with snow, its sharp peak haloed in a brilliant swirl of clouds. It was a trompe l'oeil lift-off, an enormous white-coned missile on a launch: my first sight of the Rocky Mountains rising. It took my breath.

Grand Junction, Colorado, sits in a river valley on the mountain's western foot. I stopped there for gas. "This ain't 'cold country' yet," the pump boy told me, directing my gaze to the lofty peaks ahead. We were at 4,600 feet, higher than many noble mountains in the East. "This ground around here ain't low," he proclaimed. "But it ain't high enough to freeze your blood or make ya dizzy, neither." His tiny rhinestone earring glinted.

I tried to chat him up. I said, "I was born in the Appalachians myself."

"Those ain't mountains!" he spat. "If it ain't got snow at the top year-round, it ain't no mountain. What you got back east is *hills.*" He tossed that homeward phrase that westerners love to use, whether or not they've ever been past the Mississippi. The real mountains were "fourteeners," he tutored me—snowbound and 14,000 feet. "We got fifty-six of 'em in this state." He was indignant.

The initial climb was more gentle, in fact, than inclines I had driven the day before. It took seventy miles and a couple of hours to ascend 1,200 feet. The Rockies allowed the road such erotic languor: they swelled and throbbed for 250 miles west to east—no hurry at all to reach a climax. Past a town named Montrose, the sharp climbs began. In time, overproud mesas stretched and reached and at the greedy height of hubris shoved a river and its valley into a deep ravine. The highway looped and clung and in all its desperation had the surprised effect of a giant ribbon wrapping a gift box of lavish landscape. An abandoned ranch sat bone gray and leaned with the wind like a weather vane. Occasional silk brown horses switched their tails behind white fences—counting cars like impassive bureaucrats—while bemused, pampered sheep flocked on knolls in rich beige coats and black cashmere stockings, pornographic. Higher yet, spruces so richly green they were black spiraled from cliffs inlaid with snow like ivory. Neon streaks of snow drew mountaintops in the east, where treeless peaks were too high and cold to ever melt.

At 8,000 feet the fragile air made me euphoric. Enormous clouds constructed schooners in the sky, which, sailing heedlessly high, wrecked themselves on cliffs and shadowed a turquoise lake with flotsam mist. I watched. A dinosaur fish unthawed, I thought. (The windy sunlight gave it scales.) Maybe a fishy idol of lamé, a lost tribe's jeweled god. Dopey in the altitude, I nearly dozed—saw visions—laughed madly at the schizophrenic beauty of the heights.

And it seemed to me that the mountains too went mad, as if, above all laws, they could mock gravity, turn liquid, and fly. The highway skimmed the edge, where a high wave of earth rolled up one side, sliding away like vertigo. (On a hairpin curve, I picked up a hippy hitchhiker and his mongrel dog.) Steep slopes folded into one another, gave way apocalyptically to valleys, heaved like high seas, throwing dirt, rock, lakes, and trees against the sky. The car whined and almost died, kicked in, turned its tight-lipped lament into a victor's whistle as it sprinted up to a struggling line of traffic. Ecstatic, I sped past a sluggish truck, then took on a Cadillac and its Airstream camper. (The mongrel growled till I sobered up.)

The air was cold and clear. There was nothing but rock and snow and sky here among sparse, scrawny firs. Slowly, coldly now, the bright gold dome of a mountain ascended into place, glorious as a crown. "That's Monarch," my awestruck passenger stated. A few hundred feet below its peak, its shoulder was collared with snow. Spruces, like emeralds in ermine, made an approach, but all stopped breathless at the treeline. A ski lift, dangling chairs like costume jewelry, gaudily ran on to the top. An engraved sign along the road announced the Continental Divide. Monarch stood in a lineage of summits that ruled the continent's rivers, decreeing which would pour into the Atlantic Ocean, which into the Pacific. Here, where America's rapid waters were divided and the land lay summarily cut in two, the icy wind blew fierce and unrelenting. Still, but for its gasps in the curls of my ears, the forceful world was strangely silent. One wonders, at times like these, at the petty differences we humans devise to divide us.

When I arrived in Colorado Springs, the sun had dropped behind the mountains. Their monstrous silhouette tore the evening ragged and erupted with dying orange rays. The vast Midwest's Great Plains lay walled off from light. Dr. Tom O'Reilly's house sat in dusk on a treeless knoll some distance outside the city. It was built from a pattern that repeated itself throughout the new subdivision. They were bi- or trilevel gabled frames with panels of cedar or redwood around the windows—American chalets.

I knocked on the door. Tom opened it with a hard army smile and barked, "Let's get your things inside." He was tall enough to play pro basketball and broad across the shoulders. He was handsome and blond and barely thirty. Neither pleasant nor unpleasant, he was anxious above all. Not once did he look in my face. He kept his eyes on my car, evaluating the personnel by the hardware. I'd been driving thirteen hours. I was tired and wished for a welcome with some warmth to it, perhaps a handshake. Instead he bounded past me on the stairs and out into the driveway where I'd parked, holding out his hand for the trunk key. A good guest, I pretended to be undistressed and scampered after him.

The surrounding houses were under construction yet, except one at the bottom of the driveway. There, a neighbor couple were on their deck, trying to get the barbecue lighted. "Great night for a barbecue," Tom yelled, and saluted brusquely. A breeze carried the greeting away. The man cupped his ear. Tom grabbed all five of my bags and began to march them in. The snow on the mountaintops mirrored the darkening sky, while a galaxy of lights flickered on in the city. "I can't imagine living around such beauty," I said honestly, trying to gain his confidence. I laughed. "And I'm so used to New York, I can't even imagine gay people living in such big *houses.*"

"*Shh!*" he demanded, snapping his gaze from side to side. It halted briefly on his neighbors, who were well out of earshot. "You're gonna have to watch what you say while you're here," he warned beneath his breath. "All of my neighbors are military. And there're still men doing construction on these houses." He poked his chin toward the empty shells, then seemed to catch himself. I was noticing the tiny lights that flashed on along the fresh red gravel of his drive and sidewalk. He manufactured a smile. "Aren't those *fun?*" he sang dully.

Two other guests watched the news in the "family room," which was beyond a spacious kitchen counter. Gino—who might have been as young as twenty, as old as twenty-five—had been an enlisted man and was recently discharged from the army. He was staying with Tom until his new apartment was ready. Derek, who looked more than thirty, had been in the air force—cadet, commissioned officer, an English instructor here at the academy. Now he taught remedial reading at a junior college. Tom telegraphed all these data sternly standing on the stairs. Dinner was almost on the table. He showed me to my room and stood there with an eager posture that seemed both to demand my first impressions and to insist that they be positive.

The wall-to-wall carpet was plush. The windows were covered with Levelor blinds. The walls were a smart shade of beige. The woodwork was natural. The furniture was Scandinavian modern and brand new, except in my room, where the dresser and bed were turn of the century. "From my grandparents' house in Nebraska," he stated. He clapped his hands once and rubbed his palms, like a man who had won something. "A few nice pieces they wanted me to have," he said.

"You have a beautiful house!" I overenthused. There was an overwhelming sense of newness about the place. Even the towels in my bathroom smelled of the store.

"*Fun* home!" he agreed, and ordered me to have a look around. He kept an eye on me as he started downstairs, as if to see whether I'd continue to examine his house admiringly or boorishly start unpacking. As uncomfortable with him as he seemed with me, I snooped and tried to learn something about him fast.

Tom's bedroom had a king-size bed, which was unmade from the morning. The vanity top in the bath was littered with shaving gear and expensive after-shaves, colognes, deodorants, moisturizers, and astringents. Dirty slacks, socks, workout shirts, and nylon shorts made a path from the tub to a hamper in the walk-in closet, the door to which stood open. *The Naked Ape* lay open on the tousled covers of his bed. On the wall above a nightstand hung a poignant drawing by Peter Kunz Opfersei. Two male figures stood face to face in a box. They were featureless except for flaccid penises. Each reached for the other's embrace but were frozen at a distance.

Fine art photography hung everywhere. Otherwise, books predominated in Tom's house. The spacious hall at the top of the stairs held a brand-new desk and PC and a basket of *Interview* magazines. There were shelves of books from floor to ceiling. There were shelves of autographed books of photography. There were Gore Vidal and Gay Talese, Irving, Updike, and Theroux's *Mosquito Coast*—all authors of certain cachet. I wondered how much they influenced him. There was—it surprised me—a remarkable library, too, of homosexual writings of the kind that literate (though hardly militant) gay men were expected to be acquainted with. Here were Armistead Maupin's tales of San Francisco, next to which, oddly, sat a military travel guide and *The Right Stuff*. Here too were the novels of Edmund White; John Rechy's *Sexual Outlaw*; Nancy and Casey Adair's *Word Is Out*; Vito Russo's *Celluloid Closet*; *The Gay/Lesbian Almanac*; and Bell and Weinberg's *Homosexualities: A Study of Diversity Among Men and Women*. The shelf on AIDS also included *The Joy of Gay Sex*—and, curiously, *The Joy of Lesbian Sex*—as if sex and disease were the same. *Sex and the Brain* sat next to *Sexual Intercourse from Greeting to Goodbye*.

A trail of photographs on the downstairs walls led from the living room into the kitchen, where Tom was balancing a number of chores at once. An Ansel Adams poster was inscribed "For Tom O'Reilly, Ansel Adams," and Rothe's "The Poet" read "To Tom with love and thanks." I was impressed by his associations. The final picture on this path was opposite the sink—a fine, black-and-white trompe l'oeil of a country cottage painted on an urban brick wall. It was Tom's own work. "I love this picture!" I exclaimed, surprised to find it there.

Keeping busy with the meal, he darted his eyes toward the wall as if to remind himself and commented flatly, "Oh! From the Omaha exhibit," pouring one pot into another. "Fun show."

Gino and Derek still watched the news, a report on the Reverend Jim Bakker's sexual exploits with women and alleged adventures with men.

"*Assholes!*" Gino thundered at the TV. Derek hissed.

Tom seemed oblivious. "Don't these preachers make you crazy?" I asked.

"I don't understand religion," he said distractedly, pinching spice into a sauce while staring at the recipe. "Maybe it's good for people with AIDS—an opiate for the dying. I don't really know." This opened the only topic that seemed truly to interest him.

Tom was an army flight surgeon and said he had a lot of enlisted men who were positive for HIV. "We put 'em in the hospital for observation, then follow them as long as they stay in the army. So I know how those guys feel who're infected with the virus," he claimed. "You want a beer?"

He handed me a Coors. I was dismayed. For years now I had lived ghettoized in the gay community and expected any homosexual worth his salt to be "PC"—"politically correct." One lost perspective. Coors was on the gay list of bans for supporting antigay causes. It had been said that in 1976 Coors gave money to Anita Bryant, the born-again spokeswoman for Florida orange growers, to help her fight the Dade County gay rights ordinance. Drinking Coors was as traitorous as drinking orange juice. I couldn't put the can to my lips.

"Something wrong?" Tom asked. It was a tempest in a teapot of principles. I explained it to him succinctly. "I don't keep up," he said, unimpressed. A sudden wave of defiance swept over me, in this house where it didn't matter. I pulled the tab and swigged.

"Gay activists cause a lot of grief," he stated, and returned to AIDS with a case in point. He had first gotten involved with AIDS when he was stationed in San Antonio. He had helped to form a support organization there. "I helped *form* it!" he exploded. "Then a bunch of gay activists showed up. They wanted me to march in the street with them and pass out flyers on safe sex. This is a medical disease, not a political cause. I'm a military doc, not an activist. I can't be. I told them no. Activists can't accept that. That's the problem with those types. Either I did it their way, or they didn't want my help at all. I quit."

He simmered and stirred a poivrade as he spoke. The message was indignant, his voice was not. Unadept at passion, he opted for something like ebullience. Ill-suited to his words, it came off as nonchalance.

I tried to sympathize, though I couldn't get an emotional fix on him. I said, "It can't be easy to be gay in the army."

I had hit a raw nerve. "I'm not gay." Ruthlessly he chopped asparagus stalks, not looking up. "I don't like that word. It implies a life-style. I'm yuppie and nonpolitical. I'm *not* gay."

I faltered. "Maybe you *have* to feel that way—I mean, just because you're in the military. Maybe you could be less closeted if—"

"*I'm not closeted,*" he cut me off in a voice that pretended congeniality but warded off further comment. "I don't like that word, either. I'm just not 'open.' If they thought I was gay, I'd be out in three days." He tasted his beer, and perhaps thinking that he'd sounded too much like the victim, he said, "I could make three times as much if I left. So I don't care. But I don't see any reason to push it. The army put me through school. I owe them.

"They know I have gay friends. That comes under AIDS. But if it was outside of AIDS, they could boot me just for fraternizing with homosexuals, the way the regs are written."

He washed a kettle he'd been using, hung it on the big iron rack of shiny gourmet pots above the counter where I sat. He admired his cookware. "Aren't those *fun?*" he bubbled, deadpan. "I bought everything new. *Great* house. Low mortgage, good deal. Designed it myself, made a lot of fun changes in the plan." I listened absently and fingered a bump in the laminate of the countertop. "Oh," he said. "That's nothing. I got too good a deal on this house to worry about *that.*" When he called us to dinner, I saw him slowly rub his hand across the Formica, frowning as he examined its imperfections.

The dining room table was elaborately set—new linen, new china, new silverware, and new cut-crystal goblets. On the wall below the peak of the "cathedral ceiling" hung a dark oil painting in a big gilt frame, a nineteenth-century landscape of cows in a pasture. Candles gave the room a formal glow. I was seated at one side of the table, alone. Gino and Derek sat together across from me. Tom sat at the head. A silver silk kimono embroidered with roses hung on the wall behind him. He busily served each plate—filet mignon and poivrade sauce, baked potato, precise counts of asparagus, salad, and yeast rolls. He held up a bottle of Beaujolais and buoyantly announced the winery and vintage. His connoisseur's concerns were so cheery, they came off as diffident and pressed his guests into an awkward round of hmms. Having poured and sat down, he glanced at each plate as if soliciting praise. We gave it. He ate skittishly and watched our reaction to our every bite.

Tom wasn't still for long. He excused himself again and again—to find a forgotten condiment, turn the oven off or coffee maker on, check on something unspecified, *anything*, to soap a grease spot he found on his shirt, keeping a thousand chaoses under his control. Gino and Derek said little, except for some gossip intimate to them. They were longtime friends. The slow clank of silverware against the silence made me squirm. "Gay Pride Week is coming up, I think," I wedged in clumsily, hoping for some common ground. "Do you all have a parade in Colorado Springs?" The question missed its mark. They looked at each other mutely and wondered, then agreed on no. I pressed on. Were there any good gay bars in town? All of them were boring, they said. "Tired locals, queens, and old men," grumbled Gino.

What about the army and air force men? What about the *cadets*? This military question sparked interest. Servicemen drove to Denver for the bars and baths, ninety minutes away on the interstate. Going out in Colorado Springs would be *asking* for a court-martial. Army and air force intelligence men were planted here. Gino, Derek, and Tom themselves had met in Denver, in fact, not in town. Through the men they met in Denver, they found themselves hooked into a whole gay military network back in "Colo Springs," as longtime inhabitants called it. Tom, who'd finished eating, flew into the kitchen with his plate.

Derek and Gino opened up. "It's like that cadet on the train up Pike's Peak," Derek sneered to Gino. Gino grinned at a favorite story. "The center for the air force hockey team! He sat there looking me up and down in front of all his buddies. He was so horny he was crazy, cruising me all the way up the mountain. Not *one* of his jock friends noticed." Derek's voice was tight and hostile. Gino was amused. "Those guys go through life with blinders on. They just *can't* admit all those faggots exist. *Cadets,*" he rasped, "are *stupid.* The military is stupid. *Straights are stupid.*"

Tom ran in from the kitchen and swiped Derek's plate. "You're done?" he asked, affirming Derek's story in that two-sided tone of voice that admitted the injured man's grievance while allowing that the perpetrator had been right, too. "Derek *did* have problems with the air force," Tom told me. "Cadets can really be immature. You gotta be careful getting involved with them."

"*Involved?*" Derek growled toward the kitchen door, where Tom was again disappearing. "The *cadet,* Tom, got *involved* with *me.* A guy comes on to you like *that* and you're supposed to *know* he's out to frame you?"

It was Gino who addressed the puzzlement on my face. "About five years ago," he explained, smirking, "some hot cadet got Derek booted out of the air force."

Derek kept arguing with Tom. "Out of *no*where you've got a bright, gorgeous cadet telling you he's in *love* with you and you're supposed to figure it out, '*Oh,* this must be a test, a setup. He's an intelligence agent. I'm supposed to prove what a man I am and turn him in. He'll get a commendation for his work and I will, too.' That's *great!*" he mocked, punching the air with his fist. "That's the way you get to *be* somebody in the air force? We'd have helped each other's careers—*if* I hadn't failed the test."

With the slightest furrow across his brow, Tom poured the coffee. Then the sympathy passed, leaving his face impartial, the buddy role subordinated to the officer's. "Maybe they wouldn't have gone after you so hard if that cadet hadn't been your student," he uttered fairly. "They're not gonna go lenient on anything that's that big of a problem for morale."

"I never *slept* with him," Derek countered. "I wrote him *letters.*" His voice was edged with bitterness, but all of it seemed oddly directed at air force injustice and not at Tom, whose judicial distance only set the proper limits on a military friendship and maintained his right relationship to duty. Besides, their argument relied on a rhythm of opinions too precise to be spontaneous. It seemed rehearsed, a debate they'd had countless times before.

"They set you up," I figured out. "They suspected you're gay."

"*No one* suspected I was gay," Derek answered, "because I act very straight. Everyone was shocked."

At last he sketched his story in sufficient detail to make some sense. When Derek still taught English at the academy, that last year of his air force career, he grew especially fond of one quick-witted cadet. They began to spend a lot of time together. It was platonic. They talked about writing and literature. As their friendship deepened, they talked about those great mysteries that adults always indulge in with erotic protégés a certain number of years their junior: parents, school, ambition, love, the meaning of life. "What hurt most about that whole affair," Derek complained, "is that I'd helped that kid a lot."

That December Derek went back home to his folks' for the holidays. The cadet sent Derek a Christmas card that encouraged romance—though Derek declined to be specific about the language except to say, "It was enough for anyone to go on." Derek wrote back in kind, and they continued to exchange letters until January, when classes began again. During the early winter, a rumor spread across campus that three cadets were under investigation for homosexuality—all three implicated in a letter one of them had written, which found its way to the Office of Special Investigation, the air force intelligence unit. The letter further hinted at a whole secret circle of homosexual cadets, which the OSI committed itself to expose and purge. One day OSI officers showed up in Derek's office in the classroom building where he taught.

"It didn't bother me at all when I saw them," he said. "I thought they had to be there about someone else. I was just curious about which cadet or faculty member they would ask me about and why he was under investigation." The officers came inside and locked the door. "They lied. They *lied* to me!" Derek said. "They told me the cadet had signed a statement that he'd had sex with me—and we'd never done a *thing* but *hold* each other. When they showed me my name on the interrogation list, the earth opened up under my feet. My whole life was over. They said they had all the letters and had matched up the fingerprints with mine. They handed me a *confession* to sign. Either I signed it or they'd bring me up for a court-martial. I was ruined either way.

"I *thought* about suicide. I thought about that, then said, 'No! I'm gonna *get* him.' I stayed alive just to make sure he couldn't ever destroy anyone else like that again. My shrink told me to move, to get out of here and move to a bigger city. I told him the only way I could deal with this was to stay here where everyone had to face me."

The cadet resigned. Derek never saw him again. "All of that goes in my autobiography," he said. "I've written a couple of hundred pages already. They're *all* going to have to confront the truth when the book gets published—all my old air force buddies who deserted when they heard allegations like that.

"Did you ever read *1984*?" he asked. "Everyone thinks Orwell was writing a perfect description of Russia—thought police, friends reporting on one another. But it's *here*. The targets are just different. In this country, if you're gay, you live in a police state. It's that simple."

"A lot of progress has been made since that all happened." Tom felt the need to defend the military. "They've confronted the AIDS epidemic head on—so they know they've got a lot of gays in the ranks. They could clean house if they wanted to, but you don't see them doing it. They let Gino get away with it!" he said as if trying to subvert this unpleasant tack.

"I was too smart for the bastards," Gino said. "You guys could take a few lessons from the GI."

"*Girlfriend!*" Tom manically cried, like a man trying on drag for the very first time who had just slipped into heels. He abandoned himself to a fit of guffaws. I felt embarrassed for him. I think he thought that camping would prove his ease among gay men. He made a bad queen.

Derek held tight to the original topic. "You know that's not true. They go after gays as much as they ever did," he retorted.

Tom cleared dishes while Derek spoke. The very dullness of his manner announced that this would be the end of the evening. Derek kept going. "About two times every year they uncover another 'scandal,'" he insisted. "Just two months ago, the highest-ranking cadet in his class and the guy with the *next* highest rank resigned under investigation. One of them got drunk one night and spilled everything to some other cadets who didn't like what they heard. They turned him in, and the whole thing started again. And you stand there and tell us they do a good job with AIDS. There's a difference." But by this time Tom was standing at a row of rheostats beside the dining room door. In his left hand he balanced a stack of dirty china. With his right he turned out the lights.

At ten Derek was gone. Gino was taking a leak in the downstairs john with the door half-open. I was headed upstairs when a cry stopped me midway. "Yuh-uh-uk! Asparagus piss!" Gino wailed. "They oughta use this stuff for chemical warfare!"

"Asparagus come's a lot worse!" I yelled back, raunchy by reflex. Tom was standing at the bottom of the stairs, down to his skivvies and T-shirt. "Ever get that stuff in your mouth?" I laughed. He smiled feebly, like a high school boy who didn't get a dirty joke. I was chagrined. "Maybe," I fumbled, "we'd stopped doing that before you came out."

"I'm not 'out,'" he corrected me again. This time he spoke without bravado, not pleading but coldly confessional. He drew close and, for the first time since I met him, looked into my eyes. "I admit I have homosexual tendencies, but I can't say I'm gay. I've never had the experience."

I was used to closet cases, not to virgins, and I found myself as embarrassed by his sudden intimacy as I had been by his camp.

"I've never had sex. Or," he retracted quickly, "I've never had risky sex. I've kissed—maybe three men in my whole life. We held, cuddled. I don't really think of that as having sex." There were long silences between each statement but none that invited response. He stood tall and stiff, icily guarding this disclosure he forced on himself, warning me from prying. In some odd way, I thought, he was reaching out. "The gays I meet in the army are all infected. That's the only way I meet them—I'm their doc. I knew three guys who died of AIDS before I ever knew there was such a thing as 'being gay' or a 'gay subculture.' Those were three people I would've liked to develop a relationship with—if it hadn't been for their disease. There was another guy in New York. He called a couple weeks ago to tell me he had PCP"— AIDS-related pneumonia—"and KS"—an AIDS-related cancer. "Guess I'll have to watch him die, too."

It was peculiar how numb his voice was. In spite of the pain inherent in the words, he chilled it out of them. His face was diagnostic. "Those guys were my ideals, hard to find in the gay world," he said. "They were military and athletic. You don't find those guys in the bars. The kinds of guys I grew up with in Nebraska—I'm fixated on that. Maybe I'll outgrow it, maybe I won't. Guys more like me—those are the gays I feel comfortable with.

"You seen *Parting Glances?*" he asked suddenly. I had reviewed it for *Film Comment*. A gay couple, together for years, faced AIDS in the life of a friend and wrestled with the flaws in their marriage. "Maybe I romanticize," he said, "but that's the kind of relationship I want—a lover who acts like a normal man. I fantasize about having someone I'm interested in that's masculine and cute who'll be interested back in *me*. I think"—he paused—"that would give me the confidence to think of *myself* as attractive to men. Does that make sense?"

Once on a flight from New York, Tom met one of the actors. For the first time he seemed sincerely exuberant. He was adolescent with enthusiasm. "I've seen that film twelve times," he said. "I recognized him right away on the plane. He's *straight*, you know!" This pleased him. "He showed me pictures of his wife and kids. I apologized if I was bothering him—I didn't want him to think I was hitting on him. Lot of people must think he's gay just because he played a gay role. He said that didn't bother him a bit. I told him I hoped it wouldn't make him uncomfortable if I let him know how many gay men thought of him as a role model."

Tom had gotten his autograph on a napkin. "I *never* do that sorta thing," he insisted. "*Great*, meeting him. *Fun guy!*" He grew wistful. "Just makes me think a lot about this house," he said. He glanced around the living room. A picture window overlooked the lights of Pike's Peak and Cheyenne Mountain, where a massive military complex lay deep within the rock, hidden against a nuclear attack. "This place is so big. Sometimes it makes my life feel empty. All this and only me to live in it."

Then he was bullish again. I was growing used to his mood swings. "You're a gay activist," he told me, waving me toward the basement door. "This photography I've been working on is something you'd be interested in. It's a sort of psychological study of the bodies of HIV-positive men from a gay bar. I got them to pose."

The basement was a mess of construction with a single bare bulb on the ceiling. From a box in a dusky corner, Tom drew out an envelope of proof sheets. Each held twenty frames, each frame pictured a body part—shoulder, elbow, hand, knee—until a whole naked body had more or less been cataloged. They struck me as passionless, pictures for a medical textbook. "This is a radical approach to portraying the body," he told me, "beyond anything done before. The focus isn't erotic," he explained, "but sexuality and disease, eroticism and illness—the way they work in tandem. What d'you think?"

I stared, aghast. All of the joints and limbs looked healthy.

"These aren't men with AIDS or ARC," he corroborated, "just men with antibodies to the virus."

I didn't get the point. "But these guys may never get sick," I said.

"That's not our view in the army," he asserted. "We study them until they show signs of disease or get discharged." He had set up the shoots in a Denver gay bar. "I wanted the guys to have a good time," he said, "a little bit of a show. You know, the customers got to see the models take some of their clothes off.

"Getting critical attention for my work would be a hell of a lot easier if I lived in New York," he mused, putting the pictures back in the envelope and starting upstairs. "People are a lot more receptive to innovation. They're interested in AIDS. Colorado's not a stronghold for the avant-garde. I'm very goal-oriented—high school, college, the army, med school, photography. I always focused on what I wanted. Didn't think about sex. That's what saved me."

"From *what*?" I asked.

"If I'd started having sex, I'd be dead or dying, like the rest of you gay men."

"Do you mean to say that all the way through college and medical school you didn't know you were gay?" I caught myself and retreated. "That *somehow* you were attracted to men?"

"I had a buddy in college," he said, "who I had a thing for. He died in a car accident. My dad's a psychotherapist. I talked to him about losing my friend. He didn't see any problem with having homosexual feelings, which I appreciated. In med school I went to a gay bar. It wasn't for me. With AIDS and safe sex, there were too many things you couldn't do anymore. Sex and death," he said without melodrama. "I think of sex, I think of AIDS. I knew about AIDS first."

I started to ask more questions, but he was done. Still, he held me another minute on the stairs. We wouldn't have another chance to talk, he said. After work the next day, he was leaving for the Fire Island Pines, New York's exclusive summer resort for homosexuals, where he was staying with a house full of AIDS educators. Gino and I were to meet him at the base at six and take him to the airport. He invited me to stay at his house as long as I wanted. "Gino can catch you up on stuff in the Springs. I'm not the one to brief you on the gays, anyway. No way, José!" he wailed, and thrashed his head from side to side. "Anything else you need, just search around. But you bozos had better not cause a scandal in the neighborhood. I'm the one who's gotta live in this town."

I thanked him for his hospitality and started up to bed. He stopped me again. "I know you're an activist," he said again, and checked the front door, "but when you write about me in your book, I hope you'll try to understand and be kind."

I wanted to find an answer for him. But he had marched off, commanding me sharply, "Sleep tight."

I did not sleep well that night. I was beginning to understand that men, burdened by the impassive requirements of American manhood, needed someone to confess to. A traveling stranger, I became to them like the faceless priest in a booth, a sanctified ear. However different our lives might otherwise be, they knew that I would not condemn their homosexual secret—so they seemed urgently to tell everything.

My beliefs were disturbed deeply, too. For years as an activist I had concocted an uncomplex view of the world, in which "coming out of the closet" was the answer to a homosexual's every distress. I was learning that our psychic dilemmas were more intricate than that—that the tenets of gay politics were not true to life.

In the morning, the insistent grumbling of "Good Morning, America" woke me up. Gino was on the sofa in the den, sitting cross-legged in his underwear. He hadn't showered yet or shaved. Eating a bowl of Cheerios, he stared at the TV with his furry belly bulging out. He patted the hump when he saw me and said with a smirk, "Tom keeps telling me I'm too young to grow a pot. I told him this is what a man is *supposed* to look like."

"Sometimes we're hardest on the people we love," I said. I was vapid with lack of coffee, vacant in the Springs' thin air.

"Odd duck, don't you think?" Gino stated. "Doesn't even think he's gay? I just laugh at him. AIDS and the army are the only things he can get hot for."

Tom was drawn to the manly sophistication of cadets and officers. Gino went for the rough-and-tumble of enlisted men. He had been a tow gunner in the army. "I got an achievement medal for being the best damn gunner in the battalion," he said. "The straight guys were always tellin' ya what hot shit they were— gung-ho Rambo types with their guns. Well, a fag carried one, too. Miss Queen was better than them all. I liked the army okay. I just didn't wanta do it for the rest of my life."

He had enlisted to get money for school. Once he was in, he married an enlisted lesbian in order to live off base and be paid an extra stipend. She was still in and got three hundred dollars extra a month for being married, which she split with him. "You know, I don't care one way or the other about women—whether I'm ever around them or not. Except lesbians are a little different, I think. They understand. But it's worth it to me for the *money*!"

He had had a lover in the army, too—Ron—when he was stationed in Hawaii. "Two wonderful years," he said, making me coffee. Christianity had ended that for them. When Gino was in Germany playing war games, his lover was seduced by some Jesus freaks. "He was sort of raised that way," Gino explained. "When I got back from Europe he was telling me how *wrong* homosexuality is. I said, '*Wrong*? I *love* you!' He said, 'It's just sex, a perversion.' So I told him, 'Forget the sex, then. Let's just *love* each other.' But he said that wouldn't work for him. I loved being strong for Ron," he said. "I always loved just having him in my arms. Maybe I smothered him out of my life. I don't know."

Tired from yesterday's travel, I napped off and on all afternoon. Gino tried to track down an Olympic biker who had cruised him on his flight from Hawaii. The Olympic Training Facility was in Colorado Springs because of the high altitude. With the Air Force Academy there, too, the town was ripe with fantasies, if not fulfillment. Gino made calls to the guy's father, who was an Olympic coach, but could never get hold of him. He worked on finding the boy all day, until it was time to go to the base and pick up Tom for the airport.

In the late afternoon, low F-15's seared the sky with dying screams above the hilly cul-de-sacs of the subdivision's houses. Gino's new car sputtered, the ignition groaned. Gino pumped the gas until at last the motor started. "It's the altitude," he said. "Does something to the engine or jets or something." Then he confessed, "I don't know *anything* about motors!" The road to Fort Carson climbed over the last dry heaves of the Rockies before the mountains gasped out. The land to the east was becalmed in golden sunlight, like a gentle sea. "That's the way it is from here to Kansas," Gino said.

As he drove, a big class ring on Gino's left hand glinted in the sunshine. "Every time I look at this," he told me, "I think of Ron. It was his." Everything reminded him of the man he had lost—the T-shirt he was wearing, the underwear, which had been his lover's. "Maybe I suffocated him. I wanted to be with him all the time. I could have never left his side my whole life. But I'd have rather given too much than too little."

A quarter mile from the gate of the base, we joined a funereal line of traffic, each car rolling slowly past the MP's hot, bullet eyes. Gino produced his army ID and named the hospital as our destination. The MP ordered us by. He was a giant. The shiny round toes of his high black boots seemed capable of kicking in anything. A black belt and holster held his pistol at his waist. His face made a smile that could kill. I turned and watched him salute the cars behind us, fast and brutal, beautifully fluid.

"I'd like to get him facedown," Gino said, "and fuck him until he cried."

"He *is* a hunk," I replied.

"Actually, I was thinking more about teaching him a lesson," Gino answered.

At the infirmary we gave our names and waited in the lobby among GIs, who were there to get their regular "AIDS test" or to pick up results. Along one long hall there was a row of counseling rooms as tiny as confessionals.

Everything was khaki and green—walls, sofas, cabinets, bulletin boards, uniforms—a world made of camouflage. Coffee tables carried a clutter of journals from the National Rifle Association and back issues of *Decision* magazine, the "Official Organ of the Billy Graham Crusade." There was a scattered stack of thin orange pamphlets titled "What You Should Know About HTLV-III and AIDS," which still called HIV by its long-discarded name. The information was presented in dialogue bubbles floating out of cartooned military officers' mouths. One bubble asked, "What can I do to prevent HTLV-III and AIDS?" The "right" answer was, "Don't have sex with those at increased risk." "Homosexual" and "bisexual" men topped the list, casting all men who desired other men in the same infected pool. What about boys fresh from the farms of Nebraska? I wondered. What about men who had never been fucked? Or those who had been monogamous for the past twenty years? What about men who were still virgins? Labeling all homosexuals a high-risk group was never a model of science, medicine, public health prevention; it was social engineering.

Like the rest, Gino had had to take the test every six months in the army. "I was always negative," he informed me. "But I had unsafe sex once after that," he said, not wincing. "So I'm having it done again at the public health department. Just to be sure." I told him it could take years for the antibodies to HIV to show up, and that a positive test didn't mean he would develop the disease. "*I* know that test doesn't mean anything," he answered, missing the point. "The gays who get it were mostly promiscuous." He had convinced himself. "I think negative attitudes too will bring it on. It's all attitude."

When Tom took us back to his office, I studied the certificates hung on his walls—diplomas from college and med school, Phi Beta Kappa, medical boards. There was a black-and-white aerial photo of the army base in San Antonio in 1947. Hundreds of GIs stood at attention, all melded as one into the mold of an army-air force badge. Tom was carrying his uniform on a hanger like a mannequin and had put on his clothes for Fire Island—golf shirt, golf shorts, and canvas shoes, splashes of white and pastels. "You think this is too casual for the plane?" he fretted. And when we were in the car, he bullishly asked again and again, "Those fashion queens on the Island—they doing all new wardrobes this year? Gotta get some new stuff when I get there, gotta do some shopping! *Relax, Tom, relax!*" He dug a Coors from his shoulder bag and swigged.

The parking lot at the terminal was crowded with cars full of parents and handsome cadets, who had graduated from the academy that morning and were heading home. "Girlfriend!" Tom cried. "Look at that! Won't meet anything like that on Fire Island," he groaned. "Tom! Relax!"

The next day I was leaving for Denver for the gay rodeo, which I had found advertised on a poster in a New York bar the April before. Gino insisted on taking me mountain climbing first, then up to Pike's Peak. Using his old army skills, he scaled and got down the steep, rocky slope like a goat. I labored up, stiff with the fear of falling, and rode a rock slide down, shredding my ass and hands. Gino washed my knuckles clean in an ice cold creek. Driving to the Peak, he put Holst's *Planets* into the tape deck to help me forget my pain. "Mars" collapsed under the weight of its cacophony and gave way to "Venus, the Bringer of Peace," too lonely and plaintive to be consoling. "Mercury" manically chased its melodies up and down the scales and came to no more than an impish pluck in the end. When impetuous "Jupiter, the Bringer of Jollity" began, I opened my window in spite of the cold and grew light-headed on pale, frozen breaths. Dead ahead, an enormous cliff of snow white stone cut off a troop of scrawny spruce trees and forced them to climb up another way. The mountain peaks orbited around us like icy moons. Below us, an ice gray blanket of clouds covered the world. Deep panels of snow slid from the slopes. Icicles hung like stalactites over the road.

"This is slippery," Gino said. "We could die." He was grinning and watching me from the corner of his eyes.

Near the top, the amazing "Jupiter" anthem swept forth so broad and strong, it seemed it could lift the world. We grew drunk with sound and high, cold air. In the swelling joy of that one song, there lay a peace far more profound than Venus had ever offered. We parked and looked below, where the planet had become a swirling cloud, a Milky Way. Ahead, the summit rose behind a low ridge like a sun made of snow. We grabbed each other's hands and sat there laughing wildly and crying.

In time Gino remembered, "I had this drill sergeant once that was always yelling, 'Kill! Kill!' He tried to drill it into us that men are your enemy. I feel sorry for men like that. I couldn't go through life always being so afraid of other men.

"One time in the barracks, all the guys were crowded around the TV set watching a live newscast. Some old guy, sixty years old, was getting sent up for embezzlement, I think. And while they were interviewing him, he just pulled a revolver out of this envelope and stuck it in his mouth. He blew his own head off on television.

"The guys *loved* it! They had a VCR running. They wanted to watch it over and over again." From Holst came a hammering passage of goose-step rhythms that exploded in screams from the thunder of the winds and tympani. Gino said that that day in the barracks, he had left his buddies and gone into the bathroom and cried. "I think they were all crying inside," he told me.

CHAPTER 4

THE
RODEO'S
DRY
HEAT

WHEN GINO AND I CAME DOWN FROM THE MOUNTAIN, I ATTENDED
to my wounds, then headed out for the Denver rodeo. I had
called Charlie's, the rodeo's host bar, before I left San Francisco.
Wayne Jakino, the manager, had been proud that a writer from
New York took an interest in Wild West gay life and offered to
find me a free place to stay. "A buddy to bunk with," was how he
put it. He said he would set me up with Scotty, his deejay. I would
find him in the deejay's booth when I got to the bar. Wayne's
voice was low and leathery. Full gospel music from the dance
floor nearly drowned him out.

"*Would you be free from your burden of sin? There's pow'r in the
blood, pow'r in the blood?*"

Someone in the bar hooted like a cowboy who had roped a
steer or just got saved.

I had bought basic cowboy gear in a San Francisco western
store after I talked to Wayne—boots, a straw cowboy hat, and
crisp new Levi's. I got myself up in them now to ride into town
like a ranch hand on a roundup. I was gone from Colorado

Springs by sundown. The road took me past the Air Force Academy. Swarms of blond bombshells cruised for cadets, gunning by in sleek sports cars, jetting exhaust. One cut me off at the fender. I used my mouth and horn and was unkind. Sharp as a fighter wing, the steep roof of the Air Force Chapel tore at a cloud and bled it of a thousand flaming colors. The night began to devour the mountains, leaving black mesas scattered on the plains like bread crumbs.

An hour outside the Springs, two lonely radio towers pierced a black storm and blinked like the bloody eyes of an eagle. Here the highway curved up a gentle rise. A sprawl of lights glittered in the dark distance like a comet shower. This was my first glimpse of mountain-high Denver. The traffic lumbered, slow as a wagon train. A bumper sticker read "Our Best Defense Is Mutual Respect Not Mutual Fear." It took me another hour to get to Charlie's.

Charlie's sat half a block up from Denver's biggest western-wear store. The corner lot was crowded with big cars. There were some old guzzlers, some new luxury models, a bevy of Cadillacs. Mud-caked pickup trucks crowded a side street of quiet houses, their license plates boasting the whole Southwest and several farther states. The entrance to the bar was through the back, where a two-peaked tent had been erected for the overflow. In the night air it glowed like a campfire. Its flaps tongued the air with the rustles of cowpokes inside and the two-stepping twang of the music. A big-bellied cowboy manned the door and checked ID's. With a simmering grin, he nodded the wings of his mustaches to let you in and swiped the sweat from beneath his hat.

I sidled through a straw white maze of bobbing cowboy hats. My stiff brim just missed a hundred wrecks. Midway to the bar, a slap bee-stung my ass, and a thin cowboy long-legged past me, smirking as he caught my eye. I watched him disappear in clouds of cigarette smoke and sawdust kicked up from the floor. But before I lost him altogether, he turned and I saw him wink between two sunburned faces that puffed cigarillos. I followed. He was leaning against a picnic table when I found him and had already bought me a beer. "Dave," he introduced himself. He shoved his hat back on his crown and offered me a plastic cup of draft. Its thick, foaming head swelled over the top. We two-stepped together for most of the evening.

From the corner of the tent, a pungent fog rose from caldrons of barbecued pork and fat burgers frying on the grill. We each paid four bucks. I was telling Dave I was from New York, while the cook piled our plates. "So you're that writer we been hearing about?" the cook sang, handing back my four bucks. "I'm Mad Edna." He rubbed his hands on his grub-splattered apron, then grabbed my hand. "And *this* is Mad Edna's Cookshack!" Edna spooned another high hill of coleslaw on my plate. It kicked as hard as the barbecue, which was amber hot.

"New York City!" Dave wailed with awe. All the chawing down around us stopped. I was surrounded by a posse of scuffed cowboy boots, whose sharp toes all pointed toward mine. I gazed at the sawdust floor and rued that I'd not gotten my bullhides dirtier before I dared wear them to Charlie's.

There was a long, slow trail to the dance floor, where the fire marshal counted heads and let one cowboy in for every two who went out. Below a mirror boot revolving from the ceiling, some thirty or forty cowboys and cowgirls had shuffled into facing lines. The steel guitar of Hank Williams, Jr., was already hard in a whine when the honky-tonk piano cut in and drove the chords like a stock car engine. Right boots were poised, itching to pound. *"One, two, three, four!"* and the song let loose with the lonesome complaint, *"I got ketchup on my blue jeans, I just burned my hand. Loh-urd! It's hard to be a bach-elor man."* Riding heels and sharp-pointed toes battered the floor in flawless unison. Lightning legs bolted loose like colts', and high hips muscled the air like the shanks of Derby horses. The men's tall shoulders were suspended walking horse high. Their faces were rock hard with grins.

"Do ya wohnna da-ay-aynce? Do ya wohnna par-r-rty?"

There were split-second jumps and midair turns. Together the dancers stomped like broncos in precision stampede. Bending their chests to their prancing knees, they whacked their own butts. The air cracked like whips. "Wha-*hoo!*" they cried, and rocked their sultry asses—a slow fuck on a sweat-hot night.

"You can do anythang that you whonna do, but woman, don't you step on my cowboy boots!"

At the end of the song, a fast reshuffling began as lines broke into pairs and rounded out into a circle the size of the floor. Men shifted and reshifted arms in mute negotiations over who would lead, who would follow. I let my new friend Dave lead. Scratching the floor backward with my boots, I learned how far out to hold my head to keep our hats from crashing. On the second go around the floor I glimpsed the man in the deejay booth, whom I guessed to be my weekend bunkmate, Scotty. His face was still as stone. His huge straw hat teetered on top of his earphones.

Dave twirled me out of the circle and up to Scotty's door, where I pointed to myself and mouthed my name, waiting.

"You're Darrell," he told me when he opened up. He tipped the brim of his white straw hat in welcome. His accent was dark as molasses, his voice unsmiling but not unfriendly. In the darkness of the bar and the darker shadow of his hat, I could see only that his face was lean and seemed to be ruggedly handsome. His boots and Teton made him tall. I agreed to meet him at the front bar after closing.

At two the lights came up. The cowhands upended their liquor and staggered out. I waited on a barstool with a rusty nail in hand. Strung up above the dance floor, cardboard cutouts of the states in the rodeo dallied in the air conditioner's breeze. "Who else is here from New York?" I asked, surprised to see its oddly phallic outline wiggling there. The letters, drawn in red glitter, read "Times Square," the name of a gay and lesbian square dance group in New York City.

"That's up 'ere in your honor—far's *I* can tell," Scotty told me. "No one else here from New York City." He was chasing shots with beers. I knew his sky blue eyes couldn't lie. He was matter-of-fact, I thought, to the point of being shy. He yawned and rubbed his eyes. He had been working eighteen hours a day since rodeo week had begun on Monday.

Scotty hailed from Dallas. He invited me to join a bunch of

his hometown pals for breakfast at a nearby Big Boy restaurant. All of us were tipsy. Some of us were drunk. There were lots of slaps on buddies' backs, big laughs, and rowdy love songs. Romance got more raucous by the drink.

"*Swee-eet drea—eams of yee-ou-ou!*" they crooned.

A cowboy's thumb poked a cowboy's ass while a rustling hand lassoed a crotch and wrestled it to the ground. "*Ride* those Wrangler's!" the groped man cried, then mocked, "If there was a straight man in these blue jeans, you'd have a big ole dirty boot right up your butt!" The castigated cowboys turned around and smacked their own behinds. Scotty downed another schnapps, and we followed the boys to the coffee shop, bringing up the rear behind a weaving caravan of Texas plates.

When Scotty and I arrived, the others had already staked a claim to a banquet room in the back—past a sign that warned "This Section Closed" and a dirty mop in a yellow pail, guarding the path. A cowboy named Jerry, whose hat was pushed back, had grabbed a sweeper from the utility room and was furiously pushing it back and forth across the carpet. He hummed an aggressive gospel tune like a born-again housewife. "My work's just *nay-uh-ver* done!" he complained. The carpet was littered with crumbs.

The other boys reared their chairs and propped their boots up on the table, which was still littered with dishes and leftovers from the party before. The wide-eyed waitress watched through the kitchen door. "*Yo! Wo*-man!" yelled one of the rowdy Texans, playing the bully boyfriend. "Git yourself out here!" The others scowled, playing the redneck pals. The waitress ventured out and stood back from the table. She observed the men cautiously, then seemed to judge them unconvincing. Demure, she fumbled in her apron for her pad. One of the Lone Stars drew his nose up to her bosom and read her nametag. As earthy and kind as Miss Kitty, he asked, "Now what's your name, hon? *Lee-uhn?*" he said, stringing it out. "Lynn, I think the boys here'll be wantin' some coffee."

The cowboys drew arch circles in the air above the table, pointing out the mess. Scotty passed around a big gold ring with a giant gem embedded. One of the admirers ensconced it suspi-

ciously in his fist and nodded toward the outer room, where tables of black people sat. "I'm warnin' y'all now 'bout your jewels," he stated confidentially. "There's *tables* full of niggers out
there! They'll snatch your tiaras right off your head!" A white
man, I startled, then grimaced.

"I wear my hat over mine," Scotty sniffed, who still had his
Teton on. "If they can't see it, they won't try to steal it from you.
That's somethin' you'd better take care for in this part of town."
Suddenly he seemed dead serious. The laughter stopped. "They'll
take anything that glitters, whether it's worth anything or not," he
spat.

"We still keep 'em in line down in Texas," said the man who
guarded the ring.

The food came slowly. The scrambled eggs were dry. "Lynn,
hon," complained a poke across from Scotty, "I really do not *want*
to make a fuss. But I *must* ask you to in*form* the cook that these
eggs look like somethin' my horse drops in the pasture when he's
puny. Now, there is no need to cry. We are not blamin' you for
this unpleasant situation. But I do feel that the management of
this establishment should surely apologize."

The manager came out and apologized and offered to make
us a fresh pot of coffee.

"We'll pro'ly be drinkin' a *lot*!" a cowboy scowled, eyeing the
blacks up front. "If it gets any darker out there, we're never
gonna find our way outa here."

It was five o'clock by the time we left. Scotty dozed while I
drove, and I found it remarkable that his head never fell over—
perfect cowboy posture in his dreams. He'd open his eyes, survey
the road, and groan, "Next stoplight, left, one block, turn right,"
then would be out again. He lived in a white frame bungalow
with a cowgirl couple, who were long asleep. We tiptoed across
the porch. The boards creaked. "Be real quiet," he hushed me as
he opened the door. A dog the size of a newborn pony appeared
from the darkness of the room. "Watch out for the cats. They're
apt to be all over the floor." I found a tail. An invisible cat
screamed.

Scotty gave me my options. "You can bunk with me or sleep

on the sofa in the basement. Mama Cat's down there. She's in heat. She'll be yowlin' through the night, 'less you fuck her with a Q-tip."

Scotty's room was across from the cowgirls' room in a tiny hall. He pointed me to the far side of his bed, where I laid my bag. Silently the two of us stripped down by the street lamp's light, which sifted pale and silver through the window like a moonlit fog. When we climbed in, we lay a moment staring at the ceiling. Then, wondering about this man I was to sleep with, I whispered, "Why did you leave Texas?"

"My folks kicked me out 'cause I'm gay," he growled. He was hoarse with fatigue. "Told me to get as far outa their faces as I could figure to go. So, I came up here." He lay quiet for a minute before he rolled me on my side and put his arm around my chest. I took his hand and snuggled in. His cock fell soft on the back of my leg. With his breath warm and moist against my neck, we fell asleep.

When I woke up, Scotty was scuffling through a forest of boots that lay toppled across the floor, rummaging the room for a proper cowboy hat. Hats hung on hooks, on the back of a chair, on the knob of the closet door, on a picture frame. The crease of his new blue Wrangler jeans was razor sharp. He was wearing a crisp white western shirt, V-stitched across the back, with white pearl snaps. He whispered, "You have a good one, now," and just that quickly left for the day. It was eight o'clock. I first met the women in the narrow hall. I was wrapped in my towel for the shower. They grunted, "Mornin'," gave me a nod, and paid me no mind after that. There were three instead of two. A lesbian cousin had come from Chicago for rodeo weekend.

The events didn't start till Saturday. Friday was scheduled for a brewery tour at Coors, an hour away in Golden. The brewers saw the rodeo as a chance to mend fences with the gay rights movement and undercut the boycott of their beer. The cowboys and girls were to rendezvous at Charlie's at eleven. I stopped first by the western store to buy some more gear—a cowboy belt carved with acorn leaves; a big brass buckle with the seal of Ohio, my birth state; a red-and-white checkered cowboy shirt with mother-of-pearl snaps; a second white straw hat proud as a mountain peak. I wore my new self to the tavern.

Mad Edna was already rustling up lunch when I got to the bar at ten, but serving pans full of breakfast still steamed on the table. There were creamy scrambled eggs with scorching chile sauce (reds and greens inflaming the yellows), glistening sausage, and huge white biscuits.

"Better get yourself some of that fast," grumped an old man named Warren McKinley, "before these vultures pack the rest of it away." Warren's job was to guard the tent flap. He sat with his dung-caked boots propped on two beer kegs. His jeans fit fine on his narrow hips but couldn't contain his belly, which exploded the plaids on his shirt and ate his big belt buckle.

I had trouble with the butter. It was in a spring thaw—soft on top, frozen below. The utensils were plastic. I dug my knife, it tensed, the butter flew like a stone from a slingshot. Mad Edna stared at my head and pointed with a kettle spoon. A runny ball of butter was plastered against the crown of my new hat. I panicked. Edna patted my hand. "Now, I don't know how y'all work it back east," he sympathized, "but if you sit in the sun in Denver like that, that yellow brooch of your'n is gonna *melt*." He saw my distress. "You just take a little baking soda," he instructed with his pinky extended, "and rub it *rea-ea-eal* gentle-like with a toothbrush. That'll draw up some of that grease."

Edna's primness seemed to irk tough old Warren. "Aw, just leave it be," he grunted. "It's gonna git dirty when your ridin' in't anyways!" Edna threw up his hands and walked away. Warren swung his head, disgusted, as though he'd just had a squall with a woman. He spit out a mouthful of coffee in the sawdust. "Drunkin' ole bitch! This is sure some weak-ass coffee! Well, I suppose I'll git used to it all in time," he huffed.

"The coffee?" I said.

"The whole lot of these *gays*! I haven't been in Denver all that long. This city life is really *somethin'*!"

It occurred to me that though Warren in fact worked here, he might not be homosexual. Amazed by his candid disdain, I seized on the easiest approach to keep him talking. "Big cities *are* hard to take," I answered stupidly, and asked him where he hailed from.

"You know Illinois?" he asked.

I told him I had gone to Olivet Nazarene College in Kankakee, in the eternal wasteland of Illinois's cornfields.

"That a Pentecostal school?" he queried. "That's what I am—Pentecostal. We got some bisexuals in the faith, you know— your Jimmy Bakkers playin' both sides of the pews. I guess they're gonna drag his ass through the dust for that." He nodded and mused. A tiny replica of a Jack Daniel's bottle was pinned on the front of his hat.

"But I sure enough do like listenin' to 'em preach and sing. I drove a hundred miles outa the way listenin' to Jimmy Swaggart on a fuckin' tape one time. *He* sure don't have no use for the gays. Far as I can tell, folks that's the loudest about it have some iden- tity problem theirselves. I sure as hell know *I* was that way, always a-talkin' about the 'fay-gits': 'Fuckin' queers, somebody oughta line their sissy butts up and *shoot* 'em all!' " He chortled and dragged on the butt of his cigarette. Then he crushed the fag with his boot and hoofed sawdust over it.

I was confused. "Are *you* gay?" I asked finally, timidly.

"*Hell!*" he rasped. "I knowed from the time I was this high." His hand hit the air at the height of the two beer kegs. "I didn't do anything about it, though, till I divorced my wife. That was eight years ago. Took me another four years after that to git my- self goin' with men."

I was bemused. I wondered whether he was "out" to family and hometown friends.

"Shit, no!" His face froze at the thought of such ignorance. "In that little town of fifteen hundred people? I was in the car- penters' union," he explained. "If they'd a-knowed I was gay, I wouldn't a-worked another day." He paused and thought. "Well, all in all I expect it's a pretty good life, if you can ever git used to it. When I first came in here, someone'd touch me, I'd haul off and say, 'Keep your fuckin' hands to yourself or I'll kick your queer ass!' He swigged a mouthful of Bud and laughed. A tiny stream ran down his chin. "But I reckon the folks back home'll be findin' out pretty soon." His teenage son's school buddy was coming to stay a month in the summer, he explained, to see something of the world besides rural Illinois. "That whole gol-damn apartment building I live in's gay. 'Course, that boy likes to kiss and hug and git his belly rubbed himself," he added. "*I* found that out *myself* one time!"

Suddenly his face, which was red with a grin, turned sour. "Now *here* comes a real queen!" he snarled. A nod of his hat directed me to a slight young man mincing in. His bleached hair shined in the morning sun while his flip-flops tossed sawdust behind him like glitter. He wore an oversize T-shirt that read "If you can rope it, you can ride it." Warren clinched his jaw and glared, studying the creature like a bird of prey. "It makes me *sick* to see somethin' as nelly as that. I haven't got no use for it at all. People sees that kind of thing and they think all the queers are that way. It's enough to make you stay in a closet. Pro'ly from California anyways."

Outside, a cowboy announced that the caravan for Coors was loading up. "Will I see you at the rodeo?" I asked Warren.

"Not a-ridin', you won't!" he howled. "I'm too old for that. I ain't rode in twenty-five years. That was in the straight world, though. I never did ride gay. Hell! I wasn't even 'out' when I rode in the rodeos. I'm *still* not out, if you git right down to it," he said, chuckling as he waved me out the door.

Coors sat between two soft mountains. Among spruces, ragged slopes, and streams, this idyll might have doubled for a valley in the Alps. I had ridden out with John King, the owner of Charlie's in Denver and its Phoenix twin. His new Cadillac was as big as a subway car. We identified ourselves at the guardhouse and were directed to a company van that would take us through the inner gates to the brewery.

Some sixty of the rodeo folks were already milling around when we arrived. We were taken to a new exhibition hall to admire the Coors family history in pictures and learn the steps in brewing beer. An enormous window opened onto a glistening res-

ervoir of the pure mountain waters Coors used. The beauty and
hush of the place seemed a concoction by Madison Avenue.

There were no chairs. Like children, we sat on the floor and
ate the box lunches our hosts provided. Icy tubs held pint cans of
Coors, but the group was sober. Most drank soda. I wondered
whether this abstinence was the result of the boycott, but most of
the cowboys and -girls weren't even aware of the problems with
Coors until I brought it up. Charlie's sold Coors. It was the cowboy's favorite beer. I decided the rodeo folks must be nursing
their hangovers from the night before.

After lunch we were handed hard hats and guided on an intimate trip through the brewery's inner sanctum. Great, steaming
copper caldrons rose two stories high through a gleaming maze of
ducts and pipes. Huge vats of mash turned the hot air sweet and
sour. Our tour guide offered us more beer, fresh from the tanks.
The cowboys and cowgirls took it this time. Our hosts grinned
with the effects of their hospitality. Light-headed, we were led to
a plush auditorium.

Everyone quickly settled in. Some slouched, some sat at attention. Some took off their Teton hats, some didn't. A lot of
them rested a boot on the knee. A lot of them were dipping and
chewing. Everyone now seemed bored or sulky, unmoved by such
slick settings, like high-schoolers on a field trip.

Soon John Meadows, Coors's community relations man, took
the floor with such simmering warmth, he seemed about to take
the room row by row and squeeze our hands. He wore a pin-
striped suit, but not tightly. He was a tad loose at the tie. His
smile was winning, as some men's are by nature and others' by
management training courses. "I gotta tell you, this is a first for
us," he began, and drew a gentle dip in the air with his chin, out-
lining his sincerity. "And I think, quite frankly, when I say 'a first'
to people from the gay community, we all know that what's gone
on before between us in the last ten years was not all positive. But
for you to come out here to meet us takes some guts." He told us
what he thought a hostile group would want to hear about itself.

He gave us too much credit. Even among the few who had
known of the boycott before today, I suspected that most were like

me. I had heard somewhere that Coors gave money to unspecified antigay causes. I didn't care to whom. My response was automatic. If you were gay in America, it was easy to believe in conspiracies. I didn't ask myself what beer I could possibly drink if I boycotted every brewer whose business practices discriminated against homosexuals. Large corporations were by nature reactionary. Perhaps Coors had just been more obvious. Besides, the best of homosexuals could untangle only so much of gay politics, which was intricacy more than substance. Coors was not sold in New York City then. For gay New Yorkers, it was an easy target.

Mr. Meadows was confessional. "Certainly some of what's been said about Coors and the gay community is true. Some's not. A little background," he wooed us, "about who we are and where we fit in in terms of breweries in the United States." He began with an honest jerk of the head and a serious smile that seemed apt to divulge secrets. There were more than 650 Coors distributors, he told us, in forty-seven states, Canada, and Japan. With disappointment in his voice, he noted that the beer was not sold anywhere in Pennsylvania, Indiana, or Delaware. "Maybe," he confided, "that's because we sometimes surround ourselves with controversy." His job was to change the market's heart. He seduced us with camaraderie as he narrated Coors's corporate history and kept his distance from the gay community's wound.

He spoke to us of the competition and of marketing revolutions, of Budweiser's sales war with Anheuser-Busch, of the ups and downs of profits in beer. He was precise about the fiscal years. "Now where is Coors in all this?" he finally asked.

A few seats down from where I sat, a tall, thin Houston man fidgeted with the crimson fringe that sprouted up and down his sleeves. Sometimes he twisted the wings of the fuchsia kerchief around his neck or smoothed the long white feather growing out of his hatband. Next to him, a young man repeatedly spit on his thumb to shine up a scuff on his boots. With hats sitting low to their eyes, many in the audience appeared to be sleeping. I thought, after all, they had come not for politics, but for the ride and free beer.

Mr. Meadows himself had fixed in his mind a political brotherhood among homosexuals, which gay activists created with smoke and mirrors. Reverently he noted gay leaders' names and lost his audience, which had never heard of them before. Had Mr. Meadows simply bored the cowpokes to death, he might have kept them as loyal Coors drinkers. Instead, too sincere, he began to divulge offensive attitudes toward homosexuals and told us of offenses—Coors family contributions to extreme right-wing causes—that even the well informed had not been aware of. His audience slowly turned against him. Frowns cropped up around the room.

Mr. Meadows, impervious, dug deeper. Despite all Coors's problems with the gay market, he said, the brewery had chosen not to target gay men and lesbians for advertising. "We've wanted to keep our relationship out of the public sphere," he said condescendingly, "on account of your need for privacy. We believe advertising gay images would just cause a lot of unnecessary controversy for you and make your lives even harder than they are. We've preferred to meet you one to one, like today."

As for the facts, though, he said, he'd be honest with us. "Corporate America is afraid of gays." He said, "You'd know I'm a liar if I told you all ten thousand Coors accounts think the gay community is wonderful. But business is business"—he knuckled the air, peculiarly trying to flatter us—"and the gay community is a very large consumer base. In New York," he said, "the labor movement and the gay community have teamed up to keep us out. That translates into lost profits." The AFL-CIO, angered by Coors's strike breaking, had in fact begun the national boycott, and gay activists had grabbed it by the tail.

Now the rodeo men and women began to feel the sting. An undercurrent of grumbling passed through the auditorium as Mr. Meadows summarized. "We don't believe we're antigay," he reiterated. "We believe in gay men and lesbians as important marketing opportunities. But we've had this problem between us, and both sides have to come together to solve it." Then he lifted his brow and circled his arm to invite questions.

A young cowboy lumbered to his feet, holding his hat in front of his crotch. "Some of us here pro'ly think Coors's got some lessons to learn. If you're wantin' to market to gays, you're gonna have to show some support for gay rights and AIDS."

Mr. Meadows paused, as if catching the painful point, then derailed so direct a route to the heart of the issue, ignoring the question. Instead he offered a litany of the accounts Coors had been cut out of. His face fell with hurt disbelief. "In San Francisco, all the way down to San Jose, you've got something like three hundred fifty gay bars. We're only in thirty. We've been booed out of places there!"

Now there was a hoedown of questions from the floor. Why did Coors refuse to place ads in gay newspapers? Why were applicants for employment interrogated about their sexual tastes? Mr. Meadows exhaled into his microphone and smiled proudly. "We have a lot of gay employees working happily here," he claimed. "Several of them have wanted to defend us in the press when some of these rumors got started. We didn't want them to. It was a catch-22." He grinned as he panned the room for gay employees to corroborate his story. Everyone looked around. No one answered.

"I want to know what Coors's plan is to change the gay community's mind about them," a cowboy drawled, stretching out his words like hot taffy.

"You being here today is a start," the PR man repeated. "You can expect to see us more and more visible in the gay community. What form that'll take I can't tell you. I can tell you we're going to continue to tell our story." With that he threw out his chin and grinned, signaling that the meeting was over.

A lone cowboy a few rows back still intended to be heard. As the theater seats swung up against their backs and the noisy scuffle of departure started, he hushed the crowd by drawling loudly, "Mr. Meadows, I'd just like to have a word with you." Mr. Meadows acquiescently threw out his hands. "Well," the man began, "I'm not political like some of the city gays, but I've been listenin' to what you said, and it seems to me that you screwed up pretty bad the way you're goin' about this thang. If you're wantin' someone to drink your beer, you don't fool around with the activists. You go right to the folks that's doin' the drinkin'." He halted to swallow. Meadows nodded again, as though the man had finished speaking, and abandoned his mike on a table. But the cowboy wasn't through. "So I see a couple thangs you people can do," he came back in. "One is give out condoms at the bars." Mr. Meadows's face turned pale. "I suspect they don't cost that much if you buy 'em in bunches. You can put your name right on the package—'Coors wants you to have safe sex.' You treat us drinkers right and no activists can tell us what to do."

Mr. Meadows tried to smile. Instead he grimaced. "That's not something Coors would want to do," he said, squeezing out the words. But because he'd abandoned his mike, few heard him. He took up the mike again. "I really don't think you're ever going to see Coors get involved in that kind of advertising," he claimed, and set the crowd to muttering against his beer.

It seemed to me that a brewer had achieved in one afternoon what the gay rights movement had seldom accomplished. It had politicized a lackadaisical herd of cowgirls and cowboys and made insulted activists out of them—at least for the day.

The spirits rode high on Friday night at the Rocky Mountain Rodeo Kick-off Party. It was hosted by Tracks, a private gay club on the edge of downtown Denver. There might have been five hundred there upending plastic shot glasses. Hundreds of shots of peach schnapps were stacked in tiers—an extravagant "anniversary cake" for the rodeo's fifth year. Clogging troupes from every state west of the Mississippi danced in a chorus of chattering hooves, rattling the stage floor out of its senses. Legs, arms, neck scarves, and fringe flew and quivered.

"What I like is it's *all-American*!" exulted a patriot beside me. The Denver Country Cloggers had begun their routine, dressed in black and yellow with fuzzy yellow belt buckles like bumblebee bellies. Flapping their elbows like insect wings, they performed to a disco version of "Flight of the Bumblebee." When the drag queen bee danced out in yellow-jacket tights and stung the floor with her heels, the crowd went wild. "*All-American!*" my neighbor cried, and gave me a hearty backslap.

The revelers drank all night and slept it off the next morning. The rodeo started late. The thin skin of Denver's mile-high air blistered early. Purple mountains soared beyond the blue glass skyscrapers, making them toylike and comic. A fighter jet no bigger than a fly scratched the sky with a platinum incision. A quintet of lesbians slapped calves from the rough stock chutes. Calf roping began at eleven. In the arena, whirling lassos braided wreaths in the air. Contestant number 005 spun his rope three times and looped a neck, first try, letting the line fly free through his hand so as not to jerk the calf up short. Tornadoes of hooves, boots, and dirt swirled up from the earth. He bested the competition by four seconds.

"Ain't bad," Frank Reinhardt judged, nodding his wide-brimmed hat several times. Frank owned a ranch and a gay country-and-western bar in Oklahoma City. He was a big patron of the rodeo. "They can't do no better than that on the professional circuit!" he exclaimed. His leather face was shadowed against the sun. A wind blew across the plains, raising a curtain of droughty dust. Frank tipped his hat against the storm and moved on, having horses to attend to.

One hundred and eighty contestants had registered for the events of the weekend. They stood bone quiet at the "Parade of States," when a flurry of flags from every state passed by. The Rockies rose like a mural beyond. The Stars and Stripes shivered tight against the hot wind. Cowboys and cowgirls doffed their hats. Some covered their hearts. The bleachers scuffled to attention. The crowd exploded in cheers when the corps of rainbow-striped gay lib flags stepped off with Denver's Mile High Freedom Band. The musicians high-stepped in white suspenders and snow white hats, with a snow white tuba bellowing like a bull in the noon sun. The flag bearers spun the gay lib colors like batons or held up shields that spelled "FREEDOM." The band, with the reverence of a cranky pipe organ, played "Somewhere Over the Rainbow." The cowpokes sang it like an anthem, as if envisioning a gay kingdom of Oz.

One by one the flag corps mounted horses and, raising the states like cavalry standards, gave them a run across the field. The

U.S. flag rode solo on a black Arabian. It slapped the earth brown air full of colors.

Denver's mayor, Federico Peña, and Nancy Keene, president of the local Parents and Friends of Lesbians and Gays, were the grand marshals for the two days. Ms. Keene rode in an open jeep and carried a sign that read "We ♥ Our Gay and Lesbian Children." I was alone in the press box when the pastor of Denver's Metropolitan Community Church ascended to the mike to lead in prayer. Next over was the sponsors' box, where the "community relations" man from Miller Lite sat with his young son and the man from Coors. The box above me was the bar, which served drafts. The Miller man kept an eye on the flow and was happy. Coors was deserted. This was the reverse from the way it had been at Charlie's before we toured Coors. Randy, the bartender, had been heavily drinking both brands all morning. "Another'n for Lite!" he screamed, and delighted the Miller man. "I don't care about the politics. It's the taste!" he cried. "And us queens know taste!"

Randy was a skinny man with flyaway blond hair and a constant laugh. "Hon, you look as thirsty as a cactus," he told me. "How's about somethin' to wet that prickly pear of your'n?" His tongue traveled slowly across his lips as he gave me a beer with a foaming head on it. "Us cowboys got somethin' bigger to ride"—he grinned—"than those damn horses."

In the scorekeeper's box, the reverend had raised his hands and begun the "Cowboy's Prayer." "Will you all please rise as we approach the throne of Grace?" he requested. "O Lord!" he intoned. Everyone shuffled up. Horses galloped to a halt with whinnies like Amens. The dust cloud they'd just kicked up fell to the ground, cleaning the sky for the sun. Even the wind died down. With his fist on a beer barrel's spigot, Randy two-stepped in place to some silent ballad. His kerchief lay bullfight red against his purple T-shirt, hanging from his neck like a bandit's.

The reverend prayed: "I've never liked where churches grow. I've loved creation better as it stood that day You finished it, so long ago. . . ."

I was moved by the noble simplicity of sentiment and felt tears in my eyes. I could see that Randy was fidgeting.

"Make me as big and open as the plains . . ."

"Um-m-m," Randy hummed salaciously.

"As honest as the horse between my knees . . ."

" 'The *horse* between my knees'!" the barkeep wailed, just loudly enough to stir his box seat congregation from their meditation. Like teenagers telling stories in the back church pew, we dissolved into snorts and snickers. "Preach it, *preacher*!" Randy cried to his little parish. "A *horse* between my legs is just what I've been lookin' for. If the Lord's got *that* to give away, I'm sure as hell on his side!"

"And guide me," the reverend ended, "on the long, dim trail ahead that stretches upward toward the Great Divide."

Neither the gay nor the nongay press showed up for the rodeo either day. I wondered why. It seemed ready-made for the media. I asked Wayne Jakino, the manager of Charlie's. The urban gay press, he said, had never taken much interest in such "uncultivated" gay life. And as for nongay journalists, he stated, "we work extremely hard to keep them out. No straight reporter's gonna ruin somebody's life putting their picture all over the TV news. We're not trying to bring people out of the closet. We're trying to make these people feel their lives are as important as anyone else's. Don't you think *anyone* should have that kind of compassion?"

A few weeks back Joe Berger, a hysterical writer with the tabloid *Weekly World News,* had exploited the Los Angeles gay rodeo. The paper ran campy photographs and wrote of "sissy steer wrestlers, limp-wristed calf ropers and pretty-boy bronc busters all dolled up in lovely, lacy gowns and the most adorable pink frocks you ever saw." By the time the Denver rodeo rolled around, everyone who entered the grandstand with a camera had to sign an agreement not to photograph anyone's face without permission or use any pictures commercially. We all had to carry permit tags.

Berger's article did say this: "Gays have to stage their own rodeos because they're not welcome on the regular rodeo circuit—no matter how well they handle a rope or how tough they are in the saddle. . . . 'We can ride with the best of them, but they don't want us around,'" a bronc rider had told the reporter. Countless cowboys in Denver told me that, too. Wayne Jakino approached it inside out—from the perspective of gay men's own inhibitions. "The real problem," he philosophized, "is when gays don't try. So many of 'em felt like they were sissies, they didn't even try to participate. Now they realize it's theirs, too, and they can feel better about themselves."

Wayne leaned on the fence, intent on the event—he might have had horse blinders on. A sleek brown horse thundered around a barrel in the barrel race. The rider bent over the mane, bearding his face, creating a flying beast with four wide eyes. A white patch on its forehead gleamed at the sun like a diamond. Its silken tail shot back, streaking the air. I fiddled with my telephoto lens while Wayne spoke and watched me from the corner of his eyes. "Our times are as good as any on the straight circuit," he stated.

Number 149 had just circled the second barrel and was galloping for the third, no more than a few arm's lengths from where we stood. In the stadium, cheering fans waved their hats. A row of the rider's chums strained forward with their elbows on their knees and their chins suspended a breath above their fists, waiting to spring if he won. They exploded early, at a moment when all four of the furied horse's hooves flew off the ground like a wingless Pegasus's, a chestnut cloud of light. The rider, who'd lost his hat, levitated his crotch above the saddle and hunkered down, glaring at the barrel. Again the horse kicked out all fours, brown lightning striking the ground. In that frozen second before the turn, his front legs rose in a hail of dirt, as perfect as a rearing equestrian statue's. White-eyed with his master, he threw his forehead around like a dagger and, edging out his shadow, flew toward the sun. His flaring nostrils were on fire.

Between the bleachers and chutes, a posse of contestants banded at the gate. A cowgirl in dusty jeans and scuff-toed boots straddled the fence and read off names for the flag race. "If a bucket goes down," the gruff woman warned, "you got a *penalty*.

If the flag don't make the oats, *no time!*" She zeroed the air with her hand. The contestants dipped and chewed, sopping sweat from their sunstruck necks with filigreed bandanas. Their hats swayed like a hundred desert tents. Brilliant sunlight fell through the brims, throwing yellow lace on their cheeks.

Two cowboys, who were lovers, sat beneath a cottonwood. One trained his impassive eyes on the arena. The other dozed against his leg. The sleeping man was a veteran of the bull ride. The bull, like a tornado, had spun round and round and slammed him to the ground, ready to gore him. One clown had slapped the livid animal on the nose and turned his rage, while the second somersaulted and squealed, daring the bull to chase him back into the pen. The cowboy's hat had been smashed. His shirt had been torn. His shoulder was bleeding. His jeans were dirt white. He stretched his long legs. A breeze blew up. His pants smoked dust. The shimmering leaves of the cottonwood shattered the shade. He lowered his hat across his face. He groaned and nestled his face in his lover's thighs, to sleep more peacefully.

Sitting on the fence of a nearby chute, five cowgirls guarded a snorting bronc that hoofed the straw like a skittish queen. One—a wind vane in a prairie calm—slowly fanned away the wisps of dust and the stench of manure with her tall felt hat. Her crimson cheeks were cosmetic with heat. Her gray, boyish hair was wet with sweat and plastered flat against her skull. Sometimes she rested a hand on the knee of the cowgirl beside her, who was pretty and petite. This beau pumped her jaw. Raising a paper cup toward her lips, she spit amber streams of tobacco and picked shreds from her teeth. She'd had some trouble with her horse. She complained, "It ain't kickin', it ain't shittin', it won't move." A cowgirl on her other side hammered her spurs against the chute with a sleepy rattle.

Suddenly a mass cry arose, an orchestra of yodels sounded. Fans jumped. The stolid cowgirls stood on the chute, hooking their heels on a rung and balancing. In the arena there was nothing but man and beast in dirty chaos, like a primal remake of Creation. Two pickup men on brave, tame horses circled the furies for a rescue. Two sunlit hooves bolted the air, as though with one hard kick they would crash the sky and sweep away the shatter. Piercing the vortex on one side, the horse's head dove kamikaze-like. Its mane was electric. The threat was vacant. Within inches of impact, it nosed up and saved itself from destruction. The rider jerked in a stroboscopic blur, tethered to his demon by a single, flailing arm. When the bronc's back hooves kicked up for the hundredth time, the cowboy whirled off like a moon from its orbit, before the pickup men could save him.

An anxious silence fell. For a minute the cowboy was lost in the bronco's legs, while a high-strung clown tried to woo the crazy horse from the arena. The sharp edge of a hoof knifed the rider's forearm. One of the pickup men pulled off the flank strap to quell the kick. The other dragged the man from the dirt. Now safely on the pickup horse, he raised his hands toward the stands, sassy. He had held on to his hat and cocked it smugly. In nine seconds on the bronco's spine, he had beaten all the guys before him. In the pen he displayed the long, rough wound, where the unhappy animal had trounced his flesh. "The *trick* is to make those devils your friend," I heard him say. Suddenly he leaped up and ran to the arms of a mustached man who was quite a bit older. The fringe on his chaps quivered brightly. "I damn kicked *ass!*" he cried as the older man swept him up and swung him around. "You damn sure did all right!" said the boyfriend. His excitement was as stoic as a father's.

Among the rough stock chutes and the bleachers, animals and contestants moved about in a scorched hush, as though the high sun had burned the showman out of horse and rider. In the back lot, shiny horse trailers threw off heat like toasters. Frank Reinhardt, the Oklahoma rancher, groomed a mare with long, slow strokes, and flurries of dust and hair flew from the brush like gnats. A rustling band of flies tried to steal some moisture from the animal's nostrils, making it shimmy and snort. She swished her tail across her back but lost pettishly against the insects. A woman in a mountaineer's hat reined her horse in from a trot and, hunching over the saddle horn, whispered cool nothings in the dapple gray's hot ear. It wiggled like a rabbit's. A few yards away, three leathery horsemen leaned against the bed of a pickup truck and haggled over scores and rules. Their rawhide voices mumbled. Their lips parted just enough to twitch their mustaches. Their cheeks, which carried lamb-chop flares, remained motionless. Other than eavesdropping on some sultry conversations like these, my chances for chatting with contestants and fans were slim. Such was the intensity of the sun and the business at hand. I took pictures.

"Camp" events, more than anything else, set the gay rodeos apart from the "straight" circuit. In one, contestants tied a bow in record time on a wild steer's tail while a partner held its horns. There was a race in which drag queens and dykes in drag were to mount and ride a cow. Costume counted as much as speed here. Plenty of disgusted cowboys wanted to butch up the rodeo. "Some of our guys and gals say it's 'too gay,' " Wayne Jakino told me. Proper sex roles were as much the issue in the gay world as they ever were among straights. We were forever drawing fine distinctions. "But a lot of 'em got *their* start this way," Wayne protested. "I tell 'em, 'Don't take that opportunity away from your gay brothers.' *I* think it's educational. It helps get the greenhorns started in a softer way—especially the city boys and gals." It seemed to me that jumping a steer with a bow on its tail was a dangerous act, in any case.

The goat-dressing contest began. The billies were as dumb as dolls, passively roped in the ring to concrete blocks and tractor tires, motionless as if they'd been bought from a taxidermist. Between firm fists, a cowgirl stretched a pair of BVDs and held them taut—just so—to ram them over the goat's ass. A cowboy raised the stupid beast's back legs, as if he were going to cornhole it. The lesbian tried to slip them into the skivvies, all the while arguing with the judge over exactly what the rule book meant by "rump." The lazy animal did scissor kicks and burped. He was plaintive more than obstinate, as if trying to help.

"We get more bruises and cuts from the camp competitions than all the others combined," Wayne said, chuckling. "*Try* it! Those events ain't easy!"

In the bleachers, two robust gentlemen sat in fine felt hats, dress slacks, and high-shined boots, as regal as Texas oil barons. I asked to take their picture. They came from Waco. They didn't volunteer their line of work, and something Texas wealthy in their manner made me fear that such a question would be boorish, given that oil had crashed. They told me that they were lovers. "Together many, many years," said the one with a thick black beard, whom I figured to be the younger by a decade. The older man had snow gray hair. "Just passed our twenty-fourth. Silver one's on its way." Though he didn't take his lover's hand or otherwise touch him intimately, he smiled largely at his friend. The older man, leaning with one elbow on his knee, acknowledged this affection with the palest dip of his hat but didn't remove his eyes from the goat-dressing contest.

In the arena, a cowboy couple and a contest judge stood on either side of a goat, grumbling and gesticulating madly. The judge threw his head from side to side and swore with his hand on the goat's behind as though it were a Bible. In time it seemed the cowboys won the argument. The judge skulked away. The cowboys grinned. The goat grinned back, thin-lipped, as all goats do perpetually.

"Mr. October" from Oklahoma City's Bunkhouse Bar—it was stitched on the back of his shirt—climbed the fence to the main arena, threw one leg, and sat there for a minute, surveying the space, holding his hat to the side of his face to blind the sun. His lasso coiled around one shoulder like an albino rattler while its tail sprang loose against his belt buckle. The enormous gold oval was inset with a silver map of Oklahoma. It glinted as sharp as fangs. He chatted for a minute with a handsome, shirtless man who wore black jeans, black motorcycle boots, and a black leather armband snapped around his bicep. A yellow rodeo souvenir ribbon hung in the breeze from his motorcycle friend's well-muscled chest, fluttering from a tiny bar that pierced his nipple.

The cowboy's name, I overheard, was Gary. In time he jumped across the fence to practice. I rested my long lens on a rung to watch him. First he bent his knees and tested the bounce in his hips. (His smile engraved deep lines along the sides of his mustache.) Next he dropped the loop of his rope into the dirt and pinned it with his boot against his long, thin shadow. Then, retracting the line in tiny jerks through calfskin gloves, he recoiled his rope to get the right spring for the throw. His shoulders arched sharply, adding several inches to his height. His shadow jumped, as if it were scared. The taut white cotton of his shirt revealed a gauzy Marlboro pack. He lifted the lasso above his head, limbering his wrist in tiny revolutions as it rose. At last, with a subtle hand, he gave the loop a lightning snap and turned it into a pale whirring halo. Around the cowboy's umbral figure on the ground, a lasso's awkward twin quivered faintly.

Clowns pranced through the bleachers like floozies, daring drag queens to show their panties. The "girls" were above it all. Miss Colorado Gay Rodeo Association ignored them entirely. She was as padded as Shelley Winters and wore a silver cocktail dress, nothing folksy. Her waist jacket—a piece of Mexico—was black velveteen and embroidered with black blossoms around tiny mirrors, which refracted the colors of the rodeo into tiny particles. They shattered her breasts with their changing patterns—kaleidoscopes or cracked crystal balls. She wore them like reminiscences. Miss Rodeo's hair was vintage Kate Smith, her makeup Elizabeth Arden. She remained in the shade and comported herself with great dignity, attracting quiet conversations with a few good men.

Nearby in the bleachers, a little girl giggled at a clown who pinched her cheeks and fanned her with his big sun hat, which to her must have looked like a big top. She was a plump little child—five or six, perhaps. Her own straw bonnet was fastened with a bow beneath her dimpled chin. A bouquet of bright cloth flowers adorned its crown. Her long hair was swept up beneath the brim, but stray strands cascaded anyway, making red stripes against her freckles and splashing scarlet on her sunshine shirt. A balloon on a string bobbed from her hand, with which she also clutched a large straw purse. She was sitting astraddle one daddy's knee while resting a hand on the other's. Either of her pops—who were as plump and red-cheeked as their daughter—might have been her natural father. They wore mesh trucker's caps that read "Calgary '88" and bore the Olympics logo. Both beamed as they admired their little girl. With all this manly attention from her dads and the flirting clown, she grinned so hard she squinted. Her two front teeth were missing.

The clown led me farther into the bleachers, where a lesbian sat with her foster son, a teenager who was retarded. She squeezed his hand, a black woman protecting a white child, as if keeping a southern tradition. His face shone twice in her big round sunglasses, like a mother's vision. In the mountain peaks to the west, lightning sparked the snow, melting it down to incandescence under clouds like ingots of steel.

There was magic for me at the gay rodeo—in this crowd of alienated men and women reclaiming their past. Many of the homosexuals I knew had fled their heritage, as I had, because "queers" were not allowed a part in it. The cost of remaining in our hometowns was the brutal threat of discovery. Both fear and the bitterness of exile soured a life, leaving it scornful of a wholeness it could not know. That was the grief, I suspected, that underlay the archness of so many homosexual men and the sullenness of so many lesbians. The cowboys and cowgirls at the rodeo were flouting their banishment, just as Reno's parishioners had done in making their own spirit-filled church. If many of the rodeo folks were still "closeted" by gay urban standards, they were closer to healing their lives, it seemed to me, than a host of us homosexuals who had escaped to the cities to scoff at everything we grew up with and still live in exiled secrecy. The men and women at the rodeo taught me the joy of wider possibilities.

Certainly during those two days I got more pictures than personal stories—a thousand small impressions at the speed of a bronco's buck. It occurred to me that pictures were perhaps truer in their descriptions than a writer's notes. Words forever fall short of an instant's light. Few cowboys let me photograph their faces. "I cain't have no gay pictures of me goin' around or I'll have *hell* to pay when I git home," one young cowboy said, refusing me kindly. Like many others, he was registered under a pseudonym, just in case. "Wanna take a picture of my buckle?" he asked, offering me a concession. "Ain't it a prize!" It was—a blinding trophy from another rodeo, all gold and silver with a diamond chip in the middle. I began with him and spent a lot of time shooting pictures on my knees, resorting to back shots, asses, buckles, and crotches—which, in particular, flattered my subjects.

I didn't get to talk to many of the men I photographed. In all the horsey busyness there was often time for no more than a quick request, a wrangler's grin, and a stealthy nod of a hat brim. But any time a longer smile and leisure invited a chat, I found out where my man lived, told him my purpose, and asked if I could visit him and meet his friends when I got to his part of the country. I promised them all strict anonymity, and even the men who hid their faces from the camera seemed eager for the chance to talk about their lives. Men presented me with addresses and phone numbers from Phoenix to Atlanta, as far away as Intercourse, Pennsylvania. No one turned me down.

On Sunday afternoon when I left the rodeo, the Judds were singing on the radio. "*I know where I'm goin'. Don't you wanna come, too? . . .*" Their music had the steaming rhythm of a freedom train.

CHAPTER 5

A
BUNKHOUSE
AT
PEAK 5

THERE WERE MANY TIMES THROUGHOUT MY TRAVELS WHEN I didn't know where I was going next. The day I left Denver presented such a quandary. I might head on down to New Mexico. I might drive up to the mountains to a gay resort that Tom O'Reilly had mentioned to me, adding that neither he nor his friends would be caught dead there. I studied the map and the high, breezy clouds. How do we ever choose the route we'll take, except by the sudden angle of the sun or the speed of the wind that moves a memory? Thus we always set out in some new direction that is haunted by an old one. I had loved the sunny hilltop cabins my parents took me to when I was a boy. I phoned the gay mountain lodge, which was named the Bunkhouse. It was in Breckenridge, near Peak 5 in a rocky procession of summits. A gruff man answered the phone and said his name was Rudy. He warned me to make a reservation now or risk losing out by the evening. "We're the only gay resort between the Rockies and California," he declared. "If we're full, you're out of luck."

At high noon the snow on the mountains seared a blinding

heartbeat across the sky, tearing off the tenderest blues like the vivid, ragged line of a cardiogram. My map would have had me think that the interstate from Denver to the turnoff for Breckenridge was an easy four-lane pass, cutting a gentle swath through the Rockies. Cartographers, like other guides to life, lure us travelers with comforting illusions, lest we heel in our tracks and refuse to keep on the path.

My car was disillusioned first, groaning and shivering on the steep inclines, which started in low, round hills high enough to be called mountains back east. The slopes were a patchwork of dark spruce groves, needle-stitched with piñones and scrub oaks, like a Conestoga quilt. At Buffalo Herd Overlook, a tuft of big brown beasts grazed indistinct in the distance, situated surely enough—like samples in a zoo or Indians—on reserved land: a labeled breed. I tried to take a picture as I drove but was cut off by a bright Ford pickup with a camper in its bed. Its passengers were two fine young men who sported precise haircuts and mustaches. Their T-shirts were taut on their chests. I thought they were gay. They nodded but didn't grin or wave—and left me with even less to hang my presumptions on. A confession or a night in bed is the only way to know for sure, and even that will not yield truth sometimes.

Though accustomed to high Denver, I grew light-headed again as the atmosphere thinned out with every mile. The music on the radio died. The wind blew cold. I cracked the window and let it sing. Soaring slopes spun clouds into great, still veils, like climbers' banners flying frozen from each conquered summit. It seemed like hours before I reached a kind of midpoint at the Eisenhower Memorial Tunnel. Opening twin cold mouths into the mountain's belly, it burrowed beneath the Continental Divide, and its dark, silent descent seemed to bridge vast underworlds to the visible American nation. Beyond their reemergence into light, Dillon Reservoir—its surface a changing mottle of shimmering blue and winter gray—spread out like an arctic island against the sky and made a shoreline of the road to Breckenridge. Lofty Peak 5 rose in the north, in the midst of a string of peaks that were stark wilderness.

| | |

Rudy's fort, for it was a fort, sat desolate in the middle of a long stone quarry in a narrow valley a few miles from town. High stacks of firewood walled in his house. On the split timber gate, an antelope skull was nailed to a beam between two wagon wheels and stared down upon all who would enter.

I parked the car in front by the wall of logs, which two mammoth Siberian huskies—barking madly and brushing the sky with the plumes of their tails—had mounted to greet me. As I stepped toward the gate, they suddenly dropped from sight and reappeared below the antelope's fleshless pate, at breathless attention on either side of their master. Their eyes fixed mine.

Rudy nodded a sullen welcome, spying on me from beneath his buckskin hat. He growled—more querulous than angry—as though to confide in me about a troubled day. "You have to park over there," he ordered. The dogs seemed to regard this tone of voice as kindness and stood relaxed, while Rudy pointed to a row of trucks and tractors several yards away. "The kid in the trailer"—he jerked his head toward a dusty mobile home—"he's trying to take this land for his right-of-way. I'll win yet." And, shooing the dogs, he closed the gate and climbed in my car for the little ride.

It was when I'd parked again that Rudy continued his gripe, averting his eyes peevishly. "All these belong to the kid . . ." He scowled at the collection of dirty vehicles. His voice was clear and tenor, and though he was a stocky mountaineer of middle age, he sounded like a slight schoolboy tattling on the playground bully. "He's one of those guys," Rudy hissed, "that thinks he can get away with anything."

Rudy had owned this enclave of mountain land for twenty-five years—blissful years as long as the old man and his wife in the cabin along the entrance road owned the quarry. The old woman had even supplied Rudy with homemade jams. "Well, then," Rudy continued quarrelsomely, helping me with my bags, "this kid comes up here out of nowhere—Denver or something—and buys them out, and all I get is problems." Last winter the intruder had bulldozed six feet of snow right up to the antelope gate. "I couldn't get out of my own house! He just *laughed*! He said all the land around the wall was his and there wasn't anything I could do about it." He seemed to have breathlessly rehearsed this woe a thousand times. It was the grief of a frontiersman who, for all his claim to unimpeded passage, had been made a bridgeless, boatless island in the world. "The kid doesn't like queers," Rudy told me. "But I was here a hell of a long time before *he* was!"

The root of the trouble was the Bunkhouse deed—which "leaves out a lot," its owner conceded. "I was nothing but a boy when I bought this place. My lawyer was a hack. I just paid and signed. So now I got a *gay* attorney. He took the case, then checked into some clinic or something to dry out. Gays are all alcoholics," he sniffed. "Especially the lawyers."

This haven that Rudy fought to keep was a step back in time from the brutally strip-mined quarry around it, where a field of death-white gravel stretched toward the mountain ridge a few miles away. Inside the fortress walls, a preserve of tall spruce trees guarded the gabled cabin, while careful piles of logs stood like barricades around a huge log doghouse. A rock-paved path, strewn golden with spruce needles and broken cones, led to a low plank door and a narrow shack attached to the house. Here at the cabin's entrance, all outdoor clothing came off. Ski jackets and fleece-lined coats hung from pegs that studded the walls. Tennis shoes, ski boots, and cowboy boots were paired like gaping traps across the floor. A second door with a rusty horseshoe nailed into its lintel opened onto yet another anteroom, where a pair of steer horns and a huge set of antlers held caps, earmuffs, and an array of mountaineer and western hats. The outside wall, above a fine, old rolltop desk, exhibited a display of framed aphorisms:

"Beware of 'owner.' Don't worry about dog." This was a photograph of a rough wooden sign nailed to a tree.

"A dog teaches man fidelity, perseverance, and to turn around three times before lying down. Robert Benchley."

"May You Always Have the Freedom to Be Yourself."

Prominent among Rudy's maxims, in a sleek silver frame, was

a letter he had received a decade before on White House stationery:

November 19, 1976

Dear Rudy,
Thank you for your kind invitation to stop by the Bunk House
at Christmastime. I appreciate your thoughtful gesture but
unfortunately will not be able to join you at that time because
of other plans I have made.

Best wishes,
Jack Ford

It was autographed simply "Jack," the President's son, about
whom there had always been whispers.

The rest of the house was spacious, deep, and warm, with log
walls and dark pine ceilings and floors that glowed like copper in
the lamplight. Through a door across from the entrance, a water
bed lay in a shellacked pine box as big as a backyard pool. From
its undulating leisure one could look through a wide picture window at the firs in the yard and the darkening snow-streaked
mountaintops beyond. From this angle the walls of Rudy's fortress cut off every hint of the quarry, as though the Bunkhouse
were in fact—not illusion—a refuge lost in time in an endless virgin woods.

The rest of the rooms downstairs were a rustic clutter of
wooden benches, an old church pew, little oak tables stacked with
pornographic magazines, and overstuffed reading chairs from the
thirties. In the dining room or den—it also contained a sofa,
stereo, and family-size TV—there stood a thick-topped round
pine table big enough to seat sixteen. A triangle hung in the
kitchen doorway to call guests to meals.

A fireplace of large round stones covered the long north wall
of the living room, the side of the cabin blizzard winds struck
first. The hearth today smelled cold, of ashes. The mantel was a
rough-hewn log overrun with dusty odds and ends, some of use,
some not: antique bottles and jugs, a brass oil lamp, gears from

mine machinery, drill bits, and little stuffed toy animals. A steer-hide overlapped a rocking chair, which was angled in the corner below a deer's mounted head. A well-worn saddle straddled an antique hobby horse. Yukon, the husky male, sat in the yard and surveyed the room through the picture window. Shiloh, the bitch, lay on the floor by the hearth, her back paws curled around to meet her muzzle. Resting her face on the grizzly brown head of a bear rug, she watched me relentlessly with one brown eye and one eye ice blue. Rudy was taking messages off his answering machine. Seeing me stare at Shiloh's huge head, he presumed I admired her eyes and announced dully, "It's a natural variation. It's genetic, like being gay." Many homosexually active men thought that way. It gave them an excuse for their natural desires in a world where they were reviled. It relieved them of guilt for the sexual choices they had made.

In spite of Rudy's brusque warning that morning that I reserve a space, there was to be only one other guest for the weekend, I found. A young man from San Antonio had called to say he would be arriving late. Rudy showed me my choice of dormitories upstairs, which were entered by a ladder through a trapdoor. The cabin's second story was a large open room filled with built-in bunks, each with a private curtain along its length. One more story up, the floor of a dark attic loft was covered with wrestling mats, where guests could share their muscular sleep orgiastically. Rudy's fort was built for communal sex—a relic of the years before the plague, when forbidden desire ran free. It held the dank smell of old passions—like boxes of yellowed photographs and trunks of once youthful clothes. "It's just three of us for the weekend," Rudy repeated disbelievingly, long after I'd picked out my bed and opened my bags. "So anywhere you want to sleep is fine with me." It sounded like a plea.

"None of those rodeo cowboys from Denver ever come up here anymore," he grumbled bitterly as we climbed back downstairs. "*This* is where real cowboys come! You have to hike and ride like a man when you come up here, not just dress up. I'm up here fighting this asshole kid that wants to run me out because I'm queer—*and where are my gay brothers?*"

The room at the foot of the ladder was strewn with big sturdy pillows—the sort that had filled the orgy rooms of bathhouses in the pre-AIDS days. A video screen dominated one wall. "For hot flicks," Rudy informed me. A stale sauna sat across the room. On a workout bench—an old convenience for the quick pump-up before a quick fuck—a Ken doll knelt on his hands and knees, nude except for a miniature backpack and a tiny pair of hiking boots. His crotch arched above his bare-assed clone, who lay on his belly. They were dusty.

Rudy refused to cook for only two, but had collected a stash of "two-fer" coupons. The Bunkhouse truck was broken. I drove. In this wounded mood he was in, the vast, harsh quarry that dwarfed Rudy's fort seemed to overwhelm its proprietor, too, leaving him small and abandoned. He slumped mortally against the door. As we passed the old quarry owners' cabin, an oncoming headlight ignited the anger in his face.

"Where are the gays with balls?" he spat. "Especially ever since AIDS, when the going gets rough, you know. . . ." All along the northern shore of Dillon Reservoir, he told me the story again of the "queer-hating kid" and the drunk gay coward lawyer who had failed to fight off the bigot. He savored every nuance of his long abuse. "Get the shovel and just shovel 'em up," he said. "I'll just say that I run the only gay resort in the Rockies, twenty-five years, except for my time in 'Nam and teaching skiing in Europe, and gays don't do a damn thing to support it—*then I'm off that!*" he promised when we got to the restaurant.

Still, I suspect that he would have quickly broken his vow if the sight of a young blond man at the table beside us hadn't jarred an ecstatic memory. And except for a few brief relapses to the "kid" and disloyal "gay brothers," it was this prurient kind of remembrance that consumed Rudy's chatter that weekend. It seemed to me a perhaps unconscious ploy he'd practiced for years—tales of romance and sex to inflame the libido of his guests.

"He's *perfect*, man! *Perfect!*" Rudy proclaimed the young, blond man, who was sitting with his young blond girlfriend. They both had blue eyes. Everyone looked like skiers here. Rudy was disgusted by the woman's presence. "A woman doesn't know the first thing about taking care of a man like that. What can any girl do for a jock?" He watched the fellow's every move intensely, like an NFL fan watching a flawless pass. For a moment the man smiled back, but so subtly that his woman friend's attention wasn't even fleetingly distracted.

"I met this beautiful Dutch man right after I got to Europe, who wanted to befriend me," Rudy began a story. "He kept telling me I ought to meet his brother, who lived in Switzerland. His brother was a mountain man just like me." Rudy's voice was rapid and staccato, hushed and surprised. He was a child concocting dialogue, embellishing an adventure. "A few weeks later I got to his family's house in Amsterdam and he said, 'Let's call my mountain man brother!' All of them talked to him, and then they said, 'Here's Rudy. He's a mountain man, too!' So the brother said, 'Ven are you comin' to visit me, mountain man?' I says, 'I've got two more weeks before I start teaching.' He said, 'Then come now. Take the train to my village,' and he told me how to find him.

"Have you seen *Women in Love?*" Rudy asked me. "Well, anyway, it was just like that. You know, there was all this homosexual tension and they fought it out? Remember when they're coming down the mountain on the sleds? Well, we used those same kinds of sleds. Only we didn't fight it out, we *talked* man to man."

The waitress brought our dinners, which had to be the same to use the two-fers. Our "red snapper Florentine" was stuffed with spinach and covered with mozzarella. I tossed my parsley off. Rudy identified it as asparagus and ate it. On my orange slice he continued his story. A blizzard had blown up while they were sledding, and Rudy lost his friend. A skiier helped Rudy get to the bottom. "And who was standing right there smiling?" Rudy exclaimed. "So he said, 'Hey, man, you need a sauna.' So he took me to a place in the town and took his clothes off, this beautiful man.

"So we're sittin' there gettin' high on some wine and he says, 'Hey, we are both mountain men. You are an open person.' And

I am," Rudy interjected. " 'So can I ask you something?' I said, 'Sure, man. Shoot.' He says, 'Anything?' I said, 'Hey, buddy, we're both mountain men. We've been spending this time together. What do you want to know?' So he said, 'Okay. I am with you for a time now and I do not hear you talk about women. Are you a lover of men?'

"Can you believe that!"

"Was he gay?" I asked.

"No! But he *understood,*" Rudy protested. "He was an open, honest man, and I know men. There's that brotherhood. I had this fraternity with him. Men have that."

Our waitress intruded on Rudy's reverie to take our order for dessert. Rudy stared at her, as though he were noticing her feminine presence for the first time all evening. She was as young and handsome as the fellow diner who earlier had captured Rudy's eye. She was athletic in her stance, but coquettish when she talked. She smiled through squared-off lips, re-creating the toothy face Farrah Fawcett perfected, which contorted her speech. At the end of each question or statement, she shook out her head and set thousands of carefully ragged curls to quivering. Rudy summed her up with a glance when she left. "She looks nice. But could you put up with something like that for the rest of your life?" he said.

"There's this soccer player I met on the slopes here one time," he was reminded. "I brought him back to the house with this big body builder friend of his—Mr. Missouri or something. The soccer player—*Gene!*—was a beaut of a man. So I take them into the sauna, you know, and bring in these buckets of snow, then get out the oil and rub down Gene's buddy. That guy has a dick like *this!*" Rudy still seemed astonished at the length he'd drawn between his palms. "He'd had a really hard workout and wanted to let me take care of him. So Gene complains and I say, 'Hey, man, you're always number one. You said you're an only child. You always got all the attention.' He'd gotten himself injured in a match in Denver. So he says, 'I'm the injured one!' And I tell him, 'You *know,* man, I'm a coach. I always save the best till last.'

"I finish up with his buddy and Gene stays with me. He takes off his towel and his big ole dick was hanging there six inches soft! I rolled him over on his belly and worked his leg and wrapped his knee for him. Then I'm working his ass and thighs and I feel this knot, in the dark, you know, and when I touched it I thought, Jesus! That's gotta be rubbed down real hard. It was the head of his fuckin' cock, man, stickin' out on the side! So I climbed on top of him and rubbed down his back and shoulders. When I turned him over, his cock was still stickin' straight up there. So I did his thighs and chest and worked my way down and put some oil on his dick and started rubbing. He covered his eyes with his arm, you know, and arched and wrapped his legs around me so my cock was *right there*! Right when he started to shoot—man, it was so much, it was like he was pissin'—my prick slid right in and, two or three strokes, I blew it up his ass. He just laid there shaking. I said, 'You okay, man?'

" 'Yeah. I never did that before, man. This is just between you and me. Okay?'

"I was the coach," Rudy explained, and looked at me hard to punch in some larger meaning. "All these guys have fantasies about their asses and their coach. I said, 'Just relax. I just gave you a damn good rubdown. That's all.' I saw him a lot for a while after that, but we never talked about it. He'd always talk about loving me, but nothing about sex. From then on he always put like a buffer between us—like a date or a teammate around for protection. So, you know, after a while he moved to St. Louis to go pro, and I get this phone call. 'Hey, Rudy,' " Rudy said, recalling their dialogue. " 'You know I love ya, man.'

" 'Yeah, Gene, I know that.'

" 'Well, I gotta tell ya somethin', man. I'm gettin' married. I gotta know what you think about it.'

" 'Hey, man, you're askin' that and you know I love you. I want you with *me*!'

" 'Society just won't let us live that way. All my buddies are gettin' married.'

"She's this musician," Rudy snapped, and shoved back from his plate. "She was away at college studying Beethoven and Bach and all that, and I tell him I think he needs a jock. 'What are you gonna do with this woman who's a musician and you're an athlete, man? You need someone who understands that.' I coulda done so much for that guy. I don't mean sexually. I mean being his buddy. I understand men, real well. I've always been a jock." He sat back in his chair and fired off his résumé like commands in calisthenics. "I was all-collegiate basketball in college—the house! I taught PE, skiing, soccer. I set up the whole damn high school ski program for the American schools in Europe. I got two lifetime passes to the slopes for that!

"I've spent my life with men! Gene *needed* me. He needed someone that understood a jock like a jock does."

I had never been a man's man, as Rudy was. I had been literary, musical, histrionic, and had nearly always viewed jocks as my mortal enemies. They were the kinds of guys who ridiculed me and sometimes beat me up. Both my effeminacy and my desire for men made me an outcast. I saw them as one psychic flaw and when "I came out" tried to redeem both iniquities, making a virtue of them. I insisted that all truly self-accepting homosexual men knew in their hearts that they were sissies and "acted gay." The "straight-acting" men were fooling themselves. I posited an exclusive gay world in which, for the first time in my life, I would be the consummate insider. So despotic can the social vision be of a man who feels he's always been slighted. It seems to me now that this is the myth-making impulse that drives the gay movement—and fuels a monolithic vision of gay brotherhood.

In time, life intruded upon my opinions. (The rodeo would have been enough.) But still it was hard for me to share in Rudy's jock fraternity. There was a mystical look in his eye when he spoke of it. For Rudy, this enclosed sexual life among athletes was a profound communion, spiritually rooted in Olympic manhood. My vision of gayness would have undermined the codes of masculinity. His would proclaim them. Our homosexualities were very different.

Rudy's fantasy man at the restaurant had stood with his girlfriend to leave. Rudy caught his eye again. Again they exchanged slow smiles. The woman seemed none the wiser. This played into Rudy's story. "So one and a half years after Gene married her," he continued abruptly, "he gets divorced. Last time I saw him, he was living with this other woman—some thin little lady that wears those little print dresses and puts her hair up like, I don't know, a schoolteacher or something."

"Does he sleep with her?"

"He pretends," he hissed. "She's nothin' but a housekeeper to him."

"Do they plan to get married?"

"He won't ever make that mistake again. She's just for show."

By the time we started home, the weather had turned nasty. A strong wind grabbed the car, and in the moonlight, long, low clouds raced past great, gray, slow ones, which had settled upon the reservoir like cold ducks. Rudy checked the sky and announced a snow. "It's not too late in the summer yet," he stated.

At the stop sign where the Breckenridge road, the exit ramp, and the freeway entrance all converged, Rudy suddenly grabbed my arm. *"Check that out!"* he whispered. Just a few feet down the ramp stood a young man thumbing. "Maybe he needs a place to stay," Rudy speculated. "It could be fun."

I pulled over, and he motioned the hitchhiker to the car. The traveler's face was pleasant enough, but his hair was matted and his torn clothes stank. He was probably twenty, no older. Rudy asked him where he was going.

The poor man stared, then answered stupidly, "Anywhere I can." He emitted a dry little laugh.

"Looks like snow," Rudy warned. "You get stuck out here tonight, you'll freeze." He offered his hand to introduce himself, but the boy didn't take the offer. "What's *your* name?" Rudy asked.

"I got lots of names," he replied vacantly, and peered into the car. "Names aren't important. Call me something that makes you happy."

Rudy chose "Jake" and rolled up the window for a minute to ask me, "What do you think? He seems a little crazy." But he didn't want to leave him in the cold. I would have opted to put him in a motel room for a night. Rudy told him to jump in.

Back at the Bunkhouse, Nick, the weekend's other guest, had arrived and was waiting. Rudy took his credit card, then busied himself about Jake. Jake never so much as twitched without specific instructions. Rudy gave him a towel, pointed him to the shower, and told him to throw his clothes out the bathroom door so he could wash them. But when Rudy saw his socks and shorts in a rancid pile, he decided to throw them out. "You could never kill the lice," he stated.

While Jake bathed and dressed in a pair of Rudy's skivvies and a robe, the rest of us sprawled on the orgy pillows in the "hot flicks" room to watch a *Nightline* special, Ted Koppel's marathon on AIDS. (This was what erotic space had come to.) Jeffrey Levi, the director of the National Gay & Lesbian Task Force, was dryly decrying AIDS-related discrimination. His name flashed across the screen. Jake stood by the bathroom door and rubbed his hands like Lady Macbeth. Rudy snarled at Levi's face on television. "Look at this guy. Look at his name. What right does some big-city Jew have to speak for the rest of gays?"

Only when Harvey Fierstein, the playwright, interrupted Koppel did Jake pause to listen. Koppel had told the listening world that safe sex for gay men meant no sex or monogamy. "Ted, excuse me," Fierstein rasped in his sandpaper Brooklynese, raising his hand like a precocious schoolchild. "Can I be honest wit'ya on family television? If you practice safe sex, you can be as promiscuous as you want. You can masturbate"—he pumped the air mischievously with his hand for all of Koppel's America to see—"with a thousand men and not get sick from it."

Koppel's stunned smile froze as he tried to convince his audience that Fierstein wasn't serious. Jake, whose head had been cocked like a curious puppy's, turned his back to the screen and played with his hands again. I went upstairs for the night long before Ted Koppel's national anguish ended. Nick lay head to head with Rudy on a sex pillow. Jake was curled up asleep on a bear rug. When I got up in the morning, Nick was in his own bed, and Rudy had clothed Jake, fed him, and sent him on his way.

| | |

On Saturday I played with Rudy's huskies, and napped, day-dreaming about where I should travel next. Rudy and Nick explored back trails and a hard-to-find hot springs, where (Nick told me later) Rudy told tales about the jocks he'd "had" in that very spot. When Nick left for home on Sunday morning, he'd heard all the tales that I had. Over brunch Rudy told me more. He had fixed an enormous deep-pan omelet and fresh blueberry muffins served with homemade jams. He knew how to feed a man. The motto on the front of my coffee mug read "The answer is men. . . . It's the question that's indecent."

While we ate, he flipped through an old recipe box. On the back of each recipe card he'd recorded the name, address, and phone number of every Bunkhouse guest, with some private observations. He was looking for an unused card on which to file me. On the way he found " 'Josh Goldstein, Maywood, New Jersey.' Not far from where you live," he surmised. "You could look him up." Josh was "cream cheese–stuffed salmon. Skier! Swimmer. Hot young man—fuzzy butt. Engineer." Whatever Rudy thought of Jews' speaking for gays on national television, he obviously found some good in bed.

There was also a Denver Broncos quarterback and a second Bronco whose wife had brought him to Breckenridge for skiing. Rudy had lent her his lifetime pass for the afternoon and fucked her husband in their hotel room, where he'd stayed behind with their napping baby. Then there was the player on the Dolphins' second string. "God! That ass!" Rudy grunted. "They just don't make asses like that, except on football players. I picked him up hitchhiking after a game." Rudy had taken him into his sauna and given him a rubdown, moving his cock in place against the athlete's ass. "He didn't move," Rudy remembered, "and I pressed it against him a little harder and he still doesn't move, but I'm getting nowhere because those football players' asses . . . you know, and I'm seven inches! So now I'm all the way down and no ways near in. So he starts laughing and says, 'You haven't been around a lot of football players, have you? You basketball players don't have asses.'

"Getting fucked is a big moment in a guy's life," Rudy announced. "The first time especially." He once picked up a hitchhiker named John, who was stationed at Lowry Air Force Base. "He was a redhead," he said, "a real hot kid. He was a wrestler in high school. Great body." According to the tale, the boy had knocked up a hometown girl. His father, an Ohio police chief, had forced him into the air force to clean up his act. When Rudy met him, he was going AWOL. John told Rudy he never did anything with guys except get blow jobs.

Rudy brought him home. "He didn't have anywhere to stay, you know." A Bunkhouse guest sucked him off. "So then he comes upstairs and wants me to give him a rubdown on the mats in the loft. I start talking to him about wrestling. He's got oil all over him and I go down on his cock. You know, I'm his coach, taking care of the team. Then he rolls over on his belly and I fuck him. When he came, man, he just starts crying—he's scared to death and happy at the same time, you know, because I'm his coach and he's always had a fantasy about that. He's having a real rough time with it, though, and tells me, 'My father would kill me if he saw me like this.'

"I stayed with him there, man. I held him and we *talked* about it. When you fuck a man"—Rudy paused—"that's like going into a man's sanctuary, the most sacred part of a man. Unless you're gonna take time, you don't ever do that to one of your brothers."

Like Rudy's lonely cabin, all his stories seemed musty. The fear of AIDS and Rudy's age had long emptied out his lodge. Still, he waited. He was a man of deep religious awe, a wayfarer's high hermit priest of desire, clinging to wasted magic.

CHAPTER 6

PROCESSION
OF
SUMMITS

On monday morning when i left rudy, one slope alone lay sunlit through the slow clouds rolling across the mountains. He silently pointed it out while I packed the car. Yukon and Shiloh sat still at his feet. "An avalanche up there took four good skiiers down last winter," he told me, reverent and bitter. "*Damn!* That's hard, man. A wall of snow buried those guys thirty feet under heaven! There's lots of ghosts in these mountains." Then, hardly shaking off his sadness, he repeated the route that would lead me to a preserved ghost town between Alma and Fairplay, which a friend of his tended, and insisted I pay a visit. "He was town marshal," Rudy began, "over this ridge here toward Climax. Used to go out drinking without his wife, then show up at the Bunkhouse in his uniform for some fun—"

I interrupted. I was headed to Santa Fe, a day's drive away. I was late getting started.

Though I had always planned to visit New Mexico, this Santa Fe trip was last minute. To some extent my procrastination was deliberate. From the beginning I'd opted to depend on the unexpected, letting men I met in one place guide me to men in another. I had intended all along to avoid meeting men through gay political and AIDS organizations. Throughout my years of gay activism it had become apparent to me that activists hardly represented the mass of homosexually active Americans, not even most of that much smaller group that called itself "gay." I wanted to find the silenter lives that lay beneath a movement's pronouncements and beyond the media's unlikely images.

I had been given a couple of names in New Mexico before I left San Francisco—but none that "spoke" to me. One was a wealthy board member of a national gay rights organization; the other was a favorite French chef of Santa Fe Opera patrons. They struck me as atypical in this desperately poor, dry state. But having temporized right up to the day before I departed the Bunkhouse, I was left with no one to visit and in the end resorted to a political directory I carried with me. It was an adventureless way, I thought, to go about discovering things. One listing, though, piqued my curiosity about commonly hidden truths— "Common Knowledge," with a Santa Fe telephone number. I called from Rudy's orgy attic, where I watched the red sun fall quickly and the dusk behind the purple mountains pulse pink. A soft-voiced, hesitant man named Rand answered the phone. I told him about my project and that I would like to talk to members of his group.

"I need to speak to my partner for a minute," was the only thing he answered right away. Then there was nothing but air on the line. When he returned, he said that neither he nor his colleague, Alex, could tell me much about gay life in New Mexico. They themselves had only recently moved there. They had become the leaders of Common Knowledge, the local gay group, only by default, because no one else would agree to. "We're psychics!" Rand exclaimed suddenly. A 3,500-year-old spirit who was channeled by Alex had led them from Key West to Santa Fe, he reported. "All week long we've been feeling we were going to get a visitor. We believe you're supposed to stay with us while you're here." He gave me detailed directions.

| | |

The highway to New Mexico ran close to the sky down the spine of the mountains. At the ghost town some miles from Breckenridge, I looked up Rudy's friend, Sven Jorgenson. I assumed that the spirit-led chat I had had with Rand would intrigue him, living his life among haunts as he did. He ignored it when I told him about it. I think it didn't fit his image of the sorts of things a gay writer would sincerely be interested in, and so perhaps he felt I was pandering. "So you going down to Santa Fe for the opera?" he asked instead, watering a hops vine by the old apothecary shop, then turning the hose on a fiery yellow patch of poppies. He wanted to walk me around town. Down the dirt street, on the porch of the derelict bank, a big Persian cat crawled out of the floorboards and rolled on her back lasciviously.

"Isn't it a shame," he said, laughing, "that kittens, little girls, and cute pickaninnies grow up so fast to be pussies and prowlin' niggers?"

Sven's brazenness certainly amazed me, though I didn't challenge him any more than I had Rudy or Scotty and the prejudiced cowboys. I wasn't on the road to carry a social gospel. I was looking for America through the eyes of homosexual men. So I kept silent and learned that bigotry was one of the multitude of traits American homosexuals and heterosexuals held in common.

Sven showed me to the old law office, where attorneys had once bartered with frontier justice. Forty-eight inches of snow in two days had collapsed the roof last winter. A hole in the ceiling went through to the sky. A pair of wire-rimmed glasses lay beside a dusty oil lamp on a rolltop desk, where a lawyer had abandoned them close to a century ago. Sven brushed away the veil of splinters and plaster. He had hired a prison gang from the Buena Vista—"*Bona* Vista"—penitentiary to repair all his buildings, but they had never made it around to this one. "If you don't believe in capital punishment, you would after you worked with *them*," he insisted. "I learned so many cuss words! The old ones all change when you hear 'em with a Mexican or nigger accent."

He had made his own office here. An open window looked out beyond a stony cliff to a steep valley lush with spruces. Hard mountain backs scalloped the sky. Sven talked about the memorabilia he had displayed in the room. He slipped the tattered St. Joseph's missal of his childhood off a shelf, wanting to explain to me in intricate detail his lifelong odyssey of faith. First Roman Catholic, then Old Catholic, then Episcopal, he was Russian Orthodox now. He was looking for Christian truth, he told me. He had embraced each new antique dogma devoutly.

I half listened, staring at a photograph of two young children that hung on the wooden wall. A sepia print in an old oval frame, it might have been from the 1880s but wasn't. "These are my kids," he told me. The girl was thirteen, the boy six. "You were talking about the psychics down in New Mexico? My boy sees ghosts, too. When he was three, we were having Christmas dinner at my aunt's. She lives in a beautiful old Victorian house outside Alma. All of a sudden he just went crazy. He said he saw an old man sitting in the corner. He wouldn't calm down. So I got an old photo album out to distract him, and he pointed to one of the pictures and said, 'That's him—that's the man!' It was my great-uncle. He built the house. That same thing had happened to a couple of my friends. It's made me a real believer."

Sven himself had "Victorian dreams." No sooner would he find old, mysterious gadgets lying around town than he would dream about them. "The dreams," he said, "always show me exactly what those things were used for without me looking them up." He took me farther down the street, where a cold, yellow wind spun tops in the dust. At the dentist's office, every plier and pick lay in place, so tidily had the doctor arranged his instruments before he'd died in the 1920s, and no one had ever disturbed them. The cottage next door had belonged to Sven's great-grandmother, who had died in 1914. The windows were open. Long lace curtains writhed in the breeze. His grandmother had been born there and celebrated her golden wedding anniversary in that house when he was a boy. "She was in her seventies then," he said, "and still got on a horse to ride to Denver a couple of times of year. It took her three days each way.

"Of course I never knew my *great*-grandma, but I always felt like she shaped my life." She had immigrated from Sweden. As a child Sven had been given all her letters and books. He had majored in Swedish in college and taught it to his kids to preserve the past. "A few years ago," he said, "it dawned on me that Great-Grandma was buried up here in the mountains without a gravestone. I wanted to give her one." One night after he had ordered a granite monument from Canon City, he dreamed that his great-grandmother was standing above her grave and reading the epitaph. She slapped the stone with her hand and complained, "Vell, dis is goot, but vouldn't you know after all dese years dey spell my name wrong."

"I couldn't sleep all night," he remembered. He rose early the next morning and called the shop. They were just then beginning to cut the stone. On the order, they had misspelled the name, just as it was in his dream. "People can say what they want," he said, "but I know my great-grandmother was speaking to me from beyond the grave."

A precipice at the edge of town fell hundreds of feet into a narrow, barren valley. It was there, where there was nothing more left to show me, that he first broached his homosexuality—and then obliquely. "There's a gay bar in San Francisco," he began, then stalled. "But you probably know the one." He was naive. There were hundreds of gay bars in the Bay Area. "I go down for the opera and drop in there for a drink," he said, then abruptly abandoned the topic. He did not seem squeamish to me so much as vacant, as if he had lost himself in a vision more inscrutable than his great-grandmother's ghost.

With so narrow an entrance, I pressed the issue, curious about the way this married man and father lived his life. I was politic, merely mentioning his friendship with Rudy. "I wouldn't call myself a *friend* of Rudy's," he corrected without disdain. "More an acquaintance. Totally different life-styles. *Completely* different thing." Then his eyes turned bright and he laughed. "A couple of years ago I was in Breckenridge to testify at a trial and stopped by to visit Rudy. He had thirty people or so around that big dinner table and was standing there telling stories. He had his back to me when I came in. I was in my marshal's uniform. Everyone else went dead silent. Well, Rudy just thought he had the floor and kept on going. So I went up behind and put my hand on his shoulder and told him, 'You have the right to remain silent, but that's probably impossible.'

"Well, all those guys went *crazy!* They thought it was a raid. A couple of 'em crawled under the table. A couple more climbed out the window in the pantry. I don't know if he *ever* saw those men again."

Sven chuckled until he shook, then furrowed his brow. *"Jesus!"* he exclaimed. "I bet I haven't been by the Bunkhouse in two and a half years. You have to tell Rudy hi for me next time you're up in Breckenridge. I've had some good times at the Bunkhouse, if you know what I mean. I wouldn't want to *live* that way. Lifestyle's just too different."

It occurred to me that there were men—perhaps most men—whom sexual labels failed. Rudy seemed to think of Sven as a gay man stuck with a wife. Others might describe him as "bisexual," yet a third sexual breed. But those terms, like "straight," signify a way of life in which sex is deemed the core of identity, the single Freudian need or act that controls the psyche and determines the scope of a human being. Even this early in my journey, such a way of looking at sex was beginning to seem exotic to me, a precious myth. One might as sensibly concoct natural categories out of the sports men choose to play or the foods they eat, religious dogmas or politics—any multitude of the changeable preferences to which men and women devote themselves. I suspected, though vaguely, that if Sven's attraction to men was too incidental to characterize him as "homosexual" and if "heterosexual" cut too close a sweep, "bisexual" was too even-handed. For Sven, it seemed, devotion to the supernatural was the more summary need that he had built a life upon, less fickle than sexual taste.

Down the back of the Rockies, two narrow lanes clung to cliffs etched silver with snow. In time a narrow valley appeared, then broadened again and again into a vast meadow, a soaring spring green tableland flat as a prairie and higher by thousands of feet than the tops of the East Coast's mountains. Tan pastures sprawled polka-dotted with cows. From here Colorado's highest peaks seemed merely to hump, like river knolls or foothills. Near Salida the earth rusted and swelled—a red fossil sea, sargasso with sage-brush and piñon. Here, three black storms, hanging midair and sweeping northeast, curtained the sky with their high downpours. Mt. Shevano towered violet in the west. Under a braid of white-and-charcoal clouds, its platinum peak cracked with lightning.

On a treacherous stretch of road with no place to pass, an eighteen-wheeler began to ride my tail, trumpeting its horn when I slowed down to ward him off, rolling to within a half car's length when I sped to escape him. The pavement twisted. I eased off the gas till the car stopped almost dead and pumped the brakes in warning. But he held tight and, in order to miss rear-ending me, was narrowly forced to swerve between the cliff and precipice. In the rearview mirror I saw his face contort with curses. I fled again. He gunned it and, hard on the horn, rammed my bumper till a grade or another hairpin curve made him loose the advantage.

For twenty miles I raced just ahead of him before I found a safe place to pull off. The gas tank was close to empty. I tried to stop at a filling station in a fork of the highway, but the trucker broadsided the rig in front of me and jumped out, brandishing a bat. I floored it. In the cloud of gravel and dust that spun up as I passed, he swirled on one foot. Like lightning he kicked in my fender and pelted me with a hail of rocks that shattered the rear window. I stopped to cuss him out, but in those split seconds he was back in the cab, in gear, and thundering up behind me again, holding the bat outside like a javelin.

With the roar of his engine and the blasts of his horn in my ears, sometimes I hit eighty-five, then ninety. The car quivered with speed and the altitude. The highway was deserted. I planned as a last resort wrecking and running into the hills for cover while he trashed the car. I scanned the roadside for trails—and boulders, in case he had a gun—and depended on blind curves. The steering wheel was slick with sweat. Hunched over, I held the pedal to the floor and watched the needle edge toward Empty.

A road sign read "Saguache 19 Miles." For minutes I lost the truck beyond a bend. Then it gained again till a long, last curve near town blocked it out. I pushed harder yet—ever closer to a hundred miles per hour while the speed limit dropped to forty-five, then within a half mile dropped twice by ten. I hoped a cop would stop me, but at such times, I found, there never was one. I had sped halfway through the village past a derelict string of cement-block stores and crusty mobile homes before I skidded into the lot of an old gas station for safety. Two pumps stood in the gravel, bent and rusted. A feeble neon light glowed through the sooty window. A decrepit man stepped to the door and watched. I parked behind the garage and, scouring the road for the aggressor, ran inside. I was breathing hard. The air in the place was heavy with dust and bitter with stale gasoline.

"Not sellin' much hereabouts these days," the ancient attendant admonished me, "if you're lookin' to buy something." He grinned and spit on the greasy floor. In the dingy light he looked as incorporeal as a shadow. "There's some Coca-Cola left, but those pumps out there's all dry." There was, he guessed, a station open up the road another mile or so. He couldn't say for sure. "Don't have much use for folks in that part of town," he hissed. "Don't need to go up there to see a slitherin' bunch of snakes when all the evil in the world I never wanted to see goes on right around here." He laughed heartily but made no sound, except for the creak of his crippled rocking chair when he sat down.

I told him about my terror on the highway and asked for the phone to call the police. Just then—as he began to explain that the phone had been dead for years—the enemy truck roared by, spraying up stones against the window. The old man froze. "If you're lookin' for advice, don't go callin' the police," he said. "You cause them truckers any trouble, they'll kill ya soon's they can catch ya. There's been killin's all around over things like that. Don't fool with 'em, if you wanna know what I think." With that he scowled and spit, and creaking on the rocking chair again, he waved me out the door.

At the station down the road, the attendant watched the pump and kept whistling as the gallons flew. The police were no help at all. The jail held four cells, four yelping drunks, one dispatcher, but not one cop on duty for the afternoon. The desk clerk snapped her gum and told me that my complaint was a mat-

ter for the sheriff, not the police. "Different jurisdiction altogether," she said, "when it happens out in the county." Her radio
was broken, or she would have called him for me. If I cared to
wait, he would probably drop by in the late afternoon.

I waited an hour, then left, hopeful that the trucker was now
far ahead of me, anxious that he might have pulled off the road to
lie in wait. Soon enough I found that from here on to New Mexico there weren't any hidden places from which he could launch
an ambush. The road was straight, or rolled gently, in its imper-
ceptible descent to Santa Fe, which itself lay high and thin-aired
in the mountains. To the east across the desert plains, the Sangre
de Cristo range red-lined the sky, throbbing in the sun like an artery.

Fifty miles or so from New Mexico, the Rio Grande's paltry
waters met the highway at 7,400 feet and anemically crossed the
valley west to east. The radio crackled nothing here but Spanish.
Closer yet to the border, the earth lay parched, like bones, or
crumbled in clumps as scarlet as dried blood. Dark mesas, bristling with sage and piñones, strewed the desert like carcasses. Behind black clouds, like dinosaur birds, the sky glowed sallow. A
big orange sign framed by logs read "Welcome to New Mexico—
Land of Enchantment."

A chilling mist began to fall. The air was still. Far away on
every side, lonely peaks stood ringed with storms, purple in the
dusk like brooding temples. The highway turned to sand—the
slough of a snake—and twisted through a Pueblo Indian village.
Orange adobe houses watched the road through bright orange
doors. An orange mud Gothic church stood in a white dirt yard.
Wrapped in bright blankets on the steps, three old Indian men
raised their stoic faces and stared. Outside town, sand dunes
changed color and shape below a tantrum of clouds. The wind
turned black, blew rain, and turned the road to mud. Then, as
suddenly, the pavement reappeared through the sand as a flooded
four-lane highway. At the moment of this transformation, an Indian boy, his clothes shining wet, hitchhiked beside the road. I
picked him up. He said he was journeying twenty miles toward

Santa Fe for medicine for his mother. He said she was dying. Other than that, he said nothing.

When I let him off, the rain stopped falling. In the west the sky turned pitch blue above a silver horizon. Soon a hemisphere of stars made pinholes in the night, and the earth began to sparkle electrically, as though the storm had showered phosphorescence. Beneath the blackness, the lights of adobe Santa Fe lay camouflaged in the sand.

The street plan of Santa Fe was not rational. It was as if it followed the drifting dunes—or dunelike movements of spirit. For more than an hour I tried to find Rand and Alex's address, which, they had told me, lay close to the highway. Their meticulous directions failed. I called to receive them again, then drove various routes of my own devising. A city map I bought made me more absurd. No matter how faithful or diverse the turns I made, in the end I always found myself again in the place where my search had started. "Almost everyone has that problem when they first come here," Rand told me. "In New Mexico, you've got to stop thinking logically."

Rand Lee and Alex Lucker lived in a complex of town houses that was itself an inspired labyrinth. When I arrived they were waiting a simple dinner for me of brown rice and vegetables. They were gentle men, meditative in their pace. There was, they believed, a spiritual purpose in my coming here. Rand asked whether I had begun to discover it yet, whether any conscious need had manifested itself. For the moment, I think, I felt like a psychiatric "client" who wanted to impress his shrink and get the right answer. Still, I could say there were spiritual experiences I had vaguely hoped for. Some months before I began traveling, I had read Walter Williams's *The Spirit and the Flesh: Sexual Diversity in American Indian Culture*. The author described a Native American "vision quest" he undertook in 1982 under the guidance of a *berdache*. These androgynous tribesmen were visionaries, healers, and priests who nurtured spiritual wholeness through sex-

ual rites, both homosexual and heterosexual. One such Lakota led
Williams to an isolated sweat lodge, where he left him naked in
darkness for days, without food or water, waiting for a revelation.
A circling eagle signaled when the thing was accomplished. The
author wrote of his days in the desert as an intensely cleansing experience that he could not and did not wish to explain, "a process of being that cannot be described in rational terms."

I was intrigued by the purging nature of this Indian sexuality
that refused to respect distinct "sexualities." I longed for some irrational transformation to liberate my view of such things. I told
Rand and Alex of my desire to go on a vision quest. "Maybe this
journey you're taking across America is your vision quest," Rand
stated.

Alex was a short, trim man with wiry black hair and an elfish
beard. Throughout the meal he had eaten standing. Without explanation he began this story:

"Rand and I lived in Ireland for several months before we
moved to Santa Fe. One day a farmer took us into a forest that
bordered his land, and after we walked a while, we came upon a
clearing of beautiful pools. You entered it through two big boulders and then a drop down, a kind of vaginal opening. 'What
pools are these?' I asked. It was winter, but I felt a warm energy
in the earth as soon as I stepped on the ground around them.

"No sooner had I asked the question than the sun came out
all of a sudden from behind the clouds, and the whole forest
turned emerald—the trees, the moss on their trunks, the moss on
the ground. One of the pools was like crystal—you could see every grain of sand at the bottom. After we'd been there a few minutes, the others went off farther into the woods. But I stayed. I
had this irresistible urge to go in the water. I started taking off my
clothes and hanging them on a tree, and while I was undressing
the little man—I didn't know who he was—spoke up and said,
'Don't go in over your waist.' " Alex smiled at me quizzically. His
voice was bemused. "And I thought, *Okay*. Then he said, 'Don't
cross over to the far side.' And I thought, All right. So I followed
his instructions exactly. And when I got out of the water and was
trying to put on my clothes, there were six socks on the tree in-

stead of two. I couldn't figure out how to get them back on. I was totally confused.

"I started to sit down on the moss to sort things out, but the man laughed and said, 'Don't sit down on the moss or you'll be *more* confused.' Then he told me, 'Bring back the birds. They've been gone twenty years now.'

"It was right afterward that the others came back. They found me standing there all mixed up and asked me what happened. I just told them I went swimming. I didn't say anything about the little man. But I told the farmer I'd buy the land if it was for sale. So he took me to meet the owner. At first he wasn't interested in selling, and I finally told him the little man told me to buy it. He said, 'There's no little man,' but he seemed surprised. I said, 'Yes, there is. He told me to bring the birds back.' That amazed him. He asked me, 'How do you know about the birds?' I said, 'The little man,' and he agreed to sell it to me for seven thousand dollars." Alex had consulted Alexandra, the ancient spirit he channeled. She told him to buy it and move to Santa Fe to work until he'd paid it off. "I bought one acre of forest land," he said, "and an acre that was waist high in bluebells."

As soon as he'd finished this tale, Alex went upstairs to bed. He always went to bed early now. This had been among Alexandra's instructions to him. Rand gave me his room, opposite Alex's. Like the rest of the house, it was stark—white and almost bare. A thin cotton mat lay on the floor beneath a pillow and a gauzy cover. A large eagle's feather hung on the wall at the head of the bed. The tassle on its quill was brightly beaded. It alone ornamented the room.

On Tuesday I woke at dawn. Rand and Alex were already in meditation, preparing to read tarot cards for the day's clients. The city's central plaza was within easy walking distance of their house. I set out alone to explore town. It was a warm and brilliant day with billowing clouds, though Rand told me always to expect an afternoon rain in the desert. By the felicitous simplicity of man-to-man glances, I met a young artist named Renaldo in the park beside the cathedral, which stood from the days when the territory was newly separated from Spain and Mexico. As soon as he'd told me his name, he began to complain about his lover of six years, whom he planned secretly to abandon.

"I think I'll move to Arizona," he said. "I'll pack up when he's not home, and I won't ever have to see him again. I like that best." His grievances weren't specific, just that his lover was boring now and no longer understood him as he once had. His indictments sounded more seductive than legitimate. I wasn't a sexually interested stranger, so I found an urgent excuse to walk away.

Santa Fe was an orange adobe town, mostly one and two stories tall. In the downtown boutiques and galleries, business was brisk in arts, crafts, and pottery. Tight-faced proprietors with Manhattan accents negotiated sharply with collectors from Los Angeles, who migrated annually for the Santa Fe Opera's opening. On one side of the plaza stood the old adobe Governor's Palace, a relic of Spain's dominion, before the young United States seized the land. Its covered sidewalk swarmed with bargaining tourists—less chic than the sort who patronized boutiques—while unsmiling Indian women sat wrapped in blankets, cross-legged and laconic. Their expensive leatherwork, turquoise, and silver jewelry lay out on woolen shawls. It seemed a hundred cameras shuttered at all times. The Indians shadowed their faces and frowned, looking down. On curbs and benches around the plaza's central monument, local Santa Feans—Anglo, Latino, Pueblo Indian—sunned, read the morning news, and gossiped. On the face of the memorial stone the epithet "Savage Indian" could still be read, though barely now, in an engraved paeon to white men who had conquered the land.

"Someone's tried to chisel it out," a white-haired, red-cheeked gentleman told me as I sat down beside him on the monument's ledge. "It was still very deep in the stone when I moved here nine years ago." He introduced himself as Bill Shannon. A white straw hat shaded his face. His cream-colored dress shirt was buttoned to the neck. Like his eyes, the veins on his snowy hands were turquoise. He tapped a rolled-up newspaper in his palms. "They've had some real big battles over things like that around here," he said, then asked suddenly, "You a New Yorker?" He nodded at a *New York Times* I'd bought at a nearby hotel. "That Mayor Koch of yours sure always seems to make the news."

He unrolled that morning's *New Mexican* to Ellen Goodman's column. Edward I. Koch, then mayor of New York, had called for testing all foreigners in the United States—even tourists—for antibodies to the "AIDS virus." Goodman had pointed out the absurdity of such demagogic ploys, particularly in New York, which was the epicenter of the epidemic. "Mayor Koch," she criticized, "should know the balance of trade in this disease: his city is a greater exporter than importer of AIDS."

"It's gonna kill millions," Bill said. "I already went through one plague. *Twenty million* died in the flu of 1918—*one year!* I was living in Chester, Pennsylvania, at the time. They couldn't keep up with the bodies. A steam shovel dug a big hole outside of town for all the pine boxes. They stacked 'em up, all oozing and the flies buzzin' around like thunder clouds, then shoveled 'em over. My mother died in that epidemic. I was nine years old. Panic everywhere! Oh, people thought you could get it talking on the telephone! They'd cover it with a piece of gauze. What's gonna happen when it reaches a million cases of AIDS in this country? If these," he faltered, "these homosexuals know all about the disease like they say, why don't they change their life-style?"

I decided not to "come out" to him, expecting more honest opinions if I didn't. "It's a funny thing about gays . . ." he said.

I braced. But his proposal of celibacy was practical, not bigoted. In our fast presumptions, we activists grow narrow and stupid, overanxious to bite people's heads off. Bill, in his way, was admirably tolerant.

"There's an Indian," he told me, "that worked at a restaurant right down here—they arrested him for what they said was touching three teenaged boys' genitals. He was giving 'em beer if they let him do it. He got twenty years!

"Then there's this guy—he's around, I'll show him to you. He killed an architect in town from back east who was walking his dog down by the river. The killer's girlfriend kicked the dog, and the architect slapped her. Well, they just pulled out a chain and beat him to death, and the jury let him off. You'll see him coming by here soon, begging for money.

"Now you've got this Indian touching genitals on the other hand and he gets twenty years! The justice system is ridiculous. Of course," he added, "I don't know why you'd want to touch someone's genitals. *I* wouldn't do that kind of thing and get twenty years. *I wouldn't touch Queen Elizabeth's genitals for twenty years!*" Then, abruptly—because sex always recalled death, I guessed—he digressed to AIDS. The sun was darting in and out of rainclouds, which hissed occasionally. "All this stuff about the blood supply and new viruses," Bill wondered. "My son's a physicist out here at Los Alamos—where the first atomic bomb was made. Well, they know a lot about those things out there. He said they weren't telling people the half of it."

We scurried to the porch of the Governor's Palace, taking refuge from a sudden downpour. An Indian woman, swathed in a shawl, sat motionless as an icon on the ground. Her lap was strewn with pricey offerings of gold, silver, and precious stones.

"Have you seen much of Santa Fe since you came?" Bill asked. He pointed to the Palace of Governors. "Lew Wallace wrote *Ben Hur* inside," he said. "They've still got the room the way he used it. Down the street here—you can see it from the square—we've got the Chapel of Loretto. That's another old church the Spaniards built," he believed. "They say, way back when, it didn't have a set of indoor stairs. So the nuns decided to pray, and an old man rode up on a donkey. The steps he built for the church defy the laws of gravity—no visible means of support, no columns, no nails, just floating there.

"Well, the Catholics believe the old guy was Saint Joseph. They go in there and pray for friends who've passed away. I went in one day to take a look, and you couldn't get a word to God in edgewise because the wind kept slamming the doors shut. So I told the nun—she's always kneeling at the front—'What you oughta start praying for are some doorstops!' Well, the next time I went in, that's what they had, and I said, 'Ma'am, that's just fine, but no St. Joseph brought 'em by here on a donkey.' I was christened Catholic but raised a Baptist. We don't believe in miracles."

In the plaza, a group of tourists huddled trying to decipher the tall, desecrated monument to white men. The rain splashing upon their colorful umbrellas made bright waterfalls of them.

Alex Lucker seemed always to be lost in visions. He said little about himself. That evening after Alex went to bed, Rand told me about them both. They were both Jewish. "At least through my father I am," Rand demurred, because Judaism is inherited through the mother. "My mother was an Episcopalian, but nothing was ever enforced. She used to tell me, 'We gave you a religious upbringing so you'd have something to rebel against.' That was typical in Connecticut."

It wasn't late, nine or ten. We were talking at the table in the dining alcove off the kitchen. On the walls hung three brightly embroidered banners that, other than the feather above my bed, were the only decoration in the house. Rand watched me study the white silk one behind him. "This is a chart of our chakra flowers," he interrupted his biography to explain. There'd been long consultations with Alexandra to find the ones that corresponded with their lives. "They're personal for everyone," Rand tutored. "Spiritual development's not something you can look up in a book." Each sewn word—one for each of the seven chakras— was followed by a richly threaded blossom. Rand's was a ylang-ylang. Alex had a damask rose. Rand's licorice was Alex's passion flower.

Above my head the second chart represented the chakras themselves—the physical, health and healing, love, mind, communication, wisdom, power—the chakra tones in a chromatic scale, the corresponding body parts from root to crown, and the sympathetic colors—red through green, indigo, and violet. Rand could see that this was new to me and baffling. "That one is the 'Wheel of Creation,'" he told me, pointing to the banner across the room. Like the chakras, Creation was divided into seven categories: passion, belief, strategy, clarity of vision, action, support, and communication. "Divine Passion," Rand explained, "created the universe. Nothing is created without passion.

"I don't mean the passion of sex," he hastened to add. "Alex and I are celibate. We have been since we met. That's one of the ways I don't think I fit the gay stereotype, but there are lots of others. Until I finished college, I was fat. That's not gay. I still think of myself that way. I don't know if you ever completely get over thinking of yourself the way you did when you were growing up. I wanted to belong. So I got nelly and flamboyant, because back then I thought gay men were supposed to be like that. Now everyone's supposed to be butch and a hunk from the gym. You've always got to keep changing yourself if you want to fit in.

"I hated who I was. I hated the idea of having sex—I thought I was too disgusting. That was the 1960s, a very different time. But when I went away to college, a man took an interest in me just the way I was. Finally I went home with him."

One night when Rand was just getting comfortable with having sex—"coming to grips with that," was how he put it—he slept over at his boyfriend's house for the first time. Next morning, when he returned home, he found his dorm mates looking for him frantically. "My mother'd been calling all night long," he recalled. "My father had died of a heart attack—exactly at the time I was laying in the arms of my boyfriend. I took it for a sign, as a punishment.

"I'd met some Jesus people on the street a while before, and I went to see them. They took me in. I stopped studying or going to class, and spent all of my time at the Christian house. The next year I dropped out of school to go to Washington Bible College in Lanham, Maryland. I stayed four years, but hated it there. I confessed my 'homosexual tendencies' "—he put a spin on the words—"to the dean. They tricked me into giving them other students' names—so they could pray for them, too." Rand put his face in his hands. "I hate informants."

There was one other student there, whom Rand met later. "He was popular, smart, very masculine," Rand described him, "nothing that could be identified as gay mannerisms. We talked a lot. Both of us were devout. One day I said to him, 'You're burdened heavy.' He said, 'What do you think it is?' I said, 'You're a homosexual.' I'd never even suspected him before. It was psychic intuition. He all but fainted. His face had this frozen little smile.

He said no one else knew but his pastor and his parents—and they'd kicked him out. We became good friends, and then suddenly he disappeared. No one could find him. After graduation, I heard he had killed himself.

"The Christians taught me to codify my self-hatred," he stated. Still, he believed, in those years he also discovered talents he had never before imagined in himself. "I learned I could preach, help people find peace," he told me. "That's what Alex and I are doing here. I know I could have learned that about myself without being miserable. But in my 'planning state' "—the "dream state," he also called it—"when we consult our higher selves, I chose the hard way. We choose all our own experiences, even suffering—for what we can learn from them. We choose to be gay. And if I don't have what I want as a gay man, it's because of limits I've imposed on myself. We're all looking for the truth—there are just lots of ways to get there."

One of the decisions Rand said he had made in his dream state was to meet Alex. Some time, in fact, before they met, he had written in his journal that he wanted to find a "dark, curly-haired, balding, muscular man—a doctor or a lawyer." Alex was a medical lab tech. Otherwise he was all of those things. "This was in Key West," said Rand, "and Alex was sick, *deathly* sick. *Everything* was going wrong with him. He was seeing a shrink on a sliding scale for hardship cases, paying four dollars a time." The therapist, who involved himself in the metaphysical, told Alex about Rand. "I did psychic readings," Rand explained. "One night at a group meeting I got a communication that I'd meet the man in my diary. Then Alex came in.

"Alex won't tell you any of this. He's chosen a completely new reality and put all of the past behind him." Rand told me Alex's story.

In the four years before the two men met, Alex had lost two relationships—a wife and a male lover. He had had an "open arrangement" with his wife. "But he didn't have any idea how *much* she was fucking around," Rand said bitterly. "One day after school, his daughter was looking for a blouse and found her mother's closet bare. She'd moved in with Alex's best friend—

without any warning! Alex kept the kids . . . I should say she *left* them. He always did everything around the house anyway. It was after she was gone that he 'came out.' *She* called her mother and all their old friends, and in the divorce claimed that he was an immoral father. He lost everything—the kids, the house. The judge gave him twenty-four hours to move out. He slept on the beach for three days."

In the aftermath, Alex met a new lover. "A tall, slender kid," Rand described him. He was nineteen, only three years older than Alex's son. "He was a leech," said Rand, "but Alex loved him." Alex paid for everything. He sent the boy to college, but his juvenile lover was not a student. "He was always fucking around," said Rand, "like Alex's wife. He went through fifteen thousand dollars of Alex's money once, just blew it right out of his bank account!" Rand's fingers flew fast through the air. "Then Alex got sick, and the kid lost his free ride. Alex kicked him out. That was maybe the first assertive act in Alex's life—but it took him almost dying to finally do it for himself."

In December 1984 Alex was at work in the hospital lab when he drew a pipette of "AIDS-infected blood" into an infected tooth. The hospital, Rand said, had concealed the blood's contamination. Ten days later Alex fell sick with a cytomegalovirus infection. He ran a temperature of 104 and began going blind. The hospital denied its liability. "They blamed Alex's homosexuality," Rand said, "this man who was working for them eighty hours a week at the time! Their lawyers were all over him. He gave up and resigned. He was living in a hospital-owned apartment, and they gave him twenty-four hours to get out of it. Everything seemed to be repeating in his life. I'd met him right before that and went to help him move. He'd gotten real sick in the night and was acting delirious. That's when Alexandra spoke through him for the first time. It wasn't even Alex's voice, and the English was very strange. It was hard to understand him."

Alex's first psychic experience had been in childhood, but after a traumatic incident he'd suppressed his "gift." His grandfather, a cabalistic rabbi, had started training him in astral projection and meditation when he was four. "The old man would ask him questions," Rand explained, "and have him go out and bring the answers back to him. One day he called Alex into his study by his Hebrew name and put him on his knee. And Alex went into a long, deep trance. When he came back, his grandfather was dead. His arms were still around Alex, hugging him."

According to Rand, Alex's mother blamed him for her father's death and beat him. "When they came to take his grandfather's body to the hospital, they had to take Alex, too," said Rand. "That's how hard his mother spanked him. It wasn't until the day I helped him move that Alex let a spirit speak through him again.

"At first," Rand recalled, "I thought he'd gone psychotic. The movers were there. *Nothing* was packed. No one knew what was going, what was staying. Alex was just standing there crying. Then all of a sudden he spoke to us in a funny little voice and told the movers exactly what to do. They were freaked, but they did what he told them. They even washed dirty dishes, which were laying everywhere! Afterward Alex didn't remember a thing, a complete blackout. It's always that way. We talked about it, then I took him into another trance and called Alexandra out again. She gave him instructions about his health—how to sleep, exercise, meditate, how to schedule his day. I asked her if she could affect his appetite—he was wasting away. She said yes and during the next three days he started to eat. He knew exactly what he needed. He stopped all his medicines and got well anyway. It was a drastic change in his life. It changed everything."

We mortals choose all of our earthly experiences in the planning state—in meditation or trance or sleep, or in the world between incarnations, whenever we communicate with our own Higher Consciousness. Whatever we choose we can also change. Alex repeated these precepts again and again, not as dogmas, but as affirmations of the power we have in our lives. "Every experience leads us toward Truth," he said. "There are just different paths. In your dream state you chose to come to Santa Fe and be with us," he told me. "You're not here by mistake or accident." These were Alexandra's teachings.

"Would you argue with a three-thousand-year-old entity?" Rand asked, laughing.

We spent our week together talking not about AIDS, sex, or gay politics so much—these issues seemed irrelevant—as we did about "gay spirit." We spoke of our sexual "difference" as one of nature's gifts, a separate means of searching the soul and discovering the possibilities in this world. "We chose it in the dream state," Alex stated. "It's a role we've decided to play in this journey."

My hosts talked about "past lives." One hot afternoon we made a pilgrimage to Bandelier, the Pueblo Indian ruins north of Santa Fe. There Rand told me about a past life vision—a "regression"—through which Alexandra had guided him. We climbed a dangerous cliff and sat in the sun several feet from one another, each of us before the mouth of a separate ancient cave. The Indians had dug them out for dwellings. Far below this steep wall of stone on which we perched lay the Frijoles Canyon, cut by streams and lush with vegetation—a green oasis in the dusty bowl of a fallen volcano. All around us the Jemez Mountains made the dry volcano's rim.

A verdant mesa rose directly before the cliff. A mule train narrowly climbed its side. When the pack had gotten halfway up, a churning braid of black clouds, like a giant drill, bored through the sky above the summit, leaving the rest of the canyon in sunshine. Hail thundered through the trees. Illuminated by a silver rush of lightning, it seemed to move the earth. Then it passed, relinquishing the valley to the sudden songs of birds, which cascaded like water through the air.

"I was a child," Rand said, overlooking the ravine. "I was standing by a bush. My mother and my grandmother said, 'Listen to the bush! It's talking to you! What's it saying?' They said, 'You're speaking to the spirit of the bush. You must be trained.' They took me to the elders. I was afraid. My grandmother told them, 'You have to train him.' She was trying hard to convince them, I remember.

"I dreamed afterward I was in a cave near here, near Santa Fe, being taught by the old people of the tribe. I didn't know whether they were men or women, I couldn't distinguish their gender. I learned it didn't matter. The singing eagle came to me while they were teaching me to sing. I was afraid of not getting it right. As I was coming out of the dream, the eagle swept down and embraced me in its wings like a mother.

"Not long after I had those dreams," Rand said, "I met an Indian woman named Rebecca. She was working at a center for troubled Indians that was run by one of my friends. We'd been talking for some time and I felt like I had to ask her about my vision. I asked her if the singing eagle meant anything in her tradition. She told me yes, that she'd had a visionary experience with the eagle, too. She said, 'All the time I've talked to you I've wanted to call you "son."'' We took each other in our arms and hugged and cried like babies. Then she gave me an eagle feather. She'd made the beading on the quill. I knew it was the last gift my mother would ever give me. The cycle was completed." This was the feather in Rand's room that hung over my head as I slept.

Late that night we gathered at the kitchen table beneath the chakra banners. Rand and Alex prepared me to meet the spirit. "You have to understand," Rand explained, "that from Alexandra's point of view, we don't have to suffer or ever experience evil if we don't choose to. Everything we can learn through suffering we can learn through joy. They're just different paths to understanding. To Alexandra, death isn't evil. It's a part of the process of Greater Life, a transition to the spiritual plane. In a sense, all of our deaths are suicides, because for our own unique experience of the physical plane we choose the time and the place—and even the manner in which we die. Everything is chosen in the dream state."

Rand sat across from me, Alex in between. Rand spread the tarot cards to focus psychic energy and enable us to receive the spirit. A medieval wizardry of garish human faces, angels, demons, suns, moons, and stars stared up from the top of the table. He "read" the visions they evoked, then asked, "Alex, are you ready?" Alex's body sat erect, relaxed. His eyes were shut. "You're about to leave the body," Rand breathed softly, speaking to Alex's quiet face. "You're now departing, rising, you're rising above your body, you can see yourself behind . . ." Alex's body breathed more quietly, then seemed not to breathe at all. "You are rising through the air, you see Santa Fe below, you are moving like light, you see the earth, you are flying through the planets, you can see the solar system, it is getting small, your spirit is lifting through the Milky Way . . . you see everything.

"Alexandra, are you there?"

"Indeed, I am being with you." The voice was unlike any sound I'd heard from Alex, high-pitched and reedy, like a breath unused to speech. It was a monotone, its vowels were pure. It was both exotic and natural.

"This is the twelfth of June 1987." Rand announced it like a chant. "And it's about a quarter to midnight. Alexandra, these are questions for the benefit of gay and lesbian people."

There was deep silence. Then the spirit spoke. "In your present time, your physical world indeed is going through a great acceleration of changes. Individuals enter the physical world as visitors, and everything that is available for their development will always be there for them. You are choosing to experience fear, love, sharing, and the concerns of the physical world in a way that is unique to your growth. So do not create any limit to your creativity. You are learning who you are and growing into all of your greatness. Do not stop this growth. Do not stop your uniqueness. And I ask if there are specific questions?"

"Can you tell us anything about how AIDS began?" I asked.

"It is necessary to realize that disease itself does not start in the physical world, but in another reality. Disease enters into this reality in order to allow man to remove himself from the framework of his physical world and allow him to come into communication with his inner self and greater self. As for AIDS, understand that thousands of years before this disease, a disease very similar in concept, creation, and need entered the world in the form of cancer. This ability of the body to attack itself came through in the dream state, in communication with the spiritual plane. It was chosen because of great changes in the earth and the physical reality and in order to increase one's understanding of himself. Humans yearned to communicate the need for individuals to group together and create a harmony.

"Understand that when the body attacks itself, it can also balance this account out. An ability to cure any disease is also always available. In creating a balance for AIDS, all diseases can be balanced. Indeed, AIDS too came through in the dream state because there was a need for a group of people to change political reality—that is, in reference to the earth itself—to regroup for a new age and a new energy that was entering. Man," Alexandra stated, "is not in harmony with his reality."

On account of this disharmony, the spirit predicted, the earth would respond with catastrophic floods, hurricanes, tidal waves, and volcanic eruptions that would take hundreds of thousands of lives. She emphasized that this was not a punishment for evil, but in consequence of an imbalance man has created in life. AIDS likewise "came through" so that man would "take a look and see what he is creating, where the disharmony is, and how better to create unity in the environment. If this union with the earth does not grow," she admonished, "then indeed the earth will respond."

So first, she reiterated, came man's need for great change, then the possibility of AIDS as well. "Again realize that every individual has chosen it," she said, "to be able to communicate a harmony within the earth through an understanding of the total environment. When man is concerned with the welfare of individuals and the harmony of their environment, then indeed the changes are coming through."

From Alexandra's perspective, AIDS was not a stray disease that spread by sexual accident. It was created in a communication between the "people of the earth and the mass consciousness"—in its earliest manifestation because of "a great starvation that was to take place in Africa" and insufficient health care there. "It was needed to maintain a balance among individuals," Alexandra asserted. "But social and political changes were also needed throughout many other parts of the world. So the virus itself," the spirit stated, "accepted the ability to relocate and to communicate with other parts of the earth"—where other groups of people also accepted it.

"An obstruction in the fluid of life," was what Alexandra called the virus, "a block either in the semen or blood." She acknowledged that the virus had spread among different populations by sexual contact and believed that the pandemic came about "through individuals entering into the land of Africa and relating with infected people there." She also confirmed that infected blood had been collected "in different parts of the world" and sold in international markets. This was the illegal plasma trade pharmaceutical companies had been accused of engaging in by some renegade epidemiologists. Generally, these allegations had been suppressed in the media. I was startled that Alexandra seemed to know so much about them. I tried to explore them further. She explained that she saw essential truths but had no corner on mutable knowledge such as of the earth's intricate blood trade laws. These lay outside her understandings.

"Remember also," she then cautioned, "that when the disease entered into Africa, it was not looked upon as an evil but indeed a very sacred thing." In their great fevers, she stated, tribespeople who were sick with the virus communicated with a spiritual plane. "They indeed were understood and were separated from the group because they were able to communicate knowledge from the Great Spirit." In a kind of divine delirium, they told their tribe where to find food and water. And when the delirious were about to die, the tribesmen celebrated their departure for the spiritual world. "Needles," Alexandra stated, "were injected into these individuals, and a scarring practice took place among selected members of the tribe. Those who received the Great Spirit were isolated and considered mediums between the physical world and the spiritual."

Illness, Alexandra explained, was a distinct consciousness that was invited to become a part of the individual's consciousness and communication. Because of this, she said, there was a relationship between syphilis and AIDS. Where the consciousness of syphilis and the "AIDS virus" existed together, the body could use it more quickly to create the new disease. When the AIDS consciousness existed alone, it could communicate with the individual over a longer time—"so that the body can consider whether or not the disease could or should be created," the spirit stated. "So many individuals that have suffered syphilis have a great concern when the energy of AIDS enters into them. The body already realizes what it needs to do in order to create illness. The individual has created this need," Alexandra added, "for whatever experiences are necessary to him."

Then the spirit, blithe and enigmatic, said, "It is no different in context from when an individual understands that one plus one equals two or that there is the ability to add another one and understands that a number three is available. . . ."

Rand had been looking over at me, lost, irritated at Alexandra, it seemed. He had confided to me earlier that she sometimes got carried away in riddles and had to be intruded upon. Now he cut the spirit off. "Yes!" he scolded, testy and intimate. "That's *wonderful*! But it's not the question. You said there's a balance available for every disease. Do you mean that in time the illness will disappear in general or that an individual who's sick can be healed?"

Alexandra—or, rather, Alex's body, which the spirit had assumed—had remained impassive during Rand's rebuke. She was silent a moment more and then began. "All healing takes place in a dream reality, in a sleep or meditation. Regarding the consciousness of AIDS, the individual must be given into guided meditation, specifically and uniquely for his own growth. This meditation should allow him to enter into the dream state where the healing and the balancing process can take place. When he comes back into the physical world from the planning state, he must consider bringing the information with him for the answers in this realm. For this unique and individual healing was always available in the spiritual consciousness."

Everything Alexandra said had deep appeal for me—perhaps because my own Pentecostal past had held out the fervent hope of faith healing in the laying on of hands. I had witnessed mysteries performed by my devout grandmothers. It was something left from my childhood that I wanted still to believe. I asked the channeled being what physical practices might lead us to healing, whether we might *do* anything to aid our spirits.

"Touch therapy," Alexandra told me, "aids meditation and healing, balancing the energy of the recipient." She meant the "ancient practice," she said, which was now being rediscovered. To one who saw all, every transmission of knowledge was clear. Earthbound, Rand and I were baffled. Rand interrupted again, prodding the spirit to clarify herself.

"The first touch therapy," she replied, "took place in the light touch that indeed raised certain bumps throughout the body."

"*Bumps?*" cried Rand.

"Indeed, have you not tickled another individual? And have you not raised a sensation on the physical body? It is a great security feeling that is related to the spiritual world as well."

"Light caresses as in lovemaking?" Rand asked.

Never in such misunderstandings did the spirit grow exasperated with us. Her otherworldly voice stayed steady, Alex's body perfectly still. "What I am saying," she continued, "came through to me as the first touch therapy. I am not stating that bumps are the present case. But remember the symbol of the American flag," Alexandra stated familiarly, apparently alluding to a topic in the countless psychic sessions between her and Rand. "For many Americans there is a great emotional feeling there. And in the creation of that there is also the bridge between the physical and the spiritual. In touch therapy you must find that bridge—indeed, in various kinds of massage—that is uniquely needed for the individual."

"Massage!" Rand sighed. "*That's* what you mean!"

"Indeed. When there is a bridge between the body and the spirit," she emphasized, and proceeded with her point. "Many people who have accepted AIDS into their reality are not happy with their physical self, which is only a suitcase in which they travel in this world. The individual's love of the physical body indeed is not in balance with his needs for spiritual growth. It is so that they will no longer have to concern themselves with the physical suitcase that they have created AIDS. Touch therapy is a means of encouraging them to love their body, especially when it is experiencing an illness such as AIDS. In this we create a balance. It is the energy of the spiritual plane that they need to receive, for it is not the physical body, but the experiences with which they fill the self that they will be taking into their greater realities."

"So," concluded Rand, "the purpose of healing is not to change people's minds and keep them here, but to help them experience the spiritual plane."

"Indeed, this is correct," Alexandra answered.

"Then some may respond by deciding that they can continue to live on the physical plane and experience spiritual reality. Others will decide to leave."

"Again it is by their choice. I realize," the spirit conceded, "that it is difficult for you to understand that many individuals have entered into a physical world in order to communicate with their spiritual awareness and have chosen a certain type of lifestyle and experience for their growth. And so it is not only that the gay and lesbian experience can help an individual upon this path, for each path in your physical reality indeed is a path of spiritual enlightenment that is needed uniquely for the individual.

"And so realize that individuals in any society, in any area of the world, indeed, have the ability to communicate with the consciousness of AIDS and make it part of their reality. No one group indeed can be separated from this concern. It is for this reason it has the ability to enter the physical reality through those fluids of life where indeed it finds its environment. So allow yourself to understand that there are roads in every physical reality that can enable individuals to make the contact that they are seeking.

"And remember that what is within you as an individual can also be experienced and expressed within the individual of everyone else in the physical reality whether it be in this lifetime or in any other lifetime. So judge yourself and others with an understanding of compassion. Remember that it is by choice that you are creating your experience in the physical world. Create it with the understanding of likes. For it is when you show what the similarities are—when you create similarities in the physical reality that exist among all people—that you allow the greatest communication to be available. And it is only then that people will understand their experience and will be able to be educated and grow in accordance with what indeed is not similar within themselves. Understand that for opposites to attract they must have been united by a road of similarity. The virus of the consciousness of AIDS has opened up a road of similarities to be presented. Utilize it in its fullness.

"Indeed in its way it is unfortunate that the consciousness of the people on earth has called for this need. But this oneness that is created by AIDS—the unity of loving one another, caring for one another, and holding on to life—is a communicator of the need for sharing your physical world."

Though the spirit's voice had continued strong, Alex's shoulders began to fall. The medium seemed to be tiring. Rand checked the time. Alex had been in trance for more than two hours. "Alexandra," Rand asked, "will you check? Is Alex ready to come back now?"

Alexandra spoke mutely with Alex's spirit—a dialogue in a wordless plane where knowledge came by way of soul movements. "Indeed," she answered, "he'll be ready to come back shortly."

"Alexandra," Rand asked, "in speaking to those people who have been infected with the virus or do have AIDS, do you have a specific message?"

"Realize," proclaimed the spirit, "that you have chosen this experience in order to understand your uniqueness. Realize too that the physical reality is only one of many realities that are available to you. So allow this door to open. Allow the communication to be there. Allow yourself to bring back information so that it too can be used. Share it with yourself and with others and, as you expand your experiences, create according to what you need. In your creations, receive what is necessary for your experience. Trust in yourself, believe in yourself, and understand indeed that you are one with All That Is and all the love from your greater self is always available for you. Receive it that you may increase it. And I thank you for sharing."

"Thank you, Alexandra," Rand said, and clapped his hands sharply. Alex opened his eyes and slumped, exhausted.

CHAPTER 7

COMMON
KNOWLEDGE

ONE EVENING DURING MY STAY IN SANTA FE, ALEX TOOK ME TO A
meeting of Common Knowledge, the organization through whose
phone number I had met him and Rand. The meeting house was
the Nifty Cafe, a quaint restaurant of adobe and timber that sat
alone on the outskirts of town and overlooked the desert. We
gathered on the porch and, to the moans of our rocking chairs,
watched the late sun burn the dunes scarlet, orange, hot pink,
then lavender as bright as morning stars. In time, feeling the loss,
the sand became a vast, cold, purple blanket. Two big mutts, kind
misfits of some sort, lay beside our chairs as still as death and, angling their muzzles into the night, closed their eyes. Penned at
the end of the porch, three grand peacocks feathered the air with
a thousand gaudy eyes and tore the early darkness, keening.

Around one hushed table over dinner, there were four or five
lesbians who spoke to no one but themselves. It seemed to me
that in their stoic independence they might have been known for
lesbians anywhere. There were maybe ten men, more animated,
who had coffee and pie on the back patio. Fenced in near the pea-

cocks, they were serenaded by their cries. Alex made announcements. A Saturday morning carpool would drive to this weekend's
Gay Pride parade in Albuquerque. During the summer solstice
the following week, there would be several shamanistic celebra-
tions, and everyone was welcome. For men interested in healing,
there was also an herb walk to be held in the forest near Pecos.
There was no organizational "business," no politics, no special
concern about "gayness"—only rites to renew the spirit. Most of
these men were ranchers, carpenters, potters, or painters. They
had driven into town from the desert mountains, as far as sixty
miles away, for their weekly human intercourse—gossip and a
chat.

In time, Steve Berlyn, a psychotherapist from Santa Fe,
brought up AIDS for discussion. Most everyone at the meeting
seemed to know someone sick or dead. But the talk was neither
morbid nor hysterically angry, as it almost always seemed to me
to be in New York or San Francisco. Nor were the men obsessed
with sex, not even the desperate precaution of "safer sex," though
everyone seemed perfectly to understand what it was and the
need for it. Their concern was some other wholeness they believed could heal the universe, both physically and spiritually.

Several of the men, in fact, participated with Steve in Bonding for Health, "encounter" groups that sponsored herb walks,
ritual Indian sweats, ecstatic massage, and meditations, along with
psychotherapeutic sessions. Steve explained to me why I could not
be invited. "The guys in the different groups," he said, "build a
very special trust in one another, a close community—because
we've shared a lot of secrets, a lot of needs, over the weeks.
Someone new would throw that off balance," he explained apologetically, then went on. "We're 'sex-positive men,' but we're also
learning how to be intimate in other important ways—like non-
sexual touch and being honest about ourselves. We believe that
above all you have to have that kind of human bonding if you
want to heal yourself."

Peter Koenigsberger shuffled in late, lanky, looking lost. His
long limp hair, dishwater gray, barely tapped his narrow, sloping
shoulders. Whenever he moved his chin, his gray beard brushed

his chest. As the circle widened by one chair, Peter slunk in beside me. In the candlelight from the table, his face shone red and chapped. He folded his big ruddy hands across his lap and nodded around. He didn't say a word until there was a lull in the talk about AIDS and several of the men went out to fetch more pie and a fresh pot of coffee.

"This AIDS epidemic," he whispered to me with surprise, "is really terrible." There was something unacquainted in his voice, as if he were a sympathetic straight man. Diffident, he didn't look me in the eyes, and the topic fell. We introduced ourselves. Meeting someone new made him grin. Learning that I was sojourning from out of state, he invited me to stay at his place. "You get lonely sometimes out there where we live," he added. His lover of eleven years was an eighteen-wheeler driver, on a month-long haul to Oregon and beyond. They lived in a desert cabin outside Madrid, whose name early prospectors had anglicized, pouncing on the first syllable. The once abandoned mining town was forty miles away off the old Albuquerque highway and didn't have "much to offer," Peter told me, "but hospitality." I made a date to meet him in the morning at the Madrid country store and spend one night in his cabin.

Except for its skinny, rutted highway, Madrid was a dirt town. It sat in a trough formed by dry, tan hills measeled with junipers and piñones and the breathless, brittle twigs of unnamed vegetation. A few dry-rotting cabins faced the road. Others—in rows of four or five—ran back into the bush. These were old coal miners' shacks trekked in from West Virginia by train in the 1800s, when Madrid was still mining lead, zinc, turquoise, silver, and gold. After mining died, the story goes, the town lay derelict for decades until a gaggle of San Francisco queens, "radical faeries," discovered it in the 1970s and bought up the whole place for mere thousands.

I joined Peter at the general store, as planned, at noon. He was sitting opposite the ancient potbellied stove with his elbows on the cracked linoleum counter of the soda fountain. On the porch, a big red dog swatted flies with his desultory tail. There was only the dead dry heat and the lazy buzz of insects on the yellow air. We had an ice-cream soda and set out to see the town, which was a few minutes' walk end to end. A hippie in a pickup passed, raising a cloud of sand. Peter waved. "He lives in what they call the 'fairy house' up here," he said shyly, as he always spoke. "Every once in a while they dress up in women's clothes, dresses and so forth, with their hair piled up on their heads, and go that way through town. I'm a man," he said, lethargically defending himself, "and I like being a man. So I don't quite understand people who want to be drag queens. But some of 'em are," he concluded. "They have to do their own thing, I suppose."

I asked whether in this very gay town the village government was very gay, too. There was no government here, as he remembered—no bureaucracy of any kind. "There's a water board," he contemplated. For water was all that mattered, really. One of its members was gay. "Most people around here just don't care one way or the other who's on it."

Two horses with dusty riders clopped by. The cloudless sky was so bright that it quavered. The horses drew up to the water shed beside a line of rusted railroad tracks where a steam locomotive sat dead in the heat. The sign on a nearby cafe announced "*Licores y Comidas.*" Between two weathered totem poles and two high hills of coal a sign read "ALL PEOPLE ARE CREATED EQUAL. GOD BLESS AMERICA. *We Welcome You* TO MADRID."

I followed Peter in my car. He lived outside Madrid a ways— far beyond walking distance—and halfway up a long, gentle slope that at the top did not so much draw a line against the sky as disappear. It seemed to crest like a dusty wave—then fall as if back into a dry, hot sea on some planet whose elements were other than water, earth, and air. In the midst of this immense evaporated surf, a tin roof marked the cabin like a tiny mirror, glinting flotsam bobbing in and out of sight as we drove. Trails—there were no paved roads—burrowed in the dirt like chameleons. Withered shrubs and cactus spines engraved pale, primitive designs on my car but could hardly mar Peter's embattled truck any more than it already had been. Two big, eager dogs, barking and wagging—they were dirt brown, smoking with dust—met us at the first fork and led us the rest of the way. "Old stagecoach roads," Peter said apologetically when we'd parked in a briar-and-cactus thicket downslope from the cabin. "That last one's a hundred and twenty years old—Santa Fe to Albuquerque." Like the others, it jolted vehicles ruthlessly with its sharp, embedded rocks and the deep old ruts of wagon wheels. "They haven't repaired them once this century," Peter told me, chuckling. From the truck bed we unloaded three jugs of water five gallons each, which for a dollar a month he filled at the community spigot. There was no water in his desert.

Peter's cabin was new—raw, unweathered wood—one story with a steep attic, about sixteen feet long, no more than half that measurement wide. There were five or six fir trees of no great height and several tissue-blossomed yuccas in the "yard," insofar as his yard was distinguishable at all from the rest of the dry, hard mountainside. Close to the ground, tiny wildflowers bloomed like parched, red paper. The miniature blooms of low-lying cactuses flamed as scarlet as hearts and burst sun gold at their centers. Bells—little brass globes scattered in the firs—chimed faintly. On a clothesline between the cabin and a tree, white and pastel squares of cloth with black filigree blew silently. "Buddhist prayer cloths," Peter answered when I asked. "For the well-being of the people in this area. The wind carries away our prayers."

Indoors, Peter's cabin was as ascetic as a desert monk's. To the right against the wall sat a single bunk, which left but narrow passage to the rest of the room and not much space at all beyond the foot of the bed. On the far wall, tin pots, mugs, and cooking utensils hung on nails. An old white kitchen table held two gas burners, which were the stove, and two white enamel buckets for washing and rinsing. The north wall was windowless against the winter. There—beside a sooty oil lamp, behind the ladder to the attic loft—hung a rude timber chest and shaving mirror, on whose shelf sat a white conch shell, a bowl of royal blue and yellow feathers, mantra beads, and a picture of the high lama. Peter spoke to me of the line of reincarnating karmapas and the seat of His Holiness, the gyalwa karmapa in America, in Woodstock,

New York, but his pale speech eluded me like a soporific chant. Peter and his lover (I came to understand) had deeded their land—these seventy acres of desert wilderness—to the karmapa for a monastery, with the sole stipulation that the couple was to have free use of it throughout their lifetimes. No monks were in residence yet.

A wood stove stood in the corner. Powered by a solar panel on the roof, there were a small TV, a radio, a portable tape player, and a finicky radio phone, but there was nothing else electrical, and Peter used these sparingly. The toilet—"if you have the need," he said, and pointed out the door—was downslope, downwind of the cabin: a withered scrub oak. He made me a cup of woody herbal tea and opened his mail, which he'd brought back from town, mumbling glosses as he read each letter. Cachina, Hututu, and Homer—three bright parrots—clicked and cawed in their cages by the window, flapping skittishly and feathering the floor.

"*Hututu,* good boy, *tu-tu-tu, tu-tu-tu,*" Peter hooted at the bird absently, without lifting his eyes from the postcard in his hands. "From Richard," he told me wistfully—his lover. "He was at a salmon run, doing some fishing up north. He says he'll call me next Wednesday at the Nifty, before the gay meeting begins. That's when we talk whenever he's gone." He passed me the card. "O O O" and "X X X" were scrawled across the bottom. There was a friendly letter from his former wife and one from his oldest daughter, too. "She's just a little Richard's senior," Peter said proudly. "He was twenty-three years old when we met. Guess some people think I robbed the cradle—I guess." He tucked some money in an envelope addressed to his daughter and licked it shut. "Ten bucks isn't much," he said, abstracted, "but at least I am remembering her."

He wanted to show me his land. "Better wear your boots," he cautioned.

"Are there snakes?" I gasped.

He paused, as if that consideration hadn't been his point at all. "There are those around," he answered.

I scanned the floor and scoured the rafters. I stared at the covers on the bunk (where I was to sleep) and stepped lightly when again we went outdoors. This fear of snakes bit at me constantly in this savage geography—and I wondered how savagely Freudian it might be. In adolescence I had had wonderful, frightful dreams of falling into snakepits where ecstatic reptiles turned to penises.

Two huge macaws, Blue and Charlie, lived in the back of the cabin in an adobe hut surrounded by a chicken-wire cage. They were brilliantly plumed and sullen birds, full of sudden bitchy squawks. Peter fed them nuts and apple slices and grabbed a handful of turquoise-and-yellow feathers from their pen for the band of my cowboy hat. They flapped so furiously in protest that they lost more plumage from their wings than ever Peter could have stolen had they simply ignored the theft. "One time, Charlie got away," he said. "I was crying. Richard was crying, too. We watched him sweep across the valley over there." He pointed over a vast trough of droughty land to the bleak, rocky top of a nearby hill. "He seemed awful happy flying like that, but he'd've died. We trudged all over till we captured him, on Cedar Mountain." He baby-talked to the bird, as sweetly as a father to his infant. "Eat all your apples and nuts," he begged.

Farther up the mountainside a temple for the Buddhist monks was being built, a three-story frame with floors but no walls yet. We climbed steep ladders to the top, which overlooked the desert to a distant basin where Santa Fe lay vague and shimmering in the heat, twenty miles or so away as the hawk flies. On a tattered, faded Oriental rug, a Buddha sat in this high room, surrounded by vases of shriveled flowers and a round brass gong, which Peter struck to let me hear the call to prayer. It echoed and echoed until its resonance caught in my mind, as though it were the nature of the air. I sat at the edge of the floor, my legs dangling high above the desert, wondering at the beauty of this desolation and its sound.

Only in time did the constant bite of the sun against our faces intrude on the peace. We searched for a shady arroyo, as cool as a summer desert can provide. "You can find gold in these arroyos," Peter pointed out, "if you pan long enough." In this dried creek bed, we squatted on a rock, pitching the brims of our hats against the sunshine, scooting every now and then to catch the cobweb shadows of a piñon's limbs. Elwood, one of the dogs, cried sometimes and swept the parched earth with his languid tail. I looked for snakes. "Do you like this place?" Peter asked ingenuously. "Some bugs and insects, but no place is perfect, I guess, no matter where you go."

I still knew little about this man but stray biography, nothing to place him in the world or clue me as to what had brought him to this waterless loneliness among parrots and dogs and his occasional lover. He seemed to me infused with loneliness—or longing—but nonetheless at home here. "I get visitors every now and then, though," he reminisced. "They come up here to relax." He named one, who was "cute but completely straight and too domineering. After the uranium mines closed in western New Mexico, he came up here to do his sculptures. I gave him a place to pitch his tent, right there near the cabin. He didn't work. But he took over like it was his property, giving me orders. That's how straight men are."

He had invited others, too—gay men—even placed an ad in *RFD*, a journal for rural gay men and gay men simply intrigued by life in the country. "The straight ones always expect too much. And some of these straight guys are really awful, so many of 'em, you know!" This he told me with surprise, not anger, as though, while somehow accustomed to this recognition, the enmity of man still shocked him. His eyebrows rose, his shoulders stooped. "Like 'Paranoid Pat' who lives down the road," he told me. "He shot Ivan's dog for no reason at all. Then he started complaining about people coming up the road across his land. But that's the stagecoach road. It belongs to everybody—there's no way to get up here without it. He tried to block it off! One night Pat and his son came up here drunk with their guns and threatened to kill us and all sorts of stuff, but they didn't say what for. We were very unhappy," Peter reported sincerely. "Their guns are never more than three feet away. Now we keep our shotguns ready. I've had enough of meanness from drunks." I thought of Rudy, trying to guard a tiny entrance to his land on Peak 5 of the Rocky Mountains. It seemed to me that we all peacefully long to find safe haven in this world but are forced to secure it, when we've drawn its boundaries, only by bitter vigilance.

Still, he had created a myth, as activists also do, about the peaceableness of all homosexuals. Without it, perhaps, he had no safety. "It's a nice treat," Peter said, "having a guy like you paying a visit. The thing I like about being with gay men is I can be open with 'em. With my straight friends I have to pretend, with most of 'em, anyway. But some of the gay guys give me hugs." He smiled to himself, remembering. Then, with poisonousness as quick as the strike of a coiled rattler, he hissed, "When I think about what these fundamentalists and right-wing people want to do with us . . ." He floundered. "Take away the love we need so much to live!" Then as suddenly he dropped it and was peaceful again.

Late in the afternoon Peter took me into Cerillos to meet Will, a gay handyman who worked for "some rich folks up nearer Santa Fe, taking care of their horses and gardening." Elwood ran yelping beside us on the stagecoach road, then turned back precisely at the fork where he had earlier met us coming in. Ruts so ferociously rocked the truck that I could only grunt, but somehow the softness of Peter's voice cushioned his speech and made it possible for him to keep on talking. "You've . . . known . . . Will . . . a long . . . time?" I belched with the bumps, trying to encourage Peter's part of the conversation.

"Will's young! I was a young man in the fifties!" He stated this non sequitur neither humorously nor sadly. He dodged a boulder, ran over a cactus instead. "That's no good for the tires," he muttered. I asked him whether he'd always lived in New Mexico, hoping for the history he had been remiss in telling. Leaning over the steering wheel to watch the road, he began to fill me in, though frequently he would have abandoned the story had I not urged him on. Still, he seemed less shy than acid and anxious to let some old anger lie unexposed.

In 1950, already an officer in the navy, he graduated from Yale with a master's degree in geophysics, having produced a thesis that caused considerable attention at the Atomic Energy Commission. Soon he left New England and the sea to continue his work at the Colorado School of Mines. In 1955 he began to work for the federal government and married. His specialties— electromagnetism, underground water, air tagging, cloud seeding—were all beyond me. Senator Joseph McCarthy and J. Edgar Hoover were rooting out Commies and faggots from the government then. The FBI called Peter in. "Two men in gray suits were standing in a room to question me," he remembered. "They said, 'We have a report that you're queer.' They talked that way. I don't even know how they suspected me. I wasn't seeing anybody. I didn't even know any gay guys. I didn't even know about myself for sure. I'd never had gay sex with anyone. They used a lot of dime-store psychology.

"The floor fell out from under me. I couldn't talk for a minute. I was trying to think, was I really a homosexual? They said, 'If we don't think you're telling the truth, we'll put you on a lie detector.' So I said, 'I guess, if I'm honest about my inner feelings, yes, I'm a homosexual. But I don't know any homosexuals. And I'm not having any homosexual relationships.' So they wrote on their reports I was a queer—or however they wrote it down.

"They let me stay on at the AEC, but I lived wondering when it all would happen again and what they would do to me. I thought of ending it all. I don't know how many did commit suicide or lose their job or family. It's terrible what they did to people."

He and his wife divorced in 1978, though their breakup had nothing to do with his homosexuality. Soon after that, he moved to another government job and had to apply for a higher security clearance. A half year passed before anyone contacted him about his application. "I got a call from the Department of Energy," Peter said rancidly. There was a ruined tremor in his voice that I hadn't heard before. " 'Mr. Koenigsberger, we want you to come in and talk to one of our psychiatrists.' They asked me, 'Are you homosexual?'—or 'gay,' I don't remember what language they were using then. I said, 'I suppose I am.' So they asked me, 'Are you going to molest young boys?' I said, *'Don't go asking me that crap.'* I talked to 'em just like that!

"The security clearance came through. I don't know why. That happened, but I left anyway. I had hurt my back and took my disability pay. I got out of there.

"You know, you live your whole life being watched, and you get fed up with it. Any minute they can destroy your life. They've got their files on ya, you know. I hear some of these younger gay guys ask, 'Why don't you just be more open?' Well, a lot of us are scared to death what they can do to us. I've seen that happen. I've been through all that, and they haven't."

Cerillos lay across a wide, dusty riverbed, by way of a low, narrow bridge, a couple of feet above the would-be water. The tiny town was all dirt streets and mud construction, except for the front of the "Blacksmithing & Livery" shop, whose warped wooden planks announced "Wagon Repairing" in pallid yellow letters powdered by age. Several Mexican women, tending to a brown brigade of children, bent with their buckets at the public pump, which emerged from the slow dust of the churchyard like the neck of a goose turned fossil in a catastrophic swim.

Will's mud house sat beneath a tall tree with crisp, pale leaves. The high yellow grass on its roof was the only grass around. Its walls had been melted out of shape by winds and sometimes rains. In the yard, a bright array of laundry blew on a line, like prayer flags. Will was a thin, blond, leathery man with big, rough hands. He had made spaghetti in a big iron kettle on his old iron stove and was busily stoking wood to warm it when we got there. We ate in the living room on odd plates with mismatched flatware. The room was nearly bare. Will sat on an egg crate by the furnace, whose pipe had stained the whitewashed walls with soot. Peter and I took the sagging sofa and ate from TV trays. An elected official of the town stopped by and walked in without asking. He wanted to borrow a portion of bran with spores that carried a germ to kill grasshoppers. He was a red-headed, bearded hippie.

"He's in trouble for child abuse," Will said when the man took the poisonous bran and left. "He's got six red-headed children. 'Moral,' " he commented queerly, "is a very fickle word."

"How do they accept you here as gay?" I asked.

"This is a Mexican place. Much better you be gay than An-glo. The Mexicans are much more tolerant about that."

Will was a quiet man and after our quiet dinner played the lute. In the shadowed corner where he sat, he sight-read by a can-dle from a textbook on counterpoint, page forty. "Consonance in 2nd Species" was our delicately plucked vespers. Beside him, his yellow mongrel raised his throat and sang. Will tried to play Bach. "His music drenched the world deeper than any other man," he stated, rehearsing a passage of fingering. "I teach my-self. I think you can be self-taught if it's in your genes." Two un-steady melodies teased each other baroquely. White-gold sunlight, as pale as the evening desert and as chill, drifted in on counterpoints of dust through the open door and fell in a crooked square across the floor. At sundown Peter and I went back to the mountains.

That cold night, the tiny bells in the firs rang out against a giant crystal moon—songs broken on black winds. Crickets' wings, like tongues, and the quickened flaps of prayer flags drummed the air. Lightning entranced the sky in platinum sheets, blinding a million stars in an instant. Inside, a candle flashed in a skittish draft before the Buddha of Infinite Light, an offering to Peter that Richard had painted. Peter asked if I wanted to warm his attic bunk with him, but I slept alone on the bunk downstairs and, listening to the cabin groan, shivered beneath a stack of blankets. The curtains, drawn and repelled by the hissing breeze, licked at the windowpanes. I searched for serpents in the silvered darkness beneath the door till dawn came.

In this desert mountain's endless twilight, in this sleepless immensity that haunted me, Peter found his peace, the lonely ref-uge from his terror.

On June 28, 1969, the New York City Police Department raided a Greenwich Village drag bar known as the Stonewall Inn. New York State, like most other states back then, forbade homosexual acts and allowed search-and-destroy missions against such haunts as fostered them. There had been a long and systematic campaign against the city's homosexuals. The police had assaulted the Stonewall Inn many times before and roughed up faggots. There were reports of beatings and suspicious deaths among queers whom they jailed. On this one night some brave, pissed queen threw something back and started a three-day riot. In that melee the fervent soul of the contemporary gay rights movement came into being. There had been homosexual liberation movements before then, but none as vigorous as the politics the Stonewall queens inflamed. Gay Pride parades each June commemorate their angry courage.

Albuquerque's Twelfth Annual Gay Pride Parade, like the marches in many other towns, was held one week earlier than those in the gay metropolises. Thus distant pilgrims could also make their way to Chicago, New York, Los Angeles, or San Francisco for those cities' megacelebrations. This year Albuquerque's parade—like those in similarly small cities across the nation—launched a full week of parties, cultural displays, religious services, and political panel discussions.

A group from Santa Fe, which had no parade, was to meet at a large parking lot downtown at seven o'clock on Saturday morning to form carpools to Albuquerque. I never found my fellow travelers so drove alone. No one I knew was going, anyway: Alex, Rand, Peter, Will—in fact, none of the crowd from the Nifty. Parades were not their politics. Less representative of America's homosexual men than they, I had marched every year since 1977. Pride parades were the heady stage from which I could proclaim the sexuality the world despised me for—and for which I had earlier despised myself. They were hedonistic acts of resurrection, the most holy day of the sexual year. They publicly purged my fear and guilt and dramatized my "coming out," my erotic redemption. Each year they bonded me more deeply to the lonely community of men and women who had suffered likewise. I could not miss this one.

The trip was an hour by expressway, which followed the Rio Grande the length of the state. Albuquerque's population, a sun-struck half-million, sprawled loosely across the desert and partway up the rocky walls of short-spanned mountains at the edge of town. In this bleak spaciousness, two intersecting interstates lazily managed the sparse traffic. To the east of the road, on this Saturday, a brigade of hot-air balloons ascended hugely, brilliantly painting slow stripes on a luminous, mist blue sky.

I arrived at the Common Bond Community Center at nine o'clock. It was a small, concrete-block, gay clubhouse in front of which maybe two hundred marchers had gathered. They were a festive, urban crowd, full of wry comment and stereotypically gay exaggeration. There was more campy anger and humor here than I'd seen since leaving New York, certainly more than I'd experienced so far in New Mexico. Two tall "scag drag" queens—in "housedresses" and full beards—held a floral-patterned banner lettered "MOMS FOR GAYS." Chiffon scarves covered their bouffant wigs. Posing and re-posing for photographs, they incessantly adjusted their winged sunglasses with delicately winged fingers, while behind them hazy blue mountain backs hardened against the morning sky. A beaming, bearded young man carried a handmade sign, "I'd rather be gay than *grim*!" A stout and straddle-gaited lesbian: "I may be butch, but I'm all woman." One man's placard placed his homosexuality in a long, anachronistic genius history: "Tchaikovsky, Julius Caesar, Leonard Bernstein, Alexander the Great, Walt Whitman, Aristotle, Leonardo de Vinci, Allen Ginsberg, Michelangelo, Alan Turing, Horatio Alger—and Me." Another man's sign was as delusory—"We're gay and we have gay money"—coopting the old ruse that, unencumbered by the expense of families, homosexual men are privileged by wealth.

There were several enormous motorcycles mounted by women and scattered bicycles to which towering bouquets of pink and lavender balloons were tethered. Several costumed dogs bounced balloon bouquets from their collars. There was a small contingent of disabled lesbians in wheelchairs and babies in buggies—all anchoring balloons. Children cartwheeled at the head of the march. Others bashfully clutched their moms or dads—or, what was all the same, their moms' or dads' lovers.

The parade kept to the westbound lanes of Loma

Boulevard—a broad, hot thoroughfare to the state fairgrounds, where the postparade rally was to be held. I ran alongside and shot pictures. A nervous woman with a press badge snapped pictures from the sidewalk but seemed to keep her distance from the march. In time, as fellow journalists, we spoke. She told me that she free-lanced for the *Albuquerque Journal* and that she envied me the freedom I displayed at the parade. "Those are my friends out there," she said, "and it scares me to death to get too close. You know—someone might yell or give me a hug or something. If anyone else from the paper is covering this thing, it'll be all over the office Monday morning."

"Would that be a problem?" I asked. New Mexico had up till now struck me as a tolerant state.

"A problem?" She arched her brow. "It's hard enough being a *woman* at that paper. Journalism is *guys*' territory! I have to listen to the sexist trash they say about 'the girls' at work and keep my mouth shut. If they found out I was a lesbian," she said, "I wouldn't survive. They'd can me."

She and I were the lone spectators, but for a few stray pedestrians in this vehicle town, and occasional, startled eyes in shop windows. Now and then a car or motorbike passed through the empty streets and an invective—or, rarely, a cheer—would be hurled. Then, suddenly, at the stoplight at San Mateo Boulevard, a ravenous coven of born-again Christians appeared below the Octopus Car Wash sign. The men wore ill-fitting suits as black as bats and narrow, black ties like rancid tongues. The women were as makeup free as radical lesbians but dressed in midcalf skirts and steep high heels instead of biker's boots and jeans. Tugging small children behind them, they struggled to preach at one end of the march and then the other, while their angry men stormed free. Squat demon shadows chased at their feet in the midday sun like some dark sexual need. Their placards were all askew, one of them upside down. None of their mottoes was brilliant. A grotesque cartoon of the Grim Reaper was captioned "SODOMY IS DEATH." The letters on a sign that read "HOMOSEXUALITY SICKNESS OR SIN" had squiggly lines around them of vibrating red.

In the street, castanets, gourds, tom-toms, and the delighted squeals of gay parents' cartwheeling kids raised an ecstatic ruckus. One gay marcher punched his placard in the air in elaborate syncopation with the tribal sound:

SEX is SEX
is SEX
STRAIGHTS
REPENT

At the end of a cement wall that announced "S P E A K E A S Y" stood an obese Christian woman shrouded in a tent-size dress. Like an enraged Charybdian monster, she bellowed perpetually, *"Got AIDS yet?"* Her cavernous mouth consumed her face. Her husband (or so it seemed) stood behind her, skinny and meek. The acrostic on his placard read:

G A Y
o I e
t D t
S

The children of the gay men and lesbians danced around a drum. From the sidewalk—where the loud, fat woman squealed—frightened Christian children stared, numb. They were learning that day to hate what they did not understand and destroy whatever they hated. Perhaps someday this violence would turn them against themselves. I wondered that Americans did not call such brute madness child abuse.

As an activist from "back east," I was asked to speak at the pride picnic following the parade. I spoke of the special courage it took to march in places like Albuquerque, where few men and women participated and the risk of being caught by a journalist's camera was higher than in the megaparades of New York or San Francisco. Still, I said, the big-city-based gay rights movement paid little mind to small-town activists, though urbanites could learn enormously from them about the crisis of being homosexual in America. I elaborated passionately. A "leatherman" named Matt Martinez was moved to thank me afterward. We sat on the ground and talked. He was wearing heavy biker's boots, black chaps, and a black leather cap and was shirtless. An S/M harness crossed his chest. He was slender and olive-complected, exotically handsome. A bushy black mustache shadowed his lips.

He and his lover, Brett Lane, were members of a gay biker's club, the Hijos del Sol. He invited me to go on a three-day run with other gay southwestern clubs in the mountains the following weekend. I had made plans for a summer solstice celebration outside Santa Fe and so declined. (Nor had I been more than once on the back of a big motorcycle.) He asked me instead to a dinner that night, which Brett and he were "throwing for several couples." The men lived near Bosque, forty miles south along the Rio Grande. I met one of the invited couples late that afternoon, who showed me the way.

We drove I-25. Albuquerque glimmered behind us and began to fade, a vanishing mirror tail at the end of a range of mountains. Big road signs warned "DO NOT PICK UP HITCHHIKERS IN THIS AREA." And in the desolation halfway there, prison towers and high white walls sat diminished in the desert's blinding vastness. Brett was a guard here.

Near the dusty town of Bosque, a long rough asphalt road exited the interstate. A long dirt road led off it to Matt and Brett's. Their house was pink adobe and grew up out of a pink dirt yard like a square, squat mushroom. A lonely Rio Grande cottonwood towered so high above it that its cooling shadow died before it hit the ground. Inside, the house was dark and cool, though the day had been scorching.

"Adobe is nature's perfect air-conditioning system," Matt explained. "When you live in mud houses, you never need those ugly boxes in your windows." Each night the desert chill and the dew seeped through the earthen walls, which held the coolness for the daytime. Every day, when the sun rebaked the mud, the heat worked its way inside to warm the house before nightfall. Now, at sunset, Matt and Will made their rounds, as they did each evening, to open the drapes and heavy shutters that had guarded the indoor air all day from the sunshine. "This isn't the way you guys live in New York." Matt grinned, tweaking any urban smugness I might harbor. "We *know*, 'cause we've been up there and visited. You guys think we're crude, but *our* way of life down here is *natural!*"

Old furniture of rich, dark wood—ornately carved in the Spanish style—filled the living room, or *sala*. The antique sofas were plump and the chairs upholstered in elaborate embroideries. Threadbare tapestries of Spain's New World conquests darkened the walls. Great worn rugs covered the broad pegged planks of the floor. The low plank ceiling was upheld by huge *vigas*, beams of fat barked logs. Something baroque, a concerto grosso, was playing on the radio. Old lampshades shone like candlelight.

The estate and its antique furnishings were ancestral, four generations back, when New Mexico was still Mexico. Matt's great-great-grandfather first built this house 150 years ago. The family was unadulterated Spanish—not "mixed with Indian," Matt said.

"The problem with adobe houses," Matt stated over dinner, "is they melt. You've gotta keep rebuilding them all the time." Two of the guests were quiet—Leonard and his new lover, Lee, who was from Bangkok and didn't speak English yet. The others were more garrulous and intimate. It surprised me that none of the talk was campy or "gay." No one talked mournfully of AIDS. They were longtime friends and swapped family news— marriages, births, deaths, illnesses, feuds. We spoke about the adobe house, which was a presence—the groaning language of its wooden parts, the health of its skin in the sun and rain, its temperature, its querulous daily needs, its long memory. "But you never give up on a house like this," Matt said. "It tells you who you really are. It's like a member of your family."

The kitchen, which ran the width of the house, held both a brand-new range—where Matt was simmering spaghetti sauce in a big iron kettle—and a wood-stoked cast-iron oven—where the men did all their baking. Kindling was stacked on the floor. On the shelf of the old iron stove, bread and pies were still exhaling steam. After supper we walked to the Rio Grande, past the pens of peacocks Matt and Brett raised, across dry acres of family land. The couples walked arm in arm or held hands. Matt's father, a very old man, also had a house on the acreage. He was working, on this early evening, in the estate's brick yard, where adobe for rebuilding was formed and laid out in rows to bake. He waved as we passed. The sun was almost gone. The evening wind seemed haunted. In the west, a ship of burning clouds was sinking fast. Its hull was charred, its bottom blazing. Silver torpedoes of cumulus had struck its bow. Along the river's banks, a feathery train of trees stood black against the sky and shook like mourners. In the east, the mountains were dying.

When the other guests left, I stayed. I steamed with my hosts in a hot tub in the chilly, open air, where no unnatural light faded the desert darkness or denigrated the sharpness of the stars. So baptized, I slept snugly that night between the lovers. We were three warm brothers on a giant water bed. At dawn we woke to the alarm of peacocks, which screamed beneath the window.

On Sunday morning I went to "church" in Albuquerque, a gathering of gay mystics who met weekly at Dr. Buck Rhodes's house. Buck had been a professor at the University of New Mexico medical school until he became too vocal about the AIDS epidemic. His passion had not sat well with the faculty. The bigotry there was subtle—gradual professional and social exile as Buck continued to come out of the closet. Choosing not to become a martyr to his colleagues' fear, he left the school to champion life in other ways. Free of the school, he created a company to do biomedical research on the virus.

Buck was a visionary, short, bald, round, and red, quiet with an exquisite, peaceful face. He saw the details of the house he was to build in a dream—the Place of Peace, in a garden behind a wall and a high gate across the street from the university in Albuquerque. He lived there with his teenaged daughter, who left with school friends before the "service" started. A joyful band of gay men had gathered in a circle below the arching stained-glass window of the living room. Each had brought a pot-luck dish for a kind of eucharistic brunch afterward. Every week another one of them played "God," led his brothers in a channeled ritual and meditation before they underwent the fiery waters of the hot tub in Buck's garden.

This week Roger Lanphear channeled Jesus. Sitting in the midst of our circle, Roger said almost nothing and led us in synchronized circles of breath, then transcendent, seamless pulses of breathing whose frequency carried the Jesus spirit. The presence spoke to each of us uniquely and created in us a singular vision. In a silence befitting Quakers, we shared the truths we were seeing. Jeff saw men dancing circles on an ocean and ascending from one blue field of outer space into another. They rose past constellations, brightening until each man became a sun. "We are priests and shamans," he heard within himself. "We are man and woman. We are both and neither. We stand between extremes and form the unity through which comes healing. We feel all sickness and pain and from grief create joy. We are the healers of the earth."

In time I spoke. I saw a mountain soaring from the scorched desert, green in its middle height, becoming ice and snow, then icy stone where frozen winds spun fiercely around its sharp peak. "Each one of us is everything and whole," the spirit moved me. "Searing heat, verdurous nurture, and deathly cold. We are rooted in the earth and pierce the sky. We cannot fall. We are strong."

Sunday night I shared a bed with Jeff and his recent boyfriend, John. Jeff lived in a stucco apartment row, built on the model of fifties motels, in a poor part of town. We rose before dawn, packed a basket of juices and fruits, fresh-fried tortilla chips, and humus, and trekked to the hot springs high in the Jemez Mountains. These were holy ground, Jeff told me, for spiritually minded gay men in New Mexico, though others, gay and straight, sometimes sought them out for their physical pleasures alone. The road was sinuous, narrow, walled by firs, the mossy sunlight through the woods immersed in morning dew. The mountain air was euphoric. I lost place and time.

At the top we parked on the edge of a steep, dark slope and followed a path that decayed beneath crisp leaves and the discarded scales of pinecones. Avalanches of clay, slippery new growth, and rotting logs at times carried us down. The forestal mist breathed bittersweet with death and regeneration. There was a fast, rocky stream in the ravine, which was bridged by nervous, fallen tree trunks, then a second precipitous climb, narrow foot-falls up the mountain. Far into the pines, where the hill stood up like a pyramid's wall, three stone pools, like the bowls of a scal-loped fountain, cantilevered from the cliff, poured slow silver into one another, steaming the pallid sunshine. The lowest of these reservoirs bubbled through its rocks, slicking the bosky black ground. A high pine, shaded by the opposing mountain, stood el-egant beside the water like a dark Narcissus. There, naked among the mirrored branches, sat a small son and his father, oblivious of our approach. A prosthesis for the man's knee and lower leg lay on an island rock beside him. They soaked their three feet si-lently.

The sun, rising from behind the mountain peaks and slow scrims of fog, mottled the sweeps of forest black and yellow. The breeze was chill. Jeff, John, and I bathed at the top. Above the glassy surface of this highest sultry pool, mute storms brewed in the steam, dissolving and re-creating us while we watched. Jeff submerged himself but for his face, a mask escaping a liquid-hot mirror. With a crystal resting on his heart, he focused the scald-ing energy as if through a prism, metastasizing meditations throughout his body. It was here that the spring boiled forth from a mouth in the rock, a cobalt-green niche that arched from the water, clearing and clouding as it breathed. I lay back flat and slipped my head inside its jaws, which were serrated with rocky, dripping teeth, and placed a crystal on my lips. The mountain's gullet swallowed me down to my chest, gargling hot speech, mouth to mouth with resuscitating exhalations.

There was one other spring, a hermit pool, secluded in a shady colonnade of pines farther up the mountain. When in the afternoon the sun had scorched the coolness from the air and sev-eral backpacking couples, male and female, settled in our space, I sought this hidden place alone. Wider than the others, it spread out shallow from a vaulted grotto, open before and behind, through whose crevices slivers of sunlight pierced the water, illuminating a constellation of pastel pebbles beneath. In the middle of this universe, a young, brown man sat yogilike, spotlit in an ivory column of sunshine. I stepped in. We didn't speak. In time we drew close, facing one another. He scooped a shimmering palm of pebbles from the pool and poured them over my shoulders. Round and wax smooth, they massaged me like a thousand gentle fingers, trailing liquid diamonds. In this slow-motion dream state, we bathed each other with pebbles and steaming showers, discovering ourselves in hot baptisms. When we came, we watched the semen pearls burst out and swirl, lacing the water in ecstatic confirmation of the flesh and spirit.

Jeff had tried to "read my spine" that afternoon, dragging his fingers up and down the column, sizing up my psyche by the contour of the vertebrae. It was a Native American practice, he told me. "They can tell you the stages of your life from the day you were born. Everything's recorded in your backbone." He was learning but wasn't expert yet. He urged me to meet an Indian named Felipe.

Tom Dickerson, a potter I had met at the Nifty, had told me about Felipe, too, when I visited him in Pecos, east of Santa Fe. Tom lived secluded in the Sangre de Cristo Mountains, in an adobe compound he had built thirty years ago: house, cottage, studio, Indian ceremonial buildings to accommodate the pasticcio of Native American religions he practiced. He had moved here from Kansas in the fifties—because, he said, "I couldn't come into my full power back in Wichita. Everyone else belonged. I couldn't be who I really was there."

We had a desultory chat that began with legal problems Tom was having and wound around somehow naturally to Felipe. Like Rudy in Colorado and Peter Koenigsberger in Madrid, Tom was having trouble with his deed. "A little old lady's causing me this grief," he uttered softly. "My boundaries were settled half a century ago! I've spent a *ton* of money!"

Suddenly it seemed to me that there must be some mass karma involved in all this—a psychic banishment that manifested itself in these battles to hold on to one's own land. It was as if

some overpowering, evil spirit would deny these men a small, secure place on the earth. "Why not try witchcraft?" I wisecracked.

"Oh, I know *lots* of witches," he responded. He was serious.
"All kinds. *I'm* a witch!" Tom had dove white hair and sky blue
eyes too kind, I thought, to harbor meanness, though his cheeks,
I could see, were flushed and his voice was edged with anger. His
high-topped canvas shoes were scarlet. "No, I decided to do this
all by the law," he said, "all the way to the state supreme court if
I have to. I've never once descended to pettiness. I've got a lot of
hostility in my heart. But meanness would create horrible karma
for me. Why would I want to do that when I'm dealing with this
already? Those people destroy themselves that try to take what's
yours away. Oh, she's really in trouble for what she's doing," he
declared solemnly. "But that's the choice she made."

The compound was all orange mud with green plank doors
and dark, nubby *vigas* protruding from the ceilings. The outside
walls were low and leaning, wild with flowering vines and the
blooms of spiny bushes. It was clay pot housing, like the ground
floor of Babylon. Tom's kiln stood outdoors by his studio, charred
as a dormant volcano. On a table nearby lay baked clay chips of
various surprising pigments and glazes, tints and techniques Tom
had borrowed from the Pecos Indians. "I rediscovered them," he
explained. "Everyone knew the raw materials they used but not
how to mix them together. I did it by trial and error. It took a
long time."

At sunset that afternoon Tom took me to the Pecos ruins,
down the road from where he lived. The site held the scanty evidence of a pueblo of some 660 adobe rooms and the scattered
underground chambers, kivas, that the Indians had used for spirit
rites. Tom was both knowledgeable and passionate about these
people. He was drawn to them not only for the high artistry of
their relics, but because of their ancient banished lives. He had
built a memorial kiva on his land. Pueblos had settled in this valley, he said as we walked the paths, at the turn of the last millennium. They were conquered by the Spanish and Catholicism at
the end of the seventeenth century and began to die away—felled
by arms, diseases, and alien dogmas. The survivors, fewer than

twenty out of thousands, sought refuge across the Rio Grande in the Jemez Mountains. On the first Sunday of August every year, St. Anthony's, a nearby parish, held a memorial mass for the ruined Indians. "The appreciation's a little late, don't you think?" said Tom. "It's easy to remember people you've killed off or driven away."

It was then Tom first mentioned Felipe. "He's not Pueblo. He's Apache. But you've got to talk to him if you're interested in these things. He's a survivor, in spite of the white man."

"Is he gay?"

Tom paused. "I know that's a word you use a lot," he gently chided me. "But 'gay' the way most people use it is a concept of privilege for men who can buy the things they need and be independent from their family or community. They can get the security they have to have and create a world of their own. It's a separate identity.

"Most of the people I know are poor or aren't Anglo. They can't live that way, especially Indians and Latinos. They depend on their families economically and for support in a racist society. They may have sex with men or fall in love, but their family is their identity. They can't survive without their families."

As far as Felipe was concerned, *gay* didn't comfortably fit in another way, either. "It's like the Indians that come back here for the mass once a year," Tom explained. "Their religion isn't 'either/or.' They're pagan *and* Catholic. They're both—or something between—as a way of communicating with the universe more completely. It's like saying 'man' or 'woman,' 'gay' or 'straight.' Felipe's between the extremes. That's what the Indians call *berdache*. Sex isn't the issue. It's his relationships. You really need to meet Felipe."

Felipe Ortega's voice was liquid on the phone, like a stream. I asked if we could meet. He told me he got up by four A.M. I could meet him at that hour or later. I chose eight o'clock and considered it early. He instructed me to the outskirts of Albuquerque where he lived—past the university, through the business district and Old Town, across the Rio Grande, to a left turn at the light.

"Go beyond the park," he said, "to a street called Cypress. Turn in, turn out again immediately. You'll see my house in front of you, right there."

I followed his directions to the end—though that final pirouette he demanded seemed useless. I turned into Cypress Street, then out, and suddenly the house appeared as if by alchemy, where I'd have sworn there'd been a vacant lot before. He lived in a white adobe stucco centered in a yard that was blood red. The house was in ill repair. It sat within the solitary shadow of a cottonwood tree. Felipe had heard my car and waited for me at the door. The way he hugged me when we met, we might have been lost brothers. Or I might have been a vagrant son and he my father-mother. He had an Indian madonna's face. It was not delicate, but full and ivory brown with satiny cheeks and nurturing bright black eyes. His cheekbones were Asiatic, strong and high. His mustang hair was threaded with gray and pulled back in a ponytail. He might have been in his twenties or his forties. I couldn't tell.

Inside, a phone lay off its hook on a table by the door. Felipe continued talking—in no hurry on account of my being there. Hurry was a white man's concept. I sat on the sofa and listened. A pregnant woman from a reservation was on the line. She was having labor pains. "¿Cota?" Felipe repeated. "No, cota is good." Felipe was her medicine man. "Yeah, sí, óleo is also good in pregnancies. But cota is fantastic!" He'd bring her a medicine bundle, he said, tobacco twined in sage and cedar. "El martes siguiente." Next Tuesday. Did she have a bundle left over from last time? "In your house there is no protection? You must keep doing medicines outside your door. . . . ¡Bueno! I'll be in the pueblo Saturday, too. I will pray for you while they're dancing."

When he finished, he didn't sit but did chores. Ordering his obligations for the day, he talked to me as he worked. Sometimes, as if on silent cue, he made another phone call. His bead and silver bracelets jangled on his wrists. He wore a little silver eagle's feather on a chain around his neck and a turquoise cross. It seemed to me that he had structured our talk beforehand, so powerfully did he guide me through it. The order of his thinking was elliptical, as if it were rooted in spirit rather than reason. He answered my questions before I asked them. He made delicate distinctions where before I had seen no difference.

"Political activism among Native Americans," he said, pre-empting a line of interrogation, "is simply doing what you want to do, not asking the white man for permission. Two years ago, we made a two-hundred-mile trek to commemorate the exile of our ancestors from our native lands. The newspapers all said 'celebrating.' They didn't hear our words—*'commemorating.'* We did it for *us*, not for the white man's entertainment. When we talk about political activism, we mean simply taking our spirit back into our lives and saying it is ours.

"It is also true for gays. Activism is to recover the spirit, after the oppressor has tried to take it away. There is Father Sky and Mother Earth, the male and female. Gay men and lesbians are shamans. We touch both. Among Apaches, an impotent man would sleep with a *berdache* to recover his spirit.

"White values are leaving the tribes now. We are reclaiming polygamy, getting rid of the white man's shame about our ways. My old uncle had two wives at the same time. We called them by the same names—Grandma Lisa and Grandma Lisa. The *berdache* tradition is being recovered, too. White Americans tried to kill it when they came. A lot of young gay Native American men now are refusing to marry.

"I grew up not being ostracized the way I am. My aunts dressed me up in girls' clothes." Felipe's laugh was affectionate. "I ran around thinking of myself as pretty till I went to a white school and American society said, 'You're not pretty. You're screwed up.'

"My mother was very Christian. Mom would come to me and say, 'So-and-so is going to sleep with you tonight,' and she'd bring me a male friend who understood I was special. So I'm not a misogynist, as many gay men become. My women in my family supported me, and the judgments weren't there. My grandmother, when I was born, came to visit my mother and said, 'This son of yours is going to be different. See these marks on his back?' When I was young she told me, 'I can see when you grow up, some people will whisper, "Oh, he likes boys," but these marks on your back are from the Great Spirit.' The guys I went to school with all knew my affection. I was their counselor. They asked me how to deal with their women, these macho guys."

Felipe took me to breakfast at Gabby's, a diner for truckers and cowboys. "I wear pigtails and my blanket, even in the city," he said when we were in the car. We were sitting at the stoplight at Comanche Street. Beside us with their windows down, in a wrecked and rusted Chevrolet Apache pickup, two teenaged boys drummed the dashboard to hard Christian rock. *"Holy smoke! God rules!"* the radio announcer exploded. A Ford truck sat in front of us. A bumper sticker read "JESUS—The Right Choice" and sported a cross.

"A white woman asked me once," Felipe said, transcendent, " 'Don't you ever wear a regular coat?' I said, 'Do *you* have a regular coat?' 'Why, *yes*,' she said, 'I *always* wear a regular coat!' I said, 'That's funny. I've never seen you wear one.' She was insulted."

At the restaurant we ordered huevos rancheros, which, as always in these parts, were served with tortillas instead of toast. Felipe's were laden with chunks of beef in red chile sauce. Mine were smothered in green. "In our culture," Felipe said, "braids are for both men and women. In this city, I love doing that— braids, blankets, and ribbon skirts. Two braids are so simple, so eloquent.

"Our women don't wear long nails. They don't wear makeup. Americans make their women defensive and defenseless. In Apache society, women are the best horsemen. They're empowered. So they're not jealous. They'll tell you, 'My husband is sleeping with another woman. Why not?' For us, if you deny something in yourself, you are creating disharmony in yourself, maybe in the universe. That's why among the Hickory Apaches we're allowing the white attitudes to slowly leave the tribe. We're recovering our harmony. At the pow-wows on Friday nights, there's this one dance, the men's shawl dance. Apache men don't wear shawls. In this dance, the men must dance like women. It's not 'camp,' they're authentically trying to dance as a woman. Often it's the wife who puts the shawl on the man. It's wonderful! It's amazing to see these burly Apache men being delicate. Imagine country-and-western men dancing women's roles and following. They'd say, 'What're you trying to do? Make me a fag?'

"In our tribe, you may not be too hot or too cold, too high or too low, too much one way or the other. We don't talk about male and female roles. We talk about Apache roles. The Apache way is in between. The Apache spirit is in between Mother Earth and Father Sky."

Country-and-western music had played loudly on the diner's radio throughout our meal. Now the news broke in. New Mexico, it seemed, was not understood by the mass of Americans to be one of the fifty states. So prevalent was this ignorance, a reporter announced, that even the IRS often sent back tax returns marked, "Territory outside the United States." The perturbed state legislature had approved new license plates to proclaim, "New Mexico, U.S.A."

Felipe sassed back. "They can say what they want to, but ten percent of this state is reservation land—sovereign Native American territory. Our civil law and our lives are tribal. We are not the United States. We are separate nations."

Like his friend Tom Dickerson, Felipe was a potter. Today, as once every week, he taught a senior citizens class at noon. The center sat in a barren sandy field on the far side of town at the foot of a bone dry mountain. Fifteen well-to-do elderly women were stationed around the room when we arrived, poised with sculpting stones in their hands and pots of wet, gray clay in primal states of imagination. This antique flock of potters swarmed over their arriving teacher like schoolgirls. A woman retired from Connecticut displayed a new sculpting stone—a fine piece of rock she had found in the desert. "It's *wonderful!*" Felipe sang. "Where on *earth* did you find it?" He toured the room. The students clucked and worked their clay, stepped back shyly when he came close, eager for admiration.

Most of these old women had moved to Albuquerque from elsewhere in hopes of a sunny endgame. A woman retired from Mississippi showed Felipe her bowl and, discouraged, pointed out a hole that had appeared in its side. "Leave it!" Felipe smiled. "It's artsy." She was elated.

Throughout the afternoon he continued to circle about the class—demonstrating for an entranced pupil how to use her stone to rub a nub from the vase she'd newly sculpted, offering praise, listening to the quiet griefs whispered in his ear. One overheard complaints about husbands of fifty years. A tiny woman with hands blue-laced with veins had been turning a somewhat molded ball of clay this way and that to intuit its future shape. In time she tiptoed up to me and offered this breathy confidence: "He never says much when we talk to him. But he always listens. He hears everything the girls say. That's what's important, don't you think?" They depended on him.

A similar dependence on Felipe's nurture was abundant early that evening at a weekly Roman Catholic Bible study group he led. Until only weeks before, they'd met in a room at the parish church, but the priest had become distressed by the "pagan elements" in Felipe's theology, by his Indian clothing, and by his sexuality. Now they gathered in the living room of a fellow renegade parishioner. Her home was a simple, overfurnished cottage, as intimate as catacombs. Dingy lampshades filtered the light. On this night twelve disciples, including Felipe, were gathered there. (I made thirteen.) A bright, felt folk banner of the kind commonly displayed in churches nowadays hung over the sofa: "No peace without food and drink for all."

As was their practice every week, they introduced themselves around the circle, sharing what they needed to about their lives. "Well, I did it!" a thirtyish woman exclaimed, and laughed too loudly. She was the first to speak. "I told him it was over. When I have a breakup like that, I celebrate. It wasn't right for me," she stated proudly.

"I'm not there yet," said the woman who was next. She was timid or bitter and didn't lift her head. "It's not that easy for me. That's all I have to say."

A pudgy man in blue work clothes said, "I'm a doughnut glazer—or I was until a few months back." He smiled, and his voice was kind. "I'm looking for work as . . . well, I was gonna say a glazer, but I guess it's *anything*." He chuckled at himself. "These days there's just *nothing* out there."

Next there came a couple sitting angled knee to knee. "He's my husband," was everything the woman said about herself. She pointed to the tall, broad man beside her. She was white. He was black. "I almost said 'wife.' I don't know why," she added quizzically. "Maybe some kind of compensation."

"I'm her husband," her husband answered warmly, and rubbed her hand. She laughed, contrite. "I'm also a security guard at the public schools, and I can't wait till the kids get out for summer."

Sister Marie, who wore lay clothes, introduced herself as a schoolteacher. The school nurse sitting next to her announced that she was "very single." An employment counselor said that she had a two-year-old, "which says it all about him." She said nothing about herself. A doctoral student—"at No Money U"—was studying for his comps while working nights full-time. He was pale. A tan recreation director was blond and buxom and reported that she'd been accepted into the Order of St. Ursula. Her many-hooped earrings rang out. Mrs. Lopez, who was brown and wrinkled, said with a Mexican accent, "I sell Avon. I'm really a medical secretary, which I'm not doing right now. So I guess," she added apologetically, "I'm not doing anything right now. I am going to Mexico next week. I'm taking clothes and a freezer for meat to an orphanage where I am a volunteer. I'm afraid they'll stop me at the border. They've done it before. I need your prayers."

A yellow-complexioned woman sat beside me. She had thin blond hair. Her face was drawn, her belly enormous. "I'm pregnant," she almost wept, then said acidly, "but that's obvious." She said no more.

Felipe read a lesson from the Sermon on the Mount:

" 'Therefore if thou bring thy gift to the altar, and there rememberest that thy brother hath ought against thee;

'Leave there thy gift before the altar, and go thy way; first be reconciled to thy brother, and then come and offer thy gift.'

"It says," he explained, " 'if your brother has something

against *you*,' not 'you against him.' The Scripture teaches us to forgive *them* first. That's a radical statement. Forgiveness isn't once and for all, it's a process. The first step is to accept our anger as part of being human, then work on our spirit about it. We may spin around sometimes, but we never go completely backward. But, first, we've got to accept our anger."

The pregnant woman tightened. Her hands were in her lap. She squeezed her fists. Lillian, a woman in her late sixties, perhaps, whose house this was, was trying to talk without crying. "I really need to hear this," she said. "You know my son-in-law killed my daughter, in a car wreck. He was drinking." Her mouth quivered. "I'm raising two granddaughters now, after I raised three children. I don't know what to say when someone wonders why I've got these two little girls, why such an old woman is their mother. My daughter's dead. Her murderer is free. My mother taught me not to let the sun go down on my wrath, but right now the only thing I have is my anger."

Felipe waited in the hush, then said, "Ortega is the name the Spanish gave my ancestors, a slave name. There is righteous anger. We have to let that flare. Love sometimes demands you speak the truth. Jesus never wanted us to be so passive we just let injustice happen. Confirming your anger is a healing thing. But eventually you've got to stop and take the stone out of your shoe."

"Sometimes you risk losing love when you speak the truth," said the woman who had broken with her boyfriend. "Which is hard," she gasped, "which is really difficult."

"You make it sound easy," said the unemployed glazer to Felipe, "but sometimes you're afraid to let it go for fear it'll never stop. That's what scares me a lot."

"We cannot lose true love," said Felipe. "It waits for us when we cannot find it. Anger ends. There is always love."

That evening Felipe fixed an Apache dinner for me, as altered by centuries of Spanish cuisine—wild rice in hot tomato sauce, spicy tamales. The sopaipillas—deep-fried tortillas of rice flour and blue corn meal—were served hot with honey. All of the cookware was clay pots, turned glistening black over time by kitchen flames. Other clay pots sat scattered about the dining room and crowded the dining table. They were simple and magnificently graceful. I admired one throughout our meal. "Do you like that one?" Felipe asked.

"It's mystical," I said. He smiled.

After dinner Felipe made medicine bundles, wrapping sage, cedar, and tobacco in red yarn as gifts for friends at a Hopi reservation. "You burn these to keep away spirits you're not comfortable with," he explained.

"An evil spirit?"

"In our belief, there are no good or evil spirits. There are only spirits you're ready for and spirits that create disharmony in your life. It's like foods—some agree with you, some make you sick. The AIDS virus has a place in the world, but maybe not inside *you*. In our healing ceremonies, we say to it, 'You can stay if you choose to live in harmony with this body. Otherwise, you must go.' "

He wrapped red yarn four times around a bundle of sage stems, four times at the top, and pulled it through. At the far end of the table the pale evening sunlight glazed my favorite pot. "The traditional Apache way," he continued, "may not be the most efficient way. But it works. It's like the resurrection of a corpse—uneven breathing, but it grows. Soon there will be heavy breathing, maybe to a climax. In white society you have to always define who you are in the narrowest way. A friend of mine said, 'You're not very comfortable being gay.' I said, 'I don't see myself as gay.' I'm Apache—the whole thing, not a little part of me.

"In American society you say, 'I'm attracted to Juan,' then you think, Oh, I can't be attracted to him. He's straight. My life is crazy. I have straight male friends who sleep with me, and that's strange. I have straight female friends and gay male friends who sleep with me, too, and that's strange. But if I'm attracted to them, there must be a reason. I must need some spirit from them. I met my roommate when he was sixteen. He said, 'I'm going to be your friend.' William's twenty now. He's straight, but he sleeps with me. The white gay men ask me, 'Are you trying to convince him?' Christianity has always tried to turn people into Christians. White people want everyone to adopt white ways. No one in our tribe runs around saying, 'The Apache way is best.'

"William lives with an Indian, but he doesn't try to be one. That's not his identity. He fucks his girlfriend. He also sleeps with me. Is that nonconventional? I don't try to change anybody. What I must accomplish now is be who I am. The bigger changes in the world happen at a slower pace. I feel sorry for people who stop flowing, who say, 'This is it!' In Apache culture, the prevailing spirit is chaos.

"Would you like a massage?" he asked as if it followed log-ically. "I will read your spine. I feel you asking." I stripped and lay stomach down on a table in the sitting room. Beside the divan was an old wooden stand with a picture of Jesus on it. Bibles and prayer books in English and Hebrew were strewn about. The air smoked with burning sage. Felipe's hands were small and hot, his fingertips were satin. He started at the bottom of my spine and caressed each vertebra for a moment before moving up. Every several bones he stopped and told me something precise about my past. He found girlfriends and boyfriends in my adolescence. He found my wife and the rancor of our marriage. "Do you sleep with your lover on your right?" he asked.

"Yes."

"The left is weak. The left side records your experiences with women. You fear your own femininity and fight against it. Keep your lover on your left to make it strong. When the left and right are in balance, you'll find new freedom. You'll know what you were looking for."

He kept a long and meditative silence. In the dining room before I left he led me to the table where he stored his pottery. Picking up the pot that I loved most, he gave it to me. "It was yours from the beginning," he said. "Your spirit is in it." Earth orange, it was exquisite, with low sides curved as gently as an egg's. At its rim sat a squat clay lizard, with pale green glitter streaking from its tail. It clung four-footed to the slope and, with its head above the precipice, peered into the dark abyss.

| | |

I did not want to leave New Mexico, but my lover was coming to meet me for Gay Pride Day in San Francisco at the end of June. I had little more than a week left now to visit Arizona and get back to San Francisco for the parade. The solstice occurred the week before I left. I celebrated in the desert outside Santa Fe, where "radical faeries" pitched a tipi village for the night. Bonfires lit the desolation. We were wonderfully dressed. We were hippies in embroidered jeans and tie-dyed shirts or gauzy Hindu clothing. Like Indians, we wrapped ourselves in animal hides and feathers. Or we were naked. In the arroyos we gathered sage. An altar was made on a log among the rich, low limbs of a cypress. On it we placed objects sacred to us—jewelry, crystals, herbs, photographs. I offered a piece of fool's gold Gino had given me in Colorado Springs and a love note from my lover written when we'd met ten years before.

As the year's longest day fell into darkness, we made a circle on a high, yellow knoll and watched the light lie down behind a mountain. We shared two eagle's feathers, snapped them around the outline of each body—like the flapping wings of a guardian bird. We passed a bowl of burning sage, bathing ourselves in its smoke, and drank from a common cup of water. We danced and chanted to the long evening sun. "Father Sky and Mother Earth!" we cried, and called upon the four winds and the seasons. Late in the light of a flashing ring of flames, I was the last man to be hugged at the heart of a naked swarm of arms and hands. They massaged me all at once, a Medusa of men, each man humming his tone as the wordless rumble of their chorus rushed through me.

At dawn Felipe sat in a stone sweat lodge, high in the misty coolness of a nearby mountain. A congregation of men sat around him. We cupped our hands and poured cold water on a fiery tabernacle of rocks. Great, hot clouds engulfed us. In our midst, Felipe rocked and moaned with his eyes closed gently, teaching us to invoke the spirits in Apache.

CHAPTER 8

TRUTH
OR
CONSEQUENCES

I PLANNED A CIRCLING ROUTE TO ARIZONA THROUGH THE SOUTH-
ernmost desert of the United States. There were no direct
roads, in any case. I gave myself two days to get to Phoenix,
where I expected to visit several men I had met at the Denver
rodeo. On Monday after the solstice, I drove the three hundred
empty miles that separated Santa Fe and Las Cruces—an ugly,
white hot town on the Rio Grande not far from the Mexican
border—to spend the night there with a man I knew from the
Gay Pride parade.

The bright sky was dust dry, 105 degrees, an airless blanket.
The altitude dropped 2,500 feet between Sante Fe and Las
Cruces. I drove without air-conditioning to feel the unrelieved
power of the low desert. Stark stone mountains rose from the
vast, tan flatness like miniatures. In the electric heat, the earth
squirmed—an infantry of silver hairpins. I tried the A/C, which
was tepid, and, drugged by the temperature, pulled into a roadside patch of sagebrush to sleep, but I couldn't breathe. In the
shimmering east, a huge blue plate of water lay luxuriously

miragelike. The sign pointed to "Truth or Consequences." I turned off, thinking I might go swimming.

The road was miles of fuming dirt. Truth or Consequences sat by the lake. I stopped at a desolate cinder-block diner for iced tea. A potbellied man with skin like a sun-dried tomato sat backward on a kitchen chair and was telling a story. "Had a head 'bout like that," he said, forming a triangle with his thumbs and forefingers. "All coiled up there in the sand and achin' to spring."

The waitress watched my face and chuckled loudly. I must have been white-eyed. "Not from 'round here, are ya?" she asked me.

"New York City."

"*Ha!*" cried the stove-bellied man. "*People* are meaner than snakes up there!" Then he continued. "There wuz that one ole rattler out at Elephant Butte as big around as a stovepipe. And forty or fifty feet long." He kept pausing to corner his eyes on my reaction. "May here knows what I mean." He nodded at the waitress. "*How* long wuz it, May?"

"O-o-oh," she pondered. "It wuz *long*! Lives back there under some rocks by the lake, I think."

"The lake?" I swallowed.

"Goin' swimmin'?" The old man grinned. "You'll see a nest of 'em yourself, coilin' right there on top of the water to get some sun."

"Maybe I should rent a boat instead," I muttered.

"*Boat?*" he rasped. "I seen 'em crawl right over the side of a boat when they had a mind. *May* over there," he claimed, "had to throw a big one outa her lap a few weeks back. How big *wuz* that one, May?" he yelled.

The town seemed aptly named. I tiptoed back to the car, then flew out of there like an outlaw. Outside Las Cruces, the Organ Mountains shimmered hot pink in the sunset. Their enormous rock walls rose like gaudy ranks of theater organ pipes, as if to accompany a silent western.

My stay in Las Cruces was too brief. I went with Andrew Washington, my host, to a prayer meeting in the evening, at the black Baptist church where he was a member. Afterward he took

me to El Paso and Ciudad Juárez in Mexico as an added treat. I
bought a bottle of tequila with two worms in it and a colorful
peasant blanket for five dollars. A ruined legion of Mexican families and their children slept in the lurid light of the bridge between the nations to be first in the morning for American day
jobs. It was three o'clock when we got home. I slept late. When
I got up, Andrew was gone. I scoured his bookcases, which were
crowded with Bibles and hymnals and Sunday school pamphlets.
Nor was there anything "gay" around. Andrew was "closeted"
among his fellow parishioners.

"In our denomination, the church choirs is *full* of us," he
told me gleefully. "And *most* of 'em are married mens, too. We
have our choir conventions and just get by ourselves when we're
out singin'. But *nobody* gonna say anyting." He depended for sex
on this surreptitious network of choristers and on fast, anonymous encounters in the town's one porn shop. (There was no gay
bar here.)

"Moses cain't stay hid for long in the bulrushes," he stated.
"He start gettin' tired of where he's at, his lungs fill up, and he
cry to do somethin' about it." He had had a white lover once who
had insisted on "coming out" in the church and to his parents.
"Then he went straight again," Andrew said, "after causin' everybody all them troubles. My mamma and daddy spent their whole
life pickin' cotton. They both of 'em died hard. Nobody but the
church folk got 'em through. I *love* my church too much to go
around stirrin' things up when *nobody* don't wanta hear about it.
No, no!" he exclaimed. "The church is where I get my strength."
On the wall above his bed there hung a plaque that read:

Never Be Ashamed of What You Are.
(By the Way, What Are You?)

Early in the afternoon, I visited Iosh Levy, whom I had also met
at the Gay Pride parade. A devout Jew, he wanted to show me the
town's small synagogue and the tabernacle for which he had designed the Hebrew calligraphy. As a doctoral student at the University of Chicago in the sixties, Iosh had moved here first as

therapy for his asthma. His apartment was gloomy and too cool with air-conditioning. Sheets of plastic covered the windows. A forest of brown prescription bottles crowded the kitchen table. Iosh was lonely. He knew of "the Andrews" in Las Cruces. "But I've given up trying to associate with them," he told me. "For one thing, I can hardly go to their churches!" Nor did he approve of their sexual conduct. "I don't need a lot of sex," he said. "If it's sex without affection, I can't function. Besides, I'm involved in safe-sex education here. How would it look if I went to that bookstore?"

Iosh was a man of ardent causes—poverty, peace, religious tolerance, Israel. A recent bishop in this Roman Catholic diocese had often preached against Jews as *asesinos*, Christ killers. Not long ago the local university where Iosh taught math had placed an ancient Navajo symbol on the front of its yearbook. It resembled a swastika, though for Indians it evoked brotherhood, not nazism. A Jewish student had protested, bringing separate painful histories into conflict. A barricade of police vans had had to be stationed at the synagogue.

"There's not a critical mass of Jews here," Iosh said, "or gays. A lot of people are afraid to be out of the closet either way. And maybe they're right. They've settled their lives, and what do they have to gain? People like me are an anathema to them." Still, in spite of a very public stance on AIDS, he himself had not announced his sexual identity among his congregation's members. "Though when their intolerance got to me once," he recalled mischievously, "I *did* threaten to come to Purim as Queen Esther. So I think they know. In a place like this, you change people's minds one to one, instead of big public statements. The most important thing I can do when they tell me I don't belong is to say, 'Yes, I do. I'm a part of this, I'm a part of *you*.' I stay because I belong here."

The shul was simple, except for the beautifully ornate doors before the Ark of the Covenant. Iosh led me to them quietly. For a moment he stood to one side, then translated for me the Hebrew calligraphy that had been his gift to his people. It began, "Know Before Whom You Stand . . ."

But noble, public causes had taken their toll. In his meditative hours, Iosh was a poet. When I was about to leave, he gave
me a poem to read later. It was titled "Personal":

QJM, 43, 5'9", 140
BRIGHT, WITTY,
NOT SARCASTIC OR MALICIOUS,
BUT I DRAW THE LINE AT
CATS, TOBACCO, OPERA
EXCEPT MAYBE *DON GIOVANNI*;
EARNED RESPECT IN A REDNECK TOWN
STANDING UP FOR MARTIN LUTHER KING
    ERA
PEACE SOVIET JEWS
AND OTHER QUEERS;
HAVE STOOD UP BEEN COUNTED
TOO OFTEN,
WANT TO SPEND MORE TIME
LYING DOWN.
YOUR ARMS: MUST FIT AROUND ME
YOUR FINGERS: MY SHOULDERS
YOUR NECK: MY LIPS
I WILL REMIND YOU OF YOUR STRENGTHS
    AND VIRTUES
WHEN YOU DOUBT THEM.
YOU MAY HAVE TO REMIND ME
TO LET GO OF CAUSES;
YOU MAY NEED TO REMIND ME AGAIN.

At two o'clock that afternoon a bank thermometer flashed 105
degrees. In the sunlight its pale digital numbers seemed about to
melt. I headed west. The air-conditioning blew a fuse. Bottles of
cold mineral water I had brought with me were hot before I got
out of town. In Deming, an hour out, the temperature was 110
degrees. There was no shade—just white sky above white dust
and adobe and one-story concrete block buildings. A railroad
track cut through the main street, as though cauterizing it. "Trixx

Adult Books" was the only entry in the *Gayellow Pages* for this desolate population of nine thousand. Two pickups were parked in the front. In a hot back room, a bleached-out sixteen-millimeter porn flick quivered on the plywood wall of an empty booth—a hippie and his chick fucking in a truck bed like nervous ghosts. From the gummy floor there came the occasional must of come. A three-by-five card on a bulletin board read "Latin Couple! Contact us, couples & very discrete singles. 'Being clean a must.' No drugs, pain, or Booze." Another, also with erratic spelling, read "MALE—MARRIED WOULD LIKE TO MEET SAME OR SINGLE WHO ENJOY SENUOUS GET-TOGETHERS FOR GREEK OR FRENCH—ONE WAY OR RECRIPOCAL OK. CLEAN, WELL BUILT, AND DISCREET." I wondered at men and women's arid accommodation to life here.

It was close to 5:00 P.M. when I crossed the Continental Divide this final time—at only 4,600 feet as it descended into Mexico. A voice on my dying radio gasped 110 degrees, but that was back in Deming. I knew it was hotter here and growing hotter still. I drank hot bottled water in anxious gulps, while the torrid air sapped the sweat from my skin before it had time to glisten. I stayed salty and dry. A passenger train raced across the hot sand like a snake and was swallowed—silver, red, and blue—by the shimmering horizon. A hand-painted sign at a rest stop warned of snakes. Beside a parched corral, a windmill stood dead. Pale sagebrush lay strewn across the desert like doomed battalions. Ancient, worn mountain peaks sat in the dust—dim remembrances of themselves or of a time when solar winds whipped the molten earth with whitecaps. A butte jutted from the desert like the wing of a bird petrified in a second as a primeval storm tore its feathers. In the west, the fallen sun charred a ridge and left a flimsy silhouette. Above it, the orange-and-yellow sky seemed to liquefy, while the rest of the breathless world turned blue.

I knew nothing about homosexual life in Arizona, except that the governor, Evan Mecham, was a Republican, a Mormon, and an archbigot who had canceled the state holiday honoring Dr. Martin Luther King, Jr., and had waged a campaign to root homosexuals out of the government. Arizona was among the states that took its sodomy laws seriously. I had looked forward to driving through the moonlike landscape but reserved a vague animosity toward Arizona's people, who had elected Mecham in the first place. Such all-consuming judgments are easy.

Around midnight I hit Tucson and stopped, nearly prostrate with heat. I found the Motel at Fineline listed in a gay guide to lodging and went directly to the motel bar. Almost no one was there. Disco from a tape throbbed vacantly while a mirror ball splashed light chips across the floor. "Summertime isn't our season," the bartender said. "You really gotta come back in the winter." A lonely row of men was perched on stools. I took a seat at the end. I was sullen, cranky.

"Vacation?" the man beside me queried cheerfully. He was thin, and even in the darkness I could see he had a weathered face. His gray hair was barbershop cut. I thought he looked a hell of a lot like my father.

Cynical with fatigue, I grunted to ward him off. He was not tipsy yet, but glowing brightly. Two downed rock glasses sat at his elbow on soggy napkins. Another Scotch was in his hand. Was he trying to pick me up? It seemed like incest. I was in no mood for surprises.

"Herb Skinner—" He stuck out his hand and asked me, "Whatcha drinkin'?" as he signaled me out to the bartender. "Down here on business?" he asked.

Obliged, I snapped. "*Yes*, sort of."

My testiness didn't take. He drawled, "Where from?" and grew more friendly yet when I mumbled, "New York City." He himself had moved to Tucson from *Sea*caucus, New Jersey, as he pronounced it, and was thrilled to find that we had been "neighbors" once. "Yep! Me and m'son," he added wistfully, "lived right across the river there. Went up there for work. I'm a renderer— renderin' fat from meat parts?" He said it like a question. His speech was slow and gristly. "From Oklahoma orig'nally. 'We're from *OK*,' he used to say, m'boy Newton did. 'If you're gay, OK's a good place to be *from*!' ' "

This startling confession woke me up and intrigued me. I wondered, was this a gay father and his gay son? a gay father and his straight son? straight father, gay son? and if so, what's the dad doing here alone? I asked about Newton.

"Oh," he said with longing, "I lost him about two years ago. He got AIDS. He went out with style and grace, though. What else could a father ask for? He was a country boy, you know, and he saw the way animals died when they got slaughtered. He didn't think *that* was very graceful. So at the end, he just kinda went to sleep. The doctor told him, 'I don't think you're gonna live through the night.' He had a lot of pain with the cancers and thrush and all. He always said, 'I can *stand* the pain. I just can't stand bein' sick.' But he had to decide about all them machines they had him hooked up on, and that night he went peacefully.

"Now I always come back here to the bar to see his friends when I got something I wanna celebrate?" he almost asked. All his statements seemed full of doubt, as if he had learned that every absolute in life must end with a question mark. He pushed a sheet of paper at me. "I'm celebratin' Father's Day a few days late. I got this letter today from *George Bush*! He gave a speech about AIDS. So I wrote him what I thought about it. He wrote me back!" Mr. Skinner handed me a copy of his letter, too, and wanted me to read them both right there by the dingy glow of his key chain flashlight. Herb's, full of typos and handmade corrections, was written on stationery from TAP, the Tucson AIDS Project, dated June 4, 1987. It was queerly, improbably eloquent:

Dear Vice-President Bush,
On June 14th, 1984, Father's Day, My son Newton John, a gay person, suspected correctly that he had full-blown A.I.D.S. He made three related decisions. He was going to show the Gay Community of Tucson that you can have A.I.D.S. with dignity (whatever dignity may mean). He was going to fight "the monster" with every means at his disposal. He was going to be public about what it is like to have A.I.D.S.

On June 17th, 1985, he made his final public appear-
ance at a forum held by the Tucson A.I.D.S. Project, an or-
ganization he had been instrumental in starting. He ended
his talk by saying: "Reach out to your friends, forgive your
enemies and you can begin to find peace and courage and hap-
piness and some day we will be the victor. We will conquer
A.I.D.S." He died August 5th. . . .

Here he explained, in the most clear way, how the "AIDS virus"
was believed to do its deadly work—how it was transmitted, how
it inexorably spread—then quaintly surmised its role in "Darwin-
ian evolution." He wondered whether only the fittest of all man-
kind would survive and how the survivors would go on to start all
over again. Then he posed these questions:

But start again from where and with what? We need to
ask: What social institution can survive? Will it be said that
"Our Democracy" was a victim—a victim of the AIDS vi-
rus? Where is or are the American leaders capable of leading
us in such a way that when the smoke has cleared Democracy
is not only alive and well but better for the dignified and hu-
man way in which it faced "this monster"? . . .
Newton John was fond of saying, "I may be a sissy, but
I've got spunk." He fought "The Monster" and in one sense
he lost. But in another sense he beat it. He redefined what
dignity means, and his "spunk" is alive and well in many of
those who watched him face up to what for all is an intoler-
able situation. The ability to reach out to his fellow man when
he himself hurt so badly is catching. When I go about speak-
ing, I point out that the government can legislate money for
AIDS (reluctantly), but no government can legislate human
kindness, nor can it legislate compassion, nor can it legislate
the respect and love sick people so badly want. . . .
We as a nation may have been blessed in that AIDS
struck the homosexual community first. They have not given
in to fear and panic. They have not shirked the unpleasant
tasks that come up as someone or another goes through the

process of dying. They do not ask first who or what you are when you are in trouble—they just reach down one more time and do the impossible. . . . These people have not spoken the word compassion—*they have acted in a compassionate manner. For me they have listened to my nonsense—they have picked me up when I have been down. They have done the things Newton would have done had he lived. Father's Day for me will not go unnoticed—and I am grateful to this segment of our society.*

A species survives because it presents variation to an environment. Yet our society for some reason or another believes the variant called homosexual is in some sense inferior. Democracy has in many ways passed them by. . . . As this virus finds the heterosexual world we will turn to these people who have seen their friends melt away—have met the challenge and did not come up wanting.

In the end will it be said of democracy that "it reached out to its friends. It forgave its enemies—it began to find peace and courage and happiness and it was the victor—it did conquer AIDS"?

Like it or not, we are about to find out—so fasten your seat belt, it's going to be a bumpy ride.

Sincerely,
Herb Skinner

The vice-president, known for his personal correspondence, replied:

THE VICE-PRESIDENT
WASHINGTON
June 12, 1987

Dear Mr. Skinner:
That was a very moving letter, yours of June 4. How it must hurt to have a grown son wrenched from your arms.

Enclosed is a speech I gave recently on this ghastly disease, AIDS. I would like you to give me a frank critique on this speech. What should I have left out? What should I have added?

I firmly believe we need a knowledge base—some disagree. I firmly believe we need more education and research—none disagree. This is not a problem that will be solved or even salved by the "extremes." Reasonable people must be out front trying to find the way, then trying to lead. I hope I am such a person.

I have been out to the National Institutes of Health. I have talked several times with Dr. Koop, for whom I have a high regard. A leading doctor at the prestigious Sloan-Kettering Cancer Center in New York City has been advising me. Now I am asking the loving father of an AIDS victim to help me.

Thanks so much for taking the time to spell out so beautifully your feelings.

Sincerely,
George Bush

When I had finished reading, I took Mr. Skinner's hand and held it, speechless. He ordered us each another drink and surprised me again. "To tell you the truth," he began, "AIDS is the secondary issue for me now—because my son is dead and he was the only son I ever had. But I never was one to make any bones about gay people or whatever, even as a Baptist. The *gay* issue is very important to me now. I got nothing to lose anymore." I gave him back the letters. He held the vice-president's up to the blood pink light spilling out of a neon beer sign and read it over once again in this demidarkness. He propped a warped pair of reading glasses on his nose and pushed them up now and then with the third and fourth fingers of his right hand. One and five had been amputated at the palm. I imagined a grisly mistake with a cleaver while he rendered fat.

"I don't agree with his first couple sentences, though." Uneasily Mr. Skinner shook the letter in his hand. "Newton and I didn't want sympathy. We wanted respect and love—a dialogue. We wanted people to talk about it. Newton always liked the battle." He grinned, peering into his Scotch, and shook his head. "I can tell you a *lot* about Newton!" The bartender brought him two more drinks and patted his hand as a son might. Newton was, Mr. Skinner said, a good musician, a *trom*bonist in the McDonald's All-American Band. "*All-American*," he exclaimed, "like the football team!" That was when Newton was seventeen. "When we lived in *Sea*caucus, he got a job at Radio City Music Hall! He was just an usher," he said, then corrected himself. "He was an usher." He beamed.

"You would've liked him a lot! Newton was a *master* of metaphor. He used to say, 'Comin' out used to be what rich girls from Philadelphia did, but now they're being upstaged by pretty blond boys from New York City! He went to all those fancy places in New York—Fire Island and the Hamptons and Studio 54." Mr. Skinner was proud, his speech as slow as a mouthful of Red Man. "It was exciting just to *watch* him! You know, he was so conscious about his looks. That's when I got a lot of respect for him—he was vain, but when he got the cancers on his face, it didn't bother him. I thought it would. He even stopped usin' the makeup to cover 'em up.

"I think the smartest thing he ever said, he was very far along in his disease. 'We know a lot of things the day we die, but before we die we don't know much of anything.' " Mr. Skinner seemed always to speak more slowly when he quoted his son, as though reciting Scripture. "He'd always say, 'I have to live in a fantasy land—because if you believe what you read in the newspapers, you couldn't live. It's irrational to be rational.' But if you extend it," Mr. Skinner explained, "that's true of all of us—gay or straight or whatever. If you took what the world was really like, you'd just have to jump off the first bridge you came to. That's prob'ly the smartest thing he ever said," he mused, and drank. "Does that make sense to you at all? I mean, we couldn't survive, could we? *I* could, maybe." He giggled. "But because I got Newton still in my head to keep me going!"

He slipped the letters back into a paper bag, bottomed up, and said again, "My biggest problem is the gay issue, though. The thing is, it's so difficult to talk about—only because the issue is so stupid there isn't any issue at all! I know one thing—straight people'll let you make a fool out of yourself, but gay people'll *tell* you, with *kindness*. Newton'd always let me know." Mr. Skinner snickered, sort of. "Like when I'd get outa control and go pinch some woman's titties at a bar. Does that make sense? I hope it does. It does to me. I couldn't've survived without gay people—with any style or dignity, anyways.

"You know, I didn't love Newton in *spite* of what he was, but *for* what he was. I guess some people don't understand that. Newton was my friend. Maybe I never realized it so much until he died."

It was late and I was soggy, but I wanted to talk more. We agreed to meet in the morning for breakfast. He wanted to show me a videotape of Newton's last public speech, if I could stay in town till the afternoon. I shuffled my schedule again, instead of going on to Phoenix.

It was 102 degrees at ten o'clock when we met at a Big Boy restaurant. The desert sky, the earth, the concrete and glass of Tucson, all glared like a hot cosmic fog. Herb Skinner drove up in a waxed gray Oldsmobile. ("I wanted a small one, but I got this one used," he told me apologetically. "Now I kinda enjoy this size.") He was dressed to speak at the University of Arizona Medical School in the afternoon—brown polyester slacks and short-sleeved brown shirt. A white pack of Kent cigarettes and two mechanical pencils stretched the pocket. "It's not often a father gets to follow in his son's footsteps," he said, grinning. "Kinda *hard*, too. 'Course at times Newton thought he was Cleopatra. And being Cleopatra's father wasn't ever very easy."

He told me he spoke regularly at the medical school. "My purpose," he explained slowly while cutting into a link of sausage, "is to render their good parts outa their homophobia. Some of 'em are so hostile, but that's okay. Like Newton used to say, 'People don't mean to be cruel.' Even if stupid things are said and people's feelings get hurt, there's no other way. You know," he said, cocking his head to one side, "Newton was gay and that was the end of it. I wasn't interested in readin' everything about it. People'll ask me what it's like to be the father of a gay. I say to 'em, 'You aren't askin' me a question. You're *tellin'* me somethin'. I don't feel *anything* about it.' I try to just tilt people toward *thinkin'* a little and get 'em to actin' with compassion.

"It's everybody's own choice, isn't it?" Mr. Skinner stated, sinking the tines of his fork into his eggs, letting the yellows run free. A faded navy tattoo on his forearm sharpened in the restaurant's fluorescence. "It's like comin' outa the closet. Ronald Reagan's son's gay," he announced, "but he keeps quiet. It's not to his credit or discredit, it's the choice he made. That's the way it oughta be."

When the TAP office opened, we went there, to a paste blue stucco cottage on the seedy side of downtown, across from a police construction site. There were two small rooms and a dilapidated kitchen. In the back room sat a TV and VCR between two soiled couches. Mr. Skinner deftly snatched the right cassette from a dusty box of videotapes and put it in the machine. First an odd array of clips flew by—old PSAs on AIDS from TAP and segments featuring other men's sons on the local evening news. With computerlike precision he fast-forwarded past all other speakers to the seconds before Newton's last speech, the one he had written the vice-president about. Then, perching sideways on the edge of the sofa, he sank the two remaining fingers of his maimed right hand into the cushion and braced himself anxiously. His glasses sat smudged at the tip of his nose. A disco diva's background song began, *"So little time, how can I lose . . ."* His eyes were wide while he waited. Above the music Newton spoke.

"I realize I made myself sick," he stated shockingly. "No one else did but me." He was a slender boy, blond and wan, with a fine midwestern timbre in his voice. Mr. Skinner edged forward again and raised his brow, anticipating—as he had countless times before—the next surprise. "And I'm responsible for making myself well." The father's leathery face shined.

"The choice was always mine, and mine completely," he continued. "I could have any prize that I desired. I could burn with the splendor of the brightest fire. Or else—or else I could choose time. . . ."

Mr. Skinner tugged the collar of his shirt, grooming for his son. His eyes never strayed from the voice on the TV screen.

"With a name like Newton, I was marked as an oddball from the very beginning. I have been gay since I saw Dorothy in *The Wizard of Oz*. . . ."

"He used to say that." Mr. Skinner laughed and shook his head.

"For anyone who gets AIDS . . . death is everywhere. Not only death, but guilt. And worst of all, fear. If the patient continues in this state of mind for too long a period, then he must surely die. But if he has the courage and the stamina to make the decision that he will fight this monster, then maybe . . . maybe miraculously he will live. . . ."

Herb Skinner sat entranced, cocking his head quizzically when yet another of Newton's ideas struck him fresh again. "He was just twenty-six when died," he said.

"There's a small handful of men who were diagnosed in 1979 who are still alive . . . survivors. . . . We must look to them if we are to survive. . . . They possess . . . hope. . . . Hope . . . is not a cure for the masses immediately, but a cure for the individual. And if we are to be cured, then we must pay attention not only to the body, but to the mind and to the spirit."

Mr. Skinner wrinkled his cheeks, concentrating anew on Newton's meaning.

"The government is only too glad to ignore the homosexuals. We are considered an eyesore," Newton taunted.

The father lowered his chin, suspiciously eyeing his son over the tops of his murky lenses, seeming to wonder—again—how far this time he would go.

"We have been barraged with only negative information. But if we are to survive, then we must look to the positive aspects—no matter how slim they seem to be. We must reach out to whatever source that will contribute to our own individual wellness. . . . Reach out to your friends"—Mr. Skinner arched his back and lifted his chin, his face lit up in expectation of the climax— "forgive your enemies, and you can begin to find peace, and courage, and happiness. And someday we will be the victors. We *will* conquer AIDS."

The father grinned. His eyes were fixed. He seemed not to breathe as his son disappeared like a ghost in the midst of applause and the snowy rush of silence overcame the screen. Before he lifted the wand to reset the machine, he drawled slowly, "Thank you, Newton. That was very powerful." He laughed proudly to himself. "You did a good job."

The stray remains of mountains wasted in the desert along the hundred miles between Tucson and Phoenix. This late afternoon they glowed as pink as hearts and seemed to throb in the heat. On the slopes of the hills, giant saguaros, like bristling fingers, saluted the sky. The hot, sandy wind blew passionate with sunshine.

The day was still bright when I drove into Phoenix, the streets shined yellow. The glistening buildings were all glass and white, like a sultan's oasis. Towering palms stood guard in willowy rows—wild green heads with bulging eyes, gray parchment bodies. I went first to Charlie's, twin of the bar in Denver, and arrived in time for the weekly free spaghetti dinner. Worn with my travels, I decided to take the night off to two-step and drink. John King, who owned the bars, was there, but only briefly, as busy now as he had been when I'd met him at the Colorado rodeo. He seemed to me a man who saw his proprietorship as a calling and his taverns as a kind of mission. Middle-aged, he was recently divorced and had "come out" late. And I think I had never met a man, heterosexual or otherwise, who was so straight. He was stolid, as full of no-nonsense machismo as a rancher, though he did seem mightily pleased that I had come all this way and stopped for a visit.

"How d'ya like our crowd?" he asked on a breather, a can of Coors in his hand. "Plain, ordinary farm kids," he answered himself, nodding his chin to take in every cowboy in the bar. "Major part of the boys who come in here are out of place in the gay world—they expect us to give up our boots and get citified! At

Charlie's you can be the exact same way you were growin' up and still be accepted for it." John was especially proud of the sexual pace of the place. "Here, you meet one week, dance the next. If you like each other okay, maybe you'll go home the third time 'round. We may be slow by New York or San Francisco standards. That's the way we've always been. It's not because of AIDS, either," he added briskly. "We learned our manners at the Saturday night barn dances. We court our beaus. Not a lot of kissin' on the first date."

I ate, had a few beers, got my boots high-shined in the boot slick's chair, took a couple of turns around the floor. On a whim I headed out to find the city's other gay night life. I met a young man named Peter at a little raw downtown bar called Cruisin' Central. It catered to drag queens and hustlers and scuffy-jeaned young men who were sexually needy. Peter was a wide-eyed, eager type—handsy, and he liked to talk.

"I *love* Phoenix, I *really* do!" he exclaimed when he learned I was a tourist. "Phoenix has changed me a lot!" He had just moved here from Fort Myers, Florida. "My mother even says, 'What's *happened?*' She can't believe it!"

"Why?" I teased. "Were you hyper before, or what?"

"Well, *yeah!*" He was oblivious of the gibe. "I used to need to always get up and go drinking, doin' things and stayin' out all night. Now, I always go to work, come home, and go right to bed." Tonight was a work night and already late. "*Sometimes* I go out. I don't go out too much. I'm not looking for sex. I don't want a lover. I used to have lovers, though. My old roommate from back home—he's coming out here to live with me. *He* was my lover a while. We just broke up after two and a half years. I was twenty-one when we met."

Men my age had often "come out" late and after a marriage, as I had. And although I had learned again and again that America was a much freer place than in the early seventies, I still always found myself startled at such early sex and romance. Was that his first sex with men? I asked.

"Oh, *no!*" he sang. "I had a lover before that for five years. He's six feet under now—*dead!*"

I hated these reports of death. They were a fixture of gay men's lives in New York, a staple of gay bar talk. I think I had hoped to escape them on the road. I gave him my sympathy and said something angry about AIDS.

He twisted his face into a puzzle. "It wasn't *that*," he spat, as if stupefied that I could even think so. "He was in a car accident, killed in the line of duty. He was a cop. He was in his cruiser, and I was following him in our new car I just drove off the lot. I don't know whether he was watching me or what. He drove right under the back of a semi. I wrecked, too. I was in the hospital a couple of months. He'd have been real pissed if he saw how bad I was. We'd still be together if he hadn't died.

"He hated the way I drove, you know—that's how we met! He stopped me and wrote me a ticket in front of the gay bar. The next week I went to the same bar and he was *there*. I didn't recognize him. He came up and said, 'Don't I know you?' And I said, 'I don't know *you*.' And he says, 'I wrote you a ticket for a hundred and five in a fifty-five.' I said, '*You* wrote me that ticket?'

"So he tells me to come out to the car and says, 'Go get your ticket.' I went and got it—and I don't know what he did, but he took care of it for me. We dated a couple of months, then he asked me to be his lover—on my *birthday*! I turned sixteen. I was sweet fifteen when I met him! I wish he coulda come with me out west. I always had this fantasy of being in a snowstorm in the Rockies with him. I always wanted to make love with him above the treeline."

I was staying at a large motel on the opposite side of town. That morning before dawn—I think it was somewhere around four o'clock—I had been asleep three hours when there came a gentle, persistent knock at my door. Groggy, I pulled the drapes back and peeked. On the other side of the glass, a small brown man with pin-straight, jet hair was peering at me. I dropped the curtain and simply waited for him to disappear. He knocked again. I cracked the door. (I remember thinking I would never have done such a risky thing in New York, but Phoenix struck me as safe and I grew curious.) Sternly I informed him that he had the wrong room and told him to go away.

"No," he answered me. He was shy and confident. "This is the one." He stared.

"What do you want?"

"I have come to sleep with you." His speech was clipped and exotically accented. I could see in the slice of light from the open door that he was an Indian. He might have been twenty, but I doubted it. In the sliver of space, he slid in but did not introduce himself. "I saw you come in in the afternoon," he explained. "I knew I could come here to see you." He laid his cheek against my chest. I sat at the foot of the bed.

"Are you *gay*?" I asked, too confounded to know what I was saying.

He didn't reply, as if the question were meaningless, but told me he was staying in a room across the courtyard with thirteen of his cousins. Navajo, they had come here from a reservation in the northeast corner of the state, looking for jobs. He had waited until they were all asleep to pay me this visit. He wanted me to kiss him on the lips and asked with such blue hot curiosity that I supposed he thought a simple kiss a rarity.

"Have you ever had sex with a man?" I interrogated.

He shook his head yes. "On the reservation. Many men."

"Then you've been kissed before," I ventured. He had not. "Then *how* have you had sex?" I cried stupidly.

"They take me." He was matter-of-fact, not appalled. He crawled up onto my bed and I held him. He snuggled and lay still. He was quiet for half an hour, then suddenly sat erect. "My cousins are waking up now," he stated. "I will have to go to them." On a notepad on the nightstand he wrote his name and a post office box number at the reservation so that I could write. Then, saying nothing else, he left. His name was Gone-Gone.

About a hundred miles northwest of Phoenix, a lonely Babel rises from the sands, harsh white stone patched with stark cactus groves. A winding road etches a fine line up its wall. Clouds swim continually around the pinnacle but don't obscure the sun. A tiny village sits on the slope of the peak. It has one street. "A brown spot in the road," Salvatore Vitelli and Bertrand Williams had thought when they first saw it a decade ago. A local married couple they had met on a Caribbean cruise had introduced them to this isolated mountain village when the two men came to Arizona on a visit. Soon afterward the gentlemen lovers purchased an old clapboard motel in a covert of oaks in the middle of town and made it their home. John Herschhorn, an old friend of my family's who lived in suburban Denver, had given me an introduction to them.

Bertrand and Salvatore were not to be home the day I arrived but had promised to leave a room along the veranda unlocked. A bristly family of boarhogs traipsed across the porch as I pulled up. Late the next morning, when my hosts got back from a supply run to Phoenix, Bertrand wanted to gossip about our mutual friend John and his twenty-three-year-old son Billy, who still lived with him. Salvatore was attentive. In Bertrand's presence attentiveness appeared to be his pastime. " 'She' doesn't think anyone knows 'her' story," Bertrand camped about John. " 'She' doesn't even think that son of 'hers' knows!" He swirled his eyes, which were opulently socketed above plump, bright, rosy cheeks. On his T-shirt, on the hump of his tummy, a pink rhinoceros rode a tiny bike. A canary was the fat beast's hat. A wreath of clouds surrounded its head. "When we go up to visit, John makes dinner for twelve—*all* of us 'ladies of the night' sitting around the table—and Billy'll come in. John'll go, '*Sh-sh!* Billy doesn't know!' "

"What d'ya *mean* he doesn't know?" Bertrand hooted, remembering. "That boy's not some kind of *moron*! He can *see* when all the men at his dad's dinner parties are his *aunts*! There's that *one*—that Catholic organist—with the flaming red hair piled up on his head. *Wonderful* person, but no way to keep a secret from the family." His voice trailed away. Then suddenly he was up off the sofa plucking groceries from an old plastic shopping bag. "My purse," he quipped. "But the ones from the K mart are much stronger."

Bertrand put groceries away and tidied. Salvatore drove me out to a nearby field in a new Ford Ranger to see their horses. He was a taciturn, smiling man with salt brown hair and the handsome head of a Roman emperor. The hysterical clown emblazoned on his shirt screamed, "No-o-o-o!" Salvatore pointed out the great tree in the pasture, a two-hundred-year-old walnut with an enormous shady reach of wise, gnarled limbs. Brown Mare—a cutting horse—Mr. Blue, Strawberry, and Sunshine—rock horses—and the horses' pet cat galloped up, each in overlapping turn nuzzling Bertrand's hand. "Look at that rump!" he said, slapping Strawberry's. The mare raised her ankle high. "Her legs are glorious!"

He motioned to where this pasture disappeared beyond a woods into another, higher field far away. "We ride out there to round up cattle," he said, "sleep under the trees. Every now and then I ride Sunshine thirty, thirty-five miles up in the mountains. The earth up there is all white granite—so fragile that when the horses walk over it, it breaks like china under their hoofs. I've been a horse person all my life."

Still, it was only here and now, living late in life in this mountaintop haven with Bertrand, that Salvatore had ever indulged his passion so fully. "Nature is God," he told me. He found the divine more intimate in this lofty wilderness. And their own relationship, which had begun so shortly before they'd moved here, seemed to bring them ever nearer to their natural selves, to a godlike truth about their affections that both men for most of their lives had denied.

Salvatore told me about his previous life. He was from New York. He had been married and had a daughter who was in her twenties now. In his late forties he had left his wife. He was in his sixties now. He spoke comfortably but briefly of his ex. They had met when he was an executive with *Playboy* in Los Angeles and she was a Playboy bunny. "She was one of the early centerfolds," he said. "Beautiful. Stunning. We were married eight years. We had a good thing going, good relationship. It was no great love. I loved to be seen with her. Everyone would turn when she walked in—men and women. I loved that, though sometimes I felt like I was using her.

"But we grew apart. When we got divorced, everything

seemed to go wrong, the whole world fell in on me. I had an emotional breakdown and couldn't function. So I went to Central America for a year just to straighten out. I never did fool around on her with other men," he said. "I had vague feelings, but it just goes to show if you keep busy and all involved all your life, you can go a long time not noticing. If you're real good at it, maybe forever."

When he came back from the tropics, there was a pool club he patronized a lot. He met Bertrand there. "I didn't go to cruise or pick people up," he emphasized, wanting me to understand. "I just happened to get introduced to him."

"Love at first sight?" I asked.

It had not been. Bertrand had had to grow on him, but it would have been that way with any man. "I'd never thought of things that way before," he answered. "I had a lot of trouble with the idea of a man in a relationship with another man, a sexual one. I felt intimidated. Sex by itself didn't mean anything to me. I need a relationship and sex. After a while I fell in love with him."

Bertrand was in the kitchen when we got back. "Did he tell you I'm his first affair?" he lilted accusingly. A wiry, brown dachshund danced at his feet. "Misty, sit like a prairie dog," he begged, bending down. His short, thin hair was silver white. "Ah, *see!*" he cried. "They *know* when they're being cared for and everything. That's how it ought to be.

"Did he tell I'm his First Lady, too? Salvatore is president of the town council. It doesn't matter *who's* there—even the senator, when he comes. He's president and I'm First Lady. *I'm* the butch one, though." He flashed his eyes and knocked his knuckles on the kitchen counter, where he was preparing an afternoon snack. "All these years up here and not one problem. We don't hide anything—we never lived in separate houses and sneaked in to each other at night. I don't care who knows. But we don't go around *screaming*, either," he seemed to scold. "We live normal lives. Isn't that what we all want, really? Except," he demurred, "for those gay activists in the cities."

We retired with a tray of pastries, fresh juice, and coffee to a parlor in the back, a quaint, cluttered room with linen antimacassars on the chairs and end tables strewn with half-read books and magazines. "There *is* Miss Roberts down here now," Bertrand resumed while Salvatore sat, amused. "*She* has to make a big deal out of it. She's going around saying, 'Those two, they're gay, and those women moving into town are lesbians.' But *no one cares*! They don't want to *hear* about it, but if they don't get it thrown in their faces, they just accept it for what it is.

"Listen!" he exclaimed with a vertiginous flourish of the hand. "I have a *right* to be here. I don't want to be discriminated against because I'm gay, fat, or balding. And I'm *not*," he reported. "When there's something going on in this town, they always invite the two of us. It's the *two* of us, *always*. Up here, it's *who* you are, not *what*. In the city, people cause a lot of problems for themselves, with the public sex and the cruising. I don't want gay rights—or *straight* rights. I want the *civil* rights that belong to me. And I'd damn well better have 'em." He squinted on the right and arched his left eyebrow. A flame flashed in his blue eyes.

It was just like the problem the town had had over the children in the local Catholic orphanage, Bertrand announced, sighing. "They always boarded five or six Mexican kids out there—for *years*. Fed 'em, gave 'em a place to live, got 'em on their feet, and sent 'em back to Mexico. Then they decided to bring in twenty more. *Well, every*one got in a tizzy! 'All those Mexican boys—they'll destroy the town. Rape and pillage!' You *heard* that sort of thing—after the orphanage had been here all these years without any problems! But bringing more kids in seemed to throw it up in people's faces, and they got scared.

"It's the same with this whole *gay* thing. I mean, *we*'ve been here all this time being who *we* are." He fluttered his lashes and laughed. "And *we're* accepted. As long as you don't make people think about it or put a *name* on it, they're just fine. All those Mexican kids are living here now, you know! And not *one* old lady's been raped or pillaged!" He patted his hair on the side like Mae West.

It was late in the afternoon when Salvatore took up a similar theme. "Scared people do dangerous things," he stated. He was boyish with animation, having grown comfortable with me now, I guessed. We had been sitting outside, watching the *javalinas*, the wild pigs that safaried through their yard with twelve or fourteen babies trailing. Small in other habitats, they grew big in the spacious freedom of the high country, to as much as eighty pounds. "They're frightening," Bertrand had explained, "if you don't know what they are." Their tusks were razor sharp, and they snorted and grunted. "But they're harmless if they don't think you're attacking them. They're a part of our community. We had a family that moved in once who wanted to get rid of them, start killing them off. No one here was about to do that. So finally those people left. They couldn't live in the world up here the way it was.

"Or that old guy who kept those hounds," he added with shock. "Going out for a kill, to get some cougars. Said he found out where a mother and her cubs lived in the rocks. So he rounded up his dogs and climbed on his horse and died right there of a heart attack. 'What goes around comes around' is what I say. *Or* that cowboy and the rattlers," he recalled, passing the story to Salvatore. I sat frozen.

There were lots of western diamondbacks in these hills, Salvatore reported. "But they leave you alone if you don't bother them. Some cowboy riding up here last summer saw one from his horse and he shot it. When he got down to pick it up, another one sprang out of a pile of rocks and bit him right here on his finger." He chuckled. "Are you all right?" he asked me.

"I *love* it!" Bertrand exploded. "He's going to kill an innocent snake and that rattler's brother jumps out and nabs him. Nature puts everything back in its place."

"It *is* wonderful!" Salvatore stated. "That snake comes out from his rock and says, 'Oh, no, you don't! We're all sharing this place. We all have a perfect right to be here.' "

Salvatore tried to explain to me the strange winds up here. "They're pure," he said, "from the high stratosphere. They move in a funnel around the peak." They were ventricular. "This is one of the few places in the world where that happens." He named the Andes and the Himalayas and the air above a Guatamalan lake. "Sometimes the wind changes behind you when you're out riding. It's like someone taps you on the shoulder. They say we'd be safe in a nuclear war."

On the evening before I left, I sat on a stony cliff alone high above the desert. I felt all-powerful and small. The sunset sky, like a wizard's mouth, blew flaming clouds of orange and pink that died in cold breaths of blue and purple. The darkening terrain seemed endless, gathering brown mists and resting them at the feet of small, strewn mountains. A river and a road scratched fading outlines in the dirt. Tempests brewed thunderheads below me. In the east, lightning seared the ground and made it roar, while the clear heights stayed quiet. In the two months since I'd come west, this savage topography—this wilderness map—had lured me through its planetary transformations, through cold and heat, light and darkness, through spirits divine and human.

Intimate friend, have we not traveled far together now? Count the time, the miles, the lives, that hand in hand we have trespassed. Like nomad confessors, we have heard men's deep secrets. We have shared the private happiness of strangers and been privy to their cries. How can we describe the human mysteries we have witnessed? Every heart receives its truths distinctly. Perhaps, however, we will come to agree more than before on the meaning of the marvels we have seen—and nurture greater respect for our differences of opinion.

None of our dogmas are pure. So, while we champion one belief, we are always oddly haunted by its opposite or something in between. When I was young, American religion and the common man universally condemned homosexuality as a matter of immoral choice, even as psychiatrists demeaned the desire as a terrible innate disorder, a "constitutional" flaw. Against these malevolent myths gay liberation rebelled. In time, sympathetic clerics and shrinks joined us activists to create our own fantastical explanations. Foremost, we argued that homosexual desire was probably a genetic trait that surfaced in only a few men and left the rest untainted. We claimed, in fact, that homoerotic need created a separate breed of human being, a distinct community of sensibility and social obligation. We nurtured a "gay identity," which fluctuated with cultural whims, and declared it to be the only legitimate homosexual expression. We viewed our sexual lifestyle as a mandate of our nature.

"Straights" who questioned us were bigots. Homosexually active men and women who ignored our dictates were condemned as traitors to the "gay community," "closet cases." I swallowed these tenets whole. Whether you are "gay" or "straight," my fellow traveler, can you honestly tell me now that you had not as thoughtlessly accepted these commonplace beliefs? I was looking for brotherhood—a certainty that among some tribe of American men I could claim to belong. And can you honestly say, dear reader, that you have not traveled far distances in search of such assurances, too? Perhaps your pain is different—it is racial or ethnic, or because you are a woman whose life will not fit the woman's role. For ten thousand human reasons might we be shut out. We spend a lifetime searching for others like ourselves whose common lives inexorably bind us to them, whose community we cannot lose.

For a long time before I began my travels, I doubted the gay articles of faith, even as I was one of the movement's most ardent propagandists. At the least, AIDS had horribly revealed that more men engaged in homosexual acts than any of us had ever acknowledged. Many of them, I came to understand, were happily, heterosexually married or had sex with other men only occasionally. Others had sex only with men but did not choose their friends among other homosexuals. They did not fit the mold. They were not "gay." Still, in a guilt-ridden time in my life, the creeds of gay liberation had set me free. And absent any other benign explanation of my sexuality, I continued to cling to them.

Perhaps, good reader, our travels together will have again raised doubts about men's lives in your mind, as they have in mine. The boundaries of desire no longer seem so neatly drawn on the sexual map. High in the Rocky Mountains, Rudy's jocks and his friend Sven allowed their need for men to ebb and flow, to change places sometimes with their love for women. I came to wonder whether, in fact, their liberated needs were not like most men's. Nor could I so confidently declare, as I once did, the superior rightness of my brand of "gay identity." In New Mexico, Felipe, my Apache friend, taught me about a noble tradition of homosexual expression that long had predated the white man's "gay life-style." I learned that some men harbored conflicting needs more vital to their lives than "being gay."

Schoolbooks, when I was a boy, proclaimed the wilderness dead and settled. Journeying across these magnificent, impetuous western lands, I learned otherwise. It seemed to me now that America's wilderness was in fact eternal, a world whose every part will not be tamed. So, too, I was learning about the lives of American men, about whom I really knew little beforehand. The desert roads were a beginning. I came to perceive that the heart is its own geography. A wild place, we try to civilize it by laws of love and hatred. We create social roles to govern our fiercest needs, rituals of obedience and rebellion. It is a limitless land. We draw borderlines and settle terrains where we can. They grow crowded, like cities.

And still there remain, for all our hard taming, the vast unconquered outlands of the soul. In them, each of us struggles alone, uncomforted by conventions of psychology, politics, sex, and religion. The men I met in the West lived in such environs. Some were embraced by the men and women among whom they dwelled. Some, feared, were hunted down. Some hid or ran scared. Others fought back. Like you and me, they sometimes waged war with themselves. All of them dared to know the love of other men, but each in his own way. Sexual tastes bonded them far less inexorably, I came to believe, than their courage to resist and survive.

And so, too, I came to this: Most of the men I met held more in common with their neighbors than with all the other homosexual men I had ever known. And although I found intimate communities of homosexual men throughout the West, whose shared lives made them brothers, I found no trait that surely united all homosexual men in a single gay community.

I can confidently state these insights now. Still, my friend, you will be lenient with me when I say that my heart could not quickly give up its faith in gay brotherhood. We build our very lives around such ideas. Have you not done the same, loyal to old concepts of God or politics, friendship, romance, or family? They are not painlessly abandoned. And so I set out to search for proof of the gay creed elsewhere in America—in Louisiana and the District of Columbia, in Alaska and the Midwest—hoping to find it in the midst of some other odyssey.

Even as I sat on this mountaintop debating myself, hundreds of thousands of gay men and lesbians were gathering throughout the nation to celebrate Gay Pride. And when I arrived in San Francisco again, both the Castro and City Hall would be draped with gay liberation's fluttering rainbow flags. Such exuberance leaves no place for questions. It is like religion. But now I was anxious only for this: My lover was already waiting there to take me home again before I returned to my travels. This time apart had been a sore place in my heart. I had missed him dearly.

I descended the peak to the highway west. A wilderness twilight of stars settled down on the desert.

PART TWO

A
CONFEDERATE
SUMMER

CHAPTER 9

THE
OLDEST
CONFEDERACY

Pop had just gotten a haircut when he and my mother picked me up at the Charlotte airport. "Whitewalled ya!" I teased.

"Damn barbershop," he snorted. "Takes all day long just to get a few hairs clipped. That old man cuts a little, then quits and tells a story. This mornin' he was tellin' everybody that the Jews up in New York are in cahoots with the Japanese to buy up all our cows. *That's* what's drivin' the cost of milk up. They're gonna starve our little babies in the South, then them and the *coloreds*'ll buy everyone out and punish the whites for the war."

"*What* war?"

"The Civil War."

"He said '*niggers*,' didn't he?" I goaded.

"I *think* he did, son," Dad pondered. "Pretty sure he did."

Along the road, kudzu vines devoured the South—their big leaves veiling the woods, smothering the trees, their fat stems coiling up through the tops like water moccasins in the hot breeze. My folks lived near Shelby, North Carolina, then, on a lake in the sultry foothills of the Smoky Mountains. The July sky was white with haze the day I arrived, and the air was heavy. We stopped at the farmers' market to buy a watermelon. "Test 'er with a broom straw t'see if it's ripe," said a young farmer. He sent his boy to fetch a broom.

Red faces encircled the melon bin. "Hadn't never worked for *me*," mumbled an old gentleman in a white straw hat. He was wearing a white shirt and a wide, old tie to go to town in. His face was a Fourth of July balloon in rimless glasses.

"Lay't crosswise." Pop did. It quivered, spun around, then stopped dead, pointing to the ends of the watermelon.

"I swar!" burped the old gentleman.

"Try this here'n! T'ain't ripe, I *know*!" The straw didn't budge. "I *told* ye so," the farmer said, beaming. "Works ever' time!" The South is hot with half-believed truths.

I spent two days with my parents. Pop fished from his "party barge"—a platform boat with a fringed canopy. Mother puttered about and cooked and tried to remember family news. In the evenings we went out on the boat for drinks and drifted until the sun set, our faces shadow-striped by the surrey fringe. Dad was lending me his pickup truck for my southern journeys. He was proud of me and the odyssey I had undertaken. It wouldn't have always been so. We had spent long years hostile to one another over my homosexuality. I had badgered them, sometimes viciously, with my gay liberationist views, demanding that they accept not just me and my lover, but the changeable political way in which I thought about myself. They had infuriated me with their open disgust, and later with the pretense that my sexual life didn't warrant being spoken about. But my relationship with my lover, Michael, had lasted, and in time they grew to think of him as a good son-in-law. I think my life seemed more to them now than mere sexual indulgence. We all had changed, maybe in spite of ourselves. Deep family love set our differences in their place. We tried hard to accommodate our conflicting needs.

The morning I left, Dad kicked the tires, which were balding, and checked the brakes, which grabbed. He checked under the hood, squinting through his bifocals. "You drive safe, Bud," he said, and squeezed my shoulder. When we went inside, Mom was reading a letter. Her mouth had spread tight, the way it always did when something awful was hurting her. My uncle, whose namesake I am, was degenerating horribly. He was only in his fifties. He'd been strikingly handsome and fit till this began. Now he was emaciated and full of pain, though the doctors had given him no sure diagnosis. Maybe a rare cancer, maybe multiple sclerosis, as hideous as AIDS. I took my mother in my arms. "He's dying too young," she cried.

"Maybe he's ready to go," I told her. "Maybe it's time."

"But *I'm* not ready to let him go." She sobbed. Her tears were hot on my neck. "Everybody's dying too young." That moment was the first time I felt my mother's terrible fear for me. Like many other young homosexually active men, I was greatly at risk of an early death in the AIDS epidemic.

Dad grew quiet after breakfast, then looked at me and said, "You're blessed with a wonderful relationship, son. Michael's a wonderful fella. I know it'll get lonely out there on the road, but with all this AIDS going around, it's not worth any chances. Your mother and me have had a long, beautiful life. Don't do anything to jeopardize your old age with Michael. We love you both very much."

Pop hugged me hard and hurried off to pack the truck while Mom, with her sewing shears, snipped off the little braided tail I'd grown on the back of my head, Nuyorican style. She stood watch to see that I discarded my earring. "Where you're going, people aren't going to take to those things," she warned. "You *forget*! People aren't liberal down here the way you've gotten used to up in New York."

They watched me from the driveway, the two of them—I watched them in the rearview mirror—till I'd disappeared down the road that led to the highway. Every man who passed me in a pickup truck lifted a forefinger from the steering wheel in greeting—eyes ahead, faces set, the bill of their caps, like mine, barely nodding. Behind the wheel of my father's truck—which like most on the road was Japanese made—I joined the brotherhood of rednecks.

| | |

An acquaintance of mine in New York was reared in rural Alabama. "Lord," I'd heard him say, "those folks down home still think they're living in the Confederacy." He'd arranged for me to visit. So I was headed to Alabama west of Columbus, Georgia, driving on back highways through the South as I had known it as a child. I drove at an Old South pace, luxuriating in countryside that northern manners hadn't touched and was too far from "new" cities like Atlanta to have become corrupted by suburban tastes. Bean and tobacco fields hugged the road between rolling forests of pines at the North Carolina–South Carolina border, where the earth turned red as a sinful blush and red brick Baptist churches sat askance on the land. A church billboard warned, "If you don't want to taste the fruits of sin, then stay outa the Devil's orchard." Gospel Connection Radio played the top twenty. "*Keep your wicks all trimmed and burnin' 'cause the Bridegroom is returnin'.*"

Fat white women sat swinging in the deep shade of farmhouse porches, back off the road on grassy knolls. Their high-roofed houses sat low to the cool of the ground. More tawdry yet, families of barefoot black children played in the blood red clay around sharecroppers' cabins—raw, rough-hewn clapboard, timber brown glinting golden in the humid sunshine, leaning every which way. Shrieks of hide-and-seek flew into the truck as I passed. Antebellum mansions dominated towns like Spartanburg, high fluted columns on three sides, canopied by ancient walnut trees and dark forests of magnolias.

Near the Georgia border, a skunk lay dead and fuming on the highway. A dog dried in a pool of blood with its jawbone bared. The Zion Episcopal Chapel was hidden in a stand of pines. It was built, said a historical marker, in 1848 through the contributions of rice planters. Slaves had worshiped in the gallery "prior to the conflict which many believed temporarily destroyed Southern Culture"—peculiarly wistful language, both pointed and discreet. Not far away, a deserted sharecropper's cabin sat off the road in a kudzu-laden woods. The high branches of trees, the underbrush, the split rail fence, the shed, the house itself—

everything stood gruesomely festooned by a deep green strangling beauty. The branches of two, tall, smothered pines reached skyward, like men drowning.

I dawdled across Georgia in the hot twilight and stopped in Macon around midnight. At noon the next day I made my way across the border to the state where Henry Meadows lived.

The Chattahoochee River, wide as a lake, washed the Georgia-Alabama line. Henry Meadows lived across the bridge from Columbus, Georgia, on the road to Hatchechubbee, where he'd lived in an old plantation house since 1949. That was the year he married and his daddy died of a cottonmouth bite. "I think it was the horse serum that killed him," he claimed. His voice was as slow and soft as a breeze through the pines. He explained that his house had been built before the war—"the Disagreement with the North," he meant. It was laid out on the "dog trot plan." A wide central hall ran front to back with symmetrical rooms on either side. "That way," Henry stated, "the dawgs could ru-un through it all without any bother." It sat down a white sand road in a deep pine forest. "White sand and clamshell rock, just like when the ocean was up here—but that was a long time ago—up to the fall line, where the river flattens out." His daddy had bought it in 1928, "right befo' the stock ma'ket crashed." In 1949 it had been a wedding gift.

Henry was fretting about his "little boys" when I arrived. "They're nelly little things, just like two little women. But Steven's a *whole* lot nellier than Scott." When the phone rang, Henry scurried—not running, not walking, either—his tall, slender back erect, his white hair sailing through the room like a summer fowl. His shoulders dipped. It wasn't Scott.

Young, dumb Scott was in Florida with Henry's old car. "He called last week and told me it broke *down* on him. I sent him money to get it fixed. I haven't had a *word* from him since." Scott didn't have a driver's license. He'd been jailed countless times for drunk driving. "I sho' do miss him when he's gone."

It was Thomas Way, Henry's old friend, who had introduced him to the boys. The elder gentlemen often shared their tricks from the park in "Mill Town," that poor part of Columbus where the cotton mill workers lived. "Scott was in the Russell County jail," Henry said. "*He* got out and came up here late one night lookin' like a wet puppy, cryin', 'Steven's in jail!' " Henry mimicked Scott's sob and whine, as an overindulgent, exasperated father might. "Went up there to bed with me." He tossed his eyes toward the attic bedrooms. "And *that* was *that!*"

We took chairs on the back veranda. The hard sand surrounding the house tom-tommed erratically with falling pecans, and the heavy air seemed to swell and fall with the late, moody cries of birds and crickets. A cardinal, feather light on the end of a branch, peered through the screen, his fine head nervous. A deer gazed from the edge of the clearing. "They *are* lovely, aren't they?" Henry commented. "But when they come in closer, they eat up my begonias and every impatiens plant in the yard." Baskets of scarlet-and-white impatiens hung from the eaves out of reach.

Henry sipped a gin. He was wearing fresh khaki slacks and a pressed short-sleeved white shirt, one button open at the neck. His penny loafers were in high polish. He'd been well educated in the South, an architect like his father. He crossed his long legs at the knees and thought, looking way beyond the deer. His white face was lined and gentle. Steven and Scott had been roommates. Steven had sold all their furniture for extra cash when Scott went to jail. "Steven decided he'd stay here with me," said Henry. "Sometimes I lie in bed with that little boy a-wonderin' *why* I like this so much. I think I'm crazy. This doesn't make *any* sense. But I guess that's the way the book was written.

"There's a wasp's nest in that bedroom and a piece of driftwood. There used to be a snakeskin hangin' up there, too, but Scott said it gave him the *shivers*. That thing scared him to death! I've been sleepin' up there in my son's room since my wife died. Those were the children's bedrooms."

That evening we met Thomas Way for dinner, picked him up at his condo in Columbus. Columbus fed off Fort Benning, its antebellum and Reconstruction buildings converted into pretend nostalgic shops and eateries to cater to the military and the New

South's businessmen. We ate at the Bombay Bicycle Shop, that ubiquitous sort of suburban-rustic restaurant ensconced in a parking lot. Its ceiling was dark with hollow "hewn beams," hung with antique bicycles. Thomas was a small, smiling gentleman who walked with a cane—a wound from the Second World War. Henry pined for Scott over dinner and spoke of him often. Thomas said, "Our young waiter is 'on the committee,' too, Henry, did you know? I overheard him talkin' 'ugly' to a boyfriend in here the other day." He paused and watched his plate. "Did you read the story in the Sunday newspaper about our old trickin' grounds on upper Broad Street? The chief of the po-lice said they could not do anything about it. There certainly was an abundance of po-lice cars around when the Miss Georgia Pageant was in town. I suppose they wouldn't like to be embarrassed by our po' children of the South earnin' their spendin' money that way. Of course, with the newspaper talkin' about such things, I suspect the fancier cars will make themselves scarce fo' a while."

Henry drove past the park to take Thomas home. A loose troop of skinny adolescents milled in white jeans and tight, white T-shirts in the orange aura of the street lamps. A few propped an arm on a dark parked car or pickup truck, negotiating. Henry didn't patronize the park himself. "Thomas sends 'em over to me when he's tired out on 'em," he said, chuckling, and turned to Thomas. "Yo' Timmy, by the way, did call, but *never* showed his face."

"I imagine he's right tied down with his wife and his granny. They're *both* poorly, you know."

After Henry let Thomas off, he circled the block where the county jail sat by the old stockades, half singing "The Columbus Stockade Blues," trying to remember long forgotten lines. *"Way down in Columbus, Georgia.* Wantin' to be back in Tennessee . . ." Curtis, a man who did odd jobs for Henry, had been in jail last year, he said. "I'd go to visit him, and Steven would stand outside by the stockades there and yell up at Scott. They won't let you in if you've been in the pokey yourself in the last six months. Well, they had Steven in jail fo' six whole months last year! I brought him back from a trip to Florida once and his mother came out to the house and said the sheriff was lookin' fo' him. *Oh,* he started *cryin',* 'It's jist *terrible* to go to jail if you're a homa-sexual! They all gang up on me!' I said, 'Then *why* don't you request a cell by yourself?' He said, 'Oh, I don't want *that*! I'd never *see* nobody!' 'Well,' I said, 'you *cain't* have everything.'

"I guess he's a-scared they're goin' to *fuck* him. He certainly *likes* big dicks! That's precisely what landed his ass in the pokey this time—that and *forgin'*. And hittin' some po' man he was trickin' with over his head. But they're all nigger men in the county jail. He *won't* like that! Scott was with his first lover seven *years,* till he came home one day and found him in bed with a nigra. But I suspect they put Steven in their homo bin. They're all too *nelly* in there to have sex with one another. I do believe Steven is a *true* homa-sexual," he suddenly said with surprise. "I don't think either one of 'em—Scott *nor* Steven—ever even *tried* sleepin' with a woman!"

In the middle of the block by a street lamp, Henry slowed and craned his neck at a child who sat on the curb. "*Look* at that pickaninny eatin' a watermelon! If that ain't a sight, I ain't seen it!"

Henry's son had planted all the magnolias in the yard. A huge lavender crepe myrtle ruffled the front of the house. Young pecans grew on the side. "Volunteers," Henry said. "They come up on their own." The hummingbirds were frenzied, sapping the red bells of the salvia, which tantalized them on their long stems. Henry whiplashed a catalpa branch, casting off the worms from its big, heart-shaped leaves, which were already scalloped with bites around the edges. "Big ole juicy things, good fo' fishin'." A rat snake undulated up the steps to the veranda. Henry clapped his hands sharply. It scurried. "I suspect he's tryin' to make his way up there to the bird's nest in the chimney. I found him in the house all curled up in the toilet one time—climbed up to the roof and down the stand pipe." There was this odd accommodation to contrary creatures in the Old South.

Henry moved onto the veranda and dragged a phone from the house as far as it would go. "I sho' do wish Scott would get on up that road today," he said with a sigh. Over breakfast his ear seemed always cocked. He poured char black coffee, pungent as lye. "One thing I've discovered," he went on, "about these boys who trick, is they all have '*trick* names.' I met this boy named Robert; one day, he said, 'My real name's Mark.' I said, 'Why, *Lawd*! Why do you call yourself "Robert," then?' And he said, 'Well, Robert is my "trick name."'' This other boy he brought over here one day—*cutest* thing—his name was *Tim*. Then I saw his picture in the paper a bit later and his name was Joey. He'd had a con-fron-tation with the po-lice—fightin' with his girlfriend because her father had been molestin' their little girl. He was sit-ting up here on top of a hill with a big ole *butcher* knife threat'nin' to slash himself. Well, they just hauled his ass off to the jail-house." Henry's brows gathered darkly. "He told me he wanted to marry her. He already has two kids. I said, 'Then *what* do you want to get *married* fo'?' "

The hot morning air was wet with the commingled perfumes of countless blossoms, blanketed with the sweet, warm scent of pines. A pair of bluejays catcalled to one another. The crickets were loud. "They usually shut up when it gets so hot." Henry looked about, stray gray hairs quivering on top of his head be-neath the slow hot breath of the ceiling fan. "But everything is singin' out loud this mornin'.

"I cain't keep up!" He furrowed his forehead, then smiled. "This *other* Tim—I *reckon* that's his real name—Thomas saw him walkin' in the park with his wife and three kids. He wants Thomas to *fuck* him—I *think* in front of his wife—and Thomas *won't*! So the man called me up and I thought, Lawd! Do I want to get into a scene like *that*? I said, 'Call back Sunday.' He never did. I guess they thought better of it, or they couldn't get a baby-sitter."

Henry had planned a day for me, a lazy route that took us back toward Phenix City and north along a tiny road to Beulah and the antebellum plantation one of his clients was restoring. He brought a plastic travel glass of gin and set it by the gearshift of his red Porsche. He put down the top. "Of *course*," he said, on the white sand road from his house to the highway, "Scott has disappeared *befo'*. One Sunday mornin' he called, I said, 'Whatcha doin'?' He was supposed to be there workin' fo' me. He got sorta testy and told me he'd been down there by the lake in back of the house checkin' on Curtis. That boy *despises* Curtis! Scott said he was comin' by, but I never saw a hair of him fo' three days and he showed up at the office. I said, 'Where *have* you been?' He said, 'I needed to get away and think.' I said, 'What you got to think so hard fo'?' He said, 'I've been cryin' fo' three days!' '*Why's* that?' He said, 'You and Curtis. Soon's I leave, he's down there at your lake on another fishin' expedition.' I had tried to call his daddy at the mill. They don't have a phone at the house. Nobody has a telephone these days. It's the *strangest* thing!

"Scott brought some little Jimmy out here to the house one day. He looked like jail bait to me, about twelve years old. I said, 'How do you know that boy?' He said, 'He used to trick with my father.' At any rate, Curtis doesn't think anyone knows about his other life. His oldest son just turned fifteen. His daughter's nine or ten. The man's been married three times and has one kid by a woman he was never even married to. I *know* what happens, he just cain't stay true to one woman. He's either got to find himself another woman or find some man. One time he said, 'Why don't *you* marry me?' I said, 'That doesn't sound like any fun a-tall!' He's thirty-five years old, same age as my son, and never acts like he's mo' than fifteen or sixteen. Maybe my only salvation is fo' his probation officer to throw his ass back in jail." His gin glass paused right before his mouth. He said, "I *never* cheated on my wife."

Henry was lost. The road was one car wide, pine woods breaking open to dry, grassy fields on either side. "How did I get back here?" he murmured, and took a sudden, woozy turn onto a roughly paved lane. Then he saw it, the high noble roof. Chimneys rose on both ends. Eight Doric columns fronted the porch and balcony. A long dirt drive between split rail fences snaked in and out of view through a pasture where brown horses grazed. "They *ought* to be playin' that 'Tara' theme on the radio!" Henry exclaimed.

Malcomb Dudley, probably fifty, and Jim Perot, no more

than thirty, had moved only months before from Washington, D.C.—had not quite finished moving yet. Malcomb was an Annapolis graduate, had been high-ranking military at the Pentagon and then a "corporate consultant," Henry had told me.

"We *retired* down here," Jim said, "so Malcomb could be near his mother." He spoke sweetly. "We have lunch with her every day now." He was freshly groomed in white linen slacks, a pastel shirt, and spanking white canvas deck shoes. "Malcomb was raised down here. *I'm* from Maryland originally. I taught foreign languages at the high school level. I'm studying piano now," he announced like a wife. A new mahogany concert grand sat at one end of the ballroom, an adult beginner's method open on the music stand.

"He's always practicing," Malcomb stated squarely. "Working up the Christmas carols now." Malcomb was a tan, fit, sandy-haired man with a large hard jaw and a full baritone. He was wearing a pair of regulation hiking shorts and boots. He'd been working on the old slave quarters, making them into a guest house. "We're leaving the outside rustic," he explained, "for historical purposes."

"His father owned cotton mills," Henry whispered to me.

The new swimming pool was centered at the back of the mansion. Three sides were surrounded by a covered colonnade, with hanging baskets of red impatiens and big white urns of vines. At the far end it overlooked a long, wooded valley. "It's theirs as *far* as your eye can see," Henry said, still hushed, though the couple had gone inside to pour fresh lemonade. "They *moved* this big ole house and all the slave cabins from a hundred and forty acres four and a half miles away—because the property was too small. *That* was a sight to see on a country road. The telephone company had to take all their wires down!"

High on the front balcony—across the white marble foyer floor, past rooms full of eighteenth-century English mahogany, beneath lavishly molded ceilings, up the circling central stairs—we sipped lemonade from tall, thin glasses, watching the estate in the shade of columns pocked with a century and a half of white paint. News from the North—the Irangate hearings—

was on Malcomb's mind. "Ollie North *should* be running for the House," he reported suddenly. "He'll just need to establish himself in the right district."

"Congress is just grandstanding," Jim added with a conjugal air of perturbation. "I just can't stand to watch it!"

A large American flag flew from the porch. The metal sleeve for a second flagpole was screwed into the bannister. "We have a Confederate flag on order," Jim said. "It goes there."

"Lawd!" Henry cried. "Two-thirds of the Georgia flag is 'stars and bars,' which is as much as anyone needs. We have quite *enough* controversy in the South already."

On the road out he remarked, "These old plantation houses, you know, were actually very simple indoors, not all that *moldin'* and marble. And those hangin' *baskets* by the pool! Well, Malcomb's mother *was* born and reared in 'Mill Town.'" He sighed, then slowed down to admire the kudzu covering the woods. Long, leafy arms reached for the car from a wall of dead trees. "I swear it's goin' to take over the world!"

Curtis lived in a cabin in the woods near Enon. A shanty, really. It leaned. The screen door, burst and rusted, hung limp on one hinge. The little windows were covered inside with old blankets and sheets. The living room was shadowy. A tattered old rug of Henry's lay wrinkled on the floor. On feeble shelves, on top of warped tables, on rotted windowsills—*everywhere*—old bottles, milky with age, caught the pallid sun and emitted a kind of twilight. "Beer, sodar," as Curtis said it, "medicine. I like bottles." He nodded once, tenacious with his eyes, and grinned slowly. His eyes were startling. A halo of shining brown surrounded an ice blue center—rather like the dark outer waters of a thawing pond washing its frozen core. Maybe he was handsome when he was younger. The skin on his face was raw and scaly now, and he carried a big beer gut. "I collect things," he told me. His voice was as thick as river bottom mud. Mildew sat on the air. An old phonograph scratched a forty-five—Ray Brown's "Round About Midnight." In the kitchen, a shipwreck of Melmac plates, gluey with food, rose from the murky water in the sink. Tomatoes and unshucked corn lay on the rusty drainboard—"waitin' for me to pickle 'em," Curtis said.

Curtis had just come back home from fishing with his buddy, Bones. The grass-eating carp were good in Henry's lake. Around his cabin, the grassy sand was strewn with fishing pails and squirming buckets of worms. Wrecked car bumpers, fenders, and hubcaps lay about, entwined with weeds and wildflowers. Rainbow the red setter, Rubble the bull dog, and Nigger Baby—"a ole hound pup"—twitched under clouds of gnats in the shade. A second mutt was nameless. "That's mean Rubble's girlfriend." Curtis laughed and scared her away with his foot. "She don't *need* no name. Had to shoot my other ole dog. She got too wild."

Henry had stocked his lake with two-hundred carp some weeks before. Curtis griped, "An' I only seen three the whole time!" These lay decapitated on the gate of the truck Henry had lent him for an afternoon two weeks back and hadn't seen since. "I don't know whar the other hundred and ninety-seven has went to." Henry listened, distracted. The windshield of his truck was newly shattered. "Ole Bones blew it out *blind drunk* with his shotgun," Curtis said dismissively, and offered us iced tea.

"I think he was bein' on his best behavior, offerin' iced tea," Henry said at the Piggly Wiggly, picking out peaches for dessert—he'd invited his old friend Colonel Mott to supper. "My sister sho' is afraid of him, *runs* him off if she sees him on the other side of the lake by her house." The first time Henry rescued Curtis from jail, for a DUI, he was back in two days in another county. "Fo' failure to pay child support. I told the judge he was workin' for me on the farm and could pay it up in time. It was two thousand dollars. The judge was disgusted, he'd had Curtis in that courtroom before. So sent him back out to the work camp. I went to see him off and on. *Oh, I missed him so much!* I finally paid it up for him to get him out. He was there at the house clearin' the garden fo' a few days, then he found himself a woman with money. I thought, I'm not gonna see *him* anymo'! I *didn't* fo' a long time."

It was just a year ago on New Year's Eve, Curtis had sneaked into Henry's house and stolen a pistol. By the night's end he'd wrecked an ex-wife's house, threatened her girlfriend "fo' meddlin' in his affairs," shot the front door off a black man's shack. "He said that nigger man owed him ten dollars," said Henry. Curtis spent the better part of that year in jail—five counties in three states.

When Colonel Mott arrived for supper that night, he asked, "Why don't you find someone who *works* fo' a livin'?" He was nursing a rock glass of gin on the dusky veranda. He was little and strong with a chest like a barrel and a white blushing face. Khaki shorts and knee stockings set off a pair of short, strong legs.

"I'm not bankrupt *yet*," Henry wailed. He seemed wounded. The waiting telephone sat beside him, trailing a hopeful line into the kitchen. "I *give* 'em *jobs*! They work here! They're just all *gone* fo' a little while. But *Curtis* is wearin' thin," he considered, and sipped his gin. "The last time he camped out here by the river, he had some hitchhiker with him to fuck, said he was an old friend. Late of the night, he came knockin' at the house, askin' me, 'I want your bottle of Rush. We got some bitch down here.' That big old huntin' knife was stickin' out o' his pants. My sister was unhappy." Henry then eyed the colonel sharply, smiling and accusing. "You just use your energies fo' different things."

Colonel Mott lived some ways south of Hatchechubbe near Eufaula, on old family land by the Chattahoochee. He'd fought in the First Cavalry Division in World War II, which, he said, "unfortunately fought on the Union side durin' the late '*Unpleasantness* between the States.' We spearheaded for MacArthur on the Philippines. I was settin' up bivouac, you've seen that famous picture of MacArthur wadin' through the water there. I issued him the pants he changed into afterward."

"Why did he change pants?" Henry asked in the tone of a man who'd been betrayed.

"*Because*," drawled the imperious colonel, "he was wet up to his navel and they'd already taken his picture."

After the war the colonel had married "a fine southern girl." They'd spent most of their lives stationed in Hawaii. "When my wife died," he said, "in 1968, I retired. We had not had children. I love children. I came back home and took up teachin' *po'* children in schoo'. We were havin' some *terrible* problems down here, with in-tegration beginnin', bringin' in the colored folk from various places. They couldn't read—although some of my little nigra children did real well. The dummy blacks never did any worse than the dummy whites. Of course, more white children did know their letters. There's *always* problems when people who are different start *mixin'* together of a sudden. It's like the Japanese, who are *won*derful in Japan, but they are takin' *over* Hawaii. My wife's family visited once and did not *ever* come again. They're like cockroaches, you know, the Japanese. They don't make good neighbors, crowdin', bumpin' into everybody, takin' their snapshots."

The phone rang. Henry snatched it from its cradle, with startled expectation on his face. The colonel kept going, though notably louder, as if perhaps politely to shield Henry's call from eavesdropping. "Certainly I am biased," the colonel said. "I *fought* the damn people. Of course, what they did puttin' them in those camps out west was terrible, no sense in that, treatin' people unfairly just because they come from a different place or look different, or their color or what not. Henry," he said abruptly, seeing Henry's conversation ended, "was that your boy callin' in?"

"Just Thomas." His voice was empty, doing only what it must. "Wantin' to know if Malcomb and Jim had gone and niggered that fine plantation house all up."

"Humphrey Mott," Henry lamented serenely over coffee in the sitting room the morning I left, "does not approve of my little boys. He prefers gentlemen of independent means. An old friend of his lives in Three Notch, seventy-five years old, and married a wealthy widow lady. He had a pe-nile im-plant put in so he could fuck her. Now his dick is semihard all the time. He comes over to Humphrey's to watch pornographic movies of men together. Humphrey sees a nice widow lady in Montgomery. He dates her to save face. He said he wanted me to marry a gal friend of mine I see in Atlanta when I'm up there. I told him, 'I don't know if she's interested in me. I'm not interested in her except fo' her condo and her money.' But I don't want to be married anymore. I said I'm havin' too much fun."

No one in Henry's family knew of his new life since his wife's death, though a certain freemasonry of gentlemen from fine old families had always been privy to each other's secrets in the counties surrounding Columbus. Henry's architect partner was a "member of the committee," and all those years Henry hadn't known it—and Peter, the young designer who worked for them. Peter had been Mason's lover. Mason was a newspaper editor in Columbus. "Of course," Henry explained, "everybody around knew about them. Mason started at the paper in the forties and remained a bachelor. When he threw Peter out fo' another boy, it was quite a scandal in town. Everyone here was accustomed to seeing them together."

It was Mason and Peter who'd decided that Henry was one of them and had thrown the party for him after his wife died. "I got there and everybody I knew came crawlin' out of the woodwork! I decided, 'Well I must be gay.' I'd never thought of it much befo' that time."

The room where we talked that morning was full of silver shadows that marbled the air. A high wind churned the morning sky. A forest of dark-framed photographs stood everywhere on old lace-covered tables. Henry stared past one on the table by his chair. "There's never a picture of her ever taken that she doesn't have a cigarette in her hand," he said of his wife. "Alcohol and cigarettes killed her. Livin' just like my little boys." He sighed. He was as distant as the wind. "She died sittin' in this very room. We were married thirty-five years! The year befo' she passed on, she had an operation fo' a tumor on her brain. Her heart was awfully bad. The doctor told her she couldn't drink or smoke at all, but she wouldn't give up *either* of them. She sat here all day long from the hospital smokin' and drinkin' her gin.

"That night, I took her to a dinner fo' the Georgia Trust. She looked lovely, I bought her a new gown. I went on to bed when we got home. I could hear her in here with the television on. I woke up about four in the mornin'. I could still hear that buzz from the television set. I found her facedown on the floor. She'd been sittin' there in some alco*h*olic stupor, I suspect, when she had her stroke and her cigarette caught her gown. She must have had enough of her mind about her to try to put it out—it looked like she'd been rollin' around a bit on the carpet. I called the sheriff. When he came out from lookin' at the front of her, he said, 'Mr. Meadows, you *don't want* to see your wife again.'

"It's a *won*der it didn't burn the whole house down!" There was slight and new amazement on his face. He couldn't have known how fully such tragedy would change his life, inducting him, as it did, into the oldest of confederacies.

CHAPTER 10

DIVIDED
STATES

ALABAMA IS DIVIDED INTO SIX PARTS BY ITS INTERSTATES, WHICH
wall family from family, farm from farm. It is a state of sundered
intimacies that now must be engaged through cloverleafs, like
checkpoints. Avoiding superhighways, I passed through three of
these regions on the back road that led to Tupelo, Mississippi, to
visit two young lovers. The morning, gray and cool, grew white
and steamy. The back half of a mobile home lethargically trailed
its front half up the road. A house trailer in a field had been
turned to brick, rather like Lot's wife. At a Tyler's in Opelika,
white people gathered for breakfast for $2.79—ham, eggs, bis-
cuits, grits, OJ, a plastic cup of coffee—at tables screwed into the
floor. The women's hair was ratted into nests. The men's faces
were shadowed by straw hats. A young black man stood stiff and
nodding behind the counter, grinning, it seemed to me, because
he was the manager here.

In Tallapoosa County, a Trailways bus had broken down. Its
passengers stood in the hot noon haze gaping at the opened rear,
which exposed its oily viscera. Red dust and smoke rose from hot

blue hills, which lay low and sleepy all around. Trucks groaned under the weight of logs on the way to Birmingham. Birmingham, gray and dirty in the white noon sky, was drowned in the stench of paper mills.

The road crawled block by block through the crumbling grayness of downtown. Working women, ruby with makeup and yellow with haystacks of curly hair, walked in steep heels, in the dead, wet heat, along the sidewalks. White men carried their jackets across one shoulder and loosened their ties. A gaggle of old black men changed tires in a dingy garage. On the other side of Birmingham, kudzu lavished the pines like gaudy ball gowns. Two tall pines wore kudzu cut at the root and withered, like desiccated veils.

The welcome sign to Mississippi stood side by side with an orange road sign announcing "End Construction," and it seemed to me that an era had passed. The land was flat here. On this July afternoon the trees lay below the sky like moss at the bottom of a white-warm pond. U.S. 78—which ran across the railroad tracks in Tupelo near Elvis Presley's birthplace—was named the Elvis Aaron Presley Memorial Highway for the hundred miles or so to Memphis. The silvered cupola atop the county courthouse was nearly blinded by the sky's bright haze. Pickups slowly circled the courthouse square like exhausted worshipers. On a shady street a few blocks north, Tom Kirk and Len Coker lived in a bright yellow bungalow, a modest house. An urn of crimson begonias bloomed on the front porch steps. Len wasn't home from work yet. Tom had been napping. Now it was time for him to take his dose of the AIDS drug AZT, which he took every four hours.

I'd gotten Tom's name from Eddie Sandifer, Mississippi's most prominent gay and AIDS activist, whom I'd read about in the *Advocate*. Eddie had founded an AIDS hospice in a quiet neighborhood in Jackson and was under a barrage of death threats on account of it. I'd arranged to visit the Jackson hospice but wondered too what living a homosexual life with AIDS was like in places smaller than the capital. Eddie sent me to Tupelo, where Tom now took his pill and swallowed. "It's really kind of a pain, but I gained twenty-five pounds," he said. "I was down to one forty. That was the only sign. The doctor just thought I was over-working." In spite of the rewon weight, Tom still looked slight, very young. He was only twenty-six, a preppy kid in a pink knit shirt and white-and-pastel-blue-striped shorts. His oak brown hair was very short, cut boyishly. He spoke with a soft accent, salted with the South but not deeply southern. Though he'd been raised in Tupelo, his parents were from the North. "I'd been with Len two years when I moved away, to Jacksonville, Florida," he began quietly. "That's where I got sick. But it was worth it," he claimed, "going there. If I hadn't, I would have still been sitting here in Tupelo wondering what it was like outside of here. You find out life's the same everywhere."

The sitting room, where we sat, was cloud gray with satin white woodwork. Ginger jars and vases of pastel silk flowers clut-tered the mantel. The bookcase was full of records—Patti LaBelle, the Weather Girls, Manhattan Transfer. Above the man-tel hung a deco-styled framed poster, a tuxedoed gentleman danc-ing with a pink-clad lady. This was a certain design statement I'd seen most often in Chicago in the seventies, by which time it had filtered down from New York and become midwestern: a look that was strong but not unfeminine, a code as precise as camp, unmistakably gay. It had reached Tupelo belatedly.

A large vase of fading scarlet gladiolas stood beside the fire-place. "Our flower bill last month was a hundred and fifty dol-lars," Tom said shyly. "We give them so much business they give us two for one." His voice was pleasing and monotonic as he sat on the sofa sipping a glass of soda pop, though often enough he became pensive, lost. In these moments his speckle-green eyes dimmed, and he'd fix on the acorn tree shading the window. There was the tiniest bit of gray in his hair. His cheeks blushed perpetually, as if they were fevered. When he'd come back from Jacksonville sick, he said, he'd moved back in with Len on Len's folks' farm. "The same bed Len slept in when he was little," he told me. "Before he even came out to his parents, he took one-night stands there. His father says he thinks it's wrong in God's eyes, but he wants to see Len happy. They've always treated us like we're married.

"I wouldn't mind if we started going to church again," he said suddenly, "but someplace where Len and I could be together." He knew, he said, of a Metropolitan Community Church in town, the "gay" denomination, but he and Len were leery of that. "I'd be afraid that they'd preach gay rights and stuff, instead of the gospel. Maybe the Catholics. Aren't they real liberal? Don't they have gay priests?"

On the coffee table by the sofa where Tom sat, a picture album lay open to a blank page. A stack of color photographs stood beside it, which Tom seemed to have been arranging in the cellophane pockets earlier in the day. The picture on the top was of a tall, thin, swarthy drag queen in shimmering red. Tom was holding "her" hand. "Sometimes my lover dresses in drag." He grinned cautiously. "His mother made dresses for him before she even knew he was gay. She just had to get his father out of the way when he got dressed up. Would you like a drink?" he asked, then brought me a glass of Pepsi.

Tom would rather, it seemed, talk about Len than himself and lost himself in thought less easily that way. Len was also sick. His illness, which had been diagnosed three years ago, seemed to plague Tom more than his own did. "They found out he had Hodgkin's disease," Tom explained, "when he went in the hospital for hemorrhoids." They'd done a chest X-ray in prep for surgery and found a tumor there so big it had cracked the bone. The doctors had said it was funny, if he hadn't gotten such a bad case of piles, he'd probably soon have been dead. He was twenty-one then. "My doctor said it was AIDS," Tom said, recalling the controversy. "His doctor said it wasn't, but they didn't have the AIDS test then."

In the winter of 1986 they found another suspicious lymph node and started Len on chemo. Tom hadn't been feeling well himself, so he went to stay at his parents' house, where he spent all his time reading copies of his doctor's reports on his damaged health. "I got real curious about what all the things on the charts meant about me." Two days later Len called to say he'd been taken to the hospital. That night Tom's parents took him out to eat. He got short of breath, then couldn't breathe. The next day he was in the hospital, too, with PCP, AIDS-related pneumonia. Now, remembering, he grimaced as though at the weirdness of it, then stared out at the old, strong acorn tree. "It was April when I came home. The flowers were blooming. Then we got two inches of snow. That was unusual—the flowers blooming and then the snow came and killed everything.

"A lot of rumors got out about Len; so we've both had to live with rumors. The gay guy down the street died of a heart attack two years ago—I *know* he died of a heart attack—but as far as everybody else was concerned, he died of AIDS. We've got five gay couples on this block. This is the oldest section of town. A lot of gay people are moving in and fixing up houses." He looked ahead squarely. "I don't know if that's something gay people are prone to do?" he asked with a wrinkled brow. "I feel like such an old man. Everyone 'coming out' these days looks so young. I was really worried when I was in the hospital last time. I tried to talk to Len about it, that we ought to get matters settled and all. But he doesn't like to talk."

Len himself never talked about his cancer. He was a dark, svelte young man with thick mahogany hair and black, brooding eyes. His face was beautiful, like some bird's, an eagle's. He had a long slender nose. He all but ignored me when he came in—not unkindly, carefully. He was very religious, Tom had said. "Not a believing Southern Baptist anymore, but he gets mad if I say 'goddammit'—I think because of the way he was raised and because he's dying. He might think God doesn't want him to be gay, but he's real open about it. I wouldn't have chosen to be gay, either, because of all the problems it makes."

Some time ago, Len and Tom had thrown a "gay" party at Tom's parents' house for 150 or so. A neighbor man had stood next door yelling, "Faggots!" then assaulted a lesbian. "She beat him up!" Tom exclaimed. He seemed astonished. "But it ruined the rest of the night for me, frankly. My cheek and nose got broken. Two guys were sitting on top of me hitting my face, and Len started pounding them with his penny loafers. He's good with his shoes! One time two guys beat up some lesbians at the bar. They were straight, but they get drunk and go to bed with anyone out there, there're so many redneck bisexuals here! So Len pulled off his pumps and went after them. When they went to the hospital, they had all these little high-heel holes in their heads. Len still has that pump as a souvenir, with the bloody heel." Tom put on a record by Manhattan Transfer. *"Here in the twilight zone . . ."*

So silent about his illness, Len would talk on and on about drag. In the bookcase beside the records, there was a silver-framed picture of him dressed and standing by Patti LaBelle in the lobby of the Peabody Hotel in Memphis, looking for all the world like an overdone woman. "Nobody really cared," he recalled, flat-voiced about his cross-dressed glory in the rock-and-roll heart of the South. His accent was a cracker's. "We met her three or four times there. The first time, she had her hair fixed up like fans." He fanned his hands. "I started cryin', I just couldn't help it. I begged her, 'Take me up to your room!' She said, 'I cain't do that!'" She'd registered under Patricia Edwards. He called her in the morning at ten and woke her up. "She called me back at one, *sittin' in her bathtub*, and said, 'Meet me in the lobby.' The security guard tried pushin' us away. She just told 'em, 'They're with *me!*'"

"Does she ever come to New York?" Tom asked.

In the bedroom, by a Fit for Life workout machine and a bedstand cluttered with prescription bottles, Len displayed his dresses. The closet was jammed with sequined jackets and gowns he and his mother had fashioned. He hung a red satin evening dress over his arm, while suspending a pair of satin dust rose heels and a purse from the tips of his lanky fingers. "Isn't that a piece of work!" he insisted, his dark eyes widening. Tom suggested going to the night's tawdry drag show at Tulip Creek, the one gay bar, which was out in the country. Len's face went sour. "I wouldn't be well for that at all!" he snapped.

That night we went to the weekly lip-synch contest at the Ramada Inn instead. It was full of "singles." A wilderness of philodendrons hung from a wooden ceiling darkly lit by faux stained-glass lamps—the corporate standard imposed as down home style throughout America. A radio deejay emceed, hip and sassy, dressed in tails and designer jeans, thumb-nose chic. Like most announcers' voices now on the South's TV and radio, his was northern. There was a crisis, I had noticed, brewing between the Old and New South over the flavor of speech, a civil war of sounds.

Tonight the Ramada's contestants, who sang with no voice of their own, mimed Elvis and several disco divas. Most of them were white girls respectfully pretending to sing like black women. "Natasha Touché," a black queen stuck in the ladies' room too long, missed her call and was pissed at the deejay for not waiting for her. Another black queen stumbled around the bar with unraveling hair and a shoulder strap across the elbow, exposing her bra. "Looking for a dance to dance and a song to sing," Tom quipped with an air of admiration. Below the spotlit mirror ball, a fine young man danced with self-conscious ease. He attended to his girl with that perfect reticence that cued some need to prove himself more than erotic interest. "It gets real cruisy here sometimes," Tom said. "Guys dance with the girls, then go home with each other. It's safe, in a way, because no one in here thinks you're gay—unless you're a drag queen. My friend Brian picked up a straight man here and took him to the park. The guy kicked sand in his eyes after he came. Now Brian carries a gun everywhere he goes—with those blunt-nosed bullets that'll blow your chest off. Len and I keep a gun behind the bed. Like that guy who broke my nose at the party, I'd kill him if I could. I want to see them dead."

In the car going home he asked, "In New York, can guys hold hands on the street? Do you all have Kroger's?"

"*Tupelo!*" spat Bubba Milk, handing his lover, Daniel Rae, the menu at a Chinese restaurant. "Fast-food capital of the world!" His lips wrinkled, like the drawstring of a purse. Bubba was a slender, drawn man whose short-cropped hair lay at odds with itself. His short-sleeved shirt of faded plaids was too small for his shoulders, as if it had been salvaged from his distant adolescence.

Tom Kirk had met them at Tulip Creek and introduced them to me as another gay Tupelo family facing AIDS. Bubba had fled Tupelo many years ago, when he was young, for Chicago and Atlanta. Then life took a bad turn, even before Daniel was diagnosed. *"Plain* and *simple,"* he drawled thickly, his blue eyes squinting, "my brother-in-law shot and killed my sister, then killed hisself. I moved back here five years now to raise my nephew and two nieces."

The nephew had married young and moved across the road. "Oh, not to be close by on account of Daniel's sickness," Bubba said. " 'Cause he *wants* somethin' from me! Get 'im a horse, then six months he'll ask me for a dog, forget the horse. He *thinks* my heart will weaken, and it won't."

The middle girl was also gone, a junior at Mississippi State, but she'd been on her own since high school anyway. "Well, her boyfriend said he wouldn't go out with her anymore 'cause he heard *I* had AIDS, and *I* don't. He coulda treated the whole thing more intelligently—he *did* get outa high school and bought hisself a fancy truck. Well, she sided with him and we just moved out and left her alone to make her pay the consequences of her actions." Now she lived next door with Bubba's father and stepmother. "Who are serious Baptist," he said, "but they're the most sympathetic, really."

The youngest, who was yet with Bubba and Daniel at home, had a tendency to be religious, too. She'd grown fearful of what her friends would think of her foster fathers, especially since Daniel fell ill. "Bein' Miss Booneville High and all!" Bubba's voice was stung with sarcasm. "Such a center of culture and wisdom around here! But try mentionin' *In'erview* magazine or *The Village Voice* or *Film Review* or somethin' and just see how much they know. Tell 'em they're *country*, though, and they'll get spittin' mad."

"They all wear those designer jeans," Daniel added meekly. He sat scrawny and bowed.

Bubba ran on. "Now she won't even use the same *towel* anymore, 'fraid she'll *get* somethin' from it. Oh, these Tupelo elite! Don't even know who Divine is!"

Bubba and Daniel lived some ways outside Tupelo, really,

north toward the Tennessee border, out in the country where they rented trailer spaces on their land. This too had been trouble— obnoxious queens, Bubba said, had rented from them. "You live on my land," he said, "you're gonna live clean. And these gay guys was fuckin' girls, fuckin' everyone! It's by far the wildest thing! And I sit up there thinkin', This is *not* the time to be doin' this!"

Still, Bubba's worst problems had begun with the rumors over Daniel's health, which had begun last May when Daniel had had to go into the hospital.

"Well," Daniel offered quietly, "I had the pneumonia in . . ."

"September 1985 was the first time," Bubba finished.

"September 1985," echoed Daniel, "but I'd gained up weight. At work ya had to do anything not to lose weight, 'cause that's what they picked up on from TV and—"

"Nothin' is confidential in Mississippi," Bubba entered. "One of our neighbors said she was scared to death to get out here and mow her lawn 'cause she was afraid a mosquito was gonna bite her and give her AIDS."

Daniel had been picking feebly at a bowl of rice. Now he folded his hands in his lap with a short-lived sigh. He was thirty, with the crinkled yellow skin of a very old man and the thin fuzzy hair of a newborn baby. His shapeless knit shirt had been bleached lifeless, as emaciated as his body. The bend of his elbow was brown and blue. "From the transfusion," Bubba stated, and pushed up Daniel's sleeve. An enormous bruise also wrapped his upper arm. "The cancer. Like I say, this has not been easy."

Then Daniel had gotten fired from his bartending job at the Hilton. "People had said they wouldn't work with him," Bubba said.

"Well," Daniel interceded softly, "there were other good people there, too. . . ."

"Well, *you* may have got used to it, Daniel, 'cause you're not from here, but the truth is, it was your life-style they did it for. Honey, I was raised up down here and I can scrap like the best of 'em! But if they wanna shun me, I've been in Chicago and Atlanta, I can *move* on!' 'Cause I am very up-front about who I am.

Bein' gay and straight is just who you go to bed with. You still have to do your shoppin'. You still have to work. And there shouldn't be any difference made. I'm a Christian like the rest of 'em.

"But we've two been together now ten years April last, and I will say this, it's not been ten years of fightin' and cross words. As I said, he's managed his own business all along, except, as I say, lately because of the sickness and his memory hadn't been right. *I* go a-scratchin' and a-clawin' for him now." Bubba's fog blue eyes narrowed.

Daniel raised his head. "Yeah, he's took real good care of me," he said weakly. His shoulders slumped farther.

Bubba paused. His purse-string lips began to quiver. "And I'm gonna *keep* on takin' care of ya, too, till you're gone!" he cried.

The town's gay bar, Tulip Creek, sat along the wooded stream from which it took its name, positioned at the far end of a long, fenced-in gravel lot. It was a windowless, rectangular one-story fortress of drably painted concrete block. Bubba, who sometimes spun records there, had said there'd been lots of trouble of late, with preachers and their crusading disciples invading the place. Tupelo, after all, was home to the Reverend Donald Wildmon, who had terrified network television with his boycotts of iniquitous programming—shows tainted with feminism, homosexuality, evolution, and the like. It was local Preacher McCustion, though, who advanced the frontline war against the bar. His churchy troops had taken up position in the road out front and recorded the patrons' license plates—then sent notices to the owners of the tags, often unwitting parents, wives, or employers.

"Some of those kids got kicked outa their house when their folks found out," Bubba had told me. "I got criticized by a lot of the gay community for workin' out there. I said, *hay-uhl*, I wasn't quittin' just 'cause trouble was a-startin'. But I can't say a word about AIDS on the mike, like where's to go get help or anything.

The preachers send in their spies, then put it on the radio we're all just *eaten up alive* with it.

"Well," Bubba went on, "the preachers called the po-lice one night and they came out and told 'em, '*You* all's breakin' the law'—blockin' up the road like they was. And they chased 'em right out, I might say at high speeds, and I do know one preacher was told to get on another subject or get hisself another congregation."

Tom Kirk also told me about posses of impious rednecks. He especially remembered two from a time when he had worked at Tulip Creek. "They rode up," he recalled, "and said, 'I hear you got a queer bar here.' The owner just told them to get off the property. So they pulled out their dicks and wagged them around and started peeing. They said, 'You like it, don't you?' So my boss pulled out his pistol and told them he liked it so much he was going to shoot them off and give them away at the drag contest for trophies."

Tom had argued Len into going to the bar tonight, on the chance that "Dina," a black queen and a friend of theirs, was performing. The cover was a dollar, setups a dollar each—no liquor license. We took a table in the musty darkness by the vacant dance floor and drank gin. "Reba," an enormous white queen in tights, sidestepped to and fro in a little spotlight, savoring the steep tremulousness of her heels. She was mouthing "Sweet Dreams," pirouetting oxlike on forgotten phrases. Black "Natasha Touché Tampon," who'd missed her chance at the Ramada Inn the night before, had stripped to a teddy and fishnet stockings now and sidled up behind Reba with droopy wrists dripping red claw nails. She was a dazed and wordless backup girl, a dark, disappearing vision. Above them, two mirror balls glittered slowly.

On a bar stool, "Darvon" watched them blankly. He had a tiny egg-shaped head that grew like a thing being born from his bulbous, amoebic body. Lazily kicking his little feet against the bar, he sat like Humpty-Dumpty on his stool, silently applauding the show and sniffing poppers. "My name is Darvon," he lisped, grinning breathless through toothless gums. "The patron saint of sick queens."

"He fried his brains taking acid and Darvon in New Orleans," Tom announced sympathetically, as though poor Darvon weren't there.

Reaching into his open shirt with a chubby little paw, Darvon retrieved some sort of ticket from the tubby cleavage and extended it toward the table. "Did you save your tee-kit?" he fluttered. "The winner gets a free . . ." "Sweet Dreams" drowned him out.

"Free what?" Tom asked politely.

Darvon cornered his eyeballs in their sockets and thought. "A job!" he exploded airily. "Do you want some poppers?" he asked, pretending to upend and drink them. Circling the table, he puffed fumes into each man's face. "That's *co*-caine in the bottom!" But it was only a cotton ball. He passed around a little tin of Darvon as a cure for "poppers headaches."

On the dance floor, Reba now had lost the words to "Crazy." Rubbing her hips lasciviously, she suddenly approached our table. "See that blond boy strippin' over there?" she asked. A drawling, gravelly basso whispered upon her scarlet lips. "He was over at my house with this little girl last weekend, cryin' to have a threesome. Hon, he fucked her every way but loose! And her all over me, too! I told her, 'Girl, I don't *want* it,' and she still wouldn't leave me alone. I just climbed right on top of her and twisted her titties real hard, and, baby, that was the *wrong* thing to do 'cause that was like stickin' a lit match in her gas tank. And him runnin' all over with that great big ole hard-on." Reba's long, sharp, middle fingernails drew twelve or fourteen phallic inches in the air. "I said, 'There ain't no way, honey, I'm puttin' that thing in my mouth after it was stuck up there inside that pussy.' "

In the spotlit space by the deejay's booth, Natasha had struggled with "Memories" while Reba talked, but the words hadn't come, and Darvon, who'd been stunned with poppers, resurrected now in a lisping flurry. "We're real embarrassed," he huffed, suspending his little egg head in the darkness above the table. His face pouted as though it would tear. "We're *real* embarrassed! Well, we know what it's like up there in New York and you can see what this is. We're real sorry. So embarrassed."

| | |

Reba had just gotten out of prison for heisting twenty-five thousand dollars' worth of another queen's costume jewelry. On the morning after her performance at Tulip Creek, she was receiving guests for the first time since her imprisonment. She lived in a little tar shingle house in tiny Amory, south of Tupelo. Her two cousins, queens, too, leaned against a skinny column on the porch, whose floorboards lay rotting inches above the earth. Their curly permed hair was bleached anemic. In sleeveless knit tops and women's knit shorts, they'd been doing the morning chores. Their glossy legs were splattered with dirt and fresh chips of grass. They chatted with neighbors across the yard. Mostly they waited and watched while Reba changed into women's clothes for me. Like most queens, "she" was "he" most of the time.

This prison term had cost Reba's manhood dearly—separated him from his fifteen-year-old son in Alabama, lost him his security guard job at Sears. Now he earned his living catching water moccasins: "Sell 'em for two hundred fifty dollars a piece at the pet shops and three hundred fifty dollars for those little lizards?" he seemed to ask, checking my familiarity with such things. "Oh, I do all sorts of butch things!" His mother, who'd just turned eighty-five, had stayed loyal to him, though, through this whole ordeal. She had regularly visited him and two others of his convicted "girlfriends" in jail and asked of the inmates, "You treatin' my girls right?" And the men would reply, "Yes, *ma'am*! We're treatin' those girls just fine!"

His old daddy had always been good to him, too. "He saw me perform on that song 'It's Rainin' Men,' right before he died," Reba remembered. "I just kept a-singin' 'banana, banana, banana' over and over 'cause for the *life* o' me I couldn't think o' them words. I was so poor I had made me this gown out of a garbage bag? And he told me, 'I think that's *real* perty!'"

Reba had now stepped onto the porch, grand in "her" huge platinum wig, steep white heels, and a glistening, tiger-striped jumper, tautly cinched. She pivoted precariously, daring her stiletto heels—hands heavily, delicately, suspended midair. So modeling, she turned through the door and sat on a big brown Naugahyde chair propped up on four bricks in front of a plywood wall.

"I was incarcerated a hundred days," she told me. "And it *wuz* an experience! My boyfriend was in there, too, he's basically straight, but he goes to bed with drag queens? Well, I grew a mustache and it caused problems. I wouldn't go to bed in drag with him anyway. I don't do drag in bed for *no*body.

"We had sixteen people in a cell and one time twenty-five. You had to bring your own sheets and towels from home! And when I went to that jail cell the first time, they was all this whistlin' 'cause this jailer that knowed me from back home told them I was queer. Honey, I just turned on 'em and told 'em true, 'I'm a sissy,' and if they was havin' any problems about it, they'd better get it out right there! I was only with two of 'em the whole time I was in. One of 'em was there for rape and sexual battery. I was only with him 'cause I was mad at my boyfriend."

For a time Reba interrupted herself to take me into the backyard and show me her pet hen. She was sudden in her whimsies. "One day it just walked up here in the yard," she explained. She stood beneath a big shimmering maple tree, bejeweled in sun and shadows. Softly she lifted the snow white bird up to her chest, nesting it in the heavy padding of her palms. It was a small hen, its head like a ruby, and in a brilliant moment spread its wings, throwing sunshine like white gold on Reba's hair and face. She glowed as though something magic burned inside.

"I educated them men, though," she continued, still holding the hen, "had 'em callin' each other 'girl' before I left. One night I had them playin' poker for a blow job! But, baby, I *learned*!" she declared as a cloud of sadness blew across her face. "I got to see what the other side of life was all about. I heard a number of 'em screamin' in the middle of the night with that cattle prod on 'em or them gettin' thrown in there in solitary with no bed and just a hole to pee in the floor. After a time, you know, I got to be sorta Dear Abby for 'em. I wrote 'em their letters for 'em and let 'em talk things out. Oh, yeah." She sighed.

"I didn't eat for eight days when they threw me in, gonna starve myself to death. I lost *sixty* pounds! From a forty-eight- to a thirty-eight-inch waist, *I stopped that*! But I cried a lot o' tears at night. Do you ever go through that?"

That afternoon, the day I left for Jackson, Tom Kirk took me out to Dina's house. Dina was a black queen who lived always as a woman. Tom hoped that she'd be home—she had no phone. We drove past long fields of tomatoes and cotton to a piney woods miles outside Tupelo, near where Len's family lived.

Dina's house stood in a clearing of weeds and white dirt. It was a tiny, two-story black tar-paper shack, rather like two unequal matchboxes taped together. Odd window frames, draped inside with sheets, hung cockeyed in the walls. Upstairs, two French doors opened out into the empty air. The high weeds between the road and the wooden steps parted to make a path.

Her sister and brother-in-law lived in a trailer in the back. Their five kids, whom Dina helped raise, were playing in the pines. Dina's own man wasn't home from the factory yet. She sat alone sewing rich gowns. Shimmering sequins covered the raw floor instead of carpet. Dina's eyes were coal black, as shining as her jet skin. They were shy and confident, dark jewels displayed below the fine arch of her brows. The deep lines of a slow, constant smile etched her close-shaved cheeks.

The gown she was working on now was for a woman in town, she told me. Dina earned a living that way, sewing for white women. She was meticulous and cheap. She sometimes made dresses for herself or as gifts for her "girlfriends" at the bar, when she'd saved enough excess material or money. She climbed the rough ladder upstairs and held up her finished creations to the light pouring through the precarious French doors, draping them over her small breasts. She designed them all herself. They were exquisitely shaped and stitched, classic taste and crafting.

Richard, her "husband," had built their house. He'd met Dina on the street seven years before, the day Richard came into town with the carnival. Dina was diffident in talking about it. When Richard came home from work, he was energetic. Peeling off his sweaty shirt, he sat to tell the story. He was slender, like Dina, and muscular, as Dina might have been but for the female hormones she took. His stomach and chest were chiseled tight, like the sculpture of an Olympian runner. His mahogany skin was diamonded with perspiration. He'd been driving the lead carnival truck the day they met, he said, when he saw this lady sitting at the drive-in diner in the back of a car. "She have the do' open," he recalled deliciously, "and I see dose legs, bro', and I be askin' who dat lady *wuz*! I say, 'Stop dis vehicle now! I be fallin' in love!' " It was months before he knew she was a man.

They had dated—church and the movies, mostly. "We sat there all that time," Dina explained, eyeing Richard seductively, "every night, smokin' joints and lookin' in each other's eyes. He waz gettin' *awful* close. But I made him keep his hands to himself." Her voice was as soft as Mississippi's air, so quiet. "*Bad!* He went and got it in his head to marry me! I *had* to tell him what it was. He said, 'Baby, I can't stop it now! I'm already lovin' you!' Well, he was *involved*," she chided, arching a brow.

"But we be *clean*!" cried Richard. He caressed her with his eyes. "We be the sharpest thang in Tupelo! Now, I don't know *what* it would be like if she wuzn't Dina." His forehead knitted darkly. The thought seemed to confuse him. "I mean, I don't know about a *dude*. 'Cause I don't never wanna kiss no *mus*tache. Maybe dat be because dat happen to me one time when I wuz a little kid—and I didn't *go* fo' dat shit! But I don't care what *any*body be sayin', *Dina ain't no man!* Dat be a *whole woman* sittin' over there!

"And baby"—he grew contrite toward her—"I be tryin' not to be drinkin' so much. I got a whole half bottle o' whiskey in there fo' a *week* and I ain't drank none of it fo' ya."

Dina compressed her lips in a sad smile, a plea, really. She almost whispered, "I cain't stand an alcoholic. You know you're an alcoholic when you get up in the mornin' and want that drink."

Then it passed, this pain between them, and Richard pulled from his billfold two snapshots of Dina taken with his folks at their home in Alabama. "*Dey* know," he said, "and dey not sayin' nothin'. Dey *love* dat girl!"

"But there is folks around here," Dina answered, her face gone hard, "that'll call me 'punk,' 'sissy,' 'faggot.' "

"Dat be gittin' me good when dey be sayin' 'faggot.' " Richard scowled. "I *hate* dat word. Dey don't be runnin' into yo' face with it. Dey be stealin' around to say it when yo' not there."

"I *am* the way I feel inside," Dina stated quietly, defiant. "When I had first started doin' this, they'd think it was some kind of phase. But this is the way it was."

"Her cousin be givin' her trouble," Richard explained, "and I tell him, '*I* know what time it is and *you* know what time it is, and my relationship with Dina hadn't got nothin' to do wit' you. Yeah"—he grinned and growled—"he got tight right away when I say dat. You know, dey always be tryin' to tell ya what yo' about. *I be tellin' you about dat,*" he shared intently, propping his elbows on his knees, confidential and matter-of-fact. "God make you outa nothin'. Idn't dat da trut'? And he make you how you are. When you comin' out o' yo' mamma's womb, you be gay if yo' want to be or you *don't*. What *yo'* thinkin' about it make no difference at all. But you *may* take a lo-o-ong time to git yo'self straight about dat in yo' head. Dat's why you got dese women folk sayin' sometin' be *wrong* wit' da sex dey havin'. And yo' sayin' to her, 'He be lookin' fo' a man jist like you are.'

"I wuz in da army wit' dis sergeant, big old dude, buildin' tunnels in 'Nam. Great big old scar on his face, he got all dat macho in him—hold hisself back." Richard squared his shoulders and made a condescending face like a white man. "Barkin' out he commands. But at night, he wuz da o-only woman. Dat dude'd do anythang you want fo' him to do. *What's dat fo'—hidin' from yo'self?* I'm sho' glad I got myself all figured out. Oderwise you spend yo' whole life bein' crazy wit' yo'self over sometin' dat you *supposed* to be."

He was down and preaching. Dina grinned with her mouth shut tight and sewed. "I trip 'em out down there at da church," Richard continued, pushing his lips toward Dina, as if to say she knew what he meant. "The Reverend Booker T. Ruff welcomin' the visitors and he turn his eye on me and the lady and say, 'And da sinners, too!' I put my elbow in 'Ernestine' over there and she say, 'I'm hearin' 'im, baby!' "

Dina lifted her face and beamed. "I'm the only drag queen in Tupelo that has enough nerve to live like this and go outside. This is the way I am *all* the time. I don't have any men's clothes at all. I don't want any."

"*Oh! Dat's da way she is!*" Richard cried, and turned to hold her eyes with his as he spoke to her alone, now barely above a whisper. "Dat's da way you are, queeny. She don't be hearin' *nothin'* 'cause she know who she is and she put it right out there. *She's* why I'm here! I wuz still goin' to leave fo' dat carnival and I jist keep stayin', 'cause she keep me stickin' around.

"Dat be why I love you, baby, why I be wit' you now—'cause I *respect* you so much."

Her sewing stilled. Her eyes were filled with tears.

When Tom had gotten out of the hospital with PCP in the winter, he was fired almost immediately. "I came back to work on Wednesday, turned in the insurance papers on Thursday, they fired me on Friday," he said. "The personnel manager said he didn't know I had AIDS, but when I told him I thought that's why they were letting me go, he said, 'That's a big matter! I'm afraid to be sitting in this room even talking to you.' " The man wouldn't shake Tom's hand. That had made Tom mad, he said, but the anger was passing. "When I called to ask about the insurance payment, he was real nice. He said, 'They'll find a cure.' "

Len, Tom thought, didn't have much to worry about where he worked. "I think they suspect him being gay, but they wouldn't fire you for it." Len worked at a bank, where a woman had just embezzled $15,000. They hadn't fired her for the theft, and Tom took heart in that. "They just moved her to a department where she couldn't do it anymore. They wouldn't fire Len. Maybe it's bad publicity for a bank to fire people. Up in New York, are the people with AIDS accepted?" he asked oddly. Then his mind leapt quickly. "Do only the low-class people ride subways? Do you take taxicabs?"

Tom's older brother had flown down from Boston with his

wife when Tom got sick. But then he had used Tom's sickbed for a pulpit, intimately enumerating the evils of the homosexual life as only a straight man could, worrying aloud about Tom's destination when he died. "I just agreed with him," Tom said with a sigh.

Tom had been driving through the very oldest part of town as he spoke about his family, through a neighborhood where old mansions stood in the shadows of huge maple trees, distant from the street. At one, he slid up to the curb and breathlessly said that a very old "gay guy" lived there. The house hid behind high, bristling privet hedges, in the darkness of enormous maples. For twenty-five years the old man had kept his mother's deathbed just as it was the moment she died. Tom seemed amazed as he edged back into the street and returned to his brother's story. "He came down to be close to me," Tom explained, "and I was happy about that. He was into drugs and then he met a Christian group, is why he's so religious. *He's* real happy now. Good for him! But then I started thinking about what he said and I got real mad.

"My mother puts a Bible out when he comes home. She really believes she's religious, whenever he's around. She's anything you want her to be. Like whenever she's with people from the South, she gets a southern accent. I think they drink too much, my folks. I think they're alcoholics. My father has three martinis every night and falls asleep on the couch. He goes along with anything that happens. Now he wants to take me around the world with Len. He's trying to get close because I'm dying.

"My mother's open-minded, though." Tom pondered this. "She's funny. She'll tell me, 'I met So-and-so. You probably know who he is.' Because she thinks he's another homosexual. I don't like to talk to her about it, but if it makes her happy, I will. She wants to talk about the other gays in town. Sometimes she slips and says 'queer.' But she thinks being gay is my life. I don't consider it my *life*. I don't really know what the gay life-style is. Going out getting drunk and having sex every night? Len and I don't live that way; so I don't know.

"We've been absolutely monogamous since I got back from Jacksonville—or at least I *think* we are." He startled and seemed suddenly distraught. His voice grew distant. "I know I am."

It was well past six. I'd planned to leave for Jackson at four, to have a leisurely trip. Tom kept stalling me. Couldn't I stay over another night? Wouldn't I at least have an early dinner? Within a block of the house—my truck was already packed—he turned onto the road toward Tulip Creek. "You ought to see it at day," he stated. "The woods are really pretty."

We walked along the creek. He deluged me with questions about New York, about the gay bars, the sex clubs, the social life of men with AIDS, the grocery stores. "Do you carry a gun at night?" he asked. When we got back to the car—whose tags were still from Jacksonville, Florida—a tiny tiger-striped kitten meowed, dazed, beneath the rear license plate. Nothing but fur and bone, it could hardly keep its balance. Its eyes were full of puss. Tom gently picked it up and drove it to the vet, who treated it for ear mites, chlamydia of the eyes, and starvation. "She *might* make it," the doctor assessed. Tom said he would nurse her back to health, then give her away, though he seemed brokenhearted by the prospect. He'd already named her Tulip.

"Keep her," I urged him. "She's a gift life sent your way!"

"I can't," he said sadly. "They live eighteen or twenty years sometimes. Len and I'll die before the cat—then I wouldn't know who would take care of her." When I left him that night, he was feeding her milk through an eyedropper.

Eleven months later, back in New York, I got an announcement in the mail shaped like a diaper. It said "Just arrived" and inside read:

Name: Tulip 1, Tulip 2, Tulip 3, Tulip 4, Tulip 5 (in heaven)
Date: June 18, 1988   Time: 1:46 A.M.–3:15 A.M.
Weight: Not much
Length: Short
Proud Parents: Tulip, Tom Kirk & Len Coker

CHAPTER 11

MISSISSIPPI
MENACE

BEFORE WHITE MEN, INDIANS TRAVELED A TRAIL FROM WHAT BE-
came Nashville to what became Natchez, down along the Mississippi. The route is now the Natchez Trace, a narrow two-lane
parkway, which, from Tupelo to Jackson, some two hundred miles
away, lies like a riverbed between deep walls of pines. Tonight it is
almost empty. The moonless, starless universe is as black as the asphalt highway. The trees are blacker, like jagged holes knifed out of
the sky. Explosions of dark wind whiplash their ragged outlines. In
slow, blind white pulses of lightning, huge black clouds rumble and
rise, shaking the ground. The car quakes. The headlights, on a
long, slow curve, flash the orange teeth of lime green tractors, all
grinning in a clearing in a row. A sudden wind groans beneath its
breath and rustles the forest, which sighs. This wind is flannel hot
or cold and moist. In a lull, white covens of moths shine like death.
They rush in waves into the long bright beams penetrating the
blackness in front of the car and phosphoresce like mocking confetti
spirits before they dissolve. Lightning bolts from a high black cloud
and electrocutes the earth. The sky cracks, as though broken in two,

and thunderheads moan in a chorus. A bat swoops and suspends its rodent face in the pallid light above the windshield, until heavy pellets of rain shatter the vision like glass.

I stop dead in the middle of the highway, stop the engine and the lights. For moments, like a man possessed, I chant, crying out the furious sounds of words I've never heard and do not understand, in the manner that Felipe, the Apache in New Mexico, taught me. I grow hot and wet and hoarse with chanting, until this exorcism passes.

A storm has risen from the south.

"Can I have this bat on your hood?" drawled Eddie Sandifer, greeting me in the driveway, surveying the front of my pickup truck. On the trip down the Natchez Trace, two sheer black wings—long, scalloped capes—had burned onto the grille of the hood, perfectly placed, like an emblem or a warning. "How did you *do* that?" He sounded conspiratorial. "*Somethin'* went dead wrong with *his* radar!"

Eddie was almost sixty. On the sweltering morning I met him in Jackson, he felt old, he said. A life of radical politics and, now, caring for dying young men had drained his youth. But not his will. This antebellum cottage where we stood was shadowed below tall maples in a neighborhood near the Capitol, next door to the Daughters of the Confederacy. It housed the AIDS hospice he'd founded. There had been petitions against it, fire-bomb scares, death threats. Eddie was a rural Mississippi native, a Southern Baptist preacher's son, a Communist since his twenties. He had always waged war against evil of some kind.

"I'm a strong believer in armed revolution," he announced, stepping into a decrepit parlor to take the chair behind the desk, from whose surface slivers of veneer were missing. "I'm a Trotskyist. Revolution is contin-yal, *never* ends. You're forever gonna be fightin' someone's oppression somewhere." This belief had earned him 104 arrests for civil disobedience and an FBI file forty pages deep, a chronicle of surveillance since the forties. "It ain't shit," he sniffed. "Ain't shit to it. Only thing they really got in all those papers is the seven people from Mississippi that snitched. Not even their names, just numbers for 'em. They ain't got shit."

A hairbrush lay on the desk, bristles up, like a big dead hard-shelled insect with ten thousand decaying legs. Three times he swiped it through his barbershop flattop, which was tepid brown and graying. He often groomed this way—as he spoke, on the run, old habit. His jumpsuit—blue worker's clothes that he wore for business, like a car mechanic or a sanitation man—held a soiled plastic pouch in the chest pocket for pens. He drew out a ballpoint to scribble a note on his palm when the phone rang. A little man, short and slender, he had a softly wrinkled face. His lips had long ago collapsed. He had no teeth, because he didn't want any. They'd given him some trouble some years back; he'd had them pulled. In an unjust world, teeth were an expendable problem.

The phone rang again. It was always ringing. The cradle was red, its gloss worn dull. The cord and receiver were yellow and dirty, like dried blood and guts. Eddie picked up, dragged the brush through his hair, took a swig from a Ball jar of Pepsi. "Last night in Meridian," he announced at the end of the call, "the community folk took up baseball bats against the gay bar."

On the AIDS hot line, which the hospice ran: a new divorcée wanted to charge her "AIDS test" to her ex's corporate health insurance, in case she was positive; could she? From the local TV news: "Is this channel three or twelve?" Eddie laughed. "Well, then they're bullshittin' ya. *No* one's gonna admit they know the owner of a gay bar. What's your name? You new in Mississippi? They're both of 'em owned by a Klan family. It's all a deliberate setup—to segregate the races. The mama takes the door money at the white place. The pappy works at the black one down the street. At least they've been gracious enough to collect a dollar at the door for AIDS—if *gracious* is the right terminology." As he hung up he reported, "Sounds like a real riot last night in Meridian."

Eddie had been fighting the Klan since 1945, around the time he became involved with the American Communist party, and passed out antiracist literature in McComb, his hometown, just north of the Louisiana panhandle. He found out he was "queer" about then, too. "I cain't say 'gay,' " he explained, "because I grew up in a time when no one thought of gay as an oppressed group. Where I came from, the word *gay* wasn't in existence. And I cain't say 'came out,' because I never was in. I was from the farm. All the boys were doin' it with some other boy or the cows." At the restaurant where he'd worked back then, he'd overheard that his boss was queer. "Then some black people in the kitchen," he recalled, "started teasin' me about bein' like him. I was about sixteen. I said, 'Well, that must be what I am. I'm glad to find that out.' It was out and about town that I was a Commie, a queer, and a nigger lover. The Klan did come around and warn me, but nothin' ever happened.

"My family surely never talked about it or got embarrassed. When I was in the service, someone sent my father a letter with suggestions in it about me. He just asked me what they were talkin' about and I said, 'Well, the fact is, I'm a homo-sexual.' He said, 'Oh, we've known that for years!' And that was the last I heard of it. He always was a man to defy authority—even Baptists." This defiance—a terror, really, of tyranny—Eddie inherited. His brand of homosexual activism was rooted in it. Now there was AIDS hysteria to battle, more hatred. "I do worry about our legislators," he lamented. "There's talk about jailin' positives in Georgia and Louisiana. We're buildin' a new prison to hold five thousand men and with these World War Two camps still around, it makes it perty easy for the president to use his power of preventative detention. That's a very scary thing, what they call 'preventative detention.' "

Ironically, now, he was having trouble with gay AIDS activists, too, of the kind who had ignored gay liberation, stayed closeted in the pre-AIDS years, but whose fear of the deadly disease had driven them into public. "Reagan Republicans," Eddie said, more sad than hostile. "With AIDS, you need 'em on your board to raise money and make connections, but they're votin' me out of all my other causes. Just a few weeks back, I brought it up to them that the Mississippi Gay Association"—which he led—"had *always* supported African Liberation Day, and we'd always talked out against the state-supported terrorism of the United States and Israel in the Middle East. They won't have it, though, because they don't think any of it's gay-related. Bein' gay and a Reaganite is a contradiction in terms," he told me, "and it ain't as easy to keep from bein' gay."

A dark, old painting of magnolias hung above the fireplace.

In front of it, on the mantel, sat an urn of human ashes. "An Andrew-in-the-box," Eddie had called it. "All his family ever wanted to know was who was payin' for him to stay here and ever'thing. If he'd lived to 12:05 A.M. on the first, he'd still have gotten his Social Security check—that's what they wanted. Well, when you're poor and livin' in public housin', those little bits count. But they ain't gonna get his ashes!" An enfeebled young black man and a young white man who helped him walk had seated themselves on the sofa below these remains, having entered the room as Eddie vented his dismay over homosexual politics. The white man, who did not look affluent, said softly and politely, "Well, I voted for Reagan the first time. But it was the lesser of two evils. The second time I just didn't vote. I guess the Soo-preme Court might be a problem now. Is that right?"

Eddie, though, distracted, had left to take stock of the kitchen, his leisure ended. Miss Betsy, his sister, was sitting in the driveway in her Buick, waiting to take her brother to the AIDS food bank at one o'clock. Her honking grew persistent. Inside, the slow blades of the ceiling fan labored like a child's spinning wheel in a dead breeze. The wet hot air dulled the sound of the horn. On his way outside, Eddie stopped to pride himself on three baseball trophies, which stood on a table in the hall among old hospital beds and naked mattresses. "My son's," he said of the sports awards, while Miss Betsy blasted her horn. "*Oh*, not my biological son! But I've had him since he was six weeks old. He's sixteen now. His father was a former boyfriend. We were together twenty-five years. A bisexual. He had four wives and four kids. I left him because he was an alcoholic. He left the boy with me. I raised the other three, too. And a fifth boy. I dated *his* daddy back in 1959. Both of the parents were addicts. So they left him with me."

As he turned toward the door, he seized the red, ringing phone by its yellow tail and said, when the conversation ended, "Well, the lawyers in Meridian are threatenin' to go to court in drag. I suspect that'll move things one way or t'other."

Miss Betsy now had fairly cast herself upon her horn. She was ancient, tiny, frail, and gray. Her parchment cheeks were as red as roses. She wore a crocheted top and cotton slacks, summer whites. Her tight perm was new. Her car was old and enormous. She squinted cloudy eyes to see above the steering wheel, which she grasped at ten and two o'clock with little brown-and-blue-veined hands as delicate as autumn. I seated myself in the back. Eddie didn't have the front door shut yet when Miss Betsy gave it the gas, spinning hurricanes of gravel into the air, slinging me and Eddie back against the seats like sacks, though she stayed erect, sending traffic into torrents of swerves and squealing stops and blaring horns like oaths.

"First time she's been in the car since she got her hip replaced," Eddie stated, unperturbed, and sniffed the A/C vent. He smelled exhaust, he said.

"You have the sharpest nose! I never did see the likes of it in my life," she harrumphed with a quaver, stretching her neck and glowering at his nostrils through the bottoms of her bifocals, wheeling blind around the corner. "How's that Richard Hays doin' that's been so sick?"

"Still worryin' with his nuts," Eddie said, guarding the street ahead with his gaze.

"What's wrong with 'em? Itchin'?"

"Herpes. They're both of 'em all cracked open."

"Well, that must hurt, I suspect," she sympathized as her scowl retreated.

In the back on the floor by an old wooden cane sat a small black patent-leather purse with a white lace hanky draped neatly across its lip. One end of this handkerchief fell lightly upon a paperback book, a Harlequin romance, *A Time to Love*. On the front, a blond and boy-faced hunk held a sulking brunette beauty in his arms in the garden of a Gothic mansion. "She had never liked surprises," the cover read. Suddenly Miss Betsy gunned her Buick past a little car that had driven along beside us for a block. "I don't like ridin' by people I cain't see what they're doin'," she huffed, "or what their intentions are. We got places to get to."

Late that afternoon, in a lecture hall at Jackson State University—far across town from the food bank—a professor had written these enormous white letters across a chalkboard:

HOMOSEXUALITY:
A NORM OR A MENACE TO SOCIETY

She was black. Her students were all black, all from the University Medical Center, all in biomedical fields. Everyone was dressed in suits and ties or summer cotton dresses, groomed and adorned with great particularity, as though for church. This was a panel debate. Ten debaters and a moderator, blue-faced in the room's fluorescence, sat grimly at a table at the front, their names announced in tidy, particolored letters on cardboard nameplates. Reporters and photographers from the student paper were present. In fulfillment of course requirements, the panelists had chosen the topic and the format themselves, modeling their presentation after the "Oprah Winfrey Show." "Each student will have to sub-stan-tu-ate their arguments," the professor informed the audience. Eddie, as the best known homosexual in Jackson, had been invited to observe and offer his criticism afterward. He sat fiddling with the wires of a drag queen's earbobs he'd promised to fix.

"Is it a cause and effect or is someone born that way?" began Nicole, the student moderator.

Knight, a tidy young panelist, said, "It *is* hormonal"—some imbalance. "If your parent was a homosexual, you might pick that up." He fairly rapped as he shuffled his note cards, scoring points with quotes from "medical experts" as far back as the 1930s—crumbling textbooks on the library's social science shelves.

Polk added that "Sigmund Frude," as he put it, "says that some *do* grow out of it."

Audrey was confused and passionate. "What are we supposed to say to people who are ho-mo-sexual?" she cried. "Don't we *have* to give them a reason why they are that way?"

Dunbar was frightened. He relied on an article he'd found "by a doctor and a M.D.," who'd written that every homosexual was a product of "premature seduction in childhood." "So this article," Dunbar continued, "has proved that if you get overexposed to them, you can become a homosexual, too. What if they start botherin' on you?"

Tanya, a sassy member of the audience, stood up and moaned

"*Hum-um!*" causing howls and giggles. She scolded, "Then, honey, you aren't very secure in your sexuality. If I'm workin' with some guy who's after *me* and I don't want him, then, sugar, he's not gonna get it. You got *so-o-ome* kind of problem if you've been worryin' about that! How do you know you're his type, *any*way? Besides, we are not homosexual, we're not here to decide what homosexuals think, like white people sittin' around sayin' what black people feel."

This latter statement roused a magnificent flood of audience confessions regarding family and friends, which the moderator tried solemnly to put a stop to. "Y'all are gettin' hung up," she warned, "and Oprah wouldn't let you do that."

Everywhere I'd traveled across America, citizens were obsessed with homosexuality—the great debate on radio and TV talk shows, in churches and schools, across the counter at luncheon-ettes. Newspapers in places as small as Tupelo published long features on the "local gay community." They were almost always sympathetic, if ambivalent. AIDS had certainly fired the public's interest, but the epidemic had likely become the opportunity to talk out a fascination always there, this suppressed desire that lurked close beneath the surface of most people's needs and fantasies. It was this that was remarkable: In all the urgent, often sympathetic talk, two forever distinct species were conceived— "gays" and "straights"—mythic creatures, irrevocably determined in early childhood or "born that way." But the question, it seems to me, is not how homosexual desires originate, but why some men and women overtly express them while others do not, why some fewer build a whole life around them, while the great deluded majority pretends never to have felt them at all.

As Eddie told the class, "Before gay liberation came and made a life-style out of it, I didn't know many of my friends, on the farm or in the army durin' the war, that didn't have a hankerin' for other men. There's a lot of rednecks who all along grew up doin' homosexual sex. Everybody likes to diddle!"

CHAPTER 12

BAYOU BLOOD

I MADE IT FROM JACKSON TO NEW ORLEANS IN ABOUT FIVE HOURS, with an hour's nap in a pine barren near the Louisiana border when the afternoon heat had stunned me at the wheel. By the time I crossed that stretch of interstate that spiderlegged through the cypress swamps of Maurepas and Pontchartrain, the sky had misted green with dusk. The trip on to Delcambre, where Michelle Prudhomme lived, was slow in the darkness. The narrow road through the mirroring marshlands was swept with veils of Spanish moss, eerie in the slight light of the moon. Michelle (he oddly spelled his name in the feminine way) and I had exchanged letters—earlier in the summer the phone at his house was disconnected—and agreed on an early evening hour for my arrival. But now when I called the Prudhommes' house from a pay phone in town, it was already after midnight. He instructed me to wait by the grotto of the Virgin Mary at a Catholic church downtown, where he came to meet me in the old family car. I spent a week at the Prudhommes', living and working with them as family.

There was no coolness in the air that Louisiana July, not even in the dark of the early morning. By five each day in this black, wet heat, with his wife and son, Michelle's father pointed his boat across the bay, twelve miles through the hot salt spray, wanting to make a living, wanting to keep it up as he'd begun when he was young. Jacques was proud, hard proud, of the striving. What else was there for him? This was all he knew, all he'd ever known, this old boat—or some old boat—the dinghies, the fishing, the trapping. The swamp, the marshland, the bayous, the bay, bitter in the damp cold of winter, steaming in the summer like a fish stew. He'd kept old *Père* and *Mère* Prudhomme this way when he was just a boy, raised eight brothers and six sisters. Now, for all these years, these thirty-five years since he'd married Miss Agnes, this hard, simple Cajun life had fed and clothed a wife, three girls, two sons.

Old *Père*, always sickly and disabled, had begged Jacques not to marry so young. He'd barely reached fifteen. "I tell him I raise fourteen kids an' a mama an' a deddy. I can take care of a little ole biddy wife not a hun-ed pounds!" Jacques yelled over the black wind one morning to tell this story, over the thundering groan of the old motor, over the dull thump and crash of the boat against invisible waves. A hot fishy stench swept up from the boards of the deck and the sea. The sliver of moon had set, the sun had not begun to rise. Miss Agnes, short and strong, laughed through the noise with her husband. He threw one hand up off the wheel, gesturing toward the lights of two other boats. They were like beady peering eyes racing him to Marsh Island, where alligators lay hidden in the tall grass and shallow, slimy water, angry with pain, trapped with a hook in their stomachs.

Jacques had raised his sons to these watery Cajun ways, to travailing loyalty. The older one had gone far away, to be an actor—and secretly to love men—and still lived in exile from his family. Michelle had also tried to escape—had gone to Baton Rouge and lived with a lover, had driven a truck, worked at a gay bathhouse in New Orleans—but had always come back home sooner or later. Like Jacques, Michelle knew nothing else. "Deddy cay-unt do all that fishin' by hisself. Mama help him out," he'd say with a wry, tired smile, full of gravelly indulgence. His language was the patois of the bayou. "But it *not* enough."

Michelle had just turned twenty-six. At the house on shore, in Delcambre, he slept in a room with his sister Adrienne, a year younger than he. At camp in the marsh—in the tiny screened-in shanty perched low above the bayou's water, where they lived weeks at a time to trap—his bunk was across from his mama and daddy's, below the narrow mattress for a cousin or an uncle helping out. "It *hard!*" he'd say with a grin and searching eyes, and almost laugh. "*It ain't easy!*" This time they'd been working the waters since May without a break, except for an occasional Sunday and early mass. "All dat time wit' your mama an' deddy! Ain't it a trip?" he asked.

Michelle leaned back against the gunwale, the thick brown brush of his hair blowing phosphorous green in the light of the compass. The horizon began to tremble with the flame of the coming sun. With hollow dark eyes, Michelle seemed to search the pale morning, while his daddy talked above the wind and sea and motor and his mama laughed loud against the noise. "They good people, though," he said below the chaos.

The island that morning was veiled in a warm pink mist that rose slowly, like a sleeping breath, from the low *manglier* trees and the sleek, dark grass. When we docked at camp, a cloud of mosquitoes quivered and settled to lie in wait against the rusted screens. Miss Agnes walked forcefully into their midst, her head erect, shooing them with a propellerlike motion of her arm, shaking their hold. In the other arm she grasped a box of fixings for lunch—crab from yesterday's catch, shrimp, several fine pieces of fresh fish for a stew, a loaf of bread. She would cook while we men trapped, then packed up. This was the last day of gator season. Months would pass before they returned to trap nutria "rat," muskrat, otter, coon, and mink. They would be living ashore again, until then, setting out each dark, early morning to shrimp and crab and gill net, which meager subsistence they depended on year-round. Gators were the hope of survival, though. The flesh of the captured reptiles might pay the taxes in arrears and the bill for the often disconnected phone and repairs on the outboard motors that were dead and the overdue bill at the bait shop. It might, but it hadn't this year. This season gators would lessen the weight of the debt but could not offset it. Trapping had been bad.

Jacques began to load the small aluminum fishing boat he used to negotiate the shallows of the sloughs. Soon to be fifty, he was red-faced and round without being fat, with a big, hard belly that kept the side buttons of his overalls open. The front of his T-shirt, just visible above the chest flap of his pants, read "Registered Coon Ass" and cartooned a defiant raccoon's behind. "Dat's what dey call us Cajuns down here." Jacques grinned, joshing and intimidating, his small mouth askew with chaw. "Dos politicians up in Baton Rogue don't like us sayin' dat anymo'. But I say it proud." His huge chest shook with laughter.

He was standing on the dock. He was not agile, could not bend over easily. Michelle, slender and tall, stood in the boat, taking supplies handed down from his daddy. He was not the youthful image of his father—neither the color nor the texture of his hair, nor the nose nor the shape of the head, not the girth of his frame. Michelle was someone else. He was regular in his movements, not slow, unhurried, distracted, his gaze passing through everything it fell upon. Jacques's large face was set, his narrow eyes held tight to each article he handled as though his life depended on it. He was practiced and brisk. "We gonna git dis show on de road, boy!" he said. Michelle stuffed a pack of cigarettes into the ankle of his muddy, white rubber boots and stowed the water jug and a six-pack of Pepsi, the outboard, the oars, a long pole, the black bottom of a plastic soda bottle for bailing, his fishing knives, the bullets, the gun.

The sun had broken the horizon and stunned a brilliant avalanche of clouds. The air glowed orange. The sky ascended from the marsh like fumes. Mullet leapt from the black water as though they would fly from it. "He jump up if somethin' after him, hopin' he lost 'em," said Michelle, amused and dry. Shrimp sprang through the glassy surface and left no trail. The cough of the boat's old motor alone disquieted the wide bayou, whose banks lay as long and perfectly straight as a canal's. The propellers left behind them a glinting path, like crushed mirrors.

Herons—as still as art or death—stood watch with silent squadrons of sunbirds, bitterns knee-deep in the brine. As Jacques turned into a sinuous slough along which traps were set, the motor caught on mud and underwater grass and stopped dead. He lifted and cleaned the blades, poled out to deeper water, and pulled on the ignition rope again and again, to no avail. Michelle tried, too, but the motor only sputtered and belched gas. "Don't choke it no mo', son," Jacques said. Michelle took up the oars and rowed toward the traps while Jacques stood at the stern with the pole poised above the water, ready to dislodge the boat from the muddy bottom when it stuck.

Michelle's traps were set in another part of the island. These waters we entered now were in Jacques's lease, the area consigned to him, for more than thirty years, by the state. He guided the boat through one slough into another, into farther labyrinths yet. He knew each quick turn in the banks, each of a thousand jutting clumps of high grass, as if by instinct. There, in a backwater that looked for all the world like all the others—around a grassy curl in the shore that tufted and protruded like a hundred before it—he knew he'd hung the bait. He hushed, and shoving now and then with the pole, he let the boat glide within sight of a stake and the long willowy stick that arched from its root and over the water. The line, which had swung from a notch in the stick, was down. Michelle, seeing this first, smiled and turned his thumb toward the ground to cue his father.

With a slow dig and bend of the pole against the slough bottom, Jacques lodged the boat in the grass alongside the trap, as the men rasped instructions to each other in whispers. From the bow, Michelle's bare hand grasped the stake and followed it into the mud, groping for the end of the fallen line. Still standing at the stern, his father shouldered the gun, warily suspended the barrel above the water, tensed to swing his aim precisely the second the gator's horny head broke the surface, before its steely eyes could open on its killer, before the monster could attack. Now, feeding the line through his palms, Michelle carefully, gently—in breathless motion—took up the slack, no jerk that might wrench the reptile's stomach, bring it flailing, jawing, through the water toward Michelle's outstretched arms and head. Descending slowly, his hands, one over the other, disappeared below the black surface, till half of his forearms were gone. Then, like a heartbeat, he stopped. The line was taut. He tightened his arms and, strong, slow, steady, began to pull, his shoulders drawing back into the boat, hesitating only to test, with a swift, deft tug, the pressure on the other end of the line. Jacques's gun now barreled on the spot where the trap line entered the slough. Suddenly Michelle's forceful shoulders released in a fast arc, fell back, and the line came flying, cracking the glossy water. From the bottom of the slough, a big, steel hook, like a shrimp, leapt up into the air, naked but for a glob of grass dragging on it.

Michelle gave a quirky smile. His father's lips puffed, his face burned red, his blue eyes pulsed like low flames. "Dey been runnin' dat air boat back here, o' *what?*" he growled. In slough after slough, on this last trapping day, this last chance of the year, the disappointment kept repeating itself. "Dammit!" Jacques cried. "Somebody fuckin' wid us, I believe. Never so many lines down back here before!" He spit, and an amber string of tobacco juice arced in the sunshine like lightning. Deep in the marsh, in the last of the sloughs on Jacques's land, there was a straightened hook on the end of one downed line. "Dat alligator come through here wid he big ole eyes lookin' fo' his food," Jacques sniffed, "chew off dat dirty meat and spit de hook outa dos big teet' like a toot'pick!"

Far back there, too, angling through the high grass like the poles of dreaming fishermen, there were several yet undisturbed traps, baited hooks swinging lazily—above their own dark reflections in the still water, above bright mirrored clouds—rancid in the heat. Each of these had to be cleaned, stripped of meat, to keep it from luring a gator when the season had ended, a breach of the law, a big fine. "Dis one *fu-ull* of 'em, Deddy!" Michelle half grimaced, half smiled sickeningly, suspending a greasy cow innard from the line—"melt," they called it. "It feel like liver, but it sorta bloody like a heart," he had tried to explain, "wid all dos little tubes?" Putrid with white fat and oozing black flesh, the piece he dangled crawled, rank with maggots. He swished it several times in the slough, then, grasping it, held it against the gun-wale of the stern while he cut at it with his knife, tore at it with his hands. A warm, viscous ink flew from it, spattering his pants and skin, until he worked the stinking gristle over the barb and it fell into the water, leaving his palms salved with a thick, white-clear stench like lard. "Dat *nasty!*" he hissed.

Jacques had grown quiet with the morning's failure, his eyes hard, his great, red face hard and fixed, thick like a sea wall. Al-most silently he poled the boat into a tiny inlet where his final trap was set. The melt still swung on the hook here, too. "I feel so *ba-a-ad* when Deddy scratch," Michelle whispered, gravelly. A big crab kept somersaulting from the slough, shimmering midair, clawing for the untouched meat.

"Stealin' my bait!" Jacques cried. "Dey eat anythang, dos crabs. You go down there in the bayou an' die, dey eat *you!* Dey eat each *oder!*" Then, with a prurient flash and fixing his eyes on Michelle, he quipped, "But not *dat* way, boy! Not *data* way!"

Michelle whispered, "When you scratch, you feel *ba-a-ad!* I scratch an' I feel like I wanna die."

"Alligators is gamblin'," Jacques announced, lodging the boat onto shore. "One day you git eight, nine, ten of 'em. Next day you scratch. Gamblin' is what it is. You can never tell."

Michelle Pierre Prudhomme had lied to his family about my visit. "Dey thank you jist interested in trappin'," he admonished me when I phoned. "Well, it ain't dey don't *know* about me, jist no-body wanna talk about it."

When he came to meet me at the church, his sister Adrienne came with him. They'd just gotten back from Bingo when the phone rang. They played Bingo every night of the week, nor-mally, in Vermilion Parish or St. Mary, at one hall or another. "Oh, we know all the diff'rent places!" Adrienne enthused quietly. She had a wary and diffident voice, proprietary. "Two times on Sunday!" Sometimes they added a game of putt-putt golf in New Iberia. "We got a *toor-nament* between us!" Adrienne, her lips and large cheeks meticulous with makeup, was an enormous young woman, whose crisply pressed chemise-style shirt—despite the full, long tails that overhung her jeans—could not disguise her hips. She doted on her brother as she might a boyfriend, silently admiring or fidgeting quickly with the collar of his shirt or his hair.

Their parents had long gone to bed by the time I got there, to rise at four. Since the oldest brother had fled home and the oldest sister, Anne, had married and left, it fell to Amelie to wait up to welcome me for the whole family. "Mama was gonna name *all* us kids startin' with A's," Michelle told me, smirking, "but she didn't think about it till it was too late." A tiny, grinning, energetic woman two years older than Michelle, Amelie teased her brother or paid him no mind.

Amelie sat in the garish bright, cramped kitchen—at one end of the living room of the Prudhommes' bungalow—waiting to give me my gifts: a little plaster cast alligator Miss Agnes had painted, a one-page history of *les Acadiens*, from the Nova Scotian persecution to the flight into the Louisiana bayou, and a poem called "A Cajun Welcome," in a little plastic pouch. *"Bienvenu à nôtre maison,* my friend," which promised good wine, good food, *bon temps,* and dancing—and a kiss from a "Cajun lass so fair." It ended with a warning: "If that is not enough, you can *kiss my Cajun derriere."* Michelle's mouth drew tight, constraining a sardonic comment or a laugh, as Amelie read the last lines aloud before she went to bed. She was sharing Adrienne and Michelle's bedroom for the next few nights, having given over her bed for my visit.

In the dark, early morning, while the sisters slept, Michelle stole into my room and, sitting on the bed, woke me, squeezing my shoulder gently and patting my face, leaning over my ear to whisper the time. It was five o'clock. His father had been up an hour and baked biscuits and made coffee, as he did every morning. A Ball jar of Miss Agnes's fig syrup was open on the table. Jacques, who'd already eaten, stood drying his face after shaving.

"Son," he barked as if by ritual, "it gittin' late! Gotta git this show movin' here!" Today, instead of gatoring, Jacques and Michelle had to run their crab lines in the bay.

The sun was above the horizon by the time we had loaded

the truck and driven the twenty miles to where Miss Ginny, their crab boat, was docked. "Dis po' boat seen her days," lamented Jacques, standing on the spit of the bow assembling the rake for the traps. "Named her after my first grandbaby. Now the rest of 'em want one wid *they* name on it. It ain't dat easy!"

"Dis lady made fo' calm days," said Michelle. He half chuckled sympathetically behind his father's back. "She in *trouble* when the water rough."

It was a becalmed day; the dark green water of this bay off the Gulf of Mexico lay as polished as a mirror. The air was heavy and dead. By midmorning the white sky glowed like a universe of hot gasses. Huge lily pads with misty white bouquets floated among the red decaying buoys of the crab traps, unmoved except in the slow wake of the boat. Against the tedious creak and monotonous light splash of the rake, the old boat's motor moaned steadily. Jacques stayed mostly at the wheel, with one hand on the rope that lowered the rake to catch the buoys and raise them, in slow rhythm heavily bending his shoulders against its pull until Michelle had seized the line from the water and secured the cage. Swaying from the frame of the canopy over the stern, an old transistor radio crackled Cajun songs, the hot frenzy of fiddles, twanging, mournful lyrics of French love.

"It git *bo*-rin' sometime," Michelle rasped low, out of earshot of his daddy. "I gotta git away. I been too long with them." Always in the midst of his family, Michelle had little chance to talk about himself—though he'd dare to whisper in Jacques's presence, never when Miss Agnes was around. Her gaze was constant. "She don't trust me much," he'd said back at the house with a twisted smile. It was Miss Agnes who had discovered his love of men, though perhaps she had had her suspicions all along. He had had sex in high school with two boyfriends, identical twins—whom he still saw sometimes—but that had been just sex and not romance, he'd explained. He'd been in love with his girlfriend then—a relationship his folks had considered destined—and in time he might have married her, if she hadn't broken off, left him for another boy. "I felt real *bad*," he remembered, and seemed for a moment to recollect the pain.

It was then that he'd found, through the twins, the gay bar in Lafayette, "the capital of French Louisiana," forty-five minutes away, and the bars in Baton Rouge, where he'd met a man twelve or thirteen years his senior and had a weekend affair. "He was so *hot*," Michelle drawled, his voice rocky with seduction, as he almost always spoke, his brown eyes brightening. "He wrote me dis big ole letter about it, what we did. He got real dirty in it. Mama found it." He had hidden it beneath his underwear in his bureau drawer, into which she'd been placing clean laundry. She'd confronted him with it over supper that night, with all the family gathered. "She called me *names!*" He grimaced, his eyes narrowing, still bitter with disbelief. " 'Queer,' 'faggot'—*awful* names! She tol' me I was *sick* and I jist did it with boys 'cause I couldn't keep dat girl. Deddy heard it, but didn't never said a word." Miss Agnes now blamed Randy, Michelle's lover in Baton Rogue, for luring him, turning him into a queer. "But Deddy," Michelle said, "ain't never said a thang."

On the boat in the steaming white sun in the middle of the bay, fiddles and tambourines and hot nasal twang crackled from the radio, patois as fervid and florid as Spanish. "*Pourquoi m'aimes-tu pas? . . .*" The packing crate was full now—a treasure cache of gloss-green, horn-rimmed shells, like helmets, or hearts, outlined with rivets, finely speckled white like a sign of the zodiac. Numberless pairs of tiny black eyes, like shiny glass beads in a shadow box, watched while Michelle probed among them with tongs. He pinched out a stray fish or seized a crab whose crust was warped dull green and soft, which was therefore of slightly greater value, and tossed it into the ice chest where the soda pop chilled, freezing its transformation. In the midst of this raid, a tangle of sky blue legs clacked scarlet claws, grasping frivolously. Giving Michelle time for the sorting, before raking another buoy, Jacques stalled the boat, whose exhaust sputtered and gasped in the receding wake like a drowning man. "Dis po' boat seen its days." Michelle smiled, rolling his eyes. Jacques, searching the crate himself in his orange rubber gloves, grabbed two crabs in coitus and held them up. "She a buster!" he said of the female, because she was bursting from her shell, and displayed the ivory-white wedge, like a bikini, on her bottom. "Dat her pussy! Dey *screwin'*! She soft, she got nuttin' to say. When she bustin', he pop it to her and stay on till she hard. He protectin' her! See, dey cannibals. Some oder crab eat her up when she soft if he not there. *Screwin'* "—he laughed—"and dey git caught in dat trap!"

"Dat where dat horniness git ya!" Michelle smirked. For the moment he'd quit sorting and pissed in a gleaming golden arch over the gunwale.

"Dat pussy *will* git ya in trouble," Jacques declared. "*Son!* When yo' through playin' wid yo'se'f, come on and drive.'"

The buoys were tiny in the bay, at a distance such that one could not be seen from another. The two men, father and son, traveled the waveless space between them as though submerged tracks, some invisible hold on the boat, lay below the glassy surface of the water, six concentric miles of traps, which they emptied and baited, again and again, one after the other, circling slowly toward the center. "*Somebody* been movin' *dis* one outa da way, mo' o' less," Jacques complained, angrily surveying the position of the trap in the still, vast void. When he'd grabbed and shaken out the day's last trap, he embraced it against his belly like a child. After scratching off an encrustation of barnacles, he baited it and threw it back. In the packing crate, the crabs had begun to spin slow bubbles from their gills, cloaking themselves in a watery, iridescent shroud. It was a little after noon when we sailed past the capped oil rigs in the inner bay, dead hopes that had put families out of work, and docked at the wharf near "Nigger Beach"—so-named, Michelle said, " 'cause a bunch o' niggers used to swim there." A big, bright shrimp boat crossed the harbor entrance in Miss Ginny's wake. "Damn Vietnamese!" Jacques spat.

"Dey movin' in here like rats, fishin' us all out," said Michelle with a biting voice. A federal government program, he explained, gave Vietnamese fishermen tax breaks to buy new boats and equipment, boon to immigrants, bitter insult to the Cajuns.

"A hun-ed fifty-six thousand dollar fo' a trawler like dat!" Jacques exploded. "We ain't *never* had a new boat! I tell ye, someone gonna git shot over dis one o' dese days. I find out one of 'em fishin' in my water, I smash his skull and put it in my back pocket like one o' dos shrunk thangs."

The fishery foreman on shore had pushed his chin toward the open bay and the big, new trawler and yelled, "Nobody ain't gonna let dose *Viet*-namese dock here!"

"All dis bullshit starvin' us!" Jacques growled.

"Somebody gonna git shot, I swear!" rasped Michelle.

On a scale on the back of the fishery's truck, the dockman weighed in the haul, three and a half crates, wrote out a receipt, slow day. By one the neighbor fishing men and trappers had gathered, as every afternoon, at the country store, quenching work with beer.

"Comment ça va?"

"Magnifique, may sha!"—as the Cajuns say *"mon cher." "Merci bien à la mer et à Dieu!"* exulted this old man, spicily trilling his *r*'s in the Cajun way. His chapped, happy face had been bloated by the sun. His shirt was splattered with mud and blood and fish scales. He had wild, flying whiskers and looked like a great catfish.

"Moi?" Jacques shrugged his shoulders and muttered, *"Ça va."*

Around a few old tables, and sitting on wooden crates, the bayou men told fish tales, suspended in the fascination of gossip they'd heard over and over before, then laughed uproariously, freely exchanging a kind of French for a kind of English like barter. The old man told them again about Pou-pou, the lone black trapper. "Dat ole nigger scratch till he have to quit fo' good! Git right down in da water there, try to stop dat gator snortin' puttin' he *thumbs* on da holes!"

Michelle listened to the native French uncomprehendingly, knowing, like most of the bayou's young men, words and phrases but nothing coherent.

" *'brasse mon chou!"*

"Fils putain!"

The sweat beaded on their sun-red foreheads and rolled down. They swiped it off with crushed bandannas and whistled sighs, raised their faces toward the ceiling, upending their beers. "I so hot I could fuck a nigger," one commented, belching. "Git me a little broder or a little sister! Little piece o' chocolate!"

"Sometime," Jacques said in his voice of mock, intense surprise, "*any* ass look good to me! *Looka dat ass there!*" And he swung around on the young and handsome bayou Indian who trapped with them and slapped his buttocks, while the other men whistled leeringly. "I just turn da *boys* over! You can be out in dat camp too long!" he declared with a sidewinding smile and a swig.

"In the mornin's out at de camp," Michelle whispered, and laughed, "Deddy used to grab my cousin big ole hard-on to wake him up."

On the way home, from the moving truck, Jacques and Michelle fired at bullet-riddled road signs with beer bottles as they emptied them. They could sling them up and over the roof to the opposite side of the road and hit bull's-eyes, exploding the glass. Michelle's last throw went wide. "You jist seen a miracle!" Jacques laughed and slapped his knee, swerving across lanes and crushing the shell of an armadillo. "De boy *missed!*"

This day, the last before the alligator season ended—and with it this year's chance to recoup his losses—Jacques Prudhomme caught 480 pounds of crabs, which he sold at $.27 per pound, and earned $129.60. He paid $40.00 for bait and $20.00 for fuel, on top of wear and tear on his truck and boat. Had he paid Michelle the agreed-on wage of $50.00 a day, Jacques would have made $19.60 with which to support his family and pay his bills and taxes, but Michelle wouldn't take the money. He seldom did.

That night Michelle and Adrienne, as on almost every other night, played Bingo till late. At the Knights of Columbus Hall near the town of Jeanrette, two hundred tables or more were populated beneath the fluorescent glare—French and English, Cajun whites and Creole blacks—and spread with Bingo books glued together with *bâtons de colle*, daubed with Day-Glo, sponge-tipped markers. It was an exacting, somber practice, ecstatic. Men and women, young and old, knew the letters that went with the numbers even before the letters were called, as soon as the ball was sucked into the cage and its number flashed on the digital display. Their gambling was all memorized. Their hands worked like skittish robots' as they daubed their cards, frantic to be human. The proceeds went to charity.

"I need to win me some funds," Michelle sang. "Dey say, 'Look here! Country comin' to town!' But we not very good wid our cash," he half lamented, then suddenly grew quiet, with a slow, wondering frown. "Lost *all* dat money there in Vegas. I jist keep hopin' I win big, so Deddy not have to be a fisherman anymo'."

"We wait fo' the Lawd fo' the money fo' the week," Miss Agnes had said.

The Louisiana Game Commission had allowed each trapper 110 gators this year. When Jacques set out to check his traps the last day of the season, he'd caught 53. At $50 per foot of reptile, he'd earned $19,610. The state took a full half as a gaming fee. After he'd paid his income tax, fuel and bait, and the expense of the boats and camp, he'd kept maybe $4,500 for his family. Michelle had caught forty-nine of the beasts on his own lease and earned $9,065, after the gaming fee, before his costs, which were considerably less than his father's. He'd lost $1,500 of it right away, at the beginning, when the game commission suspended the season for several days and Adrienne and he, on a lark and flush with cash, had flown away on a long fantasized weekend trip to play the casinos in Vegas. He'd lost maybe $1,000 more, maybe in fact about $1,500, on Bingo, over the couple of months. He'd given a couple of thousand to his father for survival.

By midmorning on Marsh Island, this last day, this last chance, of the alligator season, Jacques had scratched. Michelle had caught six gators on his land and still had several sloughs of traps to check.

"Here come dat seagull dat don't like us, Deddy," Michelle cried. The bird, blinding white in the rising sun, paused and whirled in a threatening rhythm above the boat, paused and whirled, with its long, sharp wings arched like a boomerang. Its siren voice pierced the hot, blue air. "He gonna start dat divin' at us again, I thank." Michelle winced. Jacques leaned back to look, his two firm chins rotating upward like movable bulwarks of stone.

The boat sat low in the water now with the weight of the catch. The rowing was ponderous. "We ain't gonna go much mo' in dis boat by itself," Michelle told his daddy. "One mo' gator gonna sink us down." Stowed in the nearby grass was a second boat, which they needed anyway to split up the work, finish the traps, and get the haul to the game warden's boat by the early afternoon, when he closed. There were tools in that spare boat, too, to fix the stalled motor.

Jacques poled the crippled boat onto shore at the "graveyard," he called it, where the small skeletons of the nutria rats they trapped each winter lay white and black and rancid in the sun. Maggots, ants, and hosts of unnamed insects plundered the tangle of bones, making it seem to quake. From this clearing walled in by the high, golden-green grass, a vile and gripping stench rose. A gator trap had been set here, too. Michelle reached into the muddy water for the line. It led, not down into the slough, but out into the marsh itself. "He take dat hook and hidin' from us back there, Deddy," Michelle said.

Jacques swiftly took up his gun, adjusting the bill of his cap to better shade his eyes from the glare of the sun. Stepping into the water almost noiselessly, he took the line from Michelle's hand and followed it gingerly so as not to tug. The gold-green growth of the marsh tufted wildly, as though it had been storm blown, then terrified in place. Side to side, with the rifle's barrel, Jacques parted the furious grass, would hesitate midpace to scour the black mud for the mud-colored reptile half-covered in it, to hear a low, mad snore or hiss. Michelle trailed him by several steps, leaving both of them room to maneuver and escape.

Suddenly Jacques tensed, slinging his eyes toward Michelle to signal a halt, then back on the spot. Like a machine, he raised the rifle to his shoulder and hunched, and laying his cheek against the muddy handle, he fired. At the crack of the bullet, screaming black birds scattered up into the sky like bugs. Then the marsh was dead still for seconds that might have been minutes or hours before Jacques, a shadow against the sun, slung the gun from his shoulder and out along his arm, like a part of his arm; curling over, with the barrel deeply invading the grass, one-armed, he fired again, but the birds had already gone. He bowed farther and for a moment disappeared. Then he stood upright, dangling the creature from a noose made of the trap line. It was a few feet long, not long, really, a few years old. From the pressure of the rope, its white cheeks puffed like an infant's. Its pouting stomach shined soft and ivory in the morning light. Except for a gentle curve as it brushed the grass, its long, graceful tail hung limp. Its legs were up and stiff against the air, the claws splayed like something stunned. Jacques strode several feet and stopped again to hold it higher with a hard, toothy grin. Silhouetted as he was, he had no eyes.

When he stood again amid the nutrias' bones, he handed the line to Michelle, who held the gator farther from himself than his father had and threw it into the empty boat. There, with the boats lodged in the mud side by side, the two men sat on the joined gunwales and tagged the tails. As one drove the knife to pierce the scales, the other held the tail tight against a sudden lash. With each new push of the knife, the animal jerked. "Dat sharp tail put a gash in yo' leg and knock yo' head silly," said Jacques. He pulled up his pant leg to show an old scar. "Even dead like he is." The bright, white mosaic of its stomach, like a lost art form, still swelled and fell, though all the others' had collapsed. "It his nerves workin'," Jacques explained. "It jist make it harder taggin' him."

Now in both boats—among plastic bottle bottoms, rusty gasoline cans, siphon tubes, oars, stray tools, a decaying life ring, and other junk of trapping all half-submerged in muddy, bloody water—the alligators lay in their death poses. A few had been thrown on their backs like discarded dolls. Several curled on their bellies like napping pets. In the sun, their shimmering, horny skin—dark, primeval iridescence—had turned as dull as chalk. Occasionally a tail, electric with the pretense of life, would whip across the metal of the boat or writhe as slowly as a body in a dream. "You better watch 'em," Jacques half warned, turning his face with one of his serious, mock looks. "Dey come alive after you shoot 'em a hun-ed times. I *seen* it!" He growled with laughter, and when I'd turned my back to him again, he gripped me on the butt with a horrendous sound and thundered with delight as I leapt from one boat to the other, wailing. "Broder, I been tellin' ye dey come alive!" he wheezed, laughing.

Michelle watched him and grinned with vacant eyes. Beside his mud-splashed boots, a big old gator curled docilely on its stomach with its long, horny snout resting on another gator's jagged tail. Its steely eyes—searing with their narrow gaze when the raging animal fought for life in the slough—stared half-lidded now, as if dazed or dozing, not quite all the light yet drained from them by death. In a ridge of the primitive creature's brow—an indentation on its green, knobby head—a brilliant pool of blood collected, fed by a wound, and, overflowing, stained its jaw crimson. Jacques had shot it, killed it with one bullet through its brain, while Michelle had worked the line and held the boat steady with the pole. Now, excited of a sudden with the several conquests of the morning or obsessed, Jacques grabbed the great gator from its rest, summoning Michelle's help to put it on display. With a hard, daring gaze and his parted lips set crooked and haughty, he grasped its bloody head above the eyes while the once powerful jaw fell agape with its useless, saw-blade rows of teeth. Michelle stood behind the beast and, with hands as strong and wide as his father's, but not so soiled with age, braced it, pulling back on its legs, the tiny scales of which glistened like lamé. He held it at a distance, his lips parted like Jacques's but with a sad smile or a half-hidden horror, as if the ruined animal were a part of him. The blinding sunlight at his back rushed through the brush of his hair, inflamed it white, a burning bush, and struck the grip of his daddy's hand like lightning. Jacques's thick fingers were sandy rough, cracked with the work of a hard lifetime. Sometime in the past, his right thumb had been torn while he fought a gator, the deep yellow nail split to its core, leaving a channel. Pressed hard as his thumb was now against the gator's wounded head, this scar ran with blood, which streamed across his hand and down his arm and drained into the slough from his elbow.

When he'd dragged the gator to the center of the boat and dropped it there for ballast, Jacques announced, "Big female." It fell belly up. "I look at 'em an' I jist know." Embedded in the ivory mosaic of the alligator's underside, above the tail, was an exquisite oval of delicate scales around a fine slit. "Dey all de same on de outside, male and female—dat same butt hole. When dey process 'em, dey stick dey finger up there inside. De oder day, some college boy gittin' his degree was checkin' 'em out, couple o' finger up dat ass. I say, '*Boy*, dat's a cold one idn' it? Dat's a *cold piece!*' An' he don't know what I'm talkin' about. Den he laugh, lookin' sorta skinned like a rat, an' say, 'Yes, sir!' " Jacques grinned, remembering that success.

"If it a male, dey feel somethin' up there," Michelle explained.

"His *pecker!*" cried Jacques. "It's a big ole thang!"

"Built-in French tickler," Michelle said, his quiet eyes teasing and lascivious.

"Dey thangs sorta fly out on de end. Sometime I wisht I had one dat big!" A laugh suspended on Jacques's face, then exploded with a roar.

"Big ole dick like dat"—Michelle furrowed his forehead and laughed—"and de po' thang's dead!"

There were twelve more traps to check, six each, before the morning ended. When Michelle at last had fixed the broken outboard, Jacques took that boat himself and disappeared into the bayou with the gun.

There was a solitary place hidden deep within the marsh Michelle loved, known as Oyster Lake. He checked his traps quickly—they were down and empty or stood untouched—and took me there. It was fed by the endless labyrinth of sloughs draining off the bayou, a place where the overflow washed. The whole of Marsh Island—a sodden demiland—seemed little more than an aberration of the sea, a lily pad that might swiftly be swept away. This "lake" was a sea within a sea, vast and mirroring, from whose center the breathless waters seemed to stretch endlessly, so invisible were its shores, burned up by the sun.

There were no sounds there—no wind across the grass, no patter of water upon the mud, no drowsy insect hums, no growl of distant motors from other trappers' boats, no terrified screams of birds. The cloudless, unending sky vibrated under the blue force of its brilliance. "It's not a bay nor nothin'," Michelle stated, hushed and enthused. "It's a lake! It's this water in the middle of the Gulf of Mexico, but completely surrounded by land!" His smile came alive here. His eyes stopped searching the empty distance as they always did when he trapped. In an instant, for this moment, he had changed—even the Cajun ellipsis of his speech, though not its sultry rhythm. At my prodding he talked some about his lover, Randy, who was a well-educated, well-off man, an economist for the state, ten years Michelle's senior. Randy had another lover, too, from a well-to-do southern family. "He spends most of his time with *him*." Michelle grimaced. "He's goin' to some college like Randy did. I *hate* that little boy," he spat. "They have all these friends that talk like college people that don't never say *nothin'* to me. Sometime he tell me, but I'm his 'cute little Cajun boy.' I hate it when he say that to me. Oh, my heart starts hurtin'." His mouth grew tight, his eyes moist and red. "I know he love me, though. I think he does," he said.

But this was not a conversation for Oyster Lake, where Michelle sought his peace, and he said no more about it. He wanted to tell me something about this place instead, then lose himself in the quiet. "I come back here all the time, all by my lonesomes," he said. He lay back in the boat, which was stopped and still. "It's so peaceful here. I roll me a joint and take off all my clothes and play wid myself." He grinned mischievously, slowly. "And Deddy, not nobody, know I'm back here. Nobody watchin' me, nobody sayin' nothin'. Jist me"—he laughed and flicked his brow—"and some cute boy in my head I'm thankin' about." The grassy tangle of sloughs around the lake had seemed too close—no way out, no way in. We smoked a joint and watched the sky for a long time.

Suddenly, as though somebody had tapped him on the shoulder, Michelle startled and checked his watch. "Deddy be waitin'," he said, a dead panic in his voice. "I don't want no explainin' to do. Maybe he waitin' fo' help." He pulled the ignition rope, and the sky and endless water shattered with sound.

Michelle knew the precise grass covert in the maze of

sloughs where his daddy would be waiting. Before we could reach it, though, Jacques came rushing toward us with a harried, irked look suffusing his red face, turned back, cast a wake so close to Michelle's boat it seemed a retribution, then sped away. In advance of the place where the last trap was set, he slowed and sternly threw up his hand. Michelle lit a cigarette, held it in his teeth with parted lips, like a hot bullet, his eyes beginning to scour the shore. Both men turned off their motors and tilted them out of the water, let the boats glide, then halted them with their poles when the trap was almost upon them.

"He in de grass there, son," Jacques snapped, hushed and rasping, with an extra scowl as if to ask him where the hell he'd been, to warn him they'd take it up later.

In this cul-de-sac of the slough, the still air rumbled with mad, low snores, a watery, death-defying anger, building, a flood unreleased yet, awaiting its time. Jacques pointed more precisely to the spot, the direction of his hand falling from the fiery golden blossoms of the grass, down the burning green stems to the shadows of mud. There, the huge, horny back of an alligator humped above the dirty water, like a moldy, stuck log, motionless but for its sound. Its dark dragon's snout lay half-submerged. Its sharp eyes glared. Around its head, the slimy water of the slough storm-clouded with blood.

"I git him once, but he *charge*," Jacques whispered.

The water shook with the reptile's breathing. Michelle slowly poled around to the stem of the trap and checked the line as his daddy grounded his own boat in the mud out of range of the powerful tail, then took up his gun against his shoulder and aimed. For the moment before he fired, there was only the sawing of mosquitoes on the air and the nervous scratchings of crickets and the wet, mad thunder that rose from the wounded monster's breast. Then the bullet cracked, and that eternal chorus of crying birds flew from the grass, like black spirits tearing at themselves. Jacques's boat rocked. The beast sprang from the water with a thunderous roar, its great pink mouth lunging, its leviathan tail beating the water and air with a fury that would bring the world down. Jacques caught his gun and fired again, but the alligator would not be subdued.

Michelle held tight on the line while the air darkened with slime and glittered with green diamonds of water against the white sun. Jacques crouched in the boat so he would not fall and shot again, then again, and for a moment the gator seemed stunned, before suddenly it began to whip about and fling itself over and over in the water, like an outraged spool, a furious machine, until it was wholly wrapped in ropes of grass and the trap line. The green water turned to carbon black with the mud the animal tore from the bottom and was laced black red with blood. The huge, webbed claws, like a diving bird's, tore wildly at the air. Then, with another explosion from Jacques's gun, they grasped and fell still. Jacques shot it again for good measure.

Michelle drew in the line, hauling the gator through the water until its head, dripping with blood and slime and grass, lay like a sea monster's beside the boat. Grabbing it by its shimmering legs, the trappers pulled their prey over the gunwale and cast it crosswise, with its jaw turned up and resting against the other side. They were slimy with weeds and mud. But no sooner had they sat down to catch their breath than the tail whiplashed and the jaw snapped again.

"*I swear, boy!*" Jacques spat, huffing with disgust and scowling, "dis'n one o' dose come *alive!*"

He swept up his gun and, with his son standing beside him, dropped the end of the barrel to the one soft place behind the animal's steel-hard skull where the shot would penetrate fully and ravage the brain. As the bullet rushed in, the huge animal leapt— arching its head and spreading its front claws, as though it would jump from the boat and run through the grass for its life—and all of a sudden Michelle groaned horribly and threw his hand to his bleeding eye, where a ricochet from the alligator's stony skull had struck him and lodged.

"Where *were* you, boy, when I needed ya here? Gittin' lost somewhere?" Jacques demanded, pulling the shard from Michelle's eye.

For supper at home that night, Miss Agnes served fried shrimp, a crab casserole—all fish they'd caught—hush puppies, onion rings, and French fries. The casserole was "pepper," Cajun hot. Anne, the oldest daughter, was there with her three small girls in bows and frilly play clothes. One of them carried a Barbie doll in a business suit with a tiny attaché and a miniature credit card. She wanted to be like that, she said, when she grew up. Uncle Michelle had played with them before the meal and had given them live crabs he'd kept from yesterday's catch. They asked him why he had a patch on his head. "Papaw"—he grinned—"thank I'm an alligator and shoot me." Which turned their faces to sad confusion till he told them he was teasing.

Around the table, Jacques told the story of the gator that didn't get away, as he would again and again at the country store, and everyone was chattering around him with frantic interest in this last day's trapping. Miss Agnes had baked a magnificent gingerbread house for her granddaughters and passed around an album of pictures of the fancy cakes she sometimes made, for friends or for sale. There was a basketball court, a military camp with bridges and a motorcycle caught in mud, and a barnyard of exquisite detail. "Ain't they *somethin'*!" Michelle beamed. "Mama a real artist!"

"*Michelle*," announced Amelie with a teasing drawl, in the midst of this chaos. Her voice was neither rank with malice nor free of hostile provocation. The family waited. "You asht me about dat beach I heerd sump'n about. Dey some *real cute boys* down there fo' ya I found."

Adrienne cast her bright, frightened eyes around the table, while Anne fussed with her children for nothing at all. Jacques had dropped his face toward his plate and dug back in, as though no one had said anything. Miss Anges's jaw went tight, and she passed the shrimp, rapidly saying things about the spices she put in her food.

Michelle looked at his sister with a sickening smile and sad, admonishing eyes. The whites were filled with blood.

At first it seemed to me that I'd never met a man whose sexuality—whose life itself—was as trapped as Michelle's. But as I drove away the next day thinking about the lives of the men I'd met in my travels—of all the men I'd ever known—his life seemed true of all of us.

CHAPTER 13

BORDERLINES
AND
WHEAT
BELTS

THE DAY I LEFT MICHELLE, I WENT TO NEW ORLEANS AND FOR three days wandered the French Quarter sampling the twenty-four-hour gay bars. There were safe-sex posters everywhere, though amid the raucous drinking and unabashed drug sales I suspected that they counted perhaps for nothing. I slept at a gay bathhouse because it was cheap. Rubbers were freely dispensed in bowls, but I saw few takers. Michelle himself had sometimes been a frequent patron there—and once had taken a job as the front desk clerk. Floating in Oyster Lake the week before, he had spoken to me of his idea of safe sex. He didn't like to fuck with condoms, preferring simply to pull out before he came—or have his partner do the same. I wondered at his trust in the timing of ejaculations, which seemed to me too much faith in the heat of passion. Still, he understood the basics—the danger of exchanging semen. Perhaps he knew enough to save his life—who could say?—though not enough to save himself from a rash of unreasonable fears. He had a friend who had once developed a persist ent case of hiccups and believed he therefore had AIDS. Michelle was terrified of getting them.

After New Orleans I had planned to visit Texas, but suddenly my would-be hosts were out of town or otherwise unavailable. I decided to roam, driving first to San Antonio to see the Alamo, then farther down to Laredo because it struck me perversely as a border place, nowhere.

Texas was a vacant land of poisonous exhaust and stinging haze. Heading south, I learned that Texans drove through their fumes in erratic herds, cantering below the limit, then, panicky, stampeding the width of the freeway. Displaying the common purpose of a breed, they surrounded and crowded in alien license plates, subjecting them to this frightful, equine sort of whimsy. Alien drivers felt the terror. I watched a car from Maryland break away, weaving shockingly. In the sweltering glare of the sun the Sunday I drove from San Antonio to Laredo, the Texan herds sped with their headlights shining, proselytizing for safe driving, a peculiarly empty American kind of gesture, warning others to do good. The highway patrol, rescuing souls from a plague of broken cars, let speeders go. Whole Mexican families stood in the steam of a furious, gaping hood or knelt on the edge of the traffic, offering up their lives to change a flat.

Deep into the Texan tip, the desert sat empty with prickly pears (which needled the cranky posts of barbed-wire fences) and yucca and bald, bony bushes that clung to the sand. A single line of train tracks glistened as though it would warp, and the traffic died in a black rubber trail of blown tires. The once grazing head of an oil well, like a heat-stunned horse's, stood unmoving in a pasture parched with white dirt. *"I've had all I can stand. . . . Dixieland,"* bristled the radio.

At the red-earth rodeo at Encinal, a white-and-silver Greyhound marked "Laredo" glinted by, exhaling bright, hot wind, and a three-car caravan of Mexicans fed their children in the blinding shade at a rest stop. Past the *No Hacer*—the "Do Nothing"—Ranch, a northbound roadblock searched for *chicanos* like contraband. A road sign gave the mileage to Monterrey, deep within Mexico. A billboard hawked "Mexico insurance" for

American cars crossing the border. In the face of the sun, a high quarter moon chicken-pocked the sky.

At that hottest hour of the Texas July afternoon when nothing was sufferable but sleep, I checked into a triple A–approved motel in Laredo. Its cracked pink concrete walls and the dusty mirrors of its windows swam in the heat by a mossy swimming pool. This was on San Bernardo Street, the thoroughfare across the Rio Grande. The furniture in the gloomy room was "Mediterranean"-styled, warped plastic and shredded veneer. The drapes were sun-cancered, the shaggy carpet dank and dirty as mold. A leaky air conditioner mildewed the air. The black nap of fungi fanned across the bathroom walls.

The gay guides I had read made no reference to Laredo. When darkness fell and colored lights beaded the night like a festival, I set out to find clues, cruising the streets for "adult bookstores" and dark plazas. In a gravel lot near my motel, a windowless cinder-block store offered triple-X movies. A sebaceous fat man with glutinous black hair took money at a wrecked metal desk by the door—two dollars for the films behind the curtain. There, in a sweltering dark room, the musty air palpitated with a woman's dubbed sighs while the blue miasma of a television screen flickered against a disarray of folding chairs.

"¿Hay películas para maricones?"—"Do you show films for fags?"—I asked the clerk.

"Aquí, no," he answered absently, his eyes fixed on a Mexican sitcom on a little black-and-white TV.

"¿Adónde van los homosexuales?"—"Where do homosexuals meet?"

Across the bridge in Mexico, he said, on the other side of the plaza. A policeman in Nuevo Laredo could give me directions.

The banks of the Rio Grande in Laredo and the entrance to the downtown bridge across the border were barricaded with chainlink fences and razor wire, the steel-and-water curtain. By night the pavement, high above the spotlit, shallow river, was bright with the stark orange light of sodium vapor lamps. Loud, white gringos passed easily in both directions, bumper to bumper in cars, crowds on foot: a ceaseless pink-faced stream of *yanqui* youngsters, burdened with back loads of bargain liquor and souvenirs, euphoric with drinking and dollars and dominance. Guards on the U.S. side, sullen as jailers, detained dark-fleshed transients longer than they did the white folk, keen for a hint of Latin accent, tedious with questions. Disheveled Mexicans hunkered sleeping on the sidewalk in the middle of the bridge, queued for day work in the morning in Laredo. Others, and ragged bands of children, begged. Competing mariachis, grinning with poverty, played for coins—a carnival of despair. Tonight, near the checkpoint on the American side, the armed guards stared down on a huddle of Mexican men who crouched on the pavement in the shadow of a customs van. The sordid orange light that leaked from the bridge fell on a young man's face that stopped me cold. His eyes held mine, erotic with desperation.

Over two hundred thousand people now lived in Nuevo Laredo, more than twice Laredo's population in less than half the space. Squat, squalid concrete facades made moats of foul streets, which lay awash in the spill of sordid light from gaping doors, rank with the stench of bitter meats, hot sewage, and stale liquor. The loud air weltered in feverish rhythms, frantic trumpet syncopations and rapid guitars, jukeboxes, and live bands. Below the tall, dark palms of the central plaza, vendors (trinkets, fried foods, minutes of sex) noisily crowded *turistas* staggering with the pleasures of decay.

On the Mexican side, I explored the town. In a corner of the plaza, an adolescent offered his brother for sale—*"tiene once años"*—eleven years old. He led me to a dark, hot alley that whispered with rats, where the child would fuck me, he said, for ten dollars, five, three, or two. The boy himself could not be fucked. *"No es un maricón. . . ."* He wasn't a fag. The older brother pled with me to make a deal while I turned away, while the younger boy stood macho and silent.

Nearby, a dirty bar opened onto the plaza. Its patrons were all poor men sweating in sawdust that rose from the floor. A haze of foul yellow light fell from the ceiling. Thirsty with the taste of salt and lime, they inflamed themselves with tequila and beer, laughed and made wagers, sang hot and alone, talked lustfully of women. Hilarious, they embraced to dance. They were not gay. Getting drunk, I watched their passionate bond and felt their need, wondered at their near fulfillment of desire.

On the plaza, a policeman in a black-patent cap gave me careful directions to the bars where *maricones* congregated. La Cava—the Cave, the most popular bar, the officer explained—was on the far side of the square. I went there directly. It was un-marked, cozy, dark, enclosed (air-conditioned), slick in design, with an alley of booths between the walls. The patrons—young, well dressed, a mixture of macho and gay—watched a mounted television playing late night movies. It was an hour earlier here than in Texas.

La Cava was crowded by midnight. The patrons' manners were flamboyant and meticulous. Standing alone in a crowd at the bar, I ordered a drink. There Eduardo slowly introduced himself to me. He was strong and masculine, dark and wonderfully hand-some, ruggedly self-possessed in cowboy boots and jeans. A wealthy Mexican, he was privileged with identification papers and offered to drive me back across the bridge when I wanted to leave. He was going to the United States anyway. He had keys to a former lover's apartment in Laredo where he sometimes spent weekends and would sleep tonight. We talked there.

In Nuevo Laredo he lived with his parents. *"No tengo esposa,"* he explained. "I'm not married." He was twenty-six. His father was a rancher and a merchant who owned department stores. Eduardo worked on the family ranch. *"Es diferente aquí."* "In Mexico," he said, "homosexuality is different." He had just turned nineteen the first time he had sex with a man. "A close friend, *de niños.*" From childhood. They'd gotten into a fistfight. His friend, who was beaten and bleeding, said, "I love you." Then they'd made love. "All of my friends are careful," Eduardo said. "Most are married."

"Do you have a girlfriend?" I asked.

"No," he said. "But no one knows about me."

"Will you marry?"

"*No sería justo a ella.*" "It wouldn't be fair to her. She wouldn't have a whole man."

"Maybe life with a man would make you happier," I answered.

My sentiment seemed to rouse in him a deeper need. He reversed himself. "No," he resolved. "Someday I will marry. I want to fill my house with children."

It was morning when Eduardo and I stopped talking. I went back to my motel and slept until the afternoon, then drove north, toward Oklahoma, where I'd arranged to be the next day. I found an old and indirect route to San Antonio that ran in an arc to the west of the interstate. This was the sole road through the nothingness fugitives must first cross when they swim the river from Mexico into the United States, and I wanted to see it, to feel its weight. Here, beneath the late sun, the heat had settled like a caustic drug and the desert lay red and stricken, a crusted pool of blood. Rusty barbed wire and gaunt, bone white posts fenced the highway for miles upon empty miles. A desolate general store sat broken in a yard of dust half an hour down the road. I wanted to call home to my lover in New York, to let him know my progress. An unsmiling, sturdy woman with ill-mannered children worked the place.

"Do you have a public phone?" I asked, standing outside the crippled screen door.

"We don't even have a *private* phone," she drawled dryly. "You seen any lines out there?"

I hadn't.

Some ways from there, when the sun burned deep into the vast horizon and the earth was veiled with flame and purple shadows, there appeared beside the road three brown faces peering from behind the branches of a cactus. In the rearview mirror, I watched them watch me pass. I turned and went back. There were five men in all. Two of them lay sick in the dust, a very old man and a young one. The three standing men froze at my approach, their shoulders crouched like frightened dogs. They were dirty, their black hair hung in oily strands, their faces were scarred with sunburn, bloodier for the deadly color of the sky. They had no provisions or bags. Their clothes were ragged. "*¿Necesitan ustedes ayuda?*" I asked. "Is there some way I can help you?" The youngest barely nodded his head, tensed to escape. "I'm not the police," I said.

The standing trio glanced at one another warily. "*Gracias,*" the youngest finally whispered.

This boy could not have been more than fifteen or sixteen years old. He was thin and stared with wan, red hunger in his eyes. His dirty hair hung to his shoulders. Several days' growth of boyish beard stubbled his hollow cheeks and his chin. Jesús was his name. He was their diffident spokesman. They'd come, he said, from Monterrey, more than two hundred miles away, and were traveling to San Antonio for work. They'd been walking five days in this parched wilderness since crossing the river, where they told me they'd narrowly fled the grasp of El Catán—the huge alligator gar said to swim the Rio Grande, snout like a gator, body like a fish. (Here the others murmured wide-eyed affirmations.) For three days they hadn't had food or fresh water, Jesús explained, except what they had scavenged from plants in the desert. Last night when they'd stopped to sleep, *el viejo*—the old one—and Jesús' younger brother had broken open a cactus and drunk its juice, which was spoiled or poisonous. It was then they'd fallen ill, though they'd been sick with thirst before this *mala suerte*, this evil luck, struck them. They'd vomited green and cried until morning. The others had helped them walk and sometimes carried them on their shoulders. "You can see," Jesús said, "still they are sick and crying, but they are not vomiting now. They are past vomiting." The men, curled like babies and grasping their stomachs, moaned feebly at our feet.

"I will take you to a doctor." The three men started, and I thought they might run. "*No!*" I hastened. A doctor might call the police. "It will be fine. What is it you want?"

"We are going to San Antonio," said Jesús. "Are you going there?"

"We're near a town." I hesitated. "I'll take you there and buy you food." I was afraid to take them farther. I'd been stopped at a roadblock in New Mexico north of Las Cruces in June and the car had been searched. I was on the interstate then, on the fastest fugitive route from Ciudad Juárez to Albuquerque. One man's warnings in Laredo were fresher yet. "They'll arrest you and impound your truck," he'd said, "if they catch you transporting aliens. They love it. It's good press."

I drove the three ambulatory men to a little store and told them to get what they needed. They gathered junk food from the shelves like shy children—processed-cheese spreads, loaves of gluey white bread, cellophane-wrapped cakes, Coca-Cola. It came to twenty dollars. Then I took them back to their felled companions and their safe place behind the cactus and left them there.

I drove for maybe ten miles, sick with my conscience, before I resolved to go back and get them again, angry at American laws that fostered inhumanity, terrified at my willingness to acquiesce. The three healthy men were eating, urging the other two to sip Coke. I was stern in my instructions to them: all but Jesús must lie flat in the bed of the truck. Soon we would be passing through small towns. They must not raise their heads. Jesús would sit with me up front. He said he'd done this before and been caught. He would help me decide what to do if we met a roadblock. More than anything, I wanted to talk to him and learn about these men's lives.

The five men had not been friends in Monterrey or, except for Jesús and his brother, even known each other before beginning their journey. Nor were they all even from the same city. They'd met on the bus to Piedras Negras, Black Rocks, where they'd swum the river and survived the alligator gar. Jesús demeaned the two *viejos*. "They are old peasants and stupid." The *viejos* had not known the laws of crossing the desert, had used up the provisions of food and water in the first two days, had been a terrible drag on the progress. These men's bond went no further than the act of their escape—from the bondage of Mexican poverty to the freedom of dollars—a slender and unequal obligation, though inexorable, inexplicable in the burden of common identity it had suddenly imposed on them. They had not belonged to one another in Mexico, they would not belong to each other after they arrived in San Antonio, only now. Arrival re-shapes our loyalties or dissolves them altogether. "My brother and I," said Jesús, "know countrymen there who will know where there is work. They have a house where we can stay. *Los viejos* and the young one must find their own way."

Jesús spoke sporadically and shyly and only when I asked him questions. He never smiled; his pale voice was raspy and ex-hausted. There were long silences when we talked. Mostly he looked straight ahead, as if searching for the tiniest danger. Some-times, though, in the failing twilight, I could see him, feel him stealing looks at me, watching my face, his eyes meeting the cor-ners of mine with some longing that was oblique and undefined. When night fell he pressed his face against the rear window and determined that his companions were asleep. He slumped and hugged the door. It seemed to me that he too had gone to sleep. For a moment I drove with only my left hand on the steering wheel, resting my right hand on the seat. I felt as though I were suspended in a flying, silent dream, in the steady hushed rush of warm, dry wind through the windows of the truck, in the rushing hot perfume of cleanliness in the black air, in the black and tor-rential emptiness of the desert night. Slowly, out of the envelop-ing darkness, I felt Jesús' hand, small and nervous, cover mine. His rough fingers reached beneath my palm and, like a lover's, closed softly.

His grasp filled me with wonder and somehow did not startle me. In the warm black solitudes where social strictures are lost and identities have no power, I had shared that kind of intimacy with other men from whom I had not expected it—there, where friendship or gratitude or sorrow or joy, the profound emotions alone, determined our need and the moment between us. I did not question whether Jesús was "gay" or his intimacy "sexual." Men and women go mad for fear of the meaning in a touch.

From San Antonio it took another day to reach the Oklahoma border. Oklahoma is shaped like a handgun. With its barrel braced on the Texas Panhandle and squeezed below western Kan-sas and Colorado's eastern extreme, it fires into the forehead of

New Mexico. Its farthest aim is New Mexico's Rockies, where even so far away one can see huge storm clouds rise from the peaks and sail toward Oklahoma like catastrophes.

In Oklahoma I was lodging with Frank Reinhardt. When I first met Frank at the Denver rodeo, he told me only that his lover had been "gay-bashed to death." He said he owned a gay bar in town and a horse farm outside Oklahoma City. He invited me to be his guest.

Now he was stark about his lover's death. He said Wayne's pickup truck was empty when he found it, but blood had been smeared like mud inside the cab. "All over. On the ceilin'. Like someone smeared it with their hands. When I opened the door, before I saw anything, I knew somethin' was wrong." That had been on a Monday, I was sure he had told me. Wayne had been missing for more than a day by then. It was a fortnight yet before some street repairmen from the city found the body. "Out to the gravel pit, December 23. It's not the kind of place they go diggin' ever' day. In retrospect, I shouldn'ta refused to go to the morgue and identify him. The corpse—well, I'll be frank—wasn't too decayed. It'd been cold for a coupla weeks, so it was perty well preserved. But I really couldn't stand to see him." It was then, right after that, that Frank had called the police himself and asked for a lie detector test.

It was on Tuesday morning, the second day of my stay, that Frank began to divulge so much to me. I'd slept late, tired from a long night dancing at Frank's bar, which was strictly a two-stepping place. Frank had gotten up early, as he always did, to tend to chores. Midmorning he fixed me breakfast. The kitchen was still a mess from the night before and Frank's own breakfast at daybreak. An iron skillet of thick yellow grease sat on the stove and a cold pot of coffee. The sink was stacked with dirty, half-rinsed dishes. Frank avoided the old chaos and instead cooked eggs and bacon in the microwave. I sat up to the breakfast counter, which divided the living room and kitchen. The brass seats of the stools were molded like saddles—a house made by the love of horses. "The plum jelly's fresh made this summer," Frank said, setting a plate of white toast before me. The jelly, sweet and pink, was from the plum trees in his yard.

"That was on a *Monday* when you found Wayne's truck?" I asked, as I often had about some detail or another these last two days, trying to allay my confusion and get the story straight.

"That would've been Wednesday, I think," he stated, as if to confirm precisely what he'd said before. He spoke with a tone of cold common sense. "There's a forty-eight-hour wait before you can file a missing persons report with the police. So there wouldn't've been any use to go and check on the pickup as soon as Monday." It was as if his grief had been moderated by state law and police regulations. But Wayne's murder was an old crime now, near-ly seven years stale. Here and there threads of the plot or anguished feeling seemed to have unraveled in the cobweb of its horror.

Frank had first begun to tell me about Wayne's death the night I got there. It was already long after midnight when I ar-rived. I'd gotten lost on the way. Frank lived northwest of Okla-homa City, on farmland that lay in a vast, flat conundrum of country roads and unpaved lanes, wooded land, and dark, turning creeks. There were no road signs. There was no moonlight. I ran into black dead ends at woods and streams. Frank had waited up, going over farm and rodeo business in his reading chair. Through the living room window, as I climbed the porch steps, he looked mustardy and warm in the light that washed through the shade of an old floor lamp. Wearing a soiled trucker's cap, he gave me a snack and a beer and had gotten only so far in the tale as to say, "The police told me I was a prime suspect," before he suggested I get some rest. I slept in the downstairs bedroom, whose window opened onto the stable yard and corral. The old four-poster bed sat across from a high, dark wardrobe topped by a tumult of frayed, straw cowboy hats and toppling stacks of trucker's caps, tucked tightly inside each other. I listened to the night and could not sleep.

The enormous acreage of Frank's farm with its Gothic clap-board house had been inherited from "Doc," the doctor Frank had once had an intimate relationship with, though their close-ness, Frank told me, was never romantic. That was 1961, and

Frank had just gotten out of the navy. "I fell in love with a horse trainer," he explained, showing me the farm the first morning of my visit. "Sold my house and chased him to Tennessee. Found a job cuttin' tobacco. *That-is-damn-sticky-back-breakin'-work!*" he percussed like the hot prairie wind. "I did it *one* day and moved back home. That's when Doc and me met. We got to be good friends, but we couldn't be lovers. I couldn't do anything about his drinkin'. He loved drinkin'. It was a year after I came home that I met Wayne. Besides, Doc didn't live all that long."

Even before Doc took ill, Frank believed, he knew he was going to die soon. "He told me," Frank said, " 'If I ever have a stroke, put me so far back in a nursing home no one can see me.' You know you get sick with ever'thing when you drink like that!" One morning in 1979, when Frank had phoned his friend's office, the nurse told him Doc had gone home with a 107-degree temperature, as Frank recalled it—though certainly a man would be delirious or comatose with such a fever. Frank said then that he'd called Doc at home and woken him from his stupor. "When I called him up again later to see how he was, the phone was busy. I went right over. I knew something was wrong before I got there," Frank said, eerily echoing the statement he'd make about finding Wayne's bloody pickup. "Doc was on the floor. He wasn't coherent at all. I called Wayne and another friend, and we took him to the hospital. The nurse at his office always said, 'He's so much better when *you're* with him.' His sisters liked to have stared daggers when they heard that. I finally went over to his clinic across the street to take a nap. They called and said he died. I cleaned all the gay stuff out of his house before the family got into it. When they checked the will, they said, 'Well, *you* got ever'thing!' They took me to court over it and bargained me down—oil leases the family'd owned. Even wanted the gifts back they had given him, some silverware. I said, 'That's ridiculous.' But I didn't want his name smeared in court." Frank had gotten all Doc's land and had begun buying horses with Wayne. The year after that, Wayne died.

Frank walked me across the inherited land. At the farm's peak, he had stabled forty-three Arabians—quarter horses and

Thoroughbreds—but now he was down to eight. A filly weanling gamboled with its mother and a skittish colt in the small corral. She coquetted with Frank and nudged his face. Nervous plumes of dust from the infant horse's hooves ascended in hot gusts of grasslands wind, ghosting the face of the sun. The mare intruded on Frank's affections and whinnied, shivering and lashing her tail against the stings of gnats and flies. He stroked her forehead, ran his fingers through her mane. In the droughty field behind the barn grazed a paint, a bay, a gray, and a dappled gray. A tiger gold cat narrowly pulsed across the fence. Bull, a dog belonging to two gay neighbors, had been killing Frank's cats, but this one—already sledged by a hammer and run over by a tractor and a car—would not die.

In the stables, a sitting hen pecked the air like a slow machine. As Frank drew near, she shrieked and stabbed the walls of the cardboard box where she nested. Suddenly, squawking, she leapt out and beat the sawdust floor with her wings. An empty egg stank in the nest like vomit. Two others lay half-hatched and chirping, protruding tiny, bloody beaks.

Frank had lost fourteen head of his dwindling stock of horses at market in Los Angeles. "Four of 'em with babies," he said, grimacing dryly. He'd paid three hundred dollars to enter each of the animals for sale, three hundred per month to board them. "Crooks neglected 'em so bad you could feel their ribs when you laid your fingers on 'em." He'd found one of the mares licking the sweat off a water pipe to survive. "Had to destroy ever' damn one."

Wayne had not been long dead then. The murder had not been solved. Rumors lingered. On the last morning of my visit, over breakfast, I tried to piece together the story. "It was a Sunday," Frank drawled, reading the *Oklahoman* for horse show news. "Pearl Harbor Day 1980." He spoke with a relentlessly distracted air, seamlessly. His voice moved with paced determination, no fissures of speech for questions. "Wayne went to church. He went every week and took his retarded sister from the mental home and his sister-in-law. Her husband was killed the year before Wayne—he was a security guard at the airport. It was a controversial thing because he wrastled an Indian woman to the ground at work and she shot him.

"We were gettin' ready to go to a party at Betsy's house, a good woman friend of ours. I went early to help her out. I got drunk. I was perty well looped by the time everyone got there and went on home to sleep. Wayne stayed. Around two A.M.—yeah, it *had* to be before two because the party had broken up—I noticed Wayne wasn't home yet. I called Betsy. She said he'd left already. I thought he must have had a wreck. It was rainin' awful bad. I drove the road, but there wasn't a sign of him. In the mornin' I called an auto insurance salesman friend of mine—he's gay—and told him I needed help. An hour later we talked again—he had friends in the police department. He told me the police couldn't do anything to help me before I reported a missing person. I asked him to stop and check the Union 76 on I-40. But he didn't see anything. I checked I-35, north of town. I figured Wayne mighta stopped at a truck stop to cruise. He was drunk. There was always lots of sex there—the truckers, in the johns. There were motel rooms.

"There was that forty-eight-hour wait and all for missing persons, and then on Wednesday I went to check out I-40 myself. I checked the toilets and the rooms. That's when I saw his pickup sittin' there, on my way back to the car. I saw the blood first, then the bullet hole in the ceiling, but it didn't go through the roof, just a bump like someone had jabbed it or stabbed it or somethin'. The police took me down to the station afterward and kept me there all day—they asked me if I'd agree to take a lie detector test. I said sure.

"The family all knew about us and ever'thing. Then I found out from Wayne's nephew—he was Wayne's age—his family thought I killed him, too. I just stopped havin' anything to do with 'em.

"The funeral made me real mad," Frank said with a hollow, dry voice, like something a long time buried. "The preacher preached against homosexuality. I think the family told him to. That church is always yelpin' for money. But let me tell ya, if they go broke, it's empty hearts, not pockets.

"My dad was great, stayed by me through the whole thing. The only thing he said was, 'Son, I wish you'd get on the other side of the fence.' I told him, 'Dad, I may be able to sit on top of the fence and do nothin' either way. But I can't go on the other side.' "

It was getting toward noon. There was paperwork for the rodeo Frank had to get done. Unceremoniously he invited me along with him to his office in the stables—a small, fluorescent-lit, windowless room. He tabulated ledger columns on an adding machine, received and made phone calls, while continuing the story of Wayne's murder. The police, he said, had checked his guns, searched the farm, and soon had dropped the case against him. Six months passed before there was any progress. "*About* six months," Frank remarked. "That's a rough guess. I was talking to Betsy a while ago and she said those are the kinds of things we try to forget." And I wondered whether I would have forgotten— whether my interest in a lover's murder could become so dull. "The guy they pinned it on was named Lucas—that's his last name. For the life of me I can't remember what his first name is." Frank furrowed his face, impassive.

Lucas, as Frank remembered, was a serial killer already in prison in Texas when he confessed to murdering Wayne with a drifter, now in a Florida prison. "I don't know whether they went ahead and accepted his confession just to clear it up and close the file," Frank began, then stalled to return a phone call (a gay cowboy pissed that the rodeo had been booked at an arena in "nigger town"). "I did wonder about it, though," he continued in the same unengaged, otherwise preoccupied voice. "Wondered whether I could have done such a thing. When I told my dad I was a prime suspect, he said, 'Is there any possibility you killed him?' He took me through it step by step, where I was, what I did. You know, could I have done it, shot him several times, brought him to the dump, then had a blackout about it? You think those things. Was I capable of doin' a thing like that?"

From the silence of the stables came a long, drawling cry—a cheer or call for help. "*Yo-o-o-o, Frank!*" A stable hand burst through the door with a sweaty wind of ripe manure and hay.

One of the mares had somehow gotten wounded and needed to be bandaged up. I stayed inside, but, craning my neck in a certain way, I watched Frank gently lift the old mare's leg and caress it while he probed a barbed-wire rip in her flesh.

When he returned he set back to work at the adding machine, a cascade of inarticulate tallies. For several minutes he said nothing. Then, with an abstract air, he raised his head. "That ole hen we saw out there?" he said. "The one with the chicks hatchin' yesterday?" The day before, while she shrieked, we had touched her eggs. Now both of her chicks were dead. Mad that we had disturbed her nest, the mother had turned her babies down into an airless clump of rags and sat on them until they suffocated.

Jim Boren and Ray Pritchett were rodeo friends of Frank's in the western Oklahoma panhandle, where Jim had been born and raised. They'd just celebrated their first anniversary when we met, though no one where they lived—neither friends nor family—knew they were gay. On the late July afternoon I visited them, we stood on a sunny, grassy knoll at the North Canadian River and, five hundred miles removed from the mountains, watched a front begin to surge across the Great Plains. A high cold surf on the distant horizon had begun to swell across a vast, yellow grass sea. Jim had watched the signs in the sky above this earth throughout his life. His family had always owned these eight hundred acres—now mostly wheat, credos of wheat—ever since this endless geography was taken from the Indians. Two iron plaques along Highway 3, in the wheatlands northwest of Oklahoma City, told part of his family's story, marking the eastern boundaries of the land runs of 1889 and 1892. His grandfather's kin had come in the first rush, his grandmother's in the second, all of them from the newly made states of Iowa and Illinois.

"Dad has one old deed," Jim recalled, "that says, 'Choctaw and Chickasaw Nations, Indian Territory, one hundred and sixty acres ceded.' " It was signed by the principal chief of the Choctaw Nation and the governor of the Chickasaw Nation in 1904 and bore the government's approval.

To the west of the knoll from which Jim surveyed his land, a plum thicket fell away, food for birds, the cows, the coyotes. Midway down, on the east side, a dilapidated house shouldered into the ground, its gaping lean-to roof and squat walls uncovering iron bed frames and woodstoves rusting there since the Dust Bowl. A buzzard cooled its wings on the ruins of the chimney, feathering the brick with shadows. At our approach a big white bird—a turkey, maybe? a wild chicken?—flapped into a cellar, skittish as a hermit. Jim lit an oily rag and descended. In the black underground its wings cast back the dirty orange glow of the flames, but its species remained indecipherable. It shrieked and huddled against the mud walls of the corner. Jim's father and grandfather had been born here. On swells in the nearby fields, two others of the family's pioneer homes leaned at wounded angles to the ground, stabbed with brush and weeds, speared by platinum sunlight, gray skeletons against the wide sky. The wind pump was pneumonic. Only the one-room school sat white and perfect off the dirt road through the fields. Jim had gone to grade school there, as had his father and mother before him. His nieces and nephews went there now, and if he had ever had any, his own children would go there, too. This land held his life like a history.

"The abstracts on some of these fields is *three inches* thick," said Ray. When Ray had moved from the city to live with Jim, he'd gotten a job with a country lawyer processing deeds. Each township carved from the old Indian nations had been documented for a century, down to the last half acre. Each owner and his mortgages and liens, the sheriff's seizures, inheritances, divorces and lawsuits, oil and mineral surveys and water rights, which over the years had often been sold off separately from the use of the surface soil: every jot of commerce and family history, every rumor that controlled the land, had to be tried and judged on the evidence of the registered abstracts before any parcel could change hands. In red dirt fields from which the wheat already had been harvested grazed the slow heads of oil wells in which Jim's family had shared. "Every place you can step your foot is stipified," Ray put it, "in the abstracts. You might own ever'thing, but there's some old lease or someone's well on a part of your land. Well, you're gonna just have to plow around it."

Black-and-yellow monarch butterflies kaleidoscoped the air and hung themselves like silk blossoms from the wiry branches of the blackjacks and the chinaberry bushes. Along a path to the pasture, Jim tore out a patch of devil's claw, whose soft, rank leaves spoiled the milk of grazing cows, whose claws wrapped their legs like chains. An unseen coven of cicadas haunted the brush with their heated chirping, like an omnivorous warning of invasion. Hidden, they ate the leaves and left behind translucent shells.

Ray's own past had been all but devoured long before he'd come to the farm to live with Jim. He'd left behind the disliked society of "queers," as he put it, in Oklahoma City. He'd left behind a sister there, too, a Pentecostal preacher's wife. He'd fled from the rest of his family more than fourteen years ago, abandoned them to their tiny hometown in the sparse panhandle, near Liberal, in Kansas, to their stifling, euphoric religion.

There was always an archness in Ray's voice, and acid suspicion of the world, though the cause of it lay largely hidden: Ray did not even talk about himself in front of Jim. "A lot of this Jim don't know," he warned me. Late in the day he began to confide in me while standing in the kitchen of their trailer home in town while Jim went to pick up a bushel of corn at his folk's farmhouse. We sat at the table while Ray stringed beans. "It isn't much fun, my life. I lost my family, I lost my wife, I lost ever'thing I owned, and it took me a long time to put it together."

Ray had gotten his girlfriend pregnant when he was fourteen. His parents had forced him to marry her. His daughter was fifteen now. "I'd had sex," he said, "exactly twice. Once't with an older man—he was my schoolteacher. Once't with her." They'd been a gospel singing team for the six years of their marriage. "I would have stayed with her the rest of my life. I had a commitment. I had a daughter. But she got so religious I couldn't take it. She quit wearin' pants, quit wearin' makeup, took off all her jewelry. I didn't like her anymore, I hated her guts. Everyone that heard our singin' said, 'Oh, you've got a perfect marriage.' We had a good testimony, and we didn't fight. But when she started

all that stuff, *I couldn't stand her*," he spat, as though a vile taste
had risen from his stomach.

"She knew I was gay before we got married. I told her folks
and my folks, too. After she divorced me, I didn't see a soul of my
family for fourteen years—till my dad had open heart surgery and
he called to see me. There's kids of my brother's I haven't *ever*
even seen. When she took me to court, she was seein' a detective
on the police force. She told him ever'thing about me. A lot of
dirt got spread. When it was over, I had to move. Nobody knew
where. I stayed drunk for six weeks. My car wouldn't run.
Ever'thing I owned was in my suitcase. In six months, she married
rich. And me with nothin' to my name. I'm still payin' off the
court and the lawyer—*four more years to go*. On top of that it took
me fifteen thousand dollars to win custody of my daughter. But I
got her.

"It's not a fun thing to be gay. It's not I don't enjoy *ever*'thing
about my life. I do. I've done a lot of things I'm proud of. But all
my life I got compared to my brother. I *hate* my brother. When
I was a kid, I did ever'thing my brother did and I did it better. But
I was different. My folks could always tell that, and they always
threw it in my face. It's like you're a complete different person
when people find out you're a queer. It's like you never knew 'em.

"You know," he said—he almost gleamed with bitterness—"I
needed them when I grew up. I was a kid and I had a kid. My
daughter and me grew up together. She was ever'thing I had. We
were friends."

Caroline, his daughter, was gone now, too. When she turned
ten she went to live with her mother again. But the move had
been Ray's idea. He'd just begun to explain his decision to me
when Jim came in, laden with corn in a bushel basket. Ray softened the edge in his voice but did not stop. Jim shucked a dozen
ears of corn at the kitchen sink and listened. One standing, one
seated, the men contrasted each other peculiarly. Oklahoma's
deep red dirt had stained Jim's baggy jeans like crimson dye. His
faded T-shirt bore a local feed store's name and emblem. A dirty
mesh trucker's cap perched high on his broad, red forehead, it's
peak spelling out "S&M Water Well Drilling." (He would have

been disdainful, I believed, of the prurient connotation in the company name, had it occurred to him.) He was an easy, sincere, straightforward guy, with blue no-nonsense eyes, which were earnest and direct when he deigned to speak. His monotone was terse. Holding his words close to his chin, he mumbled with a native farmer's caution. (Or maybe this was just a wariness with urban strangers. Not unkindly, he told me he found New Yorkers strange.)

Everything about Ray was drawn and tense. His spanking blue Wrangler jeans were as snug as new skin, his cowboy shirt was starched stiff, his filigreed boots shone like glass. His cowboy hat had imprinted a path around his skull, through waves of richly oiled hair. He had sharp hazel eyes and narrow, arched brows and sported a meticulous mustache. His handsome, well-kept face was pearly-skinned. It darkened when he talked about his past. On his callused, manicured hands, his matching wedding band was more obvious than Jim's. His exactness seemed to etch a razor line around some emptiness or need that burned within.

"Caroline was gettin' to be a woman," Ray reported, "and I didn't know anything about women. Everything women had to do, her mother always did in the privacy of the bathroom. I barely knew it was goin' on. I wanted Caroline to live with somebody she could talk to. My ex-wife is a good mother to her now, couldn't ask for better. She's well provided, she married an AT and T executive, a millionaire." Ray turned acrid. "I'm glad for her, all her money. I'm glad she got a new family. She didn't wait long. Six months. To say the least, she was seein' him before we were separated."

Jim's face had been turned to the wall the whole time. Now he cast a jovial smirk at Ray. "She had to do *somethin'* to meet her female needs," he said, "after all those years."

"*I beg your problem!*" Ray pushed back the bowl of beans he had been stringing and glared.

Jim had turned to the sink again and didn't see. "You were *that* good?" he teased, slow and salacious.

"*I was!*" Ray was enraged. "Sex once't a night, sometimes twice't—and I didn't even know anything about sex till I got married. Like I said, I'm real glad she got *her*self a new family. I'm *glad*."

Ray spoke only so much about this history in front of Jim—but more now than he ever had before, I was given to believe. It was as though he could speak more freely in my presence. I was an anonymous arbiter. Then he changed the topic. Jim said nothing remotely confidential about himself, talked only about the land and his family's life on it, but with a warmth so slow and cautious, he might have been unlocking family diaries, bloodline intimacies. After dinner, while Ray cleaned up, Jim took me back to the farm to watch the sun set. The prairie was tremulous beneath the weight of hemolytic light. For a moment the tall grass flamed like a universe of tiny torches. The skeleton of the timber house—his father and grandfather's birthplace—fell into a tidal pool of sun like char, blanched, then dissolved into the sky.

"We've been doin' perty good for a while now," Jim said, driving through a locust cloud of dust. He meant the family of Oklahoma farmers, not him and Ray. He spoke with the lingering air of a man whose life always skirted catastrophe. He'd been reared on the memory of the Dust Bowl and lived through lesser devastations. Time for him was a skittish wheel of ease and tragedy. It would quickly turn again. His oil wells helped support the farm, and because Reagan supported a freer oil market, he had voted for him. I asked whether he had not been appalled at Reagan's rhetoric and record on gay rights and AIDS.

"There are always dilemmas in the votin' booth," he mused reluctantly, "trying to weigh this thing and that thing against each other. Sometimes it's a matter of stayin' alive."

I thought he'd missed my point and repeated it less demurely. He was firm, but not unkind. "A lot of us here voted for Reagan," he stated. "Farming is my living and my family's living. I don't have to broadcast being gay—there's no reason for anybody around here to know about it. AIDS isn't an issue here. I'm not oppressed or discriminated against. We're conservative in Oklahoma. *I'm* conservative. We're private kind of people. We don't make a public issue out of private things.

"I'm not gonna turn myself into some damn label. There's a

lot of things more important to me than that. Look around! Look at this land! This all's what's kept my family alive for a century. It's my blood. It's who I am. Do you know what I mean?"

That night I drove toward Arkansas. The emptiness of the plains seemed endless as the blackness of the sky. Lonely dirt roads as straight as city streets met at right angles in fields—disorienting in their perfection, like dreams. A hemisphere of stars and the lights of distant farms pricked the darkness with the sharpness of white-hot needles: no foggy glow. Phosphorescent in the headlights of my car, a rectangle in the air announced "Kingfisher, The Buckle of the Wheat Belt." I stopped to sleep.

I was depressed. I slept deeply and dreamed claustrophobic dreams, mesh cages enclosed within mesh cages, prisons floating in airless space. The fear was anesthetic. I could see but couldn't breathe. I watched each greater place beyond me lock away. I lay numb with a terrible peace.

I woke late. The cloudless sky was blistering blue at noon. Slow glinting tractors, dwarfed by red galaxies of dirt, plowed invisible orbits until they themselves disappeared in the heat, leaving behind them expanding nebulas of crimson combustion. Monotonous oil wells, like remnant dinosaurs, sucked at the earth. Through the dark slats of a long cattle truck, a dull crowd of eyes searched the brightness. Nowhere in Texas or Oklahoma had I laughed or cried. I was anxious for the Ozarks and the humors of the hills, where the Great Plains buckled and turned green.

CHAPTER 14

THE
HUMORS
OF THE
OZARKS

IT TOOK WALT SMITH, MY OZARKIAN HOST, FOUR DAYS TO TELL ME about Billy after I arrived in Eureka Springs. The story wasn't long. It was difficult. Less for him, by now, than for me. I stopped him midstory each time. Walt had swallowed the truth. That's why he was here in the Ozarks again, maybe—to learn to live with it in his stomach. Maybe I'd been running from it, too, roaming America to deny it. Certainly I'd been searching to put it in its place. The taste of it had become too bitter to take whole. There had to be a greater truth, or some multitude of truths, that made the life Billy embodied seem smaller now somehow, less terrible in its passing. It wasn't just the disease that gnawed at our world or snatched friends away so fast and silently that we didn't even know they'd gone from us until a season afterward, too late to mourn for just one. It was the dreaming loss of youth, which a caste of us had pursued with the euphoria of religion. We'd been made invulnerable by illusion, and now it was gone, as static in its disappearance as a diary of old messages on a phone machine.

We hadn't begun our visit, Walt and I, talking about Billy.
Not at all. We wouldn't have even if we'd known then that we'd
shared him in anyway. After Oklahoma I needed to be frivolous.
I wanted to indulge in Ozark madness, the hillbilly stuff of tourists. Squealing with mock protest, Walt gave in.

FOR—TOURS
and
Weddings
Please *BLOW*
Car Horn—LOUDLY
or
Call at Mobile Home
Next Door South

Thus read the uncouthly lettered placard held to its stand by a
tiny brass hand in the vestibule of Miracle Mansion.

We returned to the car and blew the horn loudly. On cue a
clergyman descended in a ramshackle golf cart—down the gravel
road through the big stone gate at the spine of the mountain, past
a precipitous row of one-room plywood nuptial cottages. There
was a fair little girl at his side. We parked beneath a huge oak
tree, where a black and ancient fan-tailed Cadillac, the "wedding
limousine," sat rustily awaiting a groom and bride. Paul Holger
Hansen was the parson's name. He wore a ragged Panama hat and
a soiled Roman collar. A crucifix, of some alloy, dangled from a
heavy chain upon his bib. As he stepped from the cart to extend
his hand, the fly of his sun yellow slacks flew wide. Thus, unwitting, he stood. Neither the man of God nor the child was smiling,
though both seemed eager to please. "I'd guess y'all's interest is a
tour, not a weddin'," judged the reverend, eyeing Walt narrowly
and grasping my hand. His granddaughter stepped forth as our
guide.

Lillian was nine. She was quick and terribly formal. In a
voice both childish and electronically precise, she stated the fee to
view the exhibitions, liquidly converting her *r*'s and *l*'s all to *w*'s.

"*Pwease* fow-wow *me*," she announced with practiced niceness, a miniature Barbara Walters. She was bouncy with bright yellow curls, crisp in a sundress, ruffled and bowed. Her face was as brittle as a doll's. "And pwease watch your step." A little ivory hand surveyed the path.

Miracle Mansion was a dingy, concrete flying saucer of a house, stuck high on a cliff near Eureka Springs in the Ozarks of northwest Arkansas. Some two decades ago Bob Hyde, a local religious eccentric, had conceived and built it for his home. He'd named it in Greek after Christ, "Chi Rho." Hyde was a man of many talents. He also wrote. His credits included "Bonanza" episodes and *The Great Passion Play*, about the end of Christ's life, which even now played to packed bleachers down the road. He'd been an actor as well and had had a part in his own play, before he'd been run out of town. According to Walt, Hyde's penchant for displaying his penis outside ladies' bedroom windows had finally brought him down. His most passionate roles had been Jesus and Peeping Tom.

"The pwesent owners," stated little Lillian, and meaning her grandpa, "have turned the house into a shwine to the early Chwistian martyrs and given it its cuw-went name. To my wight are some two thousand pweserved bugs my gweat-gwandfather cow-wected a hundwed years ago. Also the miniatures of Pwesident Wonald Weagan and his First Wady, Nancy. They are gifts to Miwacle Mansion," she almost scolded, "by two eldewy bachewors, who made them. *Now*, fow-wow me," she commanded.

The night before, I'd insisted on seeing *The Great Passion Play* as well. The amphitheater had been crowded with Christians—a couple of thousand. They'd come great distances, from several states, in church buses with bold confessions of faith painted over their flanks: "God's Night Crawler." They'd watched the cartoon gospel onstage, spirit-struck, and jeered at the rabble Jews abusing Jesus. They'd eaten popcorn and crowed jubilantly when a beam of light broke from a hole in the set (the fallen Lord's grave), slaying Romans—but the bleachers had already begun to empty out by the time a Jell-O-bellied Christ, blood- (or cherry-) red with exertion, ascended into the heavenly branches of an enormous tree, gripped at the sides by bulky cables. Walt and I snickered and pinched each other quiet all the while.

Now, on the way home from Miracle Mansion, we laughed until we cried—giggled, sniffled—silly as schoolboys. ("Have you had quite *enough* now?" Walt wailed.) We'd been euphoric since I got there. Neither Walt nor I could say where this mutual pubescence had come from. We'd met just once before, in April in New York, the week he was moving back to live with his father in Arkansas. A friend had introduced us briefly over lunch at the Angry Squire in Chelsea. We'd been cordial then, not hysterical.

Walt was the son of a wealthy country doctor and had grown up on a gentlemanly hilltop farm overlooking the Ozarks' luxurious valleys. Like many of the local people, he'd once played an extra in the *Passion Play*—an industry crucial to Eureka Springs' economy—though unlike most he hadn't been financially or spiritually dependent on it, a child on a lark. His family were fine Episcopalians. That alone set him apart. As early as high school, he'd wanted to escape, someplace where the cultivated were appreciated. "My home ec teacher," he remembered, "told me I had to get out of here." He'd joined Up With People for a stint—now he grimaced at it—and had gotten as far as New York and Europe before he'd been booted out for breaking rules. "They'd barely let you talk to the girls—I mean, a few of 'em *had* gotten pregnant." He'd come home to graduate, then left in the fall for Columbia University. "It had to be an Ivy League school. I had to prove myself, as a southerner, and because of being gay."

Eureka Springs nested in deep, mossy shade on a mountainside, like a toy Victorian village—the gingerbread gables of one house peeping into a steep valley over the confection roof of another. It had been built as a bustling spa at the turn of the century and now maintained itself on the Disney nostalgia of its quaint hotels, boutiques, and taverns and the carnival quirk of its religious fanaticism. The great, snow white "Christ of the Ozarks" rose through the trees and stonily eyed the hoedown of boos and hillbilly music that poured from the crinkly, hewn facades of honey-colored granite downtown. Homosexuality, as far as some townsfolk could recall, had always been accepted there, an oasis in fire-and-brimstone Arkansas, long before the local circus of Christian commerce came to be.

"I grew up around gay men," reported Janet. She was a barmaid at a watering hole owned by a gay couple, where both heterosexual and homosexual interests were condoned and liaisons of both sorts were contracted for in an alcoholic haze. She was brisk in a short khaki skirt and blouse, with short, no-fuss blond hair. Attention-grabbing brass triangles quivered from her ears. "I understand there are some people who can't deal with it, they *really* can't. But it doesn't make sense to me." Fine, tar black ribbons of mascara gift-wrapped her flickering oval eyes.

"I had these two guys that baby-sat for me when I was a kid," she said. "They were lovers. My mother *loved* them! Everybody knew. Well, when I was this big"—thigh high—"she just told me they were 'married.' And that's how I always thought. You may think this is really crazy, but I used to wish my brother would be gay. Is that nuts? I just knew if he was, we'd be closer, we'd click on the same wavelength." She mixed a heavy Cape Cod. "The Springs is different, anyway, from the rest of Arkansas. *Thank* the *Law-rd*! *Yes!* You're somewhere else in the state and they ask you where you're from. You say, 'Eureka Springs,' they go, 'Oh!'" She swallowed a gasp. "They just drop it."

The native population of Eureka Springs now hovered at around two thousand. It was swollen in the summer by plump, fidgety men with pasty-faced wives going shop to shop in a daze. Middle-aged bands of married women, trading their husbands back home for vacations with the "girls," roamed coquettish. Nipping in the midafternoon, they slapsticked with boyish-slim waiters, who tended to be gay. On the day Walt and I drank iced tea at the outdoor cafe—where a wrought-iron rail barricaded the street from a precipice—a straggling surplus of lean, teen boys prowled town at the mercy of their hormones, skittish as mountain goats. One in particular—the back of whose shirt read "More Than a Mouthful"—walked about the street with hungry-eyed innocence, scratching his nuts.

The pianist was singing James Taylor: *"Oh, I've seen fire, I've seen rain. . . ."*

"How do we *always* know which ones are gay?" asked Walt.

It was here that Walt first mentioned Billy Burns's name to me—some memory in the horny boy's smile, perhaps, something kindling and inextinguishable.

"Billy?" I repeated.

Billy Burns. A New Yorker. Early thirties, the face and roundly muscled voluptuousness of a twenty-year-old. He taught high school in New Jersey (but the careers of all Manhattanites except the most fabulous are vague). He had an adolescent electricity about him, a full circuit of straight brown hair cropped like an Olympic swimmer's, soft blue eyes like low flames, a granite jaw, a wide yearning smile that took your heart away. He moved with magnetic sensuality that radiated innocence and sex. I saw him first—I don't know—on a Chelsea street, on the Fire Island beach, dancing at the Saint? Under a soaring planetarium dome, the Saint had been the temple to love-maddened pleasure—an erotic midnight riot of planets and stars, music that shook the earth and constellations, drugs like nectar, the sweat-glistening muscles of thousands of half-naked men dancing in a frenzy of worship, dark chests shimmering with salty dew like diamonds. On a high plateau above the dome, men—gods—watched the chaos of self-creation and made love. Ecstasy had been everything then, in the early 1980s, before the weight of AIDS, age, and consequence had set in. Stunned with distant passion, I'd watched Billy dance there.

"Did *you* know Billy?" Walt asked.

I was oblivious of tenses. "How is he?"

"Billy was my best friend. He died last year."

I felt grief rise in my throat. Walt looked in my eyes and stopped. For now I couldn't listen.

Though I'd seen Billy Burns maybe hundreds of times, I'd met him only once or twice. He was not a friend of mine so much as an emblem, an aspiration. Michael, my lover, had himself for some time had an unrequited crush on him. They'd met on Fire Island in 1984. I told Walt the story. It was six or so in the morning when Michael got to the Pavillion to catch the last of Saturday night's dancing. They were playing "sleaze"—slow, sweaty music for the hours when the drugs are waning. Billy was dancing alone. So was Michael. Slowly they gravitated toward one another, then hugged. Michael had once told me how he remembered first looking into Billy's startling ice blue eyes. Later that day, after a morning party, they ran into each other on the beach and ended up spending the whole afternoon together—just talking, cuddling, fondling, no outright sex. They simply lay in Billy's bed naked and touching. Billy kept saying that he didn't want to do anything sexual.

Before they parted, they exchanged phone numbers and vowed to get together in the city at the gym where they both worked out. Michael called often, but it never happened. It was autumn before they got together again. They were both spending a late season weekend on Fire Island—Michael with Bob, with whom we were engaged in a brief ménage à trois, Billy alone. Except for them, the island was almost empty. Michael often reminisced about the slow time they spent together, walking through the autumnal shadows of the seaside woods that were a summer sexual playground (and known as the "Judy Garland Memorial Forest" by the campier set). The October light was intensely yellow, he recalled, yellow orange, and everything was decaying, dying. That night Billy, Michael, and Bob made love all night long on the floor in front of the fireplace.

It wasn't until the next spring that Michael saw Billy again—one of the first weekends of the season. Waiting on the dock for the seaplane to New York, he saw a vaguely familiar man dangling his feet over the water. It was terribly hot, but the young man was wrapped in a sweatshirt and sweat pants. Then suddenly Michael remembered the former face, which was gaunt now. Billy turned to him and said, "I guess you can see I've had a rough winter, but I'm doing better now."

Michael once told me that he had put what he saw out of his mind, because the reality was too terrible. "Billy had become a symbol to me," he said, "too handsome, too magnetic, too young to die." Billy *couldn't* die. He would take too much of all our lives away with him.

| | |

Walt had come back home to live with his dad, to find something with him that he'd never had. But all his childhood reminiscences left his father out. There was a hole in his past with his father, there was only now. He spoke comfortably of his mother, though. It was she who in his senior year of high school had told him he was homosexual. "I'd been called a sissy only once in my life," he said, "at school. I was insulted and shocked, because it had never occurred to me before. They were poor farm kids and I was wealthy. Mother sat me down and just said, 'You're gay,' and told me I was gonna have to learn to deal with it. I was disgusted. I said, 'How dare you say something like that to your own son? That's the most horrible thing a mother could do!' "

Mrs. Smith had always been a dear friend to Jeremy and Jim, two gentleman shop owners who lived together. "I don't know why *that* never occurred to me," Walt stated. "She'd suggest going over and I'd *jump* in the car. Oh, yeah! I always felt 'right' with them. I never knew why, but I knew I *belonged* there." And there was Jefferson, the old pharmacist. "Old Jefferson!" Walt proclaimed sadly. "He's one of our gay martyrs. He'd never *say* he's gay. He'd never think of himself that way. He gets real drunk, then finds someone who'll let him give 'em a blow job—that's the extent of it. He's always lived with his five old-maid aunts. Three of 'em got married, but the husbands didn't live long. Jefferson took them all in. They hover over him, these five little women are his life. When I was a kid, I'd always go down to his drugstore and sit at the fountain and just talk to him. After college, I'd visit and talk about men friends, his eyes would just fog, he'd go blank. He knew what was goin' on, but there was no way in his life for him to recognize it. His whole life has been carin' for his aunts and dispensin' pills." In particular, in these reminiscing moments, Walt spoke in a soft, clipped Ozark twang that New York could never grind out of him. If anything, the alien city drove him to preserve his native speech like an heirloom.

"You know"—he gave an incredulous laugh—"I get to thinkin' about my life in New York and comin' back here. I mean, people here don't snap at you when you say 'Good mornin'.' But I can get real aware I'm livin' in Arkansas, that old closed feelin'.

"I went trout fishin' with my accountant, up in the hills. We had this guide, and I'll tell ya he was one of those guys who'd literally never been out of 'Yellville' his whole life, except for Vietnam. He took 'redneck' to new dimensions.

"Randy, my accountant, is black, *real* black, from Little Rock. His skin's like coal, there's no way you're gonna think he's *dark white*. We were boyfriends once, that's the way we met. But we *certainly* weren't lettin' on in the boat. So the guy's gettin' the lines ready and everything—that's his living—and he really wants to talk. He turns around and says, 'Did you hear the one about the three niggers who died and went to heaven?'

"Listen,"—Walt grinned, still incredulous—"Randy and I just looked at each other, and the look on our faces made us start laughin'. *What* could you say? It was like Randy wasn't there. It wasn't mean or anything—just like we were a couple of good Joes from the holler. I mean, this area is absolutely segregated, but you can't believe they see 'em so seldom they can't identify 'em when they're right there!

"So we're laughin' and *he* thinks we're goin' crazy about his joke and decides to tell *another* one! So he says, 'Did you hear the one about the two fags in the bar?' *Can you be-lieve it?* We laughed so hard we almost fell outa the boat! I thought I oughta say somethin' to him, but then I didn't sorta wanta spoil the moment. It was too rare. I kinda wonder, though, if he wasn't pickin' up on something and that was the only way he could let us know it was okay."

We were on the narrow highway outside town, just driving around. The "Christ of the Ozarks" stood pale green above the trees in the afternoon sunshine. "Did you know," Walt said, "you can suspend two automobiles from each of his hands and the arms won't fall off?"

The Smith family home was a genteel ranch style—long, low, with years of large additions. It sat on a gentle mountaintop that had been cleared for pasture. From here the dark, velvet valleys and veiled, distant hills were a kingdom. Miniature horses— mature and tiny—gamboled behind split log fences, which guarded the long road to the house. Each night new jars of jams and home-canned vegetables appeared on the kitchen counter, the work of the ancient housekeeper who'd taken care of the family since Walt was a baby. On the wall hung a needlepoint motto:

I LIKE TO SEE A MAN PROUD OF THE PLACE IN WHICH HE LIVES. I LIKE TO SEE A MAN LIVE SO THAT HIS PLACE WILL BE PROUD OF HIM.
—Abraham Lincoln

Walt sat on a stool beneath it, testing a jar of pickled corn. "In high school," he said, "the farm kids used to vandalize my car— most of 'em didn't have one. In the Ozarks you fit in, or you're out. Someone else's standard isn't somethin' people even consider here—it's un-American." He was still, and maybe forever, a foreigner to native ways, though now he was trying to break through the borders and learn. "I mean, still, once I get beyond a little circle of friends who're 'out' and comfortable with themselves ... like this guy I know. I go to a gay bar down in Fayetteville and he's always standing there rubbing his hands together. I'll say, 'Jay, what's *wrong*?' and he'll say, '*O-oh!* I don't really want to be here, I don't know why I keep comin' back. I'm really not gay. *I don't want to be.*' *He'll say that!* I started datin' this one guy—up early on Sunday mornin' to meet his fiancée for church, then spend the afternoon with her family. In the evenin' he'd be back at the bar to meet up with his buddy, who'd just dropped off *his* fiancée. I mean, they don't love these women, they don't even *fuck* 'em. They're just for cover. And *these* two'll even tell ya *they're* gay! That's the way things are down here, and nothing will ever change. That's a pretty lonely, desperate feeling."

The phone rang. The machine caught it. Yet another farmer-patient calling for his father, who was out of town. Walt stared at the nictating, bloodshot light. "The message tells 'em he's gone for the week," he said laughing, "but when they need him there's no way they can imagine he's not here. 'I need to see the doctor tonight,'" he said, mimicking the patients' molasses accent.

"Walt," I ventured, more careful of my own feelings than of his, "how was it you knew Billy so well?"

He sighed, his shoulders fell, his eyes moistened with a smile. "The day we actually met," he said, "was the most wonderful day of our friendship." Walt was at the Chelsea Gym. They'd cruised each other a couple of times before but never talked. Walt had on his Gay Pride Run T-shirt, and Billy just said, "So you ran in the Gay Pride race?"—that's all, but they hit on a crazy sense of humor, flitting around and making jokes in the middle of serious muscle. The more uneasy the muscle queens became, the more the two men giggled. They'd even giggled in the showers, a sacrilege in the watery, pumped-up hush of cruising.

"I got back to my apartment," said Walt, "and already there was this message on my machine. 'Hi, Walt, this is Billy. Will you be my best friend?' And that became a regular thing between us— Billy and the phone machine. Just crazy things, every day—the daily winning lotto number, a whole article he'd read—but always, always a message.

"It was never a sexual thing between us, even though we both recognized we were each other's type. That was one of those things that we realized from the very, very beginning—we wanted to be buddies, best friends. And that's what my relationship with Billy was, and is—the best friend I have ever, ever had."

He started to go on, but something sudden in the expression on my face stopped him. He was looking at me with the eyes of an examining physician. We said no more and went to bed.

In our forays through town, Walt had often whispered, "Queer alert." He believed he could always tell. At a hoedown one night we picked one out, the honky-tonk pianist—stereotypically handsome, overgroomed, cocky—and cornered him after the show. He fled us, overpolite and nervous, as though he'd just spilled his testosterone. Later at the tavern downtown, we met Rupert Childers, the show's clown, who'd escaped our opinions despite his routine as a hillbilly girl, which he played in a pigtail wig and gingham-and-calico dresses. He'd been far too comfortably masculine in drag, too "straight," to attract our suspicions. His big song in the show was, "My Boyfriend's Back." "*Hey li, hey li, my boyfriend* . . ." Now he was standing at the bar, arm in arm with his husband.

Rupert met us in the morning at the entrance to the holler where he lived. "Now," he instructed from his truck, "ya'll are gonna follow me just like you're the puppy and I've got the ball." His house—a finely appointed cabin, really—lay deep in the hills. He shared it with his father and a lover of ten years. He and Gene had fallen in love carving pumpkins at a hayride in Iowa, when Rupert was on tour. "Most of the people that comes to the hoedown still has tractor dust on their heels," Rupert assessed. "They come and buy tick-its and ask things like 'Does all the seats face the stage?' But there's *never* been a problem 'bout me bein' gay. They sure do ask about Clyde, the piano player, though, and he *ain't*, as far as I *know*. Some old geezer told the lead fiddler he liked ever'body in the show 'cept that queer. Well, he thought he meant *me*, so he asked him what he didn't like. And he said, 'Well, he struts up there playin' that pianer like he was God's gift, better'n ever'body. You can tell he's queer by how smooth he is.' In those dresses I'm just too obvious to be uppity."

In the afternoon I was leaving for St. Louis. I'd arranged to be there that night. Leaving Rupert's, I asked Walt about Billy again. I'd dreamed of him the night before, erotic compulsion and fear. Cool, mountain green shadows flew by as we drove, perpetual dissolution and reappearances. I resolved to listen. Loss seemed less real on the road. Billy was the son of a wealthy Long Island businessman and grew up on a large, old estate overlooking the Sound. The family was Roman Catholic. He was the youngest of ten. "It was a real comfortable, homey setting," Walt said. Billy and Walt built almost a blood kinship between them. Billy had volunteered in Walt's office at the Gay Men's Health Crisis, counseling sick and frightened men. Each summer they took a house on Fire Island together. Each Christmas they made a pilgrimage to the Metropolitan Museum to visit the tree. Rites of intimacy. "Our traditions," said Walt. "Even though otherwise our lives were pretty much separate." Sometimes, not often, they slept together—cuddling, no sex, "when one or the other of us didn't want to spend the night alone." And there were always, always, the messages on the phone machine.

"That was actually the way I found out he was sick," Walt recalled. "Sleeping with him. As a matter of fact, it was at the Fire Island house." They had taken a share together for a second season. "Billy had been doing weird things that year. The housemates had always called him Tramp." Walt laughed. "We gave him such shit! Every day he'd take some guy to his room and, you know, an hour later someone would say, 'He's still in there with that trick!' And here he'd walk out with someone different! Billy could never pass up good pecs. But all of a sudden, you know, hygiene become *super* important to him. All of us always ate out of the peanut-butter jar and Billy'd get real indignant. And he didn't want anyone to use his towels, not even to dry their hands. It got real tense.

"I mean, it was tense enough. Me bein' from GMHC, there was this constant flow of guys knockin' at the door—this was 1984—wantin' to know exactly what safe sex was. I think Billy, and everyone in that house, was *uncomfortably* aware of any 'unsafe' activity, because of my presence. And by that time he'd begun to recognize he was sick. But he didn't talk about it; so no one knew."

Early that summer Billy had oral thrush, a nubby white blanket of painful yeast on his throat and tongue, in those days a warning of sure death. Tight-mouthed, he'd kept it disguised. It was late in the season when Walt discovered signs of Billy's disease. "The last weekend," Walt said. "We were in bed, just talking, rubbing, massaging each other. We were half-asleep. I saw a KS lesion"—a wine-colored, cancerlike nodule—"on his arm. He saw me see it. Immediately he got up and walked away. That was classic Billy. The body language was very definite: 'We're not gonna deal with this right now.' One of the wonderful things about Billy was that his spirit could be so open to whatever came along. It could also be so closed. He pretty much denied his illness all along.

"I remember this one time, the spring of 1985, he was in the hospital in co-op care. You'd go down for lunch or dinner and it was clear who had AIDS, you'd see these gay couples come in. There was this one couple who came in and the guy was pretty sick. He kept falling around, he couldn't stand up. I said, 'Billy, why don't we go over and just say hello?'—because they looked like they wanted company. And he said, 'I'm sorry, Walt, I can't do it. That guy's too sick, it's too painful for me.' Sometimes he could be so spontaneous. He'd get obsessed, with treatments, something new. Then all of a sudden he wouldn't follow through."

That second summer of Billy's illness, Walt and Billy took shares in the Fire Island house again, but Billy by then had begun to lose his mind. At first his doctors believed he'd developed toxoplasmosis, a parasitic infection of the brain, but it never showed up in the blood tests. "No one could figure out *what* the hell was goin' on," Walt said. "Meantime he was losing more and more memory and getting these horrible headaches. And the funniest thing—he lost all the use of his verbs. So strange. Somehow all the verbs in his life disappeared."

It was the end of the season when Billy went into the hospital the last time. Though his family had off and on taken him in, done what they could, Walt had—in the language of the epidemic—become the "primary caregiver." "His whole family was wonderful," Walt said, "but if Billy and I had been lovers, they could have understood it more. They only understood gayness in terms of sex, genital sex. They just couldn't grasp that gay men become each other's families—because we grow up displaced from our own. This one time at the hospital, his parents were sitting there reading *The Wall Street Journal* and the *Times* and I stumbled in from the office exhausted. Billy had KS in his mouth so bad he couldn't talk. He kept trying to say something to me and I couldn't understand. I kept leaning closer and closer. I put some anesthetic in his mouth, and he was asking me to get in bed with him! I whispered, *'Billy! With your parents right here?'* I started massaging him, then finally just crawled into the bed, you know, getting into our automatic position—right side, his head on my chest. And he just sighed, *'O-o-h!'* And somehow I knew that was it. He was ready to go. Letting me hold him like that was the only way he really had left to tell me he loved me."

Walt's voice had not wavered till now. Now it cracked, a hairline. He didn't speak as he drove up the hill to the house, past the pasture of tiny horses. At the top he turned off the ignition and sat, resting his hands on the steering wheel, gazing ahead to where the furrowed field fell into a valley. "He was losing more and more cognitive attention. When people came in he just stared at them, he barely recognized anybody. But one day when I came in he reached out and grabbed my hand and held it against the IV, trying to get me to pull it out." Walt paused. *"Oh, God! This is so fucking painful!"* he gasped. "This went on for three or four days. His parents would see it and just freeze. Finally I grabbed his hand and said, 'Okay, Billy. This is it. That medicine is the only thing keepin' you alive. We take it out and you'll die. It's not like pullin' the plug. It won't happen right away. You'll feel pain. Do you understand? Are you sure that's what you want?'

"They gave him morphine. His dad and I kept a vigil—we'd stand there, staring at him. 'Is he breathing? Is he finally dead?' On September fifth, in the early morning, I'd gone home. His dad called around four and woke me up. He just said, 'Billy was really fortunate to have a friend like you. We've all gone through a lot of pain. I can understand why he loved you so much.' You know, I guess I've had a fucked-up relationship all my life with my dad, and always wanted a close one. But during that time, Billy's dad became my dad. In all that grief, I felt so much love."

Walt's voice was weak, but did not break. When he began, I believed he was telling Billy's story only for me, because I'd kept coming back to it. Now, a grieving determination had taken over. He waited a moment and took my hand and rallied. "All this from a chance meeting at the Chelsea Gym." Tears streamed his face. He laughed. "Billy was very odd in a lot of ways his family could never deal with. There was this one time we were having dinner at his family's house—like sixteen people around this huge dining room table—and Billy keeps bringing all this stuff up about being gay, and gay relationships being as good as any other kind of relationship. And his dad said, 'But it just doesn't work, it's unnatural,' and picked up his silverware and said, 'It's like you've got a fork and a knife, it won't work.' Billy took 'em out of his father's hand and said, 'Let me try!' Clang! The knife sticks right through the fork's teeth! Fine! Everybody sort of giggled. But you knew they only accepted it to a certain degree.

"It's one of those strange things. It hurts so much to lose somebody, but there's this odd, I don't know, healing that takes place. When his dad included me the way he did when Billy died, took me in like family—there was finally this realization for him about what really had been goin' on all along. Somehow Billy could never make them understand that while he was still alive. I guess, in a sense, he was finally able to make his point."

For moments now Walt couldn't speak, stifled with grief, tears straying down his cheeks. We turned toward each other. He sobbed, shattered words and barricaded anger bursting through. "I still am so pissed at him for not taking care of himself," he cried. "He knew better. He knew how to stay well! He didn't have to do that to himself!" Then, as suddenly, he laughed. "Well, *that* wasn't politically correct, was it?

"The truth is, Billy was thirty-two when he died, and he had a good time. My father is a seventy-five-year-old alcoholic and he's *never* enjoyed himself. I don't think Billy was the kind of guy who would ever live up to his potential. He'd get right up to it—a lover, whatever—and back away from it. But he *lived* for men. That was what made him happiest, and I guess he died for it.

"I had this fantasy the other day leavin' work—that I'd get home and find a message. 'Hi, Walt. This is Billy. You know the lotto number for the day? You wanta go to a movie?' I made it up and called myself. When I got to the house, I played it through. I thought, Walt, maybe you're nuts, but you really needed that. Then I stood there laughing, crazy as I used to get with Billy. *I still miss him.*"

There was a hush and a hilltop wind. Walt reached over and wrapped me in his arms, squeezing me as though he would never let go, and I cried with him that afternoon more bitterly, perhaps, than ever I had before, than I have since. I cried for friends for whom I'd never cried, who'd died too fast for crying. I cried for Billy—and for that army of lovers whose lives had dissolved silently, without my knowing. I cried for the long summer of love that now so grievously had fallen from us. Like Walt, I had had to leave New York to release the pain.

CHAPTER 15

RIVER'S
WAKE

MISSOURI ROLLS FROM THE WEST LIKE A RIVERBOAT'S WAKE—
fluorescent swells toward the Mississippi. The air, on this blue-
hot August Saturday, was dead and wet, incensed in the evening
with the forest decay of leaves and ash-black dirt. At night, as I
neared the river that holds St. Louis in its crook, a judgment of
clouds struck the hills with platinum rain. Trucks and cars stood
idling along the highway, blinking and red-eyed as penitents.

I called Andy White, whom I'd met at the Denver rodeo, as
soon as I checked into my hotel. But now he had grown nervous
about my visit. Reluctance deadened his voice. He said he would
meet me at Upside, a gay disco, at midnight, but he never showed
up. In the morning, when I called him again—and was angry—he
said he'd forgotten and already had plans for Sunday. Nor would
a rodeo friend he'd introduced me to now agree to see me—a
strikingly handsome and masculine man whose wife and teenaged
sons knew nothing of his homosexuality, whose younger son was
dying of leukemia. Assurances and reassurances of anonymity
were meaningless.

I wandered around St. Louis all day, trying to occasion something, someone. The city was as desolate as prayer. The soaring steel arch on the Mississippi's banks, "Gateway to the West," glinted through the river's mist, cathedral door to a dead sea of muggy air. All the bars were closed by Sabbath laws. In Forest Park, the largest of the city's parks, few people dared the steamy heat. Though messages were scratched, man to man, on the men's room stalls, there was no loitering. It was late in the afternoon when it occurred to me that there might be a gay Sunday mass in so silent a city. In a gay guide I found Dignity, a Roman Catholic organization. I called and caught the group's president, Mike Stanislow, at home as he was leaving for church to prepare for the service. He offered to talk to me in the parish hall before mass.

Mike was in a cassock when I met him, minusculely buttoned knees to neck. The evening sun through the high stained glass shattered against the paleness of his face. He'd moved to St. Louis more than a decade ago for seminary. He'd been ordained four years, in the Society of Our Mother of Peace, when he forsook his vows. "I couldn't live in both worlds," he said, "both the church and the gay community. My superior knew I was gay all along. There was a group of gay seminarians. Most of them didn't leave. Some of them stayed celibate. Some of them had lovers—on the side. If you're in a parish church, it demands your full time."

At the instigation of the Vatican, Dignity was being expelled from parishes across the nation in 1987—an inquisition to reclaim the Church's terror over sex and its prerogative of hypocrisy. The papal see had gone so far as to lay the blame for AIDS on homosexuality—though, worldwide, it was overwhelmingly a heterosexually transmitted disease—and to paint the epidemic violence against the homosexually identified as an understandable, if sad, consequence of their sin. So far in St. Louis Dignity had fared well by maintaining a low profile. It accommodated itself to the bishop.

"I have to be careful how I word this," Mike said with a jesuitic smile, stained light lying tentative as scruples on his lips. "We don't claim to be a 'gay mass,' but a 'parish gay outreach.' Our priests don't publicly state they're gay. We don't ask for church approval for homosexuality. You go too much in that direction, you get bucked by the goat," he confessed, curiously evoking that ancient satanic symbol.

The great Victorian facade of the Church of the Immaculate Conception sat in a once white and now poor black neighborhood. Early on this sultry August evening, black children played on the wide sweep of its steps, making useless squeals and occasionally catcalls about queers. Their giggles and noisy jeers grenaded through the tall arched doors and echoed in the lofty nave like combat. Through high, stained lancets, blasts of bright, dying light exploded and froze against the dark marble columns and floor, against the dark carved pews, where a small congregation—a hundred men, perhaps, and a trio of women, all white, well groomed, and homosexual—knelt, lost in the hugeness of the space, ready to receive the manhood of Christ in a wafer.

Two laymen, hunched with belief, assisted the priest. One I'd seen at the bar the night before, dancing sweaty with his shirt off; the other loitering in the men's room at a rest stop on the freeway where I'd waited out the rain on the highway into St. Louis. The bittersweet breath of candles and incense sweltered the wet air. Huge fans, which could not move the heat, drowned the communion hymn in the purgatorial roar of their hush. *"Come follow me, and I will give you rest."* Worshipers knelt toward the high altar fanning futilely with the backs of hymnals.

In the narthex after the mass, an aristocratically mannered man, in safari shorts and a starched cotton shirt, introduced himself to me and praised the Church. The diocese had established an AIDS task force for the one hundred cases all told in St. Louis. "I am very encouraged," he pattered softly, curling the smoke of a cigarette through his lips, thuriferous. "The diocese has been coming through in an admirable way. It gives me hope to see people responding to this tragedy with such love." He was himself a task force member, with Archbishop John May and the dean of the Episcopal cathedral. "Not openly as gay," he admonished, smiling palely. "I haven't brought it up at all. I don't think it's important to the issue here."

Beside us stood a priest, though not the one who'd cele-brated mass. He was a tall, gray, bald man of maybe sixty. At the same time obsequious and condescending, the gentleman with whom I spoke introduced him to me.

"Well, *not here,*" the father whispered when I asked if I could talk to him about Catholicism and homosexuality. "Someplace more quiet, private." Fatigue seemed to vest him like guilt. He led me back into the church's darkened nave, where the amber fires of votive candles spirited the anguished lips of plaster saints. There he directed me toward a confessional. "This is the most convenient place to chat. Do you mind?" he asked. Three spired wooden doors, medievally ornate, lead into the tiny rooms. Step-ping into the confessor's central chamber, he bade me take my place in the penitential chamber at his left. There was a chair in-stead of a kneeler. The dividing screen had been removed. In the glow of a light as faint as a candle, a crucifix hung like a specter above his head. In a weary, desultory litany, he began to confess, sometimes at the querulous distant limits of his life, sometimes approaching the soul.

"What is it like?" he said, paraphrasing what I'd asked him. "It's never easy. Never, in St. Louis. I think sometimes gay cou-ples come here to live and settle down—pretty conservative," he complained. "Once they get an old town house and fix it up, their silver pattern, their china, you never see 'em again. They disap-pear.

"It's so provincial here. You've got city officials referring to gays as 'queers' in the paper. In the diocesan news, you find ho-mosexuality associated with child abuse and murder—in general, without them outright condemning it. It's a little more subtle. The bishop's Lentan pastoral letter asked us to pray for deliver-ance from the abuses in our society—abortion, rape, homosexual-ity. I didn't read it to my parish. I couldn't.

"I have publicly defended gays and lesbians. The quote I gave to the TV news wasn't wrong—that homosexuality isn't the sin, the homosexual act is."

"Is that what you believe?" I whispered. The question weighed between us like the hot humidity.

"I say it that way or lose my job," he bemoaned. "Even that put me on the bishop's shit list. He used to write me, 'Dear Bernie.' Now it's always 'Father'—formal. If the Church at least openly admitted it had gay priests and nuns, we'd have so much less emotional difficulty—you know? I've come to believe it's better to be hated for what you really are than loved for what you pretend to be. That's the way I feel every time I celebrate mass."

"No one in your parish knows about you?"

"I've come out to a couple of close parish friends. The bishop knows, too, at least he knows my work with Dignity. He probably knows about most of the priests in the diocese who're gay. If you don't make waves, you're okay. And I'm too chicken to get too vocal. They retaliate. We don't *want* to get too militant and lose our place in the Church."

"You're celibate?"

He hesitated. "Unattached. Let's put it that way." His voice was sterile and slow. Sweat streamed the hot, pallid glow of his face, sinuate as contrition. "I did have a lover once. In the mid-sixties, for six years. It took its toll on us, the double lives. We both were alcoholics. I went away for treatment—but an alcoholic's an alcoholic. You cope with the stress by drinking more. I was in therapy for a while. It helped me get some stability in my life, but I realized I'd never be a heterosexual."

"Do you ever want a lover now?" I asked. "Is that something you hope for?"

"Never. Never again. It's too much to give yourself to a relationship *and* to a job in the Church. I'm tired now. The toll is starting to show. I say mass, but I don't feel it. This harassment from the Vatican, what they've said about homosexuals—since then I don't feel like doing a goddamn thing. It takes so much spiritual energy to always pretend. I play priest now. I don't have a whole lot of fervor. I do my job, I can't do more.

"It's going to take a martyr to change things. Most of us in this world are too afraid for crusades."

"It's too small. People are afraid to be 'out' here," said young Timothy on my first night in Vincennes, Indiana, 160 straight, narrow miles across the Illinois corn flats from St. Louis. The blinds were drawn, the porch light off. A vaulted curbside row of spruces darkened the street lamps. Even in the sanctum of his home his nervous voice was secretive.

Timothy, who would not give me his surname, lived with his lover in a white-clapboard neighborhood. Vincennes, like St. Louis, was a French Catholic town. Downtown the red-brick Church of St. Francis Xavier, the old French cathedral, predominated. Aside from that, the town was a hatch of wide, dusty streets and freight tracks. Along the fast-food strip through the center of town, high-schoolers boozed on the hoods of pickup trucks, watching their friends cruise and drag-race.

Vincennes was small and flat and hugged a convex bend in the Wabash River—the border with southern Illinois—like something being cast off. It contained the burial mounds of forgotten Indians and memorialized frontiersman George Rogers Clark with a park and colonnade for his role in capturing the settlement from the British in the Revolution. In 1814 the first play in Indiana, *She Stoops to Conquer*, was performed there—the beginning of the trouble, perhaps, if one were inclined to trace things so far back.

A century and a half later, in May of 1986, some thespians at Vincennes University, the community junior college, found themselves at the center of a scare over Knox County's physical and moral welfare. The *Knox County Daily News* and the county prosecutor, Jerry McGaughey, had deemed a party that the student actors threw at the end of the school year to be a "gay murder cult" rite. It was the last known place that eighteen-year-old Brent Brand (neither a thespian nor a student at the college) had been seen alive. His corpse had been found days later, decomposing in a drainage ditch.

"It depends on who ya talk to, who was there," stated Timothy, his wary eyes watching me as though I might have a gun. His green-eyed cat sat beside him. "Some say everybody of prominence in town. Doctors, lawyers, even the governor—and this young boy. Then later they found his body across the river in Illinois. There was rumors of him being drained of blood, a rag in his anus like he'd had anal sex and was bleedin' and they couldn't stop it, so he bled to death."

It was Timothy's lover, a college professor, whom I'd wanted to talk to, but he'd taken his two small children on vacation for the week. I'd read a report on the "murder" and witch-hunt in a gay newspaper the previous March and gotten his name from an Indianapolis gay rights group. When I got into town and called his house, Timothy answered and refused to talk. I called back and insisted. When I arrived, he only cracked the door to let me in. He'd already phoned Indianapolis to find out if I was legitimate.

"We didn't even know the party took place," he said. "I never ran across anybody who went." He hesitated, a lamb regarding a wolf. "You *sure* you're not from the Knox County paper? You're not law? I'm really uncomfortable with this. I guess you're gettin' the idea how bad it is here. We have friends that won't go out. It's not always that you experienced something. It's the fear."

That was about the extent of Timothy's reports. He pleaded that having moved to Vincennes from Kentucky when he turned twenty-two the year before, he didn't have a lot to say about the town. Then, all of a sudden, he seemed to think he'd painted too dark a picture and hastened, "There *are* some straight people you can be out to. In Kentucky I was out at work. I just started doin' that here. Like one day last week, this woman I work with walked in with this really different outfit on and saw me lookin' at it. She told me, 'When I'm done with it, you can wear it. Maybe we can go to some of those places you guys go on weekends.' I hadn't ever told her. But she's a registered nurse and married to a doctor. So she's sophisticated. I don't know, maybe I'm findin' more people that really don't care. It just takes time to start comin' out and talkin' about it to 'em."

A draft rattled the blinds. He jittered. "If you want to know more about that boy's murder," he said, "you'd better talk to Barry Bishop. I read he was at the party. I only know what I read in the paper."

| | | |

Barry Bishop was the weatherman on the local TV news. He too was away that week. The following April, on a trip to Chicago, I drove the length of the Illinois-Indiana line to see him. Spring had breathed over the fields and settled in a lime yellow mist. Barry met me at the TV station, a small square building miles outside town, in the vast, plowed middle of farmland. He was sitting in the studio when I arrived, at an old metal desk. He was short and plumpish with blond, on-air coiffed hair. He was smiling while on the telephone and glanced toward the big weather map on the wall of the set, where magnetic cartoon fronts, snowflakes, thunderstorms, tornadoes, and temperatures stuck, all askew, awaiting the latest bulletin's sensible pattern and the touch of Barry's hand. "Oh, it's variable," he was telling a caller, "frosty conditions up there tonight. That's what it looks like, and up in the fifties tomorrow. You bet." But locally, he warned, heavy storms were rolling in in the late afternoon, with a tornado threat.

The TV audience of Vincennes and the surrounding farms did call in like that, sometimes just to chat, and Denise the newscaster, Jerry the sportscaster, or Barry took the calls. "We're down-home here," Barry said. "They watch ya in their living room five nights a week, they think of ya as their famous friend, somebody they can slap on the back if they run into ya at the K mart. During thunderstorms, like later today, you get loads of calls—scared old people, especially, and farmers. You have to reassure 'em when you go on the air—'Things are fine now, everything's safe'—and they calm down and go to bed. They learn to trust ya—I guess!"

On the flimsy facade of the set, Jerry, rehearsing the athleticism of his script, looked over at Barry and flipped a limp wrist, snorting jovially. "We're good friends," Barry announced. "I wish all rednecks were as good as he is." He yelled across the studio, "He's the sportscaster who thought Brian Boitano was just some gay porn star."

On-air, Jerry and Barry were sartorial twins, bookends enclosing the desk in baggy, black sports jackets—on the recommendation of the New York media consultants the station had

hired—and the effect was of uniformed checkout boys at a macabre supermarket. This was to have "cleaned up our country image," Barry had said earlier, chuckling. Denise, young and svelte,
donned pastel plaids, with big gold earrings hooping below her
punk-teased blond hair—nothing homespun except the broadcast.
The lead story tonight was a "high-speed chase" on Wabash Avenue, a drunkard driving with his license suspended. The
"close-up" examined the perilous careers of highway workers in a
taped interview. The redneck signalman's comments were incom-
prehensibly garbled, local speech; the reporter had adjusted his
accent to match. Barry, who'd stepped off the set, winked at me
and said proudly, "*Hell-o!* We get paid to talk like this!"

Barry, who was a born-and-bred local, understood and
abided by small-town midwestern ways. His weather report was
constructed around the driving conditions to the county's high
school basketball games, with gibes at an out-of-county team. "It's
like in the movie *Hoosiers,*" he'd said before the broadcast. "My
high school has a graduating class of a hundred and twenty and
four thousand people in the bleachers on weekends. Friday
nights, every policeman in southern Indiana is busy directin' traffic. We're *all* there! You don't go to the games, you're a Commie
foreigner." Now he switched from the camera that eyed the map
to the chroma key lens, which produced spirit geographies on the
TV screen that were not on the set. Swirling his hand against a
blank blue wall and relying on a map in his head, he magically
created the weather for Vincennes. "Late tonight," he said, "we
may have trouble, some thunder movin' in. We'll be lookin' out
for funnels! More at ten."

The biggest story they'd ever done—that had caused the
greatest volume of phone calls—had been about ground moles.
"It started when Jerry just said he had a terrible problem with
moles in his yard, while we were on the air. Well, it turned into
this big ole series—'cause the switchboard lit up for days. It
nearly paralyzed us, everybody in Knox County's ideas. One old
man said, 'Run a hose from your car exhaust to the holes in the
ground'—that was the way to take care of it."

Denise had caused a stir, too, with her AIDS story—"about

our AIDS patient here," she told me. Callers had complained about her report as "dirty movies" on the air. "Then when Jerry was getting over the flu," she recalled, "there were all those people thinking how bad he looked, wondering whether he got AIDS from Barry," who necessarily must have the disease, some viewers believed, because he was gay.

"I thought"—Barry threw up his hands—"My God, I'm just gonna have to outlive this. And then some old lady called thinkin' Denise looked pregnant and wantin' to know if *I* was the father. It tries your patience, sometimes," he moaned. "It does. Surely."

Between broadcasts, while he manned the phone and ate a Big Mac with the other hand, I marveled aloud that everyone seemed to know about his sexuality. "They may not like who I *am*," he said, "but they say, 'He's a real nice guy, and that's what matters.'" The station management had known for years; the topic had just come up one day in conversation, and he'd made it "quite clear" that for any stories they did on homosexuality—or "related matters"—he was "available" to give guidance. As for the whole viewing audience of nearby counties knowing, that was a result of the Brent Brand case, the gruesome antihomosexual hysteria the county prosecutor had inflamed. "Our competing station mentioned my name as one of the men at the party who was testifying before the grand jury. With the way the case was handled, what else would anybody assume except I'm gay, if they didn't think it already?"

Barry dug out a file of photocopied newspaper clips. From them and what he told me, I pieced together something of the social toll of Brent Brand's death. The original investigation had been dropped in 1986 when a coroner in Illinois, where the body was found, reported "no physical evidence of foul play." Priscilla Wissel, Brand's mother, was not assuaged, particularly because rumors abounded that her son had attended a homosexual orgy the night he disappeared. She contacted "60 Minutes," "20/20," the FBI, and the governor of Indiana before she found the new county prosecutor, Mr. McGaughey, and the *Knox County Daily News* eager to champion her grief. The newspaper began a rash of rabid reports, liberally quoting McGaughey, who impaneled a grand jury and talked of new evidence and a " 'big break' in the case." Mrs. Wissel told the *News*, "It was a cult, and they intended to kill Brent. . . . It was a planned party, and Brent was the target." The Knox County coroner—and Mrs. Wissel's family doctor—one Dr. Rohrer, these many months later, suddenly began to suspect "foul play" and talked loosely about the "health threat to our community" through deviant sexual parties, where there was a danger of AIDS. And soon enough McGaughey uncovered "a large homosexual community here," which he couldn't help but believe was "caused" by pornography and linked to what the *News* called "the marked increase in child molestation cases being investigated" in Knox County since McGaughey had been sworn in. "Sources" pointed out "a cultish connection" in Brand's "bizarre death, possibly 'sacrificial' in form." The prosecutor was able to link one young man to the cult because he wore an earring.

"Lots of lives were ruined"—*rooned*, Barry pronounced it— "because of that grand jury. Three Vincennes University students had to add a semester, one guy tried to commit suicide when his family found out he was gay, at least three men I know lost their jobs. There was lots of vandalism. One guy had stones thrown at his car when he left the courthouse. And *he* wasn't even at the party—most of *them* had to move away. Just two or three are still left in the area, of the people that were actually at that party."

Barry had been there himself for less than an hour, he remembered. "There were thirty or forty people. I got there late and left early; it was actually so boring. So I don't know what happened before or after. But the whole time I was there the lights were on and people's clothes were on and a number of theater people from Vincennes University were standing around discussing shows. It wasn't even a gay party! There were straight people there—and *no* one that was famous! Such *ridiculous* stories! There wasn't one person there capable of a violent act—except that one man I couldn't speak for, from *Kentucky*," he spat, as suspicious as the next Hoosier of aliens.

But even that strange Kentuckian—Brand's buddy, who'd deposited the young man's corpse in the ditch—had, in the end, not been indicted for anything like murder. James Leyendecker, from near Louisville, had awakened from a drunken stupor, well after the party ended, and found Brand dead by his side. He'd panicked and driven the body to Illinois, across the Wabash—that was it. And in time—with the *News*, the prosecutor, and grand jury all swollen up in a vacuum of evidence, less real than Barry's chroma key–concocted weather—even Coroner Rohrer abandoned the case, declaring that the likely cause of death was alcohol and an overdose of perodane, a morphinelike drug. "Eighteen-year-olds do not die for no reason," he told the press warily, though now he hinted the party had been a homosexual den of narcotics.

"There weren't any *drugs*!" Barry sniffed with disgust. "Except who knows about Brand? I didn't even *see* him at that party. He was known as a street hustler, *practically*!"

Through the Indiana Civil Liberties Union, Barry had voluntarily stepped forward in the case, to corroborate the story of the owner of the house where the party took place, whom the prosecutor was trying to drive out of town. "I'm all the time testifying at trials anyway," Barry said. "Weather-related information. 'What was the flood stage when the lady's body was dumped in the river?'—that kind of stuff. But they already knew at work, because I already told 'em, '*I* know what's goin' on! Any "sacrifices" took place a hell of a long time after I was there!' When my name turned up public on our competitor's news, though, they asked me to take a few days off, till the grand jury was done. But the grand jury just kept going on and on. I went out to California. The station finally got fed up. They called me and said, 'Get your butt back here, you're back on the air.' I was off about a month. Things settled down.

"Oh, I don't hate the prosecutor for this thing! He probably just got caught up in the rush for public office and stepped out of reality a ways. He'd probably do things differently now."

But could Barry's television audience be at all so forgiving of him as he was of the prosecutor and his grand jury? I wondered. "Half a dozen occasions out in town," Barry recalled, "high school kids—and generally high school *girls*—yelled 'faggot.' I'm certain the station got a number of nasty calls. But the people I work with told me the phone was two to one in favor of gettin' me back. I'm not saying I'm unique. But it's my attitude that if you're going to be closeted, that's the way you're gonna get treated. I don't flaunt it—*no!* That would be the wrong approach. If you're truthful and people just get to know you, you're a good person first and 'gay' and 'straight' secondary. Like our viewers felt—'We don't care, we want him back.' "

After the ten o'clock news, Barry and I went for coffee in town. In the brilliance of a spotlight moon, a char-and-silver vaudeville sky rolled wild: black vortex clouds, like the stockinged legs of mad chorines, threatening to kick up the ground, then withdrawing to the applause of thunder. I asked the waitress for extra cream. She served me a plateful of tiny, plastic cups of synthetic lightener. I wrinkled my nose. Barry apologized, adding, "She grew up here on unreal things."

CHAPTER 16

THE PARTHENON'S SHADOW

THERE WERE BLUE LAWS IN VINCENNES. HOMOSEXUALS DROVE TO Louisville or even as far as Nashville on weekends to party—so I was told by a young man I met late one night at the park along the Wabash. He had a rose tattooed on his hand. His partying days were over. His sister, a single mother, had been killed five weeks before in a car wreck. He'd inherited his five-year-old niece and two preschool nephews. "I've been so consumed with everything," he said. "Like taking the kids to the doctor, all that, takes all your time. I really can't go out much anymore, not as far as Louisville."

On my way to Nashville the next day, I found no welcome sign at the Kentucky line, but even without the Ohio River, whose mud divided the states, I'd have known I was there, in the commonwealth of Thoroughbreds—beautiful horses, fast women, as Kentuckians themselves boast about their state. From behind the steering wheels of horse trucks and new Cadillacs, Kentucky Colonel gentlemen, with round red faces and dove white hair, fluttered a slow hand at the passing traffic. (The governor's proclamation making my grandfather a colonel had hung above the family Bible in his living room.) Even in tacky Henderson, hunched on the river border, a grand number of blond, lacquered belles drove Jaguars.

Western Kentucky rolled gentle and voluptuous—turquoise-tinted pastures and blue-misted ravines, wrinkly rows of tobacco. On this early August day of 1987, the soft sky above Route 41 was bright, pillowed with pink-and-baby-blue clouds; the air was newer, lighter than over the burning corn barrens of Indiana. There were no real hills till Tennessee. Near Nashville, the terrain dilated deeply, vaulting into Grecian acropolises that held the city.

The Parthenon, exact as the Athens original, sat in Centennial Park, a downtown Civil War battleground, where men of "Greek" interests sought each other out in the john across from the temple. Police, too, had been recently haunting the grounds, exposing themselves in order to entice queers to commit "crimes against nature." I'd always been intrigued by the erotic commitment of these cops who so passionately worked the masturbatory beats of America. Nearly three hundred "sex criminals" (under Tennessee law) had been captured in the park so far that year. The *Nashville Tennessean* and the *Nashville Banner*, the town's two dailies, had published names, ages, addresses, and employers. Twenty or so of the men had been put on trial the week before I got there. "Most of them," a local gay activist explained to me, "aren't gay-identified. They're heterosexual, a lot of them married. But the public still sees it as a gay problem." And I wondered again if perhaps, after all, most homosexually active men were not gay.

It was nostalgia—as much as prurient political curiosity—that drew me to the Parthenon my very first day in Tennessee. When I was in junior high, in the early sixties, my family lived in Tullahoma, a tiny town some seventy miles southeast toward Chattanooga. I'd first seen the Athenian replica back then and associated it with fig-leafed statues of naked gods, pictures of which I often sweated over in *World Book Encyclopedia*. The building was under restoration now, fenced in. A row of cars observed it from across a yard, while their drivers obliquely tolled the comings and goings at the outside men's room door. These men shopping from their cars were white, nearly all of the men in the john were black. A very general plea to the masculine world was scrawled on a toilet stall: "I love you I need you." A more desperate concession yet had been knifed in the plaster above the urinals: "Any instrument of cruelty you want used on me." I wondered if all this had been going on when my parents brought me here nearly thirty years ago and, as an adolescent, I'd been oblivious.

In a wrecked, rusted sports car, a curly-headed churl, scrawny and shirtless, watched the toilet traffic. Back in my own car, I caught his eye. He snarled, "*Wha*chulookina'?" His face was raw with hatred.

"I'm wonderin' the same thing about you, man," I barked back.

"*I ain't no faggot,*" he spat. "You fuckin' lookin' for a fight?"

"If you're no faggot," I cried, "you're hangin' around a real odd place. You *are* a mother-fuckin' queer." I strong-armed the air. He jumped from his car, then abruptly wedged himself behind the open door, as if only greater manhood held him back from pummeling a sissy. I was hooked for the moment on the power of brutality. I couldn't quit. "*Queer!*" I taunted before driving away. He stood stunned, marveling that a fag—he was sure that I was one—so violently dared to boomerang his loathing. And in that brief moment it seemed to me that what he hated most was what he feared most desperately—his own desire. Two fey young men, cross-legged on the hood of a car nearby, had been winking at the male passersby, giggling like coeds. They stared at me now. Their faces were amazed.

The only person I knew in Nashville was a lesbian bartender who'd moved from Boston on a lark. She'd offered to introduce me to her friends. She worked at a newspapermen's hangout across the alley from the *Banner* and *Tennessean*, where she knew a gay writer on staff. I met him at the bar over lunch. Randy Lynn had come to the Nashville papers from an advertising job at a Christian record company. Originally from rural Missouri, he'd refined his drawl.

"I fell into songwriting," he said. "Doing ad copy and gospel lyrics is all the same." A recent single of his had topped the gospel charts and was nominated for Song of the Year, a Dove Award, by the Gospel Music Association. "There's lots of us in the business who're gay."

As recently as his nomination for the Dove Award, Randy had been a leader in the national "ex-gay" movement, too— promoting the born-again Christian "cure." Only within the last few months had he "come out" and so suddenly become a fire-brand among Nashville's heretofore tepid homosexuals. He'd challenged the injustice of the Parthenon arrests and was rousing local support for the national gay rights March on Washington in the fall. For all his newness to the cause—perhaps because of it— Randy possessed a certain wisdom about his gay identity and the purpose of gay politics.

"I just *assume* people know. Someone'll ask me, 'Are you see-ing anyone?' I say, 'A guy named Frank.' And they'll say, 'What are you trying to tell me?' 'That Frank and I are lovers.' 'No! What are you trying to *say*—you're a homosexual?' 'No-o-o. I'm not trying to *say* that at all. Didn't you know that already?'

"I *hate* all the assumptions that go with labels. But now I'm to the point of donning a pink triangle"—that symbol the Nazis forced on homosexuals, coopted as a symbol of pride by gay lib-eration. "Somebody's got to do it. I really want to be the hetero-sexual population's worst nightmare, you know. By that I mean, *not* the stereotypical queer. I want to teach a Sunday school class and say, 'There's a higher percentage of gays in the Church, you know, because that sensitivity pulls them to God.' You've got to be somebody they like; then you drop the bomb."

That night Randy took me to dinner at Houston's, where the gospel and country-and-western music set eat—upscale hamburg-ers, French onion soup, candles. He nodded at colleagues and stopped to chat. He'd seen Marie Osmond there the week before, and Barbara Mandrell. During dinner he recalled his years in a Christian commune. "Being musical was considered feminine," he said. "So they had me working in a La-Z-Boy recliner factory to make me straight. But when it was time for services, they trotted me out to sing, because music attracted the crowds."

Uppermost in the stack of books on Randy Lynn's coffee table was *The Gay Cliché: Or How to Be a Homosexual Guy and Still Maintain Some Slight Degree of Individuality*. Randy was wearing pastel-striped Bermuda shorts with thick knitted socks and high-topped white leather tennies—gay comment on urban ghetto wear, beyond camp to dogmatic refinement. His youthful flattop was graying. He'd "turned gay" on his thirtieth birthday, he told me. "I thought," he said, " 'Here I am thirty and my life hasn't started.' There was a big joke among 'ex-gays'—they'd say, 'Who's holding out? Who's got the pill and keeping it secret?' The group here's called Promise. *Promise what?*"

Randy sat on a muslin-wrapped sofa beneath a big framed map of C. S. Lewis's Narnia, a born-again Christian fantasyland. The seven volumes of *Hymns of the Family of God* stood pinched between wooden mallard heads in the bookcase. For the evening he'd yielded his "throne," his favorite chair, to an ex-"ex-gay" friend whose liberation was even more recent than Randy's. Chris Yates was young, mid-twenties, powerfully tall, and broad-shouldered. He chain-smoked, exhaling plumes like a demon, and held tight to the claws carved on the arms of the chair. The heels of his shoes pressed hard against its front claw feet. His voice was obsessed, sometimes bitterly giddy and cavalier, sometimes trucu-lent with hatred. Randy encouraged Chris to tell me about his life. Their stories were corroborations of each other, if remem-bered with different spirits. Randy recalled his like an Exodus, Chris his like a Holocaust. Chris lifted a cigarette to his lips. His hands were as strong as a healer's, his fingernails chewed to the quick.

"I want a little white house with a picket fence and the same man for thirty years," he stated. "If I cain't have that, I don't want nothin' a-tall." He spoke with the precise country spice of a TV preacher. "My deddie's congregation is four thousand every Sun-day, the largest Pentecostal church in the Midwest. My brother and I used to sit in the first row of the choir loft, it'd be a dead service, gettin' to the last song before the preachin'. I'd tell Jimmy, 'Boy, he's dropped his watermelon! He couldn't work 'em up now if he wanted to! *Watch this!*' On that last verse I'd jump up and let out this great big whoop, and, *brother,* they'd go buck-dancin' all around that church, shoutin' and fallin' out in the spirit, for about an hour. Speakin' in tongues is a raw data dump." Chris was a gospel singer and a computer genius, too. "See, it just takes one good yelp to bring the spirit down!

"I was raised in a family I didn't know was abusive till I grew up and started dealin' with my alcoholism. I thought everyone was routinely beaten, because my parents preached that's what God expected you to do to children. Last winter, I called my parents from the psychiatric hospital and said, 'I'm gettin' outa here at five and *I'm goin' to kill you.*' They called the doctor, who they hated, and he called and told me, 'They're not worth it.' I have to say I don't know anyone angrier than I am." He took a deep drag. "I think anger is a catalyst for change. *Oh, that cigarette's good!*" He sighed defiantly, exhaling as though that forbidden jet carried a secret gospel.

From his seat below the Narnia map, Randy inserted, "People do the best they can. I call this my 'theology according to Katharine Hepburn'—all those lines in *On Golden Pond?*"

"I mean," Chris went on, "all the male children on both sides of my family and some of the women were preachers. It was just expected. I had a war inside. God called me to do something for my world, but I was Dr. Jekyll and Mr Hyde. I couldn't ratio-nalize that with my homosexual feelings." A fire burned in his eyes, fevered his cheeks. "This is very hard for me," he whis-pered. "I've buried it, I've tried to. I don't think for a long time I even knew why I was angry."

Why Chris began then to dig up his hell in front of me, I'll never know: a kind of reality check, maybe. Perhaps I was simply someone wholly uninvested in his life who in a word or a nod or with surprised eyes might legitimize the chaos of his hatred and the desperation of his same-sex love. Across the country, men I'd met had spilled their secrets to me, a man who'd soon disappear and perhaps transport some of their confused vulnerability with him and relieve them of some grievous, silent weight. They wanted to confess, to give their grief another life, independent of their souls. Chris confessed now. It tore at him. He talked and, crying, buried his face.

He had been a "problem child" whose parents had sent him away to St. Louis for junior high, to a Pentecostal boarding school. "They knew in their heart what the 'problem' was," he stated. "I was working the mall before I could ejaculate. In the seventh grade, *I* instigated a thing with one of my teachers. There were plenty of sex acts in the dorm. My RA was queer—*I had him!*" At eighteen he'd "come out" to his parents. That was 1980. They'd forced him into "cures" at a series of "deliverance centers"—Christian, pseudopsychiatric institutions. Preachers, they were also rich real estate entrepreneurs. The family home had cost half a million. "They presented it," Chris said, "as, 'Either be straight or we'll cut you off.' I was scared." His first therapist-deliverer—"a recovering homo," Chris put it—had seduced him, "then proceeded to certify to my folks that he'd made me 'straight.' " The staff taught Chris masculinity there—how to move his hands when singing gospel—he owned and sang with a Christian rock band—how to color his voice on the phone. A woman preacher, whose virile voice was her spiritual gift, had been his speech coach. He'd learned well, it seemed to me, or he'd never been a sissy to begin with. Chris was as charismatically butch as a camp meeting evangelist. His hair was whitewalled, like a marine's. He was wearing a pair of stiff new jeans. His blue eyes seemed to melt against his red-hot cheeks.

He slid forward in his chair, half kneeling. "I remember my folks waking me up at four in the morning," he said, "casting devils out of me. Shaking me, slapping me, screaming in tongues, commanding Satan at the top of their lungs, rebuking the demon of homosexuality. Sometimes in public, during a service. I can't describe the horror of having your mother look at you from across a crowded room and burst into tears for no reason, simply because you're you. My mother and father—and I need to tell you this—my parents are very big into prophecy. Mom told me she'd received a 'Word of Faith'—if I didn't go 'straight,' I'd be dead of the 'homosexual plague' in twenty-four months. So I waited the twenty-four months, and when it was over I cried all day because I was still alive."

In college, a Pentecostal Bible school, Chris for the first time sought out women. "My lifelong dream," he said, "was to be a preacher. I expected to pastor Dad's church." His family was royalty in glossolalic circles, with bloodline rights and obligations. Chris met Ruth. "She seemed to know all about me," he recalled, meaning his pedigree and destiny, not his homosexual longing. He fasted for hours in the chapel each night, to keep himself from cruising the parks and gay bars. Ruth prayed with him. "I'd pray, 'Oh, God, set me free, make me clean,' and sometimes I'd hear her praying the same thing. She had this girlfriend she couldn't go a few hours without seeing. They'd have a fight, she'd cry for days. One day I told her God had delivered me from homosexuality. She burst into tears. I said, 'I know you're fightin' the same thing.'

"My parents said God put us together so we could fight it together the rest of our lives!" His laugh was small and sour. "You know, one time I had tried to feel her breasts. She said, 'No! It's wrong before we're married.' Then I find out that bitch had been eatin' pussy for years!"

When that love failed, rumors grew that Chris's deliverance was incomplete. His parents arranged a marriage: Ellen, an older woman whom the men of the church had passed by, an accomplished gospel keyboardist, good family. They announced their decision to Chris over breakfast at the International House of Pancakes in Peoria, Illinois, when his gospel band was in town for a gig. That was August. They gave him till January to do it. Ellen lived three hours away.

"I drove down," Chris said, and crushed out his cigarette. "I think she was kinda humored by it. We went to Six Flags Over St. Louis. She was afraid of the rides, she was boring. But that night I called Dad and said, 'I did it, I'm gonna marry her.' I never asked her, I just sat down and said, 'I'm very talented, my family's prominent, I stand to be pastor of my father's church. Your dream is to be a preacher's wife; so we're going to get married.' She laughed—and on the twenty-seventh of November that same year we were married."

Chris tried to run away right before the wedding. His father caught up with him and blackmailed him back, threatened to have him arrested for stealing some family cash. Chris retold it like an altar call—in a slow-paced, tear-choked hush. "I drove Highway 74 west from Bloomington, Illinois, across the Indiana line, turned south on Route 41, kept going until I saw the sign for Terre Haute. There I found a room for the night, to sleep. . . ." He was florid with extraneous, sweat-hot detail, with an inexorable, hell-bound rhythm on his breath. He pinched the tension from the bridge of his nose, gathered his brow. His eyes glistened like blood and were dead. He lit a cigarette.

"You have to understand how afraid I was," he pleaded, as though to defend his sanity. "I had no marketable skills except gospel music and the Pentecostal ministry. My education meant nothing to the outside world. I had no money except what my parents gave me. I thought all being gay was was having sex in parks and bathhouses. My parents taught me gays were all liars and murderers—and couldn't even hold a job and earn a livin'. I lived completely in their world, I believed them. *They*," he said inclusively, as though of a collective, unseen tyranny, "want you to believe that about yourself, a whole series of self-fulfilling prophecies. If you buy into it at all, you begin to live it, you can't escape. You say, 'I can't help it. It's who I am. Everybody like me lives this way.' They told me gays were all degenerate. And by the time they were through with me I was."

He sobbed. "It's good for me to be able to feel like this," he said. "For years I couldn't cry. I was angry, I felt violent, but I couldn't feel sad. I thought I was unique—so *I hated everybody*."

Redemption Band, Chris's group, was a big success by the time he'd graduated college. *"You looked inside my lonely heart and made each fantasy come true. . . ."* He sang their theme song for me bitterly, one of those distressing kinds of lyrics with which born-agains eroticize Jesus. Redemption Band had done some two hundred gigs a year, averaged seven thousand seats, ranked at the top of the gospel charts, had been booked a number of times by Jim and Tammy Bakker for their Praise the Lord Club and Heritage, U.S.A., the mawkish Jesus-for-a-price resort. They'd grossed half a million record sales in their last year. Their transportation was a Silver Eagle bus with three bedrooms. Chris's mouth grew rank with a smile.

"There's nothin'," he said, "like slingin' up with big-time preachers in the back of that bus. I've had the best. I fulfilled my parents' prophecy. I fucked over my*self*, I fucked *every*body. I was a drunk and doin' drugs. I was ripped onstage, but the fans got high on Jesus anyway."

He tapped a cigarette from its pack and struck a match, tensed like an animal about to spring. I felt suffocated by his story. I hadn't endured his misery, but similar trials—the Church, a childhood grooming for the pulpit, "deliverances" over and over again. I'd married to escape, though that had been my choice, nothing arranged. Still, I'd somehow always seen the options—maybe because my parents had been relenting in the end, more fanatic in their love for me than devoted to the Church's punishments. None of us wholly forgives such spiritual abuse, though in time we may heal it wonderfully. Listening to Chris made the faded scars of my past inflame. I rose once to embrace him, horribly attracted to his anger. He waved me away breathlessly, crying. Randy's face, throughout the evening, never changed. It kept a knowing smile, as though he were watching the terrible, joyful progress of a soul's salvation.

In a vortex of smoke, Chris continued. His face for the first time softened, oddly, fortelling his story. On a gig in Texarkana, Arkansas, his childhood home, he suddenly began to escape his parents' control. He left his marriage. Stoned and depressed, he eluded the band and his wife to cruise the shopping mall and ran into two old friends from grade school there. Telling it, Chris was giddy, a man who had found a strange freedom. He remembered, "Almost simultaneously they said, 'Well, we *must* do brunch!' I knew right away they were fags. I just *love* queers! They'd been lovers since high school!"

That was the beginning, he said, of what he could only describe as a spiritual odyssey, the first time he'd met someone gay who wasn't a fast park fuck—"or just a story in *Newsweek* magazine," he explained. "Real people who loved each other, had good jobs, and paid their bills!" He split with his wife, went back on the road. "I never missed a beat," he reported. "The real fight was over an annulment. She still wanted to be a Pentecostal preacher's wife, and no one would touch her now that she'd been defiled by a homosexual."

The escape was incomplete. Chris owned the band, had the bus to pay for. "I *couldn't* quit," he argued. I suspected his addiction to his alienation had been deeper. He "came out" to the record company and the band. He recalled, "They told me to keep my mouth shut to the public. The fans were blessed, we were making big money." He tried several times to commit suicide and returned to his parents, prodigal and desperate. They had him committed.

In the hospital Chris overheard his father talking with the doctor, a Fundamentalist and a family friend. "Dad said, 'He got trapped after an adolescent experience. If you can make him forget long enough, God can come through.' And the doctor said, 'I assure you, Reverend, *he will forget!*' Chris paused and reflected. His face lit. "There's something I really want to say. Through all those shock treatments, I forgot my friends' phone numbers, I forgot my address, I forgot what my parents looked like. But I *never* forgot I was a homosexual."

His folks prepared a final treatment. "They wanted me to go to Mexico," Chris said. "They found this guy who 'cured' homosexuality by castration." To save his manhood, he overdosed again on pills and booze. "And something just snapped," he claimed. "I finally realized how far they were willing to go to remake me in their image." In the *Advocate* he had read about an alcoholism treatment center in Minnesota—Pride Institute—specifically for homosexuals. He decided to go. "Dad said, 'If you get on that plane, you're not my son.' Let me tell you, that was the *hardest* thing I ever did." Chris whooped, like a man falling out in the spirit. "But, oh, let me tell ya! *It was the best thing!*"

"He's gonna preach!" Randy shouted sincerely. "He's gonna speak in tongues!"

"I have to tell you the ending!" Chris proclaimed tearfully. "The fourth day I was there, the UPS man—a hunk"—he grinned—"delivered a truckload of packages. I was thinkin', I hope just one's for me. All *thirteen* of 'em were! My parents had sent me every little thing I ever owned, shipped me right out of their lives, *them bitches!* I went so crazy they had to sedate me. *Well,* when I woke up, there was a woman and an old man sittin' by my bed. She was an ordained Lutheran minister and a lesbian. The old man was her father, a pastor of some fame in those circles," Chris said. "They told their story—how she 'came out' and her father didn't understand, how he came to see that God created her the way she was. He told me something bigger than myself had kept me alive through all of this, that God didn't want me to regret or forget the past but use it to change the future, that that call I felt as a child to do God's work was still there *because* of who I am, not in spite of it.

"You know what? *I believed him!*" Chris cried, his surprised joy as great as if it had all just happened. "If I ever in my whole life had a spiritual experience, that was it! I'm sober eight months now. I'm *gay!* I'll be sober and gay tomorrow!"

"*Preach it, Brother Yates!*" Randy goaded.

"These people who hate queers are ridiculing the creation of God. I for one am not willing anymore to let that happen. When the Bible says, 'The last shall be first,' well, some of us have been last too long. Not the Church or the politicians or the fear of AIDS—nor anything you can think of—can make me turn back now." His belief was as flaming as St. Paul's, charismatic as the tongues of Pentecost. He sat back in the throne and cried, a man newly converted, his spirit gifts yet unrealized.

I was bred on the radio broadcasts of the Grand Ole Oprey. After my family moved from southern Ohio to Tennessee, we made a pilgrimage once a month to Nashville's Ryman Auditorium, the Oprey's home, for the all-night gospel sings. Country quartets crooning bound-for-Zion harmonies, soprano shouts of *"Glo-o-*

ory!" growling Amens—in a spirit fit, my grandmother almost went over the balcony at a gospel sing once. I went back to pay homage to the old brick hall, beautiful and unsophisticated, a mute museum now. That night Randy took me to the new Opreyland on the edge of the city, a "showpark" with rides and Hollywood-style musicals, sponsored this year by Toyota. Randy's connections got us tickets to sit with the singers onstage. Between Roy Acuff and Del Reeves, Minnie Pearl made a surprise visit, her beflowered hat still dangling its price tag. Arthritic and authentic, she mostly showed up unannounced now, displaced in the slick of stage makeup and TV lights. Minnie was my mother's country idol. Her painful fingers could no longer sign an autograph, but she posed with me for a picture: I was as giddy as a grandchild.

Where old Tennessee wasn't disappearing, it was being repackaged for corporate tastes. Nissan had opened a plant in the suburbs of Nashville, robot-efficient management, Japanese style. Downtown, postmodern towers crowded post-Confederate designs and housed the "Wall Street of the New South." Still, some of the old jubilant tawdry spirit was alive enough to fight. Bill Boner—homegrown, backslapping—was leading the mayoral race against Phil Bredesen, a Harvard Yard Yankee, a rich transplant. Drag queens were still heroines among gay men, unlike up north, where likely they were demeaned as political embarrassments. Randy took me to the Warehouse, where his favorites "sang." A black drag queen in a star-white gown was onstage lip-synching Anita Baker. I later learned "her" name was Pucci. I was standing in the back by the spotlight man, who'd spilled the contents of his wallet at my feet. "My son," Will said as I handed him back the picture of a little boy.

"Are you married?" I asked.

"Yes!" he drawled. Every word was twice its length. "Well, I *was*. Almost three years. But she got kilt with my boy in a car wreck." I was drinking a beer and nibbling on popcorn. I offered him some kernels with my sympathy. I didn't have a fix on his feelings. He went on, "I was comin' outa the closet the whole time we was married, though. I was, you know, *doin'* things."

He'd had two lovers since. One of them died in a car wreck, too, four years to the day—the man he'd been seeing when his wife was living. "Aren't you *glad* you talked to me? I'm *loads* o' fun!"

Will had been living in Nashville "too long," he sang, "in the buckle of the Bible belt." (He was moving to Dallas to escape.) The Baptist Sunday School Board, headquartered here, had a heavy thumb. "And the Church of Christ is like rabbits. My sister's one. *They don't like quars!* She won't even talk to me 'cept on Thanksgiving and Christmas. My mother's okay. 'Course I never *told her* anything. But I guess our mothers always know, don't they?

"They know at my job, too," by which he did not mean working the spotlight—that was a hobby. He smugly shifted the cap on his head, an ad for the water heater company where he was a repairman. "They don't say nothin' towards me. *Hay*-uhl! Some big-mouth bitch from my work come in here to see the drags one time and saw me. She went blabbin' to ever'body. I guess they seen me doin' my work so good, so they just shut her up about it.

"Besides"—and he lowered his voice and leaned into my ear—"one of my bosses is . . . I won't say 'gay,' but he is *definitely* in'er'sted. I raise Siberian huskies on my mom's farm, an' he come out to look about one. Well, there's some chug holes about eight feet. It was so damn hot! So he says he wantsa go swimmin'. I said, 'Fine, if you wanna take your clothes off, you go right ahead 'cause I don't have no swimmin' trunks to loan ya.' He was hung like a great big mule an' that ole dick just swum aroun' in the water like it was dead an' floatin' to the top. I got my clothes off just like he done—*an' I kep' my hands to myself!* He didn't get no hard-on. Honey, that water was *cold*! His thing mighta swinged around some, but it wasn't gonna *go* nowheres. He was too young, anyways, 'bout twenty-four. Besides, there is one thing I will not do. *I will not shit where I eat my food.* I'll go *up* in my job the *same way I got it.* I ain't gonna use my dick to do my work for me."

Pucci the drag queen wanted children.

"I only go out in public as a boy," he told me a day or two

after I'd seen him perform at the bar. "Most people only know me that way. We're all the same inside. It's just that some of us wear dresses for a living and some of us don't." His gowns were hung in the mess of the upstairs closet—except for the three or four he'd selected for his acts that night at the Warehouse (Anita Baker, Diana Ross). The evening's envelopes of glistening lamé were displayed on a rack on the bedroom door. One wall was furry with wigs. A zoo of teddy bears warily watched them from a shelf.

"I'm a chile!" Pucci exclaimed. Doll still, four black babies, three white babies, stared up at him from the bed. He rolled one on its stomach and patted its butt. "All adopted," he said of the Cabbage Patch kids.

Pucci was always frantically busy—rallying his friends for the gay march on Washington, helping the homeless, registering voters among Nashville's blacks, performing, *parenting*. "You gotta speak your feelings," he insisted. "That's why Lincoln made it possible. In my charity work, I always credit the gay community—so people know we're not all hanging out on street corners having sex."

He never did his charities in drag. No one would have suspected. Out of drag he was masculine and athletic. He'd just gotten back from racing his bike when I arrived at his apartment in a newish, treeless part of town. He was sporting black bike tights and a sun yellow cap with a brilliant green bill that cast a mossy reflection on his ebony face. His eyes were happy, black, round gems.

"For a female impersonator," he said, opening his hope chest to an exquisite dress whose breast bore the print of Diana Ross's lipstick, "it's not easy to find love. Being black makes it even more difficult. Black men don't like female impersonators, they don't look at them as being men. White men at least will respect you as an entertainer.

"Even as a boy, black men don't like me as much," he told me. "Maybe I'm too outspoken for black men. They're used to having black women be their housewife or mother. I believe in having a career. I don't believe in sitting home having dinner ready."

The dress in the chest had received the mark of his heroine's lips when Pucci danced with her once onstage. It had all been a fabulous mistake of timing. Ms. Ross had been announced and then delayed, as Pucci in Diana Ross drag was scurrying to his seat from the back of the auditorium. The screams and applause were thunderous.

"They thought I was her!" Pucci wailed. "So I said, 'I'm going to take *advantage* of this!' " And he'd walked all around kissing cheeks and waving his white foxtails. "Well, she came right down to my seat to get a look at me, then took me onstage. Her body felt like cotton," he reminisced. "Her perfume was so wonderful—well, you had to be there! She said, 'Damn! You got more jewelry than *I* got!' She knew I was a man. No *woman* would go in there like I did." She was singing "Swept Away." "Half of Nashville was there, going wild. Some reporter said, 'Who *are* you, miss?' " Pucci reached into the chest and touched the lip stain like a relic. "It was a wonderful year for me."

Pucci Lisenbee was raised on the vast, lost, black Southside of Chicago. Eight years earlier he had followed a man he'd just met back to Nashville; he was twenty years old then. "It was 7400 South," he said, placing the address of the childhood home. "By the interstate." He'd attended the Chicago Art Institute for a while. "I hated it." He'd modeled clothes for Carson's and Marshall Field's. "I wanted to be strictly a runway model, and I was too short. I'm only five feet six." He'd also danced. "Modern, pop, jazz." He was only thirteen when he started stealing away to the distant Northside gay bars. "I got a friend's ID, and you know what they say . . . about blacks all looking alike? So I didn't have any problem with *that*! The bouncers were white. Kinda wild. . . ." He lifted his eyes.

He'd never done drag professionally in Chicago. "My family usually flies down here once a year to see me perform," he said. "The only real problem I ever had was when I was a little bitty boy—my father saw me playing with girls. So he punished me and put a dress on me, and little girl's shoes, and made me go outside. *But I loved it!* So then he brought me in and whipped me for it. Now my parents are behind me in everything."

His babies, he suddenly thought as he talked of real life, wanted attention. He tickled their bellies. Then, pillowing them away from the edge of the bed, he led me downstairs, where three older babies sat on the couch in a quiet row, enjoying the easy listening on the radio. The room was preciously coordinated, with that elegance characteristic of a department store display: two overstuffed Deco-styled chairs and matching sofa, a lamp table draped with a cloth of fleurs-de-lis, pastel vases arranged with twigs, a potted palm. A big wicker basket was stacked with *Interview* and *GQ* magazines. At a conscientious angle on the coffee table lay Mary Wilson's *Dreamgirl: My Life as a Supreme.*

In the dining alcove, the table was always set—a glass salad bowl, brown dinner plates, and pink cloth napkins, black-stemmed champagne glasses waiting empty for the effervescence of romance, a centerpiece of heart-red gladiolas. The relationship Pucci had moved to Nashville for had not worked out. His lover had moved to Hawaii and gotten married.

"I suspected he was sort of 'that way' all along," Pucci reported with sympathy. "I mean, we *talked,* and I suspected he had tendencies. We broke up before he started dating women, though. He couldn't take me being a 'working wife.' I didn't want to be shut up in the house being loved.

"Now I'm attracted to white men more," he said, something he'd discovered since moving to the South. Chicago—an enduring northern experiment in apartheid—had been hostile to interracial couples. "I always wondered what it would be like to have someone outside your nationality," was his expression. "No, I never saw so many interracial couples as here. It really surprised me in a slave state. I *thought* it would be hard living here, especially with a white man. Then I realized it was *hard* in the North. Here I can always have a job. White, black, it's more who you know, if you really want to make it. In Chicago I didn't really *feel* prejudiced against. I went to school with all blacks, and where I lived was all black. Up there, most of my life, I never really saw anyone but black people. So you never know, do you?"

It was his career, anyway, that preoccupied him—not lovers, or sex. "I'm so busy trying to be a star," he stated. "Sex comes to my mind sometimes, but with the way things are now, I put it right out of my mind." On his sweatshirt he wore a safety pin, a symbol for "safe sex." Each of his babies wore one. He unfastened Manky's to straighten it up and kissed the doll on the forehead. Controlling the risk of infection *now* was what concerned him— not the consequences of his past.

"If it's your time, it's your time," he declared solemnly. "AIDS doesn't just happen, it's what God intends. Prayer is the only cure. You know, I *used* to believe God was punishing gays when AIDS first started. Then I realized, how could he be punishing us when we're his children? I'm definitely a person about God. Jesus comes first in my life. Then my mother."

He was dating, but only men who played by his rules. "I make it plain from the beginning it's just a good time. If they think sex—well, I don't like those kind of guys anyway. I like guys with big ideas. I'm not into teaching someone."

Baby Diana Hutton and Stephanie Wells, "goddaughters" (and namesakes) of drag performers, were wrapped in blankets now and sound asleep. Manky, Pucci imagined, had grown restless. He settled him firmly on his lap and retied a tiny shoestring. Pucci fathered thirteen dolls in all, black, white—"I have a little one from China, too," he added. "But a friend of mine is sitting him right now, because I went out of town performing. Her two and Lee like to play together. On their birthdays we always take them for a Big Mac, pull 'em up to the table in those baby seat high chairs to eat. People just *trip!*"

Pucci wet his finger with spit and rubbed a smudge from Manky's pink cheek. "Some friends dropped him on his head," he said, and winked at his baby. "That's why that mark's there. Oh, I don't think he got any brain damage! He's been acting normal lately. *I know one thing for sure*—I never get lonely. Not with my kids for company!"

That night at the Warehouse, Pucci performed three songs, each in a different dress. "Livin' for the Love of You" was royal blue. "Break Out" shined white and silver. "Show Me the Way" brought his fans to their feet. His gown was as red as a valentine.

My visit with Pucci startled me, less because of his lavish drag and his fatherly role to an intimate family of dolls than because of the ease he claimed as a gay black man since moving from Chicago to the South. Certainly I had not lived in the South since early adolescence, but my memories of blacks in the remains of the Confederacy had been terribly different from what I learned of Pucci's life.

I was born into a family of southerners who settled in southern Ohio at the end of the Second World War, in that Appalachian tristate tip along the Ohio River where the North abutts the border states. There we believed that Negroes were degenerate and also often dangerous. All the blacks I knew of lived in "Nigger Town" shanties. In this borderland of South and North, at least, we went to school together.

When the family moved to Tennessee in 1959, we went by train. Blacks were removed to the rear cars, a banishment I hardly noticed. In the grand, towered station in Nashville, the drinking fountains were racially labeled, which struck me because I'd never seen anything like it before. Two fountains—side by side though reserved separately—protruded from the wall at the top of the stairs from the train shed. The lure was irresistible. I drank from the spigot set aside for whites and felt the ineluctable power of it—a whole new geography of prerogative.

I went back to the old train station after my visit with Pucci Lisenbee. There were no passenger trains now through Nashville. The station was a stylish hotel, with the old segregated waiting room transformed into a posh restaurant frequented by businesspeople. I marveled at the number of whites and blacks eating at tables together where I'd never before seen blacks enter except as porters or redcaps. At the back of the building, the cavernous train shed sat abandoned and decayed. The fountains that had lured me were gone, though I found the place. Only the bolt and plumbing holes were left and four tinier scars where the signs

"White" and "Colored" had been torn away, like something that never happened.

How do you measure such change? By whose memory? What would Pucci's life have been as a black man in Nashville thirty years ago? As a Negro homosexual, doubly despised? How much could he have acknowledged his desire for same-sex love then, anyway? How far would his desire have even existed without permission to express it? After all, all of our needs beyond raw survival are mere products of possibility, brought to life only by the belief that this or that thing can be humanly had.

So, nearing the end of this journey through the South and that vast southern portion of the Midwest I had traveled, I wondered how to weigh what I'd experienced. Sleepless and musing, I left Nashville in the middle of the night, found a hotel for a few hours, crossed into the surging hills of eastern Tennessee at dawn, and ascended the milk-cool clouds obscuring the breasts of the Smokies. I was partial to the South, and still, for all the nostalgia of southern childhood that clung to me, it seemed a ruthless place. Violence was epidemic, both physical and spiritual. I considered men like Frank Reinhardt in Oklahoma and his lover, Wayne, who'd been shot to death in his pickup truck, probably by a fag-killing trick. In Vincennes and Nashville, antihomosexual crusades on the part of the law had destroyed men's lives, leaving many of them jobless, homeless, and terrified. Chris Yates had been emotionally brutalized by his Pentecostal parents and their church and had barely escaped their "cures" with his genitals intact. Yet in all that, he had painfully discovered his spiritual gifts.

Still, gay men did not live apart from the violence, but sometimes partook of it themselves. In rural Alabama Henry Meadows chose to live his sexual life among redneck men whose drunkenness and lawlessness often kept them jailed. Reba, the Mississippi drag queen, had been a thief, stealing jewelry from other queens. Michelle Prudhomme, the Cajun trapper, chose to stay at home in brutal poverty, loyal to his sisters and his folks. The unhappy priest I met in St. Louis remained in the homophobic Church and even so found some peace in that. Our choices all are complicated, our decisions impure. In the end it seemed to me that each of the men I met was broken or survived according to the justice exacted by his own standard, regardless of the place he lived or the nature of the society in which he found himself. Barry Bishop, the gay Vincennes weatherman, was loved by his colleagues and viewing audience because he was a good man and did not hide. No joy was unadulterated, no tragedy absolute. Religion crucified some men, but ennobled others. Politics and laws, humane or harsh, meant little against the tenor of the heart.

Yet after journeying through so many lives, I could not leave the South. It was as if I must try again to find my place in it. At the end of the day, I descended the Smokies to return to my parents' North Carolina home. I was still exploring.

CHAPTER 17

KLAN
COUNTRY

CRAIG AND RICHARD EPSON-NELMS (THEY HAD COMBINED THEIR surnames) were happy in the New South, too, though more starkly than Pucci Lisenbee. They lived in Charlotte, some forty miles east of Shelby, where my parents lived and where I'd returned with my father's pickup truck. Charlotte was another model southern city: a financiers' new skyline, as rootless with glass and steel as Pittsburgh's or Minneapolis's, whose new, solid corporate image barely belied a swamp of old-time religion that would not drain, indigenous and inexorable. This was the town, after all, that had nourished Heritage, U.S.A, the Reverend Jim and Tammy Bakker's Christian wonderworld—even if now the bedroom resort was sinking fast beneath the preacher's deceits, both erotic and fiscal. The night before I visited the Epson-Nelmses, several diners I struck up with at the New Brass Rail, a gay-oriented restaurant, defended the televangelist heatedly.

"He was the only one of 'em all that didn't condemn homosexuality," vocalized a guy named Jack. "*Lots* of us went down there for a good time. The most *no*torious rest stop on the interstate was the one nearest there—where the men from Heritage went!"

The Reverend Bakker himself, according to the Reverend Jerry Falwell, had sometimes enjoyed a good time with the boys. He was being deposed. The miry southern throne of faith was not. There were armies of preachers to take his place. The Reverend Joseph Chambers—less media polish, more backwoods grit—was rampaging against "homosexual haunts" in Charlotte as sources of AIDS. So far one porn shop after another had fallen beneath his sway (and the 7-Eleven stores had stopped carrying *Playboy*). The city council, it was said, had great respect for him, politically, and the mayor, the first black man elected, had reneged on a campaign promise to place a gay man and a lesbian on the Community Relations Board, in deference to the cleric. Mr. Chambers's disciples had lately even picketed a speech by Dr. Ruth!

There was a fledgling gay rights movement in Charlotte, a few people strong, to answer the preachers. The Epson-Nelmses were less a part of that than they were solitary warriors for respect who cast a sharp, quiet eye toward the ill-willed. There was a steely edge on their equanimity. At first they talked about nothing else but their illnesses—not disquietedly, but matter-of-factly—living proximate to death as they both did, surviving in its purlieus. "I had the fast-growing kind," said Richard of his cancer. He hadn't reached thirty yet. "If they hadn't found it when they did, I wouldn't be expecting to see 1988." The baseball-size tumor distending his adrenal gland was subsiding. He swallowed a handful of pills. "I just ate forty dollars," he said. He looked well, in spite of the morbid infestation of his flesh and its poison therapy. He was plump, little, his black skin vibrant with recuperation.

Richard and Craig lived in a new "apartment complex" (a Tudoresque town house) where not a decade ago there had been tobacco fields or cotton fields, or some such verdurous southern production. Sleepy Charlotte had swelled, protruding amoebalike over scanty country roads and skinny freight tracks that once had carried their slow interruptions across an empty, hot horizon and now blockaded steamy miles of suburban traffic. There were gaunt gardens and a swimming pool in the courtyard of this flimsy pillage of English history—modern America, the architectural plunderer. Indoors was a thin-walled series of white boxes, the kitchen a dark excrescence of the living room. Richard sat on the deep gold tufts of a crushed-velvet sofa, with Craig's blond thigh (he was wearing cutoffs) swung over his leg. The veins of Craig's sallow arms had been stippled with needles. He was at high risk for AIDS, having injected himself throughout his young adulthood, in the early 1980s, with Factor VIII. The lifeblood of hemophiliacs, the supply had already been infected with HIV back then, though no one was yet aware of the danger. Reasonably, Craig had been thoughtless of its safety. Of course, he'd had no choice. He needed the Factor to ensure that his blood would clot. Now that the purification process was believed absolute, it was too late.

"After Richard got sick, I set him up with my own hemotologist," said Craig. "I've been working with him since I was fifteen." This advantage Richard received was reciprocal. It was he who now gave Craig infusions of Factor VIII to control bleeds. Craig had pulled a muscle in his palm just the other day. Standing up, he showed me his knee, which was livid with death-slow coagulation. He displayed one box of clotting factor, a glass bottle, and the powder. "One thousand eight hundred dollars," he stated wryly. "I'll spend about a hundred and fifty thousand dollars on it this year. We're an expensive little family.

"When I had surgery on my gums last spring, my parents were there, who are not real happy about Richard and me. The doctor handed the bottle to Richard, and he infused me in front of them, just like my mother used to—because he's the one who's been giving me the stuff that keeps me alive. And it really made an impression." The lovers took to the sofa again, Craig's legs entwining Richard like albino serpents on a dark caducean staff. Pyewacket the dog—after the pet "in an old Kim Novak movie"—sat before them and scratched and whined. "*That* hospital visit cost twenty-two thousand dollars just in clotting factor," he added. "We love our insurance company."

Craig's life had been filled with this disease. He knew its sub-tleties, the haunted sense of internal rupture before a doctor could believe it was there. The apartment was full of medicines, medical files, reference books on health and disease—a current *Physicians' Desk Reference*. "I taught Richard," said Craig, "not to accept diagnoses, to read up, ask questions. His lymphoma may be AIDS-related, they don't know. Sometimes you don't have time for them to figure it out. Survival is learning to be a bitch of a patient." He lit a Merit, gave itching Pyewacket swigs of beer from a stale can on the lamp table. The pup calmed down in time. "You have to be able to scream your head off *and* know what you're talking about."

Craig believed he could pinpoint the infusion that had in-fected him—1977, the first Factor VIII he had gotten that year. "Epidemiologically," he explained, "it was the perfect time, the beginning of the epidemic." There is that need to locate the dead-ly source, that millisecond when the void passed into the blood—as if to find it were also, impossibly, to cancel it out. Multitudes of threatened men have drawn invisible flow charts, manically tracking virulent streams of semen to the one. Craig's pharmaceu-tical matrix was no less murky, turbulent with dates and symp-toms. He'd come down with severe flulike symptoms, with soaring viral titers. He'd been twelve then. But he'd been infused five hundred times before that, hundreds afterward. He'd gotten hepatitis B, Epstein-Barr, and cytomegalovirus. He'd no doubt gotten yet unnamed, unassessed germs. "I suspect," he said, "I was exposed, then reexposed and reexposed—till 1985, when they started treating the plasma to kill HIV beforehand."

Homosexual himself, Craig was predisposed perhaps to for-give the great American pool of infection from which the virus in his blood was popularly perceived to have drained—the plasma of IV drug abusers and homosexual men, unwittingly sold to plasma collectors. There was, Craig said, general anger among hemophil-iacs, a surge of animosity toward men who committed homosex-ual acts, particularly earlier in the epidemic. He quoted the mother of an infected hemophiliac infant, who'd spoken bitterly at a National Hemophilia Foundation convention. " 'These are innocent children, who didn't have a choice. The gays made a decision to engage in that behavior. It was something they didn't have to do.' I sat there the whole time and bit my tongue," Craig hissed.

The victims of hemophilia are almost invariably men. Unafflicted carrier mothers pass it on to sons and bear carrier daughters—a fifty-fifty chance with each pregnancy. Hemophiliac fathers always sire carrier daughters and normal sons. Intricate sexual transmission. Craig recalled a twenty-year-old hemophiliac who'd had an affair with a woman before he knew of his infection with HIV. "Is that any different?" he said, commenting on the mother who'd been angry at the convention.

AIDS had released a fast flood of old bigotry, Craig believed—of old intolerance dammed up. All Americans were swollen with ancient sex fears, whose streams shiveringly intercrossed. "But in the hemophilia community, there's always a special setup for homophobia," Craig put it. "Ninety-nine percent of every community wants these perfect little boys, that are macho. Then you have this son who can't play football, can't play almost any sport—if he does, he takes his life in his hands." (Brain hemorrhage is the number one killer of hemophiliacs. It turns the brain to gelatin, Craig told me.) "So, you've got a son who's often sick with bleeding episodes, dependent on the females in the family who're going to take care of him. You're all set up for thinking the kid's going to turn out gay.

"The conflict is phenomenal. Divorce is twice the national average in hemophiliac families. Guilt, a lot of guilt. The mother's guilty because she gave it to her son, ashamed that she's making him a sissy. The dad's distanced because he doesn't have the boy he wanted. *Now AIDS!*"

"His dad," added Richard, "has never given him an infusion."

"*Dig it*, I grew up in a military family and the Southern Baptist church—with all those macho boys and me gay *and* a hemophiliac. My parents had another hemophiliac son, too, he died in 1964—and Dad had *never* given him an infusion." Injections were as intimate as sex. "A typical hemophilia family."

Richard, reaching over beer-drunk Pyewacket to a brown

plastic pharmacopoeia on the coffee table, measured out a second palmful of pills. "Welcome to the world of oncology. It's costing a thousand dollars a week to treat this." He swilled. "I know it seems we spend all our time on health care. There's more to our lives than that."

Craig was a marketing expert for a hemophilia "home care" company. Richard—in this, a man like Craig's father—had been career navy. "I was still in the navy when we met," said Richard, and, untwining Craig's white snaking legs from his torso, led me to the den, where a half wall was decorated with certificates of military merit (along with a medical homeostasis chart). "I was completing my twelfth year, March last year. I really don't know how they found out that I was gay. Just suspicion, I guess. An investigation was launched. It took May to July to complete." He'd been working on Admiral Stanley Bumper's staff, Charleston, submarine group six, responsible for manning the vessels, ensuring they were ready for sea. "You've got to understand," he said, "until they kicked me out, on a 4.0 scale, I averaged 3.96 recordwise. In September I would have gotten my third consecutive good conduct medal—they give them every four years. I wanted that, twelve years of good conduct. But I got my walking papers in July." His black, mossy hair was still buzzed recruitment poster tight.

From a desk drawer he pulled out a twelve-year file of evaluations—and that last assessment of his career, August 22, 1986, which suddenly dropped his rating for "personal behavior" to 1.0, reflecting his "admitted HOMOSEXUALITY." And, on that account, his ability to counsel personnel and his military knowledge each fell a point, as if it were not so much the acts themselves—which he had engaged in vigorously for more than a decade, simultaneously with the superior performance of his naval duties—as it was the public disclosure that depraved a man's brain. It was the traitorous divulgence of the American male's erotic secrets that ruined a man.

"*Homosexuality,*"—his finger pecked the page—"is nearly always capped in military documents. It's a high crime, like treason."

Growing unsoldierly in time, he'd decided not to fight to stay in. "I started to. Then finally I asked myself, 'What would you be winning? Do you want that many more years of hiding and stress?' " He hung his head through the door to the living room, where Craig still sat. "But it made my choice easier that I met him that spring," he said with a grin. On a bookshelf and stacked in a corner on the floor were great binders of family snapshots. And on the coffee table sat wide, white-and-gold-filigreed albums of their wedding pictures, which, intrigued by the intricacy of their diseases and Richard's dismissal from the navy, I hadn't noticed.

They'd gotten "hitched," as they called it, in August of 1986. They'd met in Charleston the May before—"in a training weekend to work on a hot line," Craig explained. "I'd already been in a couple of relationships and was resigned to being a loner the rest of my life. So was he." He struck up another Merit and sipped a cup of tea. He was waiting till four o'clock to order a pizza: the parlors in Charlotte were closed between lunch and dinner. "On the last day of the training, we both ended up at a luncheon together—"

"At this point there was no attraction," said Richard.

"—at the Waffle House," Craig continued. "We talked for an hour, and something clicked. Then all afternoon in the session, little things started happening—he'd prop his head on my knee when we were sitting around the floor, or hold me."

This was proper, genteel Charleston, South Carolina, I kept thinking. "And no one was upset?" was all I could ask, burdened as I was with a view of the past.

Both of them turned stolid for a moment. "They screen people for these things," Craig said patiently. "No religious fanatics. They don't want people who'll give sermons when someone's in trouble. It's *his* dime!"

After the training that evening, Richard had taken Craig to church—the Metropolitan Community Church, a gay denomination. "I had no interest in religion," Craig said. "They started singing 'Amazing Grace,' and I shut down. I'm sorry, but when the drag queen behind me sang off key and none of the other

queens cared, I thought, Well, these people can't be too bad."
They went home together, talked all night, had sex. "It was *terrible* sex! I knew I was 'positive' "—for antibodies to HIV. "So there
were all these things we couldn't do without protection. If we'd
met in a bar and done that, we wouldn't be together."

That was at the start of the naval inquisition into Richard's
sex life. "I went to work happy anyway," he said. "Within a week
of meeting him, I knew we were going to be together for the rest
of our lives."

Most of the guests at the wedding were heterosexuals from
the hot line training. They all showed up at the house on the Isle
of Palms where the ceremony took place. Craig opened a white
wedding album and showed me first a picture of a woman friend
straightening their jackets—Craig's powdery blue, Richard's cake
white. And Richard plumbing his pocket to fetch the ring. (They
displayed their hands now to show me their bands.) There was a
snapshot of the many-plateaued and silver-confectioned cake and
another one showing the grooms twining arms to feed each other.
It was a dancing montage of dark suits, bright dresses, champagne
glasses, a representative racial mix of faces, sunny smiles.

Perhaps, I thought, this tolerance they praised was more
fluid along the coast, with its cosmopolitan population of
tourists—an economically watered pool of favorable attitudes.
Charlotte, however renewed, sat in the wooded interior of the
commonwealth of Jesse Helms, unscrupulous genital conscience
of the Senate and recovering segregationist. I was reluctant to
bring up race at all—because they hadn't, because it seemed so
alien an issue in their relationship. Surely there had been at the
least some subtle bigotry here, inside North Carolina, if not
against Richard independently, against their racial mixing, so recently have southern laws forbidden miscegenation. "No," Richard pondered, born in Texas himself. "We've not experienced
that." He grew spirited. "One of the things I like about living in
the South, if you're going to experience prejudice, it's going to be
up-front instead of a stab in the back northern style."

"In that area," Craig contributed, "you can bring on problems by being oversensitive to it—race *or* being gay."

"Whenever one of them would be an issue," Richard said, "I want it well established that it's *their* problem, not mine. Of course, where we live now, we're over here in Yuppie Town, U.S.A. Gay and black and white aren't the problems. It's 'green.' We have our fair share of BMWs in this neighborhood. We're the poor ones—we don't have a phone in our car."

"It just pays," elaborated Craig, "for us to be who we are with people. We don't go around here making *announcements* about ourselves, we put flesh and blood on 'gay.' We're *happy* when they feel free enough to ask us who's the wife!" Pyewacket, recovering from his stupor, had been accompanying his scratching with singing for some time. Craig clamped his snout. "*Silly bitch!* We still plan to send out birth announcements," he said.

"Well, he came out the right color and everything," Richard answered. "Light chocolate."

Sometime during that last week at my parents' house, I told Mom and Dad about Pucci in Nashville and about Richard and Craig: about the southern transformations in race and sex I'd seen something of, all the more magnificent because they seemed confederate—symbiotic rebellions—as if one demanded the other. "I'll tell you one thing," Mom drawled, knitting her brow, "*I* would not want to be black and live in the South." She said nothing then about "gay."

Shelby, North Carolina, sat in Cleveland County abreast of that low last heave of the Smokies—a fat continent's death gasp—before the still, sandy heartbeat of the red Atlantic plain. A cast-bronze Confederate soldier leaned green-eyed on his rifle above the courthouse square, his gaze toward modest postbellum mansions on streets fan-vaulted by centenary trees, monuments to Reconstruction. Downtown was dead. A "progressive city of home-owning, friendly, church-going resourceful people," said a Chamber of Commerce brochure, catching the New South's knack for Yankee dollars. Shelby had planted huge rural acres with the Freon-chilled atriums of shopping malls. The soft, near hills were newly cobwebbed with "subdivisions" of treeless "ranch-style homes."

My father had become a realtor in his retirement. He said (seconding Mother's sentiment) that when he got his license he'd been warned not to show "the Negroes" houses in "Caucasian" parts of the town. "Why, if I'd do somethin' like that down here, they'd burn a cross in my yard," he protested.

"Yes, they *would!*" Mother confirmed. She had gone to the recipe drawer, where she sometimes saved (and forgot) newspaper clippings she wanted me to see. These—from the *Shelby Star*—were yellowed, scavenged now to corroborate her point, if obliquely: Ku Klux Klan terror in Shelby, though against suspected homosexuals, not black, but white. In January of 1987 three white young men, assumed to be gay, had been executed—made to lie facedown on the floor, shot in the head—in Cleveland County's one porn bookstore. At first the police and the newspaper—with nothing but their own adrenal fantasies to rely on—blamed the killings on "an international pornography network linked to organized crime. . . . The trail leads all over North Carolina, throughout the United States and even worldwide," reported the winkless, wide-eyed *Star.*

Like all our worst plagues, the murderous hatred in Shelby was nothing so exotic. It was as homegrown to North Carolina as tobacco or Jesse Helms. When Mom gave me the clippings in August 1987 no killers had been caught, but Shelby's passion for global porn rings and conspiracies had wasted, with no truth to keep it alive. Numb reports had set in that the deaths had been a crusade by local Christian zealots or the KKK. Fertile Cleveland County was Christian, Klan land, had been since generations immemorial. In the spring of 1988—I was long back in New York from my travels—Mom mailed me another several months' supply of news from the *Star* and the *Charlotte Observer.* According to them, during the previous November Eugene Jackson (in his newspaper photograph his beret was emblazoned with a Christian cross) and Douglas Sheets had been indicted in the bookstore executions. They were members of the White Patriot party, a Klanish faction. Two fellow executioners remained uncaptured. According to one of their fliers, the four had enlisted for the white war against "Niggers, Jews, Queers, assorted Mongrels, white race traitors, and despicable informants"—enemies enumerated in a "Declaration of War." Some of their fliers sported drawings of lynchings. In this particular battle—the one at the Shelby III Adult Bookstore, near midnight, January 17, 1987—five of the enemy had been shot. Two survived. Travis Don Melton, nineteen, Paul Ten-Eyek Weston, twenty-six, and Kenneth Ray Godfrey, twenty-nine, died on the spot, their brains trailing blood across the concrete slab. The purpose of their deaths, stated a White Patriot manifesto, was to "avenge Yahweh on homosexuals."

Jim Baxter, editor of North Carolina's gay newspaper, *Front Page*, and Mab Segrest, an activist with North Carolinians Against Racist and Religious Violence, had documented the case. They were able to lead me to Faye and Bobby Melton, Travis Don's parents, whom I returned to North Carolina to visit in July of 1988. They lived in tiny Ellenboro, a half hour west of Shelby, where the asphalt-patch road ran scant between its dull yellow lines, rigidly followed an uncurving line of railroad tracks, where the red-plowed fields in the summer were swelteringly flat. Some miles on this side of town, before the highway wizened, you passed the cinder-block shed—floating small in a white sea of gravel, with far shores of cow pasture—where Travis Don and his friends were shot through the head. A brown van unloaded junk out front: a flea market now. In rolling woods about the same number of miles on the other side of the Meltons' house, there was a Baptist church—fire red brick and heaven white columns—with its wide graveyard in a pastoral hollow. The new Melton stone, with undying blooms chiseled in its upper corners, sat in the last new grave row before the forest. It was speckle-gray granite enclosed by two granite urns planted with plastic lilies:

TRAVIS DON

APR. 23, 1967

JAN. 17, 1987

The unaccustomed earth was still swollen, the grass dun. A fresh white basket of red plastic roses spilled across the ground.

"I know our daughter can tell you more than we can, of

course," Mrs. Melton said half apologetically on the late, hot yellow afternoon I visited them, "what Travis did with the younger generation." *Tra-ay-vis*. His liquid name lilted on her mother tongue, a drawling measure of song. Travis's teenaged sister, Diana, sat the afternoon through on the bench of the spinet, enclosed in her thoughts. Two huge pink curlers hung on her bangs. She said nothing. The Meltons could not accept that their son might have been homosexual, though throughout the afternoon it became clear to me that they tried to understand the possibility—just in case.

Among the five families, they were the only ones who still would talk, trying to settle the senselessness of what had happened. Mr. Melton—Bobby—gaunt as a fence post, smoked in the platform rocker by the sofa where his wife sat. She pulled Travis's high school picture from an album on the floor. His face was thin, like his father's, boyish fair. He wore a shy grin below a thatch of thread straight hair—this was not much more than a year before he died. There were earlier pictures of him there, grins and sibling pranks—an adolescent's home life—and some even younger. (Mr. Melton didn't look.) After graduation day the stream of pictures withered, dried, then a flood of newspaper articles took over, an inked life, a fat biography of death. "The Weston family," Mrs. Melton said—summarizing what was printed on a page clipped from the *Shelby Star*—"had claimed their son was there to testify for Christ. He was a missionary once't, said he went there against pornography.

"But no," she said, watching her hands clutch Travis's picture on the brown lap of her slacks. "If he had been goin' there to give out Bible tracts, he wouldn'ta waited till twelve o'clock at midnight to go and do it." Her frail, angry voice seemed always to fall in on itself, from the brink of tears. She pressed her fingers to her temple, through her spring-tight gray hair. She began to recite that night as "the Parris boy" had told it to her—a "boy" because at forty he still did not have a wife. She had memorized it. "They had planned," she said, "to go out and eat after Travis got off work—you know, my son—down to the Arby's and eat supper. And everything was normal, they wasn't any fight or fuss or wasn't anybody in there that was rude or nothin', and then just all of a sudden they broke in. He said, this Parris, he had heard gravel hit the driveway, and they thought, Well, who could that be at this time?—you know, about time for 'em to close. And Travis started baggin' up the money and one of 'em was sweepin' up, I think. And they come in the door and had the ski masks on and brown corduroy coats—that's the way the Parris boy described 'em. 'Two big men'—wudn't 'at the way they put it?"

"Uh-huh," Mr. Melton murmured, staring, inhaling a cigarette. His cheeks hollowed out with a ghost of smoke.

"And ordered 'em all to lay on the floor with their heads down. And then they ordered one of 'em to go back to the back and start puttin' the kerosene cans around, 'cause that's where they was gonna start burnin'. But this Parris said he heard all this commotion, and after they shot him, he *still* heard . . . stuff. And the leader man said, 'Are you another one of those *fay-gots?*'—that's what he called the Weston boy before he shot him. So they was some mention of that. But I really don't think nobody in there was gay. Them men had just been informed that, in my opinion.

"He can tell ya word for word, Parris can, what was said as the men was doin' each thing."

Travis had lived at home, in a trailer in the back—you could see it from the road—where the yard sloped down to the creek. He'd worked ever since he was old enough to hold a job and paid his share. Mr. Melton's wage at the textile mill was modest. The Shelby III had offered his son a half dollar more or so on the hour than the convenience store where he worked.

"We didn't really like it that Travis was workin' there," Mr. Melton began, then faded in smoke.

Mrs. Melton switched on a lamp to cut the pall of the draperies that darkened the picture window and picked up her husband's thought while he coughed. "We didn't *want* him to work there," she stated. "I told him a lot of people didn't like that kinda place and they had tried to set a fire to one down there in Charlotte or somep'n, and he said, 'Well, nothin' didn't never happen'—you know—'around here like 'at.' That was to ease my mind, I guess." She stopped and pondered. "But he *was* goin' to quit sure enough, 'cause on Monday after he got killed on Saturday night they called him from the Wal-Mart store to come to work. He *woulda* quit if he hada lived to quit.

"But that bookstore was not just for *gay* people. They had been a lot of *innocent* people there, too."

Her voice burned like a reed, crackling and nasal. They knew I was a writer, not that I was gay. I was "normal"—in this way just like them—so they spoke freely. "People that lived in the area, is what I mean," she added consolingly. "People from the mills—I asked my son one day. So it was the police, the only ones, that came out with the gay thing." She always spoke with a sense of tired strength, of endurance. Color pictures of the family she'd raised sat on the big, dark cabinet of the TV set, hung on the walls. There was a wedding picture of her older son and a boyhood picture of Travis playing in the front yard.

"Well," Mr. Melton counseled firmly, "there's no doctor's statement to say that any of 'em was gay. As far as we know Travis was normal like ever'body else. Except for that Billy Lamrick. *That's* where the 'gay' came in."

Billy Lamrick, who managed the Shelby III, was known to be gay. He was the one who had offered the job to Travis, was about Travis's age, a few years older. "He *says* he's gay and he's *proud* of it, uh-huh," Mrs. Melton stated, though now her emphasis did not seem deprecatory, really—just an expression of Lamrick's odd ways about things. "And Billy Lamrick is the biggest liar you'll ever run acrost," she went on rancorlessly, maybe even amused, "if he *is* gay, because he is *somep'n else*! He told my son that the principal of the high schoo' up here was his deddy!"

It was here for a moment the bitterness and sullenness that weighed on the afternoon broke suddenly. Mrs. Melton shook with laughter and covered her face. Mr. Melton mirthfully slapped the arm of his rocking chair. It would have been impossible, for any thousand reasons, for the high school principal to sire a boy like Billy, not the least of which was that normal men, in the view of this rural biology, did not breed pervert sons.

" 'Cause that man is *normal!* That just *cracks* you up," Mrs. Melton said, chuckling.

" 'Course Travis knew the boy was gay, but that didn't bother him because, he said, 'He don't bother me.' There are such things," Mrs. Melton declared, "as a person bein' a friend. There're people that are actually good friends to gay people, that don't have to be gay or anything wrong with 'em theirselves."

"Well, I don't look down on him," Mr. Melton testified. "Because if he really *is* like 'at, you know, I don't think you should take anybody out and murder 'em even if they *are* 'that way.' "

"That's like takin' someone out here," Mrs. Melton added, "because they was born without an arm and killin' em. Because there's somep'n missin' in that person's body because he was born defective some way.

"You never hear of gay people beatin' *up* nobody," continued Mrs. Melton. "You never hear of gay people doin' anything mean. You know, right now that AIDS's took over, it's a big problem and people are afraid if they get close to one that's got a disease, they'll catch it—you can understand that. But as far as 'em botherin' me, as long as they stay in their place and I stay in mine, I've got nothin' to worry about. They're not like the Klansmens murderin' people around on the street. Well"—she exhaled exhaustedly—"they have had their meetin's down below here. In the fields and places. They've marched through the towns, in their white sheets. See, nobody knowed before that they hated the gays, just the blacks."

"*They* are the gay people. They're the ones who are sick," Mr. Melton complained. "*That's true!* They are the gays and they are the sick people."

"They're messed up mentally, the KKK," Mrs. Melton explained. "That's what he was referrin' to, they're both of 'em bad disturbed." That was the comparison Mr. Melton had meant to make and chose this one word—"gay"—to do it. This one derogation harbored various meanings, though the ties among them were tenuous. Words failed.

"Well, they all live together," Mr. Melton asserted. "They don't live with their wives, they don't live with their children.

They all just live together in little places like trailers, you know. I know fifteen or twenty that belong to the Klan—some of 'em down at the mill."

"But," Mrs. Melton insisted, "their life-style's more like a pig or a animal to me, because they've got no responsibility towards their kin. That's what he means by them bein' gay, ignorin' their blood relations. See, a long time ago," she said, then stopped, staring into the lamp-gray air, "a long time ago it *was* a perty good thing. When I was growin' up when you heard of the KKK, it was like if someone beat up their wife, you know, they'd burn a cross in their yard or somep'n like 'at. It was a sort of good thing, sorta scared people up from bein' mean. And you didn't think of those people as bein' a mean bunch of people because they wasn't any killin' involved that anybody knew of. They thought they were in the right, and I think a lotta people that joined it thought they was doin' good. But now it's a different story. Now it makes you scared for your own life."

For days after the funeral, a car full of men in combat fatigues had stalked the Meltons' house and trailer, driving slowly up and down the road in an old brown Plymouth. "We got weird phone calls off and on," she said, "people we didn't none of us know, wantin' to know about Travis, you know, askin' for him when they knowed he was done dead and buried. Just sayin' things. Then they found all of 'em livin' all together in that ole dirty trailer, without their wives—just like a bunch of queers."

There were "gays," I began to understand, and there were "queers"—the one perhaps sexually maimed from birth and harmless, the other deranged, immoral, by choice, and murderous. Sometimes the terms got switched. And although Mrs. Melton insisted Travis was not gay—would not tolerate any implication of it—she sometimes went so far as to defend homosexuals. "I think the gay people have a right to stand up for their belief and what they want," she said. "And I know there are areas in California and New York and ever'where that has just streets of gay people that live in 'em. And they have their outlook to protect, because *they are put down* and they *have* to protect theirselves, to live and survive like ever'body else here on this earth. But I'm not sure what the real motive was down here."

"Thing of it is," Mr. Melton added, "most of 'em keep it to theirselves around here, but I think there're plenty of 'em around. It's just like the guy that does all the paperwork down at the auto shop, he's gay. Nobody bothers him."

"No," Mrs. Melton said more sadly than she'd spoken before. "It's never been a problem here. Except for those White Patr'ot party men," she corrected herself. "I think a lot of the gays are real good friends to other people because they grew up with 'em and, you know, it's just like I said, it's somep'n they can't help, being born that way."

"Like the detective said," Mr. Melton answered, opening the beer can that was sitting on the floor by his chair. He juggled the long, blinking ashes of his cigarette. "Even if they *were* gay— *which I don't believe a one of 'em was*—they didn't have no right to go in there and shoot those boys down like 'at and kill em, just like animals."

"I've wondered," Mrs. Melton said, still trying to find a way to undo that night, "if it wasn't drugs. 'Cause I don't think people just go killin' 'cause of someone bein' gay." Then she thought again. "Or maybe the reason why they done that is just to show homosexuals that they *could* get 'em. That's the only thing I can come up with.

"Bobby and I went down there and talked to Bill Lamrick one Sunday. He's got a little son, and the little boy, you know, is normal like. I don't think he'll prob'ly be 'that way.' And Lamrick played around there with him and talked to us, and he made the child mind. And he behaved hisself normally, too. He had about three friends with him one other time when I went with a lady friend. And he let me know right off that the other boys was like him, that 'this boy is my lover.' And you know, he just come out and said what he thought and felt.

"Now, he'll tell you Travis was gay. He'll tell you that ever'body that was *in* that bookstore just about was gay. But like I said," she hedged, "he told lies, we caught him in lies, so you cain't really depend on what he says." She drew slow tracks with her fingers up and down her lap and waited with her eyes pinched shut. " 'Course really I don't know what causes a person to be gay or what causes a person to be a lesbian"—as troublesome to her heart now as the shootings themselves, it seemed, a reality no more considered before all this than that Travis would die at the end of a Klansman's shotgun barrel—"I don't know, I'm not no doctor. . . ."

"It's like this family on television, their son was that way and they'd sent him to all kinda things—"

"Tryin' to make him different. . . ."

"—but then he went right back and they finally just accepted him."

" 'Course the Klan," Mrs. Melton said, tired and steady, "hates all kinds, anybody they can get to hate—blacks, Jew people. And I think ever'one oughta be educated about it—it needs to be taught in schoo' and churches and ever'whur else what kinda people have been belongin' to the Klan, and what they're actually out there doin' is wrong. *But it just goes on and on and on.*" Her voice broke. *"More trouble, more trouble.* And they gotta be a stoppin' point somewhur.

"I mean, none of it didn't make no sense. Them boys was mindin' their business in that bookstore, botherin' nobody. If they'd been down there beatin' up people or gettin' on to people when they come in the store, makin' fun of 'em, you could see it. *Oh, folks was tellin' stories about what went on.* Why, they even told later all them men that went there was dressed up in dresses and all runnin' up and down the highway." She laughed—not bitterly, I thought—at the absurdity of it, all the tales: how peculiar a picture they painted of this world! "They was just tellin' all kindsa lies.

"Well, *I saw my son*, he had red pants and a red sweater with those holes in it. . . ." Dusk had settled, the tawdry light inside seemed brighter, the shag green carpet deepened with a more forestal hue. "The stories just get crazier." Mrs. Melton sighed. "There're no real motives, just somebody insane like got out of a mental institution and went in there. But if they's anything in the world I could do to stop it happ'nin' again, I'd practically give my life for it."

"And them all not even gay," Mr. Melton said.

The new confederation of the South—a vast nation easily one-third of the North American continent—was still an embattled land. It was made of moss-round mountains, smoldering tidewaters, hot cobweb swamps, the humid breath of swelling red-clay fields, wide, sargasso seas of breathless plains, squatter glass-tower cities (rootless in an ancient cultured land), native drawls, like kyries, Yankee cacophonies. I'd traveled back, followed familiar, divided geographies, which were no less seismic than the conflicts that split the societies I saw and divided hearts like civil wars.

And still, that long afternoon at the Meltons'—a saffron swelter of time—I believed I would rather live among them, with their turmoil of minds, than among any thousand sophisticates I'd known who had gotten the theory of life—or race or sex—right but were unyielding in spirit. And though even the language of this family who'd lost its son and brother to bigotry sometimes seemed all wrong, like political threats, beneath it there was a generosity of heart that defied their conflicts. They seemed always to search for a place in their lives for folks whose ways they could never understand.

PART THREE

PILGRIMAGES IN AUTUMN

CHAPTER 18

ARCTIC
CIRCLES

I WAS LOOKING FOR EXTREMES. LIFE AS WE COMMONLY KNOW IT will always appear in the midst uninvited, with its guises and sleights, chameleon with myths: truths cannot so easily hide from themselves on the far, raw edge of things. I went to Alaska.

As the fat fuselage disengorged in Fairbanks, Robert Mason, my host, immediately pegged me (out of thirty or forty men on the flight) as the gay one and thereby gave me pause. It's a constant debate among the homosexually aware just what it is that so cues us to each other, to men who at all give vent to the same-sex urge whether only in fantasy or also in touch. A timbre, rhythm, some sweet archness of voice? (Robert hadn't yet heard me speak.) A certain gait? A peculiar grooming or mode of dress? A precious edge in demeanor? Perhaps it is pheromones, an instinct odor signaling the blood brotherhood that some psychiatrists and many activists believe in—something genetic, unique, and innate.

"Eye contact," Robert said. "When you were looking around for me, you looked into all the men's eyes and held it a second."

So uncomplicated is the permission men grant to one another and themselves.

A cedar camp cabin sat in the bed of Robert's truck, contingently stocked for outings. The wooden canoe rack on its roof was presently empty. We were to stop at Pat O'Malley's first, before going home, in the forest fifteen miles from Fairbanks, to water and turn her marijuana plants. Pat was wooing a possible lover in "America," as Alaskans so glibly alienate the "lower forty-eight." She'd be returning tomorrow. Robert had taken the week off work to tend to her "grass" (no small indoor garden) and his family affairs. His lover's California uncle had just gone home; Peter, his lover, a forest fire fighter, was packing to fight fires down south in Oregon; the week before, Robert's four children (twelve-year-old boy, nine-year-old girl, and twin girls who were seven) had gone back home to their mother in Sitka, on a stipple of Alaskan islands off the Canadian coast.

Robert had been married for eleven years. He'd grown up in the same small, desolate place where his children and ex-wife now lived, Baranof Island. He was native Alaskan, Athapaskan Indian, not Eskimo. "My mother used to say," he stated, " 'People think you have a sexual identity problem.' And I'd think, My God! Is it that obvious?"

Robert was a short, full-bellied, rough-and-tumble sort of guy, with chestnut hair as unkempt as a moose's pate and a tight tangle of beard like Yukon underbrush. His T-shirt was unbleached and amorphous, his heavy jeans decked with mud. Fairbanks is a muddy town when it isn't frozen, a subarctic outpost of wide, graveled streets and tawdry, crouching cabins, where cold vegetation cowers close to the ground and the spindly woods are monstrous and sparse. *Look! Look at the map!* Anchorage, the nearest city, is 360 miles south. There is nothing in the roadless north but scarce hunting hamlets and tribal villages, nothing but the private, petrol-owned, unpaved Dalton Highway, 500 miles (over mountains and tundra) to Prudhoe Bay and the Arctic Sea, where icy oil pumps gorge the pipeline to the Gulf of Alaska, to the tankers of late blackened Valdez. *Look at the atlas!* The arctic state—twice the landmass of Texas, which holds fourteen million

souls—harbors on its permafrost only half a million human beings, half of whom dwell in Anchorage, hardly Alaska at all.

Robert spoke with that fast-then-cold mania of men who
lived little among people, telling all or suddenly silent, always
shy and assertive, averting his eyes, which were as dark as a tundra lake, commanding the thaw of time between us. "There was
pressure," he said, "so I got married. She's four years older than
me, a real religious conservative. I knew I was gay *before* I got
married—*I mean*, I always knew I was attracted to men. And I
was gay while I was still married. I had a lover for two years in
camp."

The construction camp he spoke of was on an island 30 miles
from Ketchikan, some 160 miles from his wife in Sitka, were an
eagle to fly it straight. Three hundred fifty men worked there
then, no women. Robert had been a tower crane operator. "So I
had to work with everybody," he said. "I knew them all. Otherwise they kept to their own groups, very cliquish—the pipe fitters
stuck together, the iron workers—real tight. I didn't know any
other men who paired off, everything was real closeted.

"My lover and I scouted each other out. Ryan was a foreman,
so he had to room alone. Like everybody, I had a roommate. We
always got to choose, so I always chose something interesting to
look at." Robert sidewinded a smile, tainted with mischief. His
roommate went home to visit his family in Ketchikan every weekend. Then Ryan and Robert stayed together all night. Sometimes
during the week they watched TV in Ryan's room, separating
necessarily for bed when the roommate came in. "Some of the
men were suspicious, but more of him than me. I had kids, and
everyone knew that. That threw them off.

"We knew it was only for the time we were at the camp, the
relationship. We both knew that from the beginning. We had
about two years—and it stayed intense right up until the end. But
we always thought he'd go first. We thought we had about six
weeks—and one day I got offered another job. It was supposed to
start right away. In that kind of work you're used to going eight
or nine months between jobs. When you get something real sure

like that, you don't turn it down. So in one day I was gone. And that's how it ended.

"It wouldn't have lasted outside the camp, anyway. He was real closeted. He always worried someone would find out. And I had a wife and four kids to take care of. He went back to Oregon and got married. He always said his biggest goal in life was to have kids."

In the mid-1970s there were eight thousand men building the oil pipeline at the ice-locked camp of Prudhoe Bay, where the Beaufort Sea met the Arctic Ocean. Robert worked there three years, in summers of unsetting sun and winters of cryogenic darkness. "There were only four or five hundred women," Robert remembered, "and a lot of them were dykes. You had a nine-week commitment at a time before you got a leave. So the women that were straight had a real good time—the kind of women that didn't do real well with men back in town. A lot of the men were always scouting each other out. But it was always just sex up there, there wasn't any feeling to it. I'm the kind of guy who likes to cuddle—so, you know, that kind of thing gets old, if you want more than sex." Alone in the endless nights sometimes on maintenance rounds, he drove fifteen miles out over the sea on the polar ice pack to lie in the truck with his clothes off and his head out, examining the frostbitten stars, exposing himself to the black ice universe.

Back in the spring when I'd made my Alaskan travel plans, I intended to go nowhere but Anchorage. Labor Day weekend was the coronation of the "emperor" and "empress" of Alaska—one in an international annual series of charity drag balls. But I'd already scheduled a trip to Hawaii for a coronation there. Besides, the more I examined the map of the vast once Siberian subcontinent, the more Anchorage seemed peripheral, too accessible and frequented. I found a listing in the *Gayellow Pages* for the Arctic Gay/Lesbian Alliance at the University of Alaska in Fairbanks. The number rang at the women's center. The gay group was defunct, I found. The feminist who answered the phone oddly, sweetly, informed me *she* was straight, but nevertheless sympa-

thetic, and referred me to Peter Pinney, a one-man gay polar re-
source center, who warily kept a hand on Alaska's sinuous sexual
body politic.

Peter, Robert's lover, was a former Californian. Robert was
less politically defined, native to a land where such fine enamels
as "sexual identity" were known silently to crack beneath the cold
weight of erotic survival. "Gay" and "straight" were convenient
tags, of meager significance in actual practice: they could drift and
re-form like the arctic snow. As Robert understood Alaska's law,
the concept of "gay rights ordinances" was superfluous. "In
Alaska," he announced, "it's illegal to discriminate against someone for no good reason, *period*. Who you sleep with is 'no good
reason.' " He named a number of judges and high government officials who were very openly homosexual, no local secret. "There
are some crazy religious types in Anchorage"—the sort whose intolerance is always more grievously systematic in anonymous
cities. "But the only thing that really matters to most people is
how well you hold up your share of the work, how well you
shoot and fish. 'Gay' and 'straight' aren't much of a question."

It was Peter who'd invited me to stay at the cabin. But he
had to leave the night I got there, to quench America's flaming
forests: droughty 1987 was a crepitating season of fires. No
sooner had Robert picked me up at the airport and swiveled Pat's
pots of dope to the late arctic light than we drove Pete to the
rangers' compound, all duffel-bagged and green-fatigued like a
soldier. I never saw him again. We'd talked no more than an hour.
Still, their house was full and busy, though laconic as the northern
cold: they had almost silent roommates who slept odd hours.
Marjorie, a seasonal hotel bookkeeper, rented a room from them
over the summer. Her husband, Brad, hiked in from the couple's
deep-bush, riverbank cabin on weekends. Before dawn on my second day there, he made a rare weekday visit, on his way back
from a tundra trip to kill their winter's meat. The corpses of two
caribou bulls lay roped to the coroner's slab of his truck roof, autumn reindeers with blood-shattered shoulders.

All afternoon I watched Brad butcher his two caribou, which
he'd hanged like a lynching from the rafters of a shed where the

canoe lay stowed like a coffin. Their burgundy flesh bled rich as wine. Their skin and fur—like laminae of protective identity—clung useless, covering mere carcasses now. With blood-ripe hands Brad pitched a coagulating soup of viscera and broken bone to his scarlet-mouthed husky, whose huge snow-cloud tail swept the ground like a blizzard.

Brad was friendly and did not speak. His labor spoke everything he wanted me to know about him, all I needed to know—inarticulate intimacy. That evening, having discovered I was a foreign guest, he donated several of the winter's steaks for dinner at Pat's cabin. A bush contingent—couples of undetermined sexual labels, hetero or homo, friends or lovers—who cared?—hiked or three-wheel-biked in for a reindeer roast in my honor. We ate caribou filets like burgers on buns and quaffed six-packs of beer. Psychedelic on dessert mushrooms, we stripped to the buff to bathe in a rough hot tub at the twilight edge of the forest: the hairy constellations of men's chests sparkling like wet, falling stars; women's breasts suspended in black, misting water like Gemini planets. In the deepening darkness, moose, in solitaire, yipped from behind the luciferous jewels of their eyes. Wolves re-echoed a cathedral chorus of falsetto harmonies. Below a cold-white needlepoint of stars, aurora borealis, heart mad, skittered and pulsed with ribbons of color across the sky.

"Do you know any native gay men who still live in their native culture?" I asked Robert. I'd read a book about Eskimos that told of ritual homosexuality in adolescence. I wondered how it had survived the invasion of the Christian white man. He thought, and thought of none right off, though Manley Hot Springs finally came to mind, an interior fishing village where Hank Clemons lived. Hank had moved here from the lower forty-eight, in search of the liberty of isolation. Robert declined to use the word *gay* for him but said he was known to have sex with men.

There were 150 miles of empty highway between Pat O'Malley's cabin and Manley, 100 of them mud and sharp rocks. It rained continually during our slow trip; though over an ever-enfolding batter of autumn-purple desert, at a blind distance south, bald, blue Denali—old Mt. McKinley, white men called it—occasionally beaconed with its tropospheric head or, gender-switched, modeled a gaudy feminine Eskimo hood of clouds.

"I love these valleys in the summer," Robert told me, "when everything's in bloom. You sink in a couple of inches, it's like walking on air. In the fall you can stand on Denali, and under this huge sky in all directions the world turns yellow and red." Then the sudden tundra, shocked white, dies in the first snowfall. We watched the shattered, melting world through the gravel-rifled windshield. A new cracked concentric exploded in front of the steering wheel, too close behind a semi roaring lonely toward the oil camps of the Arctic Ocean. Where we turned off—mud to mud—a small wooden sign pointed north to the Arctic Circle and solitary Cold Feet, where no other but this one road of the oil companies' cut across the continental shelf of wilderness. Itinerary staples—a .44-caliber (for bears) and a .36 six-shot (for humans and smaller ferocious beasts)—lay in wait on the dashboard, loaded.

A mere few families—a disarray of loners—lived in the hamlet of Manley, which hunkered on the level banks of the Tanana, below its chill estrangement from the Yukon River. A derelict tribe of old log cabins squatted in the mud among gangrenous black spruce trees, sick with a syndrome of latitude and cold, immune deficient. "Dr. Seuss trees," Robert dubbed them, so phthisicky were they: most of Alaska was north of the respectable treeline.

At the tavern (on the submerged, gray afternoon that we arrived) gaggles of liquor-flushed Indians, in from the woods, swam around the bar, grinning and breast-stroking, with their loud, sullen children in tow. Two couples staggered an unending two-step in front of a jade (*jade!*) hearth. The log walls were ornamented with snowshoes, pelts, Eskimo masks, and a century of dead clocks. The ceiling was as low as an igloo's and dark, a bark-lined cache of unbathed, murky air. Rooms in the back were forty-five dollars (three dollars extra for a shower) and included the use of the plastic-tented, year-round, hot-spring-fed pool (swimming trunks rental, one dollar).

Robert had parked the truck in a shallow, gluey slough to the side of the tavern, where several other vehicles, spattered as sows, camped from their tailgates. There he ran into a trio of old acquaintances—from the gay bars in Anchorage, I guessed. The five of us built a fire in the mud—a half-dormant volcanic island—and ate a dinner from cracker boxes and tins while the four friends exchanged several slow years of gossip—curt explosions of enigmatic information and long shared grins. One said he'd met a "nelly native" on a Yukon River fishing trip, and there ensued one short debate over the nature of gayness. "If he fishes, he can't be *too* nelly," another of the men dissented.

"Oh, *no?*" countered the first. " 'Oh, look! A fish, a *fi-i-ish!*' " he lisped melodically, mockingly. " '*Somebody* pull it in!' Nelly comes in all packages."

A third man—with a beard like a bear's—had worked seven years in the arctic oil fields at Prudhoe Bay. "You've got to be some kind of social misfit to live all that time in a camp," he stated, matter-of-fact, neither self-deprecating nor campy. "In 1974, when I went up, there weren't any women allowed. The old construction hands, the ones in their fifties and sixties, *hated* the thought of having chicks in camp." Alcohol had been illegal there. "But you learn to hide things," he said. "Liquor, cocaine, sneak telephone calls. You had fifty-year-old men running around hiding bottles of booze under their shirts. I suppose you learn to hide sexual things, too.

"Of course, there are always things being hid back home. The old hands used to say, 'Never, *never*, surprise your wife with a visit. She don't want you to know, and you don't want to know it.' " They laughed, a crew of stags.

Hank, whom Robert had brought me here to meet, had come to Alaska in 1942 to build the Alaska Highway. He'd lived in solitary Manley now for thirty years. "He says he's had sex with everyone in Manley at some time or other, men and women," Robert explained. He left word at the bar that we were looking for him. Within an hour, mouth to mouth, he'd gotten the message. He pulled up to our camp in a muddy truck. When Robert introduced me as a writer interested in the "gay life" here, Hank's pleased-to-see-you face fell serious. Whatever he thought of himself, he knew what I meant and couldn't take us back to the house to talk because of his wife, not wanting to divulge a half century of sexcapades in front of her. He drove us around "town," a cloverleaf of mud turns: past the sparsely grassed landing strip (where beside a dead, rusted mule-drawn plow a hive of one-engine planes sat on their tails like pale cocoons), past the clapboard Manley Roadhouse (where Indians were forbidden to drink), past half-hidden log houses with gray windows blind as cataracts, past the steamy, teary tent of plastic that templed a litany of hot-spring pools, to the greater desolation of the gravel pit (where trysts were locally consummated).

Hank parked at the gravel pit, turned off the motor, and waited—we three in the cab knee to knee—urging the slow, gray, wet time with abrupt, broken bursts of dirty stories, sometimes toying with the shotgun stowed on the dashboard. ("Myself, I don't have sex with men anymore." He coughed, retracting his fingers from the ignition. "AIDS and everything—too much chance of disease.") There was the one about the fat Manley man—"English, of English extraction"—who on vacation in Molokai, Hawaii, picked up a black transvestite, thinking "she" was a woman, and, taking advantage of this first and accidental assignation with another man, got fucked. Hank's voice rasped from the back of his throat like a tumble of rocks, confidential whispers puffing out like bad breath. His eyes smiled vacantly, his face flashed smiles. He punctuated his thoughts with a quick swing of his head and a piercing gaze, as if he were trying to penetrate a tunnel of light, his palm suddenly passing across his cheek like a cloud. His knee breathed against my knee. He caressed the foreskin of the gun. I sat erect, flush with anxiety, not desire. Robert pretended a grin. The moment passed. Another came, plugging the vacuum.

"Oh, shit," Hank mused slowly and seductively, "*I can't tell you how many men around here practice gay sex.*" His exploring eyes darted over my captive body, then Robert's. We sat breathless as prey. We played dead. After several mortuary moments, stolid with pouting, he remembered, "There's *Rick.*" He rallied with a soupçon of laughter. "I got a picture of Rick and his girlfriend naked. I showed it to a neighbor woman and she said, 'Well, he doesn't even have a hard-on.' I said, *'I do!'* We fucked right there! I'm goin' over to Rick's place in a little while. For a sauna. Three times a week," ritual bath ration. "You got a towel?" he invited.

Rick had been in Alaska since 1968; he'd come with the army and never gone back. He'd moved to Manley in 1981. Since then his cabin had been in perpetual progress. He'd cut the logs and floated them himself in rafts—"two miles an hour"—down the Yukon and Tanana. It sat on a low hillside, half on log stilts, approached by a stich of hillside stairs. Rick was twenty years younger than Hank at the least, maybe in his late thirties, slim, rudely groomed, taciturn and nervous. He wasn't sullen but didn't smile. He met us at the door with a speechless nod, then led us silent out to the cool hillside and the sauna.

Tin buckets of icy spring water lined the front of the sauna shed. There was a damp, cold anteroom—the late afternoon was misting wet snow—with a two-level bench for undressing and a wall of nails for towels and clothes. We stripped to enter the sanctum of desert hot air. Rick stoked the stove below a tray of stones. Our tangy faces in our palms, we steamed mute, self-cleansing with sweat, melting into wet, wooden shadows. In time Rick said, "Ready to burn?" and threw a ladle of glassy, frigid water on the crackling rocks. *Ts-ss-ss-ss!* A stinging snake of steam coiled the room, biting our backs. *Uh-h-h-h!* Masculine whispers of pain. Rick waited and did it again, then, standing at a pail like a priest at a font, he scrubbed himself with soap and sponge and rinsed cold, scrubbed and rinsed Hank, washed us all. We recessed to the outside cold, crouched in the snow like monks—fire or ice— reentered the burning inner chamber a second time. We did this thrice, purging the flesh, secret with purification.

As always, Rick had prepared an after-sauna dinner. He said little as he heated a stew from the big iron pot on the iron woodstove—a stop-and-go ragtag of things about the weather, fishing, his eternal work on the cabin. There were gaps between the logs to be patched before winter. At last he was building an outhouse: no longer would he shit in the woods. He slept in the shallow loft above the stove and kitchen sink. The "bedroom" was enclosed with quilts of naked insulation, entered by a ladder through a tattered curtain. The one-room-that-contained-them-all was a gritty clutter of sawdust, tools, and odd, broken furnishings. I rocked like a cripple in a gimpy chair. He set out an extra oil lamp for the occasion. Its flame licked the air, whispering a willowy tale of soot. Rick dished out the stew where we sat, handing around an assortment of cracked bowls and dull, bent spoons with the etiquette of a soup kitchen, as if all us men were lost.

The stew was a khaki coagulation of rice with a succotash of unknown beans and strings of some white flesh. "Spruce hen," Rick belched when I complimented it and asked. A kind of grouse. "Road-killed meat, just this mornin'," he said. "Damn thing flew right outa the trees when I was driving back from the river—smashed my windshield!" Pancake flat. "I peeled it off and thought, Well, that's my dinner tonight! That's how I get all my poultry." I felt a big wormy apple of revulsion pulsing up my throat. I didn't choke, setting the bowl in my lap. "More?" he asked.

Sometime during our early hours there, Robert had told Rick my purpose. Rick had answered by bloating his lips and chinning the air, dropping the topic beneath him. After dinner the word— "gay"—was uttered again, by me or Robert, I don't recall why, how, probably glibly. It struck. Rick was staring through the long arctic twilight of the windowpane. "What I like best about living out here is the silence," he said. A tree, or an encircling ambush of trees, groaned toward the door, snapping plaintive twigs in approach. A succubus howled in the upper air. The oil lamps spat. In the voids we could hear our breathing. Rick didn't look into our eyes, nor did he need to. "In cities," he said, "everybody wants to talk, they want to make *you* talk. You always have to say who you are or what you are—or *they'll* tell *you*, if you don't know. I can get inside myself here, there aren't people around all the time blocking my way. I do what I want. I'm whatever I happen to be at the time. I don't have to make statements about it. I don't have to explain it. I just keep changing."

The mud road to Manley ended at the Tanana River, became

the bank itself, dissolved into the shallow water, no cul-de-sac, no sign. (Beyond it lay six hundred miles of mapless wildland and narrow sea to Siberia.) Here Robert parked his truck. Standing in the lurid light along the shore—the foreshortening subpolar sky still glowed until eleven—we clocked the dark march of winter: an exact seven minutes of elongating night each day, the ineluctable shrinking of brightness, a deepening pitiless pallor until the invisible solstice sun snuffed itself out. In endless solstitial light three summers before, a wandering wastrel had prowled the brush, waiting for whatever human crossed the sight of his shotgun. He'd greet them, then blow them away. Seven or nine had died here, one mother and her small child (there was no exact census of the living or lost in such a place). Hank certainly had known the victims. "Nothing happens for years," he'd said, "then something like that out here where help is so far away. In broad daylight." A trooper scouting the gunman from a copter had had the front of his brain shot out.

Late that night, in the whitewash of the moon, Robert and I, with his friends from camp, bathed again—in the black, steaming pools of Manley's hot springs, purling in the frost of their polymer temple, deep within a cadaverous colonnade of firs. Stolen pleasure: we were too late to wake the local who took tolls. Robert's friends, avowed men's men, were timid in their nudity. We hid each in separate, vaporous mouths of water, enveloped in low lips of concrete. Scintillant in the lunar splash of effervescence, we changed forms—shimmering wraiths or unborns.

In the morning Robert and I set out for the Kenai Peninsula, south of dull, two-story Anchorage—fourteen narrow hours over vertiginous valleys, like midocean carpets of seaweed cresting in mountains of cold foam. Sky-high Denali blinked—a mystic totem, slow strobe—the whole way.

"It's four years since we got a dissolution," Robert said, tallying the time since leaving his wife. As we rode, we talked a minuet of questions, confessions, and long silences. Over days and hundreds of miles, his gelid story waltzed out. "We stayed together an extra year for the kids. It was real important to them that we stayed friends. The nine-year-old said, 'I'm glad you both still like each other.' "

Robert's wife, at the time of their divorce, knew nothing of his homosexuality. An officious acquaintance told her later. Their son, the twelve-year-old, heard it at school. "When I asked for the kids to come up this summer, my ex said the boy didn't want to see me, he was going to spend time with his grandparents in Juneau instead. She told me I could see the kids down there. I told her that wasn't acceptable. They're my kids, and if I can't see them on my terms, I wouldn't fight her for them, I wouldn't put the kids through that. That really threw her. I told her I'd just wait to see 'em when they were adults. I knew she would talk to her psychiatrist about it. She'd led a real sheltered life.

"In three days I called back and she said okay, I could have the girls for two weeks—but only under the condition they wouldn't be exposed to any homosexuals! I let it go. And my son, Paul, wanted to come up, too. He *loved* Pete! He had everything figured out without me saying anything, and it wasn't any problem. I think he may be gay. And that's fine if that's the way he is."

It was the nine-year-old girl who had a problem about things—odd-coupled marriage, father wedded to stepfather. "She asked lots of questions." Robert did laundry for both himself and Pete. She was bothered. Which clothes were her dad's, which the other man's? Same size, they shared a wardrobe, wrong intimacy. "She's at that age when roles are really important to her," Robert stated. At an unexpected convex in the hillside road, Denali uncoiled its feminine cap of mist and was for a moment a shining enormity—same stony peak, now masculine and overwhelming. "She wanted to know why I always took his lunch to him: he was working fourteen hours a day. On Saturday, when he had some time off, he grabbed some clothes to take to the laundry, and that broke it for her, she started talking to him. Once she saw we both did chores and I didn't wait on him, well . . . then they got along fine. She just didn't like the idea I took care of him like his wife."

At midnight we stopped at an Anchorage gay bar, where the postcrowning party for the "emperor and empress of Alaska" had convened. Men-as-men, men-as-women, women-as-men, women-as-themselves: begowned woolly chests, tuxedoed breasts; rhinestoned bouffants and scarlet, mustachioed lips; masculine pallor or ruby effeminacy on whatever body. I had seen it often in "America." I would see it in Hawaii. For now this gender play seemed forced, a thin parody of radical change. We left quickly, fleeing between steep mountain walls of silver darkness down Turnagain Arm, a long, languid limb of hysterical and frigid northern sea.

The moon was high and full, the deep, domed night luxuriously spangled. Arcturus hung on the cobalt air like a cold, white insect's eye while diamond constellations swung around, worshipful broaches. In 1964 the great earthquake had muscled the snaking bay, rending the shore, lifting and warping the water's floor like a soaked slough, which now in low tide could no longer hold the flood. Amid moon-bleached pyramids of ice, earth, and stone, pale trees, standing in the salt pond of the fallen coast like a glowing host of dybbuks, wailed through the wind at the lizard skin of mud, leviathan lamé.

That icy, noiseless night we slept fully clothed within a dense spruce arbor, shadowy as a cave. Snuggling in the bed of the truck beneath a fat dermis of ratty blankets and coats, we shared our heads on a pillow.

"Jessica, my nine-year-old, figured out where Pete and I slept, smelling our pillows," Robert whispered beneath the wolf cry of silence. She had confessed this to his housemate Marjorie during a session of girl-talk one day. "Marj had told her that she was going out with some girlfriends," Robert recalled. "And Jessica said, 'You have *girl*friends? I thought you were married to Brad! Girls are supposed to have *boy*friends!' So Marj explained to her that girls have girlfriends too and told her, 'In fact, I know some girls so close they got married—and some boys get married, too.' Peter was in the other room listening to all this. Marj said, 'Tradition says girls marry boys, but not everybody follows tradition.' So later Jess came up to Pete and asked him, 'Do you know Marj said some boys get married? Does that mean you're our mom?' He said, 'You only have one mom. I'll just be your friend.'"

One day soon thereafter when her father hadn't made the bed, Jessica went into the lovers' room for a while. There were Pete and Robert's bed and a twin bed where, for expedience, Robert had told the children he slept. Jess came out, then led her father back into the room. She told him (Robert now remembered), " 'I know where you sleep and I know where Pete sleeps. I think you and Pete sleep together, in this bed, 'cause I smell Pete on this pillow and you here.' She was right. At least she didn't say"—he chuckled and squeezed me—" 'This is Pete's place, this is Dad's, but who are all these people in the middle?' "

Before the end of her stay, she'd met women wedded to each other, too, a couple whose daughter, her age, came over to play. "Cary and Ellen," Robert explained, "were married a long time before they decided to have a baby—in their forties, I think." Cary had been chosen to bear the child. In a fertile, lunar time she'd driven up the eight hundred miles of pumping stations along the oil pipeline to select a suitable father, seduced him, and left.

"He never saw her again," Robert said. "Never knew she was gay or even that she got pregnant." Now the women were split up but shared custody. "Real normal little girl," Robert stated. "A little hell-raiser! Knows *every*body in the 'community.' Our kids *love* to play together."

In the morning we woke at the broken blue toes of a glacier slippering down the black debris of a mountain out of a child's blue sky. Amputated digits of ancient snow swam numbly in a bay. Huge ankles of ice, sliding toward warmth since the last ice age, hung above the highway. This second route back home—a mostly graveled line through Alaska's lone, long loop of road—held to the path of the pipeline, which fat shaft bellied between steel fingers over the mountains, convulsing a foot at a time with its hot-and-cold ejaculate of oil, like thick black sperm. In the rapid, shattered mirror of a mountain stream, a spiny salmon, flame orange with the closeness of death, cast itself uphill against the rocks, quavering toward its high birthplace, where a pale, round moon rose. It had been gone wandering the ocean for years, had precisely found its homeward way through a thousand corridored maze of silver streams, bacteria-eaten, gasping to commit its last sex act and die. One brightly decayed fish was dead on a rock, one easily swam south.

"Maybe he got up there and got spooked," Robert said. "Maybe he didn't find a mate." Like a tongue of cold fire, it shivered with the current and ran against the crowd.

At the end of the week we returned to Pat O'Malley's cabin—"to get away from the city." *(Fairbanks!)* Pat had now returned from "America" and invited us to stay several days with her. In Alaska there seemed to be none of the segregation of lesbians from gay men that I was used to in New York and had experienced in other American cities. Men and women, like "gays" and "straights," were joint venturers in survival in this harsh land. Except that they weren't sexual with one another, I had never met a man and woman more intimate than Pat and Robert. She was one of the guys—or he was one of the girls. It didn't matter. I wanted to get to know her.

Each night after work, while Robert and I chopped wood, Pat played with Sasha, her old black Doberman, bandaged from an assault by the huskies that lived up the hill. The cripple frantically gimped under the long arc of a ball, which its mistress pitched into a birch woods. In the days since I'd arrived, the leaves had matured from sharp-clawed paws of late summer green to eczematous age spots of yellow autumn to near bare bone. Quick death was no surprise here.

Pat was an all-Irish girl—red, freckled cheeks, a curly cap of orange hair, cloverleaf green eyes. She typically wore blue jeans and a tight Dago T-shirt with an open work shirt, a tomboy by her own description. She was sedate and handsome. One evening, while Robert cooked Cornish hens and dressing, Pat propped her feet by the iron woodstove, smoked cigarettes, had a beer, and wandered. She said she missed Midge: over fifty and so twenty years Pat's senior, a wealthy Californian, owner of a guest house and an avocado ranch near San Diego. Midge's five grown kids, all spoiled, were part of the problem. They refused to let their mother continue to live so far away after she'd moved in with Pat in Alaska for one year. Pat tried living on Midge's ranch. "But I lost all my independence," she complained, like an awakening housewife or a startled househusband. "I had to give up my home, my work. She bought me a Porsche. I put up with her kids. I was 'kept.' It just never worked out." Now the women were planning yet another vacation to Hawaii, one in a repeating series of reconciliations.

Pat had had one lover in between, last year when she returned to Alaska from the ranch. Robert and Pete introduced them. Without their help, finding other lesbians had been difficult when Pat first came home from California. "Even though I'd lived here almost my whole life," she mused, "I wasn't really in touch with things." Sasha scratched her bandages on the carpet by the fire, leaping now and then to lick Pat's cheek. Now she settled her wounded haunches in her human's lap, humming from deep in the pipe of her throat with need and devotion. "But I got a job delivering mail for a while, and I started noticing the letters addressed to two men or two women."

("Pete's mom always addresses her letters to both of us," Robert contributed from the kitchen. He was stuffing midget hens. "It's a dead giveaway if you're trying to figure out who's 'family.' ")

"I got suspicious about two women on my route," Pat said. One day she left a note with their mail in the mailbox:

> My name is Patricia O'Malley. I'm from Fairbanks but just got back from living a couple of years in "America." I thought you might be able to tell me about activities around here.

They were gone, but the woman house-sitting for them called Pat. "My God! There was a whole *army* of lesbians around!"

Through a chink in the corner between two logs, a lisp of chill air intruded. Pat rose to check it out, making a mental note to repair it before winter set in. She knew this house as though it were a child; she'd conceived it and raised it herself, with the help of a few other lesbians. She'd bulldozed the timbers on a site where she worked heavy construction near town, trucked them to the lot, barked them, notched them with saw and ax, hoisted them up—a beautiful, finely crafted creation. ("There's a saying," Robert called in. " 'Alaska's the state where men are men—and so are the women.' " Pat smiled.) The logs glowed yellow in the firelight, like giant tuberous shells. Pat's cabin sat on her family's land. Her childhood home, where her parents lived still, was within easy sight up the hill.

She'd grown up here with only boys around. "I've been a big tomboy ever since I was a little girl!" she said. Momentarily she preened herself, tugging on the lapels of her workshirt and grinning mischievously. "But then"—she timidly smirked—"you get to that age where you *want* to be a lady to attract the boys. I dated the same boy in school for years." Everyone expected they'd marry: that's the way it happened on the tundra's bare market shelves. Then her parents moved to Hawaii for a year and her heart broke. "I didn't think I'd ever get over losing him." She was sixteen. "And then I found out there was always another boy to fall in love with!"

Boys! Boys! It was *boys* alone who wet her pubescent expectations, whom she fantasized a wifely life with! She never knew the frailest desire for girls—not even, she said, an occasional libidinous dream full of secret, vulval icons. "It just wasn't something that ever occurred to me," she stated. "It didn't *exist*! Girls liked boys. That was it. You only want what you know can maybe happen. I didn't know anything else." She married not long out of high school—on a summer visit to her Kansas aunt's. "Met and married," she said. "I didn't hardly know him! He turned out to be real conservative."

They lived in a big suburban apartment complex outside Topeka, where the women were all housewives. He refused to let her work outside the house. "I stayed home all day, with the other married girls. You know, we'd do the laundry, straighten up, get dinner started, then get high and sit the rest of the afternoon by the pool." The gals started taking trips—caring for the men Monday through Wednesday, getting out of town on Thursday for the weekend. One weekend they visited a woman in Kansas City, partied, got drunk and high. The hostess made a pass at Pat. "I ignored it," she said, "at first. But we ended up in bed, and everyone there knew about it."

Back home by the pool on Monday, she felt ashamed. " 'Do you all think I act different today?' " she asked her friends. "They said, 'No-o-o!' " So she asked again, " 'Do any of you have any problem with the fact I slept with that woman?' And they said, 'It doesn't bother any of us. So why don't *you* let it go?' " Pat remembered now, "I was the only one who had a problem with it." (There was, perhaps, it occurred to me then, an ubiquitous sexual sisterhood that answered the homosexual secrets of the world of men—a tight-lipped, erotic sorority.)

In a year Pat divorced and joined the navy, further breaching the uterine-tough culture wall constraining women. Still she did not think of herself as gay. What did "gay" mean? She'd engaged in nothing but sex so far. (And so it might have continued.) "Right after I got divorced," she recalled, "a lesbian cousin asked me if I was gay. I said no. She said, 'Are you sure?' " (There *was* that certain butchness about Pat, but nothing uncommon in America's blue-collar women.) "I told her it wasn't something I'd really thought about. She said, 'Well, you are!' and introduced me to some friends." One of them was a nineteen-year-old in the army. "And *she* asked me if I was gay. I told *her* no and we went to bed. I fell in love. And as soon as I did I could say I was gay. It made sense to me after that."

There was this one thing Pat could not understand about other gay men and lesbians: the angry alienation from their parents she'd often heard about. She'd called her parents right away when she "came out." They'd said, " 'It's wonderful you found someone to love.' " She'd brought her lover home to visit. "Dad met us at the door in his underwear," she recalled. "He just grabbed her and gave her a hug! I was *sorta* embarrassed." She grimaced. "I told her, 'Well, this is my family. You'll just have to learn to accept us the way we are.' " Their room was the spare room upstairs, with twin beds. Her father had spent all morning wiring the legs so the women could enjoy themselves and not fall through.

Some years ago Pat's father had told her he'd once had a male lover, in the army during the war. And her Kansas aunt, now ancient, had always lived with a "lady friend," whom Pat had been taught was family. "It's a tradition with us, I guess," she said. "I've never had anyone in my life not accept me because I'm gay. I don't know what I'd do if something like that ever happened."

In the morning I went to work with Pat, to the diesel garage she owned with her brother and father. ("No jokes!" she warned me.) A big, bearded trucker, not so old—who regularly ran the lonely road to the arctic wells at Prudhoe Bay—argued past her to her brother. The lady, he thought, couldn't begin to understand the grit-black chaos of steel and wires beneath his hood. With a dead, steady face, she paid him no mind—because she was right, of course. While he pleaded for some manly intelligence, she turned—labor blue in coveralls, lowering the thick glass of her helmet over her face—and fired the blowtorch, feeding it fuel through a long black hose. From her fingertips, a sharp, red nail of flame seared the air, scratching a white-hot line on the belly of the diesel's radiator.

How far will we go to know what we've already learned—asking questions answered over and over again, like a new catechism to practice? Point Barrow is the top of Alaska, the northernmost human habitat in North America, the atrophied nipple at the end of a continent. If you need a gauge, it is 330 vacant miles north of the Arctic Circle, 450 from derelict Manley Hot Springs. A desert horning into the Arctic Ocean, it sits for most of the year in icy solidarity with Siberia and the North Pole. There is nothing but 1,500 miles of ice between it and the quick-spinning crown of the globe, where one day becomes a nanosecond then turns into eternity.

The morning plane crossed the Arctic Circle at nine-fifteen. Steely mountains spiked through the earth below us, as sharp as teeth. They were freshly snowed in. Lines of latitude banished all trees from here—stony desolation. A bulkhead walled off half the fuselage for heavy equipment. We were tightly packed—a few day-trip tourists to Point Barrow, mostly oil field workers for

Deadhorse and the camp at Prudhoe Bay, our first stop. The oil-men were as you would guess them to be: burly, with frozen expressions on their woolly faces, their few words falling from their lips like ice cubes. Boxes marked "Mittens Hats Sox" stuffed the overhead bins. I'd dressed for early fall, not deep winter.

I scouted for "gay" men—or for men who at least might acknowledge some secret same-sex interest. It was a game I played. There were two or three of the camp men on board who seemed too carefully rugged, too tightly trimmed, displaying a self-referential masculinity that sometimes clued same-sex tastes. A salacious man behind me talked about women.

"I'm not much interested in that," said his seat mate.

"You a Mormon?" the first man asked.

"Yes, I am."

"I kinda thought so." He grinned with his voice.

A boy nineteen or twenty, skinny as a subarctic spruce tree, wore logger's suspenders and muddy boots and a frail, stolid face. Could men so slight work here? I wondered. Maybe he was a clerk. Framed posters on the bulkhead pictured beaches in Tonga and Hawaii and the sunshine of Mexico, no ski slopes. No one returned my gaze. I sat in a window seat. The man beside me slept noisily. When he woke up I was scribbling in my notepad. He watched a while and asked, "You work for a newspaper or something?"

I told him the purpose of my trip, emboldened by arctic anonymity.

He registered neither interest nor shock. I might have been answering an icebox. He seemed to fall asleep again. After several minutes, with his eyes still shut and his voice nearly drowned in the roar of the jets, he said, "I know a gay man in Alaska. I could give you his name." The flight attendant interrupted with complimentary Absolut or coffee. My row mate settled deeply into a magazine until we began our descent. His name was Henry. He was probably thirty, tall, slender overall, with a belly beginning to inundate his waistband. His straight brown hair was swept straight back. He was outfitted in a brown knit leisure suit of polyester. He repaired computers for the oil companies.

The brown tundra stretched below like oily sealskin, shivering with hundreds of ice-drop lakes. The ocean, cold liquid turning to glass, rolled slow to the earth's tattered edge. (The invisible North Pole stood over the white horizen.) An intricate web of silver pipes and towering pumps glittered the permafrost like a hot snowflake.

"Actually, I'm gay," Henry said while the jet engines thundered to protect him. Stunned, I listened. He referred to his lover as his roommate. They'd met eight years ago in Grand Rapids, Michigan. "In a 'Mary Ann' on the interstate," he told me—a "tea room," a cruisy public toilet. "He was eighteen then. I was his first."

They'd moved to Alaska in 1983 to work for the summer at a cannery camp. His roommate, Joe, was an unemployed janitor now. They'd bought a house at the foot of a glacier and lived in isolation from all upright beings but bears. A year or so ago they'd started fighting violently. Joe had ruinously run up their credit cards buying hunting and camping equipment. Henry became a "hunting widow" in deer season, left alone to pay bills. Nothing in their situation was improving. One night, after a fight, they both had to have stitches on their cheeks. Now they were splitting up. Henry's heart was broken. He needed to talk to someone about it badly.

"Joe told me I was walking away from the best thing that ever happened to me," said Henry. "He's right. He took me out of the toilets. We were 'mononomous,' " as he called it. "But he's a lackadaisi'al man. His dreams are all in the future, and I'm having trouble *now*. I can't keep taking care of him. I don't earn enough. Besides, there's this affair he's having with his sister-in-law. It's one thing too much."

Cindy, Joe's brother's wife, had come from Tucson to work for a while, leaving her husband behind. "He stayed home to work at Midas Muffler," Henry said. "His job is everything to him." One night Cindy and Joe got drunk together. He told her about his relationship with Henry—no one else in the family knew. She told him about her unhappy marriage, that she thought his brother had had experiences with men, too, that she believed herself, in fact, to be a man trapped in a woman's body. They seduced each other. "He always did like to do all the fucking," Henry complained. Now Cindy had begun divorce proceedings. "She'll just go back single," Henry speculated. "But I told him go on and move to Tucson with her. He still has straight tendencies he better take care of. He was straight until I met him. But her methods aren't real kosher, either."

Henry fidgeted with the ballpoints in his shirt pocket. The plane circled above the one runway at Deadhorse, facing, then turning its back on a silver wall of clouds where the polar ice cap was moving in. Within the month the land ice would freeze out miles to meet it and form a new ice continent, bitter cold wedding, all white. A thin snow blew over the tundra, like dust.

"I've left him before," said Henry. He spoke sadly, angrily. He seemed to plead with me. "But this time's for good." I thought he would cry. How could I give him a hug? The plane hit the runway, shuddering against the black asphalt. A man stared out the window past us. I didn't dare squeeze Henry's hand.

"I'm sorry," was all I said as he stood to disembark with his oil field buddies. He said nothing and nodded his chin, his face now frozen numb like the rest of them.

Point Barrow is a raw village of plywood cabins built of cast-off shipping crates, where the drying flesh of caribou hangs like red, tortured things on racks and their hairy, putrefied skulls stare from roofs like omens. The tundra is endlessly flat here, spongy and frosted in the early fall with tiny tufts of arctic cotton. A full-grown spruce is several inches tall. Nothing grows taller than a thumb's height.

There are no streets, only icy earthen paths. You can get in and out only by sled or plane. Every structure is built on stilts or a gravel bed to protect the frozen ground: once the permafrost begins to thaw, it thaws more deeply every slight summer until the ravenous hole, like the snowy mouth of a polar bear, swallows everything. The dead, buried erect, resurrect continually, squeezed by the cold, contracting earth from their graves.

The sky this day was blizzard gray, littered with ducks, which by custom were shot and cooked in a native soup, feathers and all. Along the paths, Eskimos hunkered against the wind, hooded in other creatures' skins, a snow cloud of gray fox's fur swirling about their faces. A stinging blizzard began to blow and blind them. The shore was abandoned with skin boats and sleds, seabirds plundering a drowned seal's body, the triumphal jawbones of whales already eaten. I poured the ocean through my pink, blue hands, feeling the surf icicle my fingers, scouring the horizon for the icy end of the world. A demon colony of sled dogs howled at me, chained since birth, chained for their lifetime. Like us human beings, they were never long free from one chain or another.

In the late afternoon, a couple of hours before the night flight, I managed to find an old friend of Robert's, Elaine, whom he'd recommended I see. White, she was the wife of a school-teacher. She sat with me at Mattie's Cafe, the old explorer's out-post that Will Rogers had frequented. She shivered with fatigue. She'd been sleepless in the summer's midnight months of sun, though now she was growing bleak with dread for the hibernating darkness that was falling. Autumn was the terrible twilight season. Robert had told me she might be able to guide me to a "gay" na-tive, though now I hardly could imagine how such a white man's concept of homosexuality would show itself in this tribal desola-tion. She knew of no one. "I don't see much of their social life," said Elaine. "Most everything goes on indoors. Besides, they keep a lot of secrets from us whites. They don't trust us."

Still, she thought and after several cups of lyelike coffee came slowly to remember a middle-aged man who worked at the "de-partment store," such as it was. "I don't know if he's *gay*," she de-murred. "I've never *thought* of him as gay. But he's certainly effeminate, whatever that tells you."

I hurried. My time ran short. The sign on the store said "Stuaqpak," in the native Iñupiak of this tribe. It was a large, clut-tered place, a fluorescent-lit dumping ground of merchandise. I searched from cash register to cash register, watching long enough to see if any clerk there might meet Elaine's description. Dry goods were on the second floor. I searched them last. It was when I'd just topped the stairs that a masculine falsetto chirped out a song from behind towering bolts of cloth, like a bird in a forest. *"Yoo-hoo! I'm* open, dear. Over here." I turned the corner and stared. Some ways off behind a register stood a birdlike Eskimo surrounded by a nest of grinning women. They *loved* him. Spinning a large bolt of some shiny cloth midair, his lithe wrists fluttered out ribbons of shimmering brightness, like dancing northern lights. "It's a lovely choice!" he cried, and tapped it with his fingertips as it fell. There was no time for me to approach him.

As I flew back to Fairbanks late that night, the sun shone like a moon on the mountains. A sunny moon rose. The sky turned black silver. The ground below became a wild glittering sea. Nothing was as it appeared to be. Rushing through the satin air above the globe, I wondered about all I'd seen since coming to Alaska, how I might interpret so foreign a place. I remembered an Inupiaq motto on the wall of Mattie's Cafe: "I walk in two worlds with one spirit." I thought of the store clerk I'd met distantly, presuming him to be a man who loved men because he was flamboyant. Fondly, I thought of him as nelly.

Then it occurred to me: How nelly could any man be and survive life in such a land? Not even nelliness, perhaps, was what it seemed.

CHAPTER 19

CAPITAL
OFFENSES

WE ALL WANT TO BELONG, OR WE ARE LIARS. WE GROW MAD IN
the craving of it. We wander the vacant tundras of our souls
searching for acceptance and love and community. I had set out
across America, I think, to find my blood brotherhood with all
homosexuals, for this is what I'd been taught that it was and accepted it with born-again faith. I had learned if you *do* this thing,
you *are* this thing, you belong to those people, not the rest of humanity, for better or worse. I was living with my parents my second year out of college when I "came out." A fourteen-year-old
boy seduced me in the woods near our house where I walked my
dog. He passed me in the dusk and asked, "Do you want a blow
job?"

"What?" I gasped, and stood breathless. I told him I'd never
had one, and I hadn't. He whistled with incredulity, then offered
me his mouth again. I took it from him.

That night, or maybe it was the next, I took my mother out
for dinner to tell her I was gay. A long adolescence of frightened
desire was behind that impulse. Certainly I was not fool enough

to think my mother, a conservative Christian, would be thrilled by the revelation. But we were an intimate, honest family—debating, quarreling, confessional Irish Protestants. We had often enough hurt each other in telling the truth and had become all the closer for it, for truthfulness was the price of belonging. Others in the family—uncles, aunts, cousins—had had their sexual scandals, had gotten women pregnant or had gotten pregnant out of wedlock. In all the iniquitous dismay, the family had nonetheless drawn its protective arm about them and reconstituted the shame as a kind of defiant honor. We did not discard our own.

My mother cried all night when I told her I liked men and so might someday fall in love with one. Stricken, I listened until dawn to her muffled sobs through the wall of my bedroom. I had asked her not to talk to my dad about it until I'd talked to him myself. It was a cruel, selfish request, insisting on her vow of silence while she hurt. But I had not known that she would mourn my homosexuality like a death. She reneged. At breakfast my father was sullen. Over the weeks phone calls came for me from men he did not know. Shortly he confronted me. We fought viciously. Did I wear a dress when I met these men on weekend nights? he asked. He disowned me and banished me from his house.

How can a father do that to his son? I wanted his love, if not his absolute approval. My loss seemed eternal, the pain all mine, because grief draws us into its cloud and makes a bleak and solitary world for us. At such times our own hurt is the only one we know. Dad lived in a man's world, with its harsh, primitive codes, a fraternity of survival that cut off the flawed from itself to die shamed. Wasn't it so? He'd learned that the product of his loins, his firstborn and only son, was a freak. Didn't that mean that he was flawed, too, had a weak and feminine gene that he'd surely never had to acknowledge, though he might have feared its existence? Now he must carry his secret about, guarding it from the strong, suspicious eyes of "normal" men. I had made my father grotesque to himself. Now he too was among the alien hunted. I can see that now. I could not see it then. I didn't want to understand him. I was consumed with vigilance for my own survival. Years of spiteful exile began between us. Such exiles are mutual things. Suddenly I belonged to the exclusive world of homosexual men, not to the family or to the masculine fraternity my mother and father had reared me to be part of.

It is peculiar how spontaneously the belief in homosexual brotherhood begins, before there is any agreement of common cause, for that seldom comes. It combusts in the sharing of the mutual secret: in the confessional meeting of eyes we've experienced with no one else, in the blinding heat of a hormonal moment and the angry first release of our taboo lust. Its fuel is our postcoital stories of fiery childhood hurt on account of this hidden desire, no matter that underneath the mere fact of the pain, for all of us the wounds are unique. It is sustained by the sense that we are ostracized among men who are tarnished by the force of this single want and so must make the best of it, though we'd never want to understand it so starkly. All men have their secrets to tell and bond momentarily with the mutually minded. Most men soon find that theirs—acceptably informed by heterosexuality—are a ticket in this world. Ours lock us out of it. We find ourselves imprisoned solitarily with other homosexuals, a community of the banned.

I'm not speaking of all homosexuals, of course, nor even of all men who've adopted a "gay" identity of some sort. I am speaking of myself—and of homosexual men who've experienced a grief at all similar, whose anger was congruent with mine. Certainly as I wandered across the continent in search of a gay brotherhood, I met many men who called themselves gay—who were comfortable with their sexuality and candid about it—who also found my angry hurt, my sense of psychic and social insult, to be mystifying because they'd never experienced it themselves. Salvatore Vitelli and Bertrand Williams in the Arizona desert, Tom Kirk and Len Coker in Tupelo, Mississippi, Robert Mason in Alaska—their community was the larger one in which they lived, unconfined by sexual identity. Their spirit seemed incompatible with gay brotherhood. When no banishment poisons homosexual love—and our sexual choices are all equal—the need for "gay community" dissolves.

My travels, of course, were not my first experience of the absence of commonality among homosexual men. The gay community, to which idea I'd devoted most of my adulthood, was refulgent with it. But if I did not belong to my family, or to the society of other "normal" men, then I must belong someplace. "Gay community" had been my salvation, the dramatic belief that among these people I found the common soul to which I was born. I reshaped my exile as destiny. I did not dwell among these fellow men because I was homeless, but because I had found my way home. We co-conspirators in this paradise agreed to wash over our rocky differences with retelling our childhood hurt and our wretched stories of "coming out"—and with great waves of brotherly sentiment. We must create an answering community to "straights," a counterweight to the evil they perpetrated against us.

But our divisions were essential and bitter. For even among this subset of men who claimed a citizenship of homosexuality, our conflicts of race and ethnicity, religion and morals, economics and social status, politics, our fundamental philosophies of life, set us acidly against one another. We humans, beneath it all, have needs and allegiances whose pull is every bit as potent as sex. Nor can we be said to share a common sexual need or even sexual practice itself. What do promiscuous gay men have in common with those who are monogamous or celibate? Or men who seek the pleasure of being fucked with those who cannot imagine such an insult to their manhood, any more than the "straightest" of men can? Or men attracted to masculine partners with those who desire the mock heterosexuality of sex with transvestites?

There always exists in our minds a solipsistic concept of what is truly "gay"—and so it is whatever most slavishly conforms to the most urgent needs of each gay man. We fight over it. The gay community is a battlefield of irreconcilable "identities." It is quite human, after all, to wish all manner of evil, even death, on those whose lives threaten our sense of belonging and well-being, or on those whose sometimes kindred lives we believe to vitiate the image of our "community." The divergences among the homosexually inclined are no different.

Gay dogma as I had known it—and preached it—was a perfect circle: if we could only *agree* about who we were, we would *agree* and end the false divisions among us. We clung tenaciously, and not uncynically, to the idea that we inexorably belonged to one another because we feared we belonged nowhere else—and because we continued to nurture a deep and righteous distrust of heterosexuals, of that vast army of homophobes who would destroy us if it could, who'd advanced against us first and most grievously in the guise of our families. We rallied our lives around our ancient fear and pain. Never again would we suffer as we had in childhood and "coming out." We could always find some ever less populous group of homosexuals whose views were more akin to ours, to take us in and shelter us when the others had issued a sentence of exile as callous as any we'd received from "straights."

But forced likenesses make us bitter. All utopias are tyrannous. And you will wonder, perhaps incredulously, why we persisted—why, as the homosexually identified, we persist—in spite of all the rancorous evidence to the contrary, in believing ourselves to be one, a separate and distinguishable race. Such loyalty to contradicted faith is a human trait. We believe what we must to save ourselves. "Gay community" had offered many of us survival in a society that was often happier to see homosexuals suicide. And for all the inimical mass of homosexual men and women with whom we had nothing in common, we also met our community of true friends there, who nurtured us and kept us alive, whom we learned to love dearly, who would be wounded deeply again by our apostasy.

I am not speaking, of course, of the vaster numbers of homosexually interested men in America. I am speaking only of myself and those like me whose terrible pain—and protective need to make a dogma of it—pushed us to the heart of the "gay community." We were the vital part of the gay rights movement. We were the world I lived in.

And so I felt I must keep traveling—more lives, more far places, retreading places I knew—to find the grail of gay brotherhood, because I could not let go of that secure idea. There was some deep buried trait I'd missed, I told myself—some underground stream that watered us all. I believed that I must find it in spite of myself, or I would be alone again in this world. I did not easily give up the faith.

In September 1987, as I returned from Alaska, homosexual activists across America were laying the last feverish plans for October's March on Washington for Lesbian and Gay Rights. Like the first one eight years before, this mass affirmation of homosexuality was conceived to be in the tradition of the great American marches of conscience—most especially the civil rights march of 1963, when Dr. Martin Luther King aroused all decent people's yearning for freedom, crying like thunder, "I have a dream." Thus the gay march evoked a single, good, and enslaved homosexual people disdaining the grip of its heterosexual tyrants, advancing into the liberty of a sexual Canaan.

I intended to make the pilgrimage with the rest. The early rumor was that several tens of thousands of us would be there, making the grueling journey by planeload and busload from every distant state (and several foreign nations) to declare, at a one day's rally, our commitment to homosexuality, then turning around sleepless to travel home again. Perhaps, I hoped, some unanimity of identity and cause would yet emerge among us in consequence of so great an effort. And the flag of my old emotions, if tattered somewhat by the storm of reality I'd been experiencing, fluttered again at the prospect of universal gay brotherhood—some innate trait that could be said to bind us and oblige us to one another like family, even more inexorably than blood.

I meandered toward the District of Columbia, feeling more old obligation to be a part of the march than any passion for the cause. Few of the men I'd met in my journeys were making the trip to Washington. Few even knew of the huge demonstration. I made visits along the way, first driving south to southwestern Pennsylvania, where Dutch stone cottages and creaking gristmills turned warm shoulders to the chilly roadside streams. Pumpkins dotted the crisp brown fields like manna. I spent the night in Intercourse, a town of a few hundred Amish farmers that lies between Compass and Bird-in-Hand. There, white farmhouses, stately in their simplicity, rose before long, golden fields of wizened corn. At night windows glowed with candles and gaslights, for the Amish scorned such demons of the modern world as electricity. Brent Allen, my host, was a young Brethren man, so less strict by dogma than his Amish brothers, less strict still since he'd left the church. He wore a workshirt, jeans, and cowboy boots in place of the Amish men's long black coats and round black hats. A carriage maker lived across the road. That afternoon Brent carried a *Playboy* to him in a sealed brown bag, because the carriage maker was forbidden by his faith to buy it himself.

Brent's homosexuality had never been an issue here, he said, though most of the townspeople would have had an inkling of it. He'd lived for several years once with a lover. He hid nothing, but, a terse man among terse people, he didn't anxiously reveal himself, either. "Life here is just what you see," he told me.

That quiet evening we ate a shoe-fly pie he'd made. The sweet ripeness of manure tingled the frosty breeze. The night air was filled with the soft, clopping paradiddle of horses' hooves on the slender highway, Amish carriages returning home from neighborly visits. That was Brent's only complaint about living among these stern people: the grooves their metal carriage wheels made in the road had sometimes thrown his motorbike. They weren't allowed to use rubber, either.

I drove southwest to Hagerstown in the mountains of Maryland—a sad place, with its old brick row houses and factories in moldy decay. The gay bar was a log cabin on the mountainside, with a fire in the fireplace. A drag queen performed Tammy Faye, squeezing gales of tears from a douche bag piped through her wig. Streaming mascara blackened her cheeks. At a porn shop in town, I met a trucker with shaggy blond hair and a rough red face whose arms were tattooed with swords and snakes. He was "straight," with a wife and little boy in Baltimore. He was also horribly drawn to men, though he still hoped someday the compulsion would leave him. "I don't know what I'd do if anyone found out," he told me, losing his consonants in a Maryland drawl that made every man a drunkard. "I'd never want that to happen to my kid. I'd lose everyone in my life. I'd shoot myself. I decided that." He showed me the stash of shotguns in his truck.

I traveled even farther west, through Civil War battlefields, to where West Virginia's autumn was on fire with the crimson orange of dying leaves and the mountains heaved like a trapped, fevered beast. It was still a week before the march on Washington. I journeyed through the bluegrass pastures outside Lexington, then back through Kentucky's misty hills to where Virginia's mountains lay against the frosty sky like violet ribbons of chimney smoke. I temporized, though I couldn't say why. Many festivities preceding the gay and lesbian march had begun already. I went to Lynchburg, where the Reverend Jerry Falwell's rich fortressed house stood guarded. Walled off, the man built inhuman dogmas and professed to understand the world.

On the Thursday before the Sunday march, I finally arrived in Ronald Reagan's Washington under a quick-moving sky. Bright, chilly sunlight and shadows spangled the ground. A bank of clouds billowed up behind the Capitol, like an alternate dome. On the Capitol grounds I met a squirrel with a nut in its mouth, who froze, furry frieze, still as stone. I looked twice. He would not be dissuaded. A big blue uniformed woman from the Capitol police glared at me stoically.

I was to meet Andrew McCabe on the Senate side at ten A.M. Andrew, a gentle man of late middle age, was a lobbyist, a Republican of importance to his party. He'd been a high-ranking adviser to the Reagan-Bush reelection campaign and planned to work for Bush as well. I had met him through another powerful Republican, Matthew Corbett, a senior vice-president at one of New York's most prestigious banks. I'd been introduced to Matthew through his eleemosynary work at the Gay Men's Health Crisis, for which institution he fund-raised, helping to sophisticate it into a cause attractive to the charity of celebrities and the wealthy. He himself, along with Andrew, was among a well-heeled, influential population of conservative homosexual men who'd been "politicized" to the gay and lesbian cause on account of the AIDS epidemic, from which no closet could hide them. Matthew had served every Republican president since Richard Nixon—in whose White House he had occupied a bright window office near the Oval Office itself—and often influenced the appointments of staff at the Pentagon, one of his most fervent interests. He had taken me with him to Washington some weeks before, for an AIDS fund-raiser among the homosexual elite. It seemed as if every high stratum of the bureaucracy had been represented there, except for cabinet members and senators. It was discreet. I had lived my adulthood as a loud and bilious activist, left-leaning. These polite men were not the kind I was accustomed to mixing with. Maybe the initial discomfort was mutual, but Andrew invited me to spend several days with him and observe his life.

On my second day with him, he took me to a Senate committee hearing on the Hill. The old hearing room had a high, elaborately sculpted ceiling, with richly paneled walls and monumental bronze torchères. It was like the great hall of a Renaissance doge. At the front, a huge, hemispheric desk with carved American eagles on each extreme awaited the committee members, who entered through a towering center doorway like dei ex machina or exposed wizards. The back of the room was crowded with the clacking, whirring, scribbling press, whose faces were unimpressed. Senate staff, lobbyists, and constituents all whispered eager greetings to one another with grand smiles and brisk hands, paying tribute to all whose status warranted it. An aide to Senator Lawton Chiles clapped Andrew on the shoulder.

"You're the real hero in all this," he said. "Things didn't start moving till *you* got a hold of that bill."

Senator Quentin Burdick, who presided, cracked the gavel twice. A greater hush fell, as if a sunspot had quieted all lesser spheres in their excited orbits. The room was electric with prerogative. I felt it and wondered at it. This Senate committee was all white, all male. Most of the aides were precisely dressed young men, all handsome as the Kennedys. Not a few were homosexual. I knew because I'd met them at Matthew Corbett's AIDS fund-raiser. There were always homosexuals in the seats of power, whether they made a public identity out of their "preference" or not, and most of them didn't. These were the sorts of men denounced as traitors by gay activists, roundly blamed because of their adamant discretion for a heavy portion of the woes American homosexuals suffered.

The bill at issue was to protect groundwater, particularly in agricultural regions. It was the socially responsible kind of legislation on which Andrew spent most of his time. "I'm an old-time conservative Republican," Andrew told me, "which means I'm pretty liberal these days. I'm a Republican who believes in the obligation to help people who can't always help themselves—the poor, the young, the old, men and women left out on account of race."

That night Andrew took me to his weekly bridge party in Arlington. Twelve gay men arrived for pot luck and cards. The living room stared across the Potomac toward the temples to Jefferson and Lincoln. The intimate political gossip was avid. One of the men would be accompanying Mrs. Reagan to an appearance—*again*—the next day and would mention to her the issue of children with AIDS. Talk turned to AIDS, not morbidly. Several of these men were staff to the Senate's most right-wing members and used their privilege to pull invisible strings, maneuvering national AIDS policy and the budget. One man told me that this one little bridge club had perhaps effected more good in the epidemic than all the gay militants combined. "Our relationship to political power is not adversarial," he stated.

On the way home Andrew took me past his church, an old society church, and a row of apartment buildings he'd convinced the parish to buy for poor families. He did *pro bono* work as well for an organization fighting apartheid in South Africa. He was a board member of a national coalition that sheltered runaway kids. As a single man, his love in life was the social good. I was deeply moved by his commitment. Still, and somewhat in spite of myself, I was disturbed by it, for Andrew—and his friends—didn't fit the hard mold of my political thinking.

He lived in a tall Georgetown town house, comfortably antique and aristocratic. In the velvet darkness of his parlor I asked him about his commitment to gay rights, for that seemed absent from his social agenda. "You're so passionate about so many *other* issues," I accused him.

"I'm not forgetting that cause," he answered. A bust of Lincoln sat behind him. On the wall hung a certificate from President Ford appointing him to the National Advisory Council on Economic Opportunity. He was meditative, not at all antagonistic, though I gave him excuse to be, I think. "I guess I'm just not consumed by that issue. Before the epidemic, when I saw gay issues I could impact in the government, I did—and now with AIDS. If I were straight, I could be a senator myself, but I won't give up my sexuality for that. And I don't think any *law* is going to make people elect me to public office. In the meantime being gay is certainly an issue in my life, but always one of many issues for me. So my thrust is to be a good citizen, so that in time being gay is *not* an issue.

"I guess you have to ask yourself what is worthy of your passion. Doesn't the gravity of a problem increase by the measure of injustice it represents? If you take an unpopular position in society, of course you're going to get lumps. But I don't see that there has been that much injustice on account of homosexuality, compared to what other people suffer. Homelessness, hunger, runaway youths—those things are for me more endemic issues. I don't ask someone whether they're gay or straight before I help them." For the first time I envied such a man the breadth of his heart.

On Friday night I took Andrew to Union Terminal to catch a train. He was not staying in town for the gay and lesbian march. He was going to his beachhouse instead. Together we stood and watched the arriving gay crowds—from Baltimore, Philadelphia, New York, Boston, beyond—all high-spirited and covered with political buttons. The continual stream of homosexual humanity disembarking the trains was astounding. My lover was arriving. I was anxious to see him. I needed his stable sense of things.

Andrew drew my attention to ranks of gay couples marching the other way, many men he knew. "No one wants to be in town for this kind of thing," he explained. "It just doesn't seem relevant to much of anything. No sane Washingtonian stays around for these demonstrations." The Reagan administration's homosexuals were bent on escape, as was Andrew.

| | |

The published goals of the March on Washington were utopianly grand: "an end to all social, economic, judicial, and legal oppression of Lesbians and Gays, and people of every race, gender, ability, class, ethnicity, faith, political ideology, transgenderal orientation"—that is, cross-dressers and transsexuals—"and sexual orientation." The march equally called for federal gay rights legislation, abortion rights, and abolishing apartheid in South Africa—magnanimity designed to legitimize the struggle against antihomosexual bigotry within the vast network of recognized oppressions. These were a French Revolution of demands. Pragmatic politics must collapse under the weight of such enormous expectation. The White House and Congress, which any such rally in Washington would seek to impress, were out of town for Columbus Day.

It didn't matter, nor was any critical attention, really, focused on the mass demonstration's methods and intents. What legislation, after all, could end the hurt perpetrated by our "straight" fellow citizens and, above all, our friends and families? What mere law could require our fellow Americans to embrace in us a desire they feared like mortality in themselves? This march, like Gay Pride parades, was a march of euphoric symbols—a search for belonging, a plea for acceptance, essentially not politics at all. Behind the scrim of the propaganda, the crowds grew infused with a cosmic sense of homosexual bonding and camaraderie. By Sunday morning, when we marchers congregated in the Ellipse behind the White House for our progress to the Mall, we had reached a half million men and women with several thousands of our children. Great bright banners shivered against the sky—from every state, from hundreds of gay and lesbian organizations. There were witty costumes, dancers, bands, and platoons of brilliant drag queens. The capital become a city for same-sex lovers, walking hand in hand.

Armies of livid placards demanded an end to AIDS—as if a compliant Congress could declare it. Others touted the specialness of homosexuality, naming thousands of geniuses and artists believed to be "gay," proclaiming talent a universal homosexual trait. The spirit of the day moved the marchers greatly. I saw embittered activists embrace who'd refused to speak for years. Today we gathered homosexuals were one people, a gay nation. *"We are a gentle, loving people,"* the marchers sang.

Michael—my lover—and I marched, arms around each other's waists, free-floating among the contingents. We had marched for years in angry celebration and protest. Now suddenly it seemed different. I seemed to watch the brotherly, sisterly jubilance at some muted distance. For the first time since "coming out," I felt I no longer belonged to all this. The great wave of gay sentiment rolled over me and left me dry.

My journey had turned inward.

CHAPTER 20

ISLANDS OF FREEDOM AND PRISON CELLS

THE SEVERAL DAYS I STAYED IN NEW YORK AFTER COMING HOME from Washington were filled with terrible anxiety. Every return home had been: this was the city that awaited me when I was done with traveling. Its decay was huge, rank with filth, rancid with its population's animosities. There was a burgeoning epidemic of antihomosexual violence and terrible racial strife. Homeless beings, reeking with degeneration, lay in the doorways of my apartment building. This was my home. I hated it.

My lover, whose nurture had always been my life source, could not console me in these returns. The obituary pages of *The New York Times* were filled now with the names of men I knew— some whom I'd loved, some who'd been well when I'd left to travel. The phone rang out with the knell of another diagnosis, another death. An editor who'd nurtured my writing—a man who'd become my dear, dear friend—had died. I had not gotten the chance to say good-bye. I could not forgive life that insult. I cried, when I was not numb, until my chest seemed to shatter.

I had no interest in this place. I could not stay. The answers seemed all to lie elsewhere, in other men's towns, in other men's lives. I still wanted to find the core of gay male identity—or discover someone who would dissolve the myth for me. I did not want the responsibility for turning renegade myself. Nor did I sleep those nights back home. I listened like a frantic mother to my breathing, madly checking my body for disease. Only the speed of the road, it seemed to me, could brighten my mind.

A journal entry
New York City
October 15

I will fly to Hawaii, then back to L.A. to cross the continent by train—one last trip. Doing the country by rail has been an old fantasy for me. But I'm growing exhausted. Michael wonders why I must go on the road again. To sew the nation together in my mind, I told him—as if the plane and train, like a needle and thread, could seam an old murmur in my heart that needs repair.

We've grown poor now on account of the telephone. I have promised to write.

Oahu, Hawaii
October 20

My love,
Forgive me for not writing sooner, but I haven't stopped exploring since I got here.

Last weekend I donned my tux and costume jewelry for the coronation of the "emperor" and "empress" of Hawaii— the annual drag ball. Such chaos! I'd guess there were more than a thousand people there, overflowing an enormous Chinese restaurant.

What's most startling is that it was a family affair! Lit-

tle Polynesian children ran around everywhere while their fathers, brothers, uncles, cousins doted over their family mahus—the native Hawaiian queens—as if the "girls" were about to be transformed into Miss Americas. The air was on fire with the flash of Instamatics.

Really, the whole evening was breathtaking. Brown adolescent boys with buttocks as sleek as ivory and pearl divers' chests trumpeted huge sea shells, then processed in sarongs accompanied by beautiful women. Some carried huge wooden bowls of papayas and pineapples along with magnificent fruits and flowers the likes of which I'd never seen before. Some balanced bowls of mountain water in their hands. Others carried platters of volcanic fire. They had crowned their heads with braids of grass and orchids. The aroma of their leis enveloped the room in a marvelous mist. A battalion of native drums followed afterward, then a long train of hula dancers—young and delicious men and women whose sinuous arms and smooth, lithe hips engraved the air with myth.

It was positively Jungian!

The queens themselves came last, parting the crowd with their giant bodies and broad Polynesian brows, which were wildly sceptered with palms and tropical blossoms. They grow to astounding size—these feminine men! All of them took a turn in swimming wear (!), then evening gowns, then huge muu-muus with leis made of shells. And each contestant sang delicately as she accompanied "herself" with a ukelele!

Tuxedoed lesbians were their escorts. I've never seen such a convoy of masculine women! They are all in the navy here, I think. (The nation is safe.)

After hours of competition, it was "Daisy Fever" who won, and the crush of music and standing ovation was deafening. Five generations of her beaming family gathered around her throne—a big red-and-gold chair carved with Chinese dragons. Last year's empress, Nilani, crowned her with gardenias and some crimson flower shaped like a bursting heart. Then all her "subjects" laid fruit at her feet while half-naked island boys danced for her pleasure.

A young Japanese man was chosen emperor while an-
other wave of food was being served—a Chinese forest of ped-
estaled dishes. A giant queen beside me plundered a plate of
chicken legs with her greasy fingers. With her mouth full, she
said, "Nine thousand chickens died for Daisy Fever's corona-
tion."

The rest of the weekend was lost in celebration—
feasting, hula dancing, and oceans of liquor. I'm still in a
stupor, but I did manage a brief "audience" with last year's
empress at a banquet on the second day. She was ever so busy
turning up her huge brown cheeks for kisses and whispering,
"mahalo!" (thank you) to all her admirers. She works as an
aide in the governor's office here—as she is! She told me that
when anyone asks if she's man or woman, she says, "What
does it matter? We're all here for a purpose, aren't we!"

I am amazed at such gentle, tolerant people. I've heard
there are a great many mahus as well, on the island of
Niihau, but no one but native Hawaiians can set foot there.
It's the last enclave of the ancient way of life. The rest is a
kind of American ruin, I think. I'm beginning to think it's the
dignity of ruined peoples that teaches us best how to live.

It's my last day here. I'm writing you from the beach—
Queen's Surf, once the playground of Hawaiian royalty and
now the cruising ground for white homosexuals. These
haoles, as they call white people here, lie nearly naked on the
grass baking on new tan lines. Mostly they're young flight at-
tendants, laying over in Honolulu, I think. They're all laden
with muscles, from pecs to thighs. Their earphones stop their
ears so they can't hear the sea. Their roving eyes are dull with
ennui. What passionless mating! Do you know, I've never un-
derstood such self-contained men. Have you ever really felt
one with them?

Enough! I'm surrounded by magnificent beauty. The sky
today is a huge mystery, blown with moist veils. It will not
hold its shape and flies by electric blue, gray, and silver. Di-
amond Head juts its stony prow into the sea, as if the island
had set sail for somewhere. A dark arm of land in the dis-

tance by Pearl Harbor seems to grasp at something, then lets go behind a curtain of emerald mist that rises from the trees. There's a volcano of clouds erupting over where the warships lie submerged with their soldier corpses, sending snowy white lava flows to the ocean.

How I wish you were lying here beside me, that we could share the magic of this place! We've let too little of such mystical beauty into our lives these last few years. I know I've made it hard for you, always battling injustice and fighting for belonging, not recognizing its face when it came. Stale rage has not brought me peace. What acceptance have I ever needed outside your love?

Pelicans sit idle in the park below the palm trees. I imagine you here with your pinions around me. Now a black storm tumbles across the mountains carrying spears of lightning, and I must go.

My plane leaves at midnight, and I haven't packed yet. I'll write from California.

Your tropical heart

West Hollywood
October 25

Dear Michael,
I'm in a foul state of mind.

I've spent the last few nights with Hal and Cleve. Things are terrible between them. They do nothing but fight. Cleve is the only wage-earner in the family now, and construction jobs have grown scarce.

Hal himself has hardly worked a day since they left New York. More than a year? Michael, he's really lost his mind! It would break your heart. He's up all night and sleeps all day, then watches football on TV like a catatonic every evening. He's become a real speed freak. I found him in the backyard yesterday hanging and rehanging laundry, twitching as if bugs were eating him, muttering nonsense things. If he's sensible at all, he talks only about AIDS—nightmarish litanies of all his dead friends. New York was a morgue for him.

Physically he's still strong as ever, I'm happy to say. But given all our sexual pasts, how could he not be infected? His L.A. friends think the virus has eaten his brain. That's to be the new excuse for all our madness. I think it's grief that's made him nuts. They so much believed this move from New York would solve their problems—and save them from AIDS. I guess they've learned that the grasp of fear can't be shaken so easily.

But listen to me—when I've done much the same thing! I think life on the road has been my antidote for the terror of returning to New York City.

I went cruising on Santa Monica Boulevard most of the night last night, and I'm exhausted. I gave a street kid— maybe seventeen—$50 to let me hang around with him. He told me he isn't gay, he just fucks men for money. He sleeps in the park. He's on parole. He was terrifyingly angry. In the car, he pulled out a needle and shot himself full of cocaine. Why doesn't that shock me? Because it seems like a reasonable way out for children destroyed already? If America can't save them, maybe at least we should let them anesthetize themselves. At one point he had me park in a rich neighborhood and was gone for about ten minutes. When he came back, he was carrying a turntable, a CD player, and a stash of other things in his arms. He'd robbed some house! He said the guy owed him. What did I learn from my night with him? That some men are desperate, that we're all accomplices.

I'm driving up the coast to the prison at San Luis Obispo tomorrow—to visit Rob Rosenkrantz, not to serve a sentence. I think I must have told you about him.

I am safe. I think I've eluded the police.

> *All my love,*
> *Your man on the lam*

A journal entry
San Luis Obispo
October 28

The fog lies everywhere—blind fog, blanching the sky, whiting out the road, dissolving houses and trees. All the mountains have vanished and the ocean has melted away in chill, white breath.

The city of San Luis Obispo lies along the Pacific coast, midway between Los Angeles and San Francisco. North of town, the California Men's Colony sits in a desolate valley like a monstrous skeleton—steel and concrete bone—surrounded by stone-bare mountains. It is a maximum security prison. Two high steel fences enclose the grounds, looped all around with razor wire and tufts of barbed wire. A concrete moat divides them. In a high square tower above the gate house, a guard paces with binoculars and a rifle, ready to kill.

Robert Rosenkrantz was just twenty years old when I went to the prison to meet him. All that I knew of the boy I had learned from several magazine articles. He had been imprisoned then for about two years, serving a life sentence for murdering a friend of his brother's.

Rob didn't fit the general image of a murderer. He was raised in Calabasas, an exclusive suburb of Los Angeles, the oldest son in an affluent Jewish family. His father was a successful attorney, and Rob himself was his father's pride, an all-American boy— good student, an athlete, into stereos, computers, and cars. He had always had a girlfriend—and a sexual secret. He harbored an attraction for other men. Except for two other boys he'd met and one young lesbian, though, his only homosexual expression was teenage chatter sent through a gay computer bulletin board, which he contacted clandestinely from his bedroom.

Around the time of Rob's high school graduation, his brother Joey and Joey's prankster buddy Steve Redman—both of whom were Rob's schoolmates—began to grow suspicious of Rob's privacy and decided to tap his telephone. The conversations they taped revealed party plans Rob had made for graduation night at the family beach house. His only guests were to be his three gay friends. Steve, in particular, hated faggots and ridiculed them incessantly, though neither boy actually claimed to know any. On the evening of the party, he and Joey, armed with the tapes, decided to launch a guerrilla attack against Rob and the other three discovered homosexuals. Dressed in military fatigues, the two boys stormed the beach house soon after the party began, roughed up Rob's friends, burned Rob's hand with a high-voltage police stun gun, and broke his nose with a five-cell steel police flashlight.

Still, the greater horror was what happened afterward. When Rob and his gay friends escaped, Steve and Joey returned to the Rosenkrantz home to "out" Rob in front of his parents. A terrible row ensued. Rob had spent what seemed like a lifetime concealing his desire for men from his father. Now all his frantic hiding counted for nothing. Mr. Rosenkrantz was both heartbroken and outraged. Rob, of course, denied the accusations. But although Joey retracted his story for a time, Steve would not back down, so livid was his hatred of homosexuals. In the morning, battered by his family's hurt and anger, Rob jumped in his car and fled for days. When he returned he was carrying a machine gun he'd bought at a shop with his Visa card. At his trial he insisted that he had only wanted to frighten Steve, to get him to take back the terrible tale he'd told. But when Rob confronted him in the street in front of the boy's apartment house, his brother's good buddy only taunted him again, and Rob raised the gun and massacred him.

I had arranged to meet and talk to Rob in two tightly timed sessions over two days. It had taken me several months to get the prison's permission. On the morning of my arrival, the warden escorted me from the outside gate. Between her office and the interview room, cavernous hallways of paired iron gates made holding pens, where the constant clang of gates and heavy keys replaced the white noise of streets and open spaces.

One of a series of guards led me into the room where I was to meet Rob and positioned me so that, from the thick glass window in the door, he could keep a constant watch on my hands and face. Rob and I could exchange nothing except words. A second guard brought Rob in; his hands were folded in front of him like a punished child's. He walked stiffly in his prison fatigues—Levi's and a blue workshirt. He was tall, very well built, and handsome, with short, thick black hair. But I'd never seen such a dead face— not hostile, really, but hardened, as if rigor mortis had set in. He waited for me to speak, then spoke to me. His voice was deep and dead, the well of emotion behind it tightly capped. He had nothing to say that wasn't to the point of our visit. I asked a question. He recited the details surrounding the murder like a well-rehearsed man on a witness stand. He sounded recorded, or as though he needed obsessively to retrace every step of his crime. "When I came home, the next morning after the party," he stated, "my dad called me in and said, 'Steve and Joey told me that you are a homosexual. Is that true?' I said no. I told him I was down there with my girlfriend, the one I took to the prom. And he just broke down and started crying. Obviously he'd been up all night sweating this out. He was crying hysterically, thanking God that I wasn't gay, just going on and on about AIDS and how terrible a life I would have if I was gay—and that kind of thing. I knew this was going to be his reaction, for years, if he ever found out. And my mom . . . that scene was repeated.

"But my dad's an attorney. So he went back to the beach house with a legal pad and made a bunch of questions for me— like, 'If it was only you and the girlfriend, how come there were more than two dirty glasses?' He wanted the name and phone number of the girl to confirm my answers. Then my brother turned on me and gave him some conversations he'd made from my phone. I was trapped right there.

"For anyone in Calabasas, being 'gay' is the lowest form of life, a fate worse than death. It was as bad as the Nazis going after the Jews. Being a faggot was scum. Fags should die. 'Kill fags!'

Especially for kids. Kids everywhere, I guess, have to have someone to look down on.

"It was all very negative, and obviously I never wanted to be
in the spotlight of my dad's thinking about it, about being gay.
My dad was someone I really looked up to."

He took a picture of his father from his wallet. He had a
sympathetic face. He was about my age, and I was startled—Rob
could be my son. While I examined the snapshot, he told me, "I
don't look at him as being motivated behind this. He was just
kind of put in a situation that he was never prepared to handle.
By which I mean, he wasn't the type of person who wouldn't rep-
resent a gay person and go into the civil rights issues, as an attorney. But when you get into it personally, he'd rather not have it.
Now he's done full circle on this.

"If I'd given him an hour or so and talked about it with
him—not an hour, but maybe a year—I probably could have gone
back to the family and said, 'Okay, I'm gay. Big deal. Let's deal
with it and get it out in the open—maybe some family therapy or
something.' If I had been comfortable with it . . . The whole
thing with me and Steve was a huge trauma for them, and this—
whether Rob's gay or straight—has become a lesser thing. Lesser
than the fact that at the time I was sitting in the L.A. County Jail
facing the possibility of the death sentence, and now I'm here
serving life."

What unnerved me was how little Rob paused, as if none of
this could stop his heart. Startling statements like insights followed triallike recitations. His soul seemed to be lost in the rush.
"But if it hadn't been Steve," he stated suddenly, "it would have
been me. My own suicide was an inevitability with me during
those years, around the time when I matured. 'If I get exposed,
I'll kill myself. There's no talking about it.' If I had completely
blown this on my own, I probably would have put a gun to my
own head—which I did many times the week before I shot him.
I mean, I didn't go into the situation wanting to kill Steve, or
wanting to kill my brother, or wanting to kill myself. I just went
into that situation wanting to put everything back the way it was.
I ended my life as I knew it when I did that. It never occurred to

me that anyone else would expose me—because I did everything I was supposed to. I was a very stereotypical 'straight,' as far as I was concerned. It was something I would be able to conceal for the rest of my life without a problem. Then this thing happened."

"But was dragging you out of the closet enough to kill a man for?" I asked. "Do you still think that?"

"Steve attacked me and he hurt me and I came back," he said. His voice was bereft of passion. Now he seemed to backpedal from the motivation for his crime. "I mean, that alone wasn't enough to obviously warrant me killing him, but it was a big part of the thing. This thing was a fag bashing, pure and simple. And Steve's violence got downplayed a lot because everyone wanted to stress the closet issue. Steve came at me with weapons. That had a lot to do with everything." A crook in Rob's nose showed where Steve had hit him with the steel flashlight. Its sharpness appeared like a still raw insult.

I asked whether he could ever forgive his own brother for the role he played. He said, "Well, we all contributed—Steve contributed, Joey contributed, and I contributed. We were all immature." His voice was dull. And his statement seemed such a well-worn recitation of remorse that I wondered whether his prison psychiatrist had scripted him to say that—practice for a distant parole hearing. He said, "They were always into commando-type activities—just on a juvenile level—guns and things like that. So I don't think there was real hatred and malice behind what they did, as an adult would have had ... I don't know."

He paused and stared through the bars on the window toward a courtyard wall of solitary confinement cells. Two brown birds played in the shadowy air, singing wildly, while a guard's stolid face watched us through the glass in the door. "It's just been a matter," he soon continued, "of not so much saying it doesn't matter anymore as saying you can only be mad for so long. I say, 'Well, I'm twenty years old. I've probably got at least fourteen or fifteen years to serve minimum before I can be paroled, and so I've lost the entire youth I had left. I just live for tomorrow and then the day after that when I get there, because that's the only way you can live in here. Otherwise you'd string yourself up. Suicide is a big thing here. Half this facility is a medical facility, just people who're constantly medicated so they can deal with this environment."

The guard knocked on the door and held up five fingers behind the glass. I looked at my watch. Rob had talked continuously, if coldly, for almost two hours, the prison allowance for an inmate interview on any given day. Anyway, I think Rob had told me everything he intended to say about the circumstances of his crime. His voice, which had always seemed passionless to me, now seemed final and perhaps exhausted. It occurred to me that there was a rawer truth to be told about his angry sorrow—or lack of it—for the murder, but I was not going to discover it that day. Anything I published about him could be used against him at a parole hearing. He seemed to me too smart to be trapped that way.

When I returned on the second day, I asked Rob about the wall of solitary confinement cells outside the window. He said, "Every prison has a 'hole,' where inmates are isolated for committing crimes within the prison." They were released from their tiny cells for only fifteen minutes a day to knock a ball against a wall for exercise. Lesser infractions—like having sex—were judged and recorded to be brought into evidence at parole hearings. A sexual relationship alone could keep a man locked up.

I wondered about "gay life" in prison. After all, Rob's secret homosexuality had been crucial to landing him here. He began to talk willingly but dismissively—as if the matter were so irrelevant that it irked him. He said, "It's not an issue—because you don't have your freedom. *That's significant!* Your values all of a sudden take a giant step into reality. It's like, I'm locked in a cell—*that's* a major problem. I'm not going to be able to have any social life for twenty years, I can't ever drive a car, there are lots of things I can't do." For the first time I thought I heard genuine anger in his voice. His torso leaned over the table. The guard watched. "Now," he said, "you're telling me this guy over here—me, whoever—is *gay?* I don't give a fuck. Outside you have a lot of leisure time to entertain these negative thoughts and worry about other people. In here you're just worrying about yourself. You're worrying about, is my cell going to get searched today? Is it going to get torn apart? Am I going to lose property? Or am I going to get into a fight? Is there going to be some major problem that's going to get me transferred to a worse prison. And whether this guy over here is gay? 'I don't care'—that's the attitude in here. People here realize what's significant in life because they have so many things taken away from them."

Then, suddenly, as if damming up a dangerous flood of emotion, he became more distant and for a while seemed removed again from what he said, as though it had nothing to do with him. "Besides, a lot of people here have been in and out of custody since their juvenile years, and I'd say a large percentage of them have had a homosexual experience in prison at one time or another anyway."

I persisted. "Who inside here knows you're gay? Guards? Inmates?"

He was brusque. "I didn't act gay out there, I don't act gay in here. *Stereotypically* I don't act gay—how's that? I don't wear eyeliner." Some of the queens inside did, he told me. He said that they made it by burning a plastic spoon and collecting the residue. "You see some relationships where the 'gay' person is obviously taking on the complete woman role. They talk, act, look, walk, and dress as much as they can like a girl. They'll get girl's pants sent in from Sears. Put it this way—there's transvestites in here that walk around in the best drag that they can put on, given the limitations of dress codes and the prison environment. They're always with their man—a big, strong daddy type, whatever you want to call it—and they're a couple. They usually try to get a cell together. No one's going to care."

I asked if he had any gay friends—if he'd found any compensation whatsoever for the horror of imprisonment. And my question sounded naive to me.

"Not any of the queens," he answered decisively. "And the guys that just fuck because there aren't any women around, I don't think of them as really gay. But I have a couple of gay friends. I can say things to them I can't say to a straight person. You can't watch the Olympics with a straight inmate and say something about the divers' butts or ask them maybe, 'Did you see that new one they just brought in?'

"But there's not much social life in here anyway. I might talk to someone five minutes a day and consider that I've had quality time with them, because between their work schedules and my work schedules and things like that, you don't have a lot of contact. My cell mate is my main social life, my best friend. And he's not gay. Other than him, if I want to talk to someone, I catch them like every couple of weeks when neither of us is working, and we might walk around the track a few times and talk about what's happened since we saw each other. The grass grows, that's basically it."

Finally I asked him about his own sex life, because it seemed to me that at least some sexual pleasure could dull the pain of life here. He looked at me as if I were trying to catch him and said coldly, "It's against prison regulations. If you're caught, it goes on your record and counts against parole." No more.

But he was more willing to speak about prison sex in general, and I found it ironic the way he used the term *safe sex*—having to do not at all with AIDS, but with eluding the constant eyes of the guards. He said, "About the only safe sex is to get a cell together. There are other very risky things you can do. I guess you could go out in the yard and sit next to each other and put a jacket over your lap. So I guess there's really nothing you can do. There are no one-night stands around here, let's put it that way. The only safe option is a relationship with your cell mate."

The life he described seemed intolerable to me, though in time we human beings seem capable of adjusting to almost any desperation, I think. I said nothing for a moment, while the guard rapped his knuckles on the glass in the door and flashed fifteen fingers, counting down. But it was what Rob said next that really startled me.

"In a way," he stated, "it's a healthier environment here than on the outside." And he seemed really to want to talk about it. "Being gay, or being bi or straight, it doesn't really take on a category, because a lot of the straight people in here have a very effeminate cell mate you know they're having sex with. It doesn't have to be labeled or talked about. It's not important. It may be hard for people on the outside to comprehend that, but those relationships are such a common occurrence that it's just not an issue in here.

"Real prison issues are, you're closer to being primitive. If you're locked in a cell in the middle of the night and you have a major medical problem, you don't have a telephone. Or am I going to get my cell searched? Everybody gets their cell searched. They can read your mail. And whether someone's gay or straight is really trivial." It struck me powerfully how terribly his life had had to be destroyed to discover that truth.

The guard was knocking again to signal five minutes just as we finished talking. But it seemed to me that now Rob wanted to say something more, as if an intimacy had ensued between us in these two days. Perhaps he deemed that I'd listened well—or somehow otherwise I'd proved myself and my efforts warranted new revelations. Rob lowered his voice and leaned into the table. He suddenly seemed tortured to me. He spoke relentlessly.

"If someone kicks you, you kick them back," he said. "If he kicks you again, you kick again. When you're both all bruised up, maybe you'll both think twice. That's the short run. I know that violence in the long run doesn't solve anything. I mean, now it would be easier for me to try to separate myself from this whole thing, pretend I didn't even kill Steve and suffer a lot of grief and remorse over his death, because Steve was someone I'd known for a long time. He was a friend of mine and I miss him. I can say that. Yeah, I have a lot of grief over Steve's death. I also have a lot of sadness that Steve was involved in this act of violence against me.

"Obviously he didn't deserve what he got. What he got was a Pandora's box he didn't even know he was tapping. I don't think people ever realize the deep-seated emotions that come out of someone when they're being beaten up just because they're gay." And even then the passion for self-recrimination in his voice seemed to waver, as if it were a record spun silently so many times that the inarticulate grooves had worn thin.

Then, abruptly, he interrupted himself and spoke with the same dispassionate anger he had generally maintained. "But I'll tell you this," he said. "There's really only one thing I care anything about now, that I think about day and night. I just want to get out of prison. I haven't ever had any exposure to gay life other than through the press and media—reading about it. I've never even been to a gay dinner party. I mean, you can look at me and everything looks like 'Okay, he can deal with it.' But I hate it. I don't want to wait to have fun out there when I'm old, when there's not much fun left for me."

A terrible sadness overwhelmed me. I wanted to be his friend and take some of the anguish from him. As we stood to leave I reached to embrace him, but he withdrew under the glare of the guard's hard eyes. He could be strip-searched for a hug. Such intimacy was an infraction.

The few brief hours I had spent with Rob, more than any other experience I'd had in crossing the nation, impressed upon me the vagueness of gay identity—and the supreme value of freedom of affection.

CHAPTER 21

CONTINENTAL
TRACKS

Los Angeles
October 30

Dear Michael,
I'm at the station waiting to board the Desert Wind. *In Salt Lake City I change trains for Seattle, then on to Chicago. I'm nearly exhausted with new discoveries, hoping the railway will be anesthetizing. I think I'm traveling more for the hell of it now.*

I do wish you could see the old terminal here. It's Art Deco with a Mexican twist—an enormous Hollywood version of a desert hacienda, something Selznic might have built. I can imagine the stars disembarking from New York—Bette Davis puffing smoke like a locomotive, Gloria Swanson holding the leashes of a hundred dogs.

How unlike airports these stations are! Their echoing grandeur makes me feel glamorous and mysterious, as if I'm about to enter a marvelous secret. A herd of trains is whispering beneath the sheds. Hot plumes of anxious breath rise from their wheels. The station master is calling us to board, naming all the stops between here and Chicago. His godlike voice makes every place seem mythic, a new creation.

My odyssey by train has begun.

Your traveler

A journal entry
Aboard the Pioneer
Salt Lake City to Seattle

November 3. The train belly-crawls like an Indian through deep ravines and tiptoes over high, tiny bridges like a tight-wire dancer. The sharp mountains are evergreen. Mists rise like mossy storms from soaring waterfalls. The tracks scream, the engine moans, pulling itself up a steep incline with a wolf howl.

The rapid Columbia River is wide and white. Its great frothing dams seem to drink it up. The train tests the water on the low stony banks, as if to wash its difficult trip from its wheels or float with the giant dreaming timber barges downstream. Passengers snap up their cameras like sudden memories, then fall back asleep or return to a tired magazine. Their fatigued, distant faces lie askew in their seats. The coach cars smell of the day's exhaustion.

It is hard getting from here to there. Our journeys contain us—no place to stop. We pass through great beauty and pain. That is what I have always loved about travel by train—the common struggle, the awful experience of moving ourselves across the same rough terrain. More than any other way to travel, it is true to our lives.

Seattle, Washington
November 8

Dear Michael,
Seattle is a gray, wet San Francisco on hills surrounded, not by ocean, but by inlets and interlocking lakes. Rising from

*rainy Puget Sound, the vague, blue Olympic Mountains bar-
ricade it from the thundering Pacific. It is a cloudy, safe place,
cloaked in a dearth of sunshine. Japan and Boston, I learned,
are about the same distance from here.*

*My host is Steve Maidhoff—a "leather topman," an
S/M activist. Like most of the leather "tops" I've known, he
is an articulate opera queen who overenunciates. He's also a
tolerant, thoughtful human being, if a bit dogmatic. I suppose he's used to having other men in his control. It's all a
game.*

*He's president of the National Leather Association and
one night this week hosted a committee meeting in his apartment to plan the national convention. The air was musky
with black cowhide. Ironically, nothing seems to worry these
people more than their acceptance by the "gay community"
and the gay misunderstanding they suffer. But it's been my
experience that only man-boy sex can arouse such gay disgust
as is directed toward S/M. Steve said gay men and lesbians
bombarded the gay paper with hate mail after the last NLA
convention. He's defensive about it. He says, "All sex is S/M.
Leather just adds theater to it."*

*Steve has a "puppy," Mark, who lives with him—a
handsome, cuddly young man who was a Trappist monk until
a few years ago, before becoming Mr. Gay Portland. On Saturday, Mark took me to a "dungeon" in the warehouse district where Seattle's "leather community" holds its parties. Its
old stone walls were black and dank. Two big rooms—one for
men, the other for lesbians—held wooden racks, fisting slings,
and crosses for "crucifixions." "Fear of Suppression" was
scrawled across a mirror. A wall of shelves was stacked with
restraints, tit clamps, whips, and electric cattle prods. In the
women's room, a lesbian was resupplying trays of rubber
gloves and razor blades. Steve said the lesbians tend to enjoy
sex involving blood more than the men. The woman said,
"When you bleed on yourself every month, you get into it—
but nothing extreme." I suppose I've known countless couples*

in my life who've done worse to each other emotionally and spiritually. Maybe this is all a harmless release for our common destructive impulses. I've learned well enough in my travels that appearances are nothing.

Still, a deep paranoia seems to pervade the S/M world. Over brunch at the top of the Space Needle just this morning, Steve and his puppy spoke of nothing else but the gay community's abandonment of the "leather community." Steve claims that because of the skinheads, white supremacists, and neo-Nazis—big movements in the Northwest—radical leathermen have been building up caches of guns to protect themselves. He insists that "acceptable homosexuals" think the bigots will stop with the gays on the fringe, like him. "Though it never happens that way," he told me. "The 'good gays' are always next. Hateful people never make such fine distinctions."

It's probably true, you know, what he says. But I wish these siege-minded men could talk to Rob Rosenkrantz before they start shooting.

This evening I catch the train across Washington State and Idaho's northern sliver to the wide desolation of Montana and North Dakota and on to Chicago—some forty-five hours. It strikes me that no vast geography can be more desolate than our minds.

Your pioneer

Journal entries
Aboard the Empire Builder
Seattle to Chicago

November 8, 9:00 P.M. Tonight there is no sky, no ground. The train ascends the Cascades through a cushion of deep black air. The wheels flutter on the tracks like wings. In the distance, the hoot of the engine decrescendoes like a midnight owl.

The train is fast asleep before Spokane. Across from me

a reclining man has laid his big bald head upon the armrest and rolled his enormous belly to one side. His little legs, tucked underneath, look like handles for a bellows. He honks and snores. Spit bubbles on his lips. A teenaged girl a few rows back chokes on a cold and never thinks to cover her cough. Two fat women can't get comfortable and toss themselves about, mumbling drowsily. Their seat backs complain. A mother walks the aisle with her whimpering baby. The train rocks us all like a cradle. Our sudden intimacy makes us family.

November 9, 6:30 A.M. Dawn lightens the layers of fog at Whitefish, Montana. The roofs of barns and log cabins are patched with new snow. In a schizophrenia of high sharp rock behind the train, the Rockies are in their death throes. To the east, the morning grasslands flatten absolutely and great plains of cows stand swishing beneath pale clouds. The flat Midwest is born in bales of hay.

It will take all day to travel through Montana, and half the night again to get to Fargo. Nothing lies in between.

November 10, 2:00 A.M. The train is late. A grain elevator shadows the white night sky. A three-quarter moon hangs over Fargo.

1:00 P.M. A fat woman downed her lunch and two desserts across from me in the dining car today, telling me all the while about her "Christian weight loss program." The overweight ladies of her church meet every noon and read the Bible aloud instead of eat. She asked me what I do for a living. I hedged, not wanting to endure a debate on homosexuality with a born-again Christian. She pressed, and in time I told her the truth, braced for an onslaught of Scripture. Instead she beamed and proclaimed for the whole dining car to hear, "My daughter's a lesbian! And she's the finest human being I've ever known!" I felt ashamed of myself on account of my prejudice.

We sat together all afternoon as the train fled flat through Wisconsin. She pointed out "pig houses"—little, peaked, individual huts where hog families sleep. The southwest part of Wisconsin, not far from Iowa, is a sea of pig houses. Silos glint across the sky like buoys.

At last, I arrive in Chicago today.

I think I had never known such fatigue as I felt by the time I got to Chicago. It was not the trip across the continent, really, that tired me so completely, but the magnificent discoveries I had undergone throughout the year—and the terrible nearness now of going back to New York. My understanding of gay identity—and so my understanding of myself—changed drastically. And going home, it seemed, required of me a radically different relationship to the "gay community" that throughout my whole adulthood I had turned to for safety. I had to learn, I believed, a new responsibility to the broader community in which I lived, which did not depend on my being homosexual.

But above all I feared going home to the culture of death that had overtaken New York since the onset of AIDS. I feared for my own survival. The terror of disease had begun to plague me.

I might have tried to lose myself in exploring new experiences in Chicago, attempting yet more distraction. But I did not, more perhaps because I lacked the energy than anything else. For several days I meandered the city. I had lived here in the seventies, until I finished graduate school. I had friends I could visit, places to go to renew old memories. I sat whole afternoons reminiscing with acquaintances and spent evenings going to gay basketball games. In no other American city, I think, do gay identified men gather together athletically as vigorously as they do in Chicago. And it struck me that that curious circumstance helped define the differences I'd experienced of gay life in Chicago and New York: Gay men gravitated to New York to make it on Broadway, to Chicago to play ball.

Still, for all my vacant wandering about the city, I carried with me a sense of dread and hoped for one last chance to resolve my fears, some peace about life and death to go home with. And it was that harsh need, I think, that, a day before I was to leave, stopped my finger on Allen Longtemps's name as I thumbed through my Chicago address book.

Allen was not really a Chicagoan in my mind. I knew him from his days in New York. He had moved to Chicago for his health and peace of mind—away from the anguished tumult of Manhattan—only perhaps two years before. We had not been intimate friends before he moved, or even frequent acquaintances, though I had always liked him greatly. I would say that I had never known much about him at all, really—except that he was sometimes a drag queen and had survived AIDS-like illnesses for nearly six years. It was his long survival that drew me to him now. And having rediscovered his name, I telephoned him obsessively until I got hold of him. I think it was as if suddenly I expected him to provide antibodies to my own fears of disease, whose titers rose and fell with my doubtful faith that any of us sexual conspirators from the gay erotic heyday would outlive, could outrun, the horror of this epidemic. Were we not all prone to seek our magic in someone else? I wanted miracles.

I'd first met Allen in the Hamptons, in 1983, where each August wealthy friends—a married couple with children, though neither was strictly "straight"—invited their lovers and bohemian intimates to share their beach house. It was a wonderful place—huge and high-towered, with a pool and formal yard—that sat in isolation from the world. We costumed ourselves and performed Shakespeare. Allen's room that year was a sunny garret, separate and quiet. He appeared only for meals, which were feasts of our host's magnificent fancy. He ate little, said little, and sat shortly before going back to bed. He was ghostly. He'd been peculiarly sick for more than a year by then but stated, gently and undogmatically, that he was getting well. We—or perhaps it was I alone—didn't believe him. It was early in the epidemic. No one had yet tracked the myriad, insidious turns the disease would take:

it had barely been named. Men died. It seemed that no one, once stricken, survived. Allen's sickness cast a terrified shadow over our sobered festivities, though he was never morbid himself. One wondered why he did not allow himself to lie passively, peacefully, to receive the afterlife—or to be more bitter that dying had been forced on him so soon.

But he would not, and though I didn't see him for a year after that, it was continuously reported by mutual friends that he was improving remarkably—"Not sick at all anymore," some said. By the time we met again he showed no symptoms of his illness. He was effervescent with health and in fantastical drag. He seemed mystical to me then and perhaps therefore unapproachable. Herald of a cure, he was the bearer of secrets.

Soon afterward he left New York for a school in rural Wisconsin, to train as a masseur. Then I heard he was living in a big old house on Chicago's Northside and working. When finally I reached him by phone, he promised to give me a good massage.

His hands were hot—not scorching, but deep and steady. I lay naked on the table in his living room and sailed into wakeful meditation, like an infant or old man rousing from a numb sleep.

"The most important thing we can do for ourselves," he said, palpating a painful muscle, "is to learn to be responsible—for taking care of ourselves in the midst of all this."

His assertion slid off me like too much oil. The issue, I thought righteously, was not any longer *our* responsibility in this plague's midst. We had radically, mournfully reformed our sex lives. We had held our sick friends. We grieved ceaselessly. We marched through the streets with demands. What more could *we* do? It was a niggardly, brutal president and a cruel nation—a callously slow research establishment, bigoted against homosexuals—that refused us a cure. I despised Ronald Reagan and the people who had elected him as I would Nazis. *Where were the nation's tears for our torn lives? Our* responsibility was not the point, I believed.

But that old bitterness had begun to burn through me. I lay

quiet and said nothing. Allen's fingers paused on my liver, where, he said, I had a block. "A lot of unreleased anger," he told me with a velvet voice like a baritone. "Are you angry?" he asked. "I never took responsibility for myself until I got ill. We're talking thirty-one, thirty-two years of resistance. I took care of other people. Other people took care of me. I was totally at the whim of the fates." I was slipping, then, into a soundless reverie beneath the wavelike surging of his palms.

Later that night he talked again. Ten coconut shells in the guise of skeletal heads—death white and black, cancerous blue, like the frights that must come to us before healing—hung spectrally in a pattern behind him. The clock on the wall was slow. I determined to listen to him, for I believed he'd made himself well. "It was 1982 and AIDS was just starting. The idea of illness was just perfect for me," he confessed. He was candid, comforting, unmelodramatic. I knew he had not been alone in such dark thinking. How many of us gay men had been searching out an excuse to escape from this world because we believed it did not want us? Allen had imagined a tragic scenario for himself—getting sick and then dying—"which fed into fantasies I'd had when I was growing up," he said. "You know, the sensitive artist, dying young. I was very attracted to the idea of suicide. Every night when I was a kid I put myself to sleep with an image of getting sick, being in the hospital—of all the people who'd come and visit me. I would just lie there and visualize all these people feeling sorry for me—then the funeral."

Allen had gone to New York from a childhood in Vermont in 1970. He'd moved there to join a dance troupe and be with his lover, Randall, who sang with the Metropolitan Opera.

Back then he was, by his own admission, a naïf. For four or five years he lived monogamously. Then he discovered Boot Hill, a gay bar on the Upper West Side, while Randall was away on tour. That was when he started drinking daily, drugging, falling through a vortex of one-night stands. Those days, he said, were alcoholic and hazy in his mind. They took him nightly through the round of back-room bars until closing at

4:00 A.M., when he'd go to the after-hours sex clubs. With two hours' sleep and the aid of coffee, he'd nevertheless make it to dance rehearsal every morning. "To this day," he told me, "I don't know how I could drink like that and still function."

In the midst of this dissipation, his long relationship with Randall began to disintegrate. One night in the fall of 1974, when Randall was singing in Europe, Allen came home drunk and swallowed thirty Seconals, swigging Sambuca. A friend found him and took him to Bellevue Hospital. Two days later he woke up in intensive care, tubes flowing from his nose and lips like the tentacles of so many obsessions that had a grip on him. For thirty days he went through detox, but it didn't last. He moved into a rooming house in Chelsea, went back to drugs and drinking. Crisis did not break him yet.

Sex in New York in those days was at its fever pitch. In a cruisy bower of Central Park, Allen met Frank, a leather topman. They started dating and then moved in together. Frank, expert at fisting, taught him how to take a man's arm up his ass. The sex lasted for hours. "I didn't even know I *had* those desires till I met this man," Allen said. "It was earth-shattering—the sensuality, the *extremeness* of it—the trust and love you have to learn to let someone take you that far in forbidden things. I don't know how to describe what that's about. . . . It bonded us in a way I'd never experienced with anyone else. At that one moment in time you're all alone in the universe with that person. Most people only see the external and judge it that way. But for me it was a transcendent, spiritual thing."

It was a search that he needed to go on, was what he said. "Not everyone's search. *My* search." I understood him and listened more intently. Hadn't the defiled extremities of sex been a search for me, too? And for vast numbers of homosexual men, perhaps, who had had to seek out the farthest reach of this fierce desire they'd been forbidden to express in order to go on living? Allen had found it in a fister's bondage.

"There were men," he said, "who found their place in that sexual community that had no place else to belong. There were no limits back then. I had no limits, either. I found I was a sensualist, a hedonist. I was discovering all sorts of things about who I was."

But nothing we conceive to be good for us can last past its time before it turns to destruction. Old roads to truth, like old highs, become deadly addictions. We reshape our lives according to our new needs, or we die. In a torrent of liquor, coke, and speed, Allen began to have terrible fights with Frank, as he had with Randall. The sexual glue didn't hold. To escape the rage, he drank alone at the waterfront bars, sleeping some nights in the tiny park by the Empire Diner, where the rooftop miniature of the Empire State Building cast a sallow light. I'd known a host of gay men in New York who'd lived like him, searching insanely to belong, addicted to their alienation. Was it also true of me? We all carry the latent antigen of that syndrome, I think. Frank threw him out. Only then, two loves gone, did Allen commit himself to get sober.

Some will say he was too late, but even our mortality, when the terror is contained, becomes our teacher. Late in the fall of 1981, before AIDS was named, Allen's health began to fail him—profound fatigue, daily fevers, night sweats, lymphadenopathy. He thought it would pass. Then men died around him, of a malady first called GRID—gay-related immune deficiency. One night a trick got sick in his arms while they were having sex. The man had a purple lesion on his chest, like a raised stain, which meant nothing to either of them. The stain was Kaposi's sarcoma, a cancerous disease growing in the ruin of his immune system.

"I wasn't afraid until he died," Allen said. "He was the first. Then there were many."

Old, black depressions set back in. "That feeling that you're a freak," he described, "that you don't really fit anywhere. Nothing I ever believed in lasted." He'd been sober two years by then, but sobriety was deficient. He waffled on life. "So AIDS, GRID," he said, "seemed like a perfect setup for me. No one would blame me. I remember lying in bed like I did as a kid, visualizing this illness becoming part of me. It seemed like a welcome thing. And the people in my life were treating me differently now, too, because I was this person who was exotically sick. I didn't have to be responsible for anything in myself. I felt loved."

Baffled doctors wanted to start cutting into him, doing biopsies of his weakening lungs and his painful lymph glands. "I was beginning to live at the hospital," Allen said. "I could see all this beginning to happen to me."

It was reality therapy. He watched close friends start dying horribly. Death startled his confounded will to live. There was nothing more certain he could say about it. The profoundest transformations in our lives bereave us of explanations. "And the doctors," he said, "these people who were supposed to take complete care of me didn't know anything more about what was going on with me than I did. I was gay, I had this weird 'gay disease.' They'd already given me up for dead—because that's the only way they could let themselves think about it—like if *they* couldn't figure it out, who could?" He made the decision not to cooperate.

Nor were his gay friends then in a position to nurture his unsure life force, though he'd never more desperately needed their community. Men drowning in whirlpools of their own fear cannot so easily reach out to be another sinking man's lifeguard. Allen joined a support group for the sick, all gay men, but got more nurture there, he said, for inevitable death than for living. "We were obsessed," he remembered, "with every new symptom—like 'And what happened to *you* this week? What are *your* blood counts?' It was sort of prestigious to be the worst." If he wanted healing—if in fact he were to decide to embrace his life—then he must strike out on his own. "I started putting all the energy I'd been using to visualize illness and death into meditating about being healthy, imagining that. Everyone thought I was crazy—defying the doctors, taking full charge of myself like that. It was the most revolutionary idea I'd had in my lifetime."

"But *how*?" I wanted to know. Our sexual abandon had been similar, if I'd not sought out the same extremes. Binges of liquor and drugs had dulled my pain. We had faced the loneliness of like terrors. Allen's life held answers for me, I'd convinced myself, if only I could draw them out. What *are* these truths we so desperately find in other men's hearts? Our longing for them is like sexual fire, flaming for the oxygen in a lover's body. Allen's vagueness angered me, as though it were a cloud guarding secret streams that could keep me alive, as if I were condemned to witness other men's healing and die. But I couldn't have admitted that then. I was grasping for hope. Hope was vague. Allen held out hope.

He tried to explain. "It's not like one day you wake up and decide you're going to be well. It was a *process*, a difficult struggle, to get back my health. It'll go on for life. I think we always have the answers in ourselves. I had to stop letting my fear drown them out." He had forced himself to stop taking his temperature hourly, madly checking over his whole body with a hand mirror. "I had to stop believing AIDS was the only possible thing in my future," he told me.

"Sometimes it seemed that the people I knew who feared it most were the ones who were getting sick—almost like the fear attracted it. Sometimes I didn't want to go on. But I'd begun to see results. It's very hard to ignore that. My blood tests started coming back nearer normal.

"And yet," he said, "I had spent so much time wanting it. . . ."

One of the men in Allen's support group was Sal, whom Allen began to take care of. He had lymphoma and a terrible variety of other illnesses. His family and friends had pulled away from him. Allen read him meditations and tried to teach him to visualize becoming well. "But the only thing he could see for himself was that he was going to keep getting sicker, then die," Allen remembered. There were tears in his eyes. "He saw death as a kind of resolve. I respected that. A lot of us have been in that place. We get to make that decision over and over again in our lives.

"I remember one night as Sal got sicker, he took my hand and asked, 'Will you stay with me until this is all over?'

"And I said yes. And I did. At the cemetery, when they were ready to put him away in the mausoleum, they gave me one last chance to tell him anything I needed to say. And I laid my hand on his casket and just said, 'Okay, my friend, I've gone with you as far as I can go.'"

I had come to take some magic from Allen. He was a model of healing. In the end, he left me to confront myself.

Chicago
November 22

Dearest Michael,
It's the better part of a year now since I left you to criss-cross the country. The adventure has been exhilarating. But I've been living other people's lives too long. My travels have become a grand distraction. I've grown scared and weary of alienation. Now it's time to come home and make sense of things. It's time to make sense of myself.

I board the Laskeshore Limited for New York this afternoon. I am waiting for your arms. I am lost without you.

Your husband

PART FOUR

THE
WINTER
OF
RETURN

CHAPTER 22

THE
GOSPEL
IN
HARLEM

I DON'T REMEMBER WHEN THE PAIN OF MY ALIENATED SEXUALITY grew to encompass all other hurts in my life and taint every joy. There are other alienations. There are compensating happinesses. Maybe it was that this banishment was the only one that received such social sanction. For a long time, I knew no place to turn to heal it. It became everything.

Hurt becomes a habit. It sustains us for a time. Then, when it cannot be contained, it eats through our lives like a cancer. Long after fights with my parents over my sexuality had ended, long after love promised to bridge our alienation, long after we had all changed and were not the mannequins of my childhood, I continued to hold my family to be the enemy, the traitor source of all my pain.

No hurt wounds us like the betrayal of our families. It breeds clones in all our relationships. We find betrayal everywhere. For years I had withheld my spontaneous love from my parents and harangued them instead with gay politics. They must say things as I would say them, agree with whatever I believed about same-sex love at the time—I was born this way, my preference was irrevocably determined in early childhood, it was a gift, it was my own choice, whatever. I held their acceptance hostage to my old pain. I think in my nurtured pain they saw my need for the love I refused to give myself and felt the shame of it.

In Chicago I met a gay activist couple whose families had thrown a "wedding" shower for them when they'd moved in together. Both pairs of parents invited their own friends and asked their sons to invite theirs. After the party one father of a groom told his son that something had puzzled him about the whole affair. "This was your wedding," he said, "and most of the men who came were couples. But all evening long I never saw one of your friends embrace his lover. They barely touched. I don't understand."

His son answered, "Dad, all through our lives we learned to disguise our love for other men. *You* taught us that. It's not easy just one day to decide those aren't the rules anymore. We were trying to respect *your* feelings."

There is always deep, old resentment in such reluctance.

On June 30, 1986—the year before I set out on my travels— the Supreme Court upheld the states' right to outlaw "sodomy." Twenty-five states and the District of Columbia were left with sodomy statutes, allowing men and women to be arrested for same-sex love, even in the privacy of their bedrooms. The Court's ruling was full of sex terror. In his majority opinion, Chief Justice Warren Burger went so far as to appeal to the morality of ancient Roman law that imposed the death sentence on sodomites.

The Court's injustice was no mere social insult to gay men and lesbians, a theoretical threat to sexual freedom. It terrified many of us. It appeared to be the beginning of pogroms. Demagogues with powerful constituencies—like Congressman William Dannemeyer and William F. Buckley, Jr., the right-wing columnist—had already called for quarantining the "AIDS infected." Buckley went so far as to propose tattooing men and women at the anatomical point the virus entered them—thus, homosexual men's asses. The president, old Ronald Reagan, was si lent. We believed a Nazi-like reign of terror was upon us. In Manhattan dinner conversations that had once scintillated with gossip, sex talk, and camp now whispered of concentration camps and underground escapes to the Netherlands or New Zealand, countries more sympathetic to homosexuals. Activist friends gathered on endless nights at my apartment that year, debating the right time to flee. Many of us had police and FBI files already. We readied our passports. We believed we would have to bitterly speak our peace, then be ready at a moment's signal to slip out of the country. We artists and writers talked of schemes to hide our work, for fear that government agents and goon squads would destroy it.

It may seem now that our fear was extreme. We no doubt did sustain it melodramatically, given a certain gay urban bent for high theater. My straight friends understood it poorly. And though my parents tried to be sympathetic, they were stupefied at my overreaction. But it seems to me now that their own earlier disdain for my affectional life, which still I could not wholly forgive them, fed my paranoia. If our parents could so brutally condemn our sexual lives, how much more brutally, it seemed, would the State crush us. Our parents had made the State's assault believable. I withdrew more completely than ever before into the protective society of homosexuals. Fear enveloped us. I turned my back on old straight friends and nurtured renewed distrust of my family. Heterosexuals were the enemy. I sought only the community of other homosexual men and women who were as frightened and angry as I was.

Months later I still ached with alienation as I set out to discover gay America. I was determined to find the safety of the universal gay bond.

I cannot say that the men I gravitated to across America were a strict cross section of the nation's homosexually identified men. In general I avoided big-city men, for I presumed, being one of them, that I knew their story well. Outside the great metropolises, I met countless men whose lives were troubled, but I was most drawn to those who appeared to me to triumph in their struggle, to have made a noble accommodation to their homosexuality in a contrary society. I had been deeply moved by men like Michelle Prudhomme in Louisiana, whose poverty and constraining filial loyalty could not daunt his happiness, sexual or otherwise. And I'd been awakened to new visions of life by men like Andrew McCabe in Washington, D.C., whose homosexuality could not divide his sympathies between the "gay" world and "straight," and others like Alex Lucker and Rand Lee, the psychics in New Mexico, and Allen Longtemps in Chicago, who sought for and found in themselves a new and spiritual identity in order to save their threatened lives. I was looking for men whose lives could show me a way out of myself.

The men I met on the road shook my world. There is a frightening thrill to disillusionment. I came back from my travels swollen with new insights, evangelistic with altered perspectives. There were ideas I could articulate and conflicted movements of my heart I could not yet speak of, with which I continued to struggle.

I had come to understand that sexual desire is a more greatly amorphous thing than I had ever before believed, that it will not confine itself neatly among one species of sexual being or another, in gay or straight "communities." I came to see that "gay" and "straight" are political divisions, not natural categories—that they serve to sum us up and limit our freedom, drawing boundaries we dare not trespass. I discovered that there is nothing I can say about all homosexuals—or most homosexuals—that I cannot also say about all men and women. I found that what is called "gay community" is a narrow affair, adequately describing few of the homosexually active among us. I came to see that there are many homosexualities, ever-changing shades of homosexual need, and I learned that although we do not wittingly choose the force of our sexual urges, we do most assuredly opt to act on them and shape them into a particular life-style—or not—and so must bear responsibility for them.

Over the course of my travels, it began to occur to me that the dogmas of sexual "communities" must necessarily be mercurial, for they do not so much declare any broad commonality among us as answer repression, whose substance and force mutate with each generation and from person to person. And it now seemed to me that as the power of oppression wanes, the enforced bonding among homosexuals likewise evaporates, though certainly until that time when America at last makes peace with erotic desire, the sexually defiant will be forced somehow to band together for survival.

I learned that America breeds hurt hearts, that there are infinite alienations. I learned that my own family had long reconciled themselves to me while I continued to think of them as my enemy—that exile is reciprocal. And journeying across this continent of magnificent geographies—through the lives of hundreds of compatriot men—I discovered how rooted I am in the wildness of America's land and the joys and conflicts of its people. I learned how American I am.

Gay New York was not eager for my overzealous wisdom. Nor, for all my ability to articulate my new knowledge, could I yet release my loyalties to hardened habits of thought and feeling. Somewhere deep I still clung to the disillusioned hope of "gay community" and to securing my place in it. So, while I preached the new gospel I'd brought home with me, for a time I became recidivist, crusading to broaden the understanding of "gayness" to include the mass of homosexually active men who naturally had no part in it and did not want one. I was a galling missionary, trying to reconcile my fresh apostasy with my terror at not having a place to belong. I set out to find in New York—as I had done elsewhere—men who lived, as it seemed to me, on the periphery of gay community. I believed I understood the included well, because I had been one of them for a time. And for all my conscious desire to belong, I think I came home still looking for old alienations.

In Santa Fe, Alexandra—the channeled spirit guide—had told me that the longest journey I would take would begin when I came home. In fact, I returned from my cross-country train trip in November, only to keep traveling, logging perhaps another twenty thousand miles in the West, the Midwest, New England, and the South. I was insatiable. That, of course, was not what Alexandra meant. I still felt bitterly at odds with my life in New York. I was yet to come to some peace with myself. Rob Goldstein, my San Francisco guide, told me one day on the phone, "The truth makes us very anxious before it sets us free."

New York was at war with itself the year I returned from my travels. In December, 1986, a gang of white boys had brutalized two young black men in Queens and chased one of them to his death in front of a car on the Brooklyn-Queens Expressway. Only the year before, Bernard Goetz had shot two black men on a Manhattan subway train, and the incident was still hot in the minds of New Yorkers. The city seemed poised for riots. All of us shared responsibility for that, it seemed to me. Though Manhattan was not so much a geographically segregated place, socially it was all the same. My world—the gay political world—was barricaded against blacks, or perhaps most homosexually active blacks simply wanted no part of it. I couldn't say which. Late that December, I briefly joined a national committee to plan for an invitation-only conference on gay and lesbian politics—the War Conference, it was dubbed. The committee was all white, mostly male, as were the issues on the proposed conference agenda. The few hundred invitees to the conference were likewise mostly white and male; there were fewer than ten racial "outsiders" among them. Nor was there any active interest in broadening the racial representation on the committee or at the conference, when I brought up the problem. Still, the discrepancy was more poignant than the gay movement's insensitivity. I knew that in this mostly nonwhite city I had no intimate nonwhite friends and had made no real effort to find any.

I decided to explore the black South Bronx and Harlem. There was hubris in that, though I didn't see it then. The black men I met invited me to visit the edge of their world but did not welcome me in.

I had read of the huge black drag balls in Harlem, a respected part of the community's history, but my timing seemed never to be right to attend. They were scarcely advertised outside the ghetto. Recently a black gay writer acquaintance of mine had told me about the Corduroy Club—an all-black gay organization scarcely known to the white gay movement. In time I was able to contact them—they were surreptitious to whites—and, in the summer of 1988, signed up for the annual boat trip. My contact told me, "Until the sixties we had primarily a white membership. Then it got too black and the whites all left. Doesn't that sound familiar?" Still, it was the largest gay organization in New York.

On the sweltering July day of the ride up and down the Hudson, more than two thousand black men and women gathered at the pier carrying card tables and chairs. Their huge picnic baskets were full of fried chicken, ham, potato salad, slaw, and liquor. I was one of four or five whites among them. All the other white men were spouses. They were a raucous, festive crew sailing on the steamy river, congregated in mingling cliques along the outside decks around their spreads. The revelers were costumed in yuppie wear or in intricate braids and swaths of African fabrics and tambourining gold jewelry. The air boomed with Motown, disco, reggae, and rap. The laughter and wild dancing never ended. The boat throbbed with the syncopated noise, rocking its way to Poughkeepsie and back to Manhattan.

I had not brought food with me, reasoning that since I had paid for a ticket, a meal must be served. "Now that's a white man's attitude if I ever saw one," commented a kind man who offered me potato salad and a chicken wing. I met two gentlemen who had been mates for forty-five years, who had fallen in love in Harlem during the war. They were smiling and chilly toward me. They refused to talk to me about their married lives and with cold courtesy dismissed me from their table. Men and women gave me food and drinks and danced with me but would not tell me their secrets.

I pursued one man long afterward—Leroy Jackson, a long-time officer of the club, who, I was told, was a public school teacher and a devout member of a huge Pentecostal church in Harlem. He was in his fifties. He seldom returned my phone calls and disappointed or offended me in that. When we did talk on the phone, he seemed reluctant to have me visit. After months of my persistence, he finally invited me to come to church with him and afterward to his apartment in the Bronx for Sunday dinner.

The subway to Harlem that Sunday was a circus of homeless men, Saturday night drunks, gold-bedecked black teens from the all-night discos, and fastidiously groomed black women with gloves and outrageous feathered hats and huge limp Bibles lying open in their laps. The church stood at the top of the subway stairs near 125th Street and Lenox Avenue, the heart of black Harlem. It was an enormous square white tabernacle, like a great barge of Zion gone aground. Inside, the front of the hall was constructed like a ship's hull upside down. The service had already begun when I arrived. The music was exhilarating—jiving piano and electric organ, electric guitars and bongo drums. The choir swayed and clapped in fugues of African rhythms. A thousand blessed worshipers shouted and flung their hands toward heaven. Leroy sat in his regular place in the wide balcony. An usher wearing white gloves took me to him. *"Great Day! God's gonna give up Zion's wall,"* the congregation sang. Tiny children, groomed like dolls, danced in their seats.

The sermon was accompanied by a continual, cacophonous chorus of amens—and other ecstatic ejaculations. A sister nodded off in the choir just as the spirit seized another obese earthly saint and sent her wailing and sailing in her all-white dress across the front of the church, like a full-rigger before a storm. Warm childhood memories sprang to my mind. I had been raised like this. Though our churches were much smaller, they were no less noisy. I knew all the songs and sang. Tears wet my cheeks, I felt one with them.

Leroy sat erect with his Bible in his hands, intent on the preacher's words, which rambled and thundered. The message was on Christian America's obsession—the nuclear family, which is to say that oily myth that greases the cogs of male domination.

"The Christian wife's duty is submission," the elder cried, while my warm emotions waned. "If she isn't what you want her to be, *you are the head*! You've got to lead her in the way—but with *love*!" He exhorted his people to gird themselves to battle Satan, just as "some of our ladies," he put it, "used to tuck up their skirts in the fields to pick cotton."

He preached about the ordained order of the Christian family and the evils that threatened to destroy America's godly family life—premarital sex, infidelity, women with careers, drugs. *"Ho-mo-sex-ual-ity!"* he roared suddenly. I grimaced and braced. He had seen a television program that very week on the previous summer's Gay Pride Day. "What a shame!" he mocked. "A day of degradation is what it is! *All of 'em talking about 'gay families' being happy!* Well, homosexuality and God don't walk together, let me tell ya. I got the *Word* on my side! *You know what I'm talking about?"*

The congregation cackled with applause. Leroy nodded beside me and said, "Amen."

After the service, trying not to offend, I asked Leroy what he thought about the sermon. He shrugged and quipped, "Oh, that doesn't bother me. I take what I need and let the rest go right over my shoulder. I keep the church and my 'social life' separate. Us black gays don't want what the white gays want. You understand me?" There was a barely concealed defiance in his voice, as if he had known all along that a white man could not understand. And I didn't.

We took the subway high into the Bronx and walked back toward the Harlem River. The raw, burned carcasses of brownstones and rotted apartment buildings, once regal dwellings, walled the sidewalks, where the stench of stale ash and water choked the air. The curbs were trashed with a pinball machine, a stripped-down car with smashed windows, musty refrigerators missing their doors, a tribe of discarded meat coolers, broken liquor bottles, dog shit, shattered glass. Only black people lived here. They sat for relief from the heat on the stoops and slept in doorways. One man, as we passed, kneeled on the landing of a second-story fire escape, plunging a needle into his flesh.

The Bronx here was rocky and steep, with ravines and winding streets. I lost my sense of direction. From the time we left the church, Leroy did not speak. When we reached the door of his apartment building, he said, perhaps a little coldly, "Come on in."

It was a handsome, middle-class building, in the Deco style, in the midst of this sea of decay. Rusted gates barricaded all the windows. "I prefer this to living in a white neighborhood," Leroy stated simply. He had been born in Harlem but had lived here his whole adult life. His apartment looked out on a dim light well and was so heavily curtained that gloom sat like a cloud inside. His living room was stashed with three plastic-covered sofas and tattered cartons of teaching aids and lesson plans. I noticed a mailing list for an AIDS foundation. From the only open window, the wan outside light cast the pale shadow of burglary grates across the floor. A dark, moldy smell sat on the air.

Washington, Leroy's young lover, came in briefly before we ate. He was ebony and tall, perhaps six feet four inches, deliciously built and handsome. He played semipro basketball. He had a wife and three children nearby in New Jersey, whom he spent a few nights with each week. He and Leroy had first met on the street in Times Square. "*Not* in one of those pornographic shops," Leroy added immediately. Washington and I spoke briefly, then he took a suitcase and left. When he had gone, Leroy said that maybe most of the men and women in the Corduroy Club were married and had secret same-sex lovers on the side. "Blacks don't 'come out' as readily as whites," he told me. "We have one strike against us already." Leroy himself was married and separated. He had grown children. His estranged wife now knew of his sexual interests but wouldn't talk about them. Leroy said, though, that she didn't care.

We had really spoken little other than this, and even then he had been sullen. He said nothing to me while he got dinner ready, though the kitchen opened onto the living room. When at last we sat down to eat, he paused and asked, "Have you been thinking I haven't been talking to you?" I looked at him. "Well, you're right," he answered. He was gentle, but there was a dull rancor in his voice. Then he said, "I'm gonna tell you a story about black and white. I don't have white friends. At my school where I teach, at my church, whatever I do, I live in a black society. I've had 'associations' with white men," he told me, raising his eyebrows to cue his meaning, "but they were always weirder than I liked.

"I had an Italian friend once. He lived across the river in New Jersey. He was wrestling with being gay. I asked him, 'Don't you know someone, *anyone*, you could try it with?' He got *all* disturbed. He thought *I* was asking to go to bed with him—and he said he didn't want to because I was black. I knew no matter how much we were good friends, the race thing was always between us.

"I went to a party at his house one time, when he had got himself a lover. It was all white and pinched collars—all of 'em telling me, 'Oh, we *love* Johnny Mathis.' I said, 'I don't bring up Frank Sinatra to *you!*' Whites always make sure you know you're black and they're white. They always find a way to bring up the difference.

"*That's* the reason the brothers won't talk to you. Right now I don't even know why I'm even letting you interview me. It's just like this study on what people think about AIDS at Columbia University. I'm the only one of my friends that agreed to do it. And you know, every time they come, they send a white man over here to interview me. *Not one black man!* All those things like that are white—white eyes looking at you. They say they want a black idea, but they ask all white questions. They say, 'How do you feel about AIDS?' and give you a choice, one to ten. I tell you I hurt. You write it in your book, 'Hurt.' But you don't understand *why* I'm hurt. You don't want to know."

At one minute he coddled me, like a teacher instructing a dense-headed student. At another his bitterness boiled. His anger seemed impersonal, so I could listen. "See," he continued, "I almost canceled out on you today. I said, Everything's on *his* terms. That's where whites always make a mistake. You told me you'd come to *my* church and *my* house. You didn't ask me to yours."

But I had wanted to understand *his* life, I told him, to experience things important to him. His perception shook me. "How about how blacks act in a white setting or meeting *your* lover?" he asked me. "We know how to use forks—because we taught white children how to use them. You got to start readin' *our* book. Why didn't you ask me to your house for dinner?

"Look," he declared, "you and I can both be gay, but we'll never socialize, for many reasons. 'Cause if I was to go to one of your affairs, I would have to watch how I talk, how I act, with everybody watching me. 'Gay' doesn't matter. Those lines between black and white—we're never gonna cross them. No one really wants to try."

"Then there's no hope," I said.

"Oh, there's *hope*, I guess," he countered. "My effort right now is having you here. And I know you took a risk, too. I might have had a group here to beat you up. It's like the elder that preached this morning said, 'You go to your brother and ask, "What have I done?"' But not the whites or the blacks want to take that extra step. Not the politicians or the white churches nor the white gays can understand till they really want to." He picked up an old picture of the board of the Corduroy Club. "These four died of AIDS. I know several others that found out they had the virus and committed suicide. You don't hear about the black gays with AIDS on television. It's a whole different issue with blacks. Do whites care about that?"

Some months later Leroy came to a reading I was doing at Columbia University. I had invited him to join us for dinner afterward. But he left as soon as the reading ended. Everyone else at the reading had been white. Every story I read was about white men. For a year afterward I kept calling to invite him to dinner, leaving messages on his phone machine. I found him at home once, and he agreed to come. I gave him a choice of dates and asked him to confirm with me when he'd chosen one. But I never heard from him again.

CHAPTER 23

MANHATTAN RESURRECTION

Miracles are both beginnings and endings, and so they alter the temporal order. They are always affirmations of rebirth, which seem to go back but really go forward. They undo the past in the present, and thus release the future.

—A Course in Miracles

IN THESE YEARS, DEATH SEEMED TO TEAR BENEATH OUR LIVES IN Manhattan like a roaring subway train. Bob, Robert, Carlos, Tim, David, Diego, Bill, Larry, Fleet, Peter, Tom, Michael, George, Joseph, Barry, Kenny, Sal, Vito, Paul, Matthew, Evan, Len, Chris, Damien, Rudy. In a dreaming moment I could believe them still alive. I could not remember all the names. They were all gone in so short a time—men I had made love to, or danced with, or fought for justice with, or only talked to in passing at the gym. Larry, who had helped me come out, died at thirty-nine of a heart attack. Kevin was stabbed to death by a fag killer. Steve was found shot through the head. Memorial cards arrived from Switzerland announcing that Marc and Nick were gone, from Chicago that

Jerry had died of AIDS. The phone rang—Martin, my dear friend in San Francisco, would be dead by the weekend. I flew to see him a final time. I have watched some men give up life for the fear of death, anesthetizing their terror with liquor and drugs or paralyzing themselves with morbidity. I've seen infected friends abandon work and joy and sink into a morbid state, though they had none of the deadly symptoms.

In 1985 the writer and translator Gregory Kolovakos and I had cofounded the Gay & Lesbian Alliance Against Defamation, GLAAD. It had risen from our anger over the media's inflammatory reporting on AIDS. As we worked together, Gregory became my dear friend. Now he was growing sicker by the day. Still, he fought courageously. Elliot, his lover, told me once that he never complained, "Why me?" He refused to feel singled out by this disease. As long as he could, he lived as if he were full of health, denying his pain and weakness. Even at the worst, he wore his wry smile. He was a stoic still amused at life. He spoke matter-of-factly, if not drolly, of suicide, should his degeneration become too great.

I wondered at him when I didn't despair. He was generous beyond good sense and had the quickest of minds. And though we met over gay politics, our sexuality became peripheral to our friendship. Gregory, at any rate, never divided the world into gay and straight, as I always had, but into fools and humane beings. He simply expected none of his friends to be bigots. And though he believed deeply in sexual justice—the freedom to choose our sexual path and not be punished for it—he believed little at all in "gay community," in the brotherhood of homosexuals. When I came to this thinking belatedly, it was his illness as much as anything that at last convinced me. Sexual likenesses and differences dissolve in the face of our mortality, for surviving life and confronting death are the experiences, at least, that we share with every man. Gregory's disease brought my gay journey to an end.

I told myself that I was prepared for Gregory's death, that I was ready to let him go. He had a lymphoma at the base of his brain and spent his last months frail and vomiting. I let his suffering numb me, because feeling it, I thought, would destroy me. His father died suddenly. Gregory had business to settle with the estate and then, he said, he would commit suicide, dying in an orderly way on his own timetable. It was as he had lived his life—by the paramount virtue of organization. He wrote the Hemlock Society. I introduced him to an acquaintance of mine who had helped a sick friend die, and in that, I believed I had fulfilled our friendship's final obligation. He chose his method, collected his pills, and waited.

He was in the hospital again on the February morning I got his call. The doctors were planning to radiate the cancer in his brain, though they held out little hope that it would help. He was terror-stricken by the threat of wasting nausea and baldness, the nuclear sickness that would overtake him. He lied to the doctors. He told them that he would need several days at home before beginning the radiation therapy in order to attend to some pressing business. But he had now set the date for dying and made all the last arrangements. On Wednesday he would leave the hospital to die at home. Elliot would stay by his side until he stopped breathing.

I was to come to see him and say good-bye on the preceding Sunday. When I arrived he seemed better than I had seen him in months—so powerful was his resolution. The vomiting had ceased. He was reading and had a stack of books yet to read at his bedside. His muscles were sometimes in terrible spasm. I rubbed his legs. I watched his face, to remember it. We were not sad, I think—could anything be sadder than his *living* this way?—but we didn't speak. In time he asked me to shut the room door and take a chair. He had a last request to make. He wanted to explain how he would die, that he would swallow the contents of thirty Seconals in a pudding. He had researched the procedure precisely. Elliot would mix the brew. Thirty was overkill. He would die quickly. Beth, Elliot's lifelong friend, would stay with him, a comforting companion. Then he said, without pausing, "I want you to help Elliot, too. I want you to be there until it's over. I've thought a lot about this. I want the three of you beside me when I die."

He was not morbid. I held back my tears. He wasn't crying himself, and I knew he would say something wry to me if I began to weep. He hated the maudlin. I said, "Of course I'll stay with you." This was the reasonable thing to do.

He had one other request. "It would be horrible," he said, "if something went wrong. This can't fail. When my breathing gets weak, if I'm struggling, I may need some help. I want you to put a pillow over my face if I need it. I know I'm asking a lot of you. But, *please*, will you do that for me?"

I searched my soul. Our vivid friendship had come to this. It was his decision, I told myself. I tried to sidestep the issue. "It'll never get to that," I answered. "You'll be gone so quickly."

He was unappeased. "I *need* to know that you'll do that for me," he stated, "or I'll never be able to get through this. Don't abandon me now."

"Yes," I told him at last. We said nothing else. I kissed him and left. It seemed to me that any other answer would be traitorous and cowardly. I felt obliged, but not courageous. Gregory needed to control the end of life, like an essay—though both of us knew how writing will not behave.

It undermined my terror, too, preparing to help him. It was vicarious, I think. Was this a rehearsal for my own ultimate death? I wanted to see if a man could die without the annihilating demon of fear reaching out to seize him. My shrink asked me, "What do you think you'll learn watching a man die?" I didn't know. I said, "That death isn't fearful if we're ready to go." And Gregory was, I insisted.

On Wednesday morning I took the crosstown bus to the hospital to pick him up and bring him home. Waiting for his release, we gossiped, catty about a hundred old enemies, as if any of them could matter on his death day. What else was there to say? He had never spoken much about his illness or his state of spirit. We followed the old script of our gossipy friendship. He was weak and wry, his voice was frail. He was belching and nauseated. Michael, my lover, had seen him the night before to say good-bye. His face was removed and uncomfortable then, as it was now. At home Michael said, "I don't like this scheme. It wasn't the face of someone who wanted to commit suicide." But Gregory's face looked sick and resolved to me.

He was methodical in his hospital bed that morning, as he'd always been about his life—signing papers for his father's estate, the mortgage company, the insurance company, the hospital. Elliot stayed at his side. He arranged for new prescriptions and signed releases for the radiation therapy—an elaborate ruse to make his doctor think he planned to go on living. He gave me notes for his obituary in *The New York Times* and carefully instructed me how to place it. "Oh, Darrell," he sighed sometimes. "What if this doesn't work? What if I throw up the pills?"

"How *can't* it?" I said to comfort him. "Rest, relax. Trust your friends now. You shouldn't go into *this* transition agitated." I avoided saying "death." "You shouldn't feel anything but a marvelous peace this morning. Everything will be fine. I promise." I was full of belief. I wanted him to feel the wonder of this final day. He took a deep breath, as if it were an odd, new experience. He exhaled, smiled, and steadied himself, then said, "You're right! *Okay!*" He dropped his hands in his lap, determined.

Elliot was mostly businesslike, but sometimes teary. He was nurturing and solicitous. He tried to hold up. He had lived with Gregory's long nights of soaking sweats and pain. *He* had never complained. "I can't see him this way. I want him to die," he once had told me, and repeated it in other sudden moments—believing it, disbelieving it, urging it on himself. We all felt that way. We had seen other friends decay with this disease and go insane. Today death was the measure of our friendship. My mind bored deep, looking for ulterior motivations. Were we also relieved that we would not bear the burden of his greater illness, had he decided to die naturally. *We*, after all, would be obligated by his suffering and degeneration, by his dementia and tantrums. Were we anxious to get rid of him?

I stared out the tight gray window and watched the traffic on the choked avenue. There was a slight rain. Umbrellas popped open on the sidewalks like flowers. The winter was springlike. I saw Gregory staring out the window, too. I wondered what *he* felt. He didn't say. My thoughts flew. Would he notice the overcast warmth of the day?

Did he care that he would never see another hospital room— the curious objects: "Oh, *this* is how we nurse sick humans!" The cranky bed, the cruel institution of glossy walls and echoing tile

floors and spigots on the walls and gadgets and windows sealed to
keep out the earth's air, and the suffocating anonymity of the hospital's healers? Did he care? What about the tumult of flowers in
his room? Their strange forms, frail-crinkled paper, freshly potted, already dying, a gift he would leave to unknown nurses now.
And this odd chair, with wheels and levers like a clock, rubber and
steel, and a high hook for tubes and fluids, which hundreds of afflicted beings had been rolled out of time in.

Did he note the eccentric elevator when we checked him
out—peculiar travel, up and down, in and out of the air and
ground, defiant of the rightful pace of gravity, buttons, lights, and
bells, coffin full of strangers, sick and well, this squeezed intimacy? Did he notice the building itself—monstrosity for healing,
jobs for thousands of fast and chilly workers? Did he wonder, preparing for his passage, why it is and how it is we humans demean
the nurture of the body and transitions of the spirit this way—as
if in a prison? *Was he thinking about these things?*

Gregory! Did you notice the wonder of life that day? The
crosstown cabbie who was polite! The terrible traffic at Fiftyseventh Street, the brown exhaust, the wailing horns, red screams
and brake lights, the huge emphysemic carcasses of buses sighing
at corners. Did you listen to the grumbling subway through the
sidewalk grates? Did you see the great carved doors to your apartment building (grand in its youthful years, now wasted—Béla
Bartok once lived here)? Did you smell the dreary maze of stale
hallways (where some tenant's air conditioner, long dead of a lung
disease, lay abandoned)? In New York we all live this way—no air,
no sky, labyrinthine entrances to our private lives, hostile, nameless neighbors. Did you pity the embattled door to your tiny
apartment space, dented with age, with its dead bolts and hundred
keyholes? Were you amused at how we barricade ourselves? You
played with your chaos of keys—openers of secrets, brass-toothed
passwords into peace. Did you think, This is the last time I'll have
to do this?

I was relieved that your dog was away for the day. Enormous,
gentle beast, he would have taken my arm off had he been there
to see me help you commit suicide. The cats played. *Look,*

Gregory, at those cats! Can you ever leave that? Brothers from a lit-ter, this was their birthday—Valentine's Day. I had forgotten. *You* noticed! They chewed each other's snouts, Skinny Atlas and Sabato, voiceless, swatting each other's ears. Skinny hid behind the rungs of a chair, palpating his paw through the bars of his cell, pretending Sabato was his jailer. Watch Sabato—full-flying fur and a storm of a tail—fall on his back like a sailor thrown to the deck and sweep the long extension of his spine across the floor like a life force. What creatures! They are slow, then suddenly fast on the table or the top of the fridge. Dead silent, they curl like seashells (tails at mouths, eating themselves), asleep in the corner. How can you ever, Gregory, give up that?

You sat on the sofa, safe in the middle, and made me put the window down (to an airshaft, your only skylight). We talked some, but nothing revealing. *How did you feel then? What were you thinking as you waited?* You slid the folded *New York Times* from the coffee table, read the headlines, then flipped it deftly to skim the bottom. (Truest of the *Times*' readers, loathing the pa-per's politics as you did.) This was your daily routine, as on any other day. You smiled curiously at the Soviets' applauding a uni-fied Germany and at U.S.-Soviet troop cutbacks. Just for a mo-ment (I wondered then), did you want to stay alive to watch the terrified world we grew up in pass? I said, "I suppose you'll be monitoring troop strength from a different perspective soon."

You raised an eyebrow and sniffed, grinned one-sided as you often did, and said (tired, sad, amused by the world's insanity), "I suppose you're right." And that was the end of our chat.

In twenty minutes' time you took three Valiums (to dull the closeness of death) and grew giddy. You giggled for a moment over some secret in your brain, then began to fall asleep. You said in a fog, "I need to relax." I was afraid you'd fall asleep before you'd committed the crime. *Then* what would we do? We *would not* feed it to you while you slept. That would be too much like murder. Elliot tapped (as spritely as tap dancing—Elliot was a dancer) thirty capsules out into a plastic cup of Swiss Miss pud-ding, and you screwed up your face. Rolling your eyes, and not without a comic sense, you spat, "Elliot, do you have to make a

Broadway number out of this?" because Elliot had danced on Broadway. I think you hated that soft tap, like a dance of death (nearly a drip, like time), and, testy, you stopped him at twenty-eight. I think Elliot—from that suspended, bemused smile of his—admired you more then than he ever had, for being a bitch. Your bitchery was always a necessary rhythm to him: it gave him his cue to allow himself to belong to you, like Burns and Allen. He said, earlier or much later, when you weren't around, "I'm trying not to say 'we.' I can't get used to that—'I,' just 'I.' We've been 'we' so long. I know this is right. This disease has been eating up *both* of our lives. *Do you know what I mean?* I just can't get used to the idea I'll be alone."

When Beth arrived at twelve-thirty sharp, you were eating test bites of unpoisoned pudding, to see if you could keep it down. Then you ate the real brew, unceremonious and unhurried, stopping only once to say, "I really want this," and turning your lip. I believed in that one moment I heard in your voice the unconvinced innocence of a child. You spooned the cup clean (with a couple of taps), smiled, yawned like a puppy. Then your head fell limp on Beth's shoulder.

We cradled you, then lifted you up—dead weight, dead, dead bundle. Do actors practice dying like this? Elliot and I tried to grasp you beneath your arms. Beth, sweet Beth—so mothering—cupped your chin, holding your head high and dignified. (That was the dance teacher in her.) But your mouth would not stay closed, as if some final silent word had stuck in your throat. Your legs were still crossed at the knee, we forgot to unwind them. Then you suddenly sprang and slipped through our hands, so fast, so heavy. The coffee table fell with the *Times* and the magazines you'd carefully stacked to read and a subscription form you hadn't mailed yet. You saw none of this. You were gone into a deadly sleep already.

"*Oh, Gregory, go!* Don't go! Stay! *No*, it's better like this. You're sick and can't live long anyway. How long? How hard? If you lived, we would only have to see you die. Now we will watch you today. *Gregory, stay!*"

We caught you at our fingertips. Why were we so calm then,

so confident of our spirits? It was right. *It was!* I didn't flinch. Gregory, I didn't flinch! I did what you asked, what I vowed, dear friend. Friend!

I righted the coffee table and held you, too. I don't know how. You lay in our arms like the weight of the world. We carried you out to your bed, a heap on the bedspread. Sweet Beth, gentle, firm-hearted Beth, arranged the posture of the pillows. No time to think. "Make him comfortable. Let him sleep." You were upright so you could belch, so you wouldn't throw up and die on your vomit. Your face was numb, your eyes were lost. I closed them. (Your mouth was still fallen.) Beth made you sit erect and balanced your head, Beth, who choreographs humans.

What were *we* thinking then? *What were we not thinking?* Elliot, your man, dumb-faced at your feet; Beth, holding your head on the window side of the bed. I felt the skin of your left hand. Old, old skin on such a young man. (You were thirty-eight!) "An old soul," you had always told me. And that pronouncement was your oddity, Gregory—man of high education and deep intellect. That self-revealing statement was your unexpected key— you, who analyzed the world so keenly but kept to yourself in things of the spirit. Those words should have been sufficient, had we been listening. Wise man! Ancient soul! Your hands seemed wrinkled then with the truths of the ages! What *did* you believe? Your wedding band—matching Elliot's—still wrapped your wedding ring finger. (You were so comic about Elliot, no one would have thought you loved him so deeply.) You said, "I want to die with it on." More of your instructions. There were so many. We were afraid your fingers would swell at death. (What did *we* know?) But we'd do as you asked. We would wait until you were dead to remove it—before the ambulance came, before the cops, before the sirens. Would there be sirens? Would we be crying? We held your hands softly and told you to let go, calling on departed spirits to guide you away.

Elliot said good-bye alone, then left for work, as you'd planned. It was his alibi. The afternoon moved slowly. "Have you ever watched someone die?" my shrink had asked me. "When the moment comes, you'll know." You had planned everything, scenarios to protect us from the law. "Officer, he was walking when we brought him home this morning. He has AIDS. There are lesions on his brain. We left him to sleep for the afternoon, then came back and found him this way." Clean crime, two hours at best. Beth and I would stay till you died, then call Elliot home to "discover" your body. He'd call 911, while Beth and I went free.

We sat that dying afternoon and talked, implicated, intimate strangers (we'd met in your hospital room only three days before). She sat on the sofa where you took your life in your hands. I sat in your rocker (like a queen). The cats rolled on the floor or stepped with their tiptoe bodies across the precipitous back of a chair. Once they slinked across our laps like snakes, then disappeared to sit guard over you, on either side of your head like Sphinxes. We spoke of life that afternoon—who we were, who we'd been, her dancing, my writing, how she and Elliot, old high school friends, had once almost married. We spoke of you, how each of us had met. I told her that our friendship had been golden. You were my "best friend," the brother I had never had.

We rapped as if we were back in the sixties, the way our generation had, stoned. I munched out on an Entenmann's and three Swiss Miss vanillas you'd left behind. (I was *starved* to death!) We rapped as if the afternoon were a common occurrence and as though it were a freak of time: living and dying, your dying, our lives. Your breathing was shallow, but you didn't stop. We debated what to do with the body.

Beth said you were listening. Your phone machine rumbled all afternoon. Did you know? A chorus of Valentine's Day calls. No one knew the day's plan, just intuition. They were messages ripe with love, friends, and old lovers! You were so loved! You were sinking deeper then, a farther peace washing over your face, your eyes, like pale sight, receding. We turned up the volume for you to hear. There was no drug numbness now. An otherworldly aliveness was setting in. You heard all your valentines.

I don't know in what rare space we swam that day while you slept, while pale gray light leaked through the window. Not in New York, not on earth, we were elsewhere. (Beth said, "This is a time and place warp.") I tried to imagine the outside world, the crowded streets, the anxious crowds and searing noise, the menagerie of wealth and beggars. The apartment was suspended in strange air. We checked you now and then, wherever you were between this realm and another. Deeper, deeper in the other world, your breathing grew shallower, softer (you *had* been snoring!), more profound. Your eyes relaxed, useless now, your skin was insubstantial, satin as baby's breath. Where had you gone? Not under the last threshold yet. Your head, rolled to one side, seemed morbid to me, uncomfortable to Beth. We tugged on you, lifted (and maybe dropped) you a little to bring you down to a final pose. Beth balanced your head. I wouldn't, couldn't, cross your hands, as morticians do. I laid them out straight beside your legs and covered them up. (You'd been so feverish when you first fell asleep, and now your fingertips were icy.) I kissed your wedding band hand, old soul. Skinny spilled out beside you like a splash of milk. We begged you to go. "It's peaceful out there," we told you. "Loving spirits will guide you through the unknown."

It was two, or was it three or four? There was a magnificent hush. Your bizarre-faced clock—with hands that dissolved and reformed in an odyssey of colors—could not tell the time exactly. *What* time? The little Braun on the opposite shelf was upside down, though I didn't notice its trick. "What's wrong with that clock?" Beth asked. "Has it *stopped?*" She stared it down and said, *"It's just wrong."* She didn't see that time was standing on its head, either.

"What's wrong?" It was five o'clock and you hadn't gone. We phoned Elliot and were amused at you, holding on as you did. We said you were holding conversations in the spirit world before you took the last step, because you depended on reason. *"Nothing yet?"* Elliot repeated, almost dumb. The wire hissed, then was silent. When he came home, past six, your skin was warm, your breath was strong (though not vigorous). Your eyes were still far away in some sunken forever. We waited, we joked, Beth meditated. I sat in a chair by your bed for a while and traveled with you. I called on my departed grandmother's spirit to help you make your transition. Elliot named a young friend of yours who had suicided. "Gregors, find Suzanne. She'll show you the way."

We ate cold sandwiches from the deli downstairs while you lay there—*cold* so the police would not catch the lingering smell of hot food and know that we'd murderously been there all along. Had you made a choice then, or were you still deciding? The evening passed. Midnight came. We changed scenarios like desperate clothes, discarding the evidence.

"What about the pillow on his face?" one of us asked.

"No, not now."

"He isn't ready yet. That would be murder."

I reneged, Gregory. I could never have lived with myself had I done that. Every minute you refused to die, we concocted new alibis. Frightened Beth called a doctor friend in Los Angeles: "If *one*, to be perfectly hypothetical," she told him, sitting like a yogi or a dancer on the floor, wrapped in the cord of the phone, "took three ten-milligram Valiums and twenty-eight Seconals and hasn't died in twelve hours, how much longer can he, or she, live?"

It was enough to kill an elephant, the physician told her, then stated, "But after surviving all this time, it could be weeks . . . or months . . . or he could still be gone any minute. You'll have to call an ambulance now, or you might be charged with criminal neglect."

We sat silent together, envisioning jail. Elliot was manic, crying, then gazing at the yellow air like a man stun-gunned. We wrote his telephone speech for the medics and police—because he couldn't remember, one minute to the next, what we told him, and *we* were so quickly changing texts: "I can't wake up my roommate. I just got home. I think he's in a coma or something."

The cats ran when the medics came in slinging torpedoes of oxygen, masking your face, clanking down the folded gurney, volleying a dry, steady fire of questions. The woman cop asked Elliot, "Who are you?"

"*I'm* his roommate," he answered.

She saw one bedroom, one bed, and said, "How long have you lived together?"

"Eight years," he said.

No mother, no father, no close blood relatives—Elliot was all you had left. "Then you two are a family," the officer stated, and in that one word helped purge the pain of this epidemic.

The midnight shift at the emergency room were baffled but asked few questions. "He has AIDS," we told them, and that was sufficient. We showed them your "living will"—no painful interventions, no intubations, no extraordinary measures, a "natural" death. They respected that and put you to bed at three A.M. to let you die. Fifteen hours had passed, and still your face was distant, like death. "He *might* wake up," an intern told us—in a gray grade of life, diminished, a paralyzed idiot. *You* had asked us to be part of this. Our terror floated over our heads but had no place to settle. We remained convinced. Our agitated calm continued. A doctor said, "He'll be gone by morning." But you weren't.

There was a gaunt young man named Julio in the bed next to yours, black-bearded, going bald, gasping for breath through a mask, clawing the sheets with his terrified hands. Were you at all aware of him, this other "AIDS case"? His torso lay motionless while his agitated head quivered, rolled to one side. His body was patched, stained with blood, sweat, and mucus, stinking of death, the heavy putrid musk of a horrible death.

A shroud of sweat washed his face, sealing his eyelids shut. He had no family, no friends. He had been there for weeks, a nurse said, with no one to visit him. I stood by his bed and held his hand, whispering my anonymous love to him. On the second day of your hospital stay, Julio stopped breathing. I had stolen a look at his chart at the nurse's station and found this: Julio had been born February 26, 1943. He was five years older than I. We shared a birthday.

Your approach to death, Gregory, was not like his. You were surrounded by quiet love. All this time you lay on your white sickbed, perfectly still, perfectly placed, like a man in a casket— your breath so pale that a breeze might have snuffed it. And then, the day after Julio died, as if you needed his space too in that room in order to live again, I saw you move your hand on your stomach. I saw it twice or maybe three times, though no one would believe me. Elliot said, "He belched, that's all, and his hand jumped." That night, twice, it moved again—with the slow unconsciousness of a dream. And still we were encouraging you to die (desperate whispers), numb afraid now of a waking drug-lobotomized creature—a monster of our complicity.

But that was not fated. On the fourth day you half opened your eyes, then fell back asleep, part conscious, pawing at the mask on your face. (Did you think that life support was saving you? Did you blame *us* that you were still living?) You pulled the catheter from your penis and wet the sheets. On the fifth day you stared foggily at our stunned trio, statuesque like three apostles beside your bed. Fragilely you began to speak—but only for water, such basic needs. On the sixth day I found you reading a new book of poetry. On the following day you started to eat for the first time in weeks—your coma had stirred your appetite. On the eighth day they let you go home. You walked down the hall on my arm, using a cane.

We had our old talks—you and I—those last two days you were in the hospital. I caught you up on the world that had passed while you were elsewhere. We started to talk of the article on Sartre in *The New York Times Book Review: No Exit.* Then we dropped it. You spoke about life more sanguinely then than I'd heard you speak in a year, about buying a new car and a new apartment, playing with the paternal inheritance you thought you'd have no chance of spending, outwitting the old miser.

"I want a place with a view and sunshine," you told me, then quipped wryly, "But I'll make all the arrangements myself. I've found out my friends are incapable of carrying out my wishes." You told me then just once (and we never discussed it) that when you first opened your eyes (and saw us standing in a pharmaceutical fog at the foot of the bed, staring in wonderment), you had been angry—"furious at you because I wasn't dead."

And you did say this, faintly, riding home from the hospital in the back of a taxi: "Three psychiatrists came to see me this morning. They were *perfect* therapists—dull and not an ounce of emotion. And *stupid*! They wanted me to name the presidents backward, after all this! I forgot George Bush and Gerald Ford, which really disturbed them." You grew soberer before you continued. "They wanted to know how they could be sure I wouldn't try killing myself again if they let me go. I told them I'd learned my body was stronger than I ever expected. That I knew I could bear the pain.

"And I told them I'd learned how loved I was—that there's too much love in my life not to go on living." We never spoke of it again.

I am a weaver of secret tales from a long odyssey. Now they are all part of me, and I am changed. One night after a Broadway show, I told Gregory's story to a photographer friend, a woman who captures the motion of life in a camera. I told her that two months later, almost to the day, he died at home in his sleep, of natural causes, and at peace. There were tears in her eyes and her voice was shaking when she asked me, "And what can you say you've learned from this?"

I rushed to find the concisest phrase. "The power of redemption," I stated, then thought better of it. Our redemptions only come in renewing the journey.

I have gone on other journeys now.